W9-AWX-029

THE PRAYER OF THE
NIGHT SHEPHERD

Phil Rickman was born in Lancashire. He writes and presents the book programme *Phil the Shelf* for BBC Radio Wales and has won awards for his TV and radio journalism. His highly acclaimed earlier novels *Candlenight*, *Crybbe*, *The Man in the Moss*, *December* and *The Chalice* are also available from Pan Books in paperback. *The Wine of Angels* introduced the Rev. Merrily Watkins, whose frightening baptism as a diocesan exorcist was charted in *Midwinter of the Spirit*, followed by *A Crown of Lights*, *The Cure of Souls* and *The Lamp of the Wicked*. He is married and lives on the Welsh border.

Phil Rickman

THE PRAYER OF THE NIGHT SHEPHERD

PAN BOOKS

First published 2004 by Macmillan

This edition published 2004 by Pan Books
an imprint of Pan Macmillan Ltd
Pan Macmillan, 20 New Wharf Road, London N1 9RR
Basingstoke and Oxford
Associated companies throughout the world
www.panmacmillan.com

ISBN 0 330 49033 8

3 5 7 9 8 6 4 2

A CIP catalogue record for this book is available from
the British Library.

Typeset by Intype Libra Ltd
Printed and bound in Great Britain by
Mackays of Chatham plc, Chatham, Kent

They had gone a mile or two when they passed one of the night shepherds upon the moorlands, and they cried to him to know if he had seen the hunt. And the man, as the story goes, was so crazed with fear that he could scarce speak . . .

Sir Arthur Conan Doyle, *The Hound of the Baskervilles*

No record in cold print can give the reader an idea of the pleasure experienced in collecting the elusive material we call folk-lore from the living brains of men and women of whose lives it has formed an integral part. In some cases, with regard to superstitious beliefs, there is a deep reserve to be overcome; the more real the belief, the greater the difficulty . . . The folk of the Welsh districts are more superstitious, as a rule . . .

Ella Mary Leather, *The Folk-lore of Herefordshire*

Under Stanner in the summer

Should have known, he really should. That morning, even though it was a fine morning, coming up to high summer, the whole valley was singing with unease.

'Oh bugger,' Jeremy Berrows said to Danny. 'You seen that?'

Up on Stanner Rocks, knobs of stone poked out like weathered gargoyles on an old church, or ancient skulls browned by the earth, half-buried, with scrubby trees in their eye sockets. From one side, you could sometimes see a whole body of rock that Danny reckoned looked like the remains of a dead giant thrown back into the greenery encrusting the cliff face.

But Jeremy wasn't looking up at Stanner – likely he blamed the rocks for taking Mary Morson away, though in Danny's view the rocks done him a favour on that one. He was staring instead at the smoky firs across the valley, the dark trees that said, *This is Wales now, boy, make no mistake.*

'What?' Danny said.

'Big black crow. Hovering.'

'No, really?'

'Just flew over real low. Then he come back, flew over again.'

'Gotter hand it to these scavengers,' Danny said. 'Awful thorough.'

Bollocks, he was thinking. You could drive yourself daft, seeing signs everywhere – even if you were Jeremy Berrows, with ditchwater in your veins and the valley talking to you all your life.

Could see where the boy was coming from today, mind. Even without crows, everything visible in the west seemed like a warning about Wales, a stiffened finger under your nose. But when you actually crossed the Border *into* Wales, the countryside relaxed into the easy, light-coloured, sheep-shaved hills where Danny Thomas had been born and bred and still lived.

Still lived. Jesus, how had that happened?

Danny was grinning in dismay, rubbing his beard, and the boy glanced at him but Danny just shook his head and tramped on down the dewy field under the fresh-rinsed morning sky, not sure any more which side of the Border they were on, or if it mattered. He was a Welshman himself, he supposed, although the way he talked wasn't recognizably Welsh either to *real* Welsh people or to the English whose country was within shouting distance, and all the shouting, from either side, done in near enough the same accent as his.

Confusing, really: if Danny was from the lighter, more English-looking country down the Radnor Valley, which was actually in *Wales*, then Jeremy, back here under the dark firs and the knuckles of Stanner Rocks, must be . . .

'You English, then, Jeremy?'

'Me?' Jeremy glanced warily at Danny, instinctively patting his thigh for Flag, the sheepdog, to come close. 'Dunno. Do it matter?'

'Matters to some,' Danny said, 'so they tells me.'

It was real confusing hereabouts, mind. For instance, the little town a mile or so behind them was in England, despite being on the Welsh side of Offa's Dyke. Even so, with its narrow main street and its closed-in feel, it *felt* Welsh.

Kington: an *anomaly.*

This was Danny's current favourite word. The naturalists he met in the pub used it about Stanner Rocks, said to be some of the oldest rocks in the country. *Anomaly* meant strange stuff going on, odd climatic things occurring up on the tops, resulting in plants that grew on Stanner and nowhere else in these islands. Local people rarely went up on the rocks these days, it being a National Nature Reserve protected by the Countryside Commission; mostly it was just the naturalists and a few tourists with permission.

But Mary Morson went up one day, and got a bit of a thing going with one of the naturalists and never come back to Jeremy Berrows, and mabbe the boy didn't want reminding.

Boy. He must be late thirties now, but he had this fresh complexion, which was rare for a farmer. Most of them had skin like old brick – like Danny's skin, in fact, what you could see of it between the grey beard and the seaweed hair. But it wasn't only that; there was an innocence about Jeremy, and that was rare, too, in a farmer, especially a good one. Jeremy also had commitment, an intense . . . *bonding* was the word they used now, with this marginal ground. The kind of bonding that hinged on knowing that if the ash came out before the oak you were in for a soak, and that kind of stuff. Whatever you wanted to call it, it had drained out of Danny Thomas long ago, leaving a bleak old desert of regrets.

'Down by there, it is.' The boy was nodding his head towards the copse at the bottom of the field, where a bunch of fat lambs was gathering. 'Other side of the ole conker tree. See him?'

They were up on a bit of a tump now, and you could see all of Jeremy's ground, almost surrounded by the huge area owned by Sebbie Three Farms, the robber baron. And you could see the big, naked feet of the giant on the side of

Stanner. Below the rock face was the main road where it turned into the Kington bypass, and a long yellow container lorry sailed past, like something out of a different time zone. Danny wondered if Jeremy even noticed the lorry – if all the boy saw wasn't just grass and trees and the plumpening lambs and the hawthorn trees sprinkled with floury blossom.

And the intrusion. The vans that shouldn't be there. Danny's gaze followed a sheep track down to the bottom field, where he could make out a cool blue roof slashed by a blade of sunlight. But no movement down there, no noise.

'Likely they won't be up and about yet,' he said. 'Always stays up late, these folks, with the booze and the dope. And music. You year any music last night?'

Jeremy shook his head, and Danny looked wistfully away towards Hergest Ridge, a long arm pushing into Wales, made famous by Mike Oldfield when he named his second album after it. Mike Oldfield was the most exciting thing that had ever happened to Kington: up on the Ridge with his kites and at home in his farmhouse with – the thought of it still made Danny Thomas catch his breath – *twenty guitars.*

Danny had three guitars in his stone barn: two acoustics and a Les Paul. He'd sold his classic Strat last Christmas. Broke his heart, but they needed a new stove, and Greta had gone without too long. And Mike Oldfield was long gone now, and Danny was left sitting in his stone barn, riffing into the night and counting all them lost opportunities to get out of farming for ever.

'No music, no,' Jeremy said. 'They was prob'ly laying low the first night.'

'You reckon?'

In Danny's experience, laying low wasn't what they did.

'It's where the ole crow was hovering,' Jeremy said. 'Direc'ly over that van.'

*

Half-past six this morning, when the boy had phoned him.

'Hippies,' he'd said.

Not Danny's favourite word. There hadn't been any hippies for over thirty years, but folks in this area loved to hang on to the obsolete. And it was what they'd always called Danny himself. *Danny Thomas? Bloody hippy. We all knows what he grows in Bryncot Dingle. If his ole man was alive it'd kill him dead.*

Danny had turned off the toaster, lowered the volume on Wishbone Ash and sought some clarification. To some of the old farmers, a hippy was anybody not wearing a tweed cap, wellies and green waterproof trousers.

'Ole van,' Jeremy said, 'with little windows at the top. And a minibus, with one of them funny stars painted on the side.'

'Pentagram?'

'Sort of thing.'

'Just the two vehicles?'

'Far's I can see. Could be more in the trees.'

'You en't been down to check?'

Jeremy had said nothing. He wouldn't have gone near, not even after dark when he was known to move around among the sheep and the cattle looking like a poacher, but in fact a guardian. Jeremy never lost a lamb to the fox; it was like he and the fox had come to an agreement.

Greta had come into the kitchen then, flip-flopping across the stained lino. Had on the old pink dressing gown, and there was purple under her eyes, and Danny thought about the stove her'd never asked for and how it wasn't enough.

He sighed and waited on the phone, until Jeremy coughed and said, real tentative, 'Only, I thought as how you might . . . you know?'

'Aye, I know,' Danny said.

It had been flattering at one time. When the New Age

5

travellers used to turn up in force, back in the '80s and '90s, the local farmers had felt threatened by the sheer numbers, and it took the police a long time to get the necessary court orders to move them on. Danny had come into his own, then – a farmer who looked like a traveller and was into their music and understood their ways. One summer night, he'd taken his Les Paul and his littlest generator and the Crate mini-amp up to this travellers' camp by Forest Inn and hung out there jamming till dawn with a bloke called Judas, from Nuneaton. Biggest bloody audience Danny ever had. He'd donated a drum of diesel for the buses and off they'd all trundled next day, no bother.

The farmers were well pleased, even Sebbie Dacre, bigtime magistrate, who'd been about to have the invaders *dealt with*. Might be a raggedy-haired druggy, Danny Thomas, but he had his priorities right when it come down to it: Danny the negotiator, Danny the diplomat. *The hippy-whisperer*, some bugger said one night in The Eagle in New Radnor. Not imagining for one moment that when Danny Thomas was up there jamming with the travellers, he'd been screaming inside, *Take me with you! Please! Get me out of yere!*

And things wasn't all that bad, then. Nowadays, agriculture was a sick joke, gasping on the life-support of EC grants. Danny wasn't hardly replacing stock, in the hope that something would come up. Prices were laughable, and he wasn't even looking forward to the haymaking, which seemed pointless. He was letting the docks grow, and the thistles. He'd even started doing the National bloody Lottery, and that was *totally* despicable.

'All right, give me quarter of an hour, boy.' Danny turned to his wife. 'Jeremy Berrows. Got travellers in his bottom field.'

'You makes it sound like a disease,' Gret said.

Danny smiled and went off to find his classic King Crimson T-shirt.

The problem was not that Jeremy was scared, just that he was plain shy and avoided the company of other men who were cynical about farming and treated their animals like a crop. Never had nothing to do with his neighbour, Sebbie Dacre, gentleman farmer and Master of the Mid-Marches Hunt. Even after his mam left the farm, Jeremy ignored the pubs, and the livestock markets when he could. Everybody thought he was coming out of it when he hooked up with Mary Morson – nice-looking girl, solid farming family. Her and Jeremy, they'd go out together, into Kington, and they had the engagement ring from the jeweller's there – Mary flashing it around, Jeremy proud as a peacock, if peacocks wore work shirts and baggy jeans.

The van was below them now, about seventy yards away, and Danny could see most of it – light blue, with bits of dark blue showing through on the roof. Hard to say what make it was – bit bigger than a Transit, sure to be. And quite old, so that would likely rule out foreign tourists who didn't know no better than to camp on somebody's ground. Foreign tourists had classy new camper vans and Winnebagos.

Jeremy was looking tense already, hunched up.

'Tell you what,' Danny said. 'Why don't I go down there, talk to the buggers on my own?'

It made sense. Jeremy looked grateful and his shoulders relaxed. Flag the dog, sensing a release of tension, lay down in the grass, panting, and Danny went down there on his own, into the dip where the bank was eroded. The stream at the bottom was almost dried up. The blossomy hedge hid the bypass, though not Stanner Rocks, and Danny could still see the faces on the rocks, and the dead giant. Way back, when he was doing acid, he'd once watched the giant's head rotting into green slime. Jesus Christ, never again.

'Hello there!' Danny shouted.

Now he was close up, he could tell this wasn't travellers in the New Age sense. The van might be old and have windows punched in the sides, but it was tidy, clean and looked-after, with nothing painted on it – no slogans, no pentagrams – and the windows had proper blinds. And it was the only vehicle here. Where was the minibus, then?

Danny stepped over a bunch of elder branches, neatly sawn and stacked and left to rot, on account of Jeremy never burned elder, which was the Devil's wood and would bring you no luck.

'Anybody about?'

He walked over to the van and peered inside the cab, remembering how, on his own farm one time, he'd found this car – posh car, BMW – tucked up against a field gate, with the engine running and a length of hose from the exhaust jammed in the window, and a man in a black suit in there, all pink-faced and well dead.

A wood pigeon came blundering out of the hedge, making as much racket as a bunch of yobs with baseball bats. Danny spun round, and saw that they were above him. Both of them.

A woman and a girl. They were standing on the bank, in full sun, and Danny Thomas could see them clearly, and they weren't exactly what he'd been expecting.

'How're you?' he said mildly. Was he a bit disappointed because they were so ordinary-looking, both in light-coloured tops and jeans and trainers? Because they wasn't wild-haired creatures with tattoos and chains and rings in their lips?

'Oh hell.' The woman scrambled down. 'I suppose we're trespassing.'

Danny shrugged.

'It was late,' the woman said, 'and we were exhausted. I'm sorry.'

Danny said, 'Where'd the other one go?'

The woman blinked, shook out her dark brown hair. The girl came down and joined her, sticking close like Flag, the sheepdog, had with Jeremy. The girl looked about fourteen.

'Minibus?' Danny said. 'Pentagram on the side?'

'Oh, yeah, right.' The woman had an English accent. 'They've gone. They left early. What happened, we met them last night – a girl and two guys. We both pulled into this garage forecourt, only it was closed, and we were nearly out of fuel and it was getting dark and I'm like, Oh Christ, what are we going to do if they're *all* closed? I mean, obviously I don't know this area too well, and I couldn't think of any-where to stop for the night. Then this girl in the bus says, "Oh, we've been round here loads of times, we can show you a good campsite." And that's how we . . .' She shrugged. 'I'm sorry. I mean, it was dark and I— We didn't light a fire or anything. We wouldn't do anything like that. Is this your farm? Can I pay you?'

Danny became aware of Jeremy Berrows up on the bank. Danny said. 'It's his farm, it is.'

'Oh.'

He watched the woman approaching Jeremy. She was very thin and her bare arms were tanned. She was real sexy, in fact, in a more *managed* way, like a rock chick of the old school.

'Hi, I'm, er . . . I'm Nat,' she said. 'Natalie. That's Clancy.'

The girl nodded and said nothing.

Jeremy didn't move at all, but he wasn't still either. He was so much a part of this land that he seemed suspended in the air currents, and his sparse, fluffy hair was dusted by the sun. When the woman moved towards Jeremy, leaving the girl by the van, Danny would swear he saw a hell of a shiver go through the boy, as if there was a sudden stiff breeze, come out of nowhere, that no one else could feel.

Danny felt an apprehension.

For over a week, the blue van stayed in the bottom field.

Then it wasn't there any more.

About a month after this, Gwilym Bufton, the feed dealer and gossipy bastard from Hundred House, told Danny Thomas that he'd seen a blue van parked up in Jeremy Berrows's yard, hidden behind the old dairy. Like it was *meant* to be hidden.

By September, people were starting to talk.

In October, Danny saw Jeremy Berrows one lunchtime in The Eagle at New Radnor, sitting at a table in the shadows with the woman with dark brown hair. Jeremy nodded and said, 'How're you?' in a nervous kind of voice, and Danny didn't push it. The woman smiled at Danny, and it was a nice smile, no question, and she was a lovely-looking woman, no question about that either, but her eyes were watchful. Danny supposed he could understand that, the way people were talking.

Next thing he heard about the van was that it had been sold – bit of irony here – to the naturalists working up at Stanner, to use as a mobile site HQ and for overnight accommodation. Serious burning of boats here, in Danny's view. Then he hears the woman's gone to work for the latest London fantasists to take over the ruinous Stanner Hall Hotel. Manager, no less.

A few days later, Greta said, when they were watching telly, during the adverts, 'Rhoda Morson – you know, Mary's mother? Well, I was talking to her, in the paper shop, see, and her says, "Oh, he's just doing it to make Mary jealous." '

'You what?'

'*Her*. Well, Rhoda Morson was mad as hell, sure t' be, when Mary blew it with Jeremy and lost the farm. Getting his own back now, that's what she reckons. Rubbing it in.'

'That's what her reckons, is it?' Danny said. *Lost the farm.* Bloody hell, it was all they ever thought about – bringing another bloody farm into the family. Where was love in the equation, or was that a 'sixties thing?

Greta looked at him, thoughtful. 'You could find out.'

'Eh?'

'How permanent it is.'

'Why'd I wanner do that? En't my affair.'

'Ah, but *is* it?' Greta said. 'Is it just *an affair*? Or has that tart got her big feet firmly under the table? The girl's going to school over at Moorfield now, 'cording to Lynne in the hairdresser's. Now *that*'s got the ring of permanent about it, isn't it?'

Danny yawned and watched a car commercial he liked because it had a soundtrack of 'Travellin' in Style' by Free. He'd never had an actual car, only second-hand trucks. He didn't mention to Greta about the van being sold; if she hadn't heard, he wasn't going to give her more gossip to spread across the valley.

'You knows Jeremy Berrows better than most,' she said. 'You could find out.'

'I prob'ly could, Gret,' Danny said. 'If I gave a shit.'

And the matter was never raised again, because that was the night of the terrible fire that wrecked Gomer Parry's plant-hire depot down the valley, killing Gomer's nephew, Fat Nev. Bit of a shock for everybody in Radnor Valley, that was, and Danny spent a lot of time helping poor old Gomer salvage what could be salvaged and restore what could be restored. Rebuilding the perimeter fence to keep out the scavengers and dealing with the particular area of the site that he realized Gomer couldn't bear to go near.

And out of the blackened ruins of Gomer's business came the glimmering of a new future for Danny. It wasn't, admittedly, the career in music he'd always dreamed of, but it would mean whole days out of the valley. New places, new people. And he was a good ole boy, Gomer Parry.

For a while, Danny Thomas was so excited that, like the great David Crosby, he almost cut his hair.

He never saw much of Jeremy Berrows again until the winter, when the trees were all rusty and the skulls of Stanner Rocks gleamed with damp like cold sweat, and the traditional stability of the border country was very much called into question.

Traditional stability: that was a bloody joke.

Part One

It occurred to a man who was cycling home to Kington late at night – he'd been working at the munitions factory during the War. Near Hergest Court he saw this enormous hound which he'd never seen before and never saw again. The hound had huge eyes – that's what impressed him most, the size of its eyes. The hound didn't attack him, and he just kept cycling and I would imagine he cycled very fast. He had a feeling that there was something that just wasn't real about it.

Bob Jenkins, journalist, Kington

ONE

Without the Song

Normally, she wouldn't think of fogging the air around non-smoking parishioners, especially so soon after a service. Tonight was different. Tonight, Merrily needed not only this cigarette but what it was saying about her.

The cigarette said, *This woman is human. This woman is weak. Also, given the alleged findings on secondary smoking, this woman is selfish and inconsiderate. This is a serial sinner.*

Only it wasn't getting through. Brenda Prosser's eyes were glowing almost golden now. Twice she'd tried to sit down at the kitchen table and been pushed back to her feet by the electricity inside her. She had to hold on to the back of the chair to stop her hands trembling, and then the joy would make her mouth go slack and she'd shake her head, smiling helplessly.

'Gone.' Maybe the fourth time she'd said that – Brenda relishing the hard finality in the word: gone, gone, gone.

'Just like it never was there, Vicar,' Big Jim Prosser said. His light grey suit was soaked and blackened across the shoulders. He stood with his back to the old Aga in the vicarage kitchen, and the Aga rumbled sourly.

And Merrily smoked and wondered how she should be responding. But the inner screen was blank. Just like Ann-Marie's scan.

'This is a miracle, sure t'be,' Jim said.

Oh Christ. Any word but that.

'And, see, like I kept saying to Jim, hardly the first one, is it?' Rain was still bubbled on Brenda's forehead like the remains of a born-again baptism. 'Not the first since you brought back the Evensong.'

'Without the song.' Merrily sat down, then abruptly stood up again and went to fill the kettle for tea. A dense curtain of rain swished across the dark window over the sink, as though it had been hosed.

They could have waited for her in the church porch, Brenda and Jim. But when the congregation was filing out, umbrellas going up, there they'd been, standing among the wet tombs and the headstones, both of them bareheaded, as though they were unaware of the sometimes-sleety rain. Like they were in some parallel dimension where it wasn't cold and it wasn't raining at all.

The truth was, Jim had said, as they followed Merrily to the vicarage, that they didn't want to talk to anyone else, didn't want to answer all the obvious questions about Ann-Marie. They thought it was only right that the vicar should be the first to know.

This was the first time that either Jim or Brenda had been to the Sunday evening service. They'd been among those older parishioners who were huffily avoiding it because they'd heard it was all changed, had become a bit unconventional, a bit *not for the likes of us*.

'I pray we'll be forgiven for ever doubting what you were trying to do, Merrily,' Brenda said now.

So much for the experiment in Mystery.

Evensong.

As in most parishes, the Sunday evening service had been killed a while ago, by falling congregations.

And then Merrily had suddenly brought it back. *Sunday*

evening in the church. Everyone welcome. Just that. Nothing about a service.

The truth was that, after what had happened with Jenny Box, she'd been feeling guilty. Deliverance work had been separating her too often from her own parish, from the day-to-day cure of souls. She'd been too busy to notice the anomalous buds in the local flower bed until they were bursting into black blossom.

When she'd put this to the Bishop, he'd waved it away. Congregations were in free fall; it was a phase. Or it wasn't a phase, but something truly sinister – the beginning of the end for organized Christianity. What about children? the Bishop asked; the new Archbishop of Canterbury was particularly worried about the absence of children in churches. Merrily had raised this issue with Jane, who seemed to have been a child like yesterday, and Jane had wrinkled her nose.

'Who *needs* kids in church, anyway? Look at it this way – kids are not supposed to drink in pubs until they're eighteen, so pubs are slightly mysterious . . . therefore cool. So like, obviously, the best way to invest in the future would be to ban the little sods from the church altogether. That way, they wouldn't turn out like me.'

'So the monthly Family Service, with kids doing readings, the quiz . . .'

'Totally crap idea, I always said that. It just makes the Church look needy and pathetic. You have to cultivate the mystery. If you don't bring back the mystery, you're stuffed, Mum.'

It was worrying: increasingly these days the kid was making a disturbing kind of sense.

OK, then. When she brought back the service, she didn't call it Evensong because there *was* no song. No hymns, no psalms. And no sermon, definitely no preaching. It was an experiment with Mystery.

She didn't even call it a service. She didn't wear the kit – no cassock, not even a dog collar after the first time – and she sat on a car cushion on the chancel steps. The heating, for what it was worth, would be on full, and pews were pulled out and angled into a semi-circle haloed by a wooden standard lamp that she'd liberated from the vestry. It was a quiet time, a low-key prelude to the working week. The first time, only four people had turned up, which partly dictated the form. Five weeks later, it was a congregation of around twenty, and growing, although *congregation* was hardly the word.

It would begin with tea and coffee and chat, turning into a discussion of people's problems. Sometimes solutions were arrived at before the villagers went home. Small difficulties sorted: babysitters found, gardeners for old people. Sometimes it would quietly feed notions into the village, and issues would be resolved during the following week.

The church as forum, the church as catalyst. The polish-scented air as balm. How it should be.

And the Mystery.

As early as the third week, more personal issues had started to emerge. The ones you wouldn't hear discussed on the street, certainly not by the people involved: marital problems, anxieties over illness and fears over kids and what they might be getting into. There was a surprising focus to these discussions, and when prayer came into it – as it usually did, in the end – it would happen spontaneously, rising like a ground mist in the nave.

Real prayer . . . and somehow this was a seal of confidentiality. None of the problems raised in the church and distilled into prayer had ever drifted back to Merrily as gossip.

She was elated. It had been *cooking*. What she didn't need at this stage was anything boiling over into myth-making.

*

Jim and Brenda Prosser ran the Eight till Late in the centre of the village. Their daughter, Ann-Marie, who last summer had been painlessly divorced, had moved into the flat over the shop, helping out there at weekends before going off clubbing in Hereford, with her mates. Ann-Marie's illness had been a rumour for some weeks. Pasted-on smiles at the checkout, whispers about *tests*. On a Sunday night two weeks ago, Alice Meek, who had the fish and chip shop in Old Barn Lane, had said, *Brenda won't talk about it, but it don't look good. En't there nothing we can do?*

'Alice,' Brenda said now. 'You know what Alice is like.'

'Calls a spade a bloody ole shovel,' Jim said.

'We met Alice when we were coming back from Dr Kent's house this afternoon, and she seemed to *know*.'

'Only by your face, love,' Jim said with affection.

The kettle began to hiss, and Merrily put tea in the pot. Brenda sat down at last. She was in her early sixties, had lost weight recently – no surprise there – and her bleach-blonde hair was fading back to white. Periodically, a hand trembled. Brenda folded both of them in her lap and stared across the refectory table at Merrily, like she was seeing the vicar in a strange new light.

'Alice told us about the special prayers you had for Ann-Marie.'

'Well, not—' Merrily looked down at the table top. Of course it was special; all prayer should be special.

'Alice said she lost track of time. She said she felt as if everybody there was together. United, you know? And that was also some of the newcomers she didn't know. All united and they were part of something that was . . . *bigger*. Said she'd never known anything like that before. Alice said.'

Emotion had brought up the Welshness in Brenda's voice. The Prossers had moved across from Brecon about fifteen years ago. Merrily felt flushed and uncertain. Happy, of

course – happy for the Prossers and Ann-Marie. It was lumi-
nously wonderful, and she'd been conscious of reaching an
unexpected level of conscious worship, but . . .

'What did Dr Kent say exactly?'

'He phoned for Ann-Marie just after lunch,' Jim said. 'He
admitted he'd known since Friday, but he was afraid to say
in case it was wrong. In case they'd somehow got the wrong
medical records or whatever. He said he didn't think it was
possible the new tests had drawn a blank, couldn't like get
his head around it. So he was trying to get the consultant
on the phone all of yesterday, and it wasn't until this morning,
see, when he managed to reach him at his home. Couldn't
believe it. Neither of them.'

'He definitely confirmed that the scan was . . .'

'Clear. Nothing there. And it *was* hers, no question of
that. No mistake here, Merrily.'

'What did the consultant say about it?'

Jim shrugged. 'You know these fellers.'

'Maybe they . . .' Merrily bit her lip. *Made a mistake the
first time.*

'See, to be frank, Merrily, I've never been what you'd call
a real churchgoer,' Jim said. 'I'm a local shopkeeper, struggling to stay in business. Sometimes I've come because it
seemed to be expected.'

Brenda sat up. 'Jim!'

'No, let me say this. I want to. It's like being a social
drinker. I was a . . . how would you put it?'

'Social worshipper?' Merrily smiled. 'That's perilously
close to martyrdom, Jim.'

'What I'm trying to say . . .' He'd reddened at last. 'Well,
if this isn't a bloody miracle, Merrily, I wouldn't recognize
one, that's all.'

Merrily tried to hold the smile. 'Big word.'

Brenda said quickly, 'Alice said you also prayed for Percy Joyce's arthritis and—'

'Yes, but that—'

'And now he's come off the steroids. You're healing people, Merrily.'

The words echoed once, clearly in her head as the kettle began to scream and shake, and the kitchen lights seemed too bright.

'I . . .' Merrily ground her cigarette into the ashtray, twisting it from side to side. 'Sometimes, God heals people.'

Sometimes. It was a crucial word, because most times people were *not* healed.

Big Jim said gently, 'We understands that. But He do need asking the right way, don't He? What I'm saying, Merrily . . . something happened during that service, to concentrate people's minds on it. Something a bit powerful, sort of thing. It's a new kind of service, and you're a new kind of vicar. Not what we was used to. Alice is telling—'

Everybody, probably.

'Where's Ann-Marie now?'

Brenda smiled. 'In the pub, I expect, with her friends. She'll be coming to thank you, have no doubts about—'

'No . . . look . . .' Merrily stood up. 'I'm really, really happy for her and for you, and it does seem like a miracle. But the body's a wonderful thing, and sometimes . . . I'd just be really glad if you didn't say too much about that aspect of it, for the moment. For the time being. Until—'

Until when, exactly?

'We'll go now,' Jim said.

'You haven't had your tea. I'm sorry . . .'

'We never wanted to embarrass you, Merrily,' Brenda said.

*

Most weeks, Lol would pull the property section out of Prof's *Hereford Times* and toss it on the pile of papers they kept for lighting the stoves.

Wood-burners in a recording studio? Prof had been unsure about this, but the punters liked it. When the sound of a log collapsing into ash had filtered like a sigh into the mix of the final acoustic song that the guitar legend Tom Storey had recorded here last week, Tom had refused to lose it. Tom, who'd left yesterday, was superstitious about these things.

Tonight, Prof would be working in here, tinkering with Tom's music perhaps until dawn. About eight p.m., Lol went out to the wood-shelter and packed a pile of blocks into a big basket, brought the basket into the stable that now housed the studio and bent to build a fire in the second stove.

Sometimes his work here amounted to little more than domestic chores and working on his own material. Prof didn't seem to mind that, but Lol did.

He was crumpling the property pages to take the kindling when he noticed a small photograph of a tiny, tilting house with a white door. He stood up and carried the paper to the light over the mixing desk.

> LEDWARDINE
> **Church Street – exquisite small, terraced house, Grade Two listed, close to the centre of this sought-after village. Beamed living room, kitchen, two bedrooms and bathroom. Open green area and orchards to rear. Must be viewed.**

He stood for a while by the mixing desk, then he tore out the page, folded it and pushed it into a back pocket of his jeans. While he was packing the rest of the property section into the stove and adding twigs, he saw himself walking in through that white door. Draped over the post at the foot of the stairs was an old woollen poncho, then you went through into the low-beamed parlour. You sat down at Lucy's desk in the window overlooking Church Street, with two lamps switched on. You heard a movement, looked over your shoulder and saw Jane Watkins, fifteen, standing in the doorway, and Jane said, desolately, *'I thought she would be here. I really didn't think she'd left us for ever.'*

Lucy Devenish: honorary aunt to Jane, mentor to Lol. Lucy had introduced him to the inspirational seventeenth-century Herefordshire poet, Thomas Traherne, and, indirectly, to Jane's mother, the Rev. Watkins.

Lucy in her poncho, face like an old Red Indian, voice like a duchess: *You have to learn to open up. Let the world flow into you again.*

He could still see Jane standing in the doorway that night at Lucy's – Lucy not yet buried after dying in the road, hit and run. Jane standing in the doorway, confused, and a pink moon hanging outside. Jane talking about her mother: *'She does like you. I can tell. I think, the way things turned out, you probably did the best thing not actually sleeping with her. It will stand you in good stead.'*

Getting to sleep with Merrily had taken more than a year. A year in which Lol had turned away from music, taken a course in psychotherapy and then turned away in disgust from psychotherapy and gone back to the music.

But neither he nor Merrily was all that young any more. They lived over half an hour apart and their lives were very different, but every day when he didn't see her seemed like a wasted day, and there was nothing like the music business for teaching you about passing time.

Lol struck a match and put it to the paper. *Ledwardine.* He'd been living there when they'd first met, but circumstances had moved him away. Now he wanted to go back. He wanted that house and everything it once had promised.

When the Prossers had gone, Merrily lit a cigarette, feeling leaden and ungracious. She was thinking, miserably, about healing.

Thinking about the corrupted Bible Belt evangelism of the former Radnor Valley minister, Father Nick Ellis. About an event called the Big Bible Fest she'd attended with a crowd of other students at theological college, where there'd been speaking in tongues and calls to the disabled to have faith and rise up out of those wheelchairs. And if they didn't rise up then their faith wasn't strong enough. Tough.

She thought about a girl called Heather Redfern – seventeen, Jane's age – who, despite prayers in at least six churches, had died of leukaemia less than a month after leading a twenty-mile sponsored walk around the black and white villages of North Herefordshire to raise money for Macmillan nurses.

And she thought about Ann-Marie Herdman – dizzy, superficial, often seen swaying across the square at one a.m., towing some bloke up to the flat over the Eight till Late. Some bloke who, in the morning, she probably wouldn't even recognize. Ann-Marie: a woman for whom the church gate was just a convenient place to wait for your lift into Hereford.

Healing was like the bloody National Lottery; the good guys rarely hit the jackpot.

Merrily stood up and went, without thinking, into the scullery/office. Because what you did now, you phoned your spiritual director.

Or you *would* do that, if your spiritual director wasn't wrestling with his own crisis in a place far away where no mobile phones were permitted – a primitive monastic community, not in the mid-Wales wilderness but on a concrete estate south of Manchester, where the police would raid flats and find guns, a place Huw Owen described as like an open wound turning septic. More suited to his condition, he said, than bare hills safe and sanitized by wind and rain.

Huw was running hard from his all-too-human emotions. He'd lost a woman, the love of his mid-life, because of a man of unfathomable evil, and the all-too-human part of Huw had sought closure through revenge. And, although – maybe *because* – this man was dead, it hadn't happened; there had been no closure, and Huw was terrified that his faith wasn't sufficient to take him beyond that.

Merrily sat down at the desk, glimpsing a dispiriting image of her own faith as a small, nutlike core inside a protective shell: too small, too shrivelled, to absorb the concept of miracles.

Jane rang from the hotel, just before ten. The same Jane who should have been home by now.

'Erm, I told Gomer I wouldn't need a lift back tonight, OK?'

'I see,' Merrily said.

'Don't be like that. There's no problem about going straight to school from here in the morning. As it happens, I've got the clobber in my case.'

'How prescient of you, flower.'

'It's as well to be prepared, you're always saying that. It looked like snow earlier. It comes down heavily up here, when it starts.'

'Being at least seven miles closer to the Arctic Circle.'

Jane's weekend job had altered the format of both their lives. It was good that she had a job, not so good that it involved overnights on Saturdays, because all they had left, then, was Sunday, Merrily's Working Day. Which left Sunday night, and now that was gone, too.

And it was the fact that Jane was working in a hotel and spending nights there. This was really stupid, but Merrily kept thinking about Donna Furlowe, daughter of the woman Huw Owen had loved. At Jane's age, maybe a little older, Donna had been working at a hotel – holiday job – and had gone missing and been found murdered, possibly one of the Cromwell Street killings. Of course that was in Gloucestershire and this was on the edge of Herefordshire, where it hardened into Wales. It wasn't even a coincidence, just paranoia.

'You all right, Mum?'

'Why do you want to stay there?' It came out sharper than she'd intended. 'Sorry. Do they want you to stay?'

'They could use the extra help, yeah.'

'Mmm.' It was wise, in this kind of situation, not to ask too many questions, to convey the illusion of trust.

'Of course, if you're lonely,' Jane said insouciantly, 'you could always give Lol a ring.'

'Jane—'

'Oh no, it's *Sunday*, isn't it? Mustn't risk having a man seen sneaking into the vicarage . . . on a Sunday. And not leaving until – *wooooh* – Monday.'

Merrily said nothing.

'When are you two going to, like, grow up?' Jane said.

TWO

Game Afoot

'And left her there . . . her lifeblood oozing into the rug.'

Pausing for a moment, lean and elegant in his black suit, he stared right through the faces watching him out of the shadows. The table lamp with the frosted globe put shards of ice into his eyes. 'Oh my God,' a woman whispered.

Jane was thinking, *Grown people*.

Now he was spinning back, sighting down his nose at the man in the wing-backed, brocaded chair. And the man was shifting uncomfortably. And the stiff white cuffs were chafing Jane's wrists.

' . . . And then you crept up to your room and waited until the entire household was silent. What time would that have been? Midnight? A quarter-past? Yes, let us say a quarter-past – twelve-seventeen being the precise time of the full moon . . . which I suspect would appeal to your sense of drama.'

With the log fire down to embers, the globe-shaded oil lamp was the only light in the drawing room, more shiveringly alive than electricity, spraying complex shadows up the oak panels. Jane dropped her resistance. She was part of the whole scam now, anyway.

'Piffle,' said the man in the wing-backed chair.

'Oh, I think not, Major. *I* think that, barely half an hour after the murder, you crept *back* down the stairs and into the

27

study, where you began to overturn chairs and pull out drawers, making as much noise as you possibly could. Finally, with the handle of your stick, you smashed not one, but *two* windows, in swift succession, so that the sound might be mistaken for a single impact.'

'Sir, your imagination is, I would suggest, even more hysterical than your abominable fiddle-playing.'

A thin hand disdainfully flicked away the insult. 'And then you moved silently, up the *back* stairs this time, and immediately re-emerged onto the main landing, dragging on your dressing gown, shouting and spluttering.'

Jane remembered it well. It had been seriously startling. She must have been in bed about twenty minutes and was half asleep when this huge roar went up. *'Who's there? Who's making all that damn noise? What the hell's going on?'*

When she'd grabbed at the switch of the bedside lamp, it hadn't come on. And then, when she got out of bed, she'd found that the ceiling light wouldn't work either. She'd gone to open the door but remembered, just in time: *Never be seen outside your room in your normal clothes, no matter what happens.* Anyhow, her jeans and stuff were in the case under the bed, so she'd thrown on the awful, stiff black dress – Edwardian maid's standard issue – before venturing out into the cold and musty darkness of the upper landing, flicking switches to find that *none* of the electric lights was functioning. Feeling her way to the top of the stairs under this eerie green glow from the smoke alarm, peering down to see most of the guests stumbling onto the main landing which was dim and full of shadows but a little brighter than upstairs because it was lit by – wow, *cool* – an incandescent thimble on a bracket. She'd noticed several of these gas mantles around the place but never imagined that they might actually work. This was like totally disorientating, a time-shift, a sliding century. She recalled a woman saying faintly, '*Is this real?*'

'You roused the entire household, Major.' A raised forefinger. The Major tried to rise but fell back into the wings of the chair. 'But you made *very sure* that you would be the first one to re-enter the study – this sombre room of death where poor Lady Hartland lay cooling in her own congealing blood. And you had to be *the first one to enter.* Is that not so?'

'Fairy-tale nonsense, sir.' But the Major's voice was slurred with guilt. Was he *really* a major? He'd been chatting in the bar an hour or so ago, explaining that he'd been based at Brecon until his retirement. Was that all made up?

The lamplight wavered. Jane felt bemused. It was *working*.

Last night, when they'd all come staggering down, the Major had been standing at the foot of the stairs, his back to the door of the study which all yesterday had been kept locked. '*Oh Lord, something terrible appears to have happened! Please, madam, you'd best not look.*' At this point, the study door had swung ajar behind him and you could see the bare lower legs of the corpse, pale as altar candles, receding into shadow. That had worked, too. *Christ*, Jane had thought, for that one crucial moment.

'So.' The man in black cleared his throat. 'We know *why* you murdered her, and now we know how. There remains only—'

'The question of proof. Of which you have none.' The Major waved a dismissive hand and turned away, gazing towards the long window. Headlamps flashed on it, tongues of creamy light distorting in the rainy panes. It was probably the Cravens, reversing out to go home. *Oh, hell*, Jane thought, *I was supposed to have drawn the curtains.* At least Ben had his back to the window, so he wouldn't have noticed.

Jane put up a hand to her white, frilly headband, making sure it hadn't slid off again.

'Proof, Major?' A faint sneer, a languid hand reaching down by the side of the chair. 'If we're looking for proof—'

'Leave that alone! How dare you, sir!'

'—Then we need hardly look very far.'

The man in black had found a walking stick, ebony, with a brass handle in the shape of a cobra's head. As he weighed it in his hands, you could hear the distant visceral scraping of a solo violin. Should have sounded naff, but it was somehow exactly right, timed to underscore the tension as the stick was proffered to the man in the chair.

'If you please, Major . . . or shall I?'

'I don't know what you're talking about.'

'Then we shall waste no more time!' Snatching back the stick and holding it over the table, next to the oil lamp, so that everyone could see him twist the cobra's head.

'*No!*' The Major sat up. 'That—'

The snake head came off, the hollow shaft of the walking stick was very gently shaken. The man in black was somehow manipulating the light so that everyone's attention was on his hands, and on the stick . . . and on this big red stone that rolled out and lay there glowing on the very edge of the table.

'Hmm. The Fontaine Ruby, I imagine.'

The Major half rose from his chair, as though he was about to make a break for it. Several spontaneous gasps wafted out of the shadows, from people who had spent most of the afternoon searching for this paste ruby – with the walking stick conspicuously propped up in the hallstand the whole time.

The man in black didn't even glance at it. Gems, in themselves, clearly held no big fascination for him; even his interest in the Major was waning now that guilt was proved. They both glanced towards the door, which had opened to reveal this guy bulked out by a huge tweed overcoat. The Major slumped back.

'I think this is all the evidence we require,' the man in black said mildly. 'You may arrest him now, Lestrade.'

Silence. And then the electric lights came up and the applause kicked in: genuine appreciation, a couple of actual cheers. A triumph. You couldn't fault it.

When the lights came fully on, everything seemed duller and shabbier, the country-house drawing room reverting to hotel lounge, the oil lamp dimming into history. And Sherlock Holmes was Ben Foley again, closing his eyes in relief.

Afterwards, when the bar was closed, Jane went down to the kitchen to collect mugs of bedtime hot chocolate to serve to the twelve guests. Earlier, she'd heard Ben saying that twelve was barely enough to make the weekend pay for itself, and they were all too old, and the whole thing was an embarrassment.

The kitchen had flagged floors and high windows and room for a whole bunch of servants, but it was dominated by the new island unit that Ben had assembled from the debris of a bankrupt butcher's shop in Leominster. If most domestic island units were the Isle of Wight this was Australia. Amber, who didn't have any staff to speak of, was on her own, bending over a corner of the unit, adding something herbal and aromatic to the cauldron of hot chocolate. She looked up.

'Is he all right?'

'Basking in adulation.'

'Yes, he's quite good at that,' Amber said. No sarcasm there; Amber didn't do sarcasm.

Last night, all wound-up before the guests came down for dinner, Ben had snarled that yeah, he might have done live theatre before, but that was over twenty years ago, and back then he didn't have to work with school pantomime props and a bunch of crappy amateurs.

'He was brilliant, Amber. Genuine massive applause – well, as massive as you can get from— Anyway, you'd have thought there was a lot more of them, to hear it.'

Amber was wearily rubbing her eyes, shoulder-length ash-blonde hair tinted pink by the halogen lights. She was probably about fifteen years younger than Ben, maybe mid-thirties, but more . . . well, more mature. She was wearing a big pink sweater and an apron with a cartoon cat on it.

'Must've taken for ever to plan,' Jane said. 'Like the gas mantles – I didn't even know they worked.'

Amber looked worried. 'Some kind of bottled gas. I don't like to think of the safety regulations he's broken. Plus messing with the trip switches last night to make sure the normal lights didn't work – I mean, what if one of those old women had fallen down the stairs?'

'Well, they didn't. It was brilliant.' Jane liked Amber moaning to her; you only moaned to people you could trust. 'Oh yeah – good news – only one of the punters correctly identified both the murderer and the motive, so that's just the one bottle of champagne to give away.'

Amber blinked. 'You did phone your mother, didn't you?'

'I did phone my mother. And there wasn't a problem about staying over.'

'Because I'd hate—'

'There was no problem.'

'It's very good of you, Jane,' Amber said. 'The girl we had before wouldn't do Saturday nights. They don't seem to want weekend jobs any more.'

'Jesus, Amber,' Jane said, 'this isn't a *job*.'

A holiday, more like. A regular weekend break, and they gave you money at the end of it. Well, usually.

At first, Jane had thought Amber was a bit like Mum, but now she saw a clear difference. Amber's modesty came out of this essential self-belief; she'd handled the food end of two significant London restaurants fronted by flash gits who treated customers like morons, knowing that she was the reason they could afford the arrogance. Flash gits faded fast, but Amber was never going to be out of work, Ben had remarked, talking about it to guests in the bar, naming names. *'I like to think I rescued her from that little scumbag. Can you bear to watch his crappy TV show?'*

To Ben, virtually everything on the box, including the news and weather, had become crap from the day he finally negotiated his severance deal with BBC Drama. A couple of weeks ago, a Face from *Casualty* or *Eastenders* – someone vaguely familiar from something Jane wouldn't have watched if the alternative was the Open University – had come to stay overnight at the hotel, accompanied by a gorgeous-looking woman who sat propping up her smile while the Face and Ben got rat-arsed and ranted on for hours about the bunch of totally talentless twats who ran the Corporation these days.

'So who *was* the winner, Jane?' Amber started setting out empty mugs on the wooden trolley.

'Oh – guy with white hair? Like Steve Martin without the humour?'

'Dr Kennedy. He's the serious expert. The others are just here for fun. Kennedy's written books on Conan Doyle and Sherlock Holmes. He knows a lot.'

'I thought Ben knew a lot.'

'Ben? All Ben's ever done is produce *The Missing Casebook* for the BBC. You're probably too young—'

'No, I think I saw a couple.'

'I'm sure you're too young to remember the fuss.'

Apparently *The Missing Casebook* had not been adapted from the Conan Doyle stories. It was this semi-serious spoof, supposed to be about what Holmes was *really* doing after everyone thought he'd died at the Reichenbach Falls. The joke being – possibly for copyright reasons – that the central character in *The Missing Casebook* was incognito. He looked like Sherlock Holmes, he spoke like Sherlock Holmes, he played his violin in the night and shot himself up with cocaine, and everyone knew who he was *really*, but he was always called something else, a different name in every episode.

'I don't actually remember that,' Jane admitted.

'The second series was cancelled. The first one didn't go down well, particularly in Holmes circles. The orthodox version's sacrosanct to those people. They want the same stories done over and over again, as if it's history, not fiction. And they don't like people taking the piss.'

'He wasn't taking the piss this weekend, though, was he? OK, the story was invented, but you can't have a murder weekend where everybody already knows who's done it, can you?'

'Murder weekends.' Amber sighed.

'No, but it worked, Amber. I was trying to be cynical, because, you know . . . But it was all beautifully done, given the—'

'Tiny budget,' Amber said.

'I mean, he really dominated it. He *was* Holmes.'

'Gave up acting when he was twenty-six,' Amber said. 'He didn't think he was good enough to be one of the greats. It's the way he is.'

'He needs to be great?'

'He needs to . . . succeed against the odds, I suppose.' Amber dipped a wooden spoon into the chocolate and tasted it. 'Anyway, the most important guest this weekend is Dr Kennedy, because he's the Secretary of The Baker Street League, and we need their conference. They're not the biggest or the oldest of the Holmes societies, but Ben knows a few members already, and obviously it would help for us to be linked with a group like that.'

Jane sniffed at the hot chocolate. You could pass out with longing.

'Amber . . .'

'What?'

'Do you *really* need this Holmes connection to make the hotel work?'

Amber blew out her cheeks, the closest she ever came to scowling. Jane knew that Ben had spotted this place in a copy of *Country Life* at the dentist's, making an impulse call and discovering that it was still on the market after five months. So there was Ben with what seemed like a decent amount of money to invest in a future out of TV . . . Ben who didn't want to go crawling to any more witless tossers who couldn't see further than cops and hospitals. Who didn't want to have to watch any more projects crash after months of hassle. Who wanted something he was *completely in control of*. He kept saying that.

And here it was, in a beautiful, atmospheric and unspoiled area less than half a day from central London. A structurally sound country house – kind of – with the possibility of twenty bedrooms if you developed outbuildings. A house with a history that, although not extensive, included a literary connection of curious significance to Ben Foley. Surely this was some kind of—

'I mean, I know he said it was an *omen* . . .' Jane said.

'Now he's finding out that the concept of total independence is a myth, especially with limited funds, and he's still having to crawl to people like Kennedy. And put on murder weekends, which he claims he does for fun, but which really are all we've got. Which isn't good, is it, Jane?'

'But this Conan Doyle thing . . .' Jane looked around the

vast kitchen, imagining a grandfatherly figure with a heavy moustache waiting politely for his mug of chocolate. The face she saw was very distinct. It was the face from a blown-up photograph framed above the fireplace in the lounge.

'We don't actually *know* if he stayed here regularly – or even once. But rumour and legend have always been enough for Ben. What he doesn't know he'll invent. Life's like television – if it's on the screen it must have happened. And that's enough to build a business image around.'

'Maybe he was just afraid you wouldn't come if you thought he had an agenda.'

'No,' Amber said sadly, 'I always go along with things.' She began to pour the chocolate into a big earthenware jug. 'I just wish it wasn't so . . . *Victorian*. There's something cold and . . . ungiving about Victorian houses. Everything's bigger than it needs to be. Too many passageways.'

'Mmm,' Jane said. Ben had shown her the 'secret passage' under the stairs, where Lady Hartland, played by Natalie Craven, had waited to die.

'Not so bad in the summer, but now I realize I don't like the forestry, and those gnarled old rocks. The way they seem to be watching you. Watching everything crumbling around you, while they've been here for ever.'

'Mmm,' Jane said again, in two minds. As a weird person, she really liked Stanner Rocks, naturally. But this seemed like a good opportunity to bring up the thing that had been bothering her a little. 'Er, while we're on the subject of everything being bigger than it needs to be, my room certainly is.'

'Sorry, Jane?'

'The tower room – I mean it's fantastic to have a room that size, but I feel a bit . . . Like, I'm not used to a room that big, that's all.'

'Oh, we thought—'

'And I keep waking up in the night. Stupid, really. So like, I . . . just wondered if I could have my old room back.'

Jane felt deceitful and a bit ashamed. She'd been switched around twice over the past couple of weekends, as the Foleys continued their winter programme of refurbishing the bedrooms one by one. Amber looked at her thoughtfully.

'Just . . . too big?'

'Stupid, really,' Jane said.

'Well, if you don't like that room, Jane—'

'It's not that I don't *like* it—'

'Then you can move your stuff back to the old one tonight if you like.'

Jane nodded, trying not to show her relief, which was kind of despicable, frankly. 'Thanks, Amber.'

Back in the lounge, Ben helped her serve the chocolate. 'Thanks, sweetheart, you've been terrific.' His hair was wisping out of the Holmes grease-slick, the curls re-forming. He bent down to her ear and whispered, 'Some of these old guys, seeing a little maid around the place in a starchy uniform, it gives them a delicious little *frisson*, you know?'

'I don't do *frissons*,' Jane said primly, and Ben laughed and went to play Holmes again for two elderly ladies, the kind that it was nice to think still existed outside of old Agatha Christie films. A few of the people here were regulars at murder weekends all over the country. There was a network of them now.

The Major came over for his chocolate. 'Terribly sorry, my dear, but I've been assuming you were Ben's daughter.'

'Just paid help . . . Major.' It felt – this was stupid – a little weird talking to a guy who'd just been exposed as having beaten a woman's brains out. It was surprising how the scenario crawled into some area of your mind and lodged there. Maybe something to do with the house. She shook herself. The maid's headband fell off, and she caught it and laughed. 'Are you *really* a major?'

He pushed his tongue into a cheek. He was stocky, sixtyish, and his tufty white moustache looked genuine. 'Frank Sampson, AVAD.'

'Sorry?'

'Arrow Valley Amateur Dramatics.'

Jane grinned. 'Had *me* fooled. Not like this area isn't full of retired soldiers.'

'Except the real ones tend to be ex-Regiment. Younger. Fitter. Not how you imagine them any more.' Frank Sampson nodded towards Ben. 'Fun, though, working with a pro. I'd like to see them make the place work. I remember the first time it was a hotel.'

'Bad?'

'Well, that was back in the sixties, when walking holidays were for the hard-up, so I suppose it was more of a hostel. After that, an old folks' home, then some sort of specialist language school, then an old folks' home *again*. Not for long, though. Elderly people hate to be dumped this far out. They want life around them, not dripping trees.'

'So what was it when Conan Doyle stayed here?'

Frank Sampson shrugged. 'Just a house, presumably. Quite a new one then, obviously. That's a bone of contention, isn't it? That's a can of worms, Clancy.'

Jane smiled. 'I'm Jane. Clancy's gone home.'

'Sorry!' He covered his mouth. 'Can't seem to get anything right tonight. Can't even get away with murder. Don't suppose there's any more of this incredible chocolate, is there? Not getting paid for this, but I'm buggered if I'm passing up the side benefits.'

The last of the logs collapsed in the grate behind them. Jane brought the earthenware jug and topped up Frank's mug. 'How do you mean, can of worms?'

'Weeeeell, you know – did he spend time here or didn't he? *I* don't know. I don't know anyone who does.'

'Why would anybody think he did, then?'

The fake major blinked. 'Well, that—'

'*Friends!*' Ben was in the middle of the room, clapping his hands together for attention. His Edwardian jacket was undone and his hair was flowing back from his shining dome. 'In case I don't see any of you in the morning, just want to say a big thanks. Thanks for being our guinea pigs.'

'Great fun,' one of the Agatha Christie ladies said. 'Hope there'll be more.'

'Well, ah . . . we've certainly learned some things.' Ben sank his hands into his jacket pockets, opening the coat out like wings, the way kids did. 'For instance, quite a few people have said that they'd rather it had started on Friday evening, through Saturday, because they really needed to leave today, to get to work tomorrow. Sorry about that. As you can no doubt guess, we're pretty much amateurs at the hotel game. But – ' he raised a forefinger ' – we learn fast. Ah . . .'

He paused and looked across at the portrait over the fireplace, the blue-tinted blow-up photo of the kind-looking man with neat hair and a weighty moustache and eyes which seemed to be focused, with a glint of mild wonder, on something in the middle distance.

'I know there's still some controversy about whether Sir Arthur spent time here,' Ben said. 'But I *feel* he did. Sometimes, when I walk through these rooms late at night or early in the morning, I like to feel he's perhaps . . . Well, we all know what an ardent spiritualist he was, so let's not get into *that*. I just feel there are mysteries about Sir Arthur which might be solved here. I don't know why I say that, I just . . . sorry . . . babbling.' Ben wiped the air. 'Apologies.'

'No, go on,' a woman said. Not one of the Agathas; this one was elegant, middle-aged, with long near-white hair and half-glasses, and Jane thought she'd come on her own. 'Are we talking about *The Hound of the Baskervilles*? Because I was rather disappointed that none of this came up during the weekend.'

'Ah, well.' Ben looked put-out. 'That deserves more than a single weekend. Can't divulge *all* our secrets in one burst, darling.'

An Agatha chuckled. 'Didn't want to waste it on the likes of us, eh?'

Ben did this camp simper, not denying it. Jane looked at Frank Sampson, the erstwhile murderer. 'Can of worms,' Frank murmured.

Later, in the lobby, with its shabby flock wallpaper and Victorian-looking wall lamps, Jane heard Ben talking to the thin man with bristly white hair. Seemed this guy Kennedy was one of those who would have preferred to leave this morning. He was leaving now, with his bottle of champagne for solving the murder.

'So we'll be hearing from you,' Ben said. 'About your conference?' He was carefully standing with his back to one of the places where the panelling had been poorly patched with stained plywood. Unfortunately, just above his head, an area of unpapered plaster was dark with damp, and he might as well have been pointing at it.

'Well, I . . .' Dr Kennedy hefted his canvas overnight bag. His voice was nasal and tinny, not a lot like Steve Martin. 'I do need to talk to my colleagues on the committee. I'll confirm my decision in writing by the end of the week.'

'Wonderful,' Ben said. 'That's marvellous, Neil.' Not exactly rubbing his hands, but aglow with satisfaction as he followed Dr Kennedy to the main door. Jane moved ahead of them and held it open for Kennedy to pull his bag through after him. Ben and Jane stood under the big brass lamp in the conservatory-porch, its long Gothic windows streaming with rain, watching him run for his car.

'Game's afoot, Jane,' Ben said.

'Sorry?' Oh yeah, Holmes-speak.

'The game is finally *afoot*.' Now he really was rubbing his hands, maybe just being deliberately theatrical.

The piece of carpet that they were standing on was soaked through. Jane hoped Dr Kennedy hadn't walked into one of the pond-size puddles on the terrace or stumbled on the eroded steps down to the car park. There was no sign of him now, anyway. Beyond the car park you could see nothing but darkness, and all you could hear was the rain in the pines.

And then a shot.

Ben was standing in the doorway, and his head twisted sharply as if he'd been hit and was about to go down. It was *that* close. A blast, loud enough to blow a hole in the rain. Jane found that she'd backed away against one of the glass panels. She was momentarily frozen, half expecting Ben to fall, but he straightened up and breathed in hard.

'*Right*.' In the golden light of the brass lamp, his eyes were bright with rage. 'That's it. That's fucking *it*.' He stepped out into the rain and splashed across to the low stone wall at the edge of the terrace.

'Ben?'

Jane followed him out, feeling her frilly headband falling off behind her. The car park was on a slope, bordered by pines and, through their tiered trunks, Jane thought she saw a blurry light moving. A car door slammed, an engine started up, and then the much brighter lights of Dr Kennedy's car shone into her eyes, and she couldn't see anything else.

This was the country. Shots happened. It was supposed to be illegal to let off a shotgun at night, and in weather like this it was seriously crazy. But it happened. It certainly happened *here*. Jane went tense, remembering last night.

'*Bastards!*' Ben climbed up on the wall, Dr Kennedy's car passing below him, the rain thudding on the shoulders of his Edwardian jacket. His fists were clenched, his long face shining with fury. 'Scumbags! Don't think I don't know who you are. I told . . . I *warned* you, not on my land! This time you're fucking *dog meat!*'

Nobody replied. Ben stood for a moment longer, with his head bowed, his back to the Hall, with its mock-mullion windows and its witch's-hat towers. Then he slammed his right fist into his left hand and came down from the wall. His hair was slicked flat to his head again, like Sherlock Holmes's hair. He walked back towards the door, taking hold of Jane's arm.

'When do you ever hear of one being revoked?'

'What?' Jane had been dredging her headband from a puddle.

'Shotgun licence. When do you ever hear of anyone's shotgun licence being revoked for misuse of firearms, Jane? Never. Because all the bloody magistrates are farmers, like this guy Dacre, and they all stand together. Bastards. I said I didn't want them on my land, disturbing my guests, killing my wildlife. I said *no*.'

'Who are they?'

Ben steered Jane back into the porch. 'Some kind of gun club. Think they can safely ignore me because I'll be gone soon, like all the others. When it all goes down, when we're declared bankrupt. It's what this area does, you see, Jane. Ruins you eventually. Nothing creative ever thrives, because it's a wilderness, a hunting ground. That's what it's always been, it's the way they like it. But they don't know me, Jane.'

'They go out shooting in these conditions?' She hadn't heard about his row with the gun club.

'I think they just saw the lights, the cars. It's a gesture – you don't interfere with us, we'll leave you alone. They think

I'm soft. Effete. Some arty bastard from London, here today, gone . . .' Ben pushed his fingers through his wet hair, wiping his shoes on the sodden carpet. '*They* don't bother me, why should they? Half of them aren't even locals. Yobs, Jane. Thick, barbaric yobs. No subtlety.' He suddenly flashed a big grin. 'Where I come from, we have *real* hard bastards.'

'Where's that, exactly?'

'Oh . . . the city. Country people think they're tough because they can pull lambs out of ewes and have to walk further for the bus. Because they can shoot things and watch foxes get torn to bits without feeling pity. Is that tough, Jane? Is that what *you*'d call tough?'

Jane wrinkled her nose. '*I* think hunting's totally psychotic, and a waste of time and money. But then, so do a lot of country people, on the quiet.'

'Do they?' Ben was either surprised or disappointed.

'Nobody really *likes* having their land churned up and their cats killed, like, by mistake. Most of them keep it to themselves, because hunt people can turn nasty when they're threatened. And country people don't like confrontation.'

Ben did, though. Ben was into drama. And although he didn't seem to be aggressive in a violent way, you got the idea that he actually needed to feel a lot of people were against him – needed this to fire him up, maintain his energy level. *Needs to succeed against the odds*, Amber had said.

Which, when you thought about it, made him a dangerous sort of person to be living here on the Border. Like actually *on* the actual Border. Jane had theories about the Border and what it meant, what it really *was*. This excited her most of the time, but now her cheap maid's outfit was blotting up the wet, and she was clammy-cold and starting to shiver and actually wish she was in her apartment back at the vicarage – how wimpish was that?

'You're a smart girl,' Ben said. 'I'm awfully glad we've

got you here. Amber's a hugely talented woman and very . . . very decent. But she needs support. And because we can only afford part-time staff, you and Natalie, you're . . .'

He didn't finish. He smiled and turned away, opening the main door for Jane, who noticed the rain coming into the glass porch through the gaps in the putty.

'They were very close last night,' Jane said.

'Who were?'

'The gun club. There was one shot . . . sounded like it was just outside the window.'

'Really,' Ben said.

THREE

What Consultants Are For

On Thursday morning in the church, the Holy Ghost was
waiting.

Alice Meek, from the chip shop in Old Barn Lane, was
doing the flowers on the altar. Dusty pillars of white light
were dropping from the upper windows and Alice's voice
was carrying like a crow's across the chancel.

'My niece, the one in Solihull, she did one of them Alpha
courses at her church, did I tell you? After the decree nisi
come through, this was – big gap in her life, usual story.'
Alice was smoothing out the altar cloth, replacing the candle
sticks. 'This Alpha, she reckoned it d' creep up on you
somehow. It don't seem like much at first, but near the end
of it she felt the Holy Spirit was in her heart like a big white
bird, and you could feel its wings fluttering. That's what she
said, Vicar. As if this big bird was trying to escape from her
breast and – ' Alice spread her arms wide ' – fill the whole
world with love and healing.'

'That's nice.' Merrily went on dusting the choir stalls,
wondering where this was going. It was the first time she'd
encountered Alice since the Prossers had told her about Ann-
Marie.

'But we prevents it happening, see.' Alice came back to
the chancel steps for the pewter vase that she'd filled with
flowers. 'We don't let it out. It's the way we are. We're all

scared to open up, so we keeps him in his cage, the poor old Holy Spirit. I never quite got that before, see.' She scuttled back and set the pewter vase on the altar. 'Nothing like freesias, is there? You en't thought of having one of them Alpha courses yere, Vicar?'

'Well, it's—'

'No. You're dead right. It's not *necessary*.' Alice came stomping back down the chancel steps, a fierce-faced little woman in a pink nylon overall. 'I yeard as how Jenny Driscoll, God rest her poor soul, used to say there was angelic light around Ledwardine Church, and now I know exac'ly what she meant. It's crept up on all of us, it has. Like me – I only come to your Sunday night service because somebody said there wasn't no hymns. Voice like mine, you don't wanner do no singing if you can help it, do you? Scare the bloody angels off the roof.'

Alice cackled. Was there a new energy about her, or was that imagination? Merrily sat down in one of the choir stalls. As with most parishes nowadays, there hadn't been a choir here for years. Some ministers even liked to condense their congregations into the stalls now. More intimate.

Alice came to sit next to her.

'I'll be honest, Vicar, some of us wasn't too sure about you at first. Bit too nervous in the pulpit. Like you wasn't too certain of what you was trying to say. But it en't all about preaching, is it? And it en't all about singin' the same ole hymns and not hearing none of the words no more. It's the quiet times, ennit? It's the quiet times when things starts to happen.'

'Things?' Merrily grew nervous.

Alice winked, like there was a great secret floating in the dusty air between them. Brenda Prosser's voice seemed to echo in the void: *Alice said she lost track of time. She said she*

felt as if everybody there was together . . . and they were part of
something that was, you know, bigger.

'It's prayer,' Merrily said, 'that's all.'

'Whatever you wanner call it's all right with me,' Alice
said. 'It's like you being the exorcist. We wasn't sure about
that either at first. But when I was talking to Mrs Hitchin,
works in the library at Leominster, she says it's all part of the
same thing.'

'Oh.'

'So anyway,' Alice said, 'I was planning to have a word
with you about my nephew, works at the tyre place in
Hereford.'

Merrily looked at her.

'Asthma,' Alice said.

Later, when the Ledwardine GP, Kent Asprey, phoned about
next year's village marathon, Merrily knew he wanted something else. This was how things were done in the sticks.

She took the call in the scullery-office, sitting at her desk
next to the window overlooking the sodden, grey garden.

'I see from my list that you haven't entered your name,'
Asprey said.

'It's next April, isn't it? Anyway, you wouldn't either, if
you had legs as short as mine.' Merrily lit a cigarette. 'But you
could put me down to be one of the people who pushes
drinks at the runners.'

'Righto,' he said. She could hear him writing.

She waited, looking across the lawn to the ancient apple
orchard which was creeping back into the churchyard so that
the church and the vicarage were enmeshed again, in a skein
of hoary branches. Apple trees were not graceful and not
pretty once the fruit was gone. In the old days, the cider
would have been made and stored by now. The cider would
see the village through the winter. The cider and the church.

But no cider was produced here any more.

'Ann-Marie Herdman,' he said. 'You'll have heard, I suppose?'

'It's remarkable, isn't it?' Merrily began to draw an apple on the sermon pad.

'At least you didn't use the word "miracle".'

'Not one of my very favourite words, Kent.'

'I . . . I know Ann-Marie pretty well . . .'

'I'm sure.' This was the man who, in the cause of preventative medicine, used to lead groups of women from Ledwardine and surrounding villages on fun runs. Until word reached his wife that, for a select few, the serious fun had begun after the run. 'So your position on this would be . . . what?'

'I'd say, let them all keep their illusions. Not often people in my profession get to impart that kind of good news. And if it helps you people fill your churches in these difficult times . . .'

'That's very generous of you, Doctor. We need all the crumbs we can get.'

'Entirely off the record, it *could* be a medical anomaly, but it's my suspicion that there was an error at the hospital with those first tests. Whether it was technical or a mix-up of names is a matter of conjecture, and we'll probably never really know, but—'

'You mean Ann-Marie Herdman never had a tumour.'

'I can't *say* that, obviously.'

'But you must've had a reason to refer her to the consultant in the first place.'

'It's what consultants are *for*, Merrily. To take the heat.'

'Of course.'

'But mistakes do occur. It's inevitable.'

'And yet you told the Prossers you'd done some checks and you couldn't find evidence of any mix-up.'

'Merrily, in these litigious times . . .'

'I see.'

'Anyway,' Asprey said, 'I thought you ought to know. I realize it can be quite embarrassing for someone in your position when people latch on to something like this and blow it up into something it isn't.'

'Yes,' Merrily said. 'That was very thoughtful of you.'

When he hung up, she was looking at the moon over Paul Klee's rooftops in the print opposite the desk. The moon was very faintly blue. She looked down at the sermon pad and saw that under the apple she'd printed the words SMUG and GIT.

At dusk, Merrily went to lock up the church, glancing, on the way out, at the prayer board on which parishioners could write the names of people for whom they'd like prayers to be said.

There were twice as many as usual. One had the final sentence underlined; it said: *THIS IS FOR SUNDAY NIGHT.*

Walking back through the churchyard, an isolated spurt of sleet hit her like grit from under lorry wheels, and she hurried under the lych-gate.

What did you *do* here? What did you do about healing? How did you explain all those times when there was no cure, when the condition worsened? What did you say to them when, after the *quiet times*, after the *unity*, after the *being part of something bigger* . . . what did you say to them when, after all that, God appeared to have let them down badly?

Back in the scullery, with about twenty minutes before Jane's school bus was due on the square, she prodded in the number for Sophie at the Hereford Cathedral gatehouse. Time to make an appointment with Bernie Dunmore.

'Gatehouse.' Male voice.

'*Bishop . . .?*'

'Merrily Watkins, as I live and breathe.' Bernie sniffed. 'Well, with slight difficulty at the moment, seem to be developing a cold. Sophie's just popped across to Fodder to get me some herbal thing which she insists is going to deal with it.'

'Echinacea?'

'What's wrong with Sudafed, I say.'

'It's a drug.'

'And?'

'Bernie,' Merrily said, 'where do we stand on healing?'

'As in . . .?'

'Spiritual.'

'We brought out an extensive report,' the Bishop reminded her. 'It's called *A Time for Healing.*'

'*A Time to Heal.* No, when I say *we*, I mean we, the Diocese. As distinct from we, the Church.'

'Bugger,' said the Bishop. 'Have you *no* pity for a man with a cold? Your department we're talking about here, isn't it? Healing and Deliverance. Remember?'

'Is it, though? My job description says Deliverance. Healing sounds like the C of E spin doctors softening it up. Less bell, book and candle, more touchy-feely caring.'

'You have a specific problem with that?'

'Possibly.'

The Bishop didn't reply. He would know better than to quote St Mark's version of Jesus's parting message, pre-ascension; as well as the Church's healing mission, it appeared to advocate picking up snakes, cause of many deaths in the US Bible Belt.

'All right, I've been doing this slightly experimental Sunday-evening service,' Merrily said. 'Loose, open-ended. I thought it was working. I mean, it brought in some of the villagers who normally wouldn't notice if the steeple fell off.

Even Jane's been a couple of times, when the weekend job allows. So . . . a modest success.'

'What I like to hear.'

'People actually saying they're reaching something deeper in the way of understanding and awareness. And discovering you can actually learn meditation for free. But it wasn't meant to be . . . I mean, it didn't start out as a healing session. We did pray, though, as you would, for a woman who'd been told she had a malignant tumour. A week later she was told that she didn't have a tumour at all.'

'Congratulations,' the Bishop said.

'Don't get me wrong, I couldn't be more delighted—'

'But you can't help wondering if it was an answer to your prayers, in the strictest sense.'

'The local GP rang to point out that it was probably a misdiagnosis. Or a technological problem with the scanner. Or an administrative cock-up, or – at worst – one of those very rare medical anomalies. Now, he could be entirely wrong, or covering something up. And he's massively out-numbered by all those people who would clearly like to think that something did happen . . .'

'Obviously.'

'But . . . Bernie, they've started to bring out their sick. They're recalling lesser ailments prayed for and subsequently eased. This morning I was asked if I'd mind curing someone's asthma, even though he doesn't live in the parish.'

'They believe you're a latent healer?'

'I stress that if it's happening it's not down to me, but I suspect there's a feeling that the Deliverance minister has a hot line. Like the fourth emergency service? The nature of the Sunday-evening service has been . . . misrepresented.'

The Bishop breathed so heavily into the phone that it was like the germs were coming down the line.

'You do have a more *exciting* ministry than most of us, don't you, Merrily?'

'Maybe I'm missing the humour here, Bishop. Young guy who gets acute asthma attacks and whose aunt is afraid that the next time it happens . . .?'

There was a long pause. Down the phone, she could hear the traffic in Broad Street, a door opening and closing, quick footsteps on the stone stairway to the gatehouse offices.

'You know Jeavons is back,' the Bishop said.

'Jeav—? Oh.'

'I mean, if you wanted to talk to someone about this. Someone who actually knows about it, as distinct from a knackered old admin bloke like me. I was only thinking, with Huw Owen being away . . .'

'I've never met Jeavons,' Merrily said.

The Bishop blew his nose. 'You're not the first to raise the question of healing lately. Healing *groups* is the normal approach. I think we all agree it's better to share the burden. It also raises ecumenical possibilities, particularly with the Catholics, and I'm quite drawn to that. Ah . . . hold on one moment . . .'

She heard another voice. She heard the Bishop saying, '*Well*, I *don't know how to work the blessed thing.*' She thought about Catholic priests she knew and how they'd react to the idea of working with a woman.

Bernie came back on the line. 'Sophie goes out for five minutes, place ceases to function. Did I mention Jeavons?'

'He's in Worcestershire, right?'

'He's been abroad. Semi-retired now, of course. Rather prematurely. Few years ago, there was a move to fast-track him into purple – view to Canterbury, one suspects. The little greaseball Blair was keen, for obvious reasons. Red faces all round when Jeavons tosses it back at them and says he'll retire instead. What he wanted, we discover, was his freedom, to pursue his specialist interests, hover over psychic surgeons in Chile.'

'At the Church's expense?'

'Dunno. My information is that he's back in the country and available as a consultant to selected clerics – although I was once told it would be unwise to refer just anybody.'

'Huw talked about him once,' Merrily recalled. 'Only—'

'Because, if anyone's on the edge of a crisis, Jeavons has been known to tip them over.'

'Only, Huw reckoned he was mad,' Merrily said.

Since the days when hundreds of medieval pilgrims had dragged their crippled limbs to the shrine of St Thomas Cantilupe in Hereford Cathedral, the Church had become increasingly uncomfortable about healing. You prayed for sick people, you might even light a candle, and if there was a cure you thanked God. Beyond that, a certain wariness crept in. *Not strictly our thing*.

In which case, what *was* the Church's thing? The way congregations were crashing, it was clear that this was a question not going unasked. While Jane was changing out of her school gear, Merrily dug out the report: *A Time to Heal: A Contribution towards the Ministry of Healing*. In his introduction, George Carey, Archbishop of Canterbury at the time, referred to 'Our Lord's injunction to heal the sick,' and suggested that the report might be studied and reflected upon and considered for action 'as appropriate in dioceses and parishes'.

As appropriate. Merrily smiled.

In relation to parishes, the report recommended that clergy involved in healing should consider combining their resources with those of doctors, community nurses and carers operating according to a 'working theology' of the Ministry of Healing.

Oh, sure. Like Kent Asprey and Lorraine Bonner, the district nurse, who maintained she'd seen too much of life to be anything but an atheist.

The report was sniffy about some healing services. *Lack of preparation, misunderstandings, unjustified claims and emotionalism leading to subsequent disappointment.* It was more supportive of what it called Intercessory Groups, in which a number of 'instructed persons' met regularly to pray for the sick.

Laying-on of hands, by the minister, in the context of a normal service or Eucharist was also accepted, as were Services of Penance, underlining the healing benefits of for-giveness.

Merrily looked up Canon Llewellyn Jeavons in the phone book. There was a Jeavons L.C.D. at Suckley.

Mad, Huw had said, without explanation.

She knew where Suckley was – a rambling hamlet not far over the Herefordshire border and not far at all, in fact, from the Frome Valley where Lol Robinson was still living out of suitcases in the granary at Prof Levin's recording studio.

Merrily sometimes caught a frightening image of herself in twenty years' time. It was in sepia: this small, monklike person in the bottom left-hand corner of the huge old vic-arage, hunched over the desk. Dark. Chilly. Cramped. Very much alone.

She saw it quite often these days. Sometimes it was so detailed, and yet so stark, that it was almost like an engraving.

That night, building a fire of apple logs in the sitting-room inglenook, Jane said, 'You don't make fires like this when I'm not here, do you? Like last weekend, for instance.'

'I was busy.'

'I think you probably didn't come in here even once. I could almost smell the damp.'

'Saturday night, I wrote the sermon. Sunday night, we had the service and then the Prossers came to tell me about Ann-Marie. Wasn't really worth it afterwards.'

The paper and the kindling flared yellow. Jane, on the heathrug in her jeans and an overstretched white sweater, looked like a little girl again. Seventeen now – scary.

'It's just . . .' The kid positioned a small log over a mesh of thorny kindling. 'I like this job. I like Stanner Hall. You get to meet people – different kinds of people. I just don't like to think of you all alone here. Like everywhere dark, except the kitchen and the scullery.'

'I've got the cat. And, of course—'

'Let's keep Him out of this,' Jane snapped. 'The point is, in under two years I'll probably be gone, whether it's university or . . . whatever. But I might be gone for like . . . for good. And you'll be kind of lodged down in that scullery like the last Jelly Baby in the jar, writing your sermons into the empty night.'

Actually, it was going to bed that was the worst time: putting out the bedside light, knowing that the attic apartment directly above you was empty. Thinking of all the empty rooms and all the people who had been and gone. Jane's dad, long gone. *Jane's dad* – that was how she thought of Sean now, as though Jane was the best thing he'd done in his foreshortened, corrupted life.

Biting her lip, she stood over Jane and bent and kneaded the kid's shoulders. 'Two years is still a long time.'

'I used to think that, but it isn't.' Jane looked up at her. 'You'll be nearly forty then. Have you even thought about that?'

'Too old for sex?'

Jane pulled away. 'Stop it.'

'It was a joke. How *are* things at the hotel?'

'Don't change the subject. You're here in this mausoleum,

on your own every weekend, and Lol's twenty miles away with no real home at all, and he can't get near half the time because of *appearances* and the Church and all that hypocritical bollocks. I mean, if you were gay – if you were a lesbian – nobody would—' Jane broke off, blushing, probably remembering a certain misunderstanding.

'*And* there's the question of restarting Lol's career,' Merrily said. 'The album out in March, the chance of a tour . . .'

The kid smiled maliciously. 'And groupies.'

'Do they *have* groupies any more?'

'Just trying to inflame the situation. Groupies and Lol doesn't arise.' Jane looked up again, an apple glow on her face. 'But you have to do something soon. Face it, most people know about you and him now, anyway.'

'Yeah, but cohabiting in the vicarage might just be a step too far. And I don't think he'd want that anyway. Now that he's finding his feet.'

'You're so . . . unimpulsive. You piss me off sometimes.'

'It's what I'm here for,' Merrily said.

Later, just before nine, she left Jane in front of the TV and slipped away to the scullery. On the blue blotter on her desk, next to the sermon pad, was a folded copy of the property section of the *Hereford Times*. Just above the fold, an advert, encircled, said:

> **LEDWARDINE**
> **Church Street – exquisite small, terraced**
> **house, Grade Two listed, close to the centre**
> **of this sought-after village.**

It could be the answer. Tomorrow, she'd call the agent. Tonight, she lifted the phone and tapped in the number of Canon Llewellyn Jeavons.

So he was mad. Maybe she could use some of that.

FOUR

The Room Under the
Witch's-Hat Tower

The pines were matt black against the blood-orange sky when Jane was walking up the hotel drive. Friday, late afternoon, and here it came again – that shivery anticipation, her senses honed as sharp as the air, as the cold tide of night swept in towards the Border.

The Border. It was *right here*. She could actually be standing on it now. The hotel was in England, but the rocks it was named after were in Wales. And here, where the track divided, was where it all coalesced in a burst of sunset.

Letting her school case and her overnight bag slip to the ground, Jane stopped at the fork. The independent working woman, on the Border.

Two witches'-hat towers were prodding up between the ragged pines. Stanner Hall was Victorian Gothic, therefore more lavishly Gothic than the original. And from this distance, at least, it looked like it belonged here, if only as a piece of skyline, on the Border. And the Border, like all borders, was more than just a political division; it was about magic and transformation, a zone out of time where things normally unseen might, for tiny, bright moments, become visible.

Some part of Jane felt this to be true and responded to it. Christianity would be like, *Turn away from the dark . . .*

shun the numinous . . . take no pleasure in the nearness of other spheres. Which was why Jane reckoned that she was always going to be a pagan at the core. OK, maybe she'd mellowed a little towards Mum's faith, but it didn't go far enough. It had no sense of place. *This* was the holy land.

Looking up the left-hand stony track that led to the top of the mysterious Stanner Rocks, she stood for a moment, feeling the night beating in like heavy, downy wings. Then she picked up her bags and took the right-hand path between the gateposts of Stanner Hall, these sculpted stone buttresses against the trespassing woods. Most of a foxhound was preserved on the top of the left-hand post, its muzzle pointing rigidly at the sky as if it was about to begin howling. On the right-hand post only the paws remained. Nothing here was completely intact. The sign at the bottom still said STANNER HALL HOTE.

'*Are we talking about* The Hound of the Baskervilles?' Voices from last Sunday. '*Rather disappointed that none of this came up during the weekend.*'

' *. . . That, ah, probably deserves more than a single week-end.*'

'*Can of worms . . . can of worms . . .*'

Well, she'd read *The Hound of the Baskervilles* years ago when she was quite young. Hadn't liked it much, always managed to avoid the films on TV. At school, when she'd raised the issue, Clancy had said, 'Yeah, I think there's some local connection,' but she didn't seem interested.

Tonight, Jane and Clancy had come off the school bus at the usual junction, at the end of the Kington bypass, but Clancy had gone off down the Gladestry road, to the farm. Clancy said her mum was coming down heavy on the subject of homework – like, it had to be done on Friday night or the kid didn't get out on Saturday. Changing schools so often, she'd fallen behind, and this was her last chance to pull back. So Jane had been seeing more of Clancy's mum than Clancy and now, when she lugged her bags into the courtyard of Stanner Hall, here was Natalie, leaning against the open kitchen door, massaging a mug of coffee.

'Hi, Jane.'

This warm, pithy voice travelling easily across the darkening yard. It was a voice that Jane imagined blokes finding very sexy. Nat, too. She was quite tall and supple, with high pointy breasts inside her black jumper. She had dense, shaggy hair, the colour of dark tobacco, and she was . . . well, very beautiful, in this enviably careless way.

'Clan *has* gone home, Jane?'

'She was certainly heading that way.'

'Hmm,' Nat said doubtfully.

Clancy had shown up for the first time at the beginning of this term. She was only about a year younger than Jane, but actually two years behind her at school – which, not surprisingly, had left her isolated, with no real friends. Jane, who knew what it was like being the new kid, had realized that Clancy's situation must be a whole lot worse, having to take lessons with little children. She'd gone out of her way to talk to Clancy at lunchtimes, and they'd become mates, kind of. Which was what had led, indirectly, to the offer of regular weekend work at the hotel where Clancy's mother was receptionist, barmaid and the person who made this joint seem halfway professional.

Nursing her mug for warmth, Natalie came out into the yard, smiling in a bruised kind of way and raising her eyes to the purpling sky.

'Like the Fall of fucking Troy in there today, Jane.'

The earthy talk was one of Nat's contradictions. Treated her own daughter like a kid and was old-fashioned about stuff like bedtimes and homework and pubs, but she'd address Jane like a real mate, a colleague. Nat had clearly been around, and not only in hotels and restaurants.

'Unexpected guests?' Jane looked over at the car park and saw Jeremy's old Daihatsu 4×4, which Nat must be using, and Ben's MG, and that was all.

'If only,' Nat said.

The letter was crinkly and discoloured, and some of the print had smudged. Amber flattened it out on the baronial island unit, slid it across to Jane and switched on the halogen spotlights.

'I had to dry it on the stove. Ben threw it in the sink on his way out.'

'Oh.' Jane looked at the letter but didn't pick it up. 'It's OK to . . .?'

'Please do,' Amber said. 'Otherwise you'll spend the rest of the night wondering why he's drinking too much and smashing things. Anyway, you're one of us now.'

Jane felt a grateful blush coming on. She picked up the letter. It was printed on what she guessed to be very expensive, fine-quality vellum, and it was brief and kind of shocking.

The Baker Street League

Dear Foley,

As expected, the management committee of The League has confirmed my decision in regard to its annual conference and the Stanner Hall Hotel.

I was mildly diverted to hear of your intention to develop the link between the hotel, Doyle and *The Hound*. However, as the majority of my members firmly reject this theory, they did not feel it would be appropriate

to associate the name of The League with your establishment.

Sincerely,

pp Dr N.P. Kennedy,
Hon. Secretary.

Jane let the letter fall to the island unit. 'PP? And it's not
even signed by anybody. That's like . . . deliberately insulting,
isn't it?'

'No, it's . . . probably just careless.' Amber's doll-like face
was squashed-in with strain, her hair pushed back over her
high forehead.

'Amber, the bastard blatantly led Ben to think you were
going to get the conference. I heard him.'

Natalie pushed the letter away with a forefinger. 'He was
hardly going to say *that* to Ben's face, was he?'

'Yeah, but he . . .' Jane felt personally hurt, remembering
the way that Ben had forced himself to smarm the guy. *That's
terrific, Neil.*

'Perhaps Kennedy had pressures we don't know about,'
Amber said. 'There's nothing we can do, anyway.'

'You did say Ben knew other members of this outfit,
though, didn't you? Maybe he can find out what the real
reason is.'

'That probably *is* the real reason, Jane. They don't believe
the story. They think we're pulling some scam.'

Jane sat down on a wooden stool. 'I don't really understand what that's about – *The Hound of the Baskervilles*.
When I read the book, it was set in Devon.'

'Dartmoor.' Amber leaned over her corner of the island,
elbows on a double oven glove with burn marks on it.

'The Grimpen Mire.' Jane shuddered. In the book, a wild
pony had been sucked to its death in the bog; she'd hated

reading that. She'd probably been about twelve. She'd hated what happened to the hound, too. She might have wept at the time. And, anyway, it was all a con. You were led to believe it was going to be supernatural, and it wasn't. 'So like, is there some suggestion that Conan Doyle wrote it here?'

Amber shook her head. 'Not exactly. The story hangs on the legend of a ghostly hound which is a sign of death for the Baskerville family. So, OK, there *was* a Baskerville family in this area. Long-established, wealthy . . . They had a castle or something at Eardisley, which is only about six miles up the road. And there's a pub called the Baskerville Arms over at Clyro, which is just over the other side of Brilley Mountain.'

'And did they have a ghostly hound?'

'No, but the Vaughan family did. They lived at Hergest Court, which is only a mile or so away from here, across the valley. There was a hound that was supposed to mean death for someone in the family if it was seen. And it has been seen. Apparently. Over the years.'

'To this day?'

Amber shrugged. 'There are no Vaughans left now. Anyway, Conan Doyle is supposed to have been related to either the Baskervilles or the Vaughans – maybe both, I don't remember – and it's believed that he stayed here, in this house, to research the story. Or he heard it while he was staying here. Or something.'

Jane was impressed. If this was true it was well worth all Ben's efforts. 'But why would Conan Doyle switch the story to Devon?'

'We don't know,' Amber said. 'As Kennedy says in his letter, a lot of Holmes enthusiasts reject the Welsh Border theory entirely, because there's also a Devon legend that fits. Maybe Doyle liked the name Baskerville enough to want to use it but didn't want to implicate the actual family, so he set the novel somewhere where there aren't any obvious Baskervilles.'

Jane thought of the stone hounds on the Stanner Hall gateposts. 'Did the Baskervilles have anything to do with this house?'

'Not that we know of. It was built by a family called Chancery. It must have been fairly new at the time the book came out in 1902. But it was built to look historic, so maybe it gave Conan Doyle an idea of what he wanted. I mean, it certainly looks more like the Baskerville Hall he describes in the book than Hergest Court does. Just a farmhouse now.'

'Honey, it's how novelists work,' Natalie said. 'You take a bit of this, bit of that, and muddle it all up so that there are no comebacks.'

Jane recalled something else. 'A woman brought it up at the murder weekend. She wanted Ben to talk about it, but he hinted he was saving it.'

'Well, of course he was,' Amber said. 'He was saving it for the annual conference of The Baker Street League. The plan was that Ben would get The League to endorse the evidence that this place is quite possibly the real Baskerville Hall, and then we'd start publicizing it. And, at the same time, Antony—'

There was a loud clink and a muted splash. Natalie had tossed a soup ladle into one of the sinks. She stood with her hands on her narrow hips, annoyed.

'It's all my fault. If I'd bothered to check out Kennedy on the Net *before* Ben had invited him, we'd all have realized that, as he was born in bloody Tavistock, he might *not* have been an ardent supporter of the theory that *The Hound* had sod-all to do with Devon.'

'How much does all this matter?' Jane asked.

'You can't do *all* his thinking for him, Nat,' Amber said. 'He gets an idea and he's off. Doesn't do his homework. He didn't even know Kennedy had scotched the Herefordshire theory in at least two of his own books.' She turned to Jane. 'Dartmoor gets a lot of Hound-related tourism – Americans, Japanese. It's like King Arthur in Cornwall: they don't exactly want to share it.'

Jane gazed around the vast kitchen. The high windows were full of pine tops and dark purple dusk. It wasn't very warm in here.

'What will you do now?'

Amber shrugged. 'Ben's still desperately trying to get hold of Antony, to put him off for a couple of weeks while he rethinks everything. He won't give up. He can't. We've very little money left, and if we sell up now we sell at a loss.'

'Who's Antony?'

'What?' Amber closed her eyes, opened them and blinked a few times, shaking her head despairingly. 'Sorry. Sorry, Jane, I thought you knew about that. Antony Largo. Old mate of Ben's from Beeb days. Independent producer, documentaries. There's a series that his outfit's putting together for Channel Four, called *Punching the Clock*, about successful people hitting hard times and having to make a new start in mid-life. So Antony approaches Ben, and Ben tells him to stuff it – I mean, he refuses to think of himself as being in mid-life, for a *start*. It's always the beginning for Ben.'

Jane smiled. It was one of the aspects of Ben she most approved of.

'But it started him thinking,' Amber said, 'and he told Antony about his plans to pinch a piece of the Sherlock Holmes tourist trade, and now he's half-sold him on the idea of a separate documentary on all of *that*. Which would have launched the whole thing nationally – brought us a lot of publicity for the hotel and some sort of fee, presumably.'

'Also,' Nat said, 'the crew would have to stay somewhere, so that would tide us over the lean period before Christmas.'

Amber looked doubtful. 'Crews aren't what they used to be. It's usually one person with a Handycam from Boots. And they'd have been doing most of their filming during the conference of The Baker Street League, when we'd be full up anyway. But that . . . obviously doesn't apply any more. We're stuffed.'

She picked up the double oven glove and slid her hands into it and covered her eyes. Jane wasn't sure if this was a comic gesture or concealment of actual tears. She imagined Ben telling Amber about the idyllic country-house hotel he'd found for them: open log fires, big, warm, traditional kitchen where she could work her magic. Cosy and romantic. Amber not realizing then that Ben's idea of romance was a howling in the night and a fiery hound on the moors.

Natalie walked over and put an arm around Amber. The worldly big sister, taller and leaner and more together. 'We can still do *something*. We can rescue something.'

'We need more time, and we haven't got it. Antony's booked in for tonight, Ben can't reach him on his mobile. He could turn up any time.' Amber lowered the oven gloves; her eyes were dry. 'Look at this place. It's like some old workhouse.'

'No, it's cool,' Jane said. 'Really.'

'It's bloody freezing, Jane. I keep on at Ben to check out this damp patch under the stairs, and he avoids it. He thinks burst pipes mystically seal themselves. This makes it four leaks we've had since the autumn. Does that augur well?'

Jane looked up through the window, moving to her right so that one of the ridges of Stanner Rocks came into view. It was a proven scientific fact that Stanner Rocks were strange, because of the Standing Wave that altered the climate, the comparative darkness of the rock itself, holding the heat, and the thin soil where plants grew that you couldn't find any-where else in Britain. Jane felt that, in ancient times, Stanner

Rocks would have been sacred, like some gloomy, miniature form of Ayer's Rock in Australia.

'I mean, until you live in a place like this you never realize what plumbing's about,' Amber wailed. 'There's miles of pipe – *miles*.'

'I mean there's an energy here,' Jane said. 'And it's right on the Border. On the edge.'

'We're all on the edge,' Amber said bitterly.

Ben, however, when he strode into the kitchen, seemed to have recovered – now apparently relishing the adversity, refocused.

'I *think* . . . we'll put Antony in the tower room.'

'You couldn't stop him?' Amber said in dismay.

'I stopped trying.' Ben, in tight black jeans and a white shirt, was swaying like a tightrope walker re-establishing his balance. 'The more I think about it, *we* don't need the bloody Baker Street League. What we have is strong enough.'

'Oh God,' Amber said.

'You don't mind going back to your old room for a couple of nights, do you, Jane?'

'She already has,' Amber said. 'Why do you want to put Antony Largo in the tower room?'

'More of an atmosphere.' Ben smiled at Jane. 'Don't you think?'

Jane must have blushed or something, because Ben smirked and said, 'Nip up and open the windows, Jane, would you, and give the bedding a shake.'

'Right.'

Oh well . . . Up the steps into the lobby, which now merged with the hall. Up the baronial stairs . . .

And when you got to the top of the first flight and turned right, through the fire doors, into the ill-lit passage towards the west, it was clear why this part of the house – although

it probably had the best rooms – had been set aside by the
Foleys as staff quarters.

The problem was, it had been dragged into the 1960s or
1970s and left there. The walls were lined with woodchip,
probably to hide the damp, and it was dim and dusty, a
languid light drifting from a tall, narrow window at the
bottom of the passage. This area of the house needed a lot
of money spending on it. Money they probably thought
they'd have to spare, but now it had gone, on the basics:
keeping the damp out and the heat in. Or trying to.

The first room, convenient for the stairs, was Ben and
Amber's own. What must it have been like when they first
arrived here, and they were the only people sleeping in this
huge house? This was Mum's problem with Ledwardine vicarage magnified about four times. A lot of the time, even
now, Ben and Amber would be alone here during the week.
Most of the part-time staff – cleaners and waiters – came in
daily during the summer, or when there were guests.

'Jane!' The fire doors clicking together. It was Ben.
'Forgot to give you the key.'

He strode ahead of her down the passage, near to the
end, unlocking the last door on the right. Actually, she was
quite glad to have him here with her. Stupid, huh?

Inside the door, there were steps up into the actual tower,
and then another door. When Jane had first started work
here, she'd been flattered and excited to be given the room
under the witch's-hat tower. OK, it was big, cold, needed
redecorating, but it was, like, you know . . . *the room under
the witch's-hat tower*.

Ben put on the light. The room had gloomy maroon flock
wallpaper, pretty old, and less than half as much furniture as
a space this size needed to look vaguely comfortable – the
three-quarter divan, the wooden stool serving as a bedside
table, the mahogany wardrobe with the cracked mirror.

The aim, apparently, was to create an en-suite bathroom at one end, and this was actually essential before you could legitimately charge anyone for spending a night here and experiencing those incredible views across Hergest Ridge into Wales.

With the light on, all you could see through the triple windows now was a thin slash of electric mauve low in the sky, like the light under a door. Ben stood in the middle of the room, rubbing his hands.

'Couldn't take it, then, Jane?'

'Sorry?'

'You wanted out.'

'Well, you know . . . look at it. It's like sleeping in . . . in somewhere too big.'

'That's all?'

'All?'

'No other reason?'

'Should there be?' Sod this; she was giving nothing away – she was going to make him say it.

Ben leaned over his folded arms, rocking slightly. 'So you had a perfectly untroubled night's sleep.'

'Don't people usually?'

'One of the builders – when we were having the partition wall taken down, between the hall and lobby – he stayed in here, and he didn't want to spend a second night.'

'Oh?'

'He thought it was haunted.'

'What happened?'

'Oh . . . noises, he reckoned. Breathing. And he said he thought he saw a woman's shape outlined against the window. Next morning, he was not a happy man. Said he thought we'd set him up.'

Jane struggled to bring up a smile. 'Did you set *me* up?'

'I thought . . . well, you're quite interested in this sort of thing, aren't you? Weird stuff.'

'So-so. Ghosts are a bit . . . I mean, they're usually just imprints, aren't they? Emotional responses trapped in the atmosphere. Nothing to worry about.' She was furious – *the bastard*. 'I mean, I wish you'd *told* me . . .'

'You'd have been expecting something then. Pointless exercise. So you wouldn't mind moving back sometime, if necessary?'

'Look, Ben, I wouldn't mind spending a night in a sleeping bag on a station platform, but I'd rather have an ordinary-sized room, thanks.'

Ben grinned. 'Ah, Jane.'

'What?'

'I should've realized the most important thing for you would be retaining your cool.'

'Look, my mother's—'

He lifted an eyebrow. Did he know? She *thought* not.

'My mother's a vicar. They're not bothered by this sort of . . . you know.'

'Right,' Ben said.

That was close. She didn't want Mum involved in anything here. This was her *separate* thing.

'So you're going to try this guy, erm . . . in here.'

'Antony Largo. If you think *you're* cool . . .'

'I don't!' Jane said, smarting, going to turn down the bed clothes.

Ben smiled and shook his head and wandered out.

Left alone, Jane shook out the duvet, remembering how, when she'd come up here to dump her case that first night last weekend, and then gone down to get something to eat, she'd returned at bedtime to find the duvet had been roughly thrown back, as if someone had started to make the bed and then abandoned it.

That could've been Ben, couldn't it? Setting her up.

Otherwise, just an imprint. Just an emotional response trapped in the atmosphere.

Jane sorted the bed and didn't hang around.

FIVE

Drink Problem

They'd moved the bed so that it faced the window and the lights of West Malvern. From this position, on a dark night, it looked as though the lights were away in the sky, big stars. And you could feel safe, for a while.

Lol said thoughtfully, 'Does this mean you get your own cult?'

Merrily sat up. The lights of West Malvern were now quite clearly just tall, narrow buildings on a hill.

'All the lanes around Ledwardine full of crutches and sticks abandoned by the roadsides,' Lol said.

'You think this is funny, don't you?'

And then she started to laugh, and it was one of those laughs that you could feel in your toes and the tips of your fingers and the pit of your stomach. Therapeutic, probably – a healing laugh. *Oh God*. Not two hours ago, she'd fed Ethel, the cat, left a second cat-meal in the timer bowl for the morning and then driven quietly away. Driven over to the granary at Prof Levin's recording studio in the Frome Valley, *for the healing* – Van Morrison sang that. Such an easy, guiltless word.

The granary was a two-room tower house reached by exterior stone steps. Lol's temporary home. Romantic. The trysting place.

He was watching Merrily, an elbow propped on the pillow to lean on. He had his little round brass-rimmed glasses on.

'Sorry. The last time we talked about this, you were a bit nervous, but it didn't seem like anything you couldn't handle.' He sat up beside her. 'What happened?'

Where to start? She told him about Alice Meek and her nephew. And about a letter this morning from a woman in Hereford whose grandchild had cerebral palsy. Nobody she knew. The letter concluding: *I said to my husband that the doctors were hopeless, so we ought to give the Church a last chance.*

'Last chance?' Lol said. 'Save my child or else?'

'Show us some action, or you're finished. And the point is, they *can* finish us. It's like if you do a gig and only two people turn up . . . no more gigs. And gigs are what the Church is about. Hence Alpha, all the dynamic, youth-oriented stuff. A good gig. You gotta do a good gig.'

'But isn't that what you're doing on Sunday nights?'

'Well, *I* thought so. Only it wasn't meant to be a *healing* gig. It was about, I dunno, helping people develop an inner life? But you discover that most people don't want an inner life. They just want a good outer life, and you need to be fit and healthy for that, and if the Church can take away your ailments, hey, that's cool. Magic. Like, if you look at the medieval Church, all those pilgrimages to the holy shrines with sick relatives on stretchers, hundreds of amazing cures attributed to St Thomas of Hereford. The Church works magic, so the Church becomes rich and influential.'

'You're still identifying more with Celtic hermits in caves?'

'Maybe they were even worse. Nothing to be responsible for.' Merrily's head sank down into the pillow. 'Healing's about taking responsibility. How can you take responsibility for something that—?'

'That you can't totally believe is going to happen?'

'God help me.'

'What about this bloke?'

'It *can* happen.' She rolled away. 'I mean, it *can*.' She was sweating. 'Jesus, am I ever going to be big enough for this job?'

'What's his name?'

'Canon Jeavons. Llewellyn Jeavons. Llewellyn with two Ls, Canon with two Ns.'

'As in loose?'

'That's what he said on the phone. He jokes around a lot.'

'*He* doesn't have a problem with it, then.'

'Evidently not.' She turned back to face Lol. 'But then he's a bloke.'

'Crass and insensitive?'

'Confident of his tradition.'

Lol said, 'What's basically wrong with this idea of a healing *group*? Responsibility shared with Catholics and Methodists and . . . whoever.'

'Pentecostalists?'

Lol sighed. 'If you must.' His parents had been out on that fevered frontier, accusing him of amplifying the Devil's music, then swapping his picture on the mantelpiece for one of Jesus Christ. This had been one of the principal milestones on the road to Victoria Ward and the syringe-wielding Dr Gascoigne, immortalized in the creepy, cathartic 'Heavy Medication Day', on the new album.

'It's probably the best solution,' Merrily said. 'But it's got to be *more* than healing. I don't want to run an all-singing, all-dancing medicine show.'

'Sometimes healing's a by-product. Like when you're in love, you feel healthier.'

'That's a good point. Holistic.'

She felt better. More complete. It should always be like

this. Yesterday, she'd thought it could be; she hadn't told him why, and there didn't seem much point now.

However, later, lying spooned on the rim of sleep, she heard Lol's voice: hesitant, feeling his breath warm on her ear in the darkness.

'There's a house. In Ledwardine.'

A hollow moment.

'For sale.' Lol said.

'Oh.'

'A small, terraced house in Church Street. Did you know?'

'Lucy's house,' she said. 'No, I didn't know, not until . . . it was in yesterday's *Hereford Times.*'

'And the week before's. I found it while I was making a fire with the paper. It kind of leapt up at me.'

'I only saw it yesterday. You'd think someone would have . . .'

But why should anyone have told *her* about it? For the past year, it had just been a weekend cottage for two solicitors from Luton. They never came to church; she'd met them, once, briefly. It was a small investment; they didn't care whose house it had been, and because they weren't there during the week no estate agent's sign had gone up.

'I'm never going to be a star,' Lol said, 'but it looks like I might make a living out of it for a while. Enough to cobble together a deposit. If I do the tour and the album sells a few. Can't stay here indefinitely, Prof needs the space. Every time somebody comes in to record, I'm back in the loft over the studio. It's not really convenient for anybody.'

'Did you ring them up about it – the agents?'

'I thought I'd better talk to you first.'

Lol was rebuilding foundations. He'd faced an audience again after many years, some of them spent on psychiatric wards. Circumstances had meant she hadn't been there for him when the unforgiving lights came up; she never again wanted him to feel alone.

'Lol . . .' Her throat was dry. 'It's gone. It's sold.'

'The house?'

'I'm so sorry. I rang the agents this morning.'

A cloudy silence. Across the room, the lights of Malvern blurred, and she realized that her eyes had filled with tears.

Lol said, '*You* rang the agents?'

'Well, I . . . It just seemed like the answer to the problem. Separate houses, just two minutes' walk away. I thought it must be meant. I thought how delighted Lucy Devenish would have been to have you living there. And I thought that if you couldn't raise the deposit, maybe we could somehow do it jointly.'

'You'd do that?'

'Of *course*.'

Lol expelled a long breath and put both his arms around her.

Christ. She closed her eyes; the last thing she wanted was for him to feel grateful.

'But it's gone,' she said.

Gone. In the paper for a whole week, and we never saw it. And then we both did, too late. Like it wasn't meant to happen at all, and the point was being underlined for us.

'It's become a very desirable place, Ledwardine,' Merrily said. She shivered slightly, unaccountably, in his arms. A goose walking over her grave.

For a time – just around the time he was realizing he wasn't never going to make it as a rock star, or even out of farming – Danny Thomas had been into some serious drinking. Never quite an alky, mind, but his name was written in big, dripping letters on the walls of half a dozen pubs in Kington and the Radnor Valley.

It ended when he got banned for a year. Greta wasn't up for ferrying him to and from the half-dozen pubs, so that was it: Danny stayed home. Cheaper than the Betty Ford clinic, and the music was better.

And it was during this period of near-abstinence that he'd come to realize that what he needed more than the booze was crowds sometimes – loud, mindless crowds. So when he'd got his licence back he'd rationed himself to two nights a week and made sure he didn't go out until half an hour before closing time, when the pubs was packed and so many folks was pissed it was almost contagious.

Which was how come Danny missed all the action tonight, down at The Eagle in New Radnor, when Sebbie Three Farms had to be escorted to his Range Rover.

They was all still talking about it when Danny arrived at twenty past ten. All familiar faces in here tonight, from Gwilym Bufton, the feed dealer, ole Joe Cadwallader, from Harpton, young Robin Thorogood, the American from Old Hindwell, with his missus and his walking stick.

'Moves like lightning, has him up against the wall, both hands round his neck, knee in his crotch,' Gwilym said. 'Never seen Sebbie move as fast – not after seven Scotches, anyway.'

'So who *was* this?' Danny asked, fetching his beer over. 'Who was Sebbie having a go at?'

'Tommy Francis, Felinfawr.' Gwilym shaking his head in disbelief. '*Tommy Francis!* Been mates since Tommy had the hunt kennels. Only feller yereabouts dares take the piss out of Sebbie. Went too far tonight, mind. Oh hell, aye.'

'Thought he was gonner kill him,' Jed Begley said. Jed, who built scrambling bikes the other side of Evenjobb, did a fair impression of Sebbie. ' "*Whadja mean by that, hey? Whadja mean?*" '

'But what did he say?' Danny asked him. 'What did *Tommy* say?'

'All he said—' Gwilym looked round for support. 'All he said was, "Must be frustratin' for you, seein' that boy comin' home to this tasty piece, thinkin' what's he got that I en't?" That right?'

'Close,' Robin Thorogood said. 'Surprised the hell out of me, way the guy reacted.'

'It's about ground, it is,' Gwilym said. 'Always comes back to ground round yere. Sebbie won't never be happy till he's lord of all he surveys, and he can't survey all his ground from any direction without he closes one eye to block out The Nant.'

'And who in his right mind's gonner close an eye, woman like that around,' Jed Begley said, and people laughed.

Not Danny, though. He'd last seen Jeremy and this Natalie here at The Eagle, when he and his new partner, Gomer, had dropped in to grab some lunch, week or so back. This Natalie with a half of lager, Jeremy with his usual limeade – and this unmistakable stiff quietness around them. Well, Danny'd been in that situation himself enough times, him and Gret. But this kind of atmosphere so early in a courting boded no particular good. Jeremy's face, for the first time ever, had seemed lined and creased and there was a brightness in his eyes that was like harsh sunshine in a leaden sky.

'Been bloody strange lately, mind,' Jed Begley went on. 'Look at them gun-boys. Did Sebbie hire them boys, or en't he?'

Danny had heard of this: shooters on the prowl. 'Welshies, ennit?'

'South Wales, aye. Hired to shoot foxes.'

'Do that make sense?' Danny said. 'Sebbie's the flamin' hunt.'

'Barry Roberts at the Arrow Valley Gun Club, he don't

get it neither,' Jed Begley said. 'And he en't happy. 'Sides, you seen more foxes than normal lately? I en't. No, see, what you got with Dacre is a drink problem. Plus, he's mad.'

'Got his own agenda, and he plays his cards close,' Gwilym said. 'Always has done. Danny knows.'

Danny nodded, said nothing. Sebbie Dacre, Sebbie Three Farms: magistrate, master of the hunt, robber baron of the Marches, with this fancy but phoney Norman coat of arms over his porch and his customized Range Rover. What passed for gentry these days – an apology for it, in Danny's view, but Sebbie was influential, supported the local shops and the pubs and the feed dealers, and he employed local labour – well, *normally* he did.

Sebbie Dacre and Jeremy Berrows had lived side by side all Jeremy's life, with no socializing but no real trouble . . . although if you stood on any one of Jeremy's boundaries you could feel Sebbie glowering like storm clouds massing. This was because Sebbie's ole man, having bought Emrys Morgan's farm, had put in a good bid for The Nant that was wedged between Emrys's farm and the Dacre estate, but the owners – Sebbie's own relations – had sold it to the Berrowses instead, for no good reason except that they *liked* the Berrowses. Which was no reason at all, in Sebbie's view.

'En't been the same since he got divorced,' Jed said. 'What's that – ten years now? Not so much losin' the wife and kid as what her cost him, plus the fees for Big Weale. Which is why he don't let women get closer than a quick bang, n' more. And here's Jeremy Berrows and this totally spectac'lar woman, delivered to his doorstep.' Jed going back into Sebbie-speak. ' "*What's this, hey? What's this about?*" Should've seen him drive off, Danny, when we finally got him in his motor. Hunches over the wheel, crunching his bloody gears. You wouldn't wanner be on the same road.'

'Like his nan,' ole Joe Cadwallader said suddenly, in his high voice.

Gwilym bent down to him. 'Wassat, Joe?'

'His nan. You're all too bloody young, that's the trouble. His nan, her used to go to the pub in Gladestry 'fore the war, this was. Idea of a woman goin' in a pub on her own, them days . . . unheard of. Idea of a woman drinkin' pints . . . *well!* Idea of a woman goin' to the pub, havin' six pints then gettin' behind the wheel of a big ole car . . .'

'Jeez,' Robin Thorogood said. 'She never kill anybody?'

Ole Joe Cadwallader didn't reply because Robin Thorogood was from Off. He just looked around – big smile, gaping mouth like an abandoned quarry.

'Whoop, whoop,' he said, and then he finished his Guinness.

The discussion died then, people drifting away. Last orders had been and gone. Danny drifted to the door and was sure he heard ole Joe Cadwallader, still sitting there behind him, going very quietly, like a whistling wind, *'Whoop, whoop.'*

Somewhere in the middle of the night, the wind came in from Wales and rattled the eaves and made the pines shiver.

Jane rolled out of bed, wrapped herself in her fleece and went to the window. Amber was right, it was freezing here, and it wasn't even December yet. But that was OK; she wasn't a guest, she wasn't expected to be warm.

She'd spent two hours helping Amber finish redecorating another bedroom. Tarting the place up, Amber had said desperately, in case they ever needed to accommodate a conference, ho, ho. Well, it was more fun than cleaning lavatories and changing bedding, and Jane was starting to take the injustice of this situation personally now. These were good people who worked hard, even if Ben *was* inclined to mess people around like he was still working in TV.

In a way, she was drawn to his philosophy. *Life's like television – if it's on the screen it must have happened.* Well, why not? It was a way of actually making things happen. Or like *amending reality.* Amber had talked about it in a disparaging way, as though she didn't understand why it was so intoxicating.

Jane understood. She'd been going out with Eirion for nearly a year now, and Eirion was obsessed with getting into the visual media. And she herself . . . well, only another year at school after this one. Decisions had to be made.

Through the window – there was a crack in the pane and a thin draught oozing through it – she could see a vague, orangey moon, and the clouds were sliding across it like they were on fast-forward.

This little room wasn't quite an attic, and there were much better views from inside the witch's-hat tower, but it was high enough to overlook some of the forestry, and you could see across to the long plateau of Hergest Ridge and the sombre conifers under the moon. And down to the Celtic Border, this seam in the earth, the secret snake which sometimes awoke and writhed. She experienced that familiar longing to *feel* the Border and all it represented: points of transition, cultures in collision.

But not from the tower room, thank you.

There was something about that room that was essentially mind-*shrinking.* Unpleasant, basically. Haunted rooms were fascinating, but not on your own. If Eirion was here – the irresistible smile, the allegedly puppy-fat spare tyre – well, that would be a whole different ball game. That could've been . . . almost fun.

Only she hadn't seen him in a fortnight. And in a couple of weeks' time, when they should be getting together for the Christmas holidays – intimate hours in candlelit corners – he would instead be on a plane with his wealthy Welsh family, bound for St Moritz or one of those other cheesy, overpriced, overcrowded playgrounds for bored tossers. It had been arranged months ago, before she had this job, and she *could* have gone with them – OK, so her mother was only a vicar on a pittance but they could have *worked something out*.

Sure they could. Could have applied for a Lottery grant. Jane felt resentful and unsettled.

A tiny light was moving somewhere below the ridge. A white light, bobbing, as if someone was carrying it. Perhaps the shooters again. The shooters who Ben had ordered off his land. Men with guns at night: bad news.

Or maybe just Jeremy. Clancy said Jeremy would sometimes creep out in the night to check on his stock. Jeremy was married to his farm, Clancy had said, which didn't hold out much hope for her mother. And Jane had thought, *Huh?* – wondering how Clancy managed to see it that way around. When you saw Natalie, this cool, careless beauty, with Jeremy, this stocky, hesitant little farmer with limited communication skills and hair like the fluff you found under the bed, you were like, *What?* However this unlikely liaison had come about, Jeremy must feel like it was his birthday every day it lasted.

The bobbing light went out, or it disappeared into the forestry or something. Shedding her fleece, Jane went back to her single bed, wishing Eirion was here. Like *here, now.* The ironic thing was that Eirion had admitted he'd rather be coming here, talking to Ben, meeting some of the telly people – not so much the stars as the producers – who, according to Ben, were likely to drop in over the festive season. Like, this documentary guy, for instance, Largo. Eirion could talk their language; he'd done work experience at HTV Wales – other kids got to hang around behind the counter in the NatWest bank, Eirion spent a fortnight with a documentary team.

Family connections, Daddy's directorships.

A distant gunshot had her springing back from the bed, back to the window.

Nothing. No lights.

They were very close last night, she'd said to Ben last Sunday when they'd come in from the rain and he'd been raging about the gun club.

Yeah. So close, one of them was right inside her head. She'd awoken in the tower room – must have been about three in the morning – with this single colossal angry bang deep inside her head . . . this swelling, echoing explosion that awoke her instantly, absolutely cold with fear, immediately thinking – the way you always thought at three in the morning – of a brain tumour or something, and she'd felt just totally . . . sick. Nauseous, headachy and – considering the size of that room – so horribly claustrophobic that she'd rushed to open the window, sliding her head under the sash into the freezing night.

There. It was out. She'd relived it.

And it was, of course, probably something for Mum.

And Mum was the reason she'd said nothing. This was what she did *separate* from Mum. The Independent Working Woman on the Border did not go crying to her mum.

Jane wrapped herself in the duvet and lay on her back with her eyes wide open to the grey window. It was crap when something awoke you in the night. You wanted to be alive to the magic in life, but all you could see was the injustice of everything, and the fragility and the darkness beyond the glass.

SIX

Beastie

The breakfast table was a battleground, and Ben was on his knees.

When Jane came in with the extra toast that nobody had asked for, Antony Largo, the independent producer, was saying. 'No, no, that is a wee bit unfair, pal, I certainly wouldnae use the word *shite*.'

Largo must have got in very late last night. He didn't look like he'd had much sleep – *that room?* – and he wasn't eating much of the food that Jane was putting out for him and Ben. Breakfast was good for eavesdropping because you could make frequent trips to and from the kitchen with fruit juice and toast and coffee, and you could hang around a lot in the doorway.

Ben was in his jogging gear, hanging back in his chair, probably thinking he was looking fit and relaxed and glowing. In fact, he looked nervous, and he was laughing too much. Jane was wincing inside for him.

The dining room at Stanner Hall was long and chilly, its end wall encrusted with a chipped and faded coat-of-arms over the fireplace where unlit logs were piled into a dog-grate. Opposite was this church-size Gothic window, which still had some stained glass in veins of cold blue and blood red. The two men were sitting under the window, next to a flaking grey concertina radiator that made more noise than heat.

'OK,' Antony Largo said, 'we're mates, we go back, I can think aloud with you.' He gave Ben this level stare, amusement in his eyes. 'You tell me: where's the contemporary dynamic? Where's the *now* drama coming from?'

Bloodied sunlight flared on Ben's forehead. He'd have done his usual run, down the drive in the early mist, up through the forestry and back into the gardens. Working up an excuse for the sweat.

'Actors,' Ben said.

Antony Largo studied the toast. The set of his shoulders said *give me strength*. He said patiently, 'We talked about that. We said we could ship over a few famous faces from your illustrious past, old friends sampling the accommodation. That is no' a difficulty.'

'That's *not*—' Ben picked up the silver pepper-pot, and Jane thought for a moment that he was going to whizz it at Largo's head, but he just brought it down again on the tablecloth to emphasize a point. 'That's not what I meant. If we have one fairly prominent actor playing Doyle, this would be the only speaking part. All the rest – Vaughan, Ellen – would be shadowy figures, half seen . . . in black and white or sepia, so that's—'

'Yeah, yeah, it'd be entirely workmanlike, and perfectly acceptable at seven p.m. on Channel Five. This is peak-hour Channel 4 and requires viscera. Sorry, pal, it still leaves me half a dozen good thrusts short of a decent climax.' Antony Largo looked up at Jane and winked. 'My apologies, hen.'

Jane grinned. Antony Largo leaned back and poured himself some coffee. With a name like that, you expected Armani and suave; what you got were faded old denims and this honed Glasgow scepticism. He was about thirty-five, and wiry, with oiled black hair. He had one ear-stud and a hard, blue-grey stubble. He looked like one of those guys who stayed fit without jogging and never put on weight – an honorary life member of the gymnasium of the street.

'Antony.' Ben laughed again, his anxiety lines deepening. 'Why do you always, *always* start off by talking everything down?'

'This is not *tactics*, pal.' Antony leaned forward, shaking his head slowly. 'Way back, when there was advertising coming out the networks' ears, money falling from the sky, we just fenced around a bit, for appearances' sake. But that was then, this is now – Independent TV drama belly-up and barely twitching.'

'Yes, but drama-*documentary*—'

' . . . Is the new drama, yeah. Doco is the new drama. But a doco with no contemporary propulsion, no plot line? OK. See it from my angle. I walk in there and I go, This is about where the Sherlock Holmes guy got his idea for *The Hound of the Baskervilles*, but hey, it's *not what you think*. And they're going, Why would we think anything? Why would we give a fart?'

'Because . . .' Ben looked up and saw Jane, who realized she must be standing there, blatantly listening, maybe with her head on one side and her mouth slightly open. She turned away and started rearranging things on her tray. 'Thank you very much, Jane,' Ben said, meaning *Piss off*. His laughter had gone tepid.

'Sorry.' Jane gave him an uncomfortable smile and slalomed away between tables that didn't match. At one time, there would have been a single banqueting job down the middle of the room; now the small separate tables looked mean and utility, kind of cafeteria. Symptomatic of what was wrong with this place.

She didn't hear Ben explaining to Antony how he thought

the TV people could be made to care. Which would have been interesting.

Passing the foot of the main stairs, Jane could hear the bagpipe wheeze of Amber vacuuming up there – staying well out of it. Natalie was bustling in from the lobby, long legs in tight black jeans, red leather coat over her arm.

'That the TV guy's car, Jane? The old Lexus?'

'Probably.' Jane glanced over her shoulder. 'Ben's struggling. I don't think he's even got round to telling the guy there's not going to be a Holmes conference.'

'Oh.'

'Essentially, they're talking at cross purposes.' Jane put down her tray on the second step; the upstairs vacuuming droned on, suggesting it was OK to talk. She brought her voice down. 'Ben's flogging his Hound line and this Largo's trying to convey that he's only interested in Ben's struggle to revive Stanner.'

When she'd first gone in, with the fruit juice, Ben had been saying how well they were doing. He said he'd altered some bookings to keep the hotel empty so he'd have time to show Largo around. The guy would have had to be blind to fall for that. Where was all the staff, for instance?

'The hotel trade looks like a pushover till you're in it,' Natalie said soberly. 'I'll be surprised if they can afford to heat this place through the winter.'

'It's *that* bad?'

Natalie waggled her fingers, suggesting borderline wonky. 'When you're full up in summer it feels like the escalator's never going to stop. In winter, the outgoings mount up. They've got three women in Kington on standby for that conference who won't be happy to stand by in the future.'

Ben ought to listen more to Nat; she had serious qualifications in catering and hotel management. Clancy said her mother had been running a big hotel at Looe, in Cornwall, before suddenly resigning (after a relationship with a man crashed). Then there'd been another admin job, at a motel near Slough, but Clancy had hated the school there and they'd moved on again. When the summer holidays came round, Nat had bought this old camper van and they'd just set off, looking for somewhere that felt right. Being gypsies, Clancy said.

Nat shifted her leather coat from one arm to the other. 'So this guy's not interested in *The Hound* at all?'

'Only as one of Ben's wild schemes to attract trade, in this *Punching the Clock* series. And that would depend on having famous faces – actors, people like that – come to stay. Like out of pity; that's how it'll look, won't it?'

'Humiliation's big,' Nat said. 'We love to see people going face-down on the concrete. Especially arrogant bastards from glamour jobs.'

Jane nodded morosely, seeing it all now, like she was viewing the rushes – meaningful cutaway shots of damp patches and peeling flock wallpaper; Stanner Hall looking half-derelict under wintry skies; Ben striding around like some manic Basil Fawlty figure. She'd neither seen nor heard anything of Antony Largo until this weekend and, call her psychic, but she guessed that shafting his old mate wouldn't leave him feeling over-gutted.

The vacuum cleaner cut out. Jane glanced up the stairs, which had a new red carpet – an important buy, according to Ben: make the punters feel special going up to their rooms.

'She shouldn't be doing that. *I* should be doing it.'

Nat eyed the tray. 'She got you to serve breakfast instead, because she wants to stay in the background. Bloody shame, Jane. A class chef.'

And you're an experienced hotel manager, Jane thought. *Yet here you both are.* But she didn't say anything about that because Ben and Antony Largo had emerged from the dining room, Largo saying, ' . . . Oh, right down the shitter, ma friend, no question there. I'm no' saying you didn't get out at the right *time*, I just think there might've been better ways of—'

He stopped. He'd seen Natalie, and he was looking at her the way male guests tended to. She was standing in a diagonal funnel of sun from the long window on the first landing. She looked typically gorgeous and typically unaware of it.

'This is Natalie Craven.' Ben took a step that put him between Nat and Antony. 'Natalie's my . . . house manager.'

Nat raised an eyebrow. Antony put his head on one side. 'I'm sorry, but you're no' an actress by any chance?' When Nat started to shake her head and he could see she wasn't smiling, he went on hurriedly, with a thickening of the accent, 'Wisnae meant to be an insult, Natalie, I just thought Ben might've called in some old . . . favour.'

'She doesn't owe me any favours,' Ben said tightly.

'Hey!' Antony put up his hands. 'No offence, pal.'

'None taken.' Ben was looking a little weary now. 'Nat, if you see Amber anywhere, can you tell her I'm taking Antony to the church to, ah, meet the Vaughans.'

'Or perhaps you'd like to join us,' Antony said softly to Nat. 'Be good to get another perspective. I, er, gather the Vaughans don't have a lot to say these days.'

Nat smiled at him. 'I've been there before. Also, there are people I need to phone. Bookings to make.' She looked at Ben. 'Like all the ones you put off this weekend?' She threw her coat over the reception desk. 'Why don't you take Jane? Jane's got a perspective on most things.'

Ben shrugged. Jane glanced at Natalie, thinking she ought to be upstairs with Amber, cleaning and redecorating. But maybe Nat wanted to find out how this situation worked out, come back with a report.

Cool.

'Time for your break, surely,' Nat said, confirming it. 'And you've never met the Vaughans, have you, Jane?'

Kington Parish Church was alone on the edge of the town. From the road it looked like a country church, walled and raised up against the cold sky. Ben didn't even glance at it, just drove straight past the entrance in his old blue MGB, with the top down. Antony Largo was beside him, Jane fleeced and huddled into the little seat behind them, her hair blown across her face.

'That *was* a church, wasn't it?' Largo said. 'The chunky grey thing with the wee spire we just passed?'

'I've changed my mind.' On the edge of the town centre, Ben had turned right, heading back into the country, raising his voice above the engine's dirty growl. 'I'm going to take the story in sequence.'

'Can we no' have the damn top up?'

'It's jammed, if you must know.'

'Great.'

'Do you good, a bit of air.'

'*I* know what'd do me good, pal, but we left her behind.' Largo leaned his head back. 'That's no offence to you, Jane, but I don't think your mother would approve of me.'

'I wasn't looking for a new dad, anyway,' Jane said.

'Hmm,' Largo mused. 'Feisty.'

They came out of a shady lane with detached houses in it, and now they were in hilly countryside. Jane had never been down here before; she had no idea where the road led. The sun was pulsing feebly, a blister behind clouds like strips of yellowing bandage.

'And you can keep your filthy paws off my staff, Largo,' Ben said mildly. 'Natalie's in a relationship, and she's bloody good at what she does.'

Largo turned to Ben. 'How would you even know?'

'What?'

Something fractured then, Largo bawling at Ben, raising himself up in the bucket seat. 'Come on, what *do* you know about the hotel trade? I mean really? What have you *done*, you maniac? You could've found something in the independent sector, no problem, like every other bastard gets dumped by the Beeb. You could've gone to Kenny and Zoë Fitzroy. You could've come to me, for Christ's sake! How naive is *this*? Find you can afford some Disneyesque mansion wi' wee towers for the price of your Dockland penthouse, and you have to grab it like it's now or never.'

Ben gripped the wheel. 'I've remarried, in case you failed to notice. I have Amber to consider.'

'Aye, and that—'

The wind made a grab at Antony Largo's voice and the folded fabric of the car's roof flapped violently behind Jane. She sank down in the little seat to hear the rest of the stuff he presumably hadn't felt able to say inside the hotel.

'—An artist and turned her into a skivvy. You had to prove you didn't need any of us: "I'm gonnae show these bastards, I'm getting out of London and create a wee paradise and get m'self fit and youthful again and make them all as sick as pigs." How naive is that? Truth of it is, you *do* need us, you arsehole.'

Ben hung grimly on to the wheel, slowing the car, breathing in deeply, swallowing something. 'The building on your left,' he said finally, through his teeth, 'is Hergest Court.'

Disappointing.

Like, it should have been bigger. Must have been bigger once, seeing it was built on a motte, an obvious castle mound above unkempt grounds and what might have been an old pond, even a moat. It was about fifty yards back from the road, part stone, part timbered. The stone end had a sloping roof, the timbered end just stopped.

'Like it's been sawn off,' Jane said.

'This is only a fragment of what it used to be.' Ben had reversed into a track of hard mud and turned the car to face the house.

It looked stark, the way buildings with timber framing rarely did. There ought to be wooded hills rising behind it, but there were only the cold fields and the waxy sky. On the sawn-off side were sporadic trees – a gloomy yew, a bent pine – and then some industrial-looking farm buildings.

'Rather forlorn now, I admit,' Ben said. 'Been let out in recent years by the owners. Lived in usually by tenant farmers, and it was even a rural art gallery for a while. You can tell by the mound it's built on that it used to be fortified, way back.'

'How far back?' Jane asked, interested now – more so than if it had been tarted up inside some mock-Elizabethan knot-garden.

'Well, thirteenth century at least. That's recorded.'

'It's no' *my* idea of Baskerville Hall,' Antony Largo said.

Ben switched off the engine, and the atmosphere between him and Largo seemed to tauten, like some invisible sheet of cellophane dividing the front seats. Jane hunched into a corner of the back seat and kept her hands in the pockets of her fleece. No other vehicle had passed since they'd arrived. No smoke was coming out of any of the three visible chimneys of Hergest Court.

'By the fifteenth century, it had become the house of the Vaughans,' Ben said. 'The most important family in the history of Kington.'

Antony stretched his legs. 'And they're your prototype Baskervilles?'

'There *is* a long-established Baskerville family in the area, which accounts for the name. But the Vaughans have the history. The central figure is Thomas Vaughan, who switched from the Lancastrian side to the Yorkists in the Wars of the Roses. Killed at the Battle of Banbury in 1469. He was known as Black Vaughan.'

'Naturally,' Antony said.

Ben frowned. 'Because of his black hair, apparently. To distinguish him from his brother who had red hair.'

'Maybe you could just not mention that.'

Jane said quickly, 'It was Hugo Baskerville in the book, wasn't it? The guy who was supposed to have brought down the curse on the family?'

'A wild, profane and godless man, according to Conan Doyle's Baskerville manuscript.' Ben turned around to face her. 'Conan Doyle brings *his* legend forward almost exactly two centuries, to the time of the Great Rebellion – the English Civil War. So both the historical background and Doyle's created one feature civil wars which tore the country apart. Doyle puts Hugo in the seventeenth rather than the fifteenth century. It's exactly how an author would muddy the waters.'

'And there was a girl, wasn't there?' Jane said.

'A neighbouring yeoman's daughter whom Hugo fancies and abducts. He drags her back to Baskerville Hall, but she escapes down the ivy from an upstairs room that night, while he and his cronies are getting pissed – the inference being that, hearing their ribald laughter, she suspects that they're all going to come up and gang-rape her. When Hugo finds that she's gone, his night's pleasure denied him, he offers himself, body and soul, to the Powers of Darkness if he can be allowed to catch up with her again. Then he mounts his horse, orders the hunting pack to be unleashed and rides off furiously across the moor, with his hounds, to hunt her down.'

'Across the moor,' Antony looked around. 'Do I see a moor?'

Ben frowned. 'For which, if we were shooting the scene, we might substitute Hergest Ridge. Which begins – ' he jerked a thumb at where the land rose steeply behind the car ' – just there. It's wild, it has its curious features. And Stanner Rocks are surely as brooding as any Dartmoor tor.'

Antony smiled.

'What happened to the girl?' Jane asked. 'I don't remember.'

'Hugo's companions go chasing after him,' Ben said. 'They're scared of what he'll do if he catches up with her. They encounter a night shepherd on the moor who's in such a state of terror that he can hardly speak. He tells them he's seen the hounds pursuing the hapless maiden, followed by Hugo on his black mare. And then, silently following Hugo, the worst thing of all.'

'*Another hound.*' Antony Largo laid on this melodramatically spooky Scottish voice, like Private Fraser in those old *Dad's Army* episodes. 'Only bigger . . . and meaner.'

'They eventually find the girl in a clearing, dead of fatigue or fear,' Ben said. 'And then they find Hugo. And, standing over him, a great black beast, bigger than any hound—'

'—*Ever seen by mortal eyes,*' Antony Largo said.

Ben finally turned to him. 'You've actually read it, then, Antony.'

'Of *course* I've read it, you tosser, I'm a pro. I do my prep – even for this sh— So, here's your beastie plucking at Hugo's throat, and then it finally rips it all away.' Antony clenched his teeth and growled until his own laughter began to choke him. 'And it turns on these guys, with its jaws all dripping with blood and flesh and its eyes on fire. And they all shit themselves on the spot and leg it. End of legend.'

Ben didn't laugh. 'Not exactly.'

'Yeah, OK. From then on, if the Hound is heard howling in the night or seen prowling the precincts, then it's no' what you'd call a fortunate omen for the Baskervilles.'

'It means death,' Ben said.

'We know *that*,' Jane said. 'But, like, how closely does that match the story of this Black Vaughan?'

Ben didn't reply. He put his shoulder against the driver's door, crunched it open and stepped out onto the edge of the road.

'Obviously, not that closely at all,' Antony murmured.

Ben leaned against the car. 'There are actually local people who won't come down here at night. Don't smile, Antony, this isn't the city, this isn't even the soft country. Vaughan was associated with a black hound, which some sources suggested was in some way satanic. Now, although the spectral black dog is a familiar motif in British folklore, the death connection is less common. But I can tell you that there are still some local people who just won't come this way for fear of meeting it on the road. I have that on good authority.'

'Say that on camera, will they, pal?'

'I don't know. Maybe.'

Jane glanced across at Hergest Court. Nothing was moving. '*Have* people seen something?'

'It's odd,' Ben said. 'You talk to people in town and they'll say, "Oh, old so-and-so's seen the Hound, he'll tell you about it. And then, when you find old so-and-so, he looks blank, never even heard of it. Which is extremely unconvincing and, in my view, the denials prove the fact of it. As I understand it, what's been seen is a big black dog that disappears into walls, solid things. And there are other related phenomena that I'll explain about later.'

'But in the book it was a fiery hound,' Jane said. 'Which turns out to have been phosphorous paint. Like, when the Hound starts appearing again in modern times – like, Victorian times – it turns out to have been an actual dog that was starved, therefore given a good reason to howl in the night. And painted with luminous paint.'

Ben nodded. 'In the novel, the fiery hound is a scam.'

'And in the end Sherlock Holmes just shoots it,' Jane said. And it was *all* coming back now. 'Why did he have to do that? The poor dog's already been deliberately starved for weeks. I hated him for that.' She was aware of both men looking at her with curiosity. 'OK, I was young. I didn't realize he needed a dramatic finale. I was just sorry for the dog, and that's all I remembered. And that's . . . that's why I've always hated the book. Sorry.'

A Land Rover Discovery came around the bend quite fast, tyres skidding in a patch of icy mud, and Ben slid quickly back into the MG. 'Jane actually makes an important point there. Why *did* Doyle give his novel such a prosaic ending? A real dog and a pot of phosphorous paint?'

'It was a Sherlock Holmes story,' Antony reminded him. 'Sherlock Holmes disnae believe in ghosties.'

'Yes,' Ben hissed, 'but Doyle did! This is the whole point: a medical man, a scientist . . . *but*, for the last twenty years of his life, also a spiritualist! *The* most famous proponent of spiritism on the planet! The guy was beyond fanatical – tours of Britain and the States, promoting what he considered to be the absolutely proven scientific fact of life after death. In fact, towards the end, Antony – ' Ben put his face to within six inches of Largo's ' – Doyle *lived* for bloody ghosties.'

Then something caught his eye and he straightened up, looking away, down the lane to where the Discovery had stopped to let two men out.

'Ah,' Ben said.

The two men both wore army-type camouflage jackets and baseball caps. One of them pulled open the back door of the vehicle, reached inside and then handed the other something that Jane thought at first was a spade.

'Them,' Ben said.

The rear door was slammed shut, and the Discovery moved on, leaving the two men standing in the road. They started walking up the lane towards the MG, heads down like they hadn't noticed it was there.

Jane thought, *Oh Christ*.

Two men, one shotgun.

'How very opportune,' Ben said through his teeth. He stepped out into the road.

Antony Largo raised an amused eyebrow, half-turning and leaning back against the passenger door for a better view. Did he know the history to this? Probably not.

'You know, one thing I've always admired about Ben,' Antony said, 'is his ability to move into a new situation and form instant and lasting friendships.'

He folded his arms, waiting to be entertained. Jane looked at Ben, already all worked-up and dismayed because he was fighting for his and Amber's life, and everything he'd thrown at Antony had been deflected – Antony in his professional body armour and Ben bare-knuckled.

'I'm just *so* much in the right mood for these scum,' Ben said. He moved into the middle of the lane and stood there with his legs planted apart, rocking slightly.

SEVEN

The Healing of the Dead

It was one of those cottages with very small windows and so few of them that it needed lamps on all day in winter. Merrily counted seven of them, on tables and in nooks, all low-wattage, white-shaded and strung out like a chain of beacons so that you navigated through the house from lamp to lamp. There was a dreamlike feel to this.

'One day, when I'm *really* old—' Canon Jeavons was leading her down a cramped passage, like a tugboat on a canal; he was balancing coffee cups and milk and sugar on a tin tray '—there gonna be a nice, plain bungalow, with windows so wide you think you living on the lawn.'

His voice was crisp and biscuity, like on high-quality FM radio. A cathedral voice, too big for a farmworker's cottage that probably had not been much updated since the wattle first met the daub.

He ducked through a doorway. 'You must be the first person in a long, long time I've never had to warn to keep their head low till they sitting down.'

They'd arrived in a room that needed no lamp. It had whitewashed brick walls, a square of white carpet and an uncurtained window, revealing a small, fenced garden, wide fields and a hoary, wooded hill. The room had a sloping ceiling, suggesting that it had begun as a lean-to. A black cast-iron flue pushed through the ceiling at a crooked angle, serving a glass-fronted, pot-bellied stove in which coals glowed agreeably. There was an earthenware coffeepot on the stove. Homely.

'This place used to be for the family cow,' Jeavons said, 'or maybe the pig. Sometimes I see just one big pig snuffling around in here – raised like a member of the family, many tears shed at the parting of the ways. Sometimes I feel the presence of a single cow, but mainly the pig. What do you feel, Merrilee?'

Unrolling her name like ribbon. His accent was a carnival – lazy Caribbean towed by old-fashioned, fruity English clerical. She couldn't decide how much of it was laid on.

'Cows are good,' she said carefully. 'And, er . . . pigs are even better.'

'Indeed!' Jeavons beamed. 'Take a seat.'

He scooped a huge grey and white cat from a fat lemon-yellow armchair and sank into it, transferring the cat to his knees. When Merrily took a matching chair on the other side of the stove, she found it was so overstuffed that her feet didn't reach the floor.

'Well now . . .' Jeavons sat back, his chins on his chest. 'Ms Deliverance. This is interesting indeed.'

'It is?' Merrily looked into the big, squash-nosed, grey-sheened face, wishing she knew more about his personal history. The established facts were that he'd been a canon attached to Worcester Cathedral; the legends told of a seeded tennis player cured of multiple sclerosis and a fire victim whose disfiguring facial scars had vanished within a week.

Canon Jeavons and the big cat both looked placidly back at her. 'Because you're still not quite sure how to handle it,' Jeavons said, 'are you?'

'I'm sorry?'

'All of this – the calling, the job. And, most of all, I would imagine, the complexities of Deliverance. It's a problem of . . . I was gonna say confidence, but it isn't that. You have a fear.'

'Lots.'

Suspicious now. When she'd finally reached him on the phone she'd learned that Sophie Hill had already called on behalf of the Bishop, to make sure that he was still available for consultation. Sophie would have told him a little about her but nothing personal. Sophie didn't do personal.

'I'd say you have a horror of being considered—' he looked at her sleepily through half-closed eyes '—*pious?*'

She thought she must have shaken, physically. 'What makes you say that, Mr Jeavons?'

'You must call me Lew,' he said. 'Now that I'm retired.'

She didn't call him anything, she just stared. He wore a linen jacket with wide blue and light-grey stripes, like for punting. Under it was something you always guessed must be available somewhere, but not in any ecclesiastical outfitters: a high necked black T-shirt with a white dog collar that was part of the design. Maybe he'd got it from a joke shop.

'See, Merrilee, most of the female clergy of my acquaintance, they all very proud of what they achieved for their sex after all these centuries. They wear the dog collar and the clerical shirt on all possible occasions. Maybe they sleep in a clerical nightdress, I wouldn't know about that. But always, when they come to see a male priest, that's when it's *extremely* important to them that they be seen as equals. You, by contrast – no collar, no shirt. Only a cross, so discreet it could even be an item of jewellery. And you're not wearing too much make-up or a short skirt, either, so . . . You're married?'

'Widowed, for some years. There is . . . a man.'

'Oh.' His eyes went into a squint. The cat purred, the coffeepot burbled on the stove.

'He's a musician. He helps out at a recording studio in

the Frome Valley. We see each other . . . not as often as we'd like, and I'm not sure what to do about that.'

'Your people know about him? In the parish?' His gut pushed out comfortably, like a flour sack, and the cat nestled into it.

'Some must've guessed by now. He used to live in the village. We thought there might be an opportunity for him to move back, but it wasn't to be.'

Wasn't to be – had she conveyed some sense of foreboding in that phrase? Defensive now; this man could pluck away your secrets like specks of fluff.

'What do your prayers tell you about this relationship?' Jeavons asked.

'I feel it's the right thing. At this moment.'

Jeavons nodded. There was a movement outside the window – a cock pheasant on the lawn. Merrily blinked. There was something about the light in here, the white clarity of everything, after the dimness of the rest of the cottage. It was like snow-light; *everything* was lit. She had the curious feeling of emerging from an initiation.

She said slowly, feeling the words drawn out of her, 'Martin Israel, in his book on exorcism, says that some degree of psychic ability is probably necessary to do this job – Deliverance.'

'And you think you don't have what's necessary?' Jeavons said.

'How did you know about me and the word "pious"?'

'I didn't.'

'Sophie didn't let it slip that "pious" was my most unfavourite word in the dictionary and that I have a fear of—?'

'Sophie?'

'Sophie Hill. The Bishop of Hereford's lay secretary.'

'Ah. A lady of evident discretion and diplomacy. No, she

didn't tell me that. But then she wouldn't, would she? You, on the other hand . . .' Canon Jeavons gripped the cat, and the cat purred fiercely. 'Merrilee, you're an open person. Aspects of you stand out as if you carrying a placard – it's in your manner, the way you dress, that big old Volvo you drive. No doubt you're capable of considerable discretion when it comes to the affairs of others, but about yourself . . . you drop sizeable clues, you know?'

'The word "pious" . . .'

Jeavons rocked back, laughing. 'You ain't gonna let this go, are you? Listen, it dropped into my mind. Things do that sometimes. If we take the time to absorb what people are telling us about themselves, directly and indirectly, and we are in a suitable state of relaxation – a contemplative state – then the clues come together and a feeling or a word sometimes drops into our minds, just like . . . like a packet out of a cigarette machine.'

She frowned. 'You can also see the nicotine on my teeth?'

'Your teeth are like pearls.'

'And it's always right, is it, this thing that drops into your mind?'

'*Hell*, no. Sometimes it's so far out I feel like a horse's ass. But when you get to my age, time's too precious to keep it to yourself and sit and wonder. This, as it happens, is at the heart of spiritual healing: taking the time to know people, making small deductions. How many doctors have the time or the patience to do that now – talking and considering and leaving time for small leaps of inspiration. No, it's, "Take two of these three times a day", or, "I'll make you an appointment to see a consultant . . . send the next one in on your way out." One time, minor ailments were resolved without the need for pills, because pills were expensive and time was cheap. And doctors – country doctors, particularly – would often be spiritual people, capable of insight. From insight to inspiration is only a small leap, which may be divinely assisted. Are you following my reasoning?'

'I think so.'

'Good. Let's have some of this coffee.' He eased himself around the cat and stood up.

Merrily said, 'What happened to your wife?'

He raised an eyebrow, as if she'd turned the tables on him.

'I'm sorry, I didn't want to—'

'God would not permit me to heal her.' Jeavons lifted the coffeepot from the stove. 'She died five years ago, around the time they wanted to groom me for bishop. Maybe if she lived I'd have gone for that, if only to see Catherine in a palace. Instead, a row. I said to them, You don't know a thing about me, you just want me 'cause purple and black go so nice together in New Labour Britain. I said, I'm going away instead. I want to find out for myself why my wife was not healed.'

'And did you?'

'Maybe. Haw, you're suspicious of me now. You thinking I'm some kind of old-time shaman out of a travelling medicine show. We should start again. Tell me what you want to know.'

'You know what I want. I was appointed as Deliverance consultant for the Diocese of Hereford. Suddenly, whichever way I turn, I'm finding the word "deliverance" linked with the word "healing".'

'And that would naturally scare you. It scares you like "pious". Because it would mean people start to see you as wonder-woman.'

'Mmm.'

'Difficult,' Jeavons said.

*

'The names,' Ben said. 'Consider the names.'

Driving back into town, he seemed re-energized, setting out his case for Arthur Conan Doyle basing *The Hound of the Baskervilles* on what had happened in Kington, talking about the way the book and this area echoed each other in unexpected ways.

And the real clincher: the remarkable coincidence of names.

'Key characters in the novel . . . look at the names. Baskerville – obviously, a prominent family in this area, as we've established. But then the others – Mortimer. Dr Mortimer is the local GP, the man who first consults Sherlock Holmes over the case. Now Mortimer – as Jane knows – is probably the most significant name in the middle-Marches. This was the core domain of the Mortimer dynasty of Norman barons. Commemorated in place names like Mortimer's Cross, which is just a few miles from here, along the Border.'

Antony Largo said nothing.

'All right,' Ben said, 'you might argue that's not such an uncommon name. But what about Stapleton? Stapleton, the naturalist who turns out to know rather more about hounds than butterflies. Stapleton, Jane. Tell him where Stapleton is.'

'Oh . . .' Jane recalled a fragment of ruined castle on a hill, a farm, a few cottages. 'It's a hamlet. Just outside Presteigne. That's right on the Border, too, isn't it? Presteigne's in Wales, Stapleton's in England – just.'

'Thank you, Jane.' Ben nodded happily. 'Baskerville, Mortimer, Stapleton. Key names strung out along the mid-Border. It *could* be coincidence, but would Holmes himself have bought that? I really don't think so. Doyle's delicately encoding the real history, the actual location of *The Hound of the Baskervilles.*'

Jane was impressed, but Antony said, 'So what about the Cabell family of Devon? What about Sir Richard Cabell who's supposed to've followed a spooky hound across the moor on his black mare after making a pact with the Devil?'

'So?'

'That story fits pretty damn well, and we know for a fact that Doyle went to Devonshire to research the terrain. We even know which hotel he stayed at.'

'And?'

'See, I found all this on the Net, very easily. Arthur went down to Dartmoor with his golfing pal, Fletcher Robinson, a Devonian. In fact, Robinson himself was said to have come up with the story – for which Doyle insisted on giving him a credit in the *Strand Magazine*, which serialized his stuff. Am I right?'

'I'm not disputing that, Antony.' Ben shook the wheel lightly. 'However – and was *this* on the Net? – the then editor of the *Strand* said that *he* understood Fletcher Robinson obtained the original story from – and I quote – "A Welsh guidebook". I can show you that reference in two biographies of Doyle. So while I couldn't deny that he borrowed elements of the Cabell legend to flesh out the scenario, all the evidence still says it starts right here.'

'And the small fact that the coachman Doyle and Robinson employed in Devon was one . . . *Harry Baskerville*? How does that equate, my friend?'

'Oh.' Jane was dismayed. 'Is that true?'

'Perfectly true,' Ben confirmed. 'And Baskerville himself assumed that his name had been borrowed. However, Stashower, in his biography of Conan Doyle, points out that Doyle mentioned the proposed title *The Hound of the Baskervilles* in a letter to his mother *before* he and Robinson went to Devon – before he even met Harry Baskerville. I can show you the reference.'

Antony didn't reply. Jane was delighted. The awkward

encounter with the shooters seemed to have given Ben a blast of confidence.

It had been almost funny – these two guys, with their South Wales accents, up from Ebbw Vale, claiming they'd been hired by a local farmer to get rid of foxes. Well, Jane had realized at once that this was bollocks; the usual situation with rough shooting was that guys like this paid the farmers for the privilege.

Anyway, the shooters had got *totally* the wrong idea, assuming that Ben, despite the jogging kit, was some local hunter warning them off his patch. And Ben, being Ben, hadn't corrected the impression, he'd played to it – Jane could hear his voice changing, acquiring this military edge. Initially, he'd just been rescuing the situation, saving face, but in the end he'd had the Ebbw Vale guys backing defensively away, up the public footpath to Hergest Ridge, bawling after them, 'Bloody cowboys! Your card's marked in this area, believe it!'

He might not have been potentially one of the greats, as Amber had put it, but he was still a bloody good actor. And now he was on a roll, his argument flowing.

'So, like, why *did* Conan Doyle transfer the whole thing to Dartmoor?' Jane asked.

Ben shrugged, lifting his hands from the wheel. 'Don't you find that interesting in itself? Also, why did Doyle decide to rubbish the concept of a *ghostly* hound in the book when in real life he'd have pounced on it with all the enthusiasm he lavished *nearly twenty years later* on those patently faked photos of the Cottingley Fairies?'

'Right.' Jane knew those pictures: close-ups of innocent young girls' faces with these archetypal Arthur Rackham-style fairies frolicking in front of them. Obvious fakes now, but convincing enough in the early days of photography. It wasn't *so* much of an indictment of Conan Doyle's gullibility.

Ben turned into the tarmac drive leading to Kington church. 'What's also interesting is that originally *The Hound* wasn't going to be a Sherlock Holmes story at all. Doyle had already killed Holmes by then – dragged over the Reichenbach Falls in the arms of his arch-enemy Moriarty. And then he writes what's become a famous letter to the editor of the *Strand*, announcing his plans for *The Hound* with the words, '*I have the idea of a real creeper.*' But you see it wasn't, at that time, going to be a Holmes adventure at all. So when Holmes was brought in, Doyle wrote the story as if it was something that had happened *pre*-Reichenbach.'

'And did he . . .?' Antony eyed Ben thoughtfully – some respect at last, Jane thought. 'I'm sorry, I know he was a fellow Scot, but my knowledge here is a wee bit scant . . . Did Conan Doyle write other stories that *were* essentially supernatural?'

Ben nosed the car into some bushes, where the ground was still furred with frost. He pulled on the handbrake with a fusillade of ratchet clicks and switched off the engine.

'Yes, Antony. Of course.'

'So when he decided to make it a Holmes tale, he knew that'd be an aspect going out the window, Holmes being the ultimate rationalist. If Holmes is gonnae solve the case, there has to be a rational explanation.'

'Yes. And what I'm wondering . . . was Doyle specifically asked by the Baskerville family – or someone else – to put in some distance? There's a traditional belief in this area that he was distantly related to the Baskervilles, who were in turn, way back, related by marriage to the Vaughans. Obviously, there's still a lot of research to be done here. Hidden connections.'

'He didn't have to use the name at all, though, did he?'

'Still, hell of a *good* name, isn't it? Where would that title be without it?' Still buzzing, like he'd been snorting coke or something, Ben stepped out onto the frosted grass. 'Come and meet the Vaughans.'

There was no tradition of shamanism or the priesthood in Lew Jeavons's family. He'd come to England from Jamaica as a teenager, his father working on the buses. As a young man he went to New York where he was ordained and met an Englishwoman, on attachment to Harvard, an academic.

'And we found our way back here. Which I always felt was my home.'

'You were . . . into healing in America?'

'Well, I've always thought I was channelling healing.' He nodded at the big cat on his knees. 'Talk to Lucius about it. He was run over on the main road at Fromes Hill in the summer. The driver didn't stop. I'm the next car along, and I pick him up, along with his exploded intestines. Take him along to the vet, who puts back the intestines, shakes his head, takes out his syringe. But I shake *my* head. Bring Lucius back here, to be my cat for whatever time he has left.'

'He looks brilliant.'

'He limps a little now, that's all. Cats respond directly to love and hands-on. People are more complex. My wife . . . she should've recovered, that was the point. It wasn't such a big heart attack, they didn't think it was a bypass situation. I was convinced she was going to recover fully, and I took my eye off of the ball, and she had a second heart attack. I was leading a healing ministry in Oxford at the time, and we were all full of it: missionary zeal – hey, this is what the Church of England's been lacking for so long! And in the middle of all this healing frenzy, my beloved wife, she just ups and dies. Happens within a month. What was that saying to me? What was He telling me?'

'You must've been . . . bitter.'

'And bewildered. I didn't *think* I was arrogant, I didn't

think I needed bringing down – and there, you see, that proves I *was* arrogant, my first thought was that it was because of *me* that she was taken away – God telling the big healer, You are *nothing*, man!'

'How old was she?'

'Forty-nine. No age. Yes, I was bitter, sure I was bitter. What do they think – we can't hate God because we're priests?'

Merrily said, 'The . . . problem I have with this is the obvious one: some people recover, some don't. Some people who are prayed for – really, *really* prayed for, by many people . . .'

'I know.'

'So all the hopes build up and, in the end . . .'

'It's a lottery?'

'Or it's not our decision. Not a decision we can – or should – try to influence, despite what the Gospel—'

'Oh boy,' Jeavons said. 'You really don't get it, do you? We do it because it's *all* we do. It's fundamental: the care of bodies, the care of souls, the care of the living earth. It's how we develop within ourselves – by suffering through our failure and trying again and suffering some more. We *suffer*, Merrilee. A doctor fails to heal someone, he says, Well, hell, I prescribed all the right drugs, I did what I could. But *we* must suffer. And that isn't what you wanted to hear, is it?'

'I . . . don't know what I wanted.'

'Maybe you just don't understand about the nature of suffering, and that suffering can be a truly positive state. We should discuss this sometime.'

'Why wasn't your wife healed?' Merrily said.

Jeavons lifted both hands from the cat, held them in the air. Sat there in the white room like a bare rock on a beach freshly washed by the tide. Was the answer one he couldn't accept? Had he been forced to conclude, in his suffering, that her faith – her faith in *him*, Lew – had been insufficient? Was that it?

He opened out his hands, a candid gesture.

'It was because I didn't understand, at the time, that there was more than Catherine in need of healing in this particular instance. I didn't know . . . I didn't know about the healing of the dead.'

EIGHT

At Home With the Vaughans

Jane was kind of tingling now. Antony Largo had demanded, *Where's the contemporary dynamic? Where's the Now Drama?* And now he had his answer: there was a totally worthwhile mystery here, deeper than the Grimpen Mire, subtler than phosphorous paint, and panting for telly. Jane carried the excitement with her, through the uncoloured, wintry churchyard to the door of the church of St Mary the Virgin.

There were quite a few churches hereabouts dedicated to Mary – a sign of Norman origins, according to Mum: the conquerors emphasizing to the conquered that they had the support of the spiritual big-hitters. From the plateaued churchyard, you had a wide view of the Welsh hills above the English town and the beginning of Hergest Ridge, a peninsula into Wales. The sky had closed in now, the clouds tightening around the sun, reduced to a hole at the end of a grey-walled tunnel.

'Used to be a Norman castle up here,' Ben said. 'Soon abandoned, though. It's thought the church itself was providing community defence against the Welsh by about the thirteenth century.'

'People shut themselves up in the church?' Jane looked up at the squat tower, with its stubby steeple.

'The tower was separated originally from the main body

of the church,' Ben said. 'It has walls a good six feet thick, apparently.'

'Now I won't have to buy the guidebook,' Antony said, as they followed Ben inside. 'Thanks.'

Jane had never been in here before; she'd been expecting stark and utility, and she was surprised at the size of it and the luminous, grotto-like darkness, the way the stained glass bestowed this old, rosy warmth. So different from the frigid dining hall at Stanner, although Ben said some of the stained glass had been put in around the same time. Heavy Victorian restoration, then, but it had worked: there was a big window with generous reds and oranges and *warm* blue and, opposite it, high up in the west, a tiny circular one with a white dove fluttering out of crimson.

The age of the place was underlined for visitors by a big modern white plaque listing all the ministers of Kington, beginning back in the days when parishioners would be putting the six-foot walls between them and the marauding Welsh.

Hugh Chabbenor 1279
Rhys ap Howell 1287
John Walwyn 1313

Ben was strolling around in the tinted gloom with his hands behind his back. 'All this was far more spectacular in the Middle Ages, we're told. Wall paintings . . . ornate screens.'

Antony was shaking his head, slipping Jane a wry smile that maybe contained just a touch of affection for Ben. Perhaps he was at last getting into Ben's groove, finding the motivation, feeling the *dynamic*.

There were only the three of them in here, or so it seemed as Ben led them back towards the door, past a table with guidebooks and magazines on it. He stood there facing them. Jane could tell that he was in Holmes mode again, a sheen on his domed forehead, the curly hair around it absorbed into the dark. Ben was excited.

'Well . . . can you see them yet?'

'Huh?' Jane looked around.

'Such a sense of drama,' Antony murmured.

He and Jane were standing by the font, to the left of the entrance. Ben stepped to one side, extending an arm into the body of the church, to their right. From the side of the chancel nearest to them a different light, a colder light, was washing between the bars of a wooden screen from a stained window beyond. This window was full of blues and whites and a thin gold, and the light was hazy.

Jane was aware of a separateness – light, colour, mood – about that whole area, evidently a side chapel. And then she saw two heads together, from behind, an alabaster couple lying on a hard white bed, the wooden screen its headboard.

'May I present Thomas,' Ben said softly. 'And Ellen.'

It was one of those still, hollow moments. The heads conveyed a superiority, an arrogance, an *hauteur*. Jane hadn't noticed them before, and now they were all she could see: two effigies on a spectacular, off-white tomb, at ease with their backs to the pews and to the door, confident of their place in the medieval Church of St Mary the Virgin and in history.

'At home with the Vaughans,' Ben was saying. 'Cosy, isn't it?'

The double tomb came up to Jane's chest. On the side nearest to her, eight anonymous carved figures, some of which might have been monks or even angels, stood behind their shields, to protect the remains inside.

Black Vaughan, in fact all white now, was nearest the altar, his effigy's praying hands projecting from its alabaster chest, its face bland and clean-shaven.

Jane noticed right away that below the feet of the effigy was a dog.

It was a disappointment, however: too small to be any kind of hound, unless the fifteenth-century monumental mason had reduced the scale to make it fit onto the tomb. A life-size hound would have spread over the whole width of it and under the feet of the woman.

Jane thought Vaughan's own feet seemed too big, like cartoon feet. 'It's like he's wearing Doc Martens.' She giggled. 'For like giving the peasants a good kicking?'

Irreverence was compulsory in this situation – the way these arrogant bastards had always claimed the place nearest to God. Like they honestly believed God was naive enough to fall for it. But as soon as she'd spoken, she was sensing disapproval, unsure of whether it was coming from Ben or she was projecting it to Black Vaughan. Or his lady.

The lady might have been beautiful; it was hard to judge from a tomb. She wore a long gown with a girdle, her slender arms bared in prayer. On her pillowed head was a small cap. Fashionable? Probably. Coquettish? Maybe not. Her face was solemn, but what would you expect?

'What does it mean that they're praying?' Jane said. 'I mean, like, are they praying for mercy because of all the corruption in their lives, all the people they shafted? All the peasants they exploited?'

'Comely wench, though,' Antony observed. 'Nice body. What's her name again?'

'Ellen.' Ben stood at her feet, his hands clasped in front of him as if he was about to join the Vaughans in prayer. 'Ellen Gethin. Also known as Ellen the Terrible.'

Antony tongued his top lip to conceal a smile. 'I trust that disnae mean she was terrible in the sack.'

Jane grinned nervously. Ben frowned. 'It was because she killed a man.'

Antony tilted his head. 'Is that a fact?'

'She came from a village called Llanbister, over the border in Radnorshire. Had a younger brother, David, of whom she was very fond. He was killed in a sword fight with his cousin, John Hir – a row over an inheritance. Ellen was shattered and bent on revenge. She was a strong woman. A formidable woman.'

'Looks maybe taller than her man,' Antony noted.

'Described as having masculine strength.'

'Sexy, though.'

'Shut up, Antony,' Ben said. Antony peered down at Ellen's breasts, then looked up at Ben and grinned.

Jane said, 'What happened?'

'There was an archery contest at Llanddewi, near Llanbister. Ellen went along disguised as a man. John Hir was the champion archer and she challenged him. John put his arrow into the target, Ellen put hers into John.'

'Feisty,' Antony said. 'Is it true or a legend?'

'It's *believed* to be entirely true, although it does rather correspond to a few classic myths about the vengeful-huntress figure. It's said to have happened in 1430, after Ellen's marriage to Thomas Vaughan. She must have been a very young woman at the time because Thomas was killed at the Battle of Banbury nearly forty years later.'

'I like it,' Antony said. 'We could've used it.'

Ben turned to Jane. 'Antony did a Channel 4 documentary series a few years ago about the psychology of women who kill. *Women of the Midnight*?'

'Aw, I hated that title,' Antony said. 'It was imposed on me. What I had in mind was to call it *My Milk for Gall*. Something like that.'

'Lady Macbeth?' Jane said. ' "Unsex me here and take my milk for gall, you murdering ministers." I . . . wow.' She stared at Antony with new respect. This man was actually the producer of *Women of the Midnight*? 'That was like . . . heavy stuff.' Not admitting that she hadn't actually seen it, having been only about ten at the time.

But she saw now why Ben was courting Antony so assiduously. She was fairly sure that *Women of the Midnight* had won some prestigious award for Channel 4, which must make Antony a seriously influential producer. Like, if *he* brought in an idea, people would listen to him, the people with money to hand out. So the main problem for Ben was convincing Antony himself, and perhaps this would be the only problem.

'Too late now though, huh?' Antony was looking down wistfully at Ellen Gethin again. Ellen's eyes were shut.

'Such a shame,' Ben purred. Jane thought, *Milk for Gall*: Lady Macbeth, Myra Hindley . . . Ellen would probably have fitted nicely into the format.

Antony moved away from Ellen and stood at the feet of Thomas, with his Doc Martens and his little alabaster dog.

'So what about this guy?'

Ben shrugged. 'We don't know very much about him. He was born in 1400, was initially a supporter of the Lancastrians during the Wars of the Roses but for some reason changed sides. One version says he was on his way to the Battle of Banbury in 1469 when he was captured by the Lancastrians, accused of treason and beheaded. His body was brought back here.'

'And was he like Hugo Baskerville? A bad guy, a tyrant?'

'We don't know. We don't know what kind of man he was when he was alive. He's better known for his activities afterwards. All the accounts say he made a very angry and destructive ghost, haunting the stretch of road between Hergest Court and Kington, often in broad daylight. Rearing up in front of women, and causing farm carts to overturn.'

'What did he have to be mad about?'

'Dunno, but it's said the town was in terror. The road to

Hergest was shunned. Taboo. Got so bad that Kington market began to suffer because nobody wanted to come. Vaughan could change shape, tormented horses as a fly. Appeared in this church as a bull, roaring through the pews during a service.'

'But not a doggie.'

'That came later,' Ben said. 'After the exorcism.'

Jane said, 'What?'

Apparently, it had taken twelve experienced ministers to deal with Vaughan, all of them gathered inside a circle drawn on the floor at Hergest Court, each with a lighted candle. There was also a woman and a young baby, presumably newly baptized and presumably representing purity. When your mother was in the trade and left books lying around, you learned quite a lot about the history of dispensing with demons.

Ben said the story had been chronicled by the Hereford-shire folklorist Ella Leather and, before that, collected by the Border diarist Francis Kilvert.

'Hell of a struggle, candles going out, slanging match with Vaughan's spirit. But they eventually reduced him to something small and manageable, and then they confined the spirit in a snuffbox.'

Snuffbox – this angle sounded familiar, and Jane figured she was bound to have read about it, at some stage, in Mrs Leather's book. It was a big book, with thousands of stories, many of which you forgot because they weren't strictly rele-vant at the time. She'd go back to it, check all this out.

'Vaughan's spirit had expressed an aversion to water,' Ben said. 'So they buried the snuffbox at the bottom of Hergest Pool.'

'As you would,' Antony said.

'It would dramatize beautifully.'

'And if you wanted some authentic stuff on exorcisms,' Jane said, 'my mother might be able to—' She broke off, her hand touching Ellen's white, shiny elbow – how broad and muscular that arm appeared now. Jane drew her hand away. Best, on the whole, not to say anything to Mum about this: she wouldn't exactly be in favour of dramatizing an exorcism, however many centuries ago it had happened.

Ben and Antony were both looking at her.

'Of course,' Ben said, 'your mother's a vicar, isn't she?'

'Um . . . yeah.'

'With a special interest in this . . . area?'

Jane sighed. Had he heard whispers? Was Mum's name still mentioned at this end of the county in connection with her run-in with the creepy evangelist, Ellis?

Whatever, it was too late now.

'She's, erm, the Deliverance Consultant for the Hereford diocese. Diocesan exorcist, as was. But like, on second thoughts, I think it would be best if she didn't know I was involved in anything like this. Dabbling? You know? They discourage it.'

'How interesting,' Ben said.

'She just got pushed into it by a previous bishop, who thought it'd be cool to have a woman operating in that area. Look, I really don't want to tell her about this, OK? If you want any information, we've got lots of books at home. I could get you anything you needed.'

'Fine,' Ben said. 'Super.'

'You really are a slippery bastard, Foley,' Antony said.

Ben didn't look at him. 'Ah . . . We don't know precisely *when* the Vaughan exorcism was, but the inference is that Vaughan was never seen again – not in person, anyway. However, as recently as 1987 two women were visiting this church when one of them distinctly saw the shape of a bull form in the atmosphere.'

'In here?' Jane glanced from side to side.

'She said it seemed to coalesce, as if it was composing itself from dust motes in the air. She was from Solihull in the Midlands, a tourist. Oddly, her name was Jenny Vaughan. The bull didn't *do* anything, it just formed and then presumably dissolved again. Like a show of strength.'

'And the Hound?' Antony said.

'It's known simply as the Hound of Hergest. It was said to appear before the death of a member of the Vaughan family. There were nine generations of Vaughans after Thomas and Ellen, and the last one to live at Hergest Court died childless at the beginning of the eighteenth century. But the phenomenon remained. Other people, over the years, are said to have seen the Hound in the lane leading to the Court. And a former tenant of Hergest used to speak of hearing what sounded like a large dog padding across the floor upstairs. This was quite recently.'

'And folk died?'

'Not as far as I'm aware. Though perhaps some Vaughan descendant somewhere . . .'

'OK, it's interesting,' Antony conceded. 'So, tell me – how important would it be to the Devon people to prove that the Conan Doyle connection here is a load of shite?'

'Well, it makes them very angry indeed. I only need to show you the terse letter I've just had from this guy Kennedy, of The Baker Street League, who's evidently poisoning a lot of people against me. It drives them crazy.'

'And you'd take them on? I mean, I'm not sure this'd be enough, but if you really got them fired up . . .'

'Look, this has become terribly important to me,' Ben said. 'It's not just financial any more – I mean, not just a question of getting publicity and an image for the hotel. Sure, it'd be wonderful to be able to afford to fully re-Victorianize Stanner, down to the last gas mantle in the last lavatory. Which is how it started, I'll admit, but it's so much more than that now. It's about winning the Border – Jane knows what I mean. The Border's a hard place, a testing place. People fail here all the time, because they haven't earned acceptance. They don't have links with the past, they're not part of a tradition. They don't *understand*.'

He was standing beside Thomas Vaughan. Black Vaughan. The white, blue and gold light was behind him. He was giving Antony Largo his piece-to-camera, framing himself in the light, the way he'd done as Holmes in the final act of the murder-mystery weekend at Stanner.

'Damn right I'd take them on,' Ben said. 'Me. And Thomas. And Ellen.' He gazed into the two white faces. 'I feel, in a strange sort of way, that we're kind of a team now.'

Following this dramatic and – Jane thought – slightly unhinged assertion, there was silence in the chapel. Just as Ben had intended.

What he hadn't intended was that it should be broken by a slow applause, the sound of two hands clapping.

Which was eerie enough, in this setting, to make Jane turn around very slowly.

NINE

Ask Arthur

She really wasn't spooky, that was the first thing. She had a well-worn sheepskin coat around her shoulders and a yellow silk headscarf and suede gloves. Jane didn't recognize her until she pulled off the scarf.

'Bravo, Mr Foley!' She shook out her pale hair. 'Golly, what a *trek* I've had. Your manager said you'd be down at Hergest Court by now, so of course I drove over there. Silent as the grave, as usual. Never mind, here we are. Yes, bravo. Awful man, Neil Kennedy, I've always thought – mean-minded and elitist. May I come in?'

Antony stepped aside to let her into the chapel, his head tilted, quizzical. Ben looked confused for a moment, and defensive, and then Jane saw his hands flick, as though he'd suddenly turned over the right page in some mental card-index.

'Of course, you were on the murder weekend. Mrs . . .'

'Elizabeth Pollen. Beth.'

'*Beth*. Yes. And you're . . . still here?'

'I'm often here, Mr Foley. I only live at Pembridge.'

'Good Lord,' Ben said weakly, as though he was bemused that anybody who lived close enough to Stanner Hall to know what kind of dump it was would want to pay good money to stay there.

But Jane was placing Mrs Pollen now: the youngest of the

Agathas – hanging out with them in the hotel bar in the evenings but clearly not a part of their weekend coach-party sleuthing scene. The only time she'd come out of the shadows was on that last night when she'd tried to persuade Ben to expand on the *Hound* reference and Ben had deflected it.

No way he could deflect it now.

Beth Pollen folded her silk scarf, like someone who didn't have too many of them. Under the heavy coat she wore a pale grey dress, and she was very slim, mothlike. Probably in her late fifties, but it was hard to be sure.

'Mr Foley, first of all, as a member of The Baker Street League, I'd like to apologize for the way Kennedy treated you over the conference. I was very much looking forward to that.'

'Yes,' Ben admitted. 'Quite a blow.'

'The membership wasn't consulted, of course. We're treated like geriatrics most of the time. I may forget to pay my subscription next year, after this. However . . . I've been speaking to your manager – Mrs Craven? – and I think we may have an alternative proposition to put to you.'

Ben blinked. 'The League?'

'*Not* The League, I'm afraid. Our coffers may not be as deep as The League's, but I hope we can strike a deal.' Mrs Pollen placed her folded scarf in the cleft between Ellen Gethin's alabaster waist and her praying hands. 'Isn't she adorable? Isn't she proud?'

'She's got *something*,' Antony agreed.

'Sorry – this is Antony Largo, an old colleague of mine.' Ben's expression had sharpened, Jane noticed, at the word *proposition*. 'We've been discussing some TV possibilities.'

'So I hear.' Mrs Pollen wore this soft, knowing smile, and Jane realized that her surprise arrival at the church had to be down to Natalie, the professional hotelier, plotting efficiently behind the reception desk to retrieve a situation which could put her out of a job. *People I need to phone. Bookings to make.* It had to have been Nat who'd told this woman about Kennedy's brutal cancellation.

Jane guessed that Ben, too, had worked all this out. 'Look,' he said, 'I'm terribly sorry, Beth, but with so much happening I'm afraid I've rather forgotten . . .'

'You haven't forgotten *anything*, Mr Foley. Don't fuss.'

'Ben.'

'*Ben.*' Her figure might be light and wafery but her voice was low and warm and soothing, like dark coffee. 'All you really need to remember is that, while I might be a member of The Baker Street League, I have a much more meaningful role with The White Company. And no . . . you aren't expected to have heard of them either.'

'One of Doyle's books, surely?' Antony said.

'It's an historical novel, of which he was enormously proud, about medieval mercenaries. And I suppose it *is* rather good. Arthur, as I'm sure you know, considered Holmes to be very much a secondary creation and always hoped to be recognized as a great historical novelist. As far as we're concerned, though, *The White Company* was simply a phrase that came through repeatedly to our Mr Hardy, and it stuck. Which gratifies Arthur, although I'm afraid most of us haven't even read it.'

'I'm afraid I haven't either,' Ben said.

'Mr Foley—' Mrs Pollen placed a calming gloved hand on Ben's arm. 'That doesn't *matter.*'

And the deal was done, more or less, right there in the cold blue Vaughan Chapel, silently witnessed by Ellen and Thomas. The White Company would hold their annual conference – or *moot*, as Beth Pollen called it – at the Stanner

Hall Hotel in the week before Christmas, effectively replacing The Baker Street League's original booking.

There would be more than twenty of them, including wives and husbands – not as many as The League and unlikely to spend as much on meat and drink, given that over half of them were vegetarians and too much drink was not encouraged, even over the festive season.

Like Ben cared, at this stage of the game – facing the cold-weather heating bills, the burst pipes and the need to keep the fridges stocked for the benefit of a handful of masochists who were into punishing winter walks and cold bedrooms. In the hollow of the night, he must surely have wondered if the Hound itself was out there somewhere, howling to herald the death of the Stanner Hall Hotel.

But now it was all turned around again. They discussed special terms, Ben meeting every suggestion with, 'Absolutely – talk to Natalie about it.' Knowing that Nat would organize the very best, most workable terms, leaving Ben to float around being entertaining and Amber to cook.

Antony Largo had been leaning against the wall between the tomb and the stained-glass window, arms folded, listening to the one-sided negotiations behind a foxy little smile which, it seemed to Jane, was fronting a deeper amusement.

'So, Beth.' Antony casually uncoiled from the wall. 'The White Company . . . is *what*, exactly?'

Jane saw Ben throw him a look that said: *Back off.* She guessed that Ben, on the threshold of the bleak season, didn't give a toss if The White Company was a society of rubber-fetishists, as long as they left a deposit.

Beth Pollen gave him a candid look. 'I think you've already guessed, Mr Largo.'

'But you could humour me.'

'Well . . . the society was officially formed in 1980 – the fiftieth anniversary of Arthur's passing.'

'Arthur's *passing*. Ah Beth, you're dropping wee clues the whole time.'

'Well, of course I am.'

Ben said, 'Antony, would you please—'

'No, no . . .' Mrs Pollen lifted a hand. 'It was originally called The Windlesham Society, after Arthur's much-loved last home in Sussex. It wasn't terribly well supported in the early days, and many of the members were rather elderly and found it increasingly difficult to get to meetings. After a few years, it faded virtually out of existence. And then, about six years ago, Alistair Hardy, of whom you might have heard . . . ? A fellow Scot?'

'Big country, Beth,' Antony said.

'*I'm* sorry. We do tend to think that because someone's eminent in our particular field he must be a household name. Alistair's a very well-known trance-medium from Edinburgh. His spirit guide, at the time, was Dr Joseph Bell, who, if you recall—'

'Doyle's tutor at Edinburgh University medical school. Impressed young Arthur with his incredible deductive skills, thus becoming the prototype for Holmes himself. Arguably a useful guy to have as your spirit guide.'

Ben whispered, 'You're *spiritualists?*'

Jane had to laugh.

Mrs Pollen said, 'Approximately six years ago, Dr Bell communicated to Alistair Hardy that a friend and former student of his was most anxious to find an enlightened audience because he didn't feel his work here was complete.'

'Now, I wonder who that would be,' Antony said.

Beth Pollen merely raised an eyebrow at him. 'In the last years of his life, Arthur's beliefs were derided. But let's not forget that when it was introduced in the West in Victorian times, spiritism was considered a science and had enormous credibility. When Arthur first applied to join the Society for

Psychical Research, in 1893, its president-elect was Arthur Balfour, who would later become Prime Minister.'

'Did I know that?' Antony wondered. 'I don't believe I did.'

'New technology was rampant. If we could pull voices from the air into a radio set, capture images on film, how long before we would all be seeing and talking to the dead?' Mrs Pollen made a wry face. 'By the twenties, we had commercial aircraft, phones, cinema, but spiritism wasn't felt to have come up with the goods, so it was considered a crank fad. Everyone's idea of a medium was Madame Arcati from Noel Coward. So it's quite reasonable to suppose that Arthur was biding his time.'

Jane thought, *And she seemed such a balanced woman.*

'The way you always refer to him as Arthur,' Antony said, 'suggests . . .'

'An affection. He's our patron, after all.'

'You're all spiritualists?'

'We're all spiritists, but we're not all mediums, if that's what you're asking – I'm not. Essentially, we're a group of people committed to furthering the work which occupied a good twenty years of a fine man's life.'

'He was – how should I put this? – a somewhat credulous man,' Antony said, avoiding Ben's agitated gaze.

'*Not* as credulous as his critics would have us believe, Mr Largo. He fought two elections. He campaigned on behalf of the wrongly convicted. He was a passionate, liberal-minded man who constantly questioned his own beliefs and fought against injustice the whole of his adult life. His only flaw – if that's how you want to regard it – was a desire to offer *hope.*'

Nobody spoke for a few seconds. Mrs Pollen turned away and spread her scarf over Ellen Gethin's face, as if she wanted to protect her from cold scepticism.

'Aye, OK, I'll buy that, Beth.' Antony leaned back against the wall. 'I'm just no' gonnae ask, if you don't mind, under what circumstances Conan Doyle became your patron.'

The short drive back to Stanner started in silence, Antony lounging against the passenger door of the MG, chewing his lip and watching Ben drive with one hand on the wheel and his hair flowing behind him. Ben's expression was so bland that Jane knew there had to be frantic action behind it. Which was understandable because, like, *Jesus* . . .

Coming up to the bypass Antony said, unsmiling, 'My friend, if this is a set-up, I think it would be wise if you were to tell me right . . . now.'

Ben didn't look at Antony. Jane had the impression he'd been expecting this.

'We go back, pal.' The open cuff of Antony's denim jacket rolled back along a muscular forearm and his forefinger came up like a knife. 'But not far enough that I wouldnae—'

He grabbed at the dash as Ben spun the MG into the side of the road, then up onto the grass, hitting the brakes hard and tossing Jane all over the small back seat.

'Sorry about that, Jane.' Ben took both hands from the wheel and half turned, as if offering his heart to Antony's blade. 'Look, I'll say this *once*. Until half an hour ago all The White Company meant to me was a *Boys' Own* adventure story that I had no particular wish to read.'

'You'll forgive me,' Antony said, 'for thinking it was all a wee bit lucky from your point of view.'

'It was quite awesomely serendipitous, but I'm telling you I knew nothing about it.'

This is Natalie, Jane thought, sliding back into the narrow rear seat, saying nothing, holding down her excitement. *Nat arranged for all this to be unveiled in front of Antony, and whatever you're paying her it isn't enough.*

'You wanted a contemporary dynamic,' Ben said. 'Now you've got one . . . *and* some.'

'And you think they'd play ball? All the way?'

'You came bloody close to asking her, matey. I was nearly soiling myself with anxiety.'

'I'm no' *quite* that stupid,' Antony said. 'I realize that to appear too eager at this stage would not be the thing.'

'No.' Ben leaned back into his bucket seat. 'Even I couldn't have dreamed up a woman with both a personal axe to grind against Neil Kennedy and a desire to prove – if only because she happens to live in this area – that *The Hound* begins on the Border. And to set it up for us like— I mean, you can *see* it, can't you? To think I was originally going to offer you, as a frame, the tired old Baker Street League debating the origins of *The Hound*. Jesus.'

'When all you needed,' Antony said, 'was for someone to . . . ask Arthur.'

'It's what they do, Antony. It's what they bloody well do.'

'So we're looking at this Alistair Hardy, who has the temerity to claim Dr Joseph Bell as his spirit guide?'

'Seems like it.'

'At Stanner.'

'You heard what I heard.' Ben slid the gearstick into second and drove back onto the bypass.

'And you think they'd let us shoot it? All of it? Like, they're no' gonnae give us any of this *privacy's crucial to the success of the operation* kind of bullshit?'

'Are you kidding? Listen. Some months after Doyle's death in 1930, more than five thousand people attended a memorial seance at the Royal Albert Hall, during which a chair was left empty for him – how private was *that*?'

'And did he, um, manifest?'

'They had a well-known medium called Estelle Roberts. And Doyle's widow Jean was on the stage. Great formal occasion, everyone in evening dress. A sign on the empty chair simply read *Sir Arthur Conan Doyle* and Lady Jean was seated next to it – though she admitted she didn't expect to turn round and see him.'

'Shucks.'

'However, Estelle Roberts began the proceedings by describing several spirits present in the hall, and their identities were confirmed by members of the audience.'

'*Plants*, Benjamin.' Antony sniffed. 'Mediums work with more plants than Alan bloody Titchmarsh.'

'Antony, I'm not making a case for the *veracity* of it, I'm simply applauding the clever building of dramatic tension. Sure, a few dozen people were unconvinced, and some of them just walked out – to the evident dismay of Mrs Roberts, who started complaining that she couldn't work under these conditions. Then somebody started playing the organ to drown out the, ah, sounds of dissent. And then, just when it looked as if it might all be falling apart, the medium suddenly shouted out' – Ben raising his voice against the buffeting air – '*He is here!*'

They rounded a bend in the bypass, and the wooded face of Stanner Rocks was up ahead, with those knobs of stone projecting like crumbling body parts.

'And there was old Arthur in the chair,' Antony said, 'placidly smoking his pipe.'

'Well, the medium claimed to have seen him. She described him as being in full evening dress, and striding with his old vigour across the stage to take his reserved seat.'

'Always keep 'em waiting.'

'Mrs Roberts said Arthur gave her a message for Lady Jean, which she promptly passed on. Unfortunately it was drowned out by a dramatic fanfare from the organist and nobody in the audience – *don't*, Antony, do not say a word – nobody in the audience heard it. But Jean maintained for the rest of her life that she was utterly convinced by its content that the message had come from her husband. Make of that what you will.'

'Doesn't matter, does it?' Antony said as they slowed for the hotel drive. 'Doesnae matter at all.'

'Not a toss.'

They glanced at one another and they both smiled.

'Well, I think I'm coming, Ben,' Antony said. 'I think I'm nearly there, pal.'

'Not in front of Jane, Antony.' Ben pushed the MG between the grey gateposts topped by damaged hounds. 'Wait till you get to your room.'

And they both started laughing, big mates again, school-boys. His room? Was this some in-joke? She was not unaware that Ben had never mentioned the room where Antony had slept or asked him if he'd experienced anything – at least not in her hearing.

Jane leaned back against the hard rear seat and wondered why she wasn't joining in. Ben glanced very briefly back at her and then at Antony, and she knew that look from a long time ago. It was like, *pas devant les enfants*. She looked quickly away from them, up through the strobing of light and pines to the turreted profile of Baskerville Hall.

'And then I'll tell you the rest,' Ben murmured to Antony. 'And that'll *really* bring you off. Pal.'

TEN

Serious Requiem

'You sound like you badly need to talk,' Sophie Hill had said when Merrily phoned.

Jeavons was right, she was an open book.

The lights were on in the gatehouse when she drove under it. Alongside, the sandstone Cathedral was crouching like a big ginger cat in the rusting remains of some late sunshine. In the office, Sophie had the kettle on. Most Saturday afternoons she'd go into the gatehouse office to sweep up the remains of the week.

'What was he like?'

'Bewildering.' Merrily sat down at the desk by the window. 'Enigmatic. Worryingly perceptive.'

'You liked him?'

'He has . . . charm.' She gazed through the window into Broad Street, where the street lights were coming on, along with chains of coloured bulbs newly hung across the road, although Christmas was still no more than a threat.

Sophie poured boiling water into the white teapot. 'I did some research. So far this year, six ministers in the diocese have made inquiries about the possibility of holding healing services. I spoke to three of them. One said, "I think we should be seen to be doing *something*." Another stressed he wanted nothing to do with Deliverance.'

'Figures.' Merrily's attempt to set up a Deliverance

Advisory Group was still in the tray marked *ongoing*. Some of them quite obviously didn't want to know because she was a woman. A month ago, after consulting her over the phone about certain technicalities, one rector had gone off and set up his own small group – all male – to deal with an alleged presence at a village shop. They'd never told her what had happened.

'Another one,' Sophie said, 'volunteered to be involved in any healing initiative if there was someone else to lead it. And as long as it wasn't – and I quote – "anyone like Jeavons". Sometimes one has to acknowledge that the clergy, as a profession, can be rather dispiriting.'

Sophie wore her mauve twinset. Her hair was white. In a dog collar she would cut a reassuring figure, but it would never happen; Sophie knew too much about the Church.

Merrily got out her cigarettes. 'There were some things I hadn't realized about Jeavons. It came out when he told me about the death of his wife, and why he couldn't heal her . . . and yet *might* have, if he'd known then what he knows now.'

Sophie turned off the main ceiling lights, switched on the desk lamp and set the teapot down between Merrily and herself.

'Go on.'

They actually went upstairs together, Ben and Antony – up the red carpet that Ben had bought instead of rewiring or a damp-proof course. Jane thought they looked like two kids who'd found a porn cache.

She found Natalie putting up Christmas lights in the cocktail bar, a room not yet fully Victorianized. It had pale green walls and colonial cane tables and fake oak beams across the ceiling, supporting nothing.

'So how long have you known about Mrs Pollen?' Jane said.

Nat was standing on the bar itself, arranging the lights between steel hooks projecting from the oak beam over it. 'Why are these bastards not coming on?'

'Maybe the fittings need tightening,' Jane said. 'Stay there.' She climbed up from a stool to the bar and picked up the end of the string of miniature bulbs.

'Beth Pollen found you, then?' Nat said.

'At the church.' Jane started turning the first pea-bulb in its plastic holder. 'She seemed OK. Surprisingly.'

'Why shouldn't she be?' Nat had her reading glasses on the end of her nose, and she peered over them at Jane. Nat looked good in glasses, would have looked good in a neck brace. 'She got into it the way most of them do. Bereavement – husband. They're not *all* cranks.'

'I just can't imagine ever wanting to contact someone who's dead.'

'Can't you?'

Jane thought about it. 'The thing is, I knew a girl at school who thought she could do it. And there was this other girl with problems who got involved, and she was like unhinged, mentally disturbed, and the whole thing pushed her over the top. It was . . . unpleasant, in the end. Horrible.'

'And your mother wouldn't like it, would she? Spiritualism.'

Jane looked up. 'That's nothing to do with it. I'm not exactly intimidated by the Church.' She tightened a second loose bulb; the lights still didn't come on. 'You do know what they're planning, don't you?'

'Yeah. I was just wondering if *you* did or if you were fishing. Pollen sounded me out during the murder weekend, so when The Baker Street League went down . . .'

'She told you *then* – at the murder weekend – that The White Company wanted to, like, seek confirmation from

Conan Doyle that this was the source of the Baskerville thing?'

'No, that seems to have occurred to them later. Pollen's late husband worked in the archive department at Powys County Council, and he was interested in Stanner. She has copies of various deeds and documents, so she knows a lot about this place. She said, how did I think Ben would feel about hosting the Company, and I said, why don't you ask him?'

Jane said. 'He's like a little kid over it.'

'It fits in nicely, doesn't it?'

All the lights had come on, a garish string of alternating sour lemon and livid blue. Natalie stared at them in clear disbelief. 'Do you think Ben got them from the County Highways Department? They look like fucking warning lights.'

Jane let go of the bulbs but didn't get down from the bar.

'Nat . . . Just now, in the car, Ben said there was something he had to tell Antony that would like . . . you know, really clinch things. What's that about?'

'Huh?'

'He gave Antony a look like, not in front of the kid. And when they came in he took him upstairs.'

'Oh.'

'You *do* know what it's about, right?'

Natalie frowned. 'Possibly. But he wouldn't have been bothered about *you* hearing it, he'd have been—' She shut up as the door opened, and then she turned and smiled and made a *ta-da* flourish towards the grim Christmas lights. 'Well . . . we got them working, Amber. We're just not sure if we're glad or not.'

Amber, in jeans and a mohair sweater, stood in the doorway with her hands on her hips. She looked horrified.

'For God's sake, they're awful! Switch them *off*!'

Natalie tweaked a bulb but the lights didn't go out. 'Where'd he get them?'

'I don't really care. Let's just get them down. I think that pipe's burst, Nat. I think the whole heating system's all to cock.'

'Oh hell,' Nat said. 'Listen, has he told you? We have a mass booking.'

Amber's eyes widened. Jane saw a certain fear there.

'I think I'm going to let Ben tell you about it himself,' Nat said. 'Not for me to pinch his glory.'

'Where is he?'

'Entertaining Mr Largo, somewhere or other. Don't panic, lovie, it's a week or so off yet. We'll get some more lights by then. We'll get the plumber. We'll make this place look almost festive. Well, the bits we allow them to film . . .'

'Film?'

'Oh, I think so.' Nat jumped down. 'Good, eh?'

And when Amber had edged anxiously away, Nat smiled and shook her head, and Jane said, 'Why *don't* you want to pinch his glory? It's all down to you.'

'Just that she may not thank me when she finds out,' Nat said. 'He'll maybe want to choose his time, Jane. She hates this place enough already. If she knew there'd been a murder, it might not—'

Jane came down from the bar top in a hurry. 'You're *kidding* . . .'

'Long time ago – before World War Two. Pollen told me, and I checked it out with that guy Sampson who played the Major. And then I told Ben.'

'What happened?'

'He decided to keep it to himself for a while. Just a domestic thing, Jane. One of the Chancery women killed her husband. No big mystery, no need to gather the suspects in

the drawing room. She was pissed at the time, apparently.'
Natalie started to bundle the alleged Christmas lights
together on the bar top, and they sent blue and yellow stripes
flaring across her face. 'On the one hand it adds to the
atmosphere of the dump, on the other . . . might put some
people off. You don't know, do you?'

Jane said, 'Erm . . . did it happen in one of the bedrooms?'

'I think it was outside, actually. In the gardens.'

Merrily told Sophie that sometimes she wished she was a
Catholic or belonged to some hardline Noncomformist sect
with strict liturgy and rules instead of guidelines.

'Just it would be nice to meet two Deliverance ministers
who operated to the same rules.'

'*Is* Jeavons a Deliverance minister?' Sophie asked.

'Not strictly. But . . . yeah, of course he is. In the cause of
healing the sick, he actually goes further into it than most
of us. This is where Deliverance meets Healing – the
healing of the dead.'

'His wife?'

'Catherine,' Merrily watched her cigarette end smould-
ering in the ashtray. 'This cool, fiercely intellectual, academic
theologian.'

Jeavons had said that he and Catherine had been married
in New York, where he was a priest and she was lecturing.
As she was English and he'd lived here too, he wanted them
to marry in England, but Catherine wouldn't hear of it. Nor
would she invite her parents to the ceremony. And when the
Jeavonses did eventually come back, as a married couple, she
didn't even notify them.

'Whatever she told Jeavons about her background, it
wasn't the truth. Some years later, Catherine's father made
contact with Lew. Someone had sent him a local newspaper
picture of the Reverend and Mrs Jeavons when Lew became

rector of a parish in Lincolnshire. The old man said he and
his wife had parted and he'd very much like to get in touch
with Catherine again.'

Jeavons had been surprised to discover that Catherine's
father was a fairly well-known Cambridge theologian, H.F.H.
Longman. Longman told Jeavons there'd been a row about
an unsuitable boyfriend while Catherine was at university.
But Catherine still refused to see her father and became very
agitated that he knew where she was – so much so that
Jeavons had to negotiate a parish-swap, which was how they'd
wound up in Worcestershire.

Merrily looked down into Broad Street: nearly dark now,
the lights misting. Sophie poured more tea, and Merrily told
her about the second time Catherine's father had been in
touch – when he was terminally ill, begging Lew to persuade
his daughter to see him one more time before he died.
Jeavons had told her she'd regret it if she didn't, and perhaps
something would be lifted if she did.

Although in the end she gave in, Catherine had refused
to have Jeavons with her at the Cambridge hospice, where
Longman was in his final coma.

Sophie leaned back into the shadows behind the desk
lamp.

'When she got home,' Merrily said, 'Jeavons was leaving
for an international conference in Cape Town. When he got
back, about three weeks later, she'd lost weight, her hair was
unwashed, she'd been drinking. He found bottles of whisky
under the sink. And she was . . . distant. Didn't want to talk
to him. And then she moved her stuff into a separate
bedroom – a temporary thing, she said. She just needed time
on her own. A few weeks later, she had a minor heart attack.'

I took my eye off the ball, was how Jeavons had put it. And
he'd done it again, after the doctors had given Catherine a
tentative all-clear and the situation between her and Lew was

gradually restabilizing. Took his eye off the ball, because this was when he was being courted by both the Church and politicians. He'd thought she'd secretly like the idea of him in episcopal purple.

When Catherine had the second heart attack, Lew had thrown himself into three desperate days of prayer and hands-on. Rarely left her bedside, never slept, the bitterness and self-recrimination lasting long after Catherine's funeral and the memorial service and Lew's rejection of the purple.

'He'd located Catherine's mother to ask if she wanted to be at the funeral, and she hadn't even replied but, some months later, he tracked her down. He said he was in a rocky mental state himself by then – could often feel Catherine's presence in the rectory. He . . . said he awoke one night and saw her in the doorway of his bedroom. But he could only hear the sobs as echoes.'

At this stage, Lew had said, he was close to dumping his ministry, having been offered a teaching and community post back in Brooklyn. He'd had his letter of acceptance in his pocket, ready to post, when the mother-in-law he'd never met had arrived without warning at the rectory and he'd finally learned the truth about his dead wife's relationship with her father.

'Oh *God*,' Sophie said irritably.

'Intellectual sparks between a father and his brilliant daughter. Her mind excited him – Longman used to say that, apparently. When she was at Oxford, he'd visit her at weekends.'

Sophie snorted.

'Jeavons said he'd often suspected there might have been someone else, someone she still thought about. Remembering the "unsuitable boyfriend". Never imagining how unsuitable the boyfriend might actually have been.'

'It's more common than we might imagine among the so-called educated classes,' Sophie said. 'They encourage their children to be "liberal-minded". Makes me sick.'

Merrily shook out a cigarette. 'The reason Catherine's mother had come to see him was that she also was experiencing problems. Maybe it was guilt at having walked away, or at her own resentment of Catherine. Understandable. It's often hard to draw a line between mental unrest and . . . and the other thing. Lew brought in another minister, a friend, to bless the vicarage, sprinkle holy water around in the room where Catherine had slept. Then they held a Requiem Eucharist for Catherine, in the presence of her mother. Which, in normal circumstances, you might expect to resolve it.'

'It didn't?'

'Got worse. He didn't go into details. But he gave back word on the Brooklyn job and just spent a lot of time praying for an answer. Also, putting himself through a kind of ritual scourging – sleeping in the bedroom that Catherine had switched to, because he felt it was . . . *their* room, you know?'

'The father?'

'Jeavons felt that the fact that she'd been there, at the hospice, when the old man died, even if he wasn't conscious – at least, she *thought* he wasn't conscious – that this might have . . . created an opening. Maybe something had been reclaimed, something renewed. Her father had wanted her back with him. You know?'

Sophie's face was hollowed behind the lamp. 'That's horrible, Merrily. Sick.'

'Lew didn't know what to do, or who to turn to for advice. Just kept on returning to that bedroom every night, with his Bible, and whenever he awoke – which was several times every night – he'd pray for help. He maintains that to heal we often have to suffer. A priest must go on suffering, without complaint, until something turns around. And you don't have to look very far into the New Testament for his sources, do you?'

Sophie looked momentarily anxious and then stern. 'I do tend to wonder if you really need this, Merrily.'

'Tell a woman about the need for suffering and you touch a *very* deep seam. Anyway, it came to Lew one night that there should be a Requiem for this person he'd grown to hate: H.F.H. Longman. So . . . Lew Jeavons, his mother-in-law, his Deliverance friend and two other colleagues gathered in the bedroom. Lew doing the honours. Part of the suffering.' Merrily paused.

'And?' Sophie said.

'He told me he went to bed that night for the last time in that room. And he awoke in the night, as he always did, but this time he didn't feel the need to pray. He simply turned over and . . . and the other side of the bed was warm. He got out of bed, pulled up the sheets and went back to their old room.'

Sophie leaned forward into the lamplight. Merrily felt the heat of her own tears and was irritated somehow.

'He gave me a copy of a book called *Healing the Family Tree* by Kenneth McFall, who was a priest and a doctor. I knew about it, never read it. It argues that your mental and physical health is often conditioned by your ancestors. They fuck you up, your mum and dad, and *their* mums and dads and so on.'

'Genetics.'

Merrily shook her head. 'Maybe related – I'm no scientist. Jeavons spent about three years researching all this, here and abroad. Visiting societies where the placating of the ancestors is still considered all-important. Which was controversial, as some of them were more or less pagan.'

'He thinks his wife was in some way destroyed by her father from beyond the grave?'

'Lew thinks if he'd known what he was looking for, if the so-called maladjusted essence had been dealt with earlier, Catherine might still be alive. Like so much of this job, it's hard to separate the spiritual from the psychological. He also talked about this tennis player, Kim Redmond, who was supposed to have been cured of MS. Jeavons said he spent a lot of time talking to Kim, and it came out that the kid's father and his grandfather were both doctors. And the grandad was furious when Kim walked out of medical school with his tennis racquet – accusing him of betraying the family and his obligations to the sick.'

'As if medicine was an ancestral obligation?' Sophie said. 'A tribal thing?'

'Mmm. During Kim's first Wimbledon, grandad dies. By the end of the week, just after the funeral, the kid's having nightmares, beginning to feel his body is no longer his to control. His game's shot to pieces, the doctors eventually start to suspect the worst. Jeavons's solution was a serious Requiem for the old man, conducted at the church where the funeral had been held.'

'And it obviously worked.' Sophie followed tennis.

'Or something did. The docs said it was probably an initial misdiagnosis. Which they would, wouldn't they? Similarly, you could say that the Requiem – the emotional weight of this ancient, solemn ritual – had an immediate psychological effect on Kim, removing the burden of guilt and related symptoms. Anyway, Jeavons says we generally do half a job.'

'Who?'

'Us. Deliverance. Because most of us don't take into consideration the true psychic weight of the family or tribe. And because we're only concerned about the dead when they're conspicuously haunting us. Jeavons's view is that the dead *always* haunt us, whether we're aware of it or not.'

Sophie sat up. 'That's untenable. He's virtually saying everyone needs deliverance.'

'To a degree.'

'And then, in no time at all you've become like that man Ellis, exorcizing everything from the demon drink to the demon—'

'Tobacco,' Merrily said. 'Not as bad as Ellis, maybe, but it's . . . perplexing.'

'It's the quickest way to a nervous breakdown, if you ask me,' Sophie said. 'My advice, for what it's worth, is to avoid this man and all he stands for.'

'He's a very influential voice in Deliverance worldwide. He showed me his computer files. He's in contact with more than three hundred priests, in the US, Canada, Africa, Australia . . . all submitting records of their work, building up this huge database on the healing of the dead. There are people out there who've been trying to heal . . . I dunno, Hitler?'

'Stop.' Sophie pointed at her, very calm, very stern. 'Stop now. Don't go near that man again, Merrily. Just *don't*.'

ELEVEN

Welshies

The smoky dusk was settling over Stanner Rocks when Gomer Parry picked Jane up in his truck, and she wondered if he could see some kind of glow coming off her.

'Cold ole night, Janey. Gonner have at least one big snow before Christmas, I'd say.' Gomer's teeth were clenched like a monkey wrench on his ciggy.

With Antony Largo as the only guest, Amber and Ben didn't need Jane to stay over, so she'd phoned Gomer and arranged for a lift home. But before she left, Antony had cornered her, and put this proposition to her and . . . it was like *incredible*.

'Me and Danny, we falled this ole dead oak for Mrs Maginn, Cwmgaer,' Gomer said. 'Then we sets up the tractor and the sawbench, cuts him up for her stove.'

Gomer was now spending most days at Danny Thomas's farm in the Radnor Valley, ten minutes from Stanner, while his yard was cleaned up after the fire and the big shed was being rebuilt. Danny was Gomer's new partner in the plant-hire business – which made all kinds of sense, with Gomer's nephew Nev dead and Danny having discovered how much he hated farming.

Rural serendipity.

In the dimness of the truck, with no dashboard lights working, Jane watched the tip of Gomer's ciggy receding towards his mouth. He had to be over seventy now, not that anybody would ever prove it. Mum always maintained that Gomer had his own organic generator, and you could sometimes see light in his glasses when there wasn't any around to be reflected.

Serendipity. Maybe Antony would change his mind. Maybe it wouldn't happen. She wouldn't be holding her breath exactly. But, like . . . *wow.*

'Hope that bugger's still paying you, Janey.'

'Sorry?'

'Foley. Word is he en't doing brilliant business. Danny's Greta's sister, she yeard as they wanted help in the bar over Christmas, and then when she gived 'em a call they said they was all right now. But there en't been nobody else took on, otherwise her'd have yeard. Don't miss a thing yereabouts, Gret and Gret's sister.'

'That's bollocks.' Jane was annoyed. It was sunk deep into the collective psyche of this area: the joy of failure. 'In fact, things are really picking up. They've just had a major conference booked.'

'From Off?'

'Of course from Off. Off's where the money is, Gomer.'

'True.' Gomer wasn't parochial himself, he just mixed with people who were.

'And Nat can handle the bar, anyway.'

Gomer slowed for the roundabout at the end of the bypass. 'This'd be Miz Natalie Craven, Jeremy Berrows's . . . friend.'

'Why, what are they saying about her?' Jane had often wondered, although she could probably guess.

'Oh . . . hippy,' Gomer said. 'Not Danny, mind. *He* don't call her that.'

That was probably because Danny was a *real* hippy, Jane thought, as Gomer cleared the roundabout and the sporadic lights of Kington were behind them, dark fields on either side.

'There was plenty folks, see, wanted Jeremy to get back with Mary Morson, after this do with the plant feller from the Rocks – well, Mary's ma, partic'ly, on account of Jeremy's worth a bob or two. This plant feller, he was just on some Government work scheme. Gone now, and never even said he was off.'

'I'm sorry, Gomer, I'm not getting this.' She was interested, naturally: the enigma of Nat and Jeremy.

'Mary Morson, her was engaged to Jeremy?'

'OK.'

'Two year or more, sure t'be. Then her goes to this rock music night at The Eagle, with some mates. Meets up with this smoothy plant feller.'

'You mean one of the botanists working on the Rocks? For the Hereford and Radnor Nature Trust?' There was a study project, Jane knew, centred on this rare plant, the Early Star of Bethlehem, found on Stanner Rocks and virtually nowhere else in Britain.

'Sure t'be,' Gomer confirmed. 'Bit of a fling. 'Course, Mary Morson reckoned her could easy go back to Jeremy on account of Jeremy, he en't going nowhere, is he? He don't never go nowhere, that boy, won't leave his stock no more'n half a day. But meantime this Natalie turns up sudden, with the kiddie, in this van. No accounting for circumstance, Janey.'

'Served the bitch right, if you ask me.'

Gomer's grin flashed in the gloom. 'Exackly what Danny d' say. Danny reckoned her was good for Jeremy, this Natalie. Bring him out of hisself.'

'Quite right,' Jane said. She stared at him. '*Was* good?'

Gomer clamped his teeth on about a millimetre of ciggy. 'Boy en't right, n'more, Janey.'

'How do you mean?'

But he just shook his head and said nothing, and Jane didn't push it. Maybe she ought to have pushed it, if only for Clancy's sake, but everything else was looking too good tonight.

The heavy stuff started for Danny not long after he got in. It started with Greta pulling off the left-hand channel of his big old Wharfedale cans and booming down his ear like her was taking over lead-vocal.

Danny sat up. 'Who?'

Greta said it again, slowly. 'Jeremy Berrows. Needs help. At The Nant. Urgent. Won't tell me n'more, but you just be careful what you takes on, Danny Thomas, because—'

'Bugger.' Danny blinked at the telly, the Foo Fighters still roaring somewhere in his brain. The telly was on, but Danny had been watching the wood-burner, like he always did when he had his music playing on winter nights, just gazing and gazing into the glass. They had these lovely barn-dried ash logs on there tonight, burning bright orange and molten gold, just coming up to perfection, and he could smell his tea, cheese toasting, and the curtains were drawn against the cold black night and . . . *Bugger!*

Danny laid the cans on the back of his armchair, where his head had been, and Greta shoved the cordless at him.

'Yeah?'

'Danny?'

'Ar.'

'They won't go away.'

'What?'

'They won't listen to me. It's like I en't yere. They're all over the yard, all over the meadow . . .'

'What you on about? Who?' Danny had Greta leaning between him and the wood-burner, trying to hear what was coming down the line. He waved at her to get out of his heat.

'Welshies,' Jeremy said.

'Where are you?'

'I'm in the house. I come back in the house, see. En't no way I can deal with all three of 'em, Danny. I got the kid with me, Clancy.'

'Well, that—'

'Don't know whatter do. Don't want no cops yere, they'd just turn it back on me or it'd get in the papers.'

'They threatenin' you?'

'Danny, I en't good in these situations, you know that.'

'Lemme get this straight, Jeremy. Welshies. This would be a raiding party come over the bloody border, is it?'

'Could say that.' Jeremy's voice had gone faint. 'I dunno, Danny, basically. I dunno what's gonner happen.'

When Jane walked into the kitchen, it was clear that Mum hadn't been in long – coat over the chair, bag on the table. Jane placed her own overnight bag very carefully by the kitchen door; she'd need to get it upstairs as soon as poss. Tried not to keep looking at it as she helped Mum cobble a meal together.

'It might snow,' Mum said from the fridge.

'Gomer said that. I bet it'll all be gone by Christmas, though. I don't remember a white Christmas.'

'There was one when you were little.' Mum came over and looked at her with evident suspicion. 'Did something happen?'

'No, why?'

'You seem . . . strangely energized.'

'It's the wonderful world of work. Invigorating.' Jane sawed hard at a farmhouse cob, keeping her head down over the bread knife. Hell, was it *that* obvious?

'Are they . . . going to want you much over Christmas?'

'Hard to say. I think there's a conference of some kind coming off. So, um, you got over to Lol then?'

'Er, yeah.'

'Good. T'riffic. Bit of a drag, though, driving all the way over the other side of the county every time you feel like a . . . proper chat.'

'Actually, we thought there might have been something—' Mum went to the sink to fill the kettle. 'Well, Lucy's old house in Church Street was for sale yet again, and we thought this time . . . Well, Lol thought he could raise the deposit.'

Jane dropped the knife, looked up in real delight. 'Wow! Really? That would be . . . incredible!'

Lucy had been Lol's mentor, had helped turn him around after Alison Kinnersley dumped him. It was what Lucy did: the nature-mystic, the keeper of the village's soul, touching all their lives when they'd first arrived in Ledwardine. Becoming Jane's fairy-godmother figure, kind of. Before dying, thrown from her moped on the road near the old Powell orchard.

'Only, it was, erm, sold,' Mum said. 'Before the agents could even get a sign up.'

'No!'

'We should've seen it earlier in the *Hereford Times*. You don't think, do you?'

'Oh God, that would've been so totally perfect. Like, for both of you. Is there *no* chance?'

Mum shrugged.

'Who's got it?'

'Looks like a weekend-cottage situation.'

'Bastards!' Jane snatched up the bread knife. 'That is *so* . . . In a country this overcrowded, there is no excuse for anybody to have more than one home. It's just like so totally unfair.

Why don't the sodding government bring in some kind of crippling second-home tax?'

'Probably because most of the Cabinet seem to have three or four homes each. I think they're lawyers, from London, these people. Well, you have to do *something* with all that money, don't you?'

Jane shook her head in sorrow. 'Mum, I'm so sorry. It would've been brilliant. And Lucy – she'd have wanted it, more than anything.' She forced a smile. 'Plus, it would've been somewhere for you to move into when I've left home and you finally come to your senses.'

'A retirement home?'

'Oh, it's my firm belief,' Jane said, 'that you'll be out of the Church within two years.'

'You wish.' Mum walked across the kitchen and scooped up the overnight bag. 'I'd better get this lot in the washer, before—'

'*No!*'

Mum turned, with the overnight bag dangling from her hand, Jane frantically aware of the bulge in the side of it. And of Mum's eyes narrowing. She thought fast.

'Put that down *at once*! Can't you *ever* sit down and relax? *I*'ll do it in the morning, when . . . when you're in church.'

There was this horrible, tense moment before Mum did her wry smile and dumped the bag.

'Sounds like you've had a lousy enough day already,' Jane said, snatching it up.

God, how close was *that*?

TWELVE

Night Exercise

Danny remembered the last time he'd had the call-out from Jeremy – a soft summer morning, the air full of warm scents, the brown-haired woman waiting in her caravan, sending out the secret siren calls that only Jeremy would hear.

Now, under an icy sky slashed by a thin moon, Danny backed Greta's old Subaru Justy out of the barn. Little grey car, discreet – don't make no Bank Holiday parade out of this. Greta was opening the galvanized farm gate for him, yowling the whole while.

'You en't called me in half an hour, I'm phoning the police! You got that, Danny Thomas?'

'Whole bloody valley got it.' Danny wound his window tight, shoving a random cassette into the player, turning up the sound cautiously, in case it was one of Gret's Jackie Collins story-book tapes. Danny had his give-away hair pushed up under his woolly hat: no need for the buggers to know who he was.

The Welshies: Sebbie Three Farm's hired guns – here, according to the popular folk-tale put around by Sebbie, to reduce the fox population.

Which was bullshit, basically, because there was never enough, and never would be enough foxes around for Sebbie Dacre and the Middle Marches Hunt. And also, seeing there was a local gun-club that would be only too grateful to be viewed by somebody as a bit useful, why had Sebbie hired from Off?

The Subaru sloshed down the track, the tape on the stereo turning out to be the Creedence collection, starting with *Susie Q*, which was all right but, if it got as far as *Bad Moon Rising* before he reached The Nant, Danny was gonner take it as an omen.

Truth was, nobody knew why Sebbie Dacre had hired shooters from South Wales to scrat about pretending to be after foxes. You didn't go out of your way to fire hard questions at boys from Off with loaded guns. But when these boys was invading what was likely the only farm along the whole border that didn't have no firearms of any description, that was seriously out of order, Danny's view of it.

At the Walton turn-off, he could see all the way to Old Radnor church, jutting up like a castle on a horizon turned jagged by quarrying. Then, just as Creedence were unrolling *Proud Mary*, the forestry rose up darker than the night sky, making him feel like some insect crawling into a yard brush.

What you had to understand first about Jeremy Berrows, see, was that he was an only child. Normal thing was for a farming family to have a spare, but Eddie Berrows was killed outright in a tractor accident when Jeremy was still at school and his mother was pregnant at the time, and her lost it, likely due to the stress. And that was that – Jeremy growing up knowing he had Full Responsibility for The Farm.

There was still farm labour to be had cheapish in them days, so they got by till the boy was sixteen and could take over official. Meantime, it was like all his ole man's know-how had come seeping into him from wherever his ole man was, and now Jeremy was truly *part* of his land, in the way Danny had felt part of the whole valley that time, way back, when he'd dropped acid in the Four Stones field. Except that with Jeremy, who didn't even drink, this was a natural chemical thing, an organic thing, ditchwater in his veins. You'd see him standing there like a little thorn tree, bristling with the breeze, Stanner Rocks behind him and the ewes around his legs. If Jeremy had played music, this would have been his album cover, and it was something close to mystical.

He just wasn't good with people, that was all. Boy was shy, and if folks thought he was just another thick-as-shit hill-farmer, that was all right with him. Let the other buggers do the talking, let Sebbie do the shouting and go on thinking he ruled the valley. Sebbie Three Farms: master of the hunt and all he surveyed – except for this thriving little holding, right in the middle of Sebbie's three farms, that belonged to Jeremy Berrows.

Danny took the Gladestry turn. Always reckoned he knew this area as well as anybody, but he still needed full beams to find the entrance to The Nant. No sign, see. Used to be one, till Jeremy's mam went into the sheltered bungalow in Kington, but Jeremy didn't need telling what was his, so when the sign fell off it stayed off, and that was that.

Full beams was a bit of a give-away, but the track was narrow and the ditches either side were four feet deep, sure to be. The headlights found some new trees that Jeremy and the woman must have planted, with strong stockades around them and chicken wire to keep the sheep off. How many farmers planted trees without there was some big environmental grant for it?

Jeremy Berrows: natural green-boy, firm custodian of the land, friend to all of—

'Christ!'

Danny slammed on, both feet hard down, the Justy's little tyres spinning and squealing like piglets in the mud.

The track had curved to the left and this big motor was blocking the whole of it like an outsize bull. No lights.

Without his own headlamps, Danny would've been up the back of it, no question.

The Justy slurped and stalled, leaving Danny slumped over the wheel, breathing heavy. Must've stayed there about half a minute, getting hisself together, switching his lights off, before pushing his hair back under his woolly hat and climbing shakily out of the Justy. Close? *Shit*.

Danny staggered up to the big motor. It was a Discovery, metallic light green, with camouflage effects sprayed on. He hated this paramilitary crap, despised these bastards already. Still, he made good and sure there was nobody inside the Discovery before setting off to walk the last fifty or so yards to the buildings, keeping to the narrow grass verge beside the ditch, aware that he'd left the Justy blocking the way out.

Too bad. He was still shaking. In the country, the worst accidents happened on farms.

In his jolted-up state, he'd forgotten to bring a torch with him, but the place looked to be well lit up already. The track ended in the farmyard, with the black and white house to the left and the old stone barn on the right, and one wall of the barn looked floodlit like an old church.

The big bay doors were shut, but Danny noticed that the small one to the side was ajar and this was where most of the light was, and there were shadows moving, and he stood there on the edge of the yard, screwing up his eyes to try and make out what was there. Then calling out, in a friendly kind of way, 'Hello there!'

This was just before the light went out and he heard footsteps coming at him from three directions, making him instinctively start whirling round, clawing at the blackness.

When the light came back on a few seconds later, it was full in his eyes, and he was near flattened by the violence of it.

*

Eirion's voice, in the phone, said, 'You total, insufferable bitch. How could you do this to me?'

Jane carried on unwrapping the package, the mobile wedged between ear and shoulder. She was smiling. She'd dug the big Jiffy bag out of her overnight case and brought it over to the bed. Mustn't drop it on the floor, an expensive and complex piece of equipment like this.

'Jane, you still—?'

'Sure.' She'd kept the overnight bag between her knees all the time she and Mum were eating, then said she'd just have to whizz upstairs to the apartment to freshen up and unpack.

'Well?' Eirion said.

'Look, it's the way it goes, sunshine. Nobody *compelled* you to go to the Alps with your creepy stepmother and a few corrupt members of the Welsh Assembly and their bimbos. I think it was John Lennon who said, "Life is what happens to other people while you're busy shooting the *piste* with a bunch of inconsequential tossers." Right, here we are . . .'

Jane released the camcorder from the bubblewrap and lay back on her bed with the phone.

'I can't stand it,' Eirion said. 'What's it look like? What sort is it?'

'Well, it's a Sony.' Jane held the camcorder over her face with one hand. She was going to have to cool this a little, or he wouldn't play ball. 'It says one-fifty and some letters. It's kind of dinky.'

'Sounds like the kind they hand out to people doing these video-diary pieces. The punter sets it up on a tripod in his room and whispers intimate thoughts at it. If it gets broken it doesn't make a major hole in the budget. Has it got one of those flaps you unfold, like a wing, and you can see the picture?'

'Hang on.' Jane sat up. 'Yep, there's a flap. Can't see anything in it.'

'That's probably because it's not switched on. Sockets for external mike?'

'Could be. Couple of those little pinhole things. In fact, there's an actual microphone as well, separate. It's longer than the camera.'

Eirion moaned.

'Piece of crap, then, is it, Irene?'

'No.' Eirion sighed. 'It's a tidy bit of kit, for the money, and it'll get very credible results on automatic setting. Jane, I'm gutted.'

'Yeah, well, I'm sorry. I truly wish you were going to be there. You'd probably get much better stuff than me.'

'Are you *trying* to make it worse? What's he like?'

'Antony? He's quite funny. Very cynical. At first, you get the feeling he really couldn't give a toss. But then he latches on to something, and you can see this steely intensity in his eyes. Of course I don't know these guys like you do, and I didn't realize he was that famous.'

'He's not *famous*, Jane. Pro doco guys are seldom famous. He's *respected*, is what counts. Which is what brings the work in. And I mean, why would a guy . . . why would a guy of his stature allow an evil little bimbo like you to . . . *shoot for television?*'

They had him backed up against the farmhouse wall, battering him with white light.

' . . . The fuck are *you?*'

Danny didn't respond. Stood there with his head bent away from the raging light, knowing that they had him wedged in. Somebody pulled off his hat and his hair came down over his face, near-wringing with cold sweat.

'Looks like one of them fuckin' travellers,' another voice

said – higher, younger. Danny placed the accent in the Valleys, somewhere down where there used to be coal mines and jobs. A good fifty miles from local, anyway.

It was them.

The light veered away from him, and he looked down and saw the lamp – one of them items you could send for out of the glossy catalogues that dropped out of local papers: ten million kilowatts, guaranteed to throw a beam halfway to Rhayader.

'Assed you a question, mun.' Hot, soupy breath in his face. 'Assed you a fuckin' *question!*'

'What I am,' Danny said through his clenched teeth, 'is a feller got hisself invited yere by the owner. Unlike some bastards.'

'Bull*shit!*' He's just a fuckin' tenant, is all. Scum, he is.'

It was blasted into his face along with some spit. The light hit him again like a big white fist, just giving him time, before he had to shut his eyes against it, to see two blokes in army-looking camouflage gear, one with the lamp, the other with something that was likely a rifle with a telescopic sight.

'Try again,' the Welshie said.

'I'm a neighbour. Who're you?'

'On your own?'

'You'll mabbe find out just now,' Danny said, and cried out as somebody grabbed his hair and hauled his head back, and they shone the light directly into his eyes, and when he shut them the night turned bright orange like the logs in his stove.

Danny!' Jeremy. His voice coming from above, probably an open window.

'Call the cops, Jeremy,' Danny said, surprised how calm he sounded, still held by his hair with his eyes tight shut.

From behind, another bloke said, 'OK, he's on his own.' Then they let go of Danny's hair, and he couldn't feel the heat from the lamp any more, and he risked opening his eyes a fraction.

The first thing he saw was the gun.

'Oh shit,' Danny said.

It wasn't what he was expecting. It had a shortish single barrel and a skeleton butt, like the end of a crutch.

'Look,' he said, nervous as hell now, 'what's this about?' If you didn't know better, you might figure these blokes for the SAS on some night exercise. All the instructions shouted, rasped out, like soldiers and armed police did on TV. A performance, designed to put the shits up you.

And it was working. No bugger in these parts had a gun like that, not even—

Danny said, 'Sebbie Dacre sent you, right?'

'Shut the fuck *up*.'

'Nathan!' The younger voice, from a few yards away. 'I can year the bastard movin' about! Fetch the fuckin' light!'

'Now, you won't move, will you, mun?' the close-up Welshie said. 'Cause if we has to come and find you we gonner beat the shit out of you, no arguments.'

'Where'm I gonner move to?' Danny just hoping Jeremy had got over his suspicions of the police and was on the phone to them right now. Failing that, it was all down to Gret. This wasn't normal, not by a mile.

'He's comin' out!' The younger voice – a shrill excitement there, you could almost hear the adrenalin crackling. Boys with guns – unstable. Danny saw one of them swing round, levelling his rifle at the half-open barn door, going into a crouch.

Behind Danny, back at the house, there was the sound of a door bolt being slammed back.

'*No!*' Jeremy. The boy bursting out of the farmhouse.

From inside the barn, there was a scuffling of straw, maybe the sound of something panting. Then a shadow was rising up in front of Jeremy, and he was going, 'Errrrrrr,' like all the breath had been punched out of him.

'You don't wanner get hurt, little man.'

'That's, that's my . . .' Jeremy, fighting for breath 'That's my *dog!*'

Danny ran out into the yard. The barn doorway was fully exposed in the bright beam, two yellow bales on end inside. He saw the butt of the rifle go back hard into the crook of the camouflage feller's shoulder. His own breath came in like ice. One of the Welshies ran over and kicked the barn door wide open and then threw hisself to the side, bawling.

'Shoot! Shoot! Shoot! Shoot the fucker!'

The gun went off twice, these crisp, tight cracks, Jeremy screaming, *'Noooo!'*

Amid the echoes, Danny heard rapid footsteps and saw something else flitting across the yard through the lamp beam to the barn.

'Stop her!' The first Welshie striding out, the lamp snatched up, beam swinging all over the place like a bar of solid light.

And then Jeremy Berrows going, 'No, Clancy, stop, Christ almighty, *no!*'

Jesus, it was the girl. Danny found himself moving fast towards the open doorway, aware of the feller with the gun coming up alongside him, his face shiny-white in the light, and Danny thinking *Oh God, oh God, oh God, what they done?*

A couple of yards from the barn, the gunman pulled ahead of Danny and twisted back, and Danny saw it coming, but he couldn't do a thing about it. His head seemed to burst apart, and he went down clawing at the frozen shit on the cobbles.

THIRTEEN

Real Personal

Spiritualism: this, essentially, was the problem. Spiritualism was the keyhole in the door to hell, and the Deliverance Ministry tended to take an inflexible line on it, so this was why Jane couldn't tell Mum about The White Company.

'Or, er . . . the camera.'

'You mean she *doesn't know you're doing this*?'

Eirion disapproved too, naturally. Rigid Welsh Chapel ethic. OK, he didn't actually go to Chapel, but it had seeped into the whole culture.

'She trusts me these days, Irene. We're into a new phase of mutual trust and support. Look, I'll tell her . . . at some stage. Meanwhile, don't be an old woman. Just give me a few, like, really basic hints, OK? *Please*, Irene.'

'You don't deserve it. You're evil and duplicitous.'

'Irene. I've had a lot of bad stuff happen to me, you know that. No father any more . . . dragged out to the sticks . . . adolescent crises . . . mother in a permanent state of spiritual angst . . .'

'You're not just economical with the truth, you're *parsimonious*.'

'Not with *you*.'

In fact, she'd told him virtually everything: the church, the Vaughans, The White Company . . . all the stuff she couldn't talk about to Mum without risking the most God-awful row, which she, frankly, did not at this moment need.

'How did Largo *put* it?' Eirion asked. 'What did he actually say?'

'Well, it . . . it was after we got back from the church, and I'd been helping Nat with these awful Christmas lights, and Amber's determined to talk to Ben, so Antony just wanders in and he's like, "Jane, could I have a wee word?" '

She told him how she'd made Antony some coffee in the lounge, and he'd said, 'Sit down a minute, Jane,' and started asking her questions: what did she think of this and that on TV, what did she have planned for when she left school?

'I mean, it was dead casual, I thought he was just making conversation. We were getting on pretty well – better than when Ben was around. And like having a laugh about how serious Ben was getting over all this. And then he goes, "Tell me, Jane, have you ever used a decent video camera?" '

'And then when you said no . . . ?'

'I didn't exactly say *no*. As such. I mean, suddenly I was getting an incredible feeling of where this might be going. Which was just . . . *wow*. So I told him that my boyfriend . . . I said my boyfriend's family was connected with television in Wales and I'd been on lots of shoots and, like, helped out . . . filled in . . . done a bit of this and that. You know?'

There was a silence. What she'd actually said was 'my *ex*-boyfriend,' wanting to keep whatever might be on the cards to herself, and she felt desperately guilty about that. Despicable. What kind of bitch did that to her guy? OK, he wouldn't be able to be involved anyway, being out of the country, but it was still . . . well, not the kind of thing Eirion would ever do to her.

'It just came out,' Jane said.

'You . . . *lied to Antony Largo*?'

Jane swallowed, realizing she was sweating.

'You didn't mention my name to him, did you?' Eirion said. 'Because when this is all over and *your* name is like something scraped off his trainers after jogging across the dog pound . . .'

'Look, it's no big deal!' She stared at the silvery little camera, panic rising. 'He'll shoot the heavy stuff himself, the seance. He just wants me to keep track of stuff happening day-to-day when he's not there. Just like point the thing at anything interesting going down around the place and especially at Ben. See, he can't afford to spend whole days *himself* around Stanner when he hasn't flogged the idea to anybody yet – which can take like weeks and weeks – and he needs to keep track of developments and he needs Ben to be in some of the pictures, so . . . Apparently, they're always getting people to do it these days. Shoot bits of stuff. There used to be hassles with the unions, but all that's—'

'So why don't you ask *Ben* for a few hints?'

'Because . . .' Jane shut her eyes. 'Because Ben's clearly not happy about me doing it. He'd rather shoot it himself and *not* be in shot. It's all so confused. Antony's idea of this project may not quite tie in with Ben's. Like, they're mates, but there's artistic friction, you know? I think, what Antony's got in mind, is that if it all crashes, at least it'll make a funny episode for this *Punching the Clock* series, about mid-life crises launching new careers.'

'And these spiritualists – the cranks who think they're going to raise the spirit of Sir Arthur Conan Doyle – they're actually going along with this?'

'Yeah, they're cool with it. Maybe they're hoping for something amazing. Irene, come on, even if nothing happens it could still be totally brilliant stuff.'

Eirion did this bitter sigh. 'I don't know why I'm doing this, but the most basic piece of advice I can give you is to use the tripod whenever possible. You've *got* a tripod?'

'Antony's having one sent over to Stanner for me.'

'Right, well, don't get carried away with hand-held stuff. Unless you've got a lot of experience and really steady hands it looks awful. Unusable, right? Also, stick to auto at all times or you'll just get in a mess.'

'Won't it look amateurish?'

'The difference will probably be minimal, and Largo can get rid of any fluffs in the editing. And make sure your shots are long enough – remember you're recording what might be a familiar scene to you for people who've never seen it before, so hang in there. Don't pan unless it's vital. Don't get carried away with the zoom. And remember that the mike on the camera's OK for ambient sound or when you're tight, but . . . What's the other mike like? Directional, or what?'

'Well, it . . . I mean you can like *point* it. Look, when you said *zoom* . . .?'

'Ration it severely. My advice is to pretend that every time you use the zoom it's going to cost you a tenner.'

'So the zoom . . . where *is* that exactly?'

'Well, it's . . . Oh, bloody hell,' Eirion said, 'suppose I just come over and show you.'

Jane fisted the air. 'I love you so much, Irene.'

'Prove it.'

'Well, maybe,' Jane said, low and sexy and exultant inside. 'Maybe later.'

This greasy, low-wattage bulb over the door. Only a feeble light, coated with dust and cobweb and dead flies, but all light was pain.

Silence in here. The only sound was in his head: the buzz-saw of pain. Standing in the doorway, he was sick with the pain.

'No. It's a friend,' Jeremy said. 'A friend.'

Danny held on to the door frame. The girl in the straw didn't move. Her hair was the same colour as the straw in the rancid butter light. She stared up at him and her eyes were full of fear and hate.

Jeremy said, 'Oh Christ, *they* done that?'

Danny's face and head were wet. He kept his hands away from it.

'Gone?' It was a tattered croak; he couldn't believe the terror in his own voice. 'All of 'em? You sure?'

On the flagged floor, a broken bale and the girl sprawled forward in the straw, looking up, covering the black and white dog with her body.

How much time had passed Danny didn't know. His head felt like the time he'd been kicked by a horse. Jeremy was staring at him.

'They was gonner shoot the dog, Danny. Clancy, she just hurled herself in front of 'em. Wasn't no answer to that. They buggered off.'

'They was gonner *shoot the dog*?'

'What they hit you with?'

'Butt of the gun, I reckon. Why the dog?'

'Dunno.' Jeremy was wearing baggy jeans and an old sweater with holes in it. He was quivering. 'Dunno what they thought.'

'Don't you really, boy?'

'I better get you an ambulance.'

'Bugger off.'

'Can you see out that eye?'

'It missed the eye. You called the cops?'

'You can't drive home in that state,' Jeremy said.

'You called the *police*?'

'No, I—'

'Why not?'

'Don't want no police, Danny. It'd all get twisted round. You know how it is.'

'This *is* Dacre, ennit?'

'They never said, not really.' Jeremy ran his hands through his sparse fair hair, his face all screwed up. 'They never ... He'll admit to hiring them, but he's gonner deny responsibility for how they done it.'

'Done what?'

'Shot the foxes.'

'Foxes, balls. He's the bloody hunt master. *He* don't wanner see no foxes shot at night, or by day. He wants 'em all decently ripped in half by his hounds. The bloody Mid Marches Hunt looks like running out of foxes to chase, Sebbie'd have a couple crates of the buggers shipped over from the city, you know that.'

Danny leaned back against the door frame, breathing through his mouth. The effort of saying all that had left him feeling faint.

'He en't an easy man to deal with,' Jeremy said.

'He's a total bastard of a man, Jeremy, we all know that.'

'He phoned me earlier.'

'Oh, *did* he?'

'Said did I know what that feller Foley was doing over at Hergest. With another feller. And a girl.'

'Why would you?'

'Well, 'cause ... 'cause Nat'lie, she d'work up at Stanner.'

'Yeah, yeah. You tell him?'

'Told him I didn't know nothin' about nothin'.' Jeremy looked down at the girl. 'You best get inside, Clancy, 'fore your mam gets in.' He smiled at her. 'Take the dog in with you. You're gonner need some tea, Danny.'

'No, I'll get off home, 'fore Gret calls in the bloody

Armed Response Unit. Give her a call for me, will you, boy? Say I tripped on the cattle grid but I'm all right now.'

In the end, it was past midnight when Danny made it home, and Jeremy had to take him in his Land Rover.

What had happened, those bastards had rammed the Justy out of the way with the bull bars on the Discovery, heaving it into the ditch. The driver's door was stove in, and Danny didn't give a lot for the sub-frame.

Bastards! Couldn't believe they'd *done* that. Couldn't believe any of this.

Knowing for a fact that if he tried to make a claim against them – even if he could find out their names – they'd deny the whole lot. Anyway, Danny avoided lawyers the same way you didn't drink sheep-dip.

'I en't fully sure what this is about,' he told Jeremy out on the bypass. 'But far as I'm concerned it just got real personal.'

'Leave it, eh, Danny. En't nothing to be done.'

'*En't nothin'*—?'

'I'll pay for the damage.'

'You bloody will not, boy!'

'Happened on my ground. Me as called you out. And I'm sorry. I shouldn't have rung you. I just didn't want nothing to happen to the girl.'

'Right,' Danny said. 'What's going on, Jeremy?'

'Nothing's going on.'

'Who are they?'

'Just some shooting yobs from—'

'Not the *Welshies*, you . . . that girl. And her mam.' Danny was talking through the pain now, so he didn't care what he said, long as he could get it out. 'What's the score there, Jeremy? Where's it goin', you and her? What's that *about*?'

Jeremy said nothing.

'All right, why'd them Welshies say it wasn't your ground? Sebbie Dacre still think he's entitled, is it?'

'I wouldn't know.' Jeremy staring straight ahead, driving slow. 'En't his. En't never gonner be his. That's all I know. I was born there, I'll die there.'

Not just an expression of intent, Danny thought, it was like he knew it for a fact – that he would die at The Nant.

Above them, the wishy-washy moonlight shone damply on Stanner Rocks, and Jeremy never spoke another word, except for 'goodnight' – not much more than a clicking of the tongue – when he dropped Danny at his top gate.

Part Two

'My friend was still looking at the coat of arms and I walked to the archway here and just looked across at the blue curtain. There was an image . . . it wasn't even a shape . . . I can only describe it as when motes hang in sunbeams. But it was the image of a bull and he was giving out the feeling of being angry . . . he was pawing at the ground but he was in the air. The inside of his nostrils – this was one of the most vivid things – were very, very red, like a racehorse when it's just stopped running. And it was wet, it was dripping moisture or something on to the ground. It was as though it was hanging in sort of strings . . . As we walked to the middle aisle it started to fade . . . I'm a hard-headed business person. But I can't deny it, I've seen it – I've experienced it.'

Jenny Vaughan, 1987

The ladies who prepare the flowers in the church did say on two separate occasions that the floral arrangement had taken the shape of a bull's head.

Alan Lloyd, local historian, Kington

FOURTEEN

Word to the Wise

So Danny went after Sebbie Three Farms.

The wisdom of this . . . well, that was in question. Jeremy phoned early Sunday morning, to see how Danny was feeling, to repeat his offer of picking up the tab for Greta's Justy and to tell Danny to leave well alone on account of Sebbie Dacre couldn't be counted on to behave like any kind of rational human being.

Danny said he'd bear that in mind.

Hour or so later, Greta bathed his head again and said, 'Leave it, you year me, Danny Thomas? You can patch him up, the little car. Leave it till tomorrow at least.'

'Longer we leaves it, harder it's gonner be.'

'You are *not* going to Dacre's place on your own. Suppose them fellers is there with their guns? You can wait till tomorrow, then you can take Gomer with you.'

'Take Gomer with me?' Danny stared at her. 'You totally cracked, woman? *Gomer?* I'd feel safer with pockets full of bloody Semtex.'

'En't as wild as he used to be,' Gret said. 'He's an ole man now. Look, you promise me—'

'I promise.' Danny went out, shaking his head at the idea that age could mellow somebody like Gomer Parry. But then, Gret had never seen Gomer at the controls of his JCB, that big gash of a smile around his ciggy, hell's own light in his glasses.

The sky was near-enough the colour of a shotgun barrel, and the cold air ripped at Danny's head wound like barbed wire as he crossed the yard to the Land Rover.

Well, no way was he gonner forget this. Couldn't live with himself. Couldn't afford another car for Greta if this one got written off.

He was on his way to Jeremy's to see if he could somehow tow the Justy home when, as it happened, he seen Sebbie Dacre in person, turning right at Walton towards Radnor Forest. Sebbie was in his mustard-coloured Range Rover, and he was on his own.

Seemed like fate.

Last in the handshaking line outside the church porch after morning service was Alice Meek, in Sunday best. Not many people wore Sunday best any more; they came to church in fleeces and jeans.

The big man with Alice wore jeans and a shiny leather jacket.

'This yere is Dexter Harris, vicar. My nephew from the tyre place? With the asthma? Didn't seem right just bringing him along tonight, for the Healing Service.'

The Healing Service?

Merrily shook hands limply with Dexter and then stood there, shivering in the cold, weak sunshine of the first day of December. When, for God's sake, had her loose prayer meeting, her meditative interlude, her quiet time before the start of the working week, become *The Healing Service*?

'I told him there wasn't nothing to be scared of. Don't wanner bring on an attack, do we?'

Alice cackled, confident that this wouldn't happen. Not on a Sunday, not at the church of the healing vicar.

Merrily looked up at Dexter Harris. He was a big, heavy man, shaven-headed, balding or both. He had a lower lip that jutted like a spout from a jug. He looked about thirty-five. He looked like he'd rather be anywhere but here, but few people argued with Alice.

Down by the lych-gate she could see Ted Clowes, retired solicitor, senior churchwarden, her mother's brother and the village's most reliable opponent of Deliverance, faith healing and anything else that was, in his narrow view, spiritually off-the-wall and fiscally unpromising. If Ted was waiting for her by the lych-gate, it was with the intention of following her home to bend her ear on neglect of crucial parish issues.

Oh well.

'How would you feel about a cup of tea, Dexter?' Merrily suggested. 'In fact, there might even be a can or two of Stella in the fridge.'

Mr Sebastian Dacre JP.

Danny Thomas and Sebbie Dacre, they was about the same age and had known one another, to a point, since they was boys. But Danny was at the local schools and Sebbie was a boarder at the Cathedral School in Hereford and riding to hounds at twelve and screeching around Kington in a Triumph Spitfire at eighteen. And Sebbie's ole man used to have close to a thousand wide acres while Danny's dad had just under forty-three acres of hillside with soil skin-deep over the rock.

And Danny was Danny Thomas, the Rock 'n' Roll farmer as was, and Sebbie was Mr Sebastian Dacre JP, Master of the Middle Marches, local organizer for The Countryside Alliance. It was like that.

Sebbie was clearly headed for The Eagle at New Radnor. Nice pub, situated just perfect in the middle of this nice quiet village – big wide street, widest in Radnorshire, sure to be, overlooked by a lot of houses and cottages and a shop and The Eagle. Danny was reminded of the streets in old Western movies, which were always very wide and quiet and just right for a shoot-out, two fellers approaching each other real slow from opposite ends.

Greta was wrong. Best to handle this on his own: Danny the negotiator, Danny the diplomat. He wanted something out of this to repair the Justy. Also it was very much time to put the arm on Sebbie to keep his muscle off Jeremy Berrows's ground. Boy looked like he'd enough to worry about right now, without lying awake at night listening for tyres creeping up the track.

Most of all, though, Danny wanted to know what was behind it. Why was Sebbie Three Farms employing these three hard-bastard shooters from South Wales?

A shedload of questions here. And if he followed Sebbie now to wherever he was going, then he wouldn't have broken his promise to Gret, would he?

Sebbie parked at the side of the road and Danny come in behind him just as he was climbing down: Sebbie Three Farms, all six foot whatever of him, tough-thin, like streaky bacon.

Sebbie put on his tweed cap. Always wore a cap because his reddish hair was sparse now and his skin was pale as watered milk. A walking invitation to skin cancer, was Sebbie, and yet he always walked tall and straight, like he was defying the sun.

Danny come right up behind him. 'Mr Dacre!'

It was how you talked to people in these parts, only real close friends using first names.

Sebbie didn't turn round at once, like a normal person would; he kept on walking towards the pub door and, when he did turn, it was only to flick a bleep at the Range Rover to lock the doors. At which point he deigned to notice Danny.

'Mr Thomas, how're you? Working with Parry now, hey? Diversification – only course open in these constricting times.'

'You happen to 'ave a minute, Mr Dacre?'

Sebbie frowned. 'People say a minute when they mean half an hour.'

His pale eyes had screwed up a bit now, cautious. Last thing he'd want would be Danny in the pub with him, where they'd be overheard, and the word spread over half of two counties by sundown.

'Cause Sebbie knew what this was about, nothing surer.

'I'll keep it short, then,' Danny said. 'Three of your boys was rampaging over The Nant last night, loosing off the kind of gun you don't normally see this side of Credenhill base. And the end result—'

'Mr Thomas—'

'End result of this bit of a farm-invasion is *this*.' Danny touched his forehead, winced.

'Doesn't look like a bullet wound to me, Mr Thomas, but more to the point—'

'More to the point, Mr Dacre, is my wife's car gets battered off the track and looks to me, bearing in mind he's eleven year old, like we could be looking at a write-off.'

'And you saw who it was, hey?'

'Your boys, it was. Like I said.'

'My *boys*? *My* boys?'

'Said you was payin' 'em to shift foxes.'

Sebbie squinted, like the sun had come out. 'That sound awfully likely to you, Mr Thomas?'

'I'm tellin' you what they said. Three Welshies from down the Valleys, sounded like.'

'And you saw them actually damaging your car, did you, these *boys*? At night.'

'Men, they was, more like. And I sure enough seen—'

'You informed the police, obviously.'

'I sure enough seen one of the buggers come over and clobber me with the butt end of his fancy gun.'

'And naturally you've told the police about that, too.'

'No.' Danny glanced down at his boots. 'Not *yet*.'

'And you're saying these men claimed to be working for me. That's an actual allegation you'd be prepared to make in front of witnesses and my solicitor?'

Danny fell silent. You forgot how hard it was getting a feller like this to put his hands up to anything. Outsiders, townies, they didn't believe Sebbie's sort existed any more, thought they was a joke – music-hall villains, feudal stuff out of history. But even now, with the countryside shrinking faster than a pair of market-stall jeans, Danny could still point you out five or six like Sebbie within twenty or thirty miles.

Sebbie gave out a look that was all but a mouthful of spit. '*I* thought you'd know better, Mr Thomas, than to come accosting me in the street with this kind of half-baked drivel.'

'It's the truth.'

'They *named* me?'

'Aw, come on, everybody knows it, Mr Dacre. Folk around yere en't daft. Nobody understands it, why you're letting foreigners in with illegal shooters, but they knows it's down to you. And they knows there's history between you and Jeremy Berrows.'

'Who does?' Sebbie was half-smiling, hadn't broken sweat. '*Who* knows all this? Give me some names, Mr Thomas, hey? Give me some names and I'll sue their arses orf in a court of law.'

Danny said nothing at all. Who was he supposed to drop in the slurry? You didn't, did you? Not to a man who never forgot a name. Danny felt ashamed. He should've brought Gomer along, like Gret said; Gomer, to put it mildly, wasn't fazed by nobs. Danny hadn't said half of what he'd planned to say, and already it was all going pear-shaped on him. His head throbbed and his vision was lopsided somehow, so that he saw Sebbie Dacre like Sebbie was some tripping image, an acid flashback: thin neck craning out of the collar of his Viyella, and his head, under the beak of his cap, like a hawk's watching a rabbit.

'Easy target, en't he, Jeremy Berrows?' Danny said.

'Mr Thomas, Jeremy Berrows would be an easy target for the Women's Institute bowling team. Now geddout of my hair.'

'I don't get it,' Danny said. 'How come you live next to Jeremy all his life, and suddenly you're turnin' the heat on?'

Sebbie just looked and half turned away like the very sight of Danny was starting to offend him.

'Or mabbe it's the woman,' Danny said. 'Nat'lie.'

Sebbie swayed just slightly and then he came out with this one, real nonchalant, like he'd just been ferreting in Danny's mind.

'You still using drugs, Mr Thomas?'

'That en't bloody fair!' Danny blurted, before he could stop hisself. His head pulsed and he felt faint.

'*Ain't fair?*' Sebbie's head shot forward like Danny's words had pressed a button. 'I'll tell you what *ain't fair.* What ain't fair is what's happening to the countryside under this fucking government. If they persist in trying to stop us hunting with hounds – make us subject to licensing and regulations, put the countryside into a suburban strait-jacket . . . if they go on trying to challenge our traditional way of dealing with *vermin* . . . then they can bloody well *expect* what one might call Less Orthodox Methods of Pest Control.'

At this point, Gwilym Bufton, the feed dealer, came across the road towards The Eagle, with another feller, and they exchanged *'ow're yous* with Sebbie, and Sebbie raised two fingers to his cap in a kind of mock-humble salute. When they'd gone into the pub, he came a bit closer to Danny, his pinky eyes shining. The street was quiet around them, and Danny had the feeling of folks at their windows, like this really was a showdown in a Western town starring the big-time rancher and the shabby dust-bowl farmer who couldn't afford a haircut. Sebbie's voice was low.

'What I'm saying *is*, if they're going to make us illegal, turn decent people into poachers, then they shouldn't be surprised to find bands of brigands roaming by night.'

Danny was thrown – this was surreal. 'What the hell's that mean? You're supposed to be a bloody magistrate!'

'And with more of our local police stations closing every year,' Sebbie said, 'they won't have the means or the manpower to counter it. Look, *I* don't know what happened to your damn car, and I expect you've got another half-dozen clapped-out wrecks in your buildings to replace it, but I can tell you one thing . . . this is only the start. And if you're not part of it, you should stay at home, get yourself quietly stoned and keep your nose out, eh? Word to the wise, Mr Thomas, word to the wise.'

He turned away. Danny didn't move, couldn't believe what he'd heard. This was a *magistrate*. He shouted after Sebbie Dacre, 'Why'd you tell them Welshies Jeremy Berrows didn't own his own farm? Why'd you tell 'em Jeremy was your tenant?'

'Don't know what you're talking about.'

'You know what, Sebbie?' Danny pointing the finger. 'I don't believe you. I think you're full of shit. I reckon you're covering some'ing up, boy.'

'And you're a faded old hippy full of pathetic, drug-induced conspiracy theories.' Sebbie stopped at the pub door. 'I'll give *you* a question, now. Why did Berrows call to *you* for help? Why didn't he call the police, hey? Give that some thought, I would, Mr Thomas, and be sure to hide your *stash* somewhere safe, because you can expect a visit in the early hours from the Dyfed-Powys Drug Squad. Good day to you.'

Then he went into the pub, and Danny saw the curtains twitching along the street and found he was shaking, like with cold turkey.

FIFTEEN

Milk into Concrete

When Merrily brought Dexter Harris into the kitchen, Jane had already made soup and sandwiches – not many big Sunday lunches in *this* household – and they'd shared them with Dexter, who at first was all shy and shambling, twice using his inhaler.

He ate steadily, glancing at Jane and occasionally at Merrily, something evidently on his mind. It took both cans of Stella to bring it out.

'They, er, they reckons you're the whatsit – county exorcist.'

'Well, nowadays, they don't . . .' Merrily's shoulders sagged. He'd have seen the movie on DVD – explanations were useless. 'Yeah, kind of. Alice told you?'

Dexter shifted uncomfortably. Maybe he was expecting her to toss holy water at him, thrust a cross in his face, instructing the demon of asthma to vacate his system. Maybe that was a course of action Lew Jeavons might even advise.

In which case, one of them was in the wrong job.

'It's probably not what you think,' Merrily said.

But what *was* she going to do? What did Alice actually expect of her? She smiled nervously at the big guy wedged into a dining chair with his leather jacket over the back. She felt worse than inadequate, she felt like someone recruited into a fraudulent enterprise, a trainee on a travelling medicine show.

And while the lager had loosened Dexter up, it didn't make the situation any more promising. He was eyeing Jane now, and claiming that today was the first time he'd been inside a church since his christening. Tell the truth, he was only doing this to shut Alice up – her nagging him and his ma about it. Dexter lived at home with his ma and his younger sister in the Bobblestock area of Hereford. Useful to have somebody around if he had an attack, look. Also it was cheaper, and most of his girlfriends had their own flats or houses, so *that* was all right.

Suppose he had an attack here, what then? Merrily looked at Jane. If Dexter's breathing changed rhythm, any laying-on of hands would take place only while they were waiting for the paramedics to get here.

Dexter started asking Jane which clubs she went to in Hereford at weekends. Jane named four, Merrily seriously hoping that she was lying. Dexter smirked at the last one, telling Jane he'd probably see her there sometime. Maybe he didn't think of himself as being twice as old.

At about two-thirty, they heard a car pulling into the vicarage drive and Jane sprang up, conspicuously relieved.

'It's Eirion.'

'Jane's boyfriend.' Merrily stood up, too, moved to the door of the scullery/office. 'Let's leave them to it, huh, Dexter?'

'Boyfriend?' Dexter looked like he'd been short-changed.

Merrily held open the office door. She was still in her dog collar and the Morning Worship kit, minus surplice, and this was probably for the best – too much informality could well convey the wrong impression to an overweight, dough-faced man of probably thirty-plus who seriously imagined someone Jane's age could fancy him.

They went in and sat down, facing one another across the desk, like one of them had come for a job. On the desk: computer, answering machine, phone, Bible, sermon book.

Now what, Lew?

This . . . is at the heart of spiritual healing – taking the time to know people, making small deductions. How many doctors have the time or the patience to do that now – talking and considering and leaving time for small leaps of inspiration?

She had a cigarette half out of the packet when Dexter blandly shook his head, making wiping motions with his hands, his lower lip projecting like an outlet pipe. She pushed the cigarette back into the packet, wondering how he survived in the clubs. Putting the Silk Cut packet out of reach. *We suffer*, Jeavons had said.

An hour passed. It was growing dark.

Dexter was talking about the collapse of his engagement two years ago – how it had really knocked him sideways to learn that his girlfriend, Farah, had been seeing another bloke for months, apparently weighing up which of them was the best bet and then deciding, for some weird reason of her own, that it wasn't Dexter.

Bitch. Made you stop trusting women, Dexter said. Made you want to start scoring a few points of your own. Dexter had hit the clubs. Shagger Harris, the foreman started calling him, down the tyre depot. Dexter grinned, looking down at the Bible on Merrily's desk.

If we take the time to absorb what people are telling us about themselves, directly and indirectly, and we are in a suitable state of relaxation – a contemplative state – then the clues they come together and a feeling – or a word – sometimes drops into our minds.

'How old are you, Dexter?'

'Me? Twenny-nine, now. Soon be thirty. Yeah, I know I look younger.'

'Nobody special since Farah? Just casual stuff?'

'Just casual sex,' Dexter said.

'Doesn't the asthma . . .?' Merrily broke off, embarrassed.

Dexter wasn't. 'Naw, they reckons it's stress brings it on, look. Well, I only gets stressed-out when I en't having no luck. Most times I can go all night, know what I mean? Don't get no problems that way.' He smiled at her. 'Funny thing, that, ennit?'

Merrily leaned back. 'You don't really think this is going to help you, do you?'

Dexter sniffed. 'Like I say, if it keeps the old woman quiet, it's something. No offence meant. I'm not much of a believer. Can't help that, can I?'

'No. If you try and force yourself to believe, that only causes . . . stress.'

'Doctor says I've gotter avoid that. People gives me stress, I don't bother with 'em no more.'

'Do you remember the first one?'

'You what?'

'The first asthma attack you ever had.'

He shook his head. 'Dunno.'

'Do you remember how old you were? Or has it always been a problem?'

''Bout twelve, thirteen.' He didn't look at her. She felt a tightening of the air between them. 'Do it matter?'

'I was just wondering what might've brought it on. If there was a particular . . . emotional problem that might've caused it. I mean, I don't know what Alice told you, but I'm not any kind of medical expert. I'm just looking for . . . maybe something we can focus on in our prayers.'

'Prayers?' He looked at her now. 'Strange, a nice-looking woman like you being a vicar and going on about prayers and that.' He looked down at her breasts. 'You must've been quite young when you had your daughter.'

'What do you think about when you're having an asthma attack?'

'Eh?'

'What goes through your mind?'

'Sorter question's that?'

'I don't know, it just came into my head. Nobody ask you that before? The doctors?'

'Why would they?'

'I'd just like to know what it's like.'

He stared at her defiantly. 'It's like you're drinking a glass of milk, and it turns into fuckin' concrete halfway down your throat. That's what it's like.'

'Thank you.' Sounded like an image that went way back. A childhood image.

'Don't you get me going,' Dexter said. 'If I starts thinkin' about it, I'll get stressed.'

He wasn't much more than a big silhouette now – wide shoulders, a pointed head. It was dark enough to put on the lamp. She reached out automatically, then paused, with a finger on the button of the Anglepoise.

'And I don't want people talkin' about me in the church,' Dexter said. 'She said you was just gonner . . . I dunno, just do the healin'.'

'It wouldn't be like that, Dexter – people talking about you. It's just, you know, to give *me* some guidance. Everything you tell me is totally confidential. Just between the two of us.'

'Nothing to tell.'

'Have you really not been in a church since your christening? No weddings? Funerals?'

He didn't reply. In the silence, she thought his breath had coarsened. She tapped the Anglepoise button, still didn't press it down. The directional light might make this seem too much like an old-style police interrogation. She thought of the basement interview rooms, opposite the cells at Hereford police headquarters, the ventilator grilles high on the walls, no windows. You didn't need to be asthmatic to feel you couldn't breathe down there.

'You ever been in bother with the police, Dexter?'

It just came out, on the back of the thought.

'Eh?'

'Look, I'm sorry if that was—'

'I fuckin' knew it.' Dexter was pushing back the chair.

'I'm sorry.' With difficulty, she didn't move. 'I don't know why I said that.'

a feeling – or a word – sometimes drops into our minds.

Dexter was on his feet, a terrifying rattle in his breath.

'It was out of order,' Merrily said, 'I'm sorry.'

'I dunno . . .' Dexter moved clumsily to the door. 'Dunno what she's been tellin' you, that ole bat.' He had his inhaler out. 'But fuck *this* for a game of soldiers.'

When Eirion tried to ease Jane back onto the bed, she just couldn't go for it. Not with Mum two floors below, doing what she was doing. Doing the business, doing the priest bit, whatever she perceived *that* was today.

'I really worry about her now.' Jane sat on the edge of the bed, with her elbows on her knees.

'It's probably reciprocated tenfold,' Eirion said.

'I'm serious. The Jenny Box thing, that whole affair, it really messed her up – this woman in desperate need of support, sitting on awful secrets, and Mum not being there for her when it came to a head.'

'She couldn't know, though, Jane, could she?'

'It doesn't *matter*, she still feels responsible. Male priests can be aloof from it all – if they can get a few bums on pews then they feel they still have a role and a bit of status. Women, everything that goes wrong they take it as their fault.'

'Isn't that slightly sexist?' Eirion said.

'And with Mum you've got this constant self-questioning – all this, "Am I doing what I'm supposed to be doing to try and fill His bloody sandals?" '

Eirion came and sat close to Jane, bending forward to peer into her face.

'I'm not upset,' Jane said, 'just in case you were thinking I might be in need of a groin to cry on.'

'So what *is* she doing?'

'Huh?'

'Down there, with this bloke.'

'I think she's been invited to cure whatever it is that's causing him to keep sucking his inhaler.'

'I don't understand.'

'OK.' Jane let him take her hand. 'It started with Ann-Marie Herdman. It's all round the village that Ann-Marie Herdman was cured of something very nasty – that she may or may *not* have had – after Mum prayed for her. Now, if it had been a regular prayer for the sick, in the course of a normal service, nobody would've said a word. But because it was at one of the mysterious new Sunday-night sessions where there are weird things like – *woooh* – meditation . . . then it must be . . . you know?'

'She's teaching meditation now?'

'In a simplistic Christian way. Nothing esoteric. I didn't realize how far it had got until I went down the shop a couple of hours ago for some stuff for sandwiches, and there were these two women talking about it to Brenda, who's Ann-Marie's mum. I mean, I knew *about* Ann-Marie, but I thought it was just another NHS cock-up. I didn't realize Mum was in the frame as . . . God, I can't bear it. And if *I* can't bear it, how does *she* feel?'

'They're saying she has healing skills?'

'It's the way people are, that's all. Always desperate for evidence of miracles. It's like when all these idiots form queues to worship a potato with the face of Jesus. One of the women said Alice Meek had brought her nephew in to have the vicar pray for him to be healed, and I'm imagining some little kid, and I'm thinking, Oh God, this is terrible, that's *all* she needs. Then Mum turns up with this big jerk with the inhaler who keeps leering at me and accidentally rubbing his leg against mine under the table. It'd be laughable if it wasn't so . . . not funny.'

'So what exactly is she doing?'

'If she's got any sense, Irene, she's explaining to him that she's unfortunately become the focus for a load of superstitious bollocks put about by old women with nothing better to occupy their minds. And then maybe suggest to this guy – *Dexter*, for heaven's sake – that they say a quick prayer together but don't expect to be throwing his inhaler into the river just yet.'

Eirion thought about this. He was Welsh; a large number of them still took religion seriously. 'But she's a priest,' he said.

'Er . . . yes.'

'Don't you see? She has to acknowledge at least the *possibility* of miracles. She has to accept that God can do it, and that she could be a channel for it. She can't just walk away from it if anybody thinks there's a small chance. You know?'

Jane sighed. 'It's a fine line.'

'It's not *that* fine, Jane.'

'The big joke . . .' Jane stared at the Mondrian walls – big plaster squares in the timber framing that she'd painted in primary colours. 'The big joke is that women think getting ordained was some huge coup for their sex. The fact is, it's the crappiest job there is, and it's getting worse all the time, as society gets more and more secular and cynical. It's obvious that the ordination of women was actually a subtle conspiracy by the male clergy, desperately searching for fall guys as everything around them collapses into some like . . . pre-Armageddon bleakness.'

'I thought you were over that.' Eirion stood up and walked to the window. It had started snowing: not much, but it always looked worse from up here, especially at dusk, white on grey.

'I have the occasional relapse,' Jane said.

Eirion sighed. 'So, do you want to know how to work this video camera, or what?'

Maybe Merrily should have realized that something was spinning out of control. Maybe, if she hadn't been thinking about Dexter Harris, she would have been curious about the extra cars on the village square. She didn't even notice them.

It was becoming unexpectedly cold – she was aware of *that*. She saw snowflakes clustered like moths around the fake gas-lamps on the square. As soon as she slid into church, wearing Jane's old duffel coat over jeans, her black cashmere sweater and her smallest pectoral cross, she made sure that the heating was on full – checking that Uncle Ted hadn't crept in and turned it down.

He hadn't, for once, but she still felt a need to do more and lugged the little cast-iron Calor-gas stove out of the vestry, wheeling it to the bottom of the chancel steps. It wouldn't make much difference, temperature-wise, but a glimpse of real, orange flames kind of warmed the soul.

She felt domestic about the church tonight, wanting to turn the House of God into a big kitchen.

How she felt about Dexter Harris – that was different. The fact that he was so charmless and unresponsive somehow made it more important to try and help him. The fact that he didn't *want* to be helped made it complicated: if there was something in his past that had caused or advanced the asthma, did she have any right, let alone responsibility, to try and find out about it?

Responsibility: where did it begin and where did it end?

Sitting alone in the choir stalls, she cleared Dexter from her mind, closed her eyes and became aware of her breathing, allowing it to regulate itself. A short meditation had become an essential preliminary to the Sunday-evening session. When she sat down here, twenty minutes before the start, she would usually have no real idea at all what form it would be taking. But when she stood up again, that no longer mattered.

It was the sounds of movement that brought her out of it. Too much movement. She knew her church; she knew her congregations and the sounds of them, familiar coughs and whispers.

When she came back into the body of the church, standing next to the faintly hissing gas stove, it was like she was in some other parish, staring out at faces she didn't recognize: a woman with a baby, two teenage girls. And in the aisles, two wheelchairs, one occupied by a boy of about eleven and the other by a woman in her fifties with a tartan rug over her knees.

There was a shuffling quiet in the church, everybody looking at Merrily, in her black sweater and her jeans, and she felt small, bewildered, desperate.

Fraudulent.

It was snowing so hard that Eirion had to leave. Jane had been hoping he wouldn't notice until it was too late, so he'd have to spend the night, but he'd borrowed his stepmother's car again, needed to get it back to Abergavenny.

Jane stood at the front door, cuddling Ethel the cat and watching through the bare trees as he drove away, red lights reflected in the half-inch of unsullied snow on Church Street. Much of what he'd told her about the camera she was sure she hadn't really taken in, but she'd made notes. She ought to practise with the gear before she went back to Stanner. In normal circumstances she could ask Mum to help, perhaps record an interview with her, with the external mike plugged in. Except that, because of the nature of what she might be shooting up at Stanner, it wasn't wise even to mention it.

Christianity was a minefield. You could talk about spirituality but not *spiritualism*, open yourself to spiritual healing but never *spirit* healing. If she told Mum about The White Company, she'd be letting herself in for one of those long, serious talks, ending with the usual warnings: *Well, it's up to you, you're intelligent and old enough to make up your own mind about what you get involved in, but* . . .

The rest unsaid, the word 'betrayal' never passing between them.

The phone was ringing. Normally, she'd let the machine grab it, but she felt like talking to somebody. She stepped back inside and shut the front door, putting Ethel down and dashing through the kitchen into the scullery to snatch up the receiver.

'Ledwardine vicarage.'

'Mrs Watkins?' Female voice.

'No, she's in church. Can I help?'

'Oh . . . no . . . It's all right, I'll call back.'

'Can I give her a message?'

'No, it's all right, really.'

The caller hung up, just as Jane recognized the voice. Was *sure* she'd recognized the voice.

She dialled 1471.

'*You were called at seven-fourteen today. The caller withheld—*'

Jane hung up. Two chairs were pulled away from the desk,

THE PRAYER OF THE NIGHT SHEPHERD

as if Mum and Dexter had left in a hurry. Jane sat down in one.

Talk about betrayal . . .

Danny tried to listen to some music, but The Foo Fighters made his headache worse. It was the first time this had happened; normally, the heavier the music the more it relaxed him. In the end he watched telly with Greta, listening to *Heartbeat* with his eyes shut, identifying the sixties numbers on the soundtrack until he fell asleep.

And Greta woke him again, with the cordless phone.

'No,' Danny mumbled. 'Please, God.'

'Gwilym Bufton, it is. I told him you wasn't well, but he said you'd want to hear this.'

'Gwilym?' Danny struggled to a sitting position. First time he'd had a call from the feed dealer since he'd given up livestock, which Gwilym saw as an act of treachery.

''Ow're you, boy?'

'Half dead.'

'That's good. Looks like we're in for some snow, ennit?'

'Sure t' be.'

'Not a problem for you n' more. In fact, it'll be contract work with the council, you and Gomer. Got your plough fitted?'

'Not yet.'

'Good business, Gomer's.'

Danny waited, his head throbbing. Bloody trouble with Border folk, took for ever to get to the point. For ever later, Gwilym gets there.

'What you been doing to Sebbie, then?'

'What have *I* been doing—?'

'You and the Berrows boy.'

'What's he saying we done?'

'En't said a thing. Havin' a go at him, though, wasn't you? Not a happy man in the pub afterwards.'

'Glad to hear it.'

'Just wonderin' what else you might've yeard.'

'Like?' This needed care; Sebbie was a valued client of Gwilym's.

'Worried man, Danny.'

'Din't look worried to me.'

'Well, he don't, do he? All bluff and bluster. You remember Zelda? Zelda Morgan, from the Min of Ag, as was?'

'Who wouldn't?'

'Sebbie been giving Zelda one for quite a while,' Gwilym said. 'Her lives in hope, poor cow. Distant relative of my good lady, see.'

'I'd make it even more distant, her becomes Mrs Dacre.'

Gwilym laughed, just a bit. 'He don't sleep much.'

'Zelda's complainin'?'

'Zelda's bothered, Danny. Wakes in the night, there's Sebbie, bollock-naked at the window. Shaking. Shaking like with the cold. And it *is* cold in Sebbie's bedroom, but it never bothers him as a rule.'

'Mabbe not as much as the price of heating-oil.'

As well as feed, Gwilym was the agent for an oil depot in Hereford.

'So he's going – this is Sebbie – he's going – "*Look, look . . .*" Drags Zelda out of bed, points down the valley, over Berrows's ground. "*See it, see it?*" '

'See what?'

'Her don't know. He won't say. And Zelda don't see nothing. Moonlit fields, that's all. Couple nights later, wakes her up again. "*You hear that? You hear that?*" Her can't year nothing, 'cept for Sebbie bleating like a ewe in labour. This is confidential, Danny.'

190

Sure it was. Fellers like Gwilym doing the rounds, farm to farm, was the reason this valley leaked like a smashed sump.

'So what's this gotter do with me?' Danny said, patient as he could manage with a bad head. 'If Dacre's losin' it, he's losin' it.'

'And then Sebbie's going, "*It's coming out of Berrows's ground . . . Berrows's ground.*" '

Danny's hand tightened on the cordless. He said casually, 'Good to know the bastard recognizes the boundary now.'

'He says, "*It's Berrows. Berrows and that bitch.*" '

'Zelda tell you this herself?'

'Zelda's pretty scared, Danny. Her asks Sebbie about it next morning, over breakfast, bugger hits the roof. Sweeps the bloody cups off the table, everything smashed. Thought he was gonner hit her. White with rage.'

'He's always bloody white, Gwilym, it's the skin he's got.'

'So, like, Zelda says to me, "Can *you* ask Jeremy Berrows 'bout this? I can't never talk to him." '

'Which is why you're askin' me,' Danny said.

'En't real sure *what* I'm asking, Danny. You're the nearest he's got to a friend – do any of this make sense?'

Danny thought about it.

'No,' he said after a bit. 'Do me one favour, Gwilym, don't spread this around. Gimme a chance to find out what I can. Or am I too late already?'

'You knows me, boy.'

'Aye,' Danny said. That was the bloody trouble.'

'What was that about?' Greta said when he'd clicked off.

'Feller Gwilym knows with a David Brown tractor for sale. I said I'd pass the word on to Gomer.'

'In other words, keep your nose out, Greta,' Greta said.

Danny stared into the reddening wood-stove.

SIXTEEN

Responding to Images

Frannie Bliss, of Hereford CID, called back on Monday afternoon, just as the light was fading.

'Not a career criminal, Merrily, I can tell you that much.'

'Didn't really think he would be.' Merrily brought the cordless and a mug of tea to the kitchen table. 'I just thought, with mention of all the clubs . . . drugs?'

'Certainly not a recognized dealer and if he *was* dealing he doesn't sound bright enough that we wouldn't know. Doesn't sound like he could run very fast, either, if we were after him.'

'Sorry.' She pulled over the ashtray, fed up now. 'Shouldn't have asked you.'

And wouldn't even have considered an approach to any other copper, but by now she and the Mersey exile Bliss knew too many of each other's flaws for him to sell her down the Wye.

As for the ethics, it went like this: she was following through on something that might help Dexter Harris with his medical condition. She had nothing to tell Bliss that might get Dexter nicked. She hadn't even told him why she wanted to know if Hereford Division had ever heard of Dexter, and he hadn't asked her.

'Mind you,' he said, 'I've known a few disabled villains over the years. Only difference is they tend to have less conscience. Feeling the world owes them. A wheelchair ramp at the town hall is often considered insufficient recompense.'

Merrily found a grin. 'It's so reassuring to talk to a man for whom the pit of human depravity can have no floor.'

'Ah, you're following your nose. You're a priest. How can you know if a gut feeling isn't a tip-off from God?'

'That's very empathetic, Francis.'

'Yeh, well . . .' Bliss was a Catholic from what was probably still the most Catholic city in England. He knew all the questions priests asked themselves with little hope of a convincing answer.

'So, how are . . . things?' Merrily said.

'Kirsty? We're not out the woods yet, but we're having what you might call a trial reconciliation. It's a start. The Job: I'm not on any shortlist for DCI as yet, but the word is that the main man in Worcester who, as you know, does *not* love me like a brother, may be on the top-detectives' transfer list, with an eye on Thames Valley. So that could be goodish news.'

'I'm glad.'

'And how's the healing coming along?' Bliss said.

'Sorry?'

'One of the DCs, his wife's had persistent back trouble. Done the rounds of osteopaths and chiropractors, getting nowhere with it. He reckoned somebody had told his missus they ought to come and talk to the Vicar of Ledwardine.'

She stared blankly out of the window at the black, spidery apple trees. This could *not* be happening.

'Might I have touched on a sore point, by chance?' Bliss said.

Merrily sighed at length, lit a cigarette, then told him about the Sunday nights, Ann-Marie and Jeavons. The whole sub-Messianic mess.

'About fifteen years ago,' Bliss said, 'when I was a young

plod, there was a noise-nuisance complaint at this chapel up near Formby. I go in, and there's one of these evangelical fellers clutching some poor bastard's head in his hands and shaking it from side to side, screaming to heaven for some action. Whole place in uproar. Well . . . no disrespect intended, Merrily, but that doesn't sound like your thing.'

'Last night, my usual congregation had doubled. *Doubled*, Frannie. Two wheelchairs in the aisle. Desperate people, and the health service in perpetual crisis. But . . . me? What *am* I?'

'What did you do?'

She blew out smoke and coughed. 'What usually happens on the Sunday-night thing is we drag out some pews and arrange ourselves into a rough circle. Too many last night for that. No spiritual calm, no intimate atmosphere – only this . . . overpowering sense of . . . *need*. I just had to stand there in front of them all, in my jeans, feeling like a useless pillock, doing my best to explain that the Diocese was currently taking steps to create a proper healing network.'

'Are they?'

'God knows. We did some prayers, but no wheelchairs were abandoned. There was a general feeling like at the pictures once when I was a kid and the projector broke down before the cavalry arrived. Never felt so inadequate – let down the Church, the Women's Ministry, the people for whom this might have been a last hope. Afterwards, this very nice little woman comes up, says how mortified she is about all these outsiders invading our lovely quiet time. What do you say?'

'Bit of a shite situation, Merrily. I'm really sorry. However, this Dexter Harris, with the asthma . . .?'

'His auntie cleans the church midweek. I'd guess she feels responsible because other people don't find him terribly lovable. What can I do? I could just pray for him, or I could try and do what Jeavons does and look for an underlying something, a hidden source. Let God in the back way.'

'Forgive me, this guy sounds like a nutter.'

'But what if he's right? What if it works?'

'All right, look,' Bliss said, 'what I'll do is, I'll run Dexter past an ancient custody sergeant called Melvyn. Melvyn's old-Force, very, *very* discreet and he's gorra brain like an antique computer – feed him a name, it goes clank, clank, clank for a few hours, and if there's a connection with anything notably unlawful over the past many years, he'll deliver eventually, like ticker tape. His specialist subject is Prostitution in Hereford since Nell Gwynne.'

'That's a big one.'

'Leave it with me,' Bliss said.

After they cut the call, Merrily considered phoning Sophie to see how soon they could arrange a meeting of all the Hereford clergy who'd declared an interest in the Healing Ministry, not including those who wanted nothing to do with Deliverance, Lew Jeavons and women.

How many would that leave? Herself, probably.

The phone went again: Jane, out of breath. Behind her, the patient rumbling of school buses.

'Mum, look . . . screwed up. Left vital books for Eng Lit at Stanner, so I . . . figured I should get on Clancy's bus and pick them up. That OK?'

Stanner. In a matter of weeks, the whole axis of Jane's life had shifted.

Merrily frowned. 'And you'd get home how?'

'I called Gomer. He's with Danny, on a blocked-soakaway crisis at New Radnor. He could pick me up around seven, which would be perfect.'

'So you do *want* to come home, eventually?' Merrily said.

'That a serious question?'

On Saturday, Jane, who didn't like killing a tree for

Christmas, had collected some dead branches, which they were going to spray silver and gold to arrange in the hall. She supposed she'd have to spray them herself now.

'I don't really know,' she said.

A few minutes later, rinsing her mug at the sink, she heard a song of Lol's in her head, the one he'd written in – she'd always supposed – a state of bitter despair about ever getting into her bed.

> Did you suffocate your feelings
> As you redefined your goals
> And vowed to undertake the cure of souls?

She wiped the mug and hung it from the shelf over the sink. And thought about Lol and told herself she was too old for one-night stands.

She needed emotional back-up, someone to hold at night, when everything else was falling away: Jane growing up, moving on, and the cure of souls – the job, the calling – wobbling on the rim of the irrational.

Snowy dusk on the Border, but the moody pines rearing behind Stanner Hall were still black and green, dark guardians. The snow had stopped after a couple of hours last night, but it had frozen by morning, and Stanner was locked into winter, the witch's-hat towers shining like white lanterns under an icy half-formed moon.

Such a lovely, lovely shot.

Jane leaned back, shoulders braced against one of the gateposts, both hands supporting the camcorder, holding it tight but not too tight. *Sure, Irene, avoid hand-held.* But if she wasted time rushing up to the hotel for the tripod, the dusk would be over and this incredible image would be history.

Jane triggered the shot, trying to breathe evenly. All day at school, she'd kept the equipment concealed in her bag to avoid attracting a crowd of sad boys with Quentin Tarantino fantasies. At lunchtime, in the school library, she'd studied her notes on Eirion's instructions and added to them, remembering things he'd said.

Make sure your shots are long enough – remember you're recording what might be a familiar scene to you for people who've never seen it before, so hang in there.

No hardship lingering on this one: pure Baskerville Hall. Was this what Conan Doyle had been picturing when he wrote about dull light through mullioned windows, holes in the ivy? OK, there was less ivy here, and it wasn't built of black granite; if he hadn't altered some of the minor details he'd have given it away.

She contained the urge to zoom in on one of the towers, holding the shot instead until she became aware of Clancy Craven shivering, kind of miserably – which, in that wildly expensive Austrian ski-jacket, Clancy was definitely not entitled to do.

Jane lowered the camera. 'You can almost hear the distant howling, Clan.' She threw back her head and howled at the cautious moon. The howl was unexpectedly resonant, echoing back off the Hall.

Clancy said, 'Don't.'

She had her shoulders hunched and her hands deep in the pockets of her blue jacket. Jane looked up to see if she was serious. Clan, though younger, was quite a bit taller than Jane. She was bony now, but you could tell she'd be like Natalie in a year or two, with a bonus of natural blonde hair. Clearly destined for serious beauty, this was a girl who really ought to be happier than she was.

Clancy shivered again, although this one was probably faked. 'You really like spooky things, don't you, Jane?'

'Doesn't everyone?' Jane squeezed the camera back into her overnight bag, Poor Irene – he'd have been gutted to the point of self-mutilation if she'd told him that Antony was bunging her a hundred a week for this. Money for jam.

'*I* don't,' Clancy said. 'I never have. All the kids are on about *Buffy the Vampire Slayer* and *Angel*. I can't watch that stuff.'

They had nothing in common, did they? Jane shouldered the bag. Of course, she'd have to tell Mum about the hundred a week at some stage. Maybe she could actually spend the money on, say, a new automatic washing machine to forestall the Second Great Flood.

'Why do they have to try and invent things to scare us, when there's so much . . .' Clancy shook her head and began to trudge up the drive, keeping out of the slippery tyre tracks in the snow, and Jane started giving her some attention, because something was very much bothering this kid.

The fact that she was here at all tonight was unusual. Normally, Clancy would go straight home to Jeremy's farm. On the bus just now, she'd told Jane that Natalie wanted her to come up to the hotel from now on, so that they could go home together in the car. Jane wondered if there could be some problem with Jeremy. Older men, teenage girls in the house – these things happened, right?

'Your mum's not scared of anything is she, though?' Jane probed, catching up with her.

Clancy stopped, fingering the drawstrings at the waist of her costly ski-jacket. Most of Clancy's clothes were expensive. 'Only thing she's scared of is something happening to me.'

'They're all scared of that. Erm, I've never liked to ask . . .' Jane zipped up her fleece. It was very cold; you didn't notice the conditions when you were working creatively. 'What happened to your dad?'

Clancy started walking again. 'I don't know.'

'Oh.'

'He wasn't anybody special. Just some guy who got her pregnant.'

'You mean like at a party or something, when everybody was pissed out of their heads?'

'Something like that. Your dad was killed, wasn't he?'

'Car crash on the motorway. With his assistant, Karen. Assistant and lover. He was a lawyer. Having a thing on the side. Both killed.' Jane was aware of the subject having been changed, but she was casual enough about this now. 'Bit of a bastard, my dad. Obviously, I remember him as being really nice, but I don't remember that much, as the years pass. I was still quite little when he died.'

'I suppose your mother hasn't been with many guys since. Being a vicar.'

'It's what makes it hard getting this thing with Lol beyond first base. She doesn't know what you're supposed to do, how you're supposed to play it. Women priests haven't been around long enough to establish a precedent.'

'Excuse me?'

With her being so tall, sometimes you forgot Clancy was a couple of years less experienced and sat in classes with little children. 'I meant, there seem to be no rules on whether it's OK for a female parish priest to be having a conspicuous relationship with a man if neither of them's married.'

'They could always *get* married.'

'Lifetime commitment? These are two very timid people, Clancy.'

Jane paused at the bend in the drive, where the Hall suddenly opened out in front of them, panels of light from the ground-floor bay windows imprinted on the clean, white lawns. Was this worth another shot?

Nah – face it, none of this was going to get used, anyway. Antony would deal with the arty stuff himself. All he wanted from Jane were snatches of what Eirion called 'actuality' – short exchanges, things happening around the place, people in motion. *Get Amber in, and Natalie, when you can,* Antony had told her. *But be discreet about it, they're not performers like Ben.*

Clancy said, 'It's the first time we've lived with a man. It's strange . . . not like I imagined.'

Jane wanted to ask, *how . . . why?* But they were getting too close to the Hall to approach an issue this big. The high pines were all around them now. It was like a medieval castle: the pines were the curtain wall and the lawns sloped up to the Hall, which was like the keep on its mound in the centre. In the dark, Stanner looked much older than Victorian. There obviously *had* been more ivy on the walls than there was now; you could see where it had been cut away for repairs, so maybe when Conan Doyle was here . . .

'Something happened at the farm, the other night,' Clancy said. 'Something horrible.'

Jane stopped, a hand on Clancy's arm. 'You mean between Nat and Jeremy?'

'*No!*' Clancy shook her off. 'Why do you always have to think of things like that? She was at work, anyway, she was here. It was Saturday night, and Jeremy and me were watching a video . . . and suddenly there was this blinding light through the window and all this shouting, and these men were outside the farmhouse, with guns and a big spot-light thing.'

'The shooters – the ones Ben's been getting hassle from?'

'I don't know. They were just . . . It was like a raid.' Clancy stood at the edge of the lawn, looking over her shoulder. 'They came out of the trees with their guns, and they were like surrounding the old barn opposite the farmhouse. They were going to shoot Flag.'

'The *dog?*'

'They would have!' Clancy's voice was raw and strained in the razory air. 'They'd have shot him. It was like they owned the place, and they could do what they wanted. Jeremy told me to stay inside, but I couldn't. I went out after Flag. And then Jeremy's mate Danny was there, and one of them hit him with his gun.'

'Danny *Thomas?*'

'Long hair and a scraggy beard?'

'That's him.'

'They hit him on the head, over an eye and made it bleed, and then they shoved his car into the ditch.'

'Jesus. Is he all *right?*'

'I think so, but—'

Jane was appalled. 'Have you told the cops?'

'Jeremy was funny about it. He didn't want to talk about it afterwards.'

'But he told your mum?'

'That's why she won't let me walk down to the farm on my own any more. I think she and Jeremy think they'll come back.'

'Does Ben know about this?'

'Don't say a word! Jane, please, you haven't to say a word! I'm not supposed to talk about it.' Clancy started walking rapidly towards the house, face splattered with light from the big windows.

Jane thought of the men that she and Ben and Antony had encountered at Hergest, who claimed they'd been hired by a local farmer to get rid of foxes. If one of his neighbours was involved, this might explain why Jeremy didn't want to cause any trouble.

'Clan, did they have Valleys accents?'

'What?'

'Were they from South Wales?'

'Might've been. I'm not sure.'

'You should tell Ben. He'll get something done without implicating Jeremy. Ben doesn't—'

'*No!*'

'He doesn't care about treading on people's toes. He *likes* that.'

'Please, Jane . . .' As they reached the Hall, Clancy was nearly in tears. 'I wouldn't've told you if I thought you were gonna go telling tales. I just . . . suddenly everything's a mess. It was OK in summer when we came, but now everything's gone crap. I don't like the people round here. Wish we could go back to Shropshire.'

'Where were you in Shropshire?'

'Craven Arms. It's between Shrewsbury and Ludlow.'

'Yeah, I know. Clancy Craven, of Craven Arms, huh?'

Clancy didn't react.

Jane said, 'Look, you've got to keep me informed of anything else that happens, OK?' And Clancy nodded, looking relieved. Jane knew what it was like in these small Border communities: you wondered whether the normal rules of Western civilization applied or if you were part of some tight, taciturn little Anglo-Welsh banana republic. Well, she'd be seeing Gomer in a few hours, and if *he* didn't know about this, as Danny's partner . . .

The very last of the daylight was soaking away into night-cloud, and Jane was glad she'd stopped to do that moody, glistening shot. Even if it never got used, the fact that she'd thought to capture it showed she was like *responding to images*.

Despite the weather, there were extra cars on the car park. Apart from Jeremy's old Daihatsu, used by Nat, and Ben's MG, covered with old carpet where the soft-top was jammed, there were three of them she'd never seen before.

'Guests? On a Monday?'

'They're not staying,' Clancy said. 'They're just here for

a meeting. Mum has to run the bar. She was moaning that they probably wouldn't be drinkers anyway, people like that.'

'People like what?' Jane could see some figures through the bay window of the lighted lounge. They were standing around like they were making small talk. Ben was one of them, and then Jane saw a woman with pale hair, and a small thrill rippled through her. 'Oh wow . . . it's *them*, isn't it?'

'I don't want to know,' Clancy said, miserable again.

'It's The White Company, isn't it?' Jane had like just *known* she had to be here tonight. Psychic or what?

'People round here are sick,' Clancy said.

This time, Frannie Bliss was calling her from his home, out near Leominster. She could hear his kids in the background, squabbling over something that made techno-bleeps.

'Merrily. Just had a call from Melvyn. He was pretty sure about this, but he likes to check his facts. There *is* a story, but it's not quite what you thought. And it goes way back. The last time Dexter Harris saw the inside of an interview room was nearly twenty years ago.'

'When he was *nine*?'

'Twelve, actually. And looked older, Melvyn says. Big lad, even then, which was how he wound up in the grown-up felons' interview room. Hang on a sec, Merrily. *I said, No . . . Daddy will fix it later . . . Gerrout, or I'll nick the pair of yer for aggravated assault.* Let me shut the door, Merrily.' Bliss put the phone down and when he came back he said, 'I had my way, the age of criminal responsibility'd be reduced to four. You might want to make notes.'

Merrily found a pen, pulled over the sermon pad.

'Right,' Bliss said, 'I'll give you the bottom line first: Dexter killed somebody.'

SEVENTEEN

Detestable to the Lord

When she was about two, maybe three, someone had given Jane this vintage nursery-rhyme book, made out of thick cloth, with serrated edges to the pages. On the front was a watercolour picture of a little girl in an apron who had the saddest face Jane had ever seen. Both the little girl and the book itself used to make her feel deeply upset, and she remembered being convinced it had been owned by a child who had been so unhappy that she'd just died of it.

This was one of her earliest memories, and it faded up when she and Clancy padded into Stanner Hall and saw Amber Foley standing at the top of the kitchen steps, wearing a vinyl apron with a watercolour-type picture on it of a cottage on a hill. Amber hadn't heard them come in, and she was staring across at the closed door of the residents' lounge. Her hair was pulled back and her skin looked like thin white eggshell about to crack.

Jane thought of life-threatening misery and a voice on the phone. She swallowed. Amber saw Clan and jumped, then blinked and smiled – weak sun reflected in a stagnant pond.

'Oh, Clancy . . . I've sorted out a table for you in the kitchen to do your homework. Your mum says—' Becoming aware of Jane, Amber looked bewildered. Like, *if this is Jane it must be Friday.*

'I left some things, Amber, on Saturday. School books.'

'Oh, *Jane*, we could've got Natalie to send them with Clan—'

Amber looked hard at her, obviously aware that Jane would have known this. One of the wall-lamp bulbs had blown, and unfamiliar shadows made the lobby look dull and brownish and semi-derelict. Good location, crap place to live. How often had Amber stood alone here, wondering how she'd ever got herself into this? And realizing, of course, that she hadn't; Ben had.

Amber flicked a glance at Clancy, who said, 'I'd better get on with it. I'll see you tomorrow, Jane,' and meekly walked past Amber and down the steps to the kitchen. *Doesn't want to know*, Jane thought. *If there's something bad or contentious going down, she just doesn't want to know about it. We have absolutely nothing in common.*

When they could hear the kid's footsteps on the kitchen flags, Jane nodded at the closed door of the residents' lounge.

'The White Company, right?'

'Ben's in there with them. And Natalie. He'd be better off married to Nat, don't you think?'

'No, that's ridiculous.'

'You know what they're doing, don't you?' Amber said.

'Well, yeah, I—You've got a problem with it?'

Amber straightened up and flattened a bulge in her apron. 'You knew they were coming, didn't you? That's why you're here.'

'Well, no, actually.'

'You couldn't keep away.'

'No, it—' Oh hell, no point in letting this fester. 'OK, if you want the absolute truth, Amber, the real reason I came is because I happened to pick up the phone last night. When you tried to call my mum?'

There was the jittery sound of polite laughter from behind the lounge door.

'And when you recognized my voice,' Jane said, 'you got off the line as quick as you could. Only I'm quite good with voices.'

'Jane, I—'

'So if it's something about me, I'd like to know, OK? Because I haven't told her anything about all this, and it could get me in a lot of bother.'

Amber's doll's cheeks were colouring.

Jane sighed. 'I suppose Ben told you what she did. Like, apart from being just a vicar?'

Amber nodded, losing what might have been a grateful smile inside a grimace.

'Only, I didn't know you were religious,' Jane said.

'I'm not. Not really. Just neurotic.'

Jane gestured at the lounge door. 'About *that*?'

There was the sound of more merriment, Ben's peal obvious.

'None of this worries him in the slightest,' Amber said. 'He loves it, for the drama. He doesn't believe in it for one minute, though obviously he won't tell *them* that – he'll be hamming it up in there for all he's worth. It's how guys like him and Antony persuade people to do things on camera that are going to get them ridiculed in thousands of homes. Because *they* don't laugh. At the time.'

Jane's eyebrows went up. 'They're not doing it *now*, are they – trying for Conan Doyle?'

'*I* don't know. I just think people like that are irresponsible, and the point is: it's not their house, is it? It's ours, God help us.' Amber moved away from the vicinity of the lounge towards the reception area. 'Look, I know it's money, much needed. I *know* it's part of Ben's Great Scheme. But getting cranks like that involved – that's the pits.'

'You rang Mum for, like, support? *Did* you get through to her in the end?'

Amber swallowed a breath. 'When Ben told me what your mother did, it seemed a bit too coincidental – like a sign. We neurotics, you know? No, I didn't try again. Not after you answered the phone.'

'Well . . .' Jane raised her gaze to the flaking frieze around the walls. 'If you'd wanted support you'd have got it, no problem. Why didn't you just ask me? I could've told you *exactly* what she'd say. Like, at some point she'd drag out a slab of the Old Testament. "*Let no one be found among you who sacrifices his son or daughter in the fire, who practises divination or sorcery or witchcraft or pisses about with spells . . .*" blah, blah . . . "*Or who is a medium or spiritist or consults with the dead. Anyone who does these things is detestable to the Lord.*" '

'That seems fairly unequivocal to me,' Amber said. 'Of course, I'm only a cook . . .'

'Amber, for heaven's sake, it's *Old Testament*. You can find bits of the OT that suggest blokes are entitled to strangle their wives for being unfaithful. It was *political* – anything paranormal, the priests of Jehovah had to keep it to them selves, or bang goes the power base. But trying to contact poor old Arthur . . . I mean, come *on*.'

'I just—' Amber folded her arms. 'Like I said, I'm not particularly religious. And, God knows, I'm certainly not psychic, although I don't entirely doubt that other people *can* perceive things that are beyond me.'

'Well, I have pagan instincts,' Jane said with relish, 'and I believe there's *masses* in this area to be sensed by anyone with the balls to . . .'

She let the sentence trail, realizing how smug and insulting it must have sounded.

'Well—' An uncharacteristic anger glowed momentarily like filaments in Amber's eyes. 'For all your pagan instincts,

Jane, you couldn't get out of that room quick enough, could you?'

'Room?'

'The tower room. I didn't particularly want to put you in that one, because we'd had a couple of people already who— But Ben said, Oh, don't worry about young Jane. Far too down-to-earth. Jane'll be *fine*.'

'So you . . . know about that.' She'd had the impression that Ben had not told Amber, who was negative enough about this place already.

'And wish I didn't,' Amber said. 'Ben laughs. He says every hotel has a room like that, and some people would even pay extra to sleep in it. If you remember, what you told us at the time was that you weren't used to sleeping in a big room.'

'Well, I—'

'Only I happened to recall you telling me when you first came how you'd turned a huge attic at Ledwardine vicarage into your apartment and painted some big coloured squares on the walls – like some famous abstract artist?'

'Mondrian.' Oh God, she couldn't even keep track of her own lies. 'All right, I had a bad night. I felt . . . not very well. I mean, I never know when it's my imagination. I'm sorry, Amber.'

'Of course, I didn't actually know at the time that it was Hattie Chancery's room,' Amber said.

Jane flung a glance into the well of the hall, where the staircase twisted out of sight. There were certain phrases you could feel like fingers up your spine – what Ben would call a *frisson* – and this was one: *Hattie Chancery's Room*. The possessive. Present-tense. *Oh God*.

'The Chancerys were the family who built this place, right?'

'I think their name was originally Chance, but they altered

it to sound more distinguished. Incomers from the Black Country. Industrial wealth, delusions of grandeur. Most of the big Victorian homes in this area seem to have been built by rich Midlanders, who wanted their own castles. The names are usually a give-away. Big houses around here tend to be called "court", from the Welsh. But they called this Stanner *Hall* to—'

'Yeah, right. So Hattie Chancery was the one who killed her husband?'

'So *you* knew.'

'Not then.'

'Because Ben only told me about this yesterday. He'd known for some time, but . . .' Amber's voice was brittle. 'He thought the little woman might be frightened.'

'But it wasn't in that room, was it?'

'Not the murder. That was in the grounds, I think. It isn't talked about much. Probably overshadowed by the War at the time, and she *was* mentally ill, apparently.'

'A madwoman?'

'No, Jane, I think we'd all prefer *mentally ill*.'

'So, like, what did people see in the room?'

'Oh . . . one man said he saw the shape of a woman against the window and smelt— Look I'm not going into this now, all right?'

'But that's the reason you're unhappy about The White Company, right?'

'I just don't think this is a happy place. But then, I'm only a cook.'

'What did he smell, this guy?'

'Alcohol . . . beer, I think.'

'You thought maybe Mum could do something about this?'

'Jane, look, it was just a knee-jerk thing. I was angry, all right?'

'She'd just warn you not to let The White Company in. And you'd go along with that, but Ben—'

'Shhh!'

Amber was looking over Jane's shoulder. Jane turned and saw the lounge door opening, and Ben gliding out, his hair sheened back, his slim, black Edwardian jacket hanging loose. His Holmes kit. He'd worn part of the Holmes kit to welcome The White Company. Well, he would, wouldn't he?

'Amber, where's—? *Jane!*' Ben looked fit, she thought, and energized, and showed no particular surprise that she was here on a Monday, only satisfaction that she *was*. 'Jane, you wouldn't by any chance have brought along that little Handycam Largo gave you to humiliate me?'

'Well, actually—'

'In which case, *fetch* it, darling.' Ben clapped his hands. 'Fetch it at once. We've got Alistair here, the medium, and we're testing various rooms to work out which is the best place to try and contact, ah . . .'

'And where are you proposing to go next?' Amber said.

'Amber, it's a positive thing,' Ben said casually.

'*Oh* no,' Amber said.

'Amber—'

'Understand this, Ben.' Something passed swiftly, like the shadow of a small bird, across Amber's white doll's face. 'Those people will *not* go into my fucking kitchen.'

'Maybe I could just describe these events to you without any comment,' Merrily said. 'And then perhaps you could just tell me what you think.' Her ear was aching from phone use.

'So formal,' Canon Jeavons said.

'I've been talking to a cop. It's all forms and recorded interviews with them, now. All about covering yourself, and isn't the Church going the same way?'

'Oh happy day,' Jeavons said. 'All right, go ahead, Merrilee. Lay it on me.'

Inside her head the chorus started up.

Forgive me, this guy sounds like a nutter.

My advice, for what it's worth, is to avoid this man and all he stands for.

If anyone's on the edge of a crisis, Jeavons has been known to tip them over.

There was no harm in listening to what he had to say. The fact was, if she'd never met Jeavons she wouldn't have dug into Dexter's history, and she wouldn't have uncovered what might be the underlying cause of his condition.

'It's about three boys from the Belmont area of Hereford.' The brief, bleak notes in the sermon book lay in the lamplight pooled next to the Bible. 'Two of them are brothers – Darrin and Roland Hook, aged thirteen and nine. Dexter Harris is their cousin. This is seventeen years ago, and he's twelve.'

Seventeen years ago. The year Jane was born. The year she quit university and married Sean. They said she could come back and get her degree, but she'd had a feeling at the time that this wouldn't happen. Law: it had never felt right – why on earth was she reading law? Parental pressure, at the time, and the influence of Uncle Ted, family solicitor. *It's a good degree to have, Merrily. Whatever you decide to do with your life, it will always be there for you.*

Wasted years.

'Belmont's an expanding suburb south of the city, close to open country. Less so now, since they built the all-night Tesco and the drive-in McDonald's and hundreds more houses and the Barnfield Trading estate, but you get the idea. You keep going and you're on the open road down to Abergavenny.'

She was seeing it as she talked: this widened country lane above the Golden Valley, which always seemed so aptly named on summer evenings with harvested fields aglow as if lit from underneath.

This had all happened on a warm evening in August, approaching dusk. The three kids were exploring a half-finished building site, where some of the houses were already lived in. Darrin had a plan.

'*Gorra wire coat-hanger down his pants,*' Bliss had told her. '*So it wasn't an impulse thing, and he chose well, just like a pro: new house with high fences. People have gone out, leaving their second car in the drive. A gift.*'

Darrin had learned the techniques from a boy at school – how to force the window and then apply the coat-hanger to the pop-up locks. Then the hot-wire bit. The only drawback was that Darrin didn't know how to drive.

Which was where Dexter came in. 'Taller than the others,' Merrily told Jeavons. 'An unusually big boy for twelve, so he could reach the pedals, no problem. Dozens of drivers must have seen this Fiesta weaving about, but there weren't many mobile phones in those days, so it was a while before the police got on to them. Not that you could miss them by now, because it was getting dark and Dexter hadn't thought about lights.'

'Already I'm sensing no happy ending,' Jeavons said.

'The police picked up the trail on the hill down to Allensmore, when they were picking up speed. Dexter subsequently told the police that he'd been afraid to brake. He was once on his bike and went over the handlebars, and he had the idea that if he did it now he and Darrin would go through the windscreen – certainly a possibility as neither had a seat belt on. By now the police are behind them, siren going. Not too close – volatile situation, car full of kids.'

'*Dexter's well hyped-up now,*' Frannie Bliss said, '*the traffic lads blasting away behind them, blue lights going. He's gorra do something. Decides the best thing is to get off the big road, dump the car and run like buggery. Sees this turning up ahead, on the other side, into this narrow little country lane, bus shelter on the corner. Decides to go for it. Just like that. No indication. Big lorry coming towards them, but Dexter reckons he's got plenty of time. An experienced motorist now – driven all of six miles on his own.*

'*Stupid little gobshite spins the wheel, sends the Fiesta whizzing across the road. Amazingly, he doesn't turn it over, but it's well out of control, as you'd expect, and naturally he's missing the turning, heading straight for the hedge. Now even at this point, if he'd left well alone, the car would just've gone through the hedge into the field where, as long as it avoided trees, it'd just be a cuts-and-bruises job.*

'*Unfortunately, Dexter panics, stands on the brakes and the Fiesta stalls on the kerb, directly in the path of the oncoming lorry. Haulage vehicle. Melvyn doesn't recall the exact tonnage, which is rare for Melvyn, but the driver was a Mr Evans, from Newport, carrying steel, and afterwards Mr Evans gives up his job, telling the coroner that he'll never drive a lorry again as long as he lives.*'

'The lorry had collided with the rear half of the Fiesta,' Merrily said, 'flattening it into the bus shelter, which collapsed. Both front doors sprang open, so Dexter and Darrin both walked away. Darrin had a broken arm, Dexter was mildly concussed. Roland, however . . .'

'*Think of the forgotten sardine in the tin,*' Bliss had said brutally, '*after the tin's been trodden on.*'

'His parents were told it was instantaneous,' Merrily said, 'meaning he didn't suffer. Which, as far as physical pain goes, may be true but disregards the state of helpless terror he'd have been in for several minutes before the crash.'

'Yes,' Jeavons said softly.

'Probably the last thing Dexter would've heard before the impact was the final screams of his nine-year-old cousin. How

213

much of the carnage he saw in the back of the car, we don't know.'

'What happen to Dexter?'

'Not much. First offence. Appeared in court as a juvenile and therefore wasn't named. Pleaded guilty to charges related to taking and driving away and causing death by dangerous driving. No previous convictions. Said very little in court apart from to apologize and burst into tears. The view of the court seems to have been that having to live with this for the rest of his life was a bigger punishment than anything the justice system could inflict.'

'Not always a good decision,' Jeavons said. 'Incarceration puts a time limit on it. Life goes on.'

'Certainly split the family. There was an awful scene at the funeral – Roland's mother screaming that Dexter was a murderer who should be in jail. Maybe forgetting that Darrin was the instigator, the one who'd learned how to break into cars. But Darrin couldn't drive, so it was Dexter who killed Roland.'

'His grandma mention any of this?'

'His auntie. Alice. Not a word, but it probably explains why Dexter's never been near a church since. His parents apparently felt compelled to move to the other side of Hereford, and he went to a different school.'

'Certainly explain why he freaks when you ask him what happens in his head when he's having an attack,' Jeavons said. 'He have any counselling at the time?'

'Not as common then as it is now, was it? Especially not for offenders.'

'And he's working in a garage now.'

'Tyre depot. But still working with cars, yes. Hasn't committed any criminal offences since, according to my friend. As far as health goes, he might always have been prone to respiratory problems, but the serious asthma attacks seem to have started within a year of the incident. So . . .' Merrily closed the pad, stared at the flat, pastel mosaic of the Paul Klee print. 'Can I help him?'

'What do *you* think?'

'I think I know what you might suggest. While the thought of it leaves me feeling exhausted already, the logic of it's almost too perfect.'

'Yes,' Jeavons said.

'Would *you* do it?'

'What? Say it.'

'The healing of the living and the healing of the dead. A formal Requiem Eucharist to bring peace to the soul of a nine-year-old boy who died seventeen years ago. And to his cousin, who has it all stored up inside him like some old video nasty that keeps replaying itself in his head . . . until it constricts his lungs.'

'Textbook,' Jeavons said. 'Unless maybe they already had a Requiem?'

'They didn't. I tracked down the minister who conducted the funeral. It was at Hereford Crematorium, they weren't practising Christians and it didn't take long. That's how I found out about the row during the service. Which didn't end there. When Dexter's dad bought a new car it was vandalized – tyres ripped, bodywork scored. Their house was also broken into twice – damage rather than theft. They suspected Darrin.'

Not without reason. Bliss had said Darrin had burgled his way through half the houses in south Hereford. The family blamed Dexter for Darrin turning bad.

'A few months ago, according to my colleague, Darrin's mother encountered Dexter's mother in the car park at Safeway . . . spat in her face.'

'The healing capabilities of time are often overrated,' Jeavons said.

'So there's a good deal more to heal here than a case of asthma.'

'You think she wanted you to find out about all this, the aunt?'

'I don't know.' Merrily lit a cigarette. 'Alice seems to be the eldest sister. She and her husband opened a chip shop in Ledwardine about twenty years ago. He died a while back. She must be well into her seventies now but still works there part-time. And does most of the cleaning in the church. And her niece in Solihull recently went on an Alpha course, which seems to have inspired Alice to come to one of our Sunday evenings.'

Felt the Holy Spirit was in her heart like a big white bird, and you could feel its wings fluttering. As if this big bird was trying to escape from her breast and fill the whole world with love and healing.

'You got yourself an enormously interesting case, Merrilee,' Lew Jeavons said. 'Why you trying to avoid it?'

'Am I?'

'Reach out! Embrace!'

He laughed hugely, the bastard.

The White Company: cool name, but . . .

Well, come on, what did you expect?

Jane stood by the stairs with Ben, watching them bunched in the hall under the blown bulb, and thinking that at least they blended with the decor. Of the three of them, Elizabeth Pollen was the most animated. There was a youngish guy with limp hair and Harry Potter glasses who had, like, *anorak* stamped across his shallow forehead, and if he didn't have spots it was only because the Clearasil was working this week.

Which meant that Alistair Hardy, the medium, the main man, had to be the heavy-set sixtyish person with pewtery hair and an intermittent scowl and a briefcase. A man clearly aware of his professional standing, like a small-town bank manager. It was laughable.

'Right,' Ben said. 'If we're all in agreement, I'd like to record some of Alistair's testing of the individual rooms. Antony Largo would have been here himself, but he's tied up on another project at the present. And so—'

And then, what Ben did, he plucked the Sony 150 out of Jane's hands, just blatantly *lifted* it.

'—I'll have to shoot this myself.' Moving away with the camcorder, he tossed her a brief, faintly rueful smile over his shoulder. 'Jane, you might like to watch how I do this. Give you a few basic ideas.'

Son of a bitch!

Jane was boiling with embarrassment. She thought she could see the Harry Potter guy smirking. She turned to look for Amber, but Amber had gone, maybe to barricade the kitchen. Natalie appeared in the lounge doorway, met Jane's eyes and shrugged, sympathetic but helpless.

EIGHTEEN

Shock of the Proof

In the dining room, Alistair Hardy said he could see a spirit.

It was all quite repulsive, Jane thought, like he was feigning a stroke. Hardy was wearing a dark grey suit and a black tie, maybe to suggest respect for the dead, and it was as though one side of him had gone numb. An arm was sticking out from his body, fingers curled, as if he was holding another hand.

He'd moved to the area where Jane had stood with her tray while serving breakfast to Ben and Antony and absorbing their edgy banter. The stained glass in the window, with only the night behind it, looked as dense as lead. The concertina radiators were silent; Ben and Amber had no heat to waste.

Ben was into a crouch, no more than a yard away from Hardy, aiming the camera upwards, probably to make the guy look more majestic; also close enough, according to Eirion's rules, to pick up usable sound through the built-in mike.

'There's an elderly lady, with a stick . . . no . . . it's a walking . . . Oh, what do you call it?' Hardy's metallic voice was pitched up, like a priest in church. If he was supposed to be from Edinburgh, why didn't he have a Scottish accent? Sounded faintly West Midlands to Jane. 'A Zimmer frame! An elderly lady with a Zimmer frame!'

Jane, standing over by the door with Natalie, murmured, 'Well, *that* sounds suitably Victorian.'

It was freezing in here. She zipped up her fleece. She hadn't yet decided if Hardy was a phoney or merely self-deluded, but the fact that the filming had been literally taken out of her hands allowed her to be as cynical and acidic as she liked.

'I believe this place actually used to be an old people's home, Alistair,' the Harry Potter guy said.

'Yes,' Hardy said. 'Thank you, Matthew.'

Jane thought, *He must have known that anyway.* It was strange, really; she had this fairly liberal acceptance of the paranormal, based on a couple of meaningful experiences of her own, but spiritualism just didn't light her candle. It was fusty and sad; it was rooms full of lumbering furniture and old ladies smelling of camphor.

'I would say the poor old dear had dementia,' Hardy said. 'She still doesn't seem to be fully aware of her own passing. And so she walks this room, around and around. I expect I can probably help her get to where she should be. When I have a little more time.'

'Meanwhile, we'll just leave her to hobble around for a few more weeks,' Jane murmured. 'This guy should be working for the NHS.'

Natalie shook her head, a little smile on her perfect, ironic lips. What, precisely, did Natalie believe in? Jane realized she had no idea. And somewhere, the incurious Clancy was quietly getting on with her homework. Jane didn't understand that, either.

Ben said, from behind the camera, 'Just the one, ah, spirit, Alistair?' His voice was conversational. You could hear it on TV already, the out-of-shot director's diffident prompt.

'I'm fairly sure this room is not the one we're looking for,

Ben.' Hardy's arm relaxed, his fingers uncurling. 'Not to worry.'

'You didn't get much in the lounge, either.'

'No. Let's go back into the hall. Perhaps upstairs?'

Jane looked at Ben. Ben said nothing. She wondered how Amber would react if he showed Hardy the 'secret' passageway under the stairs. Or if he took them up to Hattie Chancery's room. She and Nat let the four of them go through and waited. Ben had hurried ahead to get a shot of them vacating the dining room; he wouldn't want the staff in the picture.

'This is moderately naff,' Jane murmured to Natalie.

'Perhaps it's not for us to say.'

Nat was demure tonight, in a black woollen dress, the kind Mum might wear. Of course, she was responsible for this, setting it up, because it would be good for the hotel. But *would* it? If Stanner developed a reputation as the haunt of saddoes, where was the future in that?

'I mean, do you believe that guy can see anything at all?'

'I don't know, Jane – what do you think?'

'I think maybe he does – or did have – some psychic ability. But if it's not happening for him, he'll just make something up. That's where it all goes wrong. Nobody gets it all the time, but if you're a so-called professional medium, with an audience expecting fireworks, you're going to make sure they get what they want, aren't you? Like, if you know this place was once an old people's home, you invent an old girl on a zimmer.'

'And what does your mother think?'

'You been talking to Amber?'

'Ben told me about her.'

'That guy is so discreet. Amber would like it if Mum came in and scattered some holy water before The White Company gets into it.'

'And would she do that?'

'Probably. But the point is that *I* would rather she didn't get involved. Because I like it here, you know? I like this job.'

When they decided it was safe to leave the dining room, they saw Alistair Hardy moving upstairs, up the red carpet and – *oh hell* – Amber was alone at the top of the kitchen steps. Her face was blank, but you could sense the tension in the way she was standing, both hands pressing on her apron with the design of a cottage on a hill.

There was a subdued tension everywhere, the air drab with negative emotion, and it was like the fabric of Stanner Hall was moulding itself around this. Like bad vibes were part of its heritage.

If Ben was aware of this, he was pretending he wasn't, crouching at the bottom of the stairs shooting Alistair Hardy. *He loves it, for the drama. He doesn't believe in it for one minute.* Hardy had got halfway to the first landing when he abruptly turned and came down again.

'Ben, I'm being pulled the other way.'

Ben carried on recording: digital video was dirt-cheap, according to Eirion, and went on for ever. Hardy came quietly down, standing at the foot of the stairs with one arm out at an unnatural angle, his eyes not quite shut, so that you could see the whites, like the light under a closed door. Maybe he was simply telepathic and had picked up what was threshing around in Amber's head.

Slowly, like a soldier patrolling a boundary, Hardy walked away into the dimmer part of the hall, where the blown bulb was. He looked across at Amber, who looked away. Then he turned back, Beth Pollen and the others watching him in silence. Mrs Pollen had on a short grey cape, like nurses used to wear, over a long viridian skirt. Would have made better video, Jane thought, if *she* was the medium.

'*You*'re not alone, are you?'

Jane twisted round. Alistair Hardy was standing next to her. She could smell his aftershave; it seemed wrong, somehow, for a medium to be wearing aftershave; shouldn't they project a neutral ambience? Jane stiffened. It was like the way cats always chose to rub up against the one person in the room who was allergic to cat hair. She tried to move away and bumped into Harry Potter, who didn't move.

Hardy was looking at her, as if he was noticing her for the first time. She met his eyes: flat and grey and somehow leaden, like the stained glass in the dining room with no light behind it. She glanced away, found herself gazing directly into the dark lens of the camcorder – Ben on his knees on the worn rug in the centre of the hall, poised and steady and relaxed. She found they were all grouped around her now, like a coven. *What?* Jane spun, looking for a way out of this. The hall seemed suddenly full of people and shadows.

'Rather distinguished woman,' Hardy said. 'Elderly, but not at all like the poor dear in the dining room. Has your—? I'm sorry, I don't know your name.'

Jane said nothing, reluctant to give anything away to this creep. She'd been fitted up. She wanted to kick the camera out of Ben's hands. Then again, she wanted to go on working here. Possibly.

'Jane,' she said sullenly.

'Ah yes.' As if he'd known that all along and was just making sure that *she* knew who she was. 'Jane, have you a granny who's passed?'

'Not to my knowledge.'

Hardy smiled his bank manager's smile. He had a gold filling. 'She's definitely with you, my dear.'

'And you're *sure* she hasn't got Alzheimer's?'

He kept on smiling, which was unnerving. He was supposed to lose his temper with her; spiritualists had no sense of humour, everybody knew that.

'Property,' Alistair Hardy said. 'She has a message for you relating to property.' His right hand seemed to be vibrating, fingers clawed.

'I don't deal much in property these days.'

'She says . . . tell them not to give up on the house.'

Jane shrugged. Usual banal crap.

'She's taller than you,' Alistair Hardy said. 'As tall as me. Formidable, I think would be the word. She has . . . rather sharp features – strong would be a better word. Not someone to trifle with, certainly. And she's wearing . . . a shawl? Quite a large, thick shawl.'

'Don't know anyone with a shawl. Well, my mum has an old black one that she—' Jane shut her mouth. It was like with fortune tellers: you *never* went along with it, never fed them information they could build on. She looked beyond Alistair Hardy into the sepia shadow-stain around the bulb that had blown.

'It's not quite a shawl, it's – help me here, somebody – what do you call one of those garments that became very popular for a while back in the seventies? South American origins.' He lifted his good arm, started to snap his fingers in the air. 'Somebody . . . what's the word? Come on, this is quite significant.'

'Oh,' Beth Pollen said. 'You mean . . .'

The word had burst in Jane's brain before it was uttered. She kept on staring into the blown bulb, like her consciousness was being drawn into its fog, and the broken filament inside the bulb was the size of a dead tree, her hands going numb around it. She felt insubstantial, grey and vague, barely feeling her legs give way.

'You mean a *poncho*,' Mrs Pollen said.

*

Over the clanking of the van, Gomer said, 'It don't sound right to me, boy. Sounds like he was handing you a barrow-load of ole bullshit.'

'He was always full of it,' Danny admitted.

'*Bands of brigands roaming by night?*' Gomer and Danny were both staring through the windscreen at the lightless fields beyond Walton, sloping up to Radnor Forest. They were going to pick up young Jane Watkins at Stanner before Gomer dropped Danny off at home, else she'd think Gomer had forgotten about her.

'That's what he said. He d'reckon it's the only way the farmers gonner keep the fox population under control when the Government bans huntin' with hounds.'

'Ah *well*,' Gomer said, 'I can understand Sebbie comin' out with that ole wallop when he's got the MP round his place for cocktails – put the frighteners on the politicians kind of thing. But not to the likes of we.'

'So what *was* them bloody Welshies doin' in Jeremy's yard, then? They had his barn all staked out, Gomer, like they'd got the fox trapped up in there. All it was was Jeremy's ole sheepdog. They'd've bloody shot that dog if the kiddie hadn't run in. Shot the dog out of sheer spite, I reckon.'

'Should've called in the law, boy. Let them sort it out.'

'He wouldn't. He wouldn't do it, Gomer.'

'Then you oughter be asking *why* he wouldn't.'

'That was what Sebbie said. That we oughter be asking why Jeremy didn't want the cops round. And then the bastard was asking me if I was still doin' dope. Like as if Jeremy didn't want no cops round for the same reason I never did.'

'You en't still—?'

Danny coughed. 'Bit of home-grown. Strickly for personal use. And *only* a bit.' Giving Gomer a nervous glance on account of, to Gomer's generation, a twist of wacky baccy could put you on the down-escalator into hell and blacken the name of Gomer Parry Plant Hire for ever. 'Pigs don't do you for that n' more, see, long as you en't dealin'.' He was being a bit careful, though, since Dacre had dropped the little phrase 'Drug Squad'. He might be full of bullshit, but he did have contacts.

Gomer drove on steadily, said nothing. Good ole boy.

'So this woman,' Danny said. 'Miz Natalie Craven. Two ways of lookin' at that, Gomer. On the one hand, blokes is like, Lucky devil, what's he got we cn't? Whereas women's sayin' she's bewitched him, the slag.'

'And Sebbie Dacre?' Gomer wondered. 'What's Sebbie think about her?'

'Sebbie's had his share,' Danny said.

'Zelda Morgan, ennit, now?'

'Zelda, aye. Off the boil a bit, what I yeard. Zelda mabbe figurin' it wasn't worth the candle – Sebbie's moods.'

'Or mabbe Sebbie's thinkin' he can do better than Zelda,' Gomer said. 'Mabbe lookin' for a woman of means, way he got fleeced by the missus in the divorce court.'

'Have you . . .' Danny hesitating, as they rattled out onto the Kington Road. 'You yeard anythin' about Sebbie goin' strange, Gomer?'

'What way?'

'Well . . . the Welsh shooters. Settin' 'em on Jeremy. Like he's got an obsession with Jeremy, now Jeremy's got hisself a serious woman. Anything, really.'

'You reckon it's to do with the woman?'

'Dunno.'

They drove on in silence for a while, then Danny said, 'Sometimes, it feels like everything's filled up with some'ing, and it's only a matter of time 'fore it bursts. I thought it was the snow – you know that feeling you get when there's snow on the way. But it en't just snow.'

Gomer looked at him. 'Well, if you feel that way, think what it's like for Jeremy Berrows . . .'

Nat had taken Jane down to the kitchen.

There was an old flowery-patterned sofa under one of the high windows, and they sat there and Jane drank hot, sugary tea. In the opposite corner, Clancy's homework was spread over a card table; when it was established that Jane was OK, Clancy had gone back to it. She was working quietly, underlining things with a ruler.

'It's never happened to me before.' Jane shuffled to the edge of the sofa, glaring into her cup. She felt furious now at having personally created one of those *moments* for Alistair Hardy. Could imagine the Harry Potter creep relaying the story to his anorak mates, or – worse – keying it into some global spiritualist chat-room: the story of the girl who was determined to slag everything off just keeling over with *the shock of the proof.*

'It happens,' Natalie said, next to her.

'It doesn't happen to *me*. I never faint.'

Natalie said nothing. She hadn't asked the obvious question. Nobody had, not even Alistair Hardy.

'Where are they?'

'In the bar,' Nat said. 'He's still looking for what he calls a point of contact.'

'Where's Amber?'

'I don't know. Amber's in a state.'

'Wishing she'd never seen this place.'

'Something like that.'

Jane said quickly, 'When we first moved to Ledwardine, I had a very good friend who ran a shop that was devoted to the history and folklore of the area and the poetry of Thomas Traherne.'

'Look, you don't have to tell me,' Natalie said. 'Your past, above all things, is your own. You're not obliged—'

'I want to. It's going to drive me insane otherwise, and I can't tell Mum for obvious reasons. She was called Lucy Devenish, and she was killed on the road. Knocked off her moped. She was elderly and thin, and she had a face like some old warrior, and she—' The tears were like spikes behind Jane's eyes. 'Every time she went out, Nat, she wore this . . . bloody poncho.'

Nat said nothing. There was silence in the vast kitchen, except for a slow bubbling from the stove and the squeak of Clancy's fibre-tip. Clancy always pressed down too hard, as if the words might fade otherwise.

Jane clasped her hands together, squeezing tightly. 'Do you think he took her out of my mind? Stole the memory? You see, I can't believe that even if she . . . I can't believe Lucy would talk to a tosser like that. I feel he's been into my mind. I feel like he's extracted her, like some computer hacker can get into your hard disk and pull out some ancient, buried file. It's like a kind of rape.'

'I doubt that, Jane,' Nat said.

'That he took it from my mind?'

Natalie didn't reply. There were footsteps on the stone stairs, and then Alistair Hardy was standing there with Harry Potter. Hardy had his jacket off. He wore a pair of those archaic expanding armbands around his shirt sleeves. He peered at Jane, his face shiny.

'All right now, are we, my love?'

'We're fine. Just I hadn't had anything to eat since breakfast. I felt sick earlier. That's all it was. I feel fine now.'

'Good,' Hardy said. 'Mind if we come in?'

Natalie stood up. 'Well, I think you ought to—'

'Won't take a moment. This is the kitchen, is it?' He blinked. 'Or servants' quarters once, I suppose.'

'That's right,' Harry Potter said. 'I've seen the Victorian plans.'

'Where'd you get those?' Jane stood up. She was half afraid her legs would give way again, but she was OK. Plans? They had *plans of the house*? Did Ben know about this?

'Where's Ben?' Natalie said.

'Oh, he's gone outside.' Harry Potter pulled a slick of hair from his concave forehead. 'We were out near the entrance, and there was some shooting going on in the grounds, and he said it was coming through on the sound-track and ruining everything. He was really annoyed. He's gone out to – you know – remonstrate with them.'

Hell, the shooters . . .

'Oh *Christ*.' Natalie jumped up, pushed between Alistair Hardy and Potter, almost colliding with someone moving slowly down the stone steps.

Amber. She stood at the foot of the steps for several seconds after Nat had gone. Jane wanted to go after Nat, but . . .

Amber. *Those people will not go into my fucking kitchen.*

Jane saw Alistair Hardy walking in his measured, deliberate way across the flags until the island unit the size of Australia was between him and Amber.

'You mustn't be afraid, Mrs Foley,' he said.

NINETEEN

Nancy Boy

Amber said, and it was almost a wail, 'This is the kitchen. This is the heart—'

'Of the house. Yes. Precisely.'

Alistair Hardy was leaning forward over the enormous island unit, his hands splayed on the oiled hardwood: the bank manager at his desk, laying down the options.

But he and Amber weren't coming from the same direction at all, Jane knew that much. Amber meant that the kitchen was the heart of her own shrinking world. This woman was probably all that was truly professional and worthwhile about the Stanner Hall Hotel, and this was her refuge, where what remained of her confidence was located, while the rest of the house faded and dripped and crumbled and rotted and soaked up money. This was *her place*. Whereas Hardy . . .

'It's on a lower level than the rest,' Harry Potter explained. 'They had to build the foundations into the rock. This part of the house is sunk into some of the oldest stone in the country – over six hundred and fifty million years—'

'So *what*?' Amber was arching from the hips in furious incomprehension. 'I mean, six hundred million, four thousand million – *all* rock's pretty bloody old compared with the human race. I don't see the point of this.'

She backed off a little, maybe realizing that, she was shouting at the people who would be paying for Christmas.

'Mrs Foley . . .' Beth Pollen was stepping down on to the flags. 'Oh golly, what a mess. All my fault. I assumed you were *au fait* with everything. If I'd known you were at all worried, I live just a few miles away, I could easily have—'

'You don't understand,' Amber said.

For Jane, the vast kitchen had taken on a cavern-like feel: the purply-greyness, the uneven lighting, the high windows like enlarged slits in the stone. Perhaps some of that very ancient stone was in these actual walls – Amber's kitchen sanctuary formed out of Stanner Rocks. In the corner, Clancy sat watching from her card table, the pen still in her right hand.

Amber must have touched a switch somewhere because the small bank of halogen lights came on, turning Hardy's face bright pink.

He didn't move. 'Mrs Foley, I knew as soon as I came down the steps. This is where it happened.'

'I don't know what you're talking about,' Amber said.

'It's in the records.' The Harry Potter guy, Matthew, strolled into the centre of the room. He seemed older now than Jane had first figured, probably even thirtyish, not much younger than Amber. 'We know that the textile magnate, Walter Chance, who built this house, had a vague interest in spiritualism, as did a lot of people at the end of the nineteenth century. It was fashionable, state of the art – except that to them, of course, it was very much a science, with lots of gadgets. The scientific advances and the technological developments during this comparatively short period were mind-bogg—'

'We *know* all that,' Jane said, and was gratified when Matthew looked at her, irritated.

'Who *is* this girl?'

'Kitchen-maid.' Jane did a tight smile. 'With attitude.'

'Let him finish, Jane,' Amber said. 'Let's get this over with.'

'Walter retired here with his new young wife.' Matthew looked at Amber. 'I expect you know all this.'

It was clear to Jane that Amber didn't. But had Ben known? Were there aspects of this that he'd hidden? Because if there *were*, he was going to be in some deep trouble tonight.

'Mrs Bella Chance – or Chancery as they were known by then – was from London,' Matthew said, 'and Walter wanted to give her the kind of social life she was used to. He'd throw these big house parties, no expense spared. Hence a kitchen this size – loads of servants. He'd invite minor aristocracy, and some of them even turned up. But Walter Chancery was generally regarded as pretty crass and vulgar, and they were never really accepted either by the local people or by the gentry.'

Jane thought she could hear raised voices from outside, hoped to God, after what Clancy had told her about the bad attitude of the shooters at Jeremy's, that Ben wasn't chancing his arm with them. Especially while she wasn't there, with her video camera. Christ, what if he still had it with him? What if it got *broken*?

Nothing she could do. Couldn't walk out now. Besides, this was becoming interesting, stuff worth knowing, for a student of the Border. If you could put up with the anorak drone.

'So when Walter discovered that Conan Doyle had friends and relatives nearby and sometimes stayed in the area . . . You see, we just don't *have* authors now as celebrated as Conan Doyle was then. If the *Strand* was publishing a new Holmes story, there'd be endless queues for copies. Now, Doyle was told about the Hound by his friend Fletcher Robinson –

who, despite being a Devonian, was said to have come across the story in a *Welsh guidebook*. So we assume that Doyle was making inquiries about it in the area. And the Chancerys, when they learned that the great man was staying in the vicinity, well, you can imagine they just *had* to have him as their house guest.'

'I'm sorry.' Amber came into the light. 'I think this is conjecture. Ben's been all over the place, trying to find evidence—'

'Mrs Foley . . .' Beth Pollen came forward, her cape folded over her arm, looking reassuringly nice and motherly, but you never really knew with these people. 'The main reason your husband *didn't* find out about this was simply because nobody *wanted* him to. The only remaining family in this area related to the Chancerys are the Dacres, who certainly don't like to talk about it.'

'I don't know them.'

'It wouldn't help you if you did. There's only one left – Sebastian Dacre, and he's a difficult man. Ironically, the one place where your husband *might* have laid hands on useful documentation was in the very extensive records of The Baker Street League in London. Which is where I first happened upon them. Does this begin to make a certain kind of sense?'

Amber said, 'And you have copies of this . . . documentation?'

'Mysteriously – or perhaps *not* so mysteriously – when I applied to the committee to draw out the relevant papers to allow me to make some photocopies, they seemed to have . . . disappeared. I explained all this to your husband earlier.'

'You're saying this is something to do with Dr Kennedy?'

'Dr Kennedy now disputes that the material ever existed, and Dr Kennedy is now in virtual control of The League. Furthermore, he and most of the present committee very much deplore The White Company and all it stands for. They'd rather forget Doyle's obsession with spiritualism. And I'm not sure they'd go out of their way to preserve an account handwritten by a participant in the Stanner seances for a London magazine, *Cox's Quarterly* – which, it appears, paid for it in full but never, in fact, published it. Was, in fact, persuaded – we think – not to publish.'

'And you're saying this article proved conclusively that Conan Doyle based his novel on the legend of Thomas Vaughan and the Hound of Hergest?' Amber's hands were pushing down the bulges in her apron again. 'Is that what you're saying?'

'What *I* read certainly suggested that, after his evening here, Doyle was fully acquainted with the Vaughan story. We've since established that the man who wrote it, who was quite elderly at the time, died within a year of submitting it, still waiting for his piece to appear. And the magazine itself went to the wall a short time later. We don't know how or when the article fell into the hands of The Baker Street League, but I don't suppose that's important now.'

Interesting. Jane imagined Ben and Antony in London, doorstepping Neil Kennedy, for the programme: *So, tell us Dr Kennedy, why* did *you suppress documentary evidence that Arthur Conan Doyle's novel was based not in Devon but on the Welsh Border?*

She waited for Amber to ask the other crucial question – what *happened* here? But Amber didn't. Amber really didn't want to know.

Sod *that*.

'Excuse me.' Jane stood up. 'You said the writer of this article was a *participant*. Like, participant in what? What did they actually do here, in this room?'

There was a silence.

She never got an answer. In the midst of the hush, she

heard chair legs scraping the flags in Clancy's corner of the kitchen, as Beth Pollen looked at Hardy and Matthew adjusted his glasses and said, 'Should I attempt to—?'

By then Clancy was on her feet.

'*Mum!*'

Matthew was frozen into silence. Natalie had arrived at the bottom of the kitchen steps, dark brown hair tumbled over one eye, the sleeves of her black woollen dress pushed up over the elbows. Both men looking at her, because that was what men did.

'Amber . . .' The calmness in Nat's voice was like this really thin membrane over panic. 'Do we have a first-aid kit?'

The halogen lights were showing up, around her wrists, these wild, wet swatches of what could only be – *Jesus Christ* – fresh blood.

Amber's whole body jerked. 'Where's Ben?'

Jane sprang up and ran for the steps.

At the bottom of the car park, there was a small wrought-iron gate to an old footpath that Ben had cleared. The path went down through the grounds, curving through tangled woodland, almost to the edge of the bypass, facing Stanner Rocks. This was where Ben went jogging most mornings; you could go along the side of the main road and then join up with the main drive back to the hotel.

Now the gate was open. Footprints in the snow.

Jane went through hesitantly, carrying the rubber-covered torch that Amber had given her; there was no great need for it: the moon was out and the ground was bright with virgin snow.

'Careful,' Amber said, the white canvas first-aid bag over her shoulder. 'For God's sake. We don't know—'

'It's all right.' Ben's voice from some yards away – Ben's

voice like Jane had never heard it before, kind of thin and stringy. 'It's all right, Amber. All right, now.'

Just the other side of the gate was a small clearing. Jane stayed on the edge of it and shone the torch towards Ben's voice. The beam unrolled a white carpet slicked by the marks of skidding footwear. No sign of the shooters, no voices other than the Foleys'.

'Stay there, Jane.' Amber put down the first-aid bag and said to Ben, 'What have you done?'

It was like she'd asked him to stir the soup and he'd let it boil over. It was always easy to underestimate Amber: she worried about intangibles, but only because she was a practical person, controlled. She'd sent Natalie to the ladies' loo to get cleaned up and then stand by to call an ambulance.

'I'm sorry.' Ben let out a long, hollow breath that was more than a half-sob. 'I'm really *sorry* about this.'

At the same time she saw Ben, Jane heard these liquid snuffling noises, knowing as he turned into the torchlight that he was not making them. Behind him was a fence post with no fence, only shorn-off twists of barbed wire nailed to it. And a hump on the ground.

Ben turned fully towards them, rising, and Jane gasped. His Edwardian jacket hung open, exposing his once-white shirt, emblazoned now with a blotch like a red rose.

'Lost it,' Ben said. '*I* lost it.' And then he giggled. He was trembling hard. He stumbled. 'Oh Jesus.'

'Hold the torch a bit steadier, can you, Jane?' Amber looked at Ben. It was like he'd been fighting a duel and staggered back, rapiered through the heart.

'No, really, I'm all right. Don't bother about me. I'm really all right. We should see to—'

He gestured vaguely at the hump on the ground. Jane had been afraid to look at the hump. Hoping it was a dead tree. Or something. Something that didn't snuffle.

'I'm sorry about this,' Ben said again.

The man was lying with his shoulders propped against the fence post. He was wearing camouflage trousers, an army jacket. He was holding his head back against the post. You couldn't see much of his face through all the blood, but his mouth was hanging open, and there was blood in there, too, and all around his lips and nose, bubbling through a film of dirt and snot. Jane recoiled, swallowing bile. It was like he'd been bobbing for apples in a barrel of blood.

'Called me a nancy boy, you see.' Ben moved away back, so that Amber could undo the first-aid bag. 'Nat tried to stop the bleeding. Not very successfully, I'm afraid.'

'He needs to go to a hospital.' Amber's voice was crisp as the snow. 'You've broken his nose, for a start.'

'Is that really necess—? I mean, can't you—?'

'Ben, you've smashed his *face!* I can't believe you could—'

'It was *dark*, I couldn't see what I— For God's sake, Amber, they were destroying it all. Everything was going so— And then these, these bloody shots, shaking all the glass in the windows. These bast— That's illegal, that's—'

The man on the ground squirmed, as if he was trying to get up, and then he slid back down the post like he was tied to it. He tried to speak, but his voice was like a thick soup. He started to choke.

Amber said, 'Jane, leave me the torch and then go back to the house and tell Nat we need an ambulance, will you?'

'*Naw!*' The man was prising himself up, his back jammed against the fence post. '*No abulath!*'

Ben snatched the torch away from Jane, the way he'd grabbed the video camera, and held it up over his shoulder, the way police held their torches, gripping the lighted end, so they could use the thick stem as a club.

'What's he saying?'

'He said no ambulance.' Jane retched.

Amber said, 'What are you going to do now, Ben – beat all his teeth out?'

'You don't understand.' Ben shone the torch briefly round the clearing. 'There's two more of these bastards somewhere. And a gun. One of them's got a gun.'

'He's . . .' Jane backed away. 'He's right. They were at Jeremy's. They were going to shoot Jeremy's dog.'

'Then tell Natalie to phone the police as well,' Amber said. 'Jane, *go!*'

'Yes.'

Jane turned away, grateful for an excuse, and ran blindly across the clearing towards the wooden gate. Couldn't believe what Ben had done. OK, he was furious at the shooters invading his land, and it had been building up for weeks, and he was frustrated and desperate for something to work out. But this was *Ben Foley* – artistic, funny, slightly camp. You thought you knew people. You thought you *knew—*

She was pulling at the gate when the hands came down on her shoulders.

TWENTY

Not About Foxes

'So how did you find out, vicar?' Alice Meek said. Resignation there, but no big surprise. 'Who told you?'

Merrily shook her head. 'Wouldn't be fair. But it was more a question of finding out that there was something to find out. You know?'

'You was guided.' Alice put a mug of coffee in front of her. 'See, Dexter, he thought you was just gonner lay your hands on him. He said he wouldn't mind that. He come back afterwards, he says, that's it, don't wanner go n' more. I said, Dexter, I said, nothing comes easy, in this life. You want the Holy Spirit to pay you a visit in all His glory, I said, you gotter play your part, boy.'

Alice had a bungalow in a new close off Old Barn Lane, not a hundred yards from her chip shop. Alice's kitchen was bright and shiny and full of chrome. Like a chip shop, in fact. It occurred to Merrily that, of all the women who gave up their time to clean the church, Alice was probably the oldest, the busiest and the richest.

And no kids. Dexter could be in for a sizeable bequest. Whatever Alice wanted, Dexter would have to listen.

'What I was going to suggest, Alice . . .' Nervously, Merrily sipped the coffee. It was, as she'd expected, the kind you made if you needed to work all night. 'I mean, there might be something in this for more than Dexter.'

She hadn't wanted to waste any time, to dwell too much on this before taking action. She'd walked straight down to Old Barn Lane and gone into the chip shop just as it was opening for the evening. Alice wasn't working tonight, but the woman there, Sharon, had phoned Alice at home and Alice had told Sharon to send the vicar round directly.

'En't never had no kids, vicar, as you know. Used to babysit the others. Oldest sister, no kids, you spends half your nights babysitting – they think they're doing you a favour.' Alice sat herself down in a chrome-framed chair at the chrome-legged table. 'What I'm saying, I knowed all of 'em, vicar, all them kids, better 'n their own mothers in some ways, truth was known. Kids talks to the babysitter, see – when they wakes up in the night, when they're tryin' to put you off sending 'em to bed, they talks.'

'So Dexter, Darrin, Roland . . .'

'Babysitted all them boys for years. Never hardly had a Saturday night at home. Roland, he wasn't like the others. Upsets me still to think about that child. He was . . . like he didn't belong in that family. They're – I'm saying this even though it's my own family, but they're a rough bunch, vicar, en't got no social graces. En't saying there's no goodness at the heart of 'em, but you gotter dig deep sometimes. 'Cept with Roland. A true innocent, that child. He was that innocent it was like he didn't belong in this world, which is a daft thing to say—'

'I know what you mean.'

'Like he never growed a skin, vicar. Sometimes, I wakes up in the night, years him, clear as day, sniffin' his tears back. *Daddy was drunk*, he'd say. *Daddy d' come in drunk and he smelled bad.* Saturdays, see, Richie, he'd spend the whole afternoon in the pub – come back, trample on the kids' toys and laugh hisself daft about it. Then they'd go out, him and my sister, Lisa, and I'd come round and babysit and clean up the mess and dry the tears. And talk to Roland. Darrin, he was his dad's son, didn't wanner talk, got bored easy. Roland, he wasn't like neither of them. You think about what happened to him, and you think, *why?* Why was he put on this earth for that short time, for *that* to happen?'

'*You* learned something from him,' Merrily said.

'Yes.' Alice's sharp little eyes filled up – a rarity, Merrily guessed.

'What about Dexter's family?'

'That's the middle sister, Kathleen. Her ex-husband, Mike, least he kept a job longer'n a week when they was together. None of 'em was *bright*, look, no get-up-and-go. You only gotter look at Dexter. I couldn't look at Dexter for months, mind, after Roland died. I thought – God help me – why couldn't it be him instead, or Darrin?'

'Darrin's . . . been in trouble?'

'I never knows whether he's in or out of prison, vicar, been in that many times. Beyond all redemption now, that boy. His dad, *he* was always destructive, but that was just clumsy and careless, through drink mostly – he never done nothing criminal. Most he ever got done for was urinatin' in a public place – doorway of the Old House, dead centre of the city, all the shops still open, you imagine anybody that stupid? Thick as a beam-end, Richie. But Darrin – when his ma blamed Dexter for what happened to Roland, Darrin went and did damage on them, and Kath and Mike, they wouldn't put the police on him 'cause they was ashamed of what Dexter done.'

Merrily sighed.

'Problem with Dexter, look, he en't got no charm, do he, vicar? Too fat, en't too pretty to look at and not much of a way with him. Nothin' *about* him, is there? Most people, they don't know what he did – never did, even at the time; his name wasn't in no papers nor nothin', 'cause of his age.

But he always reckons everybody knows and whatever he do they en't gonner think no better of him, so he don't even make the effort. But inside, it all builds up.'

'Until he can't breathe.'

It all added up. Except, perhaps, for the Requiem for Roland seventeen years dead. This was something she wouldn't even have thought of before meeting Llewellyn Jeavons. It was unknown country. *Embrace*, Lew had said. Embrace the entire dysfunctional family? Was she big enough for this?

'Nobody got no time for the boy but me n' more,' Alice said. 'He's had girlfriends, but they drifts away. En't a good bet, is he?' She looked at Merrily. 'What you got in mind then, vicar? You gonner have to spell it out for an ole woman.'

The difficult part. Merrily looked up and saw her own face reflected, warped and stretched and crushed, in shiny things on shelves.

Danny Thomas said, '*We*'ll take him to the hospital in the van. No problem at all.' He turned to the man with the face like a bloodied waxwork. 'Nathan, ennit, as I recall?'

The guy grunted something about his mates. Amber, apparently oblivious to the cold and the carnage, had cleaned his wounds the best she could and gone calmly back to the hotel. It was all less disturbing now, in the clearing, with Danny and Gomer there.

'Looks like your mates didn't hang about, boy,' Gomer said. 'If they got a mobile, we can phone 'em from the hospital and they'll come and pick you up, mabbe.'

Everything was turned around now. The moment of panic when the hands had come down on Jane's shoulders, and then the moment of wild relief when Ben had shone the torch on the man's face and it had a beard and hair like grey seaweed around it and a puzzled expression.

'Yes, but how—?' Ben sounded worried again. 'How's he going to explain to the hospital what happened?'

'Stick to the truth, I'd say,' Gomer said. 'What happened, he slipped on the ice and snow and come down on that ole broken post with his nose. We'd just parked the van, comin' to pick Janey up, and we years the poor bugger moaning. Don't reckon our friend yere's gonner wanner make n' more of it than that.'

Jane had to smile. For a while, after what happened to his depot and to Nev, it had looked like Gomer's effective years were over; he'd been erratic, disconnected. Now he was back in gear. And bringing Danny into the business . . . that had been inspired. Mavericks, both of them.

'If you got a toilet that en't too posh, with a basin and an ole pair of jeans, that might help too,' Danny said to Ben. 'We'll stand outside, make sure he don't get away. All right, Nathan?'

Nathan might have nodded. The blood had stopped flowing, but he was still breathing through his mouth.

'This is very good of you guys,' Ben said. 'I don't know what you saw—'

'Not much,' Gomer assured him. 'Not much at all. What you wanner do now, Janey? Come with us to the hospital, or I come and pick you up on the way back?'

'That'd be out of your way,' Jane said. 'I'd better come, I suppose.'

Not exactly looking forward to sharing a back seat with the remains of Nathan, but what could she do? She waited with Gomer in the foyer while Danny escorted Nathan into the ground-floor gents and Ben ran upstairs to replace his torn and saturated trousers. There was no sign of The White Company. Were they still in the kitchen? Was she missing Alistair Hardy's first attempts to reach Sir Arthur Conan Doyle? All that stuff seemed so unreal now. As unreal as the idea of Lucy Devenish floating around her like some pagan angel.

'What did you *really* see?' she asked Gomer.

'Like I said, not much at all, Janey.' Gomer got out his tin to roll a ciggy. 'Starts off when we're just about to turn up the drive and Danny spots this green Discovery in the lay-by across the road, no lights. Had a run-in with these boys the other night, see.'

'Clancy told me.'

'*Did* she? Well, Danny's quite keen to discuss a little matter of severe damage to Greta's runabout, so he pulls in, and we waits a while. Then we sees the three of 'em running up the drive with the gun. Then there's about three shots. That's it for Danny – puts the lights on full beam, the ole fog lamps too, goes revving up the drive, windows down, bawling out, "Armed Police, stay where you are!" Seen 'em do it on the box.'

'Cool.'

'Bloody worked, too, ennit? *They* wouldn't know, that stage. They muster took to the woods, 'cause next thing we seen two of 'em back on the road behind us. Jump straight into the Discovery and off. This one – Nathan – your mate Foley likely had him cornered by then. Time we gets to the top, we years Foley shoutin' at the feller, Miz Craven trying to calm both of 'em down. He's saying to the Welshie, Just tell us what this is about, all we wanner know's what it's about. Someone payin' you to make trouble, kind of thing. Then Miz Craven, her says some'ing and then this Welshie – he don't sound too scared, not then – we years him go, "*So what you gonner do about it, you and this nancy boy?*" And that's when I reckon Foley goes for him.'

'Insult to injury.' Jane recalled Ben on the last night of the murder weekend. *They think I'm soft. They think I'm effete, some arty bastard from London.* Then he'd said, *Where I come from we have* real *hard bastards.*

Scary.

'So, what if the hospital ask questions?'

'Ah, that boy, he en't gonner say nothin'. Wouldn't look too good, where he comes from, getting hisself filled in by – pardon me – a London pansy.'

'What if the hospital tell the police?'

Gomer shrugged, lighting his ciggy. 'Could always not bother goin' all the way to the hospital – kick the bugger out, side o' the road.'

And, for a few moments, Jane thought that was what they were going to do, when Danny Thomas pulled into the bay fronting a closed and lightless garden centre on the Hereford road and switched off the engine.

'Right, then,' Danny said.

He and Nathan were in the front, Jane and Gomer sitting on bags of sand and cement on the deck of the van. Nathan had his shaven head tilted over the back of his seat. He was wearing the jeans that Ben had brought for him. They were too long. And they were white – a last, desperate joke, as Ben had accepted from Danny, with a moue of distaste, the bin liner containing Nathan's camouflage trousers.

Nathan sat up in a hurry. There was enough moonlight to show that he was very scared.

'Relax,' Danny said. 'What you gotter worry about? All you done is wrecked my wife's car and nearly put my eye out with a rifle. Do I *look* like the sorter feller holds a grudge?'

Nathan made a lunge at the door, slamming into it with his shoulder. He cried out.

'Oh, *I'm* sorry,' Danny said. 'Oughter've told you, that door's knackered, he is – only opens from the outside. You gotter wind down the window, see, lean out and do it that way. You wanner bit o' help with that, is it?'

Nathan slumped, still breathing hard through his mouth, like he had a very heavy head-cold. 'Juss fuggig . . . ged id over.'

'What – beat the shit out of you? Mess those lovely dinky white jeans? Nathan, we come to your aid, man. We're your *friends*.'

'Fuggoff.'

'And friends – what does friends do but share a few confidences?'

A lighted bus went past on the Hereford road, and you could see the scar on Danny's forehead like an angry red slug-trail. Beside Jane, Gomer took out his ciggy tin. Jane began to feel an edge of trepidation about what they were going to do to a man already in need of serious medical attention.

Nathan said, 'You lemme out now, made, we'll leave id at thad, eh?'

'Mate?' Danny said. '*Mate*? I was a fucking long-haired twat, if you recall, the other night.' He leaned towards Nathan. '*Do* you recall the other night?'

Nathan said nothing.

'Well, I recalls it in detail, Nathan, I recalls leavin' with a whole load o' questions bobbing around in my head, which also happened to hurt like hell. So where you wanner start? Let's start with who's paying you. Let's start with Mr Sebbie Dacre.'

'Dacre's . . . nod payig us nothig.'

Danny pondered this, nodding rhythmically, like he was at a gig.

'Nathan, one thing we don't do is we don't lie to our friends. Now we can have you all tucked up in Casualty in ten minutes – or at least in the bloody queue – or we can sit yere a while longer, admiring the moonlight over the Wye Valley.'

'I'm id fuggig agony, you bassard!' The sweat on Nathan's face was making the dried blood glisten like jam.

'And I feel for you, Nathan, but we en't goin' nowhere till after we has a meaningful conversation. Now . . . *Dacre.*'

'Tells us go id heavy,' Nathan said.

'On Foley?'

'Uh!' Nathan twisted his head. 'Be-ows.'

'What?'

'Beddows!'

'Jeremy Berrows?'

Nathan nodding. 'Said he was a bad tenad.'

'He en't a bloody tenant!'

'Didn' pay. Nebber fixed fences, loosed his sheep—'

'Bullshit!'

'Is whaddhe said!' Nathan coughing, phlegmy. 'Said go id hard. Beast on his ground, he won't kill id!'

'Beast?'

'Seven grand,' Nathan said.

'What?'

'Seven grand if we geds him.'

'Nathan—'

'Swearda God. We brings him a body, we geds seven, cash.'

On the back seat, Jane went rigid. Gomer carried on rolling his ciggy.

'Run that by me again, Nathan,' Danny said.

'Fuggsake . . . We brigs him a beast, it's seven thousad. Cash.'

There was a long silence. Gomer wet the ciggy paper with the tip of his tongue. Jane looked at Nathan; he wasn't as old as she'd thought, might be no more than mid-twenties. And maybe not as hard as he'd imagined he was. You could start to feel sorry for Nathan. But she still didn't understand what he was on about. Seven *thousand*?

'Forgive me – we en't talking 'bout foxes yere, are we?' Danny said.

Nathan tried to breathe through his shattered nose and the breath got caught somewhere. There was a clicky, ratchety noise, and Nathan whimpered in pain. Whatever he'd done, Jane just wished they'd get this over, get him to hospital.

'What, then?' Danny said.

'Dog.'

Jane breathed in hard. 'Clancy said—'

Danny raised a hand. 'Go on, Nathan.'

'Killid' sheep. Dacre said he'd god five, six sheep, throa's ripped out.'

'When?'

'Dunno. Recent. Didn' wad no fuss, no panig, see. Just wannid dealin' wid.'

'For seven grand? You really expect me to—?'

'Wadds id kept quiet, he does, dassa mai' thig. Don' wadda locals involved. And don' you go spreadin' dis around, 'cause dis Dacre's a hard basd—'

'*Seven grand?*'

'Swearda God! I'm not godder make ub da' kinda moddey, ab I?'

'And that's why you was gonner shoot Jeremy Berrows's sheepdog?'

'We wadder godder shoot no fuggig shee'dog!' Nathan gritted his teeth, rocking his head. 'Bigger, yeh? Down from the Ridge. Big black bugger.'

Danny turned round to Gomer. 'He on about?'

'Hold on, boy.' Gomer leaned over Danny's seat, and Jane knew what Mum meant about the light in his glasses. 'You talking some'ing like . . . for instance, there was this so-called puma down West Wales, year or two back.'

'Uh!' Nathan nodding hard, wincing at the pain. 'We was on dat . . . How Dacre god onto us, see.'

'A mystery beast? That's what you're sayin'? Dacre reckons he's got a mystery beast preying on his stock?'

Nathan closed his eyes, still nodding, sank down in the passenger seat.

Jane felt this unearthly tingle.

'Comin' out of Jeremy Berrows's ground?'

'Uh.'

Danny said, 'Let me get this right, boy. Sebbie Dacre was offering you and your mates seven thousand pound if you brought him the body of a big black dog that been attacking his flocks. Usin' you on account he didn't want no local boys involved.'

Nathan made some kind of grunt you could probably take as affirmation. Danny turned back to Gomer.

'I knew it, see. All that bullshit about demonstratin' what it's gonner be like if they bans huntin' with hounds . . .'

'The Hound,' Jane said, breathless. 'The black—'

Gomer put a hand on her arm. 'Don't get too carried away, Janey. We don't know the half of it yet.'

'Berrows's ground,' Danny whispered. 'Gwilym Bufton said Sebbie seen it *on Berrows's ground*.'

Jane said, 'Danny, I think . . .'

She was looking at Nathan struggling to sit up. A gout of fresh, bright blood flooded out over his lips. Jane stifled a scream.

'Oh hell,' Danny said, not too calmly. He turned on the engine.

Part Three

It was several years before we discovered there was any-thing ghostly about it. I'd never believed in ghosts really . . . not until we experienced it ourselves. About three years ago, walking up the stairs late in the evening, I got to about here . . . and there was a shadowy figure crossed straight across in front of me . . . sort of a crouched person, almost like a largish sort of dog . . . just passed straight in front of me and into the inner hall and . . . well, I didn't see any more after that. A prickly feeling went up my back.

John Williams, farmer, Hergest Court, 1987

TWENTY-ONE

Cwn Annwn

Turning over the apartment – this wasn't something you did lightly.

The attic door opened easily. No alarm went off, though it wouldn't have come as a big surprise to find one had been secretly installed. Merrily stood on the threshold of Jane's domain, remembering how important having her own apartment had been to the kid's acceptance, aged fifteen, of a new life in Ledwardine.

Just a child then – two years ago, incredibly, she'd been just a child. Now she was a working woman with a provisional driving licence. And *in a relationship* – was this really the new *going out with someone*? Sometimes it felt that while Jane and Eirion were in a relationship she and Lol were just going out. Even though they never did.

Merrily felt her age like a grey blanket around her shoulders. Standing in the doorway, looking up at the walls, an enormous colour chart for emulsion paint. Even on a drab day, the Mondrian Walls – currently, giant slabs of crimson, cobalt blue and chrome yellow – were startling enough to have the Listed Buildings Department chasing an injunction, if they ever found out.

Merrily went in. This visit was long overdue. It wasn't that Jane had been particularly secretive or moody or pre-occupied, or anything like that. In fact, after her long-dark-night-of-the-soul period during the autumn, she'd been unusually bright and animated.

Which had seemed to be down to the weekend job – the sense of grown-up independence it would be giving her . . . and more. Merrily remembered working Saturdays, at sixteen, in a small, indy record shop, putting on her black and purple Goth make-up like a uniform. Getting paid to be cool.

Then the record shop had closed down, the way they did, and she'd found a back-room job in an old-fashioned department store, where the merest smear of Goth and you were out. Welcome to the world of work.

What she couldn't quite understand was what was so long-term cool about washing up and waiting tables in a cold, run-down, under-financed country-house hotel run by a redundant TV executive with no catering experience and a young Delia Smith who should have known better. Naturally, she'd been over to Stanner and met them both – this being Jane's first weekend job, it was important to check it out – and Amber and Ben Foley had seemed pleasant and well-intentioned. And almost certainly doomed.

The bed was made, and very neatly. This was the bed to which Jane had brought Eirion last summer – Eirion blurting it out to Merrily the very next day, after she'd accused him of being a nice guy. *No, I'm not – I slept with your daughter.*

Merrily smiled: innocents, really, both of them.

This afternoon, under an hour ago, Lol had rung from Prof's studio, ominously hesitant.

The familiar leaden thud of a bag of anxiety landing on the doorstep.

Lol had been hesitant as long as she'd known him. Much less so with her now, obviously. No taboos between them any more. All right, one taboo. Just the single issue where hesitancy still came into it.

'This is about Jane, isn't it?' Merrily had said. 'This is one of those situations where you have to decide where your loyalties lie.'

'And what's best,' Lol said. 'Ultimately.' He paused. 'She phoned.'

'When?'

'Last night. She said it was, you know, absolutely confidential. I was to say nothing to anybody. Well, I realize that "anybody" almost invariably means you, but in this case . . .'

Merrily had sunk into the office chair, jagged neon letters spelling out PREGNANCY and ABORTION in her head. Outside, it was attempting to snow again, like it had been all week.

'She's not pregnant,' Lol said, 'as far as I know.'

'How did you—?'

'It's what you always think of first.'

'You know me *that* well?'

'Anyway, she wouldn't tell me a thing like that. The things she tells me about are the things that might offend you professionally.'

'Kid's always taken a special kind of delight in offending me professionally.'

'You're not *cooperating*, Merrily. You know you have to cooperate here, or I can't go on.'

'All right. Yes. OK. There is no way she'll ever learn you told me, as God is my—'

'We take that as read,' Lol said. 'This is about Lucy's house.'

'Oh well, Jane knows all about that.' The relief making her smile. 'We keep our secrets to an absolute minimum these days. Grown-ups. Mates. All that stuff.'

'Jane says Lucy doesn't want us to give up on the house.'

'Well, obviously, we—' Merrily paused, staring out of the window, to where the apple tree branches waved vaguely. 'Lucy says?'

'The late Lucy Devenish.'

'I see.' Merrily said.

'You do?'

'Lucy has appeared to Jane . . . in a dream?'

'No, through, um, a third party.'

'Oh.' The smile dissolving, Merrily scrabbling for a cigarette.

'She said she'd thought about it for two or three days before deciding to ring. In the end she'd decided it would be remiss of her not to pass on the message.'

'Lol, what are we talking about here? Clairvoyant, Romany shaman?'

'She kept saying things like, "Well, obviously I'm in two minds about the whole thing and it's probably bollocks anyway." After what happened with Layla Riddock, I think she'd be quite cautious.'

'I'd've thought that, too.'

'It seems to be a spiritualist medium,' Lol said.

'She went to a . . . medium?'

'I don't think it was that formal, but it was obvious she wasn't going to tell me the circumstances. So I'm just . . . I sat around and searched my conscience. And I thought, well, we *don't* know who the medium is, and there are mediums and mediums. So I decided I ought to tell you.'

'Thank you, Lol. It's appreciated.'

'Don't get me wrong,' Lol said. 'Lucy was a good friend to me.'

'So you rang the agents to see if the buyers had by chance given back word?'

'Naturally.'

'And?'

'The people can't wait to move in. Although they have two children, they find it delightfully bijou rather than small and cramped.'

Merrily wondered if he'd still have told her about Jane and the medium if it had turned out that the purchasers had suddenly backed out and Lucy's house was on the market again. She decided he would have, in the end, but maybe not until contracts had been exchanged.

'Typical spirit message, then,' Merrily said. 'Sod-all use.'

Danny wasn't sorry the job had been called off. It was too cold. The sky was tight as a snare drum, grains of fine snow collecting on the bonnet of the van like battery acid.

And Gomer was getting on in years, and excavating a wildlife pond for this posh bloke from Off, these were not the best conditions for it. So when the feller's new wife comes on the scene, going, 'No, I think it should be over *there*, don't you, darling?', Danny was relieved to hear Gomer suggesting they should both think about it for a few days.

Back in the van, Danny had asked Gomer how much he was going to charge the people for a wasted trip, and Gomer had shaken his head and said that wasn't how you kept your clients. Fair enough. Danny had shrugged, still an apprentice in the plant-hire business, and Gomer had dropped him off back at the farm.

Snow was falling, light and fine as dust motes, when Danny saw the car in front of the galvanized gate and wondered which of Greta's mouthy friends he'd have to endure before he got any lunch.

'Ah! Now! Talk of the Devil!' Greta giving it the full Janis Joplin from the living room, soon as he let himself in. 'Look who's yere, Danny!'

Danny pulled off his wellies and padded in, and came face to face with Mary Morson, Jeremy's ex, in the black business suit her wore as some kind of social services gofer at Powys Council.

'En't you at work, Mary?'

'Danny!' Greta blasted.

'Flexitime,' Mary Morson said, smug. Put on a bit of weight, Danny noticed. Pregnant? Unlikely. Accidents didn't happen to Mary Morson.

'Listen to this, Danny,' Greta said. 'Just listen to this – what did I say about that woman? Tell it him, Mary.'

'I just thought somebody should enlighten a mutual friend of ours.' Mary looked serious, light brown hair tucked behind her ears, small disapproving lines either side of her mouth. 'It's none of my business, really.'

'In which case—'

'Danny!'

'Go on, then.' Danny sighed and tried to get his bum within a yard or two of the wood-stove, but Mary and Greta both had chairs pulled up to the heat. Jerry Springer or some such earache was on the telly with the sound thankfully down, and he stood in front of that.

'That bitch is cheatin' on him already,' Greta said, big smile, and Danny turned briefly, thinking her was on about some bint on Jerry Springer. But it wasn't Jerry Springer on the box after all, it was some little blonde home-improvement tart.

'Natalie Craven,' Mary said grimly.

'Eh?'

'That blue camper van. The one Natalie Craven sold to the survey people at Stanner Rocks . . .'

'I thought you and the naturalist feller was all washed up,' Danny said.

'I still have friends there,' Mary said, voice cold as outside. 'They were using the van as a site office, and they kept the folding bed as emergency overnight accommodation for volunteers. But one day, there was evidence that it had been . . . used.'

'Mabbe one of the volunteers fancied a lie-down. It can get weary, watching little bloody plants grow.'

'At night, this was,' Mary said, 'when there weren't any volunteers on site. The van was always kept locked and the keys in a locked drawer at the Nature Trust office in town. Anyway – ' Mary's little nose twitched in distaste ' – they found suggestions of sexual activity.'

'Like *what*?' Danny raised his eyes to the big central beam. 'Pair o' pink knickers with no crot—'

'Danny!' Greta roared.

'Well, this is bloody daft, Gret. Couple o' randy naturalists nips in the ole van for a quick shag, and it's gotter be—'

'Listen, will you!'

Danny sniffed and scowled, and Mary said, 'The door hadn't been forced. It had obviously been unlocked. And if anybody might've had a spare key, nobody could think of anybody more likely than the person who sold them the van in the first place. So anyway, one of the team, he left some equipment on the site this night, see, and had to go back. And what should he find parked up there on the edge of the forestry but Jeremy's four-by-four, and nobody in it. But there was a bit of light coming from the camper van, and when he looked in the window, there *she* was, with a man, and it certainly wasn't Jeremy.'

It had all come out in a rush, and Mary Morson slumped back in her chair, lips tight. For the first time in his life, Danny wanted to physically shake the smile off Greta's face.

'*Natalie?*'

'No more'n you'd expect from a woman like that,' Greta said.

'A woman like *what*?'

'I need to spell it out?'

'So who was the man?'

'He didn't recognize the man,' Mary said. 'He couldn't see him very clearly, because he . . .' Mary looked away. 'I expect she was on top of him. But then he doesn't know many local people, anyway.'

'In which case—'

'But he *does* know Jeremy! And he knows *her.*'

Danny shut his eyes. *Shit.*

'Somebody ought to tell him,' Mary said quietly. 'Somebody who knows him well.'

'When?' Danny said harshly. 'When *was* this?'

'Night before last.' Mary Morson stood up in front of him. 'There's no mistake about this, none at all, Danny. It was her. It was Natalie Craven and a bloke, and they were—'

'All *right!*'

'We're just telling you,' Greta said, 'because you're the nearest he's got to a best friend. None of us wants to see him hurt.'

'Hurt? It'll kill him! You really expect me to go tell him? Like he don't got enough on his plate?'

'Who else is going to? You wanner wait till it's all over Kington?'

'You mean it en't already? Oh, I forgot, you en't been shopping yet, did you?'

'That's unfair!'

'Well . . .' Danny turned away. 'It's bloody upset me, it has.'

'It's upset all of us,' Mary Morson said, shameless.

Merrily checked out the pine bookcase. Not many changes here: *The Hedgewitch Almanac, Green Magic, Britain's Pagan Places,* plus another fifty or so pastel spines confirming that Jane was still a vague supporter of the Old Religion, which, as the kid now admitted, was actually not very old at all.

The shelves were all full. No room here for the Bible, which had failed to address the issue of the mystical British countryside, but there was still a corner, Merrily noted, for the 17th-century Herefordshire cleric Thomas Traherne, who'd chronicled its God-given glories at length.

This was all about the need for direct experience, a confirmation of Otherness. And, of course, there *was* an area of operation where Christianity and New Age paganism came close together.

It was spiritual healing.

It was several days now since she'd been to see Alice Meek, suggesting that if there was to be a service of healing it should initially be directed towards the soul of nine-year-old Roland Hook. Telling Alice it all came back to Roland, all the guilt and the grief . . . and the pain of a young child who had died, very afraid, in the middle of a crime. Maybe the knowledge that Roland's soul was at peace would bring some kind of harmony to the family.

'Right, then.' Alice had stood up, stiff-backed, fiery-faced. 'You leave it with me, vicar. Half of them won't understand what it's about, dull buggers, but I'll talk to my niece in Solihull, her as did the Alpha course. We'll make this happen, somehow.'

Not a word since. Sophie, meanwhile, had been compiling a list of ministers in the diocese who had a serious, practical interest in healing, with a view to organizing a preliminary meeting. But it needed someone else to organize it; Merrily wasn't good at admin.

She sat on Jane's bed. Turning over the apartment was beginning to look like a waste of time. Had she really expected to find a ouija board laid out next to the collected works of Doris Stokes? She'd looked briefly in the wardrobe, flicked open dressing-table drawers, glanced under the bed. Not even much dust under there – amazing what changes a few weekends of chambermaiding could bring about.

Through the window, she could see wooded Cole Hill, with scattered snow up there, like grated cheese. There hadn't been a serious fall this year; maybe it wouldn't come this side of Christmas. After Christmas, Lol would go on tour for the first time since . . . well, since he was hardly older than Jane. Lol finally getting a life: where would that leave them?

Don't think about it.

The only book on the bedside table was a scuffed old favourite: *The Folk-lore of Herefordshire*, by Ella Mary Leather, dead for three-quarters of a century and still unsurpassed for down-home authenticity. There was an orange Post-it sticker in the book, and Merrily let it fall open.

Cwn Annwn, or the Dogs of Hell.

Parry (Hist. Kington 205) gives an account of the superstitious beliefs of many aged persons then (1845) living in the parish.

It was the opinion of many persons then living in the out-townships that spirits in the shape of black dogs are heard in the air, previous to the dissolution of a wicked person; they were described as being jet black, yet no one pretends to have seen them. But many believed that the king of darkness (say the gossips) sent them to terrify mankind when the soul of a human being was about to quit its earthly tenement.

Kington: the final frontier, the least known, most hidden, of Herefordshire's six towns, in appearance more like the Radnorshire towns of Knighton and Rhayader, but with streets more cramped than either. It was even on the Welsh side of Offa's Dyke. It was entirely understandable that Kington folk, even in the nineteenth century, should have felt under the dominion of Welsh mythology. And inevitable that Jane, working weekends in the area, would be interested. Mrs Leather added:

Hergest Court was, or perhaps still is, haunted by a demon dog, said to have belonged to Black Vaughan and to have accompanied him during his life. It is seen before a death in the Vaughan family. A native of Kington writes: 'In my young days I knew the people who lived at Hergest Court well, and they used to tell me strange things of the animal. How he inhabited a room at the top of the house, which no one ever ventured to enter; how he was heard there at night, clanking his chain; how at other times he was seen wandering about (minus the chain!) His favourite haunt was a pond, the "watering place" on the high road from Kington. The spot was much dreaded, and if possible avoided, by late travellers. I knew many who said they had seen the black dog of Hergest.'

Right. This was the legend alleged to be the source of *The Hound of the Baskervilles*. Ben Foley hosted murder weekends at Stanner, appearing as Sherlock Holmes, on the basis – unproven – that Arthur Conan Doyle used to stay there.

This would be Jane helping out with background research.

Of course, despite being a doctor, a man of science, Conan Doyle had been very deeply into spiritualism and psychic matters in general. Merrily recalled reading how he was convinced that the escapologist, Harry Houdini, was using psychic powers to dematerialize, which Houdini denied to the end. Doyle had also championed the Cottingley Fairies photographs – fakes.

Hmm.

Merrily shut the book and arranged it carefully on the

bedside table, the way she'd found it. She went back to the bookcase, crouched down and re-inspected the titles, one by one this time. Definitely nothing here suggestive of a new interest in spiritualism.

When you thought about it, the only place Jane could realistically have encountered a medium – the only place, apart from school, she'd been to in weeks, in fact – was Stanner Hall.

Was, or perhaps still is, haunted by a demon dog.

But that was Hergest Court, not Stanner. Stanner wasn't old enough to be haunted by a demon dog. A 'demon dog', anyway, was probably no more than an imprint, or a projection. Nothing demonic about dogs.

Merrily checked out the little room which, due to cash flow, was still only halfway to becoming Jane's private bathroom. Found herself lifting the lid of the toilet cistern.

Nothing but brownish water. Feeling stupid and treacherous, Merrily replaced the cistern lid. As she left the apartment she looked around the upper landing, full of shadows even in the early afternoon, and a few trailing cobwebs she ought to get around to removing. She cleared her throat.

'We're all right, you know. We can manage, Lol and me. And you must have things to get on with, Lucy. A woman like you.'

She went downstairs, shaking her head. Madness. All priests were prey to madness.

And then, on reaching the bottom, she immediately turned and went back up and said a small prayer outside Jane's door. Paranoia.

*

That night it all came back, like something she'd eaten, when the kid said, 'Would it be OK if I spent *all* next weekend at Stanner? Friday till Sunday?'

Merrily went still, hands in the washing up bowl. She didn't turn round.

'Weather doesn't look too promising, flower.'

'Well, I can always cadge a lift with Gomer in the truck if it looks bad. The thing is, they really need me – there's a conference on.'

'An actual *conference*.'

'Don't be like that. They're doing their best.'

'What kind of conference?'

'Oh. . . . something called The White Company. It's the title of an historical novel by Conan Doyle so I expect they're into, like, the non-Holmes side of it. Which sounds boring, but Ben thinks it's great. Like, anything at all to do with Conan Doyle, he's up for it. And the money, naturally.'

'Interesting man,' Merrily said, 'Conan Doyle.'

'Er . . . yeah.'

'Progressive thinker. Although he lost a lot of credibility towards the end of his life through his support of spiritualism.'

'Well, he would wouldn't he?'

'Would he?'

'It was all bollocks.'

'Ben Foley's not interested in that side of him, then?'

'Ben's got *his* credibility to think about.' Jane stood up. 'Tell you what . . . just to make sure it's OK for the weekend, how about I walk down to Gomer's and ask him if he'll be around Kington, with Danny. And the truck.'

'Why don't you just give him a ring?'

'I've tried. Always leaves his answering machine on at night. Look, if you light the fire, I'll be back in no time.'

Through the half-open kitchen door, Merrily watched Jane throwing on her fleece and slipping out the front way. Oh, there was *something*.

TWENTY-TWO

Whoop, Whoop

'Comes a time,' Gomer said, 'when you gotter decide whether seven grand's worth gettin' your face stove in for. Naw, they en't been back, them Welshies, 'course they en't.'

Gomer's kitchen was still like a monument to Minnie, who had died on him: very clean and bright with shiny pots and cake tins, lurid curtains with big red tulips on them and a tea cosy in the shape of a marmalade cat. Nothing added, nothing taken away; maybe a shrine or maybe Gomer just wasn't interested in kitchens.

'I did try to phone you a few times.' Jane took off her fleece. 'I rang Danny last night, but I got Greta so I had to pretend it was a wrong number. Anything I can do while I'm here?'

Gomer gave her a sharp look. 'I en't an ole pensioner yet, girl.'

'*I* know that. It's just that when you're a weekend maid it's the way you think.' She sat down at the kitchen table. 'It's a lot of money, Gomer.'

'Oh hell, aye. Even for Sebbie Three Farms, now. Lost a fair bit five year or so back. Wife divorced him. Had to do a bit o' jugglin' to hold on to all his ground.'

'What's he like?'

'Sebbie? Standard ole Border gentry. Certain kind seems to thrive yereabouts – talk posh but rough as a sow's hide underneath. Can't say I likes the feller, but can't say I dislikes him as much as some of 'em. En't figured it out, mind, why he brung in shooters from Off.'

'Because he didn't want local people gossiping.'

'But if he's got a beast at his flocks, why en't he out there hisself? Been around guns all his life. Why en't Sebbie out there hisself takin' a pop? Tea, Janey?'

'No, thanks, I can't stay long.'

'Well, I'm gonner have one.'

Gomer went to put the kettle on. Jane looked at the crack of night between the drawn curtains. For three nights, she'd lain in bed dwelling, with no pleasurable *frissons*, upon the beast, the *participants in the event* in the kitchens at Stanner. And sometimes feeling Lucy Devenish watching her from the corner by the bookcase – this solemn, hawk-nosed figure in a poncho, rebuking her for her lies, deceit and despicable selfishness.

'Gomer . . .' She hesitated. Gomer plugged in the kettle and turned and looked at her. 'The Hound of Hergest,' she said.

Gomer came and sat down. His smile was sceptical. 'I won't say I en't never yeard of folk supposed to've seen him, Janey. But the ole Hound of Hergest – do he kill ewes, this is the question?'

'I don't know.'

'Yere's the situation. Dogs kills sheep. Sheepdogs kills sheep – one o' your big myths is that stock with their throats ripped out, that's all down to Mr Fox. Truth is, whole load of lambs gets savaged every year by sheepdogs. Thin line between snappin' at sheep to round 'em up and picking one off. Point I'm makin', Janey, if you got a mystery beast preyin' on ewes, chances are it's a big sheepdog – mabbe two – that's got the taste for blood.'

'So why's this Sebbie Dacre so scared of going out there himself with a gun?'

'I say scared?' Gomer squinted at her.

Also, at night, she'd thought of Nathan. What if he'd died? What if he'd died there in Danny's van, leaving Ben facing a manslaughter charge, at the very least, and Gomer and Danny and her as accessories?

What if he'd died *after* they'd got him to the hospital? What if he was dead now?

'I wouldn't know why Sebbie's scared,' Gomer said. 'Man like Sebbie, he don't confide to the likes of we. Don't confide to nobody, that family. He also don't scare that easy.'

'They were related to the Chancerys of Stanner, weren't they?'

'Who you year that from, Janey?'

'Woman who's booking a conference at Stanner. Mrs Pollen.'

'From Pembridge?' Gomer nodded. 'Me and Nev put her a septic tank in once. Husband used to be County Harchivist for Powys.'

'So Dacre *is* related to the Chancerys?'

'Small world, girl, terrible inbred. Sebbie's ma was Margery Davies, second daughter of Robert and Hattie Davies – Hattie Chancery as was. After Stanner was sold, Margie 'herited most of the ground on the Welsh side and some money, and her married Richard Dacre, who was the son of a farmer on the *English* side. So, overnight, like, they become the biggest landowners yereabouts. And they had just the one son and that was Sebbie, and a younger daughter. So when Richard died, Sebbie got the main farms and all the ground and a fair bit of cash. And then he bought up Emrys Morgan's farm across the valley, when Emrys died, and so that's why they calls him Sebbie Three Farms. See?'

'So Dacre is Hattie Chancery's grandson. And great-grandson of Walter Chance, who built Stanner Hall.'

'Correct. Hattie, her had two daughters, but Paula, the oldest, got sent away, and Paula was left the Stanner home farm, The Nant, which was leased long-term to Eddie Berrows, Jeremy's dad, who was Hattie's farm manager's son.'

'So Jeremy's farm was originally part of the Stanner estate, too.'

'Not much wasn't. Now Paula, after what happened with Hattie and Robert, her was brung up by Robert's sister up in Cheshire. Growed up and married a feller up there and just took the income from the lease. But her died youngish, see, and Richard Dacre, he kept trying to buy The Nant off Paula's husband, but Paula, her had a soft spot for the Berrows from when her was little, and her husband knew the Berrowses didn't want the Dacres as their landlords, 'cause the Dacres'd likely have 'em out on their arses first possible opportunity. So he signs another lease with Eddie Berrows – under Richard's nose, so to speak. And the Dacres was blind bloody furious. So that split the family good and proper. Plus, it explains why Sebbie Dacre got no love for Jeremy.'

'It's not short of feuds, is it, this area? You need an up-to-date feud-map just to find your way around.' Jane was imagining a large-scale plan of the Welsh Border hills, with arteries of hatred linking farms and estates, pockets of old resentment, dotted lines marking tunnels of lingering suspicion.

''Course, quite a lot of folk don't think too highly of Sebbie,' Gomer said. 'Do he care? Do he f— No, he don't, Janey. He don't care.'

'So, what happened – I mean I really think I ought to know this, working at Stanner – what exactly happened with

Hattie Chancery? Or is that something people don't talk about?'

'They don't *talk* about it,' Gomer said, 'on account there en't that many folk left round yere remembers it.'

'What about you?'

'I was just a boy then. Just a kiddie at the little school.'

'So you're saying you don't remember it either?'

Gomer dug into a pocket of his baggy jeans and slapped his ciggy tin on the kitchen table. ''Course I remembers it. All everybody bloody jabbered about for weeks.'

Jane beamed at him. 'Maybe I will have a cup of tea after all, if that's all right.'

And she sat quietly and watched Gomer making it. Could tell by the way he was nodding to himself, lips moving, that he was replaying his memories like a videotape, and maybe editing them, too.

While the tea was brewing, Gomer brought down Minnie's bone-china cups and saucers, and it was touching to watch him laying them out with hands that looked like heavy-duty gardening gloves. Jane waited. If she was going to be of any use to Antony Largo, she needed more background information. This wasn't simply curiosity, it was need-to-know.

Last night, from the apartment, she'd rung Natalie to ask how things were going, like with Ben. Nat hadn't been all that forthcoming. 'He's all right.'

Jane had pressed on anyway. 'But *is* he? That guy thought Ben was going to kill him. He was terrified, he— It's like . . . it's a side of Ben I've never seen.'

'He's a man,' Nat had said, offhand. 'Men can't be seen to back down. I really don't think he meant to do that much damage.'

'Nat, was he—?'

'It happened very quickly, Jane. I didn't really see anything.'

'Well, obviously, that's what you'd tell the police.'

'Police?'

'I mean *if* the police were involved. If that guy's injuries—'

'Jane . . .' Nat's voice had gone low. 'That really isn't going to happen. So I think it's best we all forget about this incident. It was a one-off, and if it gets round . . . you know what this area's like. We don't want Ben to get a reputation. Best if we don't talk about it *any more*. All right?'

Nat had sounded nervy. Not herself at all.

And Jane was still hearing, *Thick, barbaric yobs. No subtlety . . . Where I come from, we have real hard bastards.'*

Time to investigate Ben's history. This morning, Jane had got up early, gone down to the scullery/office, switched on the computer and fed *Ben Foley* into Google. Hard to remember what life had been like without the Net. Now everybody was a private eye.

The results had been disappointing. All she'd found were references to the various TV series Ben had been involved with, no personal stuff at all. It had been mildly amusing to discover a website for *The Missing Casebook*, his series about what had really happened to Sherlock Holmes post-Reichenbach. It had become a very small cult, the website set up by a hard core of fans furious that it hadn't run to a second series. But the site didn't seem to have been updated for a while.

Jane also looked up Antony Largo. Most of the references were to his documentary *Women of the Midnight*. The words most often applied to Antony were *committed* and *tenacious*. To understand what drove women to kill without mercy, without pity, inverting their need to nurture, he was said to have spent weeks in Holloway prison and had corresponded with Myra Hindley, the moors murderess. After *Women of the Midnight*, Antony never seemed to have been out of work, but he didn't seem to have done anything since that had been quite as massively acclaimed.

It was becoming clear that Ben had known exactly what he was doing – connecting with old triumphs – when he'd introduced Antony to Hattie Chancery.

'Hattie Chancery,' Gomer said, lighting up. 'Her was as big as a cow. Her could skin a rabbit with her teeth. Her could ride all day and drink strong men under the table.'

'Really?'

'Prob'ly not, but it's what we was told as kids. "Eat up your sprouts, boy, else Hattie Chancery'll come for you in the night and put you under her arm and take you away." You woke up in the night, bit of a creak, it'd be Hattie Chancery on the stairs.'

'This was while she was still alive?'

'Sure t' be.' Gomer nodded. 'Master of the Middle Marches, see, for years. The hunt, Janey. Used to year 'em galloping up Woolmer's pitch of a Saturday, hounds yowlin' away, but the loudest of all'd be Hattie Chancery. Like a *whoop, whoop* in the air, urgin' on the fellers. Hattie Chancery: *whoop, whoop*.'

Gomer leaned back in his chair, into the smoke from his ciggy and the clouds of his childhood.

'Was that unusual,' Jane asked him, 'having a female hunt master in those days?'

'Was round yere. But Hattie, her was a dynamite horse-woman, and had this authority about her. Big woman, see. Weighed a fair bit, in later years. Drank beer. Pints. Big thirst on her.'

Jane knew girls at school who drank pints, but that was more about sexual politics than big thirst.

'You still gets huntswomen like that now, mind,' Gomer

said. 'Loud. I remember folks used to jump in the ditch if they yeard Hattie's car comin' round the bend from the pub at Gladestry. *That* was a fact – into the bloody ditch, no messin', and they'd year her laughing like a maniac as her come beltin' past, well tanked-up, all the windows down. No big drink-driving thing in them days, see. Least, not for the likes of Hattie Chancery.'

Jane was surprised that Gomer could remember so far back, but she supposed you did when you got older; it was just the more recent events that became a haze.

'What about the husband?'

'Robert? Kept well out of it, Janey. Never hunted. Couldn't ride, for one thing – they reckoned he had an injury from the Great War, but I also yeard it said he had a bit of a distaste for all that. For blood. Bad time, they reckoned, in France, and he come back a changed man: quiet, thoughtful, never talked about what he'd seen. Son of a doctor in Kington, Robert was. Good-lookin' feller, caught Hattie's eye, and that was that. Her was young, eighteen or so, when her married Robert. Hattie's ole man had died by then, and so Robert come to Stanner. Hattie wouldn't never leave Stanner. Brought Robert back like a bride. That's what they used to say. Like a bride.'

Jane sipped her tea, forming this picture of Robert as some kind of poetic Wilfred Owen type, sickened by the horrors of the trenches. Maybe even a Lol type.

'Serious mismatch,' Gomer said. 'Went wrong early, got worse.'

'You ever see him?'

'Mostly, he stayed round the house and the grounds, but I seen him once or twice. Every now and seldom he'd go for a walk on his own, along Hergest Ridge, with a knapsack. And I was with my ole man this day – I'd be about seven – and we seen Mr Robert, and he give me an apple. And I remember my ole man watching him walk off, head down into the wind, and the ole man sayin', "Poor bugger." Always remember that. *Poor bugger.*'

'So how long was that before . . .'

'Oh, mabbe a year or two. 'Course, there was a lot o' gossip 'fore that, about Hattie and her men.'

'She had other men?'

'Oh hell, aye. Any number, you believed the stories. *Any* number. Good-lookin' woman, see. Golden-haired and statuesque, like. There was tales . . .' Gomer looked into his cup, cleared his throat. 'Like, you'll've yeard how a new huntsman gets blooded, from his first kill. They reckoned the Middle Marches had its own . . . test. For a new boy. See if he was up to it, like.'

'What – up to Hattie?'

'Her was said to be . . . I suppose today you'd have a name for it.'

'Generous?'

'Nympho,' Gomer said. 'Appetites like a feller, my mam used to say – not to me, like, but I overyeard her and Mrs Probert from the Cwm once. Well, naturally, after her done what her done, they all had their theories. More like a feller. Used to get in fights in the pub. Smash an ole pint glass, shove it at you.'

'She *glassed* people?'

'All kinds of stories went round after her killed Robert. Stories I wouldn't rush to repeat.' Gomer sniffed, stirring his tea, ciggy in his lips. 'Not to a young woman.'

'Oh, *Gomer.*'

'Janey, it was gossip. We was kids. Young boys. 'Sides, it was five or six years after her was dead I yeard this. Durin' the War. Young lads talkin', the way young lads talks at that age.'

Jane had an image of Gomer in adolescence: thin as a straw, hair like a yardbrush.

'Gomer, I'm like . . . seventeen, now? You know?'

Gomer stirred the dregs of the tea in the pot and filled his cup with it – tea like sump oil. 'It was Stanner Rocks,' he said. 'Used to take 'em up Stanner.'

'Men?'

'Funny place, see. Scientists now, they reckons it's down to what they calls a Standing Wave. Meteological stuff. Gives it a rare climate up there, like in Italy and them places. Nowhere like it, 'specially not on the edge of Wales.'

'Mediterranean.' Jane nodded. Ben had gone on about it, bemoaning the fact that the rocks, with their odd climatic conditions and their rare plants, didn't belong to the hotel. A national nature reserve now, so you had to have special permission to go up there, which meant Ben couldn't even build it up as a tourist attraction.

'They din't know the scientific stuff then,' Gomer said, 'but everybody said it was a funny place, what with the Devil's Garden where nothing grew – just thin soil, more like, but they always called it the Devil's Garden. Soil's that thin on them ole rocks that in a good summer you'll have a drought up there as kills off half the trees and the bushes. See, what—'

'And she used to take men up there?'

Gomer sucked the ciggy to the end, carefully extracted the remains. 'Boys' talk. No matter what the weather was like, see, you'd always find a warm spot on top o' Stanner.'

'Like for sex?'

'Bloody hell, Janey! Can't get to it fast enough, can you?'

'Sorry.'

Gomer drank his tea. 'Her'd make 'em go right to the edge. Right to the edge of the rocks. The cliff edge.

Hundred-foot drop or more, onto stones. And her'd have 'em right on the edge, more ways than one. *Whoop whoop.*'

'Oh.'

'Boys' talk, Janey. Stories, that's all.'

'So like, did *you* know anybody who . . . ?'

Gomer stared into his teacup; it was empty.

'*Gomer!*'

'Pal o' mine – his older brother. He was one.'

'And what happened?'

'Men wasn't experienced back then, Janey, not quite the same way they are now. Her gets him . . . overwrought.' Gomer's face went dark red. 'And then, when he can't think proper, her's got him hanging half over the edge. Thought he was gonner go over the top and he . . . he din't care, see. Din't care if he went over or not.'

'Bloody hell, Gomer.'

'Boys' talk,' Gomer said. 'They used to say her liked 'em to be real scared. This was the thing for Hattie. Take the boys to the edge, show 'em who was boss.'

'Domination? Like, she got off on it?'

'Mabbe.'

'So it wasn't just boys' talk at all, was it?' Jane said softly.

Gomer coughed. 'Mabbe not all of it.' He started rolling another ciggy, then stopped and shut the tin and looked past Jane into a corner of the kitchen as if he thought Minnie might be there, watching him with disapproval. 'Afterwards, her'd make 'em bring a rock back for her. A stone. Mabbe the size of half a brick.'

'What for?'

'Kept the stones on the mantelpiece. In a line.'

'I don't get it.'

'Trophies,' Gomer said. 'Every time her had a different feller up the top he'd have to fetch a new rock back. All laid out on the mantelpiece in the big drawing room, all in a line, where poor Robert could see 'em – watch the line of stones gettin' longer. He wasn't a well man by then. Chest. Spent a lot o' time in the lounge in front of the fire. Under this line of stones, gettin' longer.'

'What a total bitch.'

'We had all the gossip from the servants, see – local people. Her used to scream at him that he was weak – a malingerer. He was ill, was what it was, but Hattie din't wanner know 'bout that. Not her idea of what a countryman should be – a countryman was *healthy*. When her was out huntin', he'd go to bed, try to build up his strength, mabbe fall asleep and then her'd come back and find him . . . rip all the bedclothes off him, leave him shiverin'. Always made her angry, the drink. Some folks gets merry, some— What's wrong, Janey?'

'She pulled the bedclothes off him?'

Jane moistened her lips. In her head, a memory of being in the doorway of her first bedroom at Stanner, looking in at all the duvet pulled off, its cover gathered in a heap like a flaccid parachute.

'If he was still up,' Gomer said, 'there'd likely be a fight – a real fight: bruises, split lips. *His* lips. *That* was talked about, oh hell, aye. Can't cover up a split lip, can you? Can't pass it off as how you fell over the grate.'

'How could he stand it?'

'Her house, her money. Where's he gonner go? Pitiful, Janey.'

'Yes.'

'And that was how it come to the end. Night of the day of the hunt. Hattie real fired up, as usual. Her'd ride like the devil, and if they ever come back without a kill . . . not a happy woman.'

'You make her sound like . . .'

'Ar?'

'Doesn't matter, go on.'

'This night – round about now on the calendar, night of the Middle Marches Hunt Ball . . . See, Robert, he wouldn't go to the Hunt Ball, couldn't get on with these country sports types. Hattie goes alone. Comes back alone around two or three in the mornin', but whether her was alone between leavin' the ball and gettin' back to Stanner, that's anybody's guess.'

'Slag.'

'Ar. So he's still up when her gets in, mabbe asleep in the chair. Then, all this noise, shoutin' and screamin'. Servants yeard it, but they was used to it, see. It was only when it carried on out in the garden – and then it all goes quiet – that a couple of 'em comes out, the servants. Found Robert out in the garden, down near this ole seat where he used to sit and stare out at the hills. They reckoned he'd tried to crawl up onto the seat, but he'd just fallen back, down on the grass. And Hattie – her was just standin' there, a few yards away, like a marble statue, arms down by her sides. A rock in each hand. From the mantelpiece.'

'Jesus.' Jane wondered how much of *this* Ben had told Amber. How much Ben himself knew. If he knew *anything* when he was planning his cute little murder-mystery weekend.

'Then Hattie, her drops the rocks and walks calmly past 'em, up the path and into the house. Servants carries Robert in, lays him out on the long sofa. One of 'em rings for the doctor, though they knows it's too late. Hattie's movin' around upstairs, but nobody's brave enough to go up there. And then one of 'em notices the desk drawer's hangin' open. This is where Robert kept his service revolver, locked away.'

'Oh hell, Gomer.'

'No sooner they seen the drawer's open than it's too late. Echoes through the whole house like . . .'

Oh. Oh G—

' . . . thunder. Took a while 'fore one of 'em was up to goin' up them stairs. Ole Leonard, the butler, it was. Had a bit of a job getting the bedroom door open on account of Hattie was on the floor behind it. Big woman, see, like I say.'

Jane heard her own voice saying, 'Was she dead?' Like from a distance, like it was someone else speaking, because she didn't think she could move her lips.

'Her'd put the end of the ole revolver in her mouth, Janey.'

She wanted to scream aloud. She wanted to leap up and go screaming down the lane. Anything to take her out of her own head, where an explosion had happened in the early hours.

'Not the nicest way to go,' Gomer said. 'But I s'pose it's what you'd expect, kind of woman her was. No nonsense. You chews on the barrel, en't nothing gonna go wrong. Hexpedient. How much them kids saw, nobody knows – mabbe it's what messed Paula up in the head.'

'She doesn—' Jane's lips were rubbery. 'Doesn't seem like a woman who would kill herself.'

'What's the alternative, Janey? Even if her didn't get hanged, her'd've gone to jail for life. Go to jail? Leave Stanner? Lose it all for a few moments of black madness? Naw, her took the man's way out – that's what they used to say. And took Stanner Hall with her. You inherited Stanner, would you wanner live there after that? Not like it was ancestral – two generations? Never was a house again. Commercial premises from then on. Grounds all overgrown. Us kids tellin' stories of Hattie's big ghost, gliding through the tangled ole gardens with a rock in each hand.'

Gomer gathered the teacups and the pot on a tray and took them to the sink.

'Goin' *Whoop, whoop*,' he said over his shoulder. '*Whoop, whoop*.'

TWENTY-THREE

Showdown Time

Danny had awoken in the dark with this sense of something closing around him like a fist. Like during the Foot and Mouth – filthy smoke from distant pyres of flesh and hide, mostly unnecessary, an uninvestigated crime perpetrated by the wankers of Westminster, and all you could do was turn away and weep.

In the end he'd got up, leaving Greta rumbling warmly, happy as an old Rayburn. Half-past three in the morning, and he'd gone downstairs and shoved a block into the stove, putting on his cans and letting in the soaring fury of The Queens of the Stone Age. There were times when only heavy music could blank out the foundry of your thoughts.

Even though he'd resisted rolling a joint, he awoke before seven with a mouth like the deck of a New Age traveller's bus, and Greta bending over him, lifting off the cans, closing his hands around a mug of tea.

'You en't *got* to, Danny.'

Danny sat up, spilling the tea.

'Like you said, it en't really your business,' Greta said.

'But . . . ?'

'But nothing.'

'But you think I *should* tell him. Don't you?'

'You can tell me. If you want to.' Greta sat down next to him, in her old pink towelling robe. Danny remembered a seventeen-year-old rock chick in a kimono, and how he used to picture her with him in a beach house overlooking the Pacific Ocean, knowing – totally bloody *knowing* – that one day that was where they'd be, him and Gret. And here they still were, after thirty years, and it was too cold for kimonos and always would be now.

'Tell you what?'

'The rest of it,' Greta said. 'There's more to it, en't there?' Mabbe years since her'd spoken to him like this – this *quiet*.

'Dunno what you mean.'

'Look at me,' Greta said.

He did. Always looked good with her hair down, but it was only ever down in the mornings. Danny felt a sense of loss and sadness.

'He's different is what it is, Gret. *You* know that. Different from the rest of 'em, different even from me. But at least I can see it.'

'Different how?' Greta said, holding his gaze with her big brown eyes. *You, my brown-eyed girl*. The young Van Morrison. How long ago? *God*.

'Look,' he said, 'I'm sorry what I said about you gossipin'. I was distraught.'

'You don't tell me things n' more, Danny. Think I'm gonner spread everything round Kington market. It's like Gomer's your wife now.'

'Don't be daft.' And yet he knew this was partly right. There was things that Gomer understood, though you wouldn't think it to look at him with his ciggy jammed in and his glasses alight. You'd think Gomer was a bit touched. But mabbe that was it – you needed to be a bit touched to understand some things. Greta and him, folks used to say they was both touched, back in the wild ole days.

'You were right about one thing,' Greta said. 'Mary

Morson was never the one for Jeremy. No sensitiveness there at all.'

'No.'

'Jeremy's mother used to say he had the Sight.'

'Even his *mother* did? You never told me that before.'

'Din't wanner set you off. Visions and stuff.'

'That was acid. I wouldn't do that now.'

'Wouldn't you?'

Danny smiled. Greta continued to sit there. *Bugger*, Danny thought, *it's too early for this*.

'Never loses a lamb, do he?' Greta said. 'Never loses a lamb to the fox. It's like he's come to an agreement with the foxes. His mother used to say that, too. When he was real little, he'd creep out at night and they'd find him sitting with the sheep. Catch his death, his mother used to say.'

Funny phrase that, Danny thought. *Catch his death*. Funny how a familiar saying could sound new and full of meaning, if it caught you in the right mood. Aye, if death was coming, Jeremy would see it, mabbe have a chance to catch it in both hands, his eyes wide open.

'He's part of that farm,' Danny told Greta. 'The land, the stock, Jeremy. A whole organism, see, and he's the part as *thinks*. And he keeps it all balanced, and in that way I always feel the boy's good for this whole area. Balance – don't ask me to explain it. It's the way he works, goes quietly on . . . if they'd leave him alone.'

'People?'

'He just en't good with people. They don't get to know him easy, and he don't know them. Hard to go quietly, nowadays.'

'Mary Morson made all the running,' Greta said.

'Her'd have to.'

'He was a catch. A good, sound farm.'

'Mary Morson's a cold-hearted little bloody gold-digger.'

'And this Natalie?' Greta said. 'Where's the difference there? Got it made now. Single parent in need of a home. Where's the difference?'

Danny drained his mug. 'There *is* a difference. All I can tell you is, the first time they met, it was in the air. Like some'ing he'd been waiting for all his life. I can't explain it. It didn't seem right, but then it did – later. I don't know why.'

'She's beautiful, Danny, how else would he be?'

Danny bowed his head. 'This *is* gonner kill him, Gret.'

'It'll kill him if he gets it from somebody else.'

'Mary.' Danny sighed. 'Aye, Mary'll spread it.'

'Only thinks of herself.'

'Shit.' He stared at the light on the stereo, a little red planet. 'See, the rest of it . . . I can't figure it out, but some'-ing's gone unstable. Sebbie Dacre feels it, I'm sure of that. Sebbie feels threatened – big farmer, big magistrate, Master of the fucking Hunt, and he feels threatened. By Jeremy? How's that possible? Lived side by side with Sebbie all his life, no trouble – no pally-pally either, but that's a class thing. Yet here's Sebbie sending his Welshie shooters to terrorize the boy. Why?'

Greta put a hand on Danny's thigh. 'You got a job today, with Gomer?'

'Nope.'

'Then you better go talk to him, en't you? You go this morning. Get it over.'

'Aye.' Danny put his mug on the floor and then he put his arms around her, his eyes full of tears that he couldn't have fully explained.

Around mid-morning, it finally started to snow. Real snow, the kind you knew wouldn't stop. Flakes the size of two-pound coins, and it was already an inch deep on the vicarage drive when Merrily opened the front door to Gomer Parry.

'Vicar.' The end of Gomer's ciggy was the only warmth out there. He had his old cap on and his muffler. When you looked up, the snow was almost black against the sky.

'You must've heard the kettle.'

'Ah,' Gomer said, '*that*'s what it was.'

He sat down at the kitchen table, with his cap, his muffler and his ciggy tin in a little mound by his elbow, and she made him tea and put out chocolate digestives for him to dunk. When the phone rang, she let the machine take it.

'You talked to Jane last night?' She switched on the lamp on the dresser.

'Difficult,' Gomer said.

'Goes without saying.'

'Don't wanner break no confidence.'

'You're not the first to say that, in relation to Jane.' Merrily came and sat down opposite him. 'Vicars aren't good for much these days, but we're good at keeping confidences. Take it all with us to the grave.'

'*I* know that, Vicar. 'Sides, this prob'ly en't confidential.' He glanced around. 'Her's at school?'

Merrily nodded. 'Last day of term tomorrow. If it carries on snowing like this, she may not even make it tomorrow.'

'So this . . .'

'This could be our last chance to talk about her behind her back, yes.'

'See this—' Gomer broke a chocolate digestive in half. 'Her's likely told you about it already, but if her en't . . .' He stared up at the snowy window.

Merrily said, 'It isn't about spiritualism, is it?'

'Eh?'

'Contacting the dead?'

Gomer blinked. 'No, it's about this Ben Foley beating seven bells out of this feller the other night.'

'*What?*'

Gomer nodded slowly. 'Her never tole you 'bout that, then.'

Danny turned the Land Rover around and parked him up against some holly trees on the edge of the farmyard at The Nant. By the time he'd unbuckled and climbed down, the windscreen was already thick with snow. It had to come, and he was glad; it was like some of the tension had been released from the drum-skin sky. Just from the sky, though, not from Danny Thomas.

Jeremy was already at the gate, like he'd been watching out for something. He had on one of those tea-cosy woollen hats – Badly Drawn Boy job.

'Just passin',' Danny said. 'Reckoned you might need a bit o' help gettin' the ewes down from the hill.' He looked up at the teeming sky. 'Way all this come on – sudden, like.'

'Had 'em down last night.' The snow was all over Jeremy, confusing the pattern on his blue and black workshirt.

Well, he would know this was on its way, wouldn't he? His friends the clouds, and all that.

'Jeremy, we . . .' Danny stood and faced him over the gate, pulling his denim jacket together over the baggy old Soft Machine sweatshirt he was wearing over his King Crimson T-shirt: the layered look. 'I reckon we gotter talk, boy.'

Jeremy said, 'We don't 'ave to.' He started waggling his hands, embarrassed. 'What I mean . . . the way he's comin' down you could easy get blocked in back at your place.'

Danny rested his arms in the soft snow on top of the wooden gate. 'Do I give a shit, boy? This partic'lar moment, mabbe not.' He pointed at the farmhouse door. 'Inside, eh?'

What was strange was that nothing had changed from when Jeremy's mam was in charge: the same dresser with some of the pots the old girl hadn't been able to take with her to the sheltered bungalow in Kington, the same flowery wallpaper between the beams, the same dark green picture of Jesus Christ in the Garden of Gethsemane.

Blocks of wood were turning into glowing orange husks on the open fire in the cast-iron range. The kettle hissed on the hob. Flag the sheepdog lay on the same old brown and green rag rug that had been here likely thirty-five years. Damn near as old as Jeremy, that rug.

All of which was odd, when you knew there'd been a new woman here for nigh on six months now, a smart woman who'd be expected to make big changes.

Danny sank into the old rocking chair and told Jeremy about the Welshie, Nathan, what Ben Foley had done to him and what he'd told them on his way to hospital. Just in case Miz Natalie Craven hadn't given him the full story.

'No problem at the hospital, in the end,' Danny said. 'Gomer knowed the nurse from when his missus died. 'Sides, even if they'd wanted to keep the boy in, they'd've had nowhere to put the poor bugger. Seen bigger bloody sheep sheds than that new hospital.'

Jeremy stood his wellies on the stone hearth at the foot of the range. Jesus Christ looked miserably down from over the fireplace, waiting to get betrayed by a bloke he reckoned was his mate. Danny looked up at Jesus, who seemed to be saying, *Make this easy, can't you?*

'See, these fellers from Off, you never knows what baggage they brung with 'em,' Danny said. 'That feller Foley – big chip on his shoulder, Greta reckons. Had his nose pushed out down the BBC in London. Lot of anger built up inside him. Coulder killed that boy, see. Goes at him like a bloody maniac. And he *was* a boy. No more'n twenty-four or -five. Thought he was hard, thought Foley was soft. Bad mistake.'

Danny leaned back and rocked the chair, which creaked. Reason he was going into this episode, apart from buying time to think, was to find out exactly how much Natalie Craven was telling Jeremy about day-to-day – and night-to-night – life up at Stanner. And if this Foley had some unknown degree of violence in his London past, who knew what other secrets might be there?

Specifically: what were Foley's relations with Natalie? If something *was* on the go, it wouldn't be easy for Foley and Nat to get it together in the hotel – not with Mrs Foley around and young Jane at weekends. But a nice camper van within easy jogging distance . . . and Foley *did* jog, apparently. Well, the question needed asking, that was for sure. Not that Danny would make the suggestion to Jeremy, bloody hell, no. Not directly, anyway.

'So what do, er, Nat'lie think about him?'

'Nat?' Jeremy scratched his head through his hat. 'Well, her thinks . . . thinks mabbe he was provoked. Not the first time the shooters been on his land. Had guests in at the time. See, he's worried they en't gonner make a go of it – that's the top and bottom of it. Desperate situation.'

'Least you won't see those boys again.'

'Hard to say, ennit?' Jeremy had sat himself on a wooden stool, away from the fire, like he was determined not to get comfortable, lulled into saying too much. There was a sprig of holly on the mantelpiece but no mistletoe anywhere: old Border lore reckoned it was unlucky to bring in mistletoe before New Year.

'So we had a chat with this Nathan before we took him to the hospital,' Danny said. 'Not a chance to be missed. And he was quite forthcoming, that boy, 'bout how Sebbie

Dacre was gonner bung 'em seven grand when they proved they shot the beast.'

Jeremy didn't react to this.

'So mabbe that was why they was gonner shoot Flag yere. Paint him black all over, with luminous bits and—'

'I know what you're sayin'—'

'The Hound of Hergest, Jeremy. Sebbie hired the Welshies to shoot some'ing bearing a close resemblance to the famous Hound of Hergest.'

Jeremy looked down at his light blue socks.

'It make any sense to you, boy?' Danny said.

Jeremy didn't look up. 'Can't shoot what en't there, can you?'

Danny pondered this, noting how clean the room was, everything polished that needed polishing. Outside the window, the snow fell real quiet and in some quantity. The only sound was the dog's breathing.

'By *en't there*,' Danny said carefully, 'do you mean en't there as in, like, imaginary? Or en't there as in . . . *en't there*? If you secs what I mean.'

They were getting close to matters that Jeremy didn't talk about, not so much because he was suspicious or embarrassed but because they were hard to put into words. He pulled off his Badly Drawn Boy hat and pushed his fingers through his hair.

'Sebbie Dacre, he won't have it talked about.'

'Well, that's pretty obvious, Jeremy, else he'd've been down the gun club and wouldn't need to offer them Welsh boys a penny.'

Jeremy said, 'Foley, he was supposed to be goin' round askin' people if they'd ever seen it. And Dacre said if any of his employees – or anybody workin' for the hunt or their relations – which I reckon covers most folks in this area – if they said anythin' to Foley they'd have the sack.'

'Tole you that?'

'Ken, the postman. We was at school together.'

'So who are they, these folks reckons they seen it?'

'Just folks. Over the years.'

'Like?'

Jeremy looked at Danny, then looked away into the red fire. 'Me.'

'I see.' Danny felt his beard bristle. 'When was this, Jeremy?'

'It en't what you think,' Jeremy's face creased up, mabbe more with sorrow at Danny's unease. 'En't like in the films, all red-eyed. En't n'more'n a shadow most times. Might be there, just before dark, see, bounding down off the Ridge, corner of your eye. Might be close up, but real faint, a cold patch against your leg. But you knows.'

The fire was pumping out heat, but there was places it couldn't reach.

'It *is* a dog?'

'Kind of thing.'

'Sebbie reckoned he'd had ewes savaged. What en't there can't savage ewes.'

Jeremy said, 'The beast they was huntin' round Llangadog year or so back? All over the papers – police marksmen, helicopters, the lot? It killed a dog, a whippet. Tore his throat out. Folks swore they seen a big cat, but when the police done DNA tests on the dog it killed they figured it was another dog did it. Yet you still had folks swore blind they'd seen this big beast, puma, whatever. Nobody ever found a puma, though, dead or alive. Or a big dog.'

'What's your point?'

'Things . . . happens. Things as en't meant to be explained. Why try?'

Danny found Jeremy meeting his stare now. Anybody else,

he'd suspect a wind-up, but all he could see in Jeremy's eyes was sadness and acceptance.

'All right . . .' He held on to the chair so it wouldn't rock, wouldn't creak. 'What about Sebbie Three Farms?'

'He believes,' Jeremy said. 'He just don't want nobody *thinkin'* he believes. So he makes a big noise. Bigger the noise, scareder he is, I reckon.'

'Why's he scared?'

''Cause most folk seen it, it don't matter . . . not to them.'

'You mean Sebbie . . .' Danny held on to the chair arms, trying to anchor himself down. You hung out with Jeremy you lost hold of reality, felt yourself slipping into Jeremy's fuzzy world. It was like dropping acid again and, same as he'd told Greta this morning, Danny didn't see himself going there no more.

'Personal,' Jeremy said.

Danny sagged back in the chair. This was getting well out of his ballpark. Wouldn't be a bad idea, mabbe, to get Gomer to go and have a quiet chat with his lady vicar over in Ledwardine, whose specialist subject appeared to be fellers like Jeremy Berrows.

We keep our secrets to a minimum now, she'd said to Lol. *Grown-ups. Mates.*

So this was the kid's idea of a minimum.

Gomer, like Lol, had clearly done a lot of agonizing before shopping Jane. '*See, when you first told me her was working at Stanner, I din't make much of it, 'cause things change, places change . . .*'

It seemed that, on the way back from taking a smashed-up man to Hereford hospital, Jane had suggested to Gomer that it would be best not to talk about the incident, not even to Mum, because Ben was in a difficult enough position and if this got out . . .

Merrily stood by the window, watching the apple trees becoming stooped and shaggy with snow. The probable truth was that the kid had concealed the incident not out of loyalty to her employer but because of what *else* she might have to disclose – like, for instance, an alleged predatory beast carrying a £7,000 bounty.

Which made no sense. Not yet, anyway.

The clock above the old Aga said 2.30. Couple of hours before Jane was due home, and in this weather it would probably be longer. Merrily could hear traffic grinding up the hill to the village square, the futile sound of tyres spinning. If Herefordshire Council's foul-weather rapid-response was as rapid as usual, they wouldn't see a snow plough or a gritter until around lunchtime tomorrow.

In the interim, showdown time.

So there'd been a domestic murder in the garden at Stanner Hall in the year before World War Two.

Well, that was a long time ago, but seeing what Ben Foley – a man with no known history of violence – had done to the intruder, Nathan, in that same garden had brought the superstitious side of Gomer Parry squirming uncomfortably into the light. Superstition was never far below the surface along this Border: the most rural county in England lying back to back with the most rural county in Wales.

'*Just if I had a daughter, Vicar, and her was working at Stanner, these is things I'd wanner know.*' Gomer had still seemed embarrassed. He'd refused a second cup of tea and gone shuffling back into the snow, pulling on his old tweed cap and leaving her to examine all the features of country-hotel life that Jane had been concealing.

That *bloody* kid. Did nothing ever change?

Merrily leaned against the Aga rail, pondering the options. If she couldn't reveal either Gomer or Lol as informants, there was at least one person she could shop with impunity.

She would admit to Jane that she'd raided the apartment. She would produce the copy of *Folk-lore of Herefordshire*, with the relevant pages marked. It wasn't much, but it was a way in. And in the course of the subsequent bitter quarrel the whole truth would, with any luck, come pooling out all over the unforgiving flagstones.

What was good about this weather was that, the way things were looking, Jane would not be returning to Stanner this weekend. Big fires, CDs of Nick Drake, Beth Orton . . . Lol Robinson, even. Mother-daughter quality time.

All the same, Merrily watched the ceaseless snow with trepidation. They made jokes about the council and the grit lorries, but they were jokes best made over a mug of hot chocolate in front of a blazing fire. This was a part of the county that had often been cut off, lost its electricity and its phone lines, reverting for whole days to a semi-medieval way of life.

When the phone rang, she grabbed the cordless from the wall.

'Mum.'

'They let you out?'

'Erm . . . they sent for the school buses early.'

'Because of the snow.'

'Otherwise about five hundred of us would have been spending all night fighting over the sofa bed in the medical suite.'

'Understandable. So you'll be home early, then.'

'And we don't *have* to come back tomorrow, if it's bad.'

'And then it's the holidays.'

'Right.'

'Well, that's very thoughtful of the education department. I'll go and light the fire.'

'Yes,' Jane said. 'Do that. It's just . . .'

'Something wrong?'

'Not exactly *wrong*. It's . . . like, the snow's coming down so hard, they reckon all the minor roads in the north of the county could be . . . difficult, by tonight. So that would mean I probably wouldn't be able to get to Stanner at all tomorrow, maybe not even with Gomer.'

'Can't be helped, flower.'

'No.'

'Act of God. Never mind, I expect the conference will have to be called off as well.'

'So, like, I thought the best thing to do would be to get on Clancy's bus.'

'What?'

'So, like, that's what I did. Kind of a spur of the moment . . . thing.'

Merrily said tightly, 'Where are you?'

'I'm at Stanner,' Jane said. 'And it really was for the best. The snow's *much* worse here.'

TWENTY-FOUR

Necessary Penance

Looking out from her room over, like, Siberia, Jane phoned Eirion on his mobile and was invited to leave voicemail. 'We need to talk,' Jane said menacingly.

She sat down on the bed, cold. Even turned up full, the radiator was like a cheap hot-water bottle the morning after. Stanner needed more money spending on it than Ben and Amber were ever likely to make, this was clear.

It was also clear, when she'd walked in with Clancy an hour or so ago, shaking the snow off her parka, that Ben and Amber had had words. Amber was tense, Ben fizzing with anger. Ben always turned anxiety into anger – according to which equation, desperation became rage. Nathan the shooter had found that out.

Amber had frowned. 'Jane, this is crazy. You should *not* have come.'

'You need me,' Jane had said.

But it had been Ben who'd needed her first, waiting until Amber had gone down to the kitchen before producing a folded sheet of A4 that had obviously been dried out. 'You undoubtedly know more about the Internet than me. How do I find out where this stuff originates?'

Jane spread the paper out on the bed. *Yuk*. 'Haven't the faintest idea,' she'd told Ben, 'but my boyfriend might be able to find out.'

Ben had found it drawing-pinned to the hotel sign at the bottom of the drive. It didn't have to be at all relevant to Ben or Stanner; the area had its share of weirdos. But the Stanner board wasn't exactly a convenient place to pin anything, and if it was a joke it could have been funnier.

i was just a kid about 15 when the case was on. i remember seeing the picture of her in the Mirror in her school uniform and it knocked me out. i had it up in my bedroom but my mother made me take it down so I stuck it up inside my locker dore at school. i have offen wondered what happened to her and what i would do if i met her. does anybody know where she is now. I have never been able to forget her. CHRIS.

'Might be rubbish, but with a conference on this weekend, if someone's trying to tell us something, I'd quite like to know what,' Ben had said when Jane had identified it as a printout from some kind of sad, obsessive Internet chat room or message board.

I gather Brigid is very popular in Germany. I also read in a Dutch magazine that she was living in the South of France. She is grown up now and is said to be absolutely gorgeous. *Drop dead gorgeous* ha ha. When she came out she spent some time in Italy, where she is supposed to have done two men but the police did not know who she was until she had left the country, and there was no evidence. So it looks like she's still doing it. They can't stop. It's a physical need. HOWARD
I think that is all rubbish about Brigid going abroad put around to slop us looking for her. i have it on good authority that she's here but may have had plastic surgery. I think I would know her whatever she'd had

done to her. I have been dreaming about her for about 20
years. she still makes me swet. GAVIN.

At the bottom, it said:

full explicit details: sign in and see what Brigid REALLY did

Sick, or what?

If anybody could track it down, Eirion could. If he hadn't
left for the *piste*.

Jane went to the window. You could see the forestry across
the valley, and Hergest Ridge, mauve against the sky. Yes,
you could even see a sky, of sorts. Did this offer some hope
that the snow was actually thinning?

Mum, on the phone, had said things like *I see*, calmly
conveying an acute sense of betrayal. This morning, over the
breakfast, Jane had kept glancing at her, thinking, *I ought to
tell you everything. I ought to do it now.* After what Gomer
had revealed, it hadn't been her easiest night's sleep. But if
she'd laid the Hattie thing on her, Mum would have seen to
it that she didn't get here tonight. She might even, on
hearing about the explosion in the head, have kept her off
school. Which wouldn't have helped.

Because what could Mum have done about this, anyway?
Exorcists worked by invitation only.

Clancy had gone to watch TV in Ben and Amber's private
sitting room, some bland early-evening soap. On the bus,
Jane had said, on the subject of The White Company,
'Doesn't it interest you *at all?*' And Clancy had been like,
'What's the point of wasting your life imagining you go to
some spooky place when you die?'

Huh? They really didn't have much to say to one another,
her and Clancy, did they? Jane sat on the bed and scowled

and then dialled the mobile number that Antony had given her.

'Antony, it's Jane. I'm sorry to bother you. I don't know what it's like with you, but it's fairly bad here . . . well, not *that* bad. I mean, I managed to get in tonight on the bus, and Ben reckons enough of the key people from The White Company are around for it to go ahead. Alistair Hardy's staying with Beth Pollen, and she's going to meet some more of them at Hereford Station in a four-wheel drive tomorrow. So like . . . *are* you going to make it all right? And if not, what do you want me to do? If you could like let me know. I've got some really nice shots of Stanner in the snowstorm. So, like . . . bye.'

She sat on the bed, huddled inside her fleece. The snow wasn't thinning at all, was it? Most of the time you just lied to yourself because if you then repeated the lie to someone else it wouldn't *seem* like a lie.

Why *had* she gone out of her way, in the face of the weather and her mother's dismay, to come back?

Because she was a working woman and, with a conference on, Amber needed all the help she could get. Because she was retained by Antony Largo, on the promise of *considerably more* money, as a cameraperson. Because if it turned out that The White Company made some historic contact tonight and she'd *missed it* . . .

Yeah, mainly that.

Why had she *not* wanted to come? Why had she actively *dreaded* being here? Because, on the other side of this unlikely but nonetheless compelling psychic odyssey there was the bloated ghost of Hattie Chancery, her repellent life, her sordid and hideous death.

She gave Eirion another five minutes to call back, then stood up and snapped on the light. No good putting this off any longer. She took off her fleece, pulled her overnight bag from under the bed, found her warmest sweater and put that on, dragging the fleece over the top. She felt a little better, got out the Sony 150 and checked the charge. Then she put out the light and went out onto the top landing, down the second flight of stairs and left at the fire doors.

Had to do this. Had to dispense with it before she could move on. Before she could stop waking up in the morning waiting for the bloody bang.

This morning at the breakfast table, at her most pathetic, she'd nearly cried out to Mum to take it away, to exorcise Hattie Chancery from her subconscious. Like Mum could really do this with a sign of the cross and a pat on the head. Bonkers.

She had to do this – walking down the passage with the Sony held in front of her like an automatic weapon – because it made the difference between being a woman and a child. Because she'd never been in that room with any knowledge of whose room it had been and what she'd done – i.e. the knowledge that Hattie Chancery was the kind of woman, basically, who, in life, Jane would have hated even more than she did as some sick possible *presence*.

And also the knowledge of the stains under the maroon flock wallpaper, the blood dribbling down the windows.

She intended to walk into the room under the witch's-hat tower, bring the Sony 150 to her shoulder, demanding, *Imprint yourself on that, you brutal bitch*. This was a necessary penance.

'Couldn't do it.' Danny had his head in his hands, a bowl of tomato soup cooling on the table at his elbow. 'In the end, I couldn't tell him.' He looked up at Greta. 'Pathetic, eh?'

'Could be it's for the best,' Greta said, but he could see she didn't believe that, not for one second.

'Suppose he's mad? Suppose he's ill? Suppose that what we

reckoned all these years was perceptiveness, *knowingness* . . . suppose that was just signs of his . . . mental dysfunction.'

'Big words tonight, Danny.'

'I en't thick,' Danny said. 'Might've lost a few brain cells to acid and metal, since the ole grammar school, but it en't taken it all away.'

'Have your soup.'

Danny swallowed some tomato soup. Through the kitchen window, he could see the snow ghosting the farmyard that was foggy-grey with old stone and dusk. No stock out there no more, nothing in the sheds except for his own tractor and Delia, Gomer's new JCB. Need to have the tractor up and ready tonight, with the snowplough bolted on; this could go on for days.

'Know what I was scared of back there, suddenly, Gret? That mabbe, if I told him, he'd kill her. Like Geoff James did when his missus—'

'Danny, this is *Jeremy.*'

'Can't just say that n' more.' Danny put his spoon down. 'People goes funny. Same disease: isolation, EC form-filling, stock-tagging, signing all your beasts over to the bureaucrats. No independence, no pride, no satisfaction, no money. You reads the bloody papers, you'd think all country folk's worried about is what the government's doin' to bloody huntin' with hounds – like it's fundamental to us all in the sticks, 'stead of just a rich man's expensive pleasure intro-duced by psychotic Norman barons. *Shit.*'

'You got out,' Greta reminded him, that soothing tone again. 'You're with Gomer now. You sidelined, you en't part of it n' more.'

'Jeremy en't never gonner get out, though, is he? It's part of *him.* Part of him's in the land. Uproot him, he's dead.'

'Why should he be uprooted? He's got a good, solid farm. He's respected. He's got—'

'A good woman? Ole days, see, there was farming marriages, and they lasted. Now you got *partners* . . . temp'ry. All right in cities, mabbe, where it's all temp'ry and you can move on, swap around. In the country, you don't have *continuity* – there's another big word, see – if you don't have continuity, you're fucked. Jesus Christ, did I just say some'ing *Conservative*?'

'Look,' Greta said, 'he won't be out of his yard at all for days, if it keeps on like this, so unless somebody rings him and tells him about Natalie, he en't gonner find out nothin', is he?'

Danny stared into his soup, a pool of blood. He was thinking about Natalie Craven and her mousy little partner, and Ben Foley and his mousy little wife.

Ben Foley, saviour of Stanner. Incomer with attitude, smooth Londoner widely said to be driven by irrational obsessions. Man who showed up on your doorstep asking if you seen the Hound of Hergest.

'Sign of death.'

Greta gave him a hard look. 'What is?'

'The Hound of Hergest.'

'Let's not get silly about this,' Greta said. 'Jeremy's ma used to say he was always seeing things that wasn't there. It's the way he is. His condition.'

'That's what it's supposed to be, though, ennit, the Hound: an omen of death.'

'If your name's Vaughan.'

'The Vaughans've all gone.'

'Nothing to worry about, then,' Greta said.

'Just be honest,' Merrily said. 'Tell me what you think I need to do. Tell me I'm overreacting. Tell me it's time to let go of the leash, cut some slack, sever the umbilical, make some space, chill out. *Tell me, Lol.*'

'You know I can't do clichés.' Lol took the mobile out into the passage and went across to the stable door, unbolting the top half and pushing against a crust of snow. The section of door opened with a sound like splintering plywood. Somewhere out there was the Frome Valley, as white and cold and barren as an old psychiatric ward he used to know.

'Tell me there's nothing to be afraid of,' Merrily said into his ear, serious now. Snow talk. Unexpectedly severe weather could do this to you. You were no longer in control. Nobody was.

'I'll come over,' Lol said.

'No. You can't. Really. It's just been on the radio: go home and stay home. Stay off the roads unless it's an emergency, and even then—'

'It's not bad here.' Lol looked for his car, couldn't see it. It was nearly dark, and the snow was like a wall.

'I've got enough to worry about without the thought of you stuck all night in a snowdrift in an ancient Astra with a heater that hasn't worked in years.'

Music started up in the studio behind Lol: a slow, growling twelve-bar blues from the album that Prof Levin was mixing for the guitar legend Tom Storey. A relentless, chugging momentum: life going on.

'It's Gomer, that's all,' Merrily said. She'd already told him about Ben Foley and the violence and the woman called Hattie Chancery. 'Gomer's worried; how often does that happen?'

'You could phone her. She's got her mobile?'

'I could do that, yes. I could go on to her very carefully, stepping on eggshells, knowing that at any time she could lose her temper and cut the call and switch off the mobile, and that's the link gone for the duration. I *could* do that. Would *you* do that?'

*

There was a gas mantle projecting from the wall, just inside the fire doors. During the murder weekend, Ben had propped the doors open so that you could see the mantle from the stairs, and you were back in Hattie Chancery's young days, enclosed in a hollow glow.

No mention of Hattie Chancery during the murder weekend. There were murder games, with the scent of mystery, and there was real murder, with its sadness and its stink.

The mantle, unlit, was utility-looking, without romance. No doubt it would be working again when The White Company were in residence. The passage, meanwhile, was lit by electric wall lights – dim vertical tubes under amber-tinted glass. The walls, with their recessed doors, were lined with woodchip paper. The lights turned them yellow.

Jane stood at the entrance to the passage, legs apart, and lingered on the shot. Ought to have brought the tripod really, but she guessed that if she'd gone downstairs to look for it she wouldn't have come back. As it was, she kept wanting to turn back but wouldn't permit herself to stop or even to hurry, to get it over with.

Oh, don't worry about young Jane. Far too down-to-earth. Jane'll be fine.

He really didn't care, did he, as long as he came out a winner.

Called me a nancy boy.

A winner against the odds. Whatever it took.

But was she really so different? Jane Watkins: research and second camera. Using Eirion, deceiving Mum. Snatching every new experience to further her own ambitions, hoovering up the dirt on Hattie and the tragic Robert, while despising The White Company as naff and sad.

Capricious and contrary, this Jane Watkins, not a nice person.

Still shooting, Jane walked on, with sour determination, along the passage, where the sharp smell of recent painting failed to obscure the odour of damp and quite possibly rot.

She stopped in front of the last door on the right, the image wobbling. Through the lens, with the recording signal aglow, it was both more exciting and less scary because it was less personal – a professional thing.

The door was like all the other doors in the passage except that it didn't have a number on it. When she opened it – reaching out to the handle, giving it a quick push and then stepping back, with the camera still running – she realized that it was too dark in there to shoot anything. She put the camera on pause and lowered it, recalling that there were a few steps to a second door that was oak and Gothic-pointed.

Jane stopped briefly at the bottom of the steps. She remembered a pot lampshade hanging from the ceiling. There was a switch somewhere, on an old-fashioned pewter box. But when she hand-swept the walls on either side she couldn't find it. Perhaps it was at the top. She located the first step with the toe of a trainer, went up carefully, one, two, three, four – was that it?

No – she stumbled – five.

Jane remembered how it had seemed so cool at first, having one of the tower rooms, sleeping under the witch's hat, with views across the Border.

A shocking cinematic image flared unconjured in her mind: the heavy old service revolver clunking on the floor as Hattie's head exploded, blonde hair snaking with blood and wet brains, and a splatting on the walls and—

What was it like to have killed? To have done – publicly, without hope of concealment – the one thing you could never reverse, put right, make recompense for. One way or another, your life was over, wasn't it?

No more *tally-ho*, no more *whoop-whoop*.

She felt for the handle of the bedroom door, catching an acrid waxy smell. Furniture polish? The cold clawed through her chunky sweater as though it was cheesecloth, and she thought of Robert Davies lying here in a fever, Hattie hauling the bedclothes from his sweating body. What had Hattie felt like as she carried the service revolver up here? How had she known it was loaded, unless she'd loaded it herself? So was this an outcome that had always been at the back of her mind? Because it really wasn't a woman's way of suicide, was it, to blow all your beauty to fragments?

Jane's hand found the doorknob, cast-iron and globular, grasped it angrily, turned it and went into the bedroom, standing there panting out some kind of mixed-up defiance into the darkness.

Only, it wasn't dark at all. Hattie Chancery's room was delicately rinsed in ochre light.

Jane's senses swam.

She saw a mustard-shaded oil lamp standing on a dressing table of polished oak in front of the central window with its floor-length purple velvet curtains. The light lured a dull lustre from the gilt frames of pictures on the flock wallpaper.

The polish-fumes seared her throat. This was wrong; everything was wrong, many years wrong. She reeled back against the door and it closed behind her with a heavy *thunk* and an efficient click. The triple mirrors on the dressing table reflected a high, claw-footed bed, and a woman's figure rising.

And Jane just screamed, high and piercing, like she never had before, at least not since she was very little, as she saw, in the middle mirror, a broad face, with thick fair hair piled up and twisted and eyes that were small and round and pale like silverskin onions.

TWENTY-FIVE

Shifting Big Furniture

The White Company was a band of English mercenaries formed by Sir John Hawkwood in the fourteenth century, best known for its campaigns in Italy. It was also a firm supplying bathroom-related fluffy goods through mail order and two fancy-dress historical re-creation societies.

Close to the bottom of the first page, Google finally identi-fied *The White Company* as Sir Arthur Conan Doyle's classic historical novel, and Merrily clicked on it.

Motley group of English mercenaries led by Sir Nigel Loring . . . assiduous attention to historical detail . . .

Nothing, however, to suggest that the novel in any way reflected the central obsession of Doyle's last two decades.

In under an hour, she'd gathered a mass of background on this: Sir Arthur's tireless tours of Britain and America, promoting his conviction that spiritualism would alter mankind for ever by making life after death a scientific fact. His blind defence of obvious fakery. His insistence that he'd spoken, at a seance, with his son Kingsley, a victim of the Great War, and his brother Innes. His belief that his sister Annette, over thirty years dead, had communed with Jean, Arthur's wife, through automatic writing. Eventually, Arthur had acquired his own high-level spirit contact, Phencas, a scribe from the Sumerian city of Ur, dead for over four thousand years.

A kindly, decent, deluded man.

In the snow-padded silence of the scullery, the phone went off like a burglar alarm. Two phone lines had become a necessary extravagance. Merrily plucked it up, wedging it under her chin while tapping on *next*, for Page Two.

'Ledwardine Vic—'

'Vicar?'

'Alice.'

'Vicar, will you be in if I comes round later on?'

'I . . . yeah, sure. Wear wellies, though, Alice, because I haven't bothered clearing the drive.'

'With Dexter,' Alice said.

'Oh.'

The digital clock on the desk said 7.18 p.m. The snow had turned the apple trees outside the window into cartoon wraiths. Page Two came up, with its highlighted words: *white, white, white* . . .

'Sorry I've been so long getting back to you,' Alice said, 'My sisters, they said yes, they'd like to have the Eucharist. Dexter, he en't so sure.'

'He's with you now?'

'Does two nights a week in the chip shop.'

In a steamy chip shop? With asthma?

'I en't letting him go back to Hereford tonight – what if he got stuck in the snow and he couldn't breathe? How would they get him to the hospital? Will you talk to him, vicar? Will you make him see some sense?'

'Well, you know, I'll . . . I mean, I can try and explain, but I don't want to—'

''Bout half an hour, then?' Alice said.

On the screen, near the top of Page Two, it said:

The White Company. *Established to further the mission*

*of Sir Arthur Conan Doyle to prove that the spirit world
is an incontestable fact.*

Oh.

'OK,' Merrily said, 'fine.'

Replacing the phone with one hand, she clicked the mouse
with the other, watching a bulky figure fading up: sagging
white moustache, pinstripe suit, watch chain, watchful eyes.
Encircling him, like some tragic Greek chorus, other faces
less defined – misty faces blinking on and off, like faulty street
lamps, in shades of white and grey. And then:

The White Company welcomes you

Walter was this fat and beaming old git, with a moustache
that curled. His wife, Bella, might have been his daughter:
turned-up nose, big hair gathered on top of her head. And
the kid, this flat-faced kid clutching her hand, could have
been Walter's granddaughter.

In fact this was Hattie Chancery, apparently the earliest
obtainable photograph of her. It was on the wall next to the
door, one of four framed photos in here: Walter and his
family in the garden – Walter, formal in wing collar, and
his wife Bella in some kind of flouncy crinoline. Also, two
scenes of what, presumably, was the Middle-Marches Hunt
hounding some poor bloody fox into a badger set. And, over
the bed, so she might see herself reflected in the mirror when
she awoke . . . the adult Hattie.

'Where did they get them?' Jane's voice was still unsteady.
Shock, it seemed, could carry on pulsing through your body
for whole minutes afterwards. Already she was despising
herself, but that didn't take it away.

'On loan from the museum at Kington.' Natalie lay on
her back on the claw-footed bed, smoking a cigarette. 'A

deal. Ben found a really old washtub and stuff like that in one of the outhouses and donated it all. The pictures can go back after this – we'll get them all copied when the snow goes. But Ben thought the originals might give off the strongest vibrations.'

'For Hardy?'

'I mean, Ben thinks it's all shit really, but if it makes The White Company feel more inspired . . .' Nat rolled over and off the bed, stood up and stretched – just the way she had when Jane had first walked in, rising up alongside the gilt-framed portrait hanging over the high mahogany headboard. She wore tight jeans and a black shirt open to a silver pendant. 'I'm shattered, Jane. Shifting big furniture takes it out of you.'

Jane went to the bottom of the bed and looked up at the woman in the sepia photo-portrait: the coils of glistening hair, the broad face with unsmiling lips like segments of soft white pear, and those pale, pale eyes gazing over your shoulder as if Hattie was disdainfully contemplating the mess left by her own blood on the wall between the windows.

'How old was she here, do you think?'

'I wouldn't know. Thirty?'

'And Alistair Hardy actually wants to sleep in here?' Jane could no longer imagine doing that. And the thought of waking up on a wintry morning to those silverskin eyes . . .

'I don't think he knows about it yet. It's Ben's idea. He's become obsessed with the Chancery woman and this room – Stanner's haunted room – and he's thinking televisually. So we have to recreate the room pretty much as she'd remember it. Which, I have to tell you, has taken all day. The dressing table, we pinched from Room Seven – I spent about an hour polishing the foul thing. The bed – we had to bring that down in sections from one of the attics.'

'This was her actual bed?'

'God knows. It had enough dust on it.'

'It bloody scared *me*, Nat. It's . . . just unhealthy.'

'Your face when you first opened the door, Jane, will live with me for a long time.'

'It was just a big shell when I was last here.' She looked around again. 'Rather Hardy than me.'

In fact, Hardy deserved all he got. Jane was still furious at him for using Lucy Devenish. An affront; Lucy's spirituality was well in advance of all this.

Natalie walked past her and opened the bedroom door. 'Well, if we find him dead of a heart attack in the morning, it's an occupational hazard. I can't say I like him. Let's go and have some tea.'

Jane looked at her with something between shock and respect. *Dead of a heart attack?* It was the sort of thing a kid would say, oblivious of the rules of adult decency that obliged you to airbrush your thoughts before you exposed them. Nat was just so cool. It certainly took some kind of cool – or a complete absence of sensitivity to the numinous – to lie there alone on that bed, under that very eerie picture of Stanner's murderer.

'Nat . . .'

'Huh?'

'Does Amber know about this . . . refurbishing?'

'Some of it. She's been very quiet all week. I mean, the idea of them summoning spirits in her kitchen – the only place she can really bear to spend time in . . .' Nat glanced outside, down the dark steps to the passage. 'Sometimes I think she might surprise us all and leave him to it.'

'Leave *Ben*?'

'Leave Stanner and give Ben the big option. Could you blame her?'

'Nat, it would destroy him. He thinks he's doing all this for Amber.'

'Yeah.' Nat smiled with no humour. 'Aren't men danger-ously delusional sometimes?'

'And dangerously aggressive,' Jane said.

Nat eyed her, a warning look. *It was a one-off. We don't want Ben to get a reputation, do we?*

'Look . . .' Jane glanced away from her, determined to get this out. 'I've been thinking about it a lot . . .'

'Well, don't. It won't help anybody.'

'Been finding out about Hattie Chancery.' Jane glanced warily at Hattie's reflection in the dressing-table mirror. 'I mean . . . you *do* know what she did in here, don't you?'

Natalie came back into the room. 'Ben's still letting Amber think she shot herself outside somewhere. I mean, Christ, they sleep just up the passage. Who told you?'

'Gomer. And he told me about Hattie and all her men. What she did with them on the top of Stanner Rocks. All the aggression she had inside her. And the booze.'

'If you believe all that.'

'I kind of do.' Jane looked at her. 'Don't you?'

'You're asking me what I believe?' Natalie supported her bum against the dressing table, stretched her long legs out, stared at Hattie. 'I believe you don't let anybody fuck you about. That's it, really.'

Jane, her back to the door, looked at the bed. It had a faded old mauve coverlet on it, with a fringe. She said, not looking at Nat, 'When I was here, for that one night, I came back and found the quilt and the sheets had been pulled off and thrown back against the headboard. No, really, it happened. And I didn't even know whose room it had been then.'

Nat made no comment.

'OK.' Jane turned to Natalie. 'Maybe Amber or somebody had been about to change the bedding and forgot and went away and left it. There could be a whole bunch of rational explanations, and I hope one of them was the truth. But I also had a really bad dream in here. I mean *really* bad. And also—'

Nat said quietly, 'Um, Jane . . .'

'I mean, if you consider what happened last weekend . . . put that together with Hattie – goes up Stanner Rocks, shags some guy, comes back and smashes her sick husband's head in. With a couple of the rocks she kept as like *trophies*? And then you think of Ben – OK, volatile, but basically this artistic, non-violent bloke – who just loses it *completely.* On maybe the same spot? It was a *horrendous* attack. If you and Amber hadn't been here, let's face it, he might've killed that guy. And you know that's true. He might be on remand now for murder.'

'Jane, I don't think this is a particularly—'

'What got *into* him? You have to ask. Because if that was the *real* Ben—'

'Jane—'

'—Then maybe it would be a good thing if Amber did leave him. Maybe he's the wrong kind of person to *be* here. You know?' Jane blinked. 'What's wrong?'

Natalie was looking over Jane's shoulder. Apologetically.

Jane stiffened, her shoulders hunching. She shut her eyes for a moment, opening them, in anguish, to a long, unsmiling face in the left-hand mirror of the dressing table.

'Erm . . .' She turned slowly, towards Ben, with her shoulders still up around her ears, forcing what she guessed would be a sick and cringing smile, holding out the camcorder like an offering. 'Like, I . . . just came to . . . to get some, like, atmos shots?'

Inaugurated in 1980, on the fiftieth anniversary of the passing of Sir Arthur Conan Doyle, The White Company was originally called The Windlesham Society, after Sir

Arthur's last home in Sussex. The name was changed
after the words 'White Company' were repeatedly
received at spiritist meetings throughout Britain,
both clairaudiently and through automatic writing.
Finally, Sir Arthur himself conveyed to the eminent
channelist, Mr Alistair Hardy, that he would consider
it an honour to be patron of a society named after an
especial favourite amongst his novels.

The Society now comprises of both committed
spiritists and Sherlock Holmes enthusiasts. In 1993,
the outline of a planned Holmes story, *The Adventure
of the White Shadow*, was channelled to Mr Hardy and
later drafted in full by Mr Mason W. Mower, of
Connecticut.

Merrily wrinkled her nose. The idea of a society combining
committed spiritualists and Sherlock Holmes enthusiasts
sounded slightly unlikely, if you considered that Holmes was
the creation of Conan Doyle's rational, scientific side.

But, then, wasn't spiritualism considered to *be* rational
and scientific? Wasn't that the whole point – that they were
proving the fact of life after death without the excess
baggage?

Meaning religion. Merrily fingered her small pectoral cross
on its chain.

It was easy to say that the Church was just jealous because
these guys were offering direct experience. There were many
people no longer scared of death because their departed loved
ones were saying, *We're here for you*. And even if it was faked,
was that all bad? The main spiritualist wave had come after
the First World War – all those grieving families who didn't
know how their sons and husbands had died, had no bodies
to bury. A means of bringing closure.

The doorbell rang. Merrily groaned. The thought of an hour with Dexter Harris was not enticing.

She stood up, pulling on one of Jane's old fleeces over her cowl-neck sweater. Half her wardrobe these days consisted of the kid's cast-offs. No fire in the sitting room, so she'd have to keep Alice and Dexter in the kitchen, and it wasn't too warm in there either, despite the Aga. She went through to the hall, meeting the eyes of the jaded Jesus hanging on to his lantern of hope in Holman Hunt's *Light of the World*, Uncle Ted's house-warming present.

To prove that the spirit world is an incontestable fact.

Slipping the catch, tugging the front door out of its frozen frame, she thought what a disappointment it must be to Conan Doyle, if he was still watching, that the great spiritual revolution had crumbled so quickly into the ruins of Crank City. The front door shuddered and the white night came in from the open porch in tingling crystals of cold.

For a moment, it was surreal. The front garden of the vicarage was like some kind of fairy-tale bedchamber, the lawn a lumpy white mattress, bushes squashed into piles of pillows, a night light glimmering from the village square through the bare trees.

Very much a part of this tableau, he unwound his scarf and a frieze of snow.

'Um, I wondered if I might sing a carol.'

'God!' She laughed in delight, looking down the drive towards the snowbound square. 'How did you—? Where's your car?'

'How would you feel about *Ding Dong M—*?'

'You're insane!'

'And there are medical records to prove it,' Lol said.

TWENTY-SIX

White High

Lol sat barefooted on the rug in the scullery, defrosting his toes by two bars of the electric fire. The lights were out, but the door to the kitchen was ajar a couple of inches. His frayed blue jeans were somehow soaked despite his wellies, and there were wet patches on the dark green sweatshirt with white stencilled lettering. He sat there alone, watching the snow widening the window ledge outside, and he felt wildly happy.

The lettering on the sweatshirt said *Gomer Parry Plant Hire*, commemorating the days he'd spent as an unskilled labourer in the wake of Gomer's disastrous fire. Another small breakthrough: if it makes you a little anxious, *do it*. A chance to shovel tons of earth with your bare hands before playing live on stage for the first time since your teens. An impossible polar expedition in a clapped-out, sixteen-year-old Vauxhall Astra, to be with the person you love? *Do it*.

The old Astra had slithered over snow-blinded hills, hugging a council grit-lorry down to Leominster. Tunnelling through the suffocated lanes, Lol had passed two abandoned cars, snow-bloated, and gone chugging on impossibly until the old girl finally gave up, rolling away into the cascading night.

But she only gave up – there *was* a God – on the hill that was already evolving into Church Street, Ledwardine, vainly spinning her wheels before sinking back, exhausted, into the Community Hall car park. Lol had climbed out like he was emerging from a trance state, and bent to kiss her cold grille thanks and goodnight before walking up to the vicarage on a white high.

On the deserted square, a Christmas tree stood in front of the squat-pillared market hall, the whole scene loaded with snow, the fairy lights reduced to gauzy smudges of colour like ice lollies in a deep-freeze. Lol had looked back for a sign – a *For Sale* sign on Lucy's old house – as if the sudden enchantment of the night might have tossed it back onto the market.

No sign there, no lights. Maybe there was a forbidding, black-lettered sign somewhere that said he didn't belong here, but right now he didn't care. He sat in the glow of two faintly zinging orange bars and half-listened to Merrily in the kitchen, dealing with some people who had arrived soon after him. Best they didn't see him; it would have been all over the village by morning. The way things had turned out, even his car wasn't here. Snow was good at secrets.

From the kitchen, he heard about arrangements for what seemed to be a memorial service. There was an elderly woman with a croaky voice that he recognized at once. *Salt and vinegar with that, is it?* And a guy called Dexter who managed to be both gruff and whiny. Sounded like routine parish stuff.

At first, idly browsing the *Cwn Annwn* passages from Mrs Leather, Lol wasn't aware of what Merrily was saying, just the soft and muted colours of her voice. Luxuriating in the proximity of her, recalling an old Van Morrison song from *Tupelo Honey*, about a woman in the kitchen with the lights turned down low.

It was quite a while before raised voices began to suggest that there was unpleasantness here.

*

'No, what's she's saying,' Alice from the chippy said, 'is that we needs a proper funeral for the boy. With the full rites.'

Merrily said, 'Well, not—'

'That's fucking creepy!'

'*Dexter!*'

'Funeral for a kid that's already been in his grave for near twenty year?'

'It's not—'

'You're telling me that en't creepy?'

'It's not a funeral,' Merrily said, 'and I honestly don't think you'd find it creepy. However, it's only an idea, a possibility.'

'You got no right. Should never've gone round askin' questions, rakin' it all up. It's in the past.'

'It's in *you!*' Alice shrieked. 'Don't you see that?' Her voice steadied. 'Been like this all night, he has, Vicar. I don't know what's the matter with him.'

Merrily said, 'Dexter, first of all, we don't have to do this, not if you don't want to. And we don't even have to do it in a church.'

'Then where's the bloody point?'

'All I'm trying to say is that the Eucharist – communion – is a very powerful way of tackling these things, in which . . . we believe that Jesus himself is personally involved. And it can sometimes draw a line under things, create order and calm, where there's been long-term unrest, ill feeling, distress . . . conflict.'

'Yes,' Alice said, 'this is what we want.'

'Alice asked me if there was any way I could help, and I'm sorry if it isn't what either of you were expecting. If you don't think it's the right thing, you don't have to have anything to do with it.'

'But,' Alice said, with menace, 'you'll be letting your family down if you don't.'

'*No!*' An ache in Dexter's voice. From the scullery, Lol could feel him wanting to beat his head on the table.

Alice said, 'En't no reason the rest of us can't go ahead without him, is there, Vicar?'

'Well, we *could*, but that wouldn't—'

'What about Darrin?' Dexter said. 'He gonner be there?'

'It might also help Darrin a lot,' Merrily said. 'It would be good if everyone was there, from both sides of the family. It can bring things out. In my experience.'

'Bring out the truth?'

'Well, it . . . it can bring peace.'

'And what if everybody don't want the truth out?'

Merrily didn't reply. Alice shouted, 'We all wants the truth!'

'Well, mabbe Darrin don't! Mabbe the truth en't what Darrin wants at all, look.'

Nobody spoke for a while. Chairs creaked, small movements of unrest. Then Dexter started mumbling. Lol couldn't make out any of it. Then Alice said, raw-voiced, 'What's this? You never—' And Dexter mumbled some more, and Alice said faintly, '*No. Dear God.*'

Dexter's voice came in again, no longer gruff, raised up in panic.

'He's like, "Get your fuckin' foot down, you big use-less—" '

'*Dexter!*'

'No,' Merrily said. 'Go on. Please.'

'I was bigger than Darrin, but he was real nasty, look. Stuck his knife in the back of my hand once. Had an airgun, shot a robin in the garden. Things people thought were nice, he'd wanner destroy. So like, when we gets into the Fiesta, there's a kiddy's picture book on the seat, and he picks it up and rips it in half, throws the bits out of the window. Roland, he starts crying, Darrin's leanin' over him and pinchin' him, telling him we're going to London. We en't stopping till we gets to London, and we en't never comin' back. Never see his mam and dad again.'

'Oh God in heaven, Vicar, *stop him!*'

'Weren't *no* stoppin' him, Alice. More the kid's screechin', more he's gettin' off on it. Excited! Gettin' more excited the further we goes. I'm like, "Don't you wanner go back now? How we gonner get back if we goes too far?" Darrin's goin', "*Keep your fuckin' foot down, you fat wanker, we're goin' on the motorway, we're goin' to London.*" '

Alice was moaning, 'Oh, dear God, no, oh dear God.' Lol sensing a rhythm, as if she was rocking backwards and forwards, doubled up in anguish.

'So Roland, he's gettin' real hysterical, starts pulling at the door handle, and Darrin's goin', "*You get away from that door or I'll give you a smacking.*" So like Roland waits till Darrin turns round again and I can year him fiddling with the handle, and then Darrin whips round, sudden-like, and whangs him in the face, *bang!* Cops is behind us by then, look, blue lights going and that, and Roland's sobbin' away, and that's when I decides I'm gonner go across the road and up this little turning, then the cops'll be able to get us. And that . . . that's how it was.'

Silence, except for creaking chairs, small sounds of unrest. Then Alice started to weep. *Routine parochial issue.* Lol tugged his wet trainers onto his bare feet.

Merrily said, 'You didn't tell the police about . . . any of this. Did you?'

'How could I? But you see why Darrin en't gonner want none of it out.'

'Or your parents? You tell your parents *anything*?'

'They know what Darrin's like. Alice knows.'

Another silence.

Then a jagged wail.

'Oh my God, that poor little child . . . his own *brother* . . .'
Like Alice's voice was bleeding. 'Oh my God, and then he
died! He— My *God*, I never knew none of this.'

''Course you never knew,' Dexter snapped. 'Darrin en't
never gonner tell you, was he?'

'Gets worse, gets worse all the time.'

'You made me, Alice, I didn't wanner—'

'How'm I gonner tell my sisters?'

'Can't, can you?' Dexter said flatly. 'No way.'

A chair creaking, someone standing up, footsteps going
nowhere on the kitchen flags.

Then Alice said, 'We surely needs it now.'

'Eh?'

'*I* can't live with this. Knowing that child's out there.'

'He en't out there, Alice, he's f— He's gone.'

'We needs it now, more than ever – the Holy Spirit, the
holy Eucharist.'

'No way!'

'Like a big white bird.'

'This is an end to it!'

'How do we organize it, Vicar? How soon can we do it?'

'Well, you know, that's up to—'

'*No!*' Sound of a big fist smashing into the table; Lol
leapt up. 'I don't wannit!' Dexter roared. 'I don't wannit to
happen, you understand me? Why you gotter—? You're a
fuckin' ole meddler, Alice, nobody assed you to start all this
shit. I only told you to fuckin' stop you, for fuck's sake!'

Putting his right eye to the crack in the door, Lol saw a
bulky guy with a petulant lower lip and a shaven head,
standing in the middle of the kitchen. He looked marginally
nearer to tears than to violence, but his fists were bunched,
and he was breathing through his mouth. He unclenched a
fist and started feeling in a pocket of his leather coat. Lol put
a hand on the door, ready to wrench it open.

Dexter brought his hand up to his mouth. There was a vacuum gasp.

'You're stressin' me out. Leave it. *Fuck it!* All right?'

Dexter walked out, banging the kitchen door hard enough to make pans rattle on shelves.

'Alice,' Merrily said, from out of Lol's view. 'Let him walk it off in the cold air.'

Now she was hunched in the office chair, hands limp between her knees. She looked bloodless. Lol's white high had evaporated. It was a powerful reminder, this episode, of how vulnerable the clergy were, feeling they had to be there, for everybody, whether it was wanted or not.

Including the dead? Even the dead?

'I don't even know how bad he is, you see,' Merrily said. 'I don't know enough about asthma. What if he's out there on the square and he can't get his breath?'

'Does Alice live far away?'

'Three minutes' walk.'

'Not a problem, then.'

'Let's hope not.' She stood up and came and sank down beside him on the rug. They sat there in front of the electric fire, with their backs to the wall, their shoulders not quite touching, and she told him about the death of the kid called Roland Hook and seventeen years of corrosive bitterness inside a family.

'I don't get it,' Lol said. 'In a way I can understand Dexter's problem with this. *Is* it normal, to have some kind of belated funeral service, in the hope that it's going to make everything all right?'

'Jeavons,' Merrily said.

'The loose canon.'

'It's not *just* Jeavons. There's a movement inside Healing and Deliverance which argues that some illness, particularly

319

chronic illness, can be the result of something unresolved in the family's past. Or the victim being in the grip of some aberrant ancestor.'

'Your ancestors are haunting you and you don't know it?'

'It makes a certain kind of sense, but that's the trouble, isn't it? We're finding hauntings where there are no actual phenomena . . . other than an illness, or an emotional crisis. We – the Church of England.'

'So, by calming the spirit of this poor kid, who died in a state of terror, you can, in theory—'

'*I* can't.'

'Sorry, forgot the protocol. By organizing this Requiem for the dead kid, you can, in theory, open the way for *God* to cure not only Dexter's asthma, but also to heal the rift in his wider family?'

'Er . . . yeah.'

'Bloody hell,' Lol said, dismayed. 'You go along with this, you could be spending every day of the rest of your life doing complicated Eucharistic services for people laying all their problems on their ancestors. Sure, let's all blame the dead.'

Merrily shrugged.

'The Church of England authorizes this? And healing?'

Merrily said, '*When evening came, many who were demon-possessed were brought to Him, and He drove out the spirits with a word and healed all the sick.*'

'What's that?'

'Matthew's Gospel, linking healing and deliverance.'

'You're not Jesus Christ,' Lol said. 'Healing could make you ill.'

'Do I look ill?'

'You look tired.'

'I'm fine. Really.' She smiled at him. 'I'm awfully glad you're here.'

Their shoulders touched. Lol took a long breath.

She laid her head wearily on his shoulder. 'I'm all mixed up. Rumours – just *rumours* – of healing, and I'm getting the size of congregation I always dreamed of. And it makes me sweat. A hint of miracle cures, and suddenly you're on the way to becoming someone with a big voice and disciples.'

'Scary.'

Yes, it was. It was the very place he would hate for her to go, because of his parents, the born-again Pentecostalists, who used to attend Bible Belt-type healing services conducted by some crazy pastor who shook people till the sickness dropped out of them. But even the pastor, as far as Lol knew, hadn't sought to heal the living through the dead.

Merrily said, 'I mean, I really, really want it to happen for people . . . for the sick. I just don't want it to be me who's seen as the significant channel. It's too early. It's somehow too early for the women's ministry. Certainly too early for me. How selfish is that? How *cowardly* is that?'

Lol felt the wetness on her cheeks and put an arm around her and held her, as chastely as he could bear. He tried to think of something he could say that didn't sound soothing or patronizing or argumentative. On one level, he simply empathized. The idea of being a Major Artist still scared him, and the thought that he would soon be too old to scale the lowest available peak was almost comforting. But there was a big difference between a career and a calling, where you had to keep asking not what you or the audience needed, but how *God* wanted you to play it.

It was a lousy, thankless job. Jane would sometimes tell Lol how much she hoped that her mum would one day see the light and, slamming the church door behind her, start running.

Merrily said, 'Lew Jeavons said this was a very interesting case, and he's distressingly right. More right than he could know. And it's all valid, even on a psychological level. I mean, some priests believe that if, say, your great-grandfather was a Satanist or a heretic or even a Freemason a century ago, it could be affecting your health today. Well, yeah, sure . . . But *this* case – even if the Requiem is no more than symbolic, it still might help. I mean, look at what it's brought out tonight.'

'It's certainly ruined any chance of Alice getting to sleep.'

'*Reach out*, Jeavons said. *Embrace*.' Merrily sighed.

'I really wouldn't like to think of you embracing Darrin Hook,' Lol said.

TWENTY-SEVEN

Five Barrels

Jane followed Ben down the red-carpeted stairs, aware of dragging her feet. Ben was silent the whole way. He wore a black fleece zipped all the way up and black jeans. He was like his own shadow.

As they came into the lobby Jane saw the build-up of snow on the window ledges and thought, *He can fire me, but he can't send me home in this.*

The office behind the reception desk was used mainly by Natalie to monitor incomings and outgoings and to deal with wages for occasional cleaners and waitresses. It had originally been some kind of cloak and boot room. There were still a dozen coat hooks on walls that were cracked, white and windowless. The desk was ebony-coloured, with gold-leaf bits and had come from Ben and Amber's London flat.

Ben sat behind the desk in a leather swivel chair and nodded at the typist's chair opposite. A strip light made his thin face white and taut. Jane sat, too. Headmaster's-study situation.

'Look, Ben, all I meant—'

He waved her into silence. Above his head was a framed print of one of the etchings from the *Strand Magazine*. It was almost entirely black, except for a white spurt of flame from a pistol. Beneath the drawing, it said: *Holmes had emptied five barrels of his revolver into the creature's flank.*

Ben said, 'This business of strange forces, curses, haunt-ings, the mystical powers of the Border, the retentive power of ancient rocks . . . It's absolute rubbish, isn't it?' He leaned back, his hands clasped on his chest, swivelling a little. 'Jane, I'm a drama man, always will be, and that's about using *real* people and *real* places to create an *illusion*.'

Jane nodded.

'When you're putting a TV production together,' Ben said, 'you have this great tangle of egos – actors, writers, money men. You have time limits, locations, weather con-ditions. And you have to contain the lot inside a budget that never seems adequate to the task. And then, when it's all over, you're competing for just ninety minutes of someone's attention. Which is fine; it obliges me to – ' Ben unclasped his hands and brought them slowly together in the air ' – condense.'

'Make it . . . controllable?'

Ben smiled.

'But what are you – I'm sorry – what are you talking about exactly? The documentary or . . .?'

'The whole thing. The big picture. Stanner, the enterprise. This place appealed to me as soon as I saw it because it's pure artifice, built to look like a Gothic manor house, on a lavish scale. A production. And then, thanks to Conan Doyle, it became Baskerville Hall, *another* creation.'

Jane thought about this. 'But if *The Hound of the Basker-villes* was based on an actual legend – a real legend – then there *is* a kind of reality here, surely.'

'A real legend?' Ben looked pained. 'How real *is* a legend? What's the so-called Hound of Hergest now but a half-forgotten local folk tale? Who's even heard about that outside this immediate area? Whereas the Hound of the Baskervilles – the creation, the artifice – is world-famous, immortal . . . a hugely powerful image. *That*'s the power I'm harnessing – I mean, stuff the Hound of Hergest. Its part was over as soon as Doyle's book was written.'

Typical. Jane's mouth tightened.

'What?' Ben said. 'Come on, spit it out.'

'Well, it's . . . you know it's been *seen*.'

'What has?'

'The Hound. Or something. Something that's killing sheep. The shooters . . . that's what they were after.'

Ben nodded slowly.

Jane blinked at him. 'You knew that?'

'About Dacre and his pathetic bounty? Of course I knew. Known about it for a while. And naturally, I love the idea of something out there. And I love the idea of people believing in it, and I want to hear their stories. As long as the bastard *stays* out there . . . something unknown.'

Ben laughed. Over his head, Sherlock Holmes pumped round after round into the flank of the poor hound, its head and muzzle outlined in white lines of phosphorus.

'Only Dacre – who I've never met, by the way, and have no particular wish to – rather shot himself in the foot. When he heard I was making inquiries about sightings of the Hound, he instructed his tenants, his employees at the farm and the hunt kennels – anybody, in fact, he felt he had authority over – to keep *shtum*.' Ben smiled, tongue prodding at the inside of a cheek. 'Fortunately, in this day and age the feudal flame burns rather lower than it used to.'

'You actually knew the shooters were working for him?'

'Well, not at first. I'd heard rumours of what they were after, but I only started putting it together after you and I and Antony encountered them in the lane at Hergest Court. Ended up meeting a very interesting old guy in Kington – no friend of Dacre's and more than willing to talk to me about a number of things, as it happens. Yes, of course I knew who they were working for.'

'So when you found that guy Nathan . . .'

'When I *lost it completely*, you mean, Jane? When I *risked facing a murder charge*?'

Jane squirmed. She looked away from Ben's taunting eyes, inevitably up at the etching. And then it was like Holmes's pistol had gone off in her head in a spurt of light. Something began, shockingly, to make sense.

Ben looked up as Natalie's head came round the door.

'Ben, Alistair Hardy's just arrived, with that guy Matthew. I've shown them up to the Chancery room. I have to take Clancy to a neighbour's for the night, OK? The drive's totally blocked at The Nant – I'll be back later.'

'Nat – do be careful. We need you enormously this weekend.'

'Yeah, I know. I'll try not to get stuck,' Natalie said, and Ben raised a hand.

For a moment, as the door closed on Natalie, the instability of the Border seemed to vibrate through the room, making everything glow, but with a cheap and garish light. Jane took a breath and came right out with it.

'The truth is that the very last thing you wanted was for those guys to come out of the pines with a dead puma. That would've blown it, right?'

'Blown it?'

'The mystique.' Jane gripped the sides of her chair. 'A whole century's worth. Like, you don't believe the story of the spectral hound, but you don't want it disproved either. You didn't want those guys coming up with anything real that they'd shot. Certainly not anywhere near Stanner. Like . . . *Oh, we've shot the Hound.* And it gets in all the papers. You really didn't want that.'

'Would've been a touch prosaic,' Ben agreed.

'And that was really . . . that was *why*?'

She heard him shouting at the shooters on the last night

of the murder weekend. '*I warned you, not on my land! This time you're fucking dog meat!*'

You thought you knew about people. She'd had this nice, safe image of Ben: clever, charming, theatrical, faintly camp.

Ben shrugged. Jane almost cringed from him.

The snow was piled like mashed potato out by the entrance of Danny's place, and Danny had his tractor out, with the snowplough attachment and the spotlights. If he got it cleared now and he was up again by five tomorrow, likely he could keep on top of it.

He climbed down and stood by the gate, looking out. The Queens of the Stone Age were giving it some welly from the stereo back in the cab, singing, as it happened, about the sky falling. If this went on, there'd be some contract work for him and Gomer, from the county highways, sure to be. Plant hire, like Gomer kept saying, never slept.

Normally he'd be excited: snow was a challenge, folk needed help. But tonight he felt weary. Biggest problem was the lane outside – passable now, with four-wheel drive, but tomorrow was another day. Danny was knackered now, and the snow was oppressive.

Back at the house, he saw a tongue of yellow light – the back door opening – and Greta shouted, 'Is it clear?'

'Clear as I can get it without two tons of grit.' Danny left the music on and trudged back up the path.

'Only Jeremy rang, see. Wanted to know if we could take the child tonight on account his track's blocked solid.'

Danny kept on walking till he reached the back door. 'Gimme that again, Gret.'

'The child. Clancy? That woman— Her mother . . . is gonner bring her down from the hotel. Drop her off yere.'

'Wants *us* to have her?'

'I said I'd make up the spare bed.'

Danny stood just short of the step, trying to figure it. This Natalie and the kiddie, here they were at a great big hotel full of empty bedrooms . . . and they wanted the spare bed in the boxroom where he kept all his albums. But even that wasn't the *most* unlikely aspect of it.

'Nothing strike you as funny, Gret?' Danny breathed in stinging air through his teeth. *'Jeremy's track?* When is Jeremy's track *ever* blocked?'

'You gonner come in or not, 'fore we loses every bit of heat in the house?' Greta backed away from the cold, arms folded.

Danny stepped inside. 'If anybody knowed the big snow was on the way . . . When I was up The Nant earlier on, he'd got a trailerload of grit all ready. Had his ewes down last night, all tucked up. And now you tell me—'

Danny's brain froze.

'Well, what you want me to say?' Greta demanded. 'I accuse him of lying, say we en't having the girl—? What's wrong?'

'He don't want the kiddie there. Why don't he want the kiddie there?'

Her stared at him, not getting it.

'Greta, how'd he sound? What d' he sound like, in hisself?'

'Sounded like he always does, to me. Half-baked. What's the—?'

'When was this? When'd he ring?'

'Half an hour ago, mabbe. You was busy out there, I didn't wanner bother you with—'

'Holy shit, Greta . . .' The jolt to Danny's senses kicked him back outside. He shut his eyes and he threw his head back, feeling the fat snowflakes coming down on his upturned face and his beard and his gritted teeth. He snapped back upright. 'Call him.' Wiping his eyes hard with the heel of his hand. 'If he don't answer, call again. And again.'

'What do I say to him?'

'Talk about the weather, talk about any damn thing.' Danny stumbled away through the snow to his tractor. 'But keep him talking.'

Jane ran upstairs and tossed the camcorder on her bed in fury. Picked up her phone and saw there was a message on the voicemail: Antony's number.

Sod *that*. She dropped the phone on the bed and sat quietly for a while with the light out, watching the snow drifting past the window, wishing she'd caught the usual bus, gone home to Mum. Someone you could count on to behave like . . . decently.

What was worst about this was that Ben didn't even seem to see anything vaguely wrong in meeting violence with violence. And all to sustain his *hugely powerful image*.

She felt sick. She wanted out of here.

With no enthusiasm, she picked up the phone, keyed in the message.

'*Jane. Listen, hen, I have a problem. We're talking white hell here. Those guys at the Highways Agency, they're never prepared for cruel and unusual weather, and it looks like they're about to close the Severn Bridge. I'm doing ma best here, but it may be tomorrow night or later before I can get over there. Looks like it's down to you, the big one. Don't worry about it, you screw up it's no' the end of the world, we can reconstruct. Just weld the wee thing to your hands and get what you can: lots of Ben, lots of the weirdos, keep in tight, don't zoom. And don't be put off; they get used to the lens, the punters and the victims both. Good luck.*'

'Sod off,' Jane said sourly. If they thought she wanted to be part of the *artifice*, they could both sod off.

It seemed likely now that they were all in this – The White Company too. Was Alistair Hardy really going to tell the viewers that he couldn't actually get Conan Doyle on the line? Was he going to tell Ben that Conan Doyle had confirmed to him that the Hound was purely a Devon myth? Not if he had any psychic sense of what Ben was about – Ben, who suddenly was no longer endearingly eccentric, but more than a little unstable.

Maybe it was simply mid-life crisis, hormonal: Ben well into his fifties now, racing the clock. Ready to hurl the clock to the ground, it seemed, and hack at it with his heel in rage. Ready to damage anybody threatening the *now drama*.

Reluctantly, Jane called Antony back. At least he was younger and therefore probably less desperate. When he answered, she could hear a car engine.

'Sorry, I didn't know you were driving.'

'Jane, is that you? Trying to get myself home, here, through the white hell, which has arrived in the soft South, and the novelty's already wearing thin. Wait a sec, let me pull into the verge.'

'OK. Sorry.' The cynical languor in his voice had a calming effect on Jane. She waited for the handbrake's ratchet. 'Antony, can I talk to you confidentially?'

'Aye, I'll switch off the recording machine.'

'Huh?'

'Joke. Go on.'

'I'm worried. About things. Well, about Ben.'

'Well, I never.'

'This is serious. You're his mate, or I wouldn't tell you – in fact, I didn't tell you, OK?'

'Jane, this conversation will dissipate in the ether.'

And so, in the face of his levity, and because there was no one else she could tell, she told Antony the shocking truth about Nathan and what Ben had done to him. Told him in considerable detail.

And then she told him why Ben had done it.

'Oh boy,' Antony said.

She told him how Ben, on another occasion, after screaming at the shooters, had said that where he came from there were *real* hard bastards.

'Knightsbridge?'

'Jesus Christ, Antony!'

'OK. Joke. Ben's from Reading and not what you'd call the most salubrious side. As I understand it, his old man was a builder's labourer, something like that. Well, fine. Not then, though – Ben came into television at a time when a good and educated background, a nice accent, was still very much an advantage, and he gave them what they felt most comfortable with, and now he's stuck with it. So, yeah, I guess he knows how to handle himself. However, next time he tears someone's face off, it would be awfully nice to have it on camera. Is the wee Sony in your other hand, as we speak?'

'Antony, I don't—'

'Jane, don't worry about it. He's no' gonnae do anything to spoil the programme, believe it. I know this guy, I promise you.'

What did she expect, common sense? God, were they all the same?

She said, slightly desperately, 'It's just . . . that it's getting weirder. It's getting out of hand. Like Hattie Chancery?'

'Who?'

'The daughter of the man who built Stanner. She killed her—'

'Oh yeah, he told me.'

'But what's *she* have to do with Doyle and the Hound of Hergest? She probably wasn't even born when Doyle was here. It's just like, Oh, *she*'s spooky, let's throw her into the pot. I just think it's getting out of hand.'

'So?'

'Well, that . . .' What was she supposed to say to this guy?

Antony, I want to believe. I want to believe in the mystical Borderland, and if the Hound's part of that, I wanted to believe in the Hound. I need this. I don't want it turned into . . . artifice.

'Jane, listen. Don't worry, it's gonnae be fine. We can sort all this out later. You're my number one girl out there, and only one rule. If it's sexy, shoot it.'

'Cool,' Jane said sadly.

After Walton, the forestry came up on both sides of the tractor, this hostile army of giants in new white armour. Danny's face felt hot with anger and anxiety. He'd even switched off his music – mabbe feel more like playing it on the way back, instead of replaying over and over in his head what Greta had said.

Sounded like he always does. Half-baked. Like he en't yere.

Danny leaned on the wheel and the tractor battered on into England. Like he'd figured, no Hereford gritters or ploughs had made it this far, and by the time he reached the turning to The Nant, the road looked like it would soon be impassable for ordinary vehicles.

However . . .

On Jeremy's ground, the snow was packed tight on either side, and there was a well-cleared channel down the middle, and the tractor rolled sweetly down this long, grey alleyway to the edge of the farmyard.

Dear God.

Danny climbed down from the cab, hissing as the night wrapped its frozen arms around him. He looked around: no lights in the farmhouse, no security lights outside. Power off already? Snow brought the lines down?

Danny hoped it was only the power that was off.

He stood there and looked at The Nant for long seconds, snow accumulating on the vinyl shoulders of his donkey jacket and already inches thick, dense as Christmas-cake icing, on the farmhouse roof.

And then, before he'd realized it, he was bawling out into the white night, like Greta doing the full Janis, 'Jeremy! Jeremy, where are you, boy? *JEREMY!*'

When he filled his lungs again, the bitter air stung his throat and he started to cough, doubled up by the gate. He leaned on the gate, tears in his eyes, panting, letting the silence re-form around him as the snow fell, all pretty and pitiless. *Come out, Jeremy, please.*

But when he pictured Jeremy, the boy wasn't coming towards him but walking softly away through the cushiony fields, off into the hollows of the deep forestry where there was peace.

Danny raised his head and thought he saw a glow behind one of the windows in the farmhouse. And it was then that it started up.

At first it was like it was coming up from the ground, from some sunken prison cell, down where there was no light and no hope. It was coming up through the snow like tongues of cold fire. It was as old as the hills, as old as the Ridge, and bone-cold, the coldest sound in the world.

TWENTY-EIGHT

The Jane Police

So much bigger than asthma now.

This was what Alice said when Merrily rang her, as Lol had known she would, before the night was out.

Alice was a force of nature. If Dexter thought that by finally coming out with the untold story he was going to make her drop it, he'd got her badly wrong. She'd discovered this powerfully mystical aspect of Christianity she'd never imagined existed. And also – as the oldest sister in a dysfunctional family – she saw it as her responsibility to *sort everything out*.

Even from across the scullery, Lol had heard everything coming out of the phone, Alice's voice crackling like an old radio. She and Dexter had had a row and Dexter had stomped off in a rage, although he was supposed to come back to do the last two hours in the chip shop – Alice saying he wasn't having his own way this time, asthma or no asthma, nothing was going to stop The Eucharist. Telling Dexter she'd find Darrin herself, make sure he was there. At *The Eucharist*.

'She's fallen in love with the word,' Merrily said. 'Sounds powerful and kind of technical. Prayer's comforting, but *Eucharist* suggests big guns.'

The computer was booting up, this row of icons extending along the bottom of the screen, Lol realizing that he didn't know what any of them meant: another religion he didn't understand.

'So where's Darrin now?'

'Well, he *was* in prison. One way or another, Alice will find him. Which is *not* what Dexter wants. But Dexter's clearly still scared of Darrin. Whereas Alice is scared of nobody.'

A face with a heavy moustache was on the screen, the expression solemn and dignified but the eyes bright with just the possibility of madness.

Illuminating Merrily's other problem.

'*If* The White Company are simply harmless, misguided, terribly British eccentrics –' she was standing next to the computer, holding her pectoral cross between her fingers ' – then why didn't Jane tell me about them?'

'Because she knows you'd have to disapprove,' Lol said. 'And she'd be embarrassed if she had to say, "I'm sorry I can't work this weekend because my mum doesn't want me exposed to evil forces." '

'You think I'm overreacting.'

'She's grown up quite a lot in the past year. I mean . . . have you actually had experience of a medium letting evil into the world, or is this received wisdom?'

'In as much as it's received from the same source we get all our—' Merrily sank into the chair, hair mussed. 'It's *all* received wisdom, isn't it? It's why they call us The Church. And if she's grown up that much, why did you feel you had to tell me about Lucy?'

He looked up at her from the rug. 'Because, in the Jane Police, I'm just a junior officer.'

She laughed. There was something that might have been a tear stain like a birthmark alongside her nose. He wanted to go over and lick it off.

'I'm trying not to get screwed up or sanctimonious about this,' Merrily said. 'There are even one or two Deliverance ministers who actually *work* with mediums and don't seem to have come to any—'

'Look, you won't rest till you find out what they're doing. Why don't you ask them?'

'What do I do – send them a spirit message?'

'Or even go back to the homepage and click on *Contacts*.'

'Oh.' She flipped back a page. '*Contact Us*.'

To apply for membership or to obtain any of our leaflets, contact Matthew Hawksley on otherside@asc.com

Merrily clicked on it. An e-mail option came up. 'Should I?'

'What's your own e-mail address? No reference to Deliverance in it?'

'Are you kidding? Jane uses it. It just says Watkins.'

'Why don't you say you're a Conan Doyle enthusiast and you've heard there's a conference at Stanner Hall this weekend. And is it still on, despite the weather? Mention the *cwn annwn* – that'll sound knowledgeable.'

'OK.' Merrily began typing.

Good evening, Mr Hawksley,

   Word has reached me of your gathering at the Stanner Hall Hotel, near Kington, in Herefordshire, this weekend. As a Conan Doyle enthusiast living not far away, I should be most interested to learn more details. In fact, given the weather conditions, will the conference still be taking place?

   As my own researches into the links between Sir Arthur Conan Doyle, the Hound of Hergest, the *cwn annwn*, etc. have shown, this is a fascinating area of

inquiry. If you could supply me with more details ASAP,
I would be most grateful.

Yours sincerely,

M. Watkins.

'Perfect,' Lol said.

'What if they *are* at Stanner, and one of them shows this
to Jane?'

'They're unlikely to make the connection,' Lol said. 'But
if they do, you'll get a call from Jane. And she'll have to tell
you all about it, in a lot of detail, and there won't be a
mystery any more, and we can get out of this cell and go
and light a fire and watch the snow build a big white wall
between us and the world.'

Merrily put on a wry smile that didn't quite work.

Jane was pacing the shabby lobby with the camera hanging
from her shoulder like a school bag – the camera and all it
represented a burden now; it had come to this. Time to talk
seriously to Nat – soon as she got back.

When the porch door slammed, it wasn't Nat but
Matthew, the Harry Potter clone, carrying a laptop in a
leather case. Just for the sake of it, Jane brought up the Sony
150 and shot him by the side of the Christmas tree in front
of the reception desk.

Matthew half turned and stuck his tongue out. Behind
him, the white lights on the tree were unevenly spread, and
it looked spindly and skeletal, like a frosted pylon. Ben had
brought the tree in himself last weekend, probably nicked it
out of the forestry. Jane didn't approve of young trees hacked
off above the roots and brought indoors to die slowly, so
that by Twelfth Night – Happy New Year – you had a
stiffened corpse. She lowered the camera, nodding at the
laptop.

'You get e-mails from the Other Side on that?'

Matthew inspected her through his black-framed glasses. 'I realize you're much too cool to be mixed up with spiritists and channellers, and I suppose I was much the same at your age.'

'What changed?' To Jane, adulthood seemed an arid place tonight.

'You don't want to know. Stick to your filming.'

'No, I do,' Jane said.

Matthew stared into her eyes, and she stared back and realized he could be as old as Mum. Glasses with big frames sometimes made people look a lot younger, like with beards and double chins.

'For what it's worth,' he said, 'what changed me was losing a mate. Beth's husband, Steve Pollen, who was my boss at Powys Council. In the Archive department. Steve died very unexpectedly.'

'Oh. I'm sorry.'

'Only, it didn't stop him coming into work. You'd find something interesting – say, some missing estate records – and you'd say automatically, "Here, look at this, Steve," and then you'd think, *Hang on, he's dead*, and then you'd realize you'd just caught a glimpse of him at the files. People who die without some degree of foreknowledge often don't realize they've passed.'

Two of the lights on the tree had gone out. Jane thought of Ledwardine, remembered the dead branches she'd collected in the orchard and brought into the vicarage to be sprayed silver and gold for Christmas, she and Mum planning to decorate them this weekend. She felt a stab of loneliness.

'Actually, I think I saw a woman once. Like, when she was dead? I didn't know she was dead until later, so it wasn't scary. I mean I was pretty sure I saw her, but . . . you know?'

Matthew nodded. 'Most of the spirits we see are complete

strangers, so we don't realize they're not there. It's only when we spot someone in a situation where nobody could possibly be at a particular time, like in a deserted theatre or a church that's been locked up, that we think, *Uh-oh . . .*'

Jane frowned; this conversation was getting too pally.

'Don't get me wrong, I still think spiritualism's naff. It's a big issue, life after death, but you see these mediums working an audience, and all they ever get is like, "Remember your dad's blue suit in the wardrobe – well, it's OK to send it to the Oxfam shop." '

Matthew looked exasperated at last. 'People who are bereaved don't want a lecture on metaphysics, they just want some evidence of survival – some small thing that sounds trivial and naff to an intellectual like you, but is conclusive proof that someone they thought had gone for ever is still around.'

So now she was just young and heartless.

'Does he . . . still come into the office?'

'Steve? No, he's gone on now. We decided, Beth and I, that we ought to try and help him. Which is how we got into the network. You help them to accept their state. They hang around people they used to know and get confused. But if it's explained to them, they'll just turn around and see the light – literally. And they'll see people – usually their relatives who've already passed – waiting to welcome them. Which is wonderful. And you've got that *look* again.'

The guy was clearly sincere. 'Just seems too easy.'

'It's not *easy*, but it's normal. What was interesting in this case, however, on a more basic level, was that when Steve died he was putting together a file of newly discovered records relating to Hergest and Stanner, and I was able to finish the work for him, with Beth. Which was how I learned about the Windlesham group and The White Company. Sometimes you're led to things.'

Jane said, 'You found out about Walter Chancery and everything – from these records?'

'It connected up.'

The phone on reception started to ring.

'So what *did* they do the night Conan Doyle came here?'

'Hadn't you better get that?' Matthew said.

'Look, I know all about Hattie Chancery . . .'

Matthew smiled, shaking his head, and walked off. Jane snatched up the phone.

'Stanner Hall.'

'Where's your mobile?'

'Irene!'

'You wanna talk, talk,' Eirion said.

'*Jane* . . .' Amber came round the corner from the kitchen steps. 'Oh, sorry . . .'

Jane held up two fingers, appealing for a couple of minutes, and fished The Brigid Document from her jeans.

'You do realize we leave in the morning,' Eirion said when she'd finished reading it out. 'I kind of thought you were ringing to wish me *bon voyage*.'

'Oh hell, I'd forgotten.'

'Thanks.'

'I didn't mean—'

'We're leaving early because of the snow.'

'Oh well, never mind this, then, I'll—'

'I'll give it half an hour, OK?'

'You're awfully obliging, for a Welshman.'

'Make that fifteen minutes,' Eirion said.

Amber was nowhere in sight when Jane came off the phone, but Matthew was halfway up the stairs, in conversation with Alistair Hardy.

These guys – it was all so cosy. Forced-cosy, like a nursing home. Did death reduce the intellect to mush? Going to work, wondering why nobody would talk to you, till one day someone like Hardy turned you round, and there were all your dead relatives lined up like for some awful retirement party. *Surprise, surprise*: all your dead relatives in paper hats, with vacant, dead smiles and party poppers.

'Jane!' Amber was standing by the eerie tree, wearing her vinyl apron. Her voice was too light and thin for this place; in Stanner, unless you projected, your words were carried off like dust. 'Come and help me, would you?'

'OK.'

But as soon as they reached the kitchen steps, it was, 'Jane, *did* you tell your mother what's happening here?'

'Well, no, I told you what she'd say.'

'I said you wouldn't tell her,' Amber said with resignation. 'Ben thought you would, but then he—'

'Ben? *Ben* knows you rang my mum?'

'It was actually Ben's idea, Jane.' This time Amber's words resounded like a smoke alarm. 'It was Ben who suggested I rang her.'

'I don't understand.'

'You'd better come down to the kitchen.' Amber looked over her shoulder and then back at Jane and down at the camera in her hands. 'Deception's not my forte, Jane, I'm just a cook.'

The back-porch door was unlocked. Normal enough. Danny went through, with his lambing lamp switched on. The usual stuff in here: shovels, rubber leggings on a peg, hard hat and face guard for the chainsaw.

He banged on the back door. 'Jeremy!'

The howling stopped. Danny rattled the handle; it turned and the door opened. Not normal, not at night. Danny shone the lamp into the kitchen: old-fashioned, green-painted kitchenette, exposed sink, old brown Rayburn.

'Jeremy?'

The Rayburn chunnered to itself. A tap dripped. No one here. He went through into the living room, where the lambing lamp found Jesus half in shadow, his face tinted by the olive light of the Garden of Gethsemane. Below the mantelpiece, behind a fireguard, little orange flames were curling quietly out of a tamped-down mix of woodblocks and coal-slack in the range.

Below that, the dog sat on the brown and green rag rug. The dog wasn't howling no more, only panting slightly, his flanks heaving, his stare on Danny but not moving from the rug that had been here all his life and all Jeremy's life. This was a good dog, Border Collie crossed with something else. Something that howled.

'Where's the boss, Flag?'

The dog didn't come to him, didn't howl, didn't growl, didn't whimper, just sat. Danny shone the light around, over the pink-flowered wallpaper that Jeremy's mam had pasted up long, long ago. Over the dresser was a picture plate of what might have been Hereford Cathedral, with a crack through the tower.

On the top of the drawer section of the dresser was a small white envelope.

On the envelope, it said *Mr Danny Thomas*.

Danny said, 'Oh God. Oh Jesus Christ.'

The envelope wasn't sealed. Danny took out the single sheet of folded paper inside and held it under the lambing light.

Danny, I've never been one for formality. You been a good friend to me, always. Please take the dog, he knows you. Please deal with the sale of my stock, and see they go to the right kind of place or keep everything yourself for nothing. Natalie will

Danny let the paper fall. Something like a sob came out of him. When he looked up, the face of Jesus had gone into full shadow.

He ran out, through the kitchen, through the porch and into the white yard. Opposite him, the big barn door was shut. The little door in the bottom right-hand corner was not quite closed.

Danny saw a glimmering of light in there.

He stopped outside the door, very afraid. Behind him, the dog was howling again, making the coldest, loneliest sound in all the bloody world. The snow was coming down harder, but he couldn't feel it. It didn't feel cold no more; its flakes might have been rose petals.

TWENTY-NINE

Twist

You forgot how isolating snow could be. At the highest point of the village, the church and the vicarage had become an island of ancient stones and crooked timbers rising out of an arctic sea into a falling sky. Merrily and Lol made a brief exploratory foray into the upholstered softness: no vehicles moving on the square, the little market hall squatting like a white-capped mushroom, lighted windows in The Black Swan reduced to shining slits by high sills of snow. The Swan was a local pub again, its car trade in retreat.

Merrily and Lol came back in, and she shut the front door and stood eye to eye with the lamp-bearing Christ, lord of weary acceptance.

'Wouldn't even get to the main road, would we?'

She brushed down Jane's fleece, kicked off her wellingtons, sending shards of snow skating across the mat and the flagstones. Lol followed her through to the scullery, where Ethel the cat dozed in front of the electric fire. He sat down in front of the computer, snow melting into his hair.

'There you go.'

She leaned against him. 'What?'

Thank you for your inquiry. To be conversant with the Stanner Project, it is clear you must have contacts in

the Psychic World, although I have not heard of you.
Accordingly, I attach our fact sheet.

The involvement of Sir Arthur himself in the events
of 1899, combined with the subsequent history makes
this, for us, a once-in-a-lifetime opportunity, and we
very much hope to go ahead this weekend. However, the
state of the weather means that we may be fewer in number
than was originally anticipated and so, if you are a
genuine person residing sufficiently close to Stanner
Hall as to be able to journey here, we would be
interested to hear more from you. We make no secret of
our work, but it is essential that only sympathetic and
like-minded people are involved as I am sure you
appreciate. Please e-mail me again if you are
interested. I shall be communicating with several other
individuals throughout the evening and therefore
shall be available should you wish to know more.

All good wishes,
Matthew

Lol looked up at her through his brass-rimmed glasses.

'Confirmation.' Merrily moved to the window, looked out
at the ghosts of apple trees. 'It looks like they're there already.
I . . . I'm just . . . Well, I'm not well disposed towards my
daughter.' Turning and throwing up her hands in frustration.
'*The Stanner Project*? Project! How long's *that* been going
on? *We make no secret of our work*. How long's the bloody
kid known about all this?'

The electric fire put a blush on the white wall under
the window – a poor defence, Merrily thought, against the
winged spirits of the night, the *cwn annwn* chasing souls.
While electricity had helped to kill off superstition, everyone
in the countryside knew it was most prone to failure when
you most needed it.

'Might as well find out the rest.' Lol clicked on the attachment.

THE STANNER PROJECT

Sir Arthur Conan Doyle seemed, in his later years, to be in a permanent state of excitement and anticipation, always believing that his field of study would eventually change everyone's life, removing all fear and uncertainty about the nature of death, dispelling centuries of superstition and removing the residual control still exercised over the less-sophisticated by the Church.

The White Company has come to believe that ACD's own certainty stemmed, in part, from an experience that occurred at the end of the nineteenth century, when he was already a successful author and a wealthy man, at a time when he was re-evaluating his life and searching for a new purpose. A 'mid-life crisis', if you like.

We believe that his initial baptism – a 'baptism of fire' – occurred at Stanner Hall, on the border of Herefordshire, England, and Powys, Wales, when he took part in what had originally been devised as little more than a party game for his amusement but which turned into something profoundly disturbing – so disturbing, in fact, that ACD, with his, at the time, limited knowledge was only able to deal with it by fictionalizing it in a way that would eliminate all paranormal implications.

We suspect it was many years before he was able to understand the true psychic and psychological implications of the Stanner experience, if indeed he reached a full understanding prior to his passing in 1930.

The Stanner Project, involving Mr Alistair Hardy and others, will attempt to re-examine the Experience in the light of more recent developments in psychical and psychological thinking and perhaps point the way to the breakthrough anticipated by ACD. The implications of this are quite awesome and any information, particularly with regard to the anomaly, which might further our inquiries even at this late stage would be gratefully received.

'Certainly explains why Jane kept it to herself.' Merrily gave the document to the printer. ' "Something profoundly disturbing." That's comforting, isn't it? I'll be able to sleep now.'

'And the breakthrough . . . would be what?'

'Always the same one with these people: final, undeniable proof of life after death. Kept Conan Doyle in transatlantic lecture tours for over twenty years.'

'Matthew implies that the real reason the Church is opposed to spiritualism is not, as *you* might say, because people might let in something dangerous, but because it would undermine your power base. I mean . . . don't you ever wonder?'

She stood there with Jane's fleece hanging open and her pectoral cross swinging free. Of course she wondered.

Lol said, 'Like, if these people were, suddenly, out of the blue to happen upon absolute, undeniable evidence of an afterlife?'

'The atheists and the physicists would still deny it.'

'What about the Christians?'

'Ah well, even if we had to accept it as fact, it would still only be the beginning for us. However far it went, it would be the beginning. But look, they won't, will they? They won't find it. Because apart from anything, I don't believe truth is ever going to come out of terror. Portents of death, the Hounds of Annwn?'

Bang, bang, bang. Front door. Ethel springing up on the desk.

Merrily flinched. 'If this turns out to be Dexter and Alice again, I don't think I can face it.'

Lol stood up. 'I'll get it.'

'No, best if—'

She watched his face fall. Another test failed. Dammit, they had to get over this stupid concealment of the obvious.

'Yes,' she said. 'If you would.'

The kitchen was empty, every surface clean, as if the house was being vacated for a while. Amber stood next to the stove, which was something French and steely grey. The smell of rich chocolate seemed inappropriate tonight. The lights in here made Amber look ill.

'As soon as they found out what your mother actually did, they thought it would be a good . . . friction point.' The size and the emptiness of the kitchen made her voice sound forced and full of fissures, like a student teacher on day one.

Jane still wasn't getting it. 'Friction?'

'If the Diocesan Exorcist jumped in with some dire warning about the risks of messing with spirits, they thought that would be a nice touch. Then they'd try and get her to express decent Christian reservations on video. And even if she wouldn't play, it would still be a nice twist. Friction, you see, Jane. Friction's sexy.'

'Amber, I'm not— *They?*'

'Ben. And Antony.'

If it's sexy, shoot it.

'They wanted to—'

'Ben knew I wasn't happy about the spiritualism angle from the start. He suggested I give your mother a ring and ask her advice. Pretend I was doing it behind his back. And if she reacted badly and tried to stop you coming here as a result, that would make another good twist. Twists are important. Conflict and friction and twists.'

Jane sagged. 'They'd have used us . . . as *a twist*?'

'Jane, love, don't get this wrong – they never think of it as any kind of betrayal. It's just television. It's feeding the monster. TV's this awful, voracious predator; if you get too near, you inevitably get eaten. I'm not saying I totally *didn't* want to ring your mother – it would've been nice to get some objective advice from someone with expertise. And if she managed to step in and stop you coming, well, I suppose that was something else I didn't have to worry about. Ben's going, "Oh, don't worry, Jane will have told her by now, we can expect another visit." '

'But I didn't. I *wouldn't*. I work here, I wouldn't—'

'I know. I said you wouldn't.'

Jane unslung the camera, very much mistrusting it now, and placed it on the island unit, backing away from it. 'Why are you telling me this? Why are you telling me now?' Trying to stay calm, work out the extent of Ben's duplicity, but aware of breathing faster.

'I was going to call you tonight,' Amber said, 'and warn you that all the roads would be blocked so don't even think of coming tomorrow. But with your youthful enthusiasm and your obvious desire not to miss anything interesting, you bloody well turned up tonight. *That*'s why I'm telling you.'

'But, like, why would you . . . why would you not want me here? I'm shooting the *video*. And if Antony doesn't make it—'

'He may very well not get through, that's true,' Amber agreed. 'Which would be leaving the lunatic in charge of the asylum.'

'Ben?'

I'm a drama man. It's about using real people and real places . . .

'I don't know whether Antony *not* being here will make him more sensible or even more irrational. All I know is, he's been busily shooting material all week – interviewing Hardy and Mrs Pollen and a man in Kington who used to work—'

'Hang on.' Jane stiffened. 'You're saying he's got a video camera? *Ben?*'

Amber sighed.

'I don't understand.'

'Jane, you—' Amber's face crumpled with this terrifyingly maternal kind of sympathy. 'You didn't *really* think they'd leave it all to you, did you?'

Jane stepped back and stared at the camcorder on the island unit like it was contaminated with anthrax.

'Well, I . . .' She felt this acute burning behind her eyes.

'I'm really sorry,' Amber said. 'I should've told you days ago.'

Jane swallowed hard. No wonder Matthew had been laughing at her. They were *all* laughing at her. All of them laughing up their sleeves at the smart-arse schoolkid prancing round with her professional video camera. All of them: Ben, Antony . . . The White Company . . . Ben . . . Antony . . .

Don't worry, it's gonnae be fine. It's gonnae be riveting, Jane.

'Antony set me up?'

You're my number one girl.

'Jane, it's— He really wouldn't see it like that. These little Sonys are so comparatively cheap, they can scatter them around like throwaway pens. And if you thought you were the only person with a camera, you'd try all the harder to get good material. You'd start seeing your name in lights. Obviously, he'll use some of what you've done, of course he will . . .'

'He *set me up!*'

'He also set Ben up. And Ben set Antony up. And you

and I, between us, were supposed to set your mother up. Television, Jane – everybody at some time gets set up, the end invariably justifying the means. When it's all over, Ben and Antony'll watch the results together and get pissed, and that'll be that. Television.'

'It's despicable.'

'No, Jane.' Amber did this brittle little laugh. 'It's art.'

'And what do we do now? Just go along with it?' Jane snatched up the camera with no reverence.

Amber said, 'If *were* thinking of hurling that thing to the flags in rage, please don't. There's been too much rage.'

Jane shook her head, letting the camera dangle from her hands on its strap. 'What should I do?'

'I think you should do what you were supposed to do in the first place. Tell your mother. Everything.'

'And what's *she* going to do?'

Amber said, 'Look, I'm only a cook, but—'

'Christ, Amber, if you say that *again*— I mean, I'm only a *schoolkid*, and if *I* can see it—'

'See what?'

'That if Conan Doyle, the John the Baptist of Spiritualism, kept quiet about what happened here – even if it was evidence of survival after death – then there must have been something fairly unpleasant.'

'Though obviously not unpleasant enough to prevent you grabbing the chance to film something similar, if you got the chance.'

Jane put the camcorder back on the island unit.

'I'm not a very nice person, am I?'

'You're a *young* person, that's all.'

'OK, I'll phone Mum. What then?'

Amber folded her arms, staring at the flags. 'Realistically, I think your mother ought to talk to the only one of them I've had much to do with. Mrs Pollen.'

'When was that?'

'Earlier today. She came looking for me. Would hate to cause offence, et cetera. Old-fashioned country woman – Women's Institute, cakes for the fête, jolly dinner parties, two golden labradors. And she's the only one of them who got into this through personal loss. And she was a church-goer.'

'All the reward you get for suffering Victorian hymns and dismal sermons,' Jane said. 'He pinches your husband before his time.'

'You must have stimulating discussions, you and your mother,' Amber said.

'Keeps her on her toes.'

'Mrs Pollen now thinks that she was somehow directed here by her husband.' Amber shrugged, looking uncommitted either way. 'My feeling is that she believes that if they can get through, she'll be . . . rewarded.'

'Get some contact with him? That really doesn't happen.' Jane looked up at the high window, through which, by daylight, you could see the top of Stanner Rocks. 'That's so sad.'

'On the surface, she's very breezy and sort of earthy about it, but underneath she's mixed up. In a way, it's rekindled her faith, but she's aware that the Church thinks it's wrong, and there's clearly some guilt about that. Anyway, I think she'd like to talk to your mother, and that wouldn't do any of us any harm at this stage.'

'Except possibly Ben.'

'Not my problem,' Amber said, and Jane looked at her, recalling what Nat had said about her calling it quits, moving out.

Amber said, 'They call it The Stanner Project, Ben calls it The Hook. The contemporary events from which they can hang a century of conjecture. As far as he's concerned whatever kind of answer they get, if any, is entirely irrelevant. What's important is that the question gets posed, on television. Did *The Hound of the Baskervilles* begin *here?* Any extra spooky bits would be a nice bonus, but the programme doesn't depend on that, now he knows what happened when Conan Doyle was here.'

'He does?' For a moment, Jane almost forgot her own humiliation. 'You mean someone finally traced the missing document?'

'Oh, Ben did better than that.' Amber's smile was twisted. 'He traced someone who was working here. Well, not then, obviously, not at the *time*. But someone who worked here sixty-odd years ago and so talked to people who *were* here at the time.'

'Wow – who?'

Amber said the contact had come through the guy who played the Major in the murder thing, Frank Sampson. When Dacre was trying to stop people talking to Ben, it had worked in reverse in some cases, and Frank had phoned on Tuesday to say an old man called Leonard Parsonage, who used to be the butler here, would be happy to talk to Ben.

'Seems Dacre's father got him sacked years ago,' Amber said. 'You know what it's like around here for old feuds.'

'Leonard.' Jane was remembering Gomer's account of the death of Hattie Chancery. *Took a while 'fore one of 'em was up to going up them stairs. Ole Leonard, the butler, it was, my mam said.*

'He lives in a sheltered bungalow now, in Kington. He's over ninety, which still means he must have been in his twenties when he was here.'

'Amber, he was the person who found Hattie's body. He's talked about all that?'

'Better than that, he's talked on videotape.' Amber bent and opened a cupboard in the base of the island unit. 'Do you want to go and watch it? You can tell your mother all about it.'

'You've got it *here*?'

Amber rose, clutching a Maxell VHS videotape in a light blue case with a gold stripe. 'This is a copy that Ben ran off for Antony to look at. I pinched it from his desk. You can take it up to our bedroom, there's a video machine in there.'

'Have *you* seen it?'

'You know which our bedroom is, don't you, Jane?'

Jane accepted the tape. 'You sure you want me to see it?'

'Jane, you're *gagging* to see it.'

Lol came back into the scullery with Gomer Parry, cap in his hands, squeezing it like a sponge as he fought for breath, ignoring the chair Merrily was offering.

'Know you en't gonner mind, Vicar. I got the truck out front. Had a call from Danny Thomas, see. You recalls Danny Thomas, of Kinnerton?'

She stared at him, puzzled, assembling the image of a bearded man with grey hair over his shoulders, a flat cap on top. 'You mean the one who's also your partner now?'

Gomer's glasses had clouded. He snatched them off, wiped them savagely on his sleeve.

'Gomer, let me get you some tea—'

'*No!* No, thank you.' He rammed his glasses back on. 'Bloody stupid. 'Course you knows the boy.' He stared at her defiantly. 'En't lost no marbles, Vicar, I just—'

'I know. You went dashing out into the cold and then back into the warm. It gets to us all.' She took his cap gently, unrolled it and hung it on the waste-paper bin near the electric fire. 'He's OK, isn't he? Danny?'

'*He*'s all right. Juss called me up. Just he got this pal, see.' Gomer sat down at last, bringing out his ciggy tin like it was part of the same cycle of movements. 'Ta.'

'Take it slowly, Gomer.'

'Bit of a loner, that's all. Hell, a lot of a loner.' Gomer shook his head, annoyed, stared in disgust at his ciggy tin. 'I en't thinkin' straight *at all* . . . You knows full well who I'm talkin' about. Boy's girlfriend's daughter, her's Jane's . . . you know, that kiddie?'

'Clancy? You're talking about Jeremy . . . ?'

'Berrows. Exac'ly. Jeremy Berrows. Me and Danny been talkin' a lot about Jeremy Berrows, the situation he's got hisself into. And a lot of other stuff. And I been thinkin' for a long time – Danny, too – we needs to ask the little vicar to take a look. And you know how it is, you lets things slide and then it all come down on you. And now Jeremy . . .'

Gomer took off his glasses, pinched his nose.

'What's he done, Gomer?'

'Boy's hanged hisself,' Gomer said.

THIRTY

The Huntress

'Where do you want me to start, Mr Foley?' Leonard Parsonage asked.

He was a very thin old man. All really old people tended to be thin, Jane thought, making themselves less of a target for all the things that could take you down.

'I'd just like to get the levels right before we start.' Ben's voice came through fainter, from one side. 'Why don't you tell us what you've been doing since you left Stanner? Have you been in Kington ever since?'

The old guy got as far as saying he'd returned to Kent, where he was born, to get married, then come back to Kington to buy an ironmonger's business. Then Ben must have cut the recording. When it came back, Ben was saying, on that same background level, 'Tell me what she was really like, Leonard. Tell me what Hattie was like – Mrs Davies.'

'Mrs *Chancery*.' Leonard had a tiny black personal microphone clipped to the mustard-coloured tie jutting out from the neck of his v-neck pullover. The mike looked like a stag beetle climbing up it. 'We hadn't to call her Mrs Davies. Mrs Chancery, it was, or Mrs Hattie.' He stopped talking and looked directly into the lens.

'No, at *me*, Leonard. Let's start again, OK? And remember, talk to me, *not* the camera. Forget about the camera.'

It looked to Jane like this had been hard going, but all Ben's questions and prompts could be edited out, and he could overlay the edits with other pictures, like the photos of Hattie and Stanner – Jane had learned all this from Eirion. For all the use it was now.

Wrenching back her anger, she looked around the Foleys' bedroom while Leonard rearranged himself. It was at the front of the house, with a bay window overlooking the car park, and it was very unfussy, with a plain wardrobe and a double divan. No dressing table, no mirror. Very Amber.

'Well, it had to be "Mrs Chancery",' Leonard said, 'because Stanner was the House of the Chancerys, you see. Robert Davies, he was just the stallion brought to the mare, that's what they used to say. Looked less of a stallion, mind you, when I first saw him than he had before the First War, according to Mrs Betts – she was the cook. Mrs Betts said they all used to fancy Mr Robert, although in later years they all felt very sorry for him, naturally, because of . . . because of the way she would treat him.'

Leonard wore false teeth which clicked sometimes, but he talked quite fluently, in the way of a man who was used to dealing with people. Ben had positioned him in front of a picture window with a view across some kind of car park to Kington market place with its red-brick clock tower.

'What was she like, Leonard? Physically. Describe her – what she looked like. Take your time.'

'She was . . . Oh, my Lord, she was like a goddess to us. Diana the Huntress – somebody called her that, I think it was the minister at the church. Diana the Huntress, yes. Because she *was*, you see – she used to go hunting every day of the week, it seemed like, in the season. Well, not that many women did, in those days. Oh, don't get me wrong, she was all woman. *All* woman. Too *much* woman, some might've said.'

Leonard smiled in what struck Jane as a surprisingly lascivious way, and there was a shiny bit of drool in the corner of his mouth. He had a thin white moustache, kind of dandyish. Jane wondered, just wondered . . .

'OK, tell me about the hunting,' Ben said. 'How did that start?'

'Oh well, old Walter, he encouraged her. That was what I was told. Walter couldn't ride and he was too old to start, but that was what you did in those days, the gentry, and so he had his daughter on a horse from a very early age, and that was how she got in with the hunt. If you rode, you hunted – pretty much the way it is today. But I would say the hunting was always more important than the riding for Mrs Hattie. Anyway, that was about when the Middle Marches Hunt was first started, and it was mainly young people back then.'

'This was before the First World War?'

'It would've been, yes. She was just a girl, but quite large, even then – you could see that from the photos, I expect. Yes, the hunt, I believe they kept that on through most of the War, although some of the young men had gone off to fight. Afterwards, after the War, it went from strength to strength. They had these hounds from France that were bred down in Glamorgan – nothing but the best for the Middle Marches. The Chancerys, they supported the Hunt in the early years – financially, that is, when they had money to spare – and they also founded a hunt supporters' club to raise more money, so it would always be *buoyant*. But Mrs Hattie lived for it, oh my Lord, yes. If there was bad snow or disease or some reason the hunt had to be called off, then she was in a *very* black mood indeed.'

'This is in your day, Leonard?'

'Oh yes. I came there in thirty-four, which was the year after the old fellow died. I was soon Mrs Hattie's right-hand man – that was what she used to say. Or "my squire". She talked about herself like a knight on horseback. "My Squire", yes. I was her squire.'

'Black moods?'

'Eh?'

'You said she'd be in a black mood when the hunting was off. What was that like?'

'Black moods . . . black hound.' Leonard bit down on his lower lip and stared into the distance. He had pale blue eyes, watery.

'What's that mean?' Ben said.

'Used to say she ran with the black hound. One of her sayings. She'd come back, and the groom would take her horse, all covered with sweat, and I'd be there, and she'd say, "Bring me a bloody drink, Leonard, the black hound was in the pack today." '

'What did she mean by that?'

'Well, it was one of her sayings.'

'But did she mean there was an actual—?'

'It meant, as far as I could fathom, that she'd been riding hard and fierce that day, Mr Foley. And if there'd been no kill, she wouldn't be in the best of moods.'

A silence, then, that went on for a long time. The television and video were in the corner of the bedroom, near the window. Jane was sitting on a bedding box at the foot of the bed, and old Leonard seemed to be looking over her shoulder. She glanced behind, uncomfortable, as if Hattie might be there with her onion eyes. The bed was unmade, as though Ben had just rolled out of it. Or as if someone had pulled all the—

'And Mr Robert would soon know about it,' Leonard said.

Jane turned back to the TV in time to catch another silence.

Ben said eventually, 'What did she do to Mr Robert, Leonard?'

'He . . .' Leonard licked his lips. 'Next day, Mr Robert might have a black eye, or a big lip. Or scratch marks down his cheek. Or all of them. That was the wounds you could see.'

'She might have done damage you couldn't see?'

Leonard nodded very slightly. 'Sometimes he'd be limping.'

'And this happened after she *ran with the black hound*,' Ben said, with a lot of emphasis.

Leonard said nothing.

'Where did they go, Leonard? Did they hunt on the Ridge?'

'Oh, everywhere. For the local farmers, it didn't do not to let the hunt cross your land.'

'The . . .' Ben broke off, struggling to form a question. 'Leonard, when she said "black hound", did you have any reason to believe she might have been making some connection with the legend of the Hound of Hergest?'

Leonard smiled.

'You do *know* of the legend?'

''Course I do.' He looked stern again. 'And all that damn silliness.'

Ben let the silence hang for twenty, thirty seconds.

'Silliness,' Leonard said again.

'What do you mean exactly?'

'There was a bit of silliness when she . . . when they died.'

'In what way?'

'Oh . . .' Leonard looked cross. 'One of the maids said she'd seen a shadow of a big black dog go across the lawn.'

'When Hattie died?' Ben keeping the excitement out of his voice. 'Robert?'

'Oh, before. Before any of it. The night before, around

dusk, before it was dark. And the night before that, too. Or so she said. Just silliness, Mr Foley. Things get repeated and exaggerated, specially in country places. You don't want that on your programme, do you?'

'And Hattie – she knew about the legends.'

'Aaah.' Leonard's face twisted in exasperation. 'She'd no time for *legends*. History, now, she was interested in history. She always said this was her place, and her roots were here – even though they weren't, of course, because Stanner was still a new house then, even if it looked old. But she'd never known anywhere else, she was born at Stanner, so I suppose that was true in a way. And she used to go to the church and look at the graves.'

'Why?'

'I was never with her, Mr Foley, I was only the butler. Never been much of a churchgoer, anyway. Lost my two older brothers in the First War, and never saw much point to it after that. Got themselves killed before they were twenty-one, and here's me, ninety-three. It's all a lottery, Mr Foley, no God in this, I'm afraid. Or if there is, you can't rely on him.'

'What about Mrs Chancery? Did she go to church?'

'Well . . . she went to the church. Not to the services much, unless it was something to do with the hunt – a funeral, a wedding. When a member of the hunt got married, they'd all form an arch outside the church, whichever church it was, with their riding crops and they'd—'

'Leonard, why did she go to the church, if not to services?'

'To look at the graves, like I say. The big ones inside the church. I never go there, but aren't there some big ones inside?'

Silence.

Ben said, 'You mean . . . the tombs?'

'Ah. Sorry. Yes, the tombs.'

'Thomas Vaughan.'

'Him, yes. Black Vaughan. And the woman.'

'Ellen Gethin. The Terrible.'

'The Terrible, yes. Mrs Hattie, she used to say, *that*'s my ancestor, there in the church.'

Jane said, '*Shit*.'

'You're saying she described Ellen Gethin as her ancestor? This . . . take your time, Leonard, this is interesting. She said that this Ellen Gethin – the Terrible – was her ancestor?'

'I think she meant they were alike,' Leonard said. 'Or she liked to think they were. Did this Ellen hunt? I suppose she would've done.'

'What else?'

'Eh?'

'Did they have anything else in common?'

'Well, I don't know.'

'Leonard, if I remind you that Ellen Gethin killed a man in cold blood . . .'

'Did she?'

'You don't know about that?'

Leonard didn't look particularly interested. 'Well,' he said, 'I expect I must've heard about it once, a long time ago perhaps, but I've never bothered much with history.'

'You mean medieval history. Old history.'

'Knights and things.'

'But more recent history . . . Walter Chancery's time.'

Leonard smiled. 'That's not history to me.'

'Good,' Ben said. 'But first, can we . . . talk in some detail about the night when Hattie killed Robert?'

'I'd really rather not, if you don't mind, Mr Foley,' Leonard said. 'That wasn't what Frank said you wanted to talk about.'

'It upset you?'

'It upsets me still, Mr Foley. No point in upsetting yourself any more when you get to my age. It's all over, it's all done, it was a very tragic business, and it didn't do me any good at all in the long run. The children were too young, and it turned out there were huge debts. Mr Walter Chancery's younger brother came to sort things out, and I think he just wanted rid, and my services were the first to be dispensed with, thanks to . . . someone I could mention but won't. Anyway, Mrs Hattie, she always *valued* my services. Oh my Lord, yes. And I cried when I found her. I was in tears. I knew it was all over for all of us.'

The water in Leonard's eyes had become pools, and he turned his head away.

'I'm sorry,' Ben said.

'Switch that thing off, would you?'

The tape cut out and the TV screen went blue.

Jane just sat there, watching it, relieved in a way, because there was an awful lot to think about. There *was* a link between Hattie and the Hound, and the link was Ellen Gethin. Ellen in her long, girdled gown, the small cap on her head. *Comely wench*, Antony Largo had said irreverently. *Nice body.* And then Ben had said, *Me and Thomas and Ellen. I feel, in a strange sort of way, that we're kind of a team now.*

The TV screen flickered, and Leonard was back. It must have been some time later because his eyes were dry and calm now, and it was a different camera angle – Leonard's chair pushed closer into the window. A shirt-sleeved arm came into view, with a mug of tea or coffee on the end.

'There you are, Leonard.' Vaguely familiar voice.

'Thank you, Frank.' Leonard's hands wrapped themselves around the mug. 'You don't mind this, do you, Mr Foley?'

Frank Sampson, Jane thought, Arrow Valley Amateur Dramatics.

Ben said something inaudible.

'Yes,' Leonard said. 'That's all right. I'll talk about that.

I wasn't there, though, you understand that. I'm old, but I'm not *that* old.'

'You don't look a day over sixty, Leonard,' Ben said heartily, and Leonard giggled shrilly, and Ben started to ask him questions about Walter Chancery and his crass attempts to become a society host in his castle by the rocks. Leonard kept stopping to remind Ben that this was only what he'd heard from Mrs Betts, the cook, and a few others of the staff who'd been there many years, and Ben kept saying, don't worry about that, just keep it coming.

Leonard said it wasn't quite right about the Chancerys building the house from scratch. In fact, they'd taken it over from a business associate of Walter's, who was an architect and had done some industrial design for Walter. He'd built the house for himself, lovingly, over many years and had been killed when some masonry collapsed.

'Here?' Ben asked.

'No, no. On a site over in the Midlands. But he'd invited Walter and Bella to see his house, and Bella had fallen in love with it. And after this chap died, she urged Walter to buy it. They'd just found out Bella was pregnant and, of course, this made Walter more amenable to the idea of a new family home.'

Leonard then told a long story about how Walter had had all these stags' heads with huge antlers brought down from Scotland, and a suit of armour from a place in Gloucestershire. There was a duke came to stay once, Leonard said, or it might have been an earl.

'And Sir Arthur Conan Doyle?' Ben said nonchalantly at one point. 'Didn't they say Sir Arthur was there?'

Leonard looked thoughtful, then he smiled. Outside the window, a woman with a black labrador walked across the car park to a silver Ford Focus.

'Oh my Lord, yes,' Leonard said. 'No doubt about that.'

Jane thought she heard Ben's sigh, and if she hadn't heard it she'd sensed it.

But Leonard's eyes narrowed, and his hands came up, a forefinger quivering.

'But he never came back, you know,' Leonard said. 'That's why it's been forgotten. He came here the once, but he never came back, and you can quite understand that. When you know what they did.'

THIRTY-ONE

Noise and Blood

The hedgerows were swollen on both sides into vast white bales, the lanes squeezed down to one vehicle width. The snow was still falling, but in a desultory way, like a handful of pebbles after an avalanche.

The cab of Gomer's truck smelled of oil and sawdust and the suspension hung down on the left, as if the truck had a hernia.

'No, she hasn't really talked much about the mother,' Merrily said over the heater's phlegmy cough. She had on Jane's duffel coat, woollen gloves, a white woolly hat from the WI Christmas Fair, and Lol's scarf. And she was still cold. And chilled, which was different.

'We always knowed there was some'ing we *din't* know, Vicar,' Gomer said, 'that's the point. First the boy was gonner marry Mary Morson, then her's gone off with this naturalist feller from the Rocks. Next thing, this Nat'lie's turned up with her camper van and the kiddie, and they've moved into The Nant inside the week, and the ole van gone to Stanner Rocks. Burning her boats kind of thing.'

They passed a barn in a field, cloaked in snow, one of the few isolated barns in this particular area not yet turned into luxury dwellings, and therefore still available for farmer-suicides. It was nearly always the barn, the engine room of the farm. Barns had fully exposed hanging beams and trusses and bales of hay you could build up, steps to the gallows. Dozens of farmers in this area had gone out this way in the past twenty years. Something ritualistic about it: a dying breed speeding up the inevitable.

'Love at first sight?' Merrily thought of Lol, back at the vicarage: '*Go*' – pushing her mobile phone into his hands – '*This situation gets you over there, with a good reason. Two birds, one stone. I'll keep talking to Matthew. Keep it switched on.*'

'Seemed that way.' Gomer dipping his lights as they made it round a bend. Ahead of them, a small dead tree poked out of a field like a stiffened hand from under a shroud.

Merrily said, 'But?'

The truck started to skid; Gomer casually spun the wheels into it; the truck rocked and steadied and shaved a few inches from the left-hand snow wall. Gomer bit down on his thin ciggy.

'Other day, see, what happens is Danny comes home, finds Mary Morson there. Says this Natalie's been seen in her ole camper van up on Stanner. With a feller. Gettin' up to things.'

'Oh.'

'Well, Mary Morson, her figured they could get back together, her and Jeremy, if it all broke up – that's Greta's view of it. Likely on Mary's terms. Her'd wanner crush him first, then pick up the bits, ennit?'

'Likeable girl, then.'

'All heart. So Greta, her says to Danny, He's your mate, you better go tell him. Mary Morson, her en't gonner sit on this potato for too long. Well, Danny, his renowned diplomat skills don't extend to tellin' his mate his woman's playin' away.'

'Difficult.'

'Near impossible, for a Radnorshire farmer.'

'Who was the man she was with, Gomer?'

'Dunno.'

'Danny didn't tell him about it, but you think someone else did?'

'Mary Morson, mabbe her rung to break the news to him as he wasn't the only fish in Natalie's stream.' Gomer went silent for maybe eight swings of the wipers. 'Well, see, the thing is, you didn't always have to tell Jeremy things. He'd know. Wouldn't let on, mabbe, but he'd know.'

'Oh?'

'No big deal, Vicar. Well, mabbe now it is, but it din't used to be when farm life rolled along with no distractions, no form-fillin', no ministry inspectors on your back.'

'You're saying—?'

'Boy's what we used to call a natural farmer. In the ole sense. A *quiet* farmer. Goin' quietly on.'

Gomer turned left, and the many-tiered lights of a transcontinental lorry came into view, like a remote cocktail bar. Merrily pulled out her cigarettes and lighter.

'My ole mam,' Gomer said, 'her'd never leave part of an onion in the house. Use the lot, else throw the rest away, or put him on the fire. First new moon in May, my ole feller used to set about the nettles. You done it then, the ole nettles'd stay down. And they wasn't *that* superstitious, see. Just that most folk, they'd have one or two things they'd stick by.'

'Mmm. I count magpies, I'm afraid.'

'Jeremy's family, they knowed the lot. Why you never watches a funeral through glass. Why it en't right for a woman to come in first on Christmas Day, 'less her slept there the night before, and definitely *not* if her's wearing new shoes. Boy growed up with all that. *All* of it. Most youngsters, it gets to the stage when they rebels against the ole ways, only Jeremy's dad died when he was young, and he took over the farm when he was n' more 'n a child. Took on the farm, took on the traditions. Small world, no distractions. Found he had a . . . *haptitude*. You followin' me, Vicar?'

'Go on.' Remembering her Herefordshire grandad, his relationship with apple trees.

'Danny d' reckon it was like it was all talkin' to him: the ground, the trees . . . the stock. He sees stuff some of us mabbe don't notice, and it tells him things. Sounds like ole wallop, don't it?'

'A touch pagan, maybe.'

'Oh hell, no. Big churchgoers, all their lives, the Berrows. That's why Danny said could *you* come, take care of things now.'

'I see.'

'He . . .' Gomer hesitated. 'He never was good with people, see, Jeremy. Church services scared him. But he'd go on his own, see, when the church was empty, take bits of stuff for Harvest Festival when nobody was about. Time of the Foot-and-Mouth, he'd be there every morning and every night, on his own – not for long, mind, just slipping in quietly. And the Foot-and-Mouth stayed well away from The Nant. The Berrows ground, see, always been in good heart, never no chemicals.' Gomer gave Merrily a quick glance. 'I en't specifically implying nothin' by this, Vicar. Boy went quietly on, that was all.'

'You said he . . . knew things, without having to be told.'

Again, Gomer didn't offer a direct answer.

'Danny was over there earlier. Boy'd already brought his sheep down, cleared his track. So when he phones to ask if Greta can take this kiddie, Clancy, for the night, Danny knowed straight off some'ing was wrong. The woman always took the kiddie back to the farm at night. Then her went back to Stanner herself if her had to work late, like doing the bar.'

'So *she*'d stay the night, but she wouldn't have her daughter stay there.'

When Merrily had asked Jane if Clancy worked at the hotel too, at weekends, Jane had said Natalie wouldn't allow it because the kid was so far behind at school. Natalie was very strict about homework and early nights. Odd really, Jane had said, because she certainly wasn't the Victorian-parent type.

'But, Gomer, Jeremy must have known that Danny would be suspicious and go rushing up there. And that Danny would have the means to get through the snow.'

'Likely the boy wanted to be sure it was Danny found him, ennit?'

'Oh.'

Gomer switched off the wipers, and Merrily saw that the snow had almost stopped. You could see low cloud now, shifting like smoke, the pale suggestion of a moon behind it. They crested a hill, and there was Kington: a snug medieval snow-fantasy tucked under the white wings of the border hills. With its brave twinkling of Christmas lights, the town looked small and cosy; the hills didn't.

There were no visible lights in the Welsh hills. Sometimes, from outside, Wales loomed like a threat. It all relaxed once you were across the border, down in the pale, quilted pastures of the Radnor Valley. All the threat was in the space between.

'It's a . . . strange kind of place, isn't it? This valley. Hergest . . . Stanner . . . the, erm, Hound.'

'They don't talk about it, none of it, you know that. Not the local people.'

'No.'

Not even whimsy for tourists, she knew that much. Hergest Court, long since relinquished by whatever remained of the Vaughan family, was apparently tenanted most of the time, but never promoted as a visitor attraction. When you thought about it, very little of anything here was for the tourists.

'Temptin' fate, see,' Gomer said. 'You asks people, they'll give you, *Ah, load of ole wallop*. But they en't gonner tempt fate, all the same.'

'But, if the Vaughan family's long gone . . .'

'Temptin' fate,' Gomer mumbled, almost angrily. 'You don't *do* that.'

'Gomer, tell me one thing: you see *any* basic connection between the legend of the Hound of Hergest and the stuff you were telling me about the other night – whatever's been killing this guy Dacre's sheep?'

Gomer grunted. 'Has it?'

'Has it what?'

'Been killin' sheep. I en't yeard of any, save for Dacre's. And Sebbie . . .' Gomer paused, chopping down to second gear. 'Sebbie's losin' it, big-time. Fact.'

They came to the traffic island on the edge of town: an iced cake, uncut. Chances were nobody would get in or out of town tonight. The truck creaked around the island and on to the bypass via a shallow gully down the middle.

'Losing it how?' Needing a firmer handle on this before she went into the Berrows farm.

'On the booze. Givin' out daft sentences on the Bench. Makin' a spectacle of hisself in the pubs. Family thing, I reckon. Mabbe it all comes down to wassername . . . , genetic. Only, you feels it's in the ground, too, weighing it down like clay. Two attitudes to the ground, see, Vicar: either you goes quietly on, tendin' and healin', like Jeremy Berrows, or you goes roarin' over it, like with the hunt. *Whoop, whoop.*'

'Domination.'

'Makes you *feel* like you're in charge, I s'pose. I wouldn't know. Mabbe it's just about noise and blood. All I know *is*, there's what feels like a terrible rage buried somewhere in this valley. You take the tale of ole Black Vaughan – mad as hell, turnin' over market carts. The Hound in the night, the bull in the church. Blood and noise all around. Yere's Sebbie Dacre, Master of the Middle Marches: blood and noise. Like his granny. And in the middle of it all, this little farmer goin' quietly on, little island of calm. Can't be easy. Mabbe Jeremy, mabbe he was yearin' all the noise and blood poundin' in his head, gettin' closer and closer, until he couldn't take it n' more.'

'Maybe someone should've—'

'Sorry, Vicar?'

Rural stress came in many forms, most of them un-recorded, unrecognized by psychiatry.

'Doesn't matter.' Merrily tightened Lol's long scarf. 'Are we nearly there?'

With the lights of Kington behind them, they'd followed the bypass into a harder, lightless landscape, ranks of snow-caked conifers forming on the hazy edges of the headlight beams.

'What *have* they been shooting at, Gomer? Do *you* know?'

She'd been here many times, and she knew that when you turned the corner and cruised down into the Radnor Valley, the landscape and your spirits usually lightened. Only tonight they wouldn't be turning the corner.

'Likely shadows,' Gomer said. 'Shootin' at shadows.'

At first, Jane had thought like, Wow, the enterprise, the bravado, *the spectacle*.

Realizing in seconds that nothing else the Chancerys might have done could have been more blatantly insane. And in that situation today they would have known it – between them, they would have seen, for heaven's sake, a dozen crazy horror movies with the same simplistic message: don't meddle. A pulp cliché now.

They'd been mature people, people of wealth and status, and they'd behaved like irresponsible kids.

But, of course, they were Victorians – at the decadent end, verging on the Edwardian. Jane had done her social history and, at this particular period, in the heat and smoke of technological revolution, superstition belonged to the more primitive corners of the Empire. The Chancerys would have felt some kind of immunity, by virtue of being Victorians.

Jane sat down on the edge of her bed, looking at the window, a blackboard dusted with chalk, and still seeing the ill-fitting dentures of Leonard Parsonage working their way around the word *exshorshism*. The beetle-like personal mike distorting it, too close to his mouth because of the way his tie bulged out of his pullover.

Jane shuddered. Sitting there in the dark, with three inches of snow on the windowsill, she finally called home.

Not thinking too hard about what she was going to say. Fairly confident, now, that she could turn this around with Mum. Because it was a fact that if she *hadn't* kept quiet, stuck around, picking up pertinent information here and there, ear to the ground . . . well, no outsider would know the full extent of it, and that—

'Knight's Frome— sorry, Ledwardine Vicarage.'

Jane stiffened for a moment, not expecting this.

'*Lol*? Is that you?'

'Jane!'

'What are you *doing* there?' Mum and Lol: a secret love-tryst. The things that went on when your back was turned.

'Not enough,' Lol said. He didn't sound happy.

'Are you snowed in?'

'Kind of.'

'You and Mum?'

'I wish,' Lol said.

*

As soon as Merrily walked into the living room at The Nant, her gaze connected with the eyes of Jesus whose face wore a bleak smile of acceptance, his halo dull with weariness. Kind of, *Just get this over*. The picture wasn't as famous as *The Light of the World*, but it wasn't any more guaranteed to engender hope.

The half-mile track hadn't been blocked. Gomer had been able to drive up to the wall around the farmhouse, where Danny's tractor was wedged.

She stood near the living-room doorway, spotting the dog next: a sheepdog, more black than white. The dog's head was pointing upwards, between the knees of the man sitting on a wooden stool. The man was looking down at the floor. Behind him, a fire roared in the range, gilding perhaps everything in the room except the picture of Jesus.

Gomer prodded her gently into the room, and Danny Thomas stood up from somewhere.

'Mrs Watkins . . . Good of you.'

Now she was here she didn't know what to say, how to go about this. It was like the strangeness of the whole area was concentrated in this square, fire-lit room. And when Danny spoke, that was also surreal, initially.

'I, er . . . I had this album once, see. In my folky days.'

'Sorry?'

'Fairport Convention,' Danny said. His hair hung over his face like wet seaweed over a rock. '*Babbacombe Lee*. Period when Dave Swarbrick was writin' the songs? Before your time, I 'spect.'

'No,' Merrily said. 'I . . . I remember it.'

She stared at Danny, in his bottle-green farmer's overalls. The dog began to whimper. A log shifted on the fire.

'Oh God,' Merrily whispered. 'John Babbacombe Lee, the man they couldn't—'

Danny Thomas looked at her helplessly, his eyes wide with

anguish. Danny had been crying. 'Hang,' he said. 'The man they couldn't hang.' He pointed at the man on the stool in front of the fire. 'And that . . . that's Jeremy Berrows, the man couldn't hang hisself. Stupid little bastard.'

THIRTY-TWO

Party Game

'But he's all right?' Jane was sounding lost, disconnected, groping for certainties. 'He won't *die*?'

'Not if he stays away from rope,' Lol said.

Hanged. A weighty word, full of ancient resonance and with only one definition: execution.

'Lol . . . *why*? Why *would* he?'

Jeremy Berrows. A harmless, benign little guy, Merrily had said, when she'd called to tell him it could be a long night. There were things, she'd said, that didn't add up. Things that even Gomer couldn't put together.

'Was it like a cry-for-help thing, or what?'

'I . . . wouldn't think it's what you do when you're hoping someone's going to discover you in time,' Lol said. 'Meanwhile, keep this to yourself, OK?'

The lemon-yellow sleep light on the front of the computer was swelling and fading, swelling and fading. Here in the vicar's study, where madness collected like dust. Flaky fantasies in the phone lines, images of the irrational only clicks away.

'Why's Mum gone to The Nant? Why did Gomer want *her* to go? I need to talk to her.'

'If you do, it might be wisest to assume that she knows too much already for you to get away with . . . concealing anything.'

'Like what?'

'The White Company?'

'Oh my God, who's been talking? She knows about the documentary?'

Lol said nothing.

'Lol, look, all it was – I swear it – Ben and this guy Antony are shooting a TV thing about Conan Doyle and spiritualism, and Antony gave me a video camera. He wanted *me* to shoot stuff, when he wasn't there. So, like, I wasn't going to blow it, just because there were spiritualists involved. I mean, was I?'

'No, you wouldn't do that.'

'Only a lot of it was total bullshit. I was very naive. I was stitched up. I'm an extremely gullible person, and I wish I'd never come here, all right?'

'I'd like to make some time to cry for you,' Lol said, 'but could you tell me about The Stanner Project first?'

She was quiet for so long, he was beginning to think they'd lost the signal.

'Oh God, you really do know everything,' Jane said.

Merrily followed Danny Thomas back into the kitchen, shut the door.

'What about a doctor?'

Danny dropped a scornful hiss. 'What's a doctor gonner do for *his* condition?'

He went and half-sat on the edge of the kitchen table, hair matted on his face. When she'd put on the electric light, he'd switched it off again, as if there was something here that had to be contained in near-darkness to stop it spreading. A tongue of flame wavered on the wick of a small hurricane lamp on the draining board. This was the lamp that had been on a ledge in the barn when Danny had crashed in. When he'd seen something that he said was like out of a black acid-flashback.

'Thought I was too late. All the beasts in there moaning.'

And Jeremy Berrows in the meagre lamplight, stoically dangling.

Danny roaring in agony and rage.

Jeremy, seeing Danny in the entrance there, had started twitching and jerking, half-spinning on the rope, staring in terror at Danny out of his bulging eyes. *Trying, for fuck's sake, to finish it.*

'Sorry,' Danny said, meaning his language. Merrily waved it away, and Danny said he must've gone temporarily insane hisself at that point, fumbling out his clasp-knife, clawing his way to the top of the scaffold of bales, slashing like a mad bastard at the oily rope.

Lucky that Jeremy was old-fashioned about rope: none of your nylon for this boy.

'Stretched under his weight, see. So his feet's reaching the topmost bales, and he don't even know it. Only wondering why it's takin' so long.'

'Has he said anything?'

Danny shook his head. He'd caught Jeremy as he fell, laying him out on the hay, the boy making this cawing noise like a stricken crow, wearing the mark of the rope like a red collar, bruises coming up under it. Long minutes passing before Jeremy would let Danny help him up and into the house.

'Can he even speak?'

'Can't hardly move his head.' Danny was intertwining his hands, like he was washing them slowly under a tap. 'I can't do n' more for him, Vicar.' He looked hard at her. 'Can I?'

'Is there a medicine chest? First-aid box?'

'En't that kind o' first aid he needs.'

'Would help if he was able to talk, though. Has someone gone for Natalie?'

'We don't know where she is. En't at Stanner.' Danny

stood up. 'Ah, damn. My idea we gets you yere, now I don't know what to tell you. I still don't know what brought him to this. Things about this boy we en't never fathomed.'

'Gomer thought maybe he'd just found out about – ' she glanced at the door, brought her voice down ' – about Natalie? In the van?'

'Couldn't *tell* him, see, Vicar. Had the perfect opportunity, couldn't do it. Can't hardly ask him now, can I?' Danny hung his head, a slow smile shuffling into his beard. 'You could, though, mabbe.'

'Thanks.'

'And then ask him who she is.'

'Natalie?'

'Ask him who she is, really,' Danny said. 'This is what we wanner know, see.'

Sounding as if there was something here that he half-suspected but didn't dare approach.

'It's hard to believe how crazy they were, the Chancerys,' Jane said to Lol. 'You know about Thomas Vaughan. Black Vaughan?'

'A bit.'

'According to the legend, he was terrorizing Kington. After his death. The full poltergeist thing. The whole economy of the town under threat because people didn't want to go there.'

'This was when?'

'Fifteenth, sixteenth century? If it happened at all. Folklore seems to work to its own calendar, doesn't it? So they call in the Church. You know about that? Twelve priests confine the spirit in a snuff-box. Which might've been a metaphor – a way of explaining it to humble countryfolk who knew sod-all about states of consciousness but had a vague idea of what a snuff-box looked like.'

'Did it work?'

'To an extent. No more actual violence, just vague mani-festations, like the Hound. Like warnings that it was only dormant. Maybe . . . hang on a mo, I'm just putting the phone down.'

Lol heard Jane moving about. There was the sound of a door opening and then closing before she was back at her mobile.

'Thought there might've been somebody around. This place is suddenly full of totally unbalanced people.'

'Where are you?' The Jane he knew would relish being around totally unbalanced people.

'In my room. If the door had a lock I'd lock it. *Jeremy* . . . I don't believe it.'

'You OK?'

'Yeah, I'm just not sure who I can trust. Lol, if you talk to Mum, tell her we . . . would appreciate some help. But tell her to ring me first, not just show up.'

'Who's "we"?'

'Amber. And me. Everybody else seems to have a finger in the pie.'

Lol guessed he was about to hear things that Jane would never have passed on if she hadn't been shafted over the video.

'This is what Ben finally got from old Leonard. Walter Chancery got hold of the Vaughan story. Or rather, his wife did – Bella – who was well into this new fad for spirit-contact. See, what strikes me about all this is that it was probably the first time in recorded history when people weren't terrified by the supernatural. Like the birth of New Age.'

'Convinced the mystery of death was being unveiled to them.'

'Totally. So when Bella hears the tale of Black Vaughan, she's like, OK, let's look at all this in the light of – *wooh!* –

modern science! Meaning spiritualism. There'd been some sightings locally, mainly the dog – but when was that dog *not* seen around? So Bella Chancery's like, Hey, let's do something for the community. Lady Bountiful. These crass incomers, money coming out of their ears, but what they wanted was status – like in Society and also locally. They wanted to be lord and lady of the manor, that was how Leonard put it. They had a celebrated medium there by the name of Erasmus Cookson, who Bella shipped up from London. And because they were into spectacle and stuff, they all dressed up. They used the kitchen, because it had stone walls and it looked like you were inside a castle. The kitchen's quite big, and they arranged it like the great hall of a castle, with candles everywhere.'

'Why would they dress up?'

'For the exorcism. They recreated the exorcism of Black Vaughan. If you look in Mrs Leather you'll see there's quite a lot to go on. The dialogue between Vaughan and the priests? Total pantomime, but that wouldn't worry them.'

'Where did they get twelve priests?'

'Well, they didn't, obviously. Just got friends in – house guests, people down from London, and dressed them up like monks or something. And servants to make up the numbers. And this Erasmus Cookson, who was like some kind of showbiz spiritualist and who may have been a charlatan, for all I know.'

'And Arthur Conan Doyle?'

'And Conan Doyle. Absolutely. Doyle was in the area with relatives, right? In fact, one theory is that it was nothing to do with helping the community, they just – this is the kind of people they were – staged the whole thing for the benefit of this big celeb.'

'And what happened?'

'And they even had an actual snuff-box? You imagine that?

They were probably going to tie a brick to it and toss it in the sodding pond.'

'Hang on, Jane.' Lol awoke the computer, brought up Matthew's last message.

We believe that his initial baptism – a 'baptism of fire' – occurred at Stanner Hall . . . little more than a party game for his amusement . . . turned into something profoundly disturbing

'So what happened that disturbed Conan Doyle enough to send him into complete denial and turn the Hound into a detective story with a weak ending?'

'This is what Ben's asking. He videoed Leonard talking about it, and Leonard's telling Ben what I've just told you, and Ben's like, "What happened?" in his calm interviewer's voice, like he really couldn't give a toss. And Leonard's sitting there with this thin little smile on his lips, and Ben's going, "*Leonard, what happened*?" You can feel him just longing to walk into shot and shake the old guy – *I* wanted to. And Leonard's just shaking his head sadly. "Stupid stories, Mr Foley, to frighten the children, I'm not going to pass on stupid stories." And that's where the video ends, with this shot of Leonard sitting there shaking his head, with a bit of dribble at the corner of his mouth.'

'So after Ben showed you the video—'

'He didn't. He doesn't know I've seen it. Amber gave it me to watch.'

'So you don't know if he found out any more after he'd stopped recording – if this guy told him the rest, off the record.'

'No.'

'You're not going to *do* anything, are you?' Lol said. Because Jane, slighted, was an unexploded device.

'Look, if they're planning to recreate the recreation of the exorcism of Black Vaughan – yeah, I know, where do you get twelve priests in a snowstorm? – but whatever they have in mind, it's got to be spiritually offensive, hasn't it? So I've said I'd go along with Amber, who thinks it's time to talk to Mum.'

'You want her to raid the joint in the name of the Church?'

'She could *talk* to people. She's the Diocesan Exorcist, that must count for ... *Lol* ...' He could almost feel the heat of her breath in his ear, as if she was cupping her hands around the receiver. 'You don't think they *want* that?'

He saw where she was going. 'Jane, let's not—'

'According to Amber, Ben's original idea was that Mum would be part of the documentary – like formally protesting on behalf of the Church? But suppose what he really wanted was that she should be involved as an *exorcist*. If you were doing it now – putting Vaughan to bed – who else would you use? Lol, they—'

'Jane—'

Jane's voice was hoarse. '*Suppose they want her to take on Vaughan?*'

'That's crap.'

'It's so *not* crap, Lol. It's the sort of thing Foley would think of as soon as he found out what my mother was.'

'Jane.'

'What?'

'Don't *do* anything. Think of all the times you've been wrong and the damage it's caused.'

'Only maybe this time I'm not wrong,' Jane said.

Pocketing her phone, holding the videotape inside her fleece, she went out onto the upper landing and down the stairs that came out near the fire doors concealing the passage that led to Hattie Chancery's room.

She imagined Alistair Hardy lying in Hattie's bed, in the dark. Silverskin eyes watching him from a corner of the room. And then, as he was close to sleep, a hissing, and something cold writhing all over him: *whoop, whoop*.

Jane smirked. He'd probably enjoy it.

At least she now had an idea why Ben wanted Hardy in that room. With Hattie Chancery identifying herself with Ellen Gethin, and all that *black hound in the pack* stuff, there could be quite a strong link here . . .

Suppose Lol was right, and Ben *had* managed to get more information out of Leonard, even if it wasn't on camera. Well, she couldn't ask Ben outright without causing a row over Amber letting her watch the tape, *but* . . .

. . . but she *could* ask Frank Sampson, who'd been there holding Leonard's hand. It was a bit late but, if they were going to try and involve Mum in this, it was very much legit to give him a ring.

Right, then.

As she walked down the red stair-carpet, the videotape tumbled out of her fleece and went bumping down the final steps ahead of her. She grabbed the box, fumbled it back under her fleece, firing glances around the reception area.

Nobody about, not even Amber.

Whom, of course, she could no longer trust either. Amber might be planning to walk out on Ben, but she was just as dependent on this crazy investment as he was. She, too, had everything to lose.

And where was Natalie? Why hadn't she come back? Did she know about Jeremy?

This was a nightmare.

The phone started ringing behind the reception desk, Jane instinctively moving to answer it, then stopping. She stood by the desk, in the shadow-flecked light from the too-small chandelier, waiting to see if anyone else would respond.

Nobody showed. Not even a demented old woman, some years dead, leaning on the ghost of a Zimmer frame.

Jane ignored the phone, ran down the steps to the kitchen to put the tape back. The snow-glare from the high windows showed her where everything was; she didn't bother to put on lights as she walked across the echoey stone flags to the island unit, stretching away like a mortician's slab. Something was on top of the unit: the video camera that was supposed to be welded to her hands.

Stuff you, Antony, with your Glasgow hard-boy chic. Jane bent to the cupboard from which Amber had pulled the videotape, opened it up and slid the tape out from under her fleece, stowing it on an empty shelf. As she came to her feet, she noticed that the light in the room was changing colour, like someone had shone a torch in here.

She stood up, backing away to the nearest wall. The light didn't go out, it swelled yellow and orange, a reflection from somewhere igniting like a match in the lens of the camera on the island unit. She looked up, and saw that it was all concentrated in the nearest high window: a billowing light around an intense core, like a gas jet.

She didn't understand. If this was the window facing Stanner Rocks, then the rocks were on fire.

THIRTY-THREE

Time Nearly Up

Merrily had her coat off: no dog collar, but the pectoral cross on display.

'Jeremy, would it be all right if I were to pray with you?'

Wearing a white T-shirt with holes in it, he was hunched forward in the rocking chair, what seemed like permanent tears, hard as plastic bubbles, on the edges of his eyes.

'You don't wanner bother 'bout me.' His voice was high and gritty, as if there was sharp sand in his throat. He turned away and winced. 'Waste of space, I am.'

Merrily put both her hands over his. 'Don't move your head, if it hurts.' On her knees, she shuffled out of his line of sight, kneeling on the rag rug next to Flag, the sheepdog, in the furnace light from the range. Danny and Gomer had gone into the kitchen, leaving her to it, just her and the dog. The heat was intense, the dog was panting, Jeremy's seared throat looked like roast ham in the firelight.

Merrily closed her eyes.

'Oh God, only you know why Jeremy was driven to try to take his own life. Bring him from this suffocating place. Calm his emotions and his fears, strengthen him, give him the help he needs to . . .'

Couldn't go on. This was trite and meaningless. She was disgusted with herself and opened her eyes because she knew that he was looking at her. His eyes were blue-grey and flecked with uncertainty like the skies in March.

'Jeremy,' she said. '*Why?*'

Jane tracked Ben out of the lobby into the porch, shooting him as he bent to lace up his hiking boots.

'Jane, what the *hell* are you doing?'

She didn't reply, but took care to stay well back so he couldn't snatch the Sony 150 from her again. She didn't even know if the battery was still active; it was the gesture that counted. Independent working woman with a video.

Beth Pollen came briskly through, dragging on her sheepskin coat, shaking out her headscarf. 'Anyone called the fire brigade? Now I think about it, I'm sure I heard an explosion about twenty minutes ago. It's hard to tell in snow.'

Ben looked up. 'Amber's seeing to it. Though I can't imagine how they could get up there in these conditions. I don't even understand how a fire's even possible on snow-covered bare rocks.'

'I was involved with a Nature Trust survey some years ago,' Beth Pollen said. 'Awfully weird place. The rocks retain heat, apparently.'

'In thick snow?'

'Strange times, Ben. Doesn't look like a threat to the hotel, but you never know. I'll come with you, if you like. If you don't know the paths fairly well, it can be jolly dangerous.'

Ben snapped, 'For God's sake, Jane, switch that thing *off*!'

'Just obeying instructions.' Jane didn't lower the camera. There was a clear image of Ben's face, twisted with annoyance. 'Antony says it's supposed to be welded to my hands.'

'Well, *I*'m telling you to take the thing away, and I'm the one who's *paying* you, in case you—'

Jane ignored him, pushing open the swing doors with her bum and backing out into the car park, still recording. She had on her boots and her nylon parka, which was a pain because it was fairly new and still crackled when she walked, doubtless getting onto the soundtrack. But at least she was equipped for the conditions, unlike Alistair Hardy and Matthew, who were hanging around the porch door now, looking up at the smoking rocks like they were being deprived of some profound spiritual experience.

Outside, ankle-deep in snow, Jane put the camera on pause while she took up a position about ten yards away, shooting Ben and Beth Pollen as they came out and then risking a pan up towards the sky, ambered now and spark-flecked, though the flames were low, as if the gas jet had been turned down. She had no idea what this was about, but neither did Ben, and he was unnerved for once, and that made her feel empowered.

'Jane!' Ben was standing in the middle of the car park, at the end of a channel of light from the porch. He had on a black Gore-Tex jacket and a black baseball cap with a reflective yellow stripe. 'You're staying here, you understand? You are *not* coming up there with us.'

'If I fall, I promise I won't sue Stanner Hall.'

'If you want to keep your job – ' and he wasn't smiling ' – you'll go back.'

Oh.

Jane didn't move, carried on shooting him. It felt warmer, as though the fire on the rocks had conditioned the ambient temperature. Speaking down the side of the camera, right under the mike, she said casually, 'You sacking me, Ben?'

'Not if you go back at once.'

Although it had stopped snowing now, Jane felt the night still swirling around her: dark energy, shifting destiny.

'Tell you what,' she said. 'Let's not complicate things. I quit.'

Lol was leaning over Ella Mary Leather under the Anglepoise. The cover of the big paperback had this warm-coloured Merrie England watercolour street-scene, with a drummer and a dancing woman in a white dress. Post-it markers projected from the top edge of the book, like little coloured flags, part of the scene.

Herefordshire, 1912, the most rural county in England, with the unknowable horrors of the Great War still two years away. An area still loosely held in a harness of medieval customs, an eerie carnival always flickering on the periphery.

> Vaughan . . . was a very wicked man, so after his death he could not rest and came back 'stronger and stronger all the while . . .' He sometimes took the form of a fly in order to 'torment the horses'. Finally, he came into the church itself in the form of a bull. It was decided that something must be done.

Ethel strolled over the open book, sat down on the lamp-base and began to wash her paws – Ethel who used to be Lol's cat, back when he was living in Ledwardine. Who was now the official vicarage cat, while Lol was still just an occasional visitor, trying to help out.

'Something must be done,' Lol said to the cat.

> 'So they got twelve parsons, with twelve candles, to wait in the church to try and read him down into a silver snuff-box. For,' the old man who told me the story explained, 'we have all got a sperrit something like a spark inside we, and a sperrit can go large or small, or down, down, quite small, even into a snuff-box.' There were present, to help

lay the spirit, a woman with a new-born baby, whose innocence and purity were perhaps held powerful in exorcism.

'Well, they read, but it was no use . . .'

Read what? Something from the Bible? The full text of the Roman Catholic Rite of Exorcism?

. . . They were all afraid . . . and all their candles went out but one. The parson as held that candle had a stout heart, and he feared no man nor sperrit. He called out 'Vaughan, why art thou so fierce?' 'I was fierce when I was a man, but fiercer now, for I am a devil!' was the answer. But nothing could dismay the stout-hearted parson, though, to tell the truth, he was nearly blind, and not a pertickler sober man.'

The detail suggesting an actual local character. But no names, no dates.

'He read and read and read, and when Vaughan felt himself going down, and down, and down, till the snuff-box was nearly shut, he asked, "Vaughan, where wilt thou be laid?" The spirit answered, "Anywhere, anywhere but not in the Red Sea!" So they shut the box and took him and buried him for a thousand years in the bottom of Hergest pool, in the wood, with a big stone on top of him. But the time is nearly up!'

The time is nearly up.
Lol leaned back. 'How nearly is nearly, Ethel?'
A thousand years would take the story back pre-Norman Conquest. And yet Black Vaughan was said to have been mortally wounded at the Battle of Banbury, during the Wars

of the Roses, in 1469. And furthermore, according to Mrs Leather:

> He and his ancestors were brave and honourable men, and history in no way corroborates the popular traditions concerning them. Still they ... were probably regarded with more awe and fear than love by the folk among whom they lived.

But a devil? And when did the Hound fade into the picture? No suggestions of a big black dog accompanying Black Vaughan's ghost, pre-exorcism.

Lol flipped to the second index sticker.

> Hergest Court was, or perhaps still is, haunted by a demon dog, said to have belonged to Black Vaughan.

Said by whom? Lol went through to the kitchen, overlaid with Aga-throb, and into the passage to the narrow back stairs, ducking his head for the low oak beam at the bottom, although he was short enough, just, to walk underneath it. He felt uncomfortable here without Merrily. He didn't belong, and the vicarage knew it. He switched on the upstairs lights and went up to the first landing: crooked walls patched with old doors.

One of them to Merrily's bedroom. *Sleep there if I'm not back.* Kissing him in front of Gomer, which had been reassuring. But he'd still come creeping up by the back stairs, because he wasn't worthy, and the vicarage knew.

'Only, time's nearly up,' Jeremy Berrows said.

His face was haloed by the fire, like a monk's face in an illuminated manuscript. Like a martyr's face.

Time nearly up. Merrily wondered where she'd heard that phrase recently.

Jeremy let out a deep sigh, as though a decision had been made for him.

'Farm's on a lease, see.'

'This farm? I thought you owned it.'

'Folk do.' Jeremy fingered his throat. 'Me too, when my dad was alive.'

He'd started to talk to her, in a half-apologetic way, as though ashamed at the ungraciousness of his early responses. Danny had rescued him from himself, therefore Danny was owed, and Danny had brought in this woman to help. Perhaps a concession was needed.

And so Jeremy had conceded that the time was nearly up. The lease was nearly up? Was his suicide attempt linked to a fear – a fear he'd felt unable to share, even with his best friend – that he was about to lose his beloved home? Farmers had hanged themselves for far less.

Merrily glanced at the Welsh dresser, with its mugs and picture plates and a gilt-framed, faded photo of two children, a boy and a girl, both fair-haired, like brother and sister. It looked as if little or nothing had altered in here in thirty or forty years. What would Jeremy do when *goin' quietly on* was no longer an option?

'I . . . heard that Mr Dacre might have been putting it around that he . . . has some rights to The Nant.'

Jeremy shook his head just far enough for it to hurt.

'No?'

'Always reckoned it *should* be his, on account of he owns the rest of the valley.'

'It's said he's been behaving in a threatening way. Hiring men with guns, Gomer says.'

'He's scared.'

'What's he scared of?'

'He's scared of what they took on. His family. What was give to 'em.'

'The Chancerys? Your family were tenants of the Chancerys, right?'

He nodded, and then – evidently relieved that he could at least do this without pain, that it didn't hurt to be positive – he nodded again. Merrily wondered if Gomer and Danny were following this from the other side of the closed door.

'What did the Chancerys think had been given to them?'

Jeremy looked at her, like, *Do I have to go into this?*

She thought she knew, anyway: a tradition, roots. Gomer had told her how the Chancerys had sought to buy into the Welsh Border heritage. Not the most stable foundation on which to build a new dynasty.

Jeremy said, 'Don't suppose you seen Nat'lie?'

'We came straight from Ledwardine. I haven't been up to Stanner yet.'

'Her won't be there.'

'Where will she be?'

He didn't answer. He looked down at his knees, between which Flag had wedged his head. Jeremy placed his hands either side of the sheepdog's head, as if in benediction. Merrily let the silence hang for maybe half a minute before trying to catch his gaze and failing and then feeling her way back into the mystery of Natalie Craven.

'People talk. People like to gossip when somebody new turns up.'

He didn't say anything.

'They're only curious. They don't realize what damage it can cause when things get twisted around.'

'No.' Jeremy lifted his hands and placed a palm either side of his face, as if to stop his head from shaking.

'And if your friends don't know the truth either, they can't help you. They can't put a stop to it.'

'No.'

'Who exactly is she, Jeremy?'

Jeremy shifted to grip the dog's fur. The silence from the other side of the door was like a balloon blown up to bursting point.

'Her's my landlord,' Jeremy said.

The door handle rattled slightly as if somebody had just let go of it.

'*She* owns The Nant? Natalie?'

He nodded. 'Her name's not Nat'lie . . . din't use to be.'

'So that would make her . . .'

'Paula's daughter. Brigid. Paula inherited The Nant from her mother.'

'Hattie.'

Jeremy nodded.

'So, is Paula dead now?'

'Aye. Long time.'

'So Natalie came back to . . . claim her inheritance?'

'And mabbe find out some . . . things.'

Merrily thought of what Gomer and Jane had both said about Jeremy and Natalie: such an ill-matched couple. Perhaps they weren't a couple at all. Was one of them a kind of . . . lodger?

'Paula . . .' Jeremy looked at Merrily. ' . . . Not many folks know this, but Paula was sick, see. Her growed up sick. In the head. When Hattie and Robert died, her was still young, eight or nine, and Margery was only three. Things wasn't too good between the kids, so Hattie's uncle who come down to sort things out, he decided it was best if—'

'How do you mean, things weren't good?'

'Oh. Well, they reckoned Paula was always jealous of Margery and when they . . . Well, there was a bit of an incident when . . . I think Paula tried to drown her in the bath one time – they was only little.'

'God.'

'Well, see, Robert had a sister up north, and they took her in. They had to sell Stanner on account of the debts, so Paula got the only house left, which was The Nant, as was rented then to my ole man. Paula had the rent. In trust. But Paula . . . her wasn't right. Got took into homes, early on. They figured her wasn't safe. Set fire to the house once.'

'Oh.' This did not sound good.

'Margery, the Dacres adopted her, and she got left a couple hundred acres of land and some money, and her growed up and married the Dacre boy, Richard. Keepin' it all in the family, kind of thing.'

'These things happened . . .'

'And they had Sebbie ten year before Paula was even married, even though Paula was five years older. Met a feller in hospital. Male nurse. Paula was real good-lookin', he . . . fell in love, I s'pose. 'Ventually, he convinces the authorities to let her out. Short stretches at first, and he looked after her, and there was no problems. Then Paula was discharged and they got wed. Her'd be well into her thirties by then. But her . . . wasn't right, see. Should never've been let out, they reckoned.'

'She had a baby . . .'

'Then . . . died. Brigid growed up with her dad. They'd come yere on holiday, on the quiet – never wanted nobody to know about Paula, how she'd turned out. One stage, see, they offered to sell The Nant to my ole man, but he didn't have the money, nowhere near. So they negotiated another lease, for twenty-five years. So like, both sides agreed it be better if they let it get round they'd sold us the farm. Keep Richard and Sebbie off dad's back.'

'But now, you think Sebbie perhaps . . . knows the truth?'

Jeremy looked at Merrily at last. 'It's possible. Deal was done at the time through Big Weale, the solicitor, in Kington.

And when he . . . when he died, sudden, leavin' his whole business in a big tangle, this other firm come in to sort it all out. 'Course, Sebbie's a magistrate, knows all the lawyers for miles around. Things gets mislaid. Documents. Can't always trust lawyers, can you?'

'And the lease . . .'

'Lease is nearly up.'

'Dacre thinks he has a chance of getting you out and buying The Nant?'

'Can't say what he thinks. Dacre's in a funny state. Things he done lately en't been that rational.'

This from a man who'd just tried to hang himself. But Merrily's understanding of that was hardening up in the light of what she was learning about Jeremy's weakening grip on everything he held dear.

'So the future . . .' She didn't know how to put it.

'No.' Jeremy shook his head so hard that Merrily winced. 'It en't about *that*.' The agony of it made his eyes water and come out like marbles. 'En't about money, nor ground. I love the Nant, course I do, every square inch of it, only . . .'

Merrily looked up at him. Her knees were starting to ache.

'When we was kids, see – twelve, thirteen – her come to stay with her dad. They had a posh caravan. Me and her, we like . . . we got fond. Wrote to each other for years. All them years, I'm dreaming mabbe . . . mabbe her'll come back. And praying, I s'pose. Prayed a lot, truth be told. Prayers she'd come back.'

'And then she did come back . . . twenty-five years later?'

'Aye.'

'All that time—'

'Things happened, see. In her life.'

Merrily reached out and took one of his hands, squeezed it gently.

'I seen the van parked . . . where they used to put the

caravan. I was scared. I seen Clancy at first in the lower field in the early morning – it was like seein' Brigid, like her'd come back near enough the same as when I last seen her. I was scared . . . couldn't go there. I called up Danny, and he come down. Then we seen this woman . . . and her hair was dark – thought it wasn't her, after all, see. And then . . .'

Tears rolled down Jeremy's face. Tears coming without any change of expression, like a crying doll's.

Merrily thought, *But she stayed. She moved in, with her daughter. She put her daughter into a local school, got a job at the hotel, the house her family used to own . . .*

There were big gaps in this story. Big issues that he wasn't telling her about. She thought about the note that Danny had shown her when she arrived, Jeremy's prosaic farmer's farewell.

Please deal with the sale of my stock, and see they go to the right kind of place or keep everything yourself for nothing. Natalie will understand.

'He could've took the farm,' Jeremy said. 'Took The Nant. Took the lot.'

'Dacre?'

Merrily thought of what Gomer had said: *Mary Morson, mabbe her rung to break the news to him as he wasn't the only fish in Natalie's stream.*

Other fish. Worst-case scenario.

She looked over to the photo on the dresser: two light-haired children in T-shirts and shorts, screwing up their eyes against the sun. Standing side by side, not touching. The girl, even then, a bit taller than the boy.

She thought, in dismay, *Dacre?*

Dacre and his cousin in the back of a camper van on the top of Stanner Rocks?

'Could've had the lot if he'd left *her*.'

Jeremy looked away, back into the fire.

THIRTY-FOUR

The Butcher's Counter

Jane stayed where she was; no backing off now. Ben took an impulsive step towards her and then abruptly turned away and caught up with Beth Pollen at the little gate at the bottom of the car park. He threw open the gate and followed Mrs Pollen into the darkness of the clearing beyond, the place where he'd pulped Nathan, the shooter.

Bastard. Jane stood for a moment, feeling the cold on her face like a contemptuous slap, and then, breathing hard, she followed them.

I quit. That simple. Perhaps part of her had known this was coming, was unavoidable after what Amber had told her about the *good friction point*, the proposed use of Mum as a *twist*.

Twist. *Hook*. *Contemporary dynamic*. She didn't have to listen to this bullshit any more and, if he wanted some *now drama*, he could have it.

She was almost at the gate when she became aware of him standing just on the other side, by the fence post where Nathan had lain. He was alone; Beth Pollen must have gone on a little way; Jane could see a torch beam bobbing.

She stopped, keeping some space between her and Ben, clasping the camera to her chest. Maybe she'd have to hit him with it.

'Jane . . .' If he was speaking quietly that was probably

only because he didn't want Beth Pollen to hear. 'Jane, whatever you just said, let's pretend either you didn't say it or I didn't hear it. And while—'

'I said I qu—'

Ben raised a hand. 'While I realize you were the first one to spot the flames, I have to stress that I *know* this track, and how dangerous it can be. Also, I think I can smell petrol, so obviously someone started that fire. All I want to do is make sure nobody's in any danger.'

'You think someone's up there?'

'You're not going to be missing anything. It's irrelevant. It's probably kids.'

'So why's it OK for Mrs Pollen to go up?'

'She's not going up. She's making sure I take the right path and waiting at the bottom of it with the mobile phone. I wouldn't trust *you* to wait anywhere.'

'*I* think you know what this is about, don't you?' Jane said. 'I think you know what's happening up there . . .'

'Don't try to be clever, Jane.'

' . . . Why the rocks are on fire.'

'And don't—' She could almost see his patience snap like a frozen twig in the air above his head. 'Don't mess with me, all right?'

'Or what – you'll beat—?' She almost felt him go rigid, knew she'd gone too far, but it was too late to stop now. 'And aren't we in the perfect place for it? Where you worked Nathan over? Where Hattie Chancery smashed her husband's head in, with the trophy stones?'

She heard the squeaking of his leather gloves as his fists tightened, and she felt a tug of fear, remembering the state of Nathan. She looked around for Beth Pollen's torch: no sign now. She was backing up against the gate and feeling behind her for the fastener, jiggling it urgently when Ben moved.

She bit off a scream.

But all he did was turn, without a word, and walk off again, only faster this time, half-jogging, his hiking boots going *phwat, phwat, phwat* in the tight fresh snow. By the time Jane was through the wicket gate, he'd disappeared into the pines.

She knew that she ought to get out of there, go back to the hotel. But it wasn't in her to back down, not tonight. She found his tracks and followed them. The independent, unemployed woman on the Border.

The moment Lol entered Merrily's bedroom, the phone beside the bed began to shrill, and he felt momentarily guilty, as though someone had discovered him prying. Snowlight greywashed the room. He glanced quickly back at the door, impelled to go rushing out of it and down the stairs to take the call in the office.

Instead, he switched on the bedside lamp. The bed was turned down. There was a nightdress case like a black and white cat curled up on one of the pillows. A white towelling bathrobe hung behind the door. A cross of dark wood was positioned in the centre of the wall opposite the bed.

The caller had a voice like a rich, organic mulch. 'I'm phoning for Mrs Watkins. I do realize it's late.'

'She's out.' Lol sat on the edge of the bed. 'I'm sorry.'

'Guess I'd be sorry, too, I was in her house and she wasn't.' The caller chuckled. 'Well now, you must be the musician who would like to spend more time with the lovely Merrilee, but the situation, alas, forbids it. A concise name that rolls off the . . . Lon?'

'Canon Jeavons?' Lol said.

'But you should call me Lew. We just two guys with short names. You think we shorten our names in the belief it gonna streamline our lives? Ah, wait . . . *Lol*. Not Lon, it's Lol, correct? You know, I sometimes wonder, if I reverted to all three syllables of my own given name, whether perhaps it would slow me down enough that I didn't give half-assed advice.'

Lol looked around Merrily's bedroom. Its white walls were uneven, bolted together with twisted ribs of ancient oak. It had a pine wardrobe, no dressing table, no mirrors.

'You mean like *Reach out?*' he said. '*Embrace?*'

'Good,' Canon Jeavons said. 'She talks to you. Yes, I guess that's what I mean. On reflection, what I should've said was, *Be reticent, go careful.* That would be a slightly different approach, wouldn't it?'

'That would be exactly the opposite approach,' Lol said.

In between the wardrobe and the window, the bedside light was reflected from polished wood, and he spotted his oldest Washburn guitar, the one he'd left here at the end of the summer when he was working on the final songs for the new album.

'Lol,' Canon Jeavons said, 'you don't *have* to tell me where she's gone, but you could reassure me it's nowhere in connection with a small boy who died in a car wreck.'

Lol saw that the Washburn was shining with new polish and had been stood reverently on a cushion. The cushion was pale blue, velvet. He was touched.

'No, it isn't anything to do with that,' he said.

'Thank you,' Jeavons said solemnly. 'Can I ask – are you a religious man yourself, Lol? No forget that. Intrusive. Only, when I said *on reflection*, I mean that this phone call came out of prayer. Which, I concede, the secular might define as a conversation with the inner self in the hope of inspiration. In any event, I sit down and we going over it all between us. And the message comes to me: better to tell her to take advice before proceeding any further in this matter.'

'She did take advice,' Lol said. 'She took advice from you.'

A pause.

'Yes,' Jeavons said heavily. 'However—'

'Let me get this right – *God* suggested you might call back. Because He wasn't impressed with the advice you gave?'

'Lol–'

'She told you about the brother?'

'The bad guy.' Jeavons sighed. 'Yes. The, ah, acts of violence carried out by the brother against the other half of the family, that did not bode well. Six years in New York, and I didn't pick up on that. Must be getting old.'

'As it happens,' Lol said, 'what we now know of him makes him seem even less of a teddy bear.'

'I'm sorry to hear that. It . . .' Jeavons hesitated. ' . . . must be hard for you, Lol.'

'It can get a bit perplexing.'

'I like a man who understates. Come *on*, it blows your head off! For instance, where is she now, on this terrible night?'

Lol watched the light shimmer from the guitar, recalling the last song he'd composed on it and its key lines: *The camera lies/she might vaporize.*

'Well,' he said, 'I hope she's having a quiet one-to-one with a mild-mannered farmer who tried to take his own life. I hope she *not* standing in for twelve priests at the exorcism of a medieval devil and a hound of hell.'

A stony place, quilted with snow.

The path was here somewhere, but Jane couldn't find it. She'd gone blundering after Ben into the white areas between the trees, looking for his tracks, until she wound up, panting, at the fork in the main drive. This was where one track sloped down to the Kington bypass, while the other, much narrower, crawled to the top of Stanner Rocks.

She'd been up there just once, when the weather was still

OK. Great views. The track wasn't too steep, and you could get a vehicle up when the ground was firm, but it went very close to the edge, where the old quarry had been, and you wouldn't be happy doing it at night, not even in the best of conditions, not even with somebody like Gomer Parry at the wheel.

She saw the stems of the pines lighting up maybe fifty yards ahead of her, like organ pipes – Ben switching on a torch? Only it seemed to be in the wrong place. Too low. So easy to get disorientated in the white hell. She headed for the beam, anyway, and—

'*Aaah!*' A thin branch whipped her cheek, pulled the camera away, and she stumbled, and the camera fell into the snow.

Not too clever. She snatched up the Sony 150 and dusted it off. Moved on more slowly, holding it in both hands. Now she could neither see nor hear Ben or Beth Pollen, and the torch beam had vanished, and if it wasn't for the snow and a lemon-wedge of moon she could be in trouble here.

Jane stopped, realizing in dismay that this actually wasn't being very adult. Being adult was about standing back and rethinking your position in the light of changing circumstances. Like, circumstances were saying that Ben Foley didn't want her here – basically, she guessed, because he didn't want any of this preserved on video. Taking on Ben, getting into his face, was probably unwise. But once you were launched on the path of *being awkward*, it was a matter of basic pride that you didn't turn away. It was like when you were a little kid, running faster and faster, giddy with it, knowing that the fall was inevitable.

Jane stubbed her toe on something very hard and stumbled and went down with her hands in the snow, throwing up a fine flurry like a cloud of frozen midges, as she pulled them out with a sucking sound.

Looking up she saw, in a moment of cold awe, the white-spattered face of Stanner Rocks, sheered off where the quarrying had been before the rocks were recognized as ancient and precious. The wall was glowering over her like a decaying cathedral, holes in its masonry pointed with snow. No flames up there now, no amber halo, only the milky mixture of snowlight and thin moonlight. And on the ground, that wet sucking sound.

Only the sucking was *nothing to do with her*.

The shock of this came at Jane like a sudden wild gust from nowhere, as she crouched, exposed, in the snow. It came at her along with something else – something close up, loping, something that came with a loose, heavy panting, with a pulsing of muscle and with a piercingly thin, raw, feral smell that ripped at your senses like barbed wire.

Jane tightened up, shrinking into a hedgehog ball. Somewhere far inside her – beneath the parka and the fleece, beneath the skin – there was a rolling orb of cold that felt no bigger than a pea and no smaller than a planet, coming to rest in her stomach and weighting her to the rock. And although she couldn't seem to move, she could still scream, with no shame, like an animal.

And cower, biting down on a second scream – also, agonizingly, on her tongue – as the ground lit up around her.

'For goodness' *sake*!' A gloved hand came out of the light. 'What's the *matter* with you?'

'Oh God.' Jane was shaking, kept falling back down.

'Are you hurt?' Beth Pollen was bulked out by the sheepskin coat, throwing off some wholesome, matronly perfume, her voice mature and strong and unafraid.

'Didn't you hear it?'

'I certainly heard *you*.'

'Didn't you *feel* it?'

'I really don't know how your mother puts up with you,' Beth Pollen said crossly.

Jane stood up, careful to stay within the torch beam, aware of holding on to Mrs Pollen's tough, sheepskin sleeve and not, under any circumstances, wanting to let go.

'Where'th . . .' The tip of her tongue swelling where she'd bitten it. 'Where's Ben?'

'Gone down to the main road to wait for the fire brigade. In the end, he didn't need to go all the way up the track to see what had happened. It was pretty obvious.'

'What was?'

'It was that old camper van, used by all kinds of people for all kinds of purposes – some idiot had contrived to set it alight, and the petrol tank blew up. Ben doesn't think anybody was in there, but if they were— Come on, we may as well go and join him; there's nothing we can do here.'

'*No . . .*'

'Jane, it's very cold and I'm—'

'You didn't hear it, then?'

Beth Pollen peered at her. 'What are we talking about?'

Jane was holding on to Mrs Pollen's arm with both hands, just couldn't seem to let go. The torch beam was dragged away over the uneven ground. They were on the floor of what had been a quarry, between the snowbound bypass and the sheerest face of Stanner Rocks, going up maybe a hundred feet then some more in jagged stages, before the summit sloped back into the forestry behind.

There was a distant warbling: fire engines. The real world. Jane sagged, relieved for maybe the first time in her life to be slipping back into a place where the arrival of fire engines could make everything all right.

She let go of Beth Pollen's arm. It occurred to her that this was the first time she and this woman had been alone together, one-to-one. On every other occasion, others had been there – Ben or The White Company, of whom Mrs Pollen was the most . . . normal.

'You . . . know my mother?'

'I know *of* your mother,' Mrs Pollen said.

'Only Amber said you might want to talk to her.'

'Did she?'

'Before you— What's *that*?' Jane grabbed at Mrs Pollen's arm again.

'It sounds like the fire brigade at last, thank God. What *is* the matter with you?'

'No . . .' Steering the torch towards the rocks. '*That*.'

Pointing to an area about ten yards away, an area of white but a different kind of white: the splodgy, pink-spattered white of the butcher's counter.

'You really are a tiresome girl,' Beth Pollen said.

And then she said, 'Oh my God . . . Oh my *God*.'

Part Four

Then, as it would seem, he became as one that hath a devil, for rushing down the stairs into the dining hall, he sprang upon the great table . . . and he cried aloud before all the company that he would that very night render his body and soul to the Powers of Evil if he might but overtake the wench.

From The Baskerville Manuscript
Sir Arthur Conan Doyle, *The Hound of the Baskervilles*

THIRTY-FIVE

Fresh Blood

She hardly recognized the place. It was like some unfinished centre for asylum seekers: cavernous and hollow, echoing with alienation and confusion. Displaced people wandering around, clusters of coppers in uniform and crime-scene technos in coveralls like flimsy snowsuits.

Merrily saw Ben Foley standing near the foot of the baronial stairs with a youngish guy in black-framed glasses and an older man in a suit. Foley had his hands behind his back, hair swept back from his long face, lips compressed. He looked defiant, which suggested that he was deeply worried. Amber Foley came past with a tray of coffees, her hair white under the chandelier.

'Lovely!' A policeman taking the tray. Amber didn't notice Merrily; Amber was keeping busy. But when the copper carried the tray away, Merrily spotted Jane.

There was this lopsided Christmas tree with wan, white lights, and the kid was standing next to it, a video camera dangling from a strap around her neck, as though this was all she possessed. She looked like some stranded backpacker whose passport had been stolen on her first trip abroad.

Merrily was about to go to her when DS Mumford faded up like the house detective in some drab old *film noir*.

'Mrs Watkins. How're you?'

'Bewildered, Andy.' If Mumford was here, it suggested Bliss was running the event, therefore care was needed.

'Remarkable how quick you made it, considering the conditions.'

'Gomer's good at snow. And I'm afraid you take risks when you're worried.'

'Gomer, eh?'

'He heard about it from Danny Thomas. Word travels fast in the Radnor Valley. So I thought that with Jane's involvement, I'd better . . .'

No need at all to tell Mumford that Jane had managed to ring Lol, and Lol had phoned her at The Nant . . . which would have meant explaining how she and Gomer had come to *be* at The Nant and . . . like Jeremy Berrows didn't have enough problems.

There had been fire engines and police Land Rovers at the rocks when they'd got here. Warblers and blue beacons in the snow, the *son et lumière* of violent death. Gomer had dropped her by the porch, gone to park the truck.

'Andy, I think I'd better have a word with Jane.'

'Well, the boss has just sent for her,' Mumford said. 'He *might* be amenable to you going in. Seventeen now, isn't that right?'

The last legal umbilical slashed – Jane was old enough to be questioned by the police without a responsible adult in attendance. Merrily saw that the kid's hair was pushed back behind her ears, like it had lost the ribbon. As usual in these extreme situations, she looked about nine.

The door marked *lounge* opened now, and a woman came out. Late fifties, well-managed white hair, sheepskin coat.

'Thank you, Mrs Pollen.' Frannie Bliss was holding the door for her. 'We may need you again. Sleeping here tonight?'

'I'll be here, Inspector, but I can't see any of us getting much sleep, can you?'

THE PRAYER OF THE NIGHT SHEPHERD

Bliss looked almost sympathetic for a moment. Then he spied Jane, and then Merrily about fifteen feet away. His small teeth glittered through the freckles. Where most police put on a severe front in the face of serious crime, Bliss rarely attempted to disguise extreme glee.

'Little Jane Watkins. And her mum, valiantly battling through the snow in the old Volvo.'

'Gomer's truck, in fact,' Merrily said, clasping Jane.

'*Mum—*' Jane's lips against her ear. '*Did Lol . . .?*'

'Gomer.' Bliss grinned, like a young dog-fox casing a chicken run. 'Of course. And me thinking God had parted the snowdrifts for you, like the Red Sea.'

'A miracle in itself, Gomer Parry Plant Hire.'

'He'll do anything for you, won't he, Merrily? Come through.' Bliss stepped aside, holding the lounge door wide. 'It's not the Ritz, but, hey . . .'

'You can handle hardship.'

'The poor Durex-suits are out playing in the snow. They may be away some time, as someone once said. Dr Grace, the Home Office pathologist, is with them, moaning pitifully. What a night, eh?'

Merrily followed Jane into the lounge.

'I do like this room,' Bliss said. 'Don't you? It's like, "I've called you all together here in the drawing room . . ." Who's that old bugger over the fireplace?'

'Sir Arthur Conan Doyle,' Jane said tonelessly. 'Ben uses this room for his mystery weekends, pretty much like you just said.'

'Perceptive of me, Jane.'

A single fat log smouldered on a bed of ash in the grate below the blue-tinted blow-up of the great man's face. Maybe it was the same picture as the one on The White Company's website: Doyle in middle age, his eyes fixed on something the photographer couldn't see.

'Mr Foley kindly agreed to us having this as our incident room – for tonight, anyway. We'll see he's recompensed, we're very good about things like that. It's bloody cold, mind.' Bliss went to peer at the fire. He was wearing an old blue fleece jacket over jeans.

'The central heating will have gone off by now,' Jane said. 'They weren't expecting so many late guests.' She nodded at the fire. 'All Ben's logs are still green. He doesn't know anything about wood-burning. It's softwood, nicked out of the forestry.'

Bliss glanced back at Jane in curiosity. The kid's face was expressionless-to-sullen. The boss no longer a hero, then. Bliss grabbed a poker, battering the solitary log in search of heat under there, and Merrily took the opportunity to whisper in Jane's ear, '*I came directly from home, OK?*'

The kid nodded briefly, maybe brightening a little, possibly even grateful at being gathered into her mum's confidence. Lol had briefly explained about the video camera, the proposed documentary. '*Go easy on her, eh? What would you have done at that age?*'

'You know, Merrily . . .' Bliss stood with his hands on his hips. 'I realize you're *peripheral* to all this – that this is Jane's show – but when you're present I always know that other angles I might've found a trifle, shall we say, *puzzling* . . . will be covered. Mrs Elizabeth Pollen, for instance. Now what on earth would that be about?'

'Mrs Pollen's a member of The White Company,' Jane said.

Merrily said, 'I don't know Mrs Pollen personally, but The White Company seems to be a spiritualist group set up to continue the efforts of Arthur Conan Doyle to prove there's life after death.'

'Thank you. Do we *need* proof, Merrily, you and me?' Bliss rubbed his hands together, kindling energy, and moved over to a mahogany writing table set up in the bay window. It had an unlit repro-Victorian oil lamp on it, with a green shade. There was a hard chair either side of the table. 'No,' he said, 'we're mates, let's go and sit by the fire. Statement later, Jane. Just a cosy chat for now. You know me.'

They sat down, mother and daughter, on a sofa. And Merrily, who *did* know Bliss, too well, became wary, because Bliss didn't *do* cosy. All she knew was that there'd been a fire up on the rocks and then a body found below. Found by Jane, this was the problem.

Merrily felt a draught on her ankles; she was still wearing Jane's duffel coat, her fingers enfolded in the white woolly hat on her knees. Through the window, she could see someone trudging across the sludgy car park towards the porch: Gomer, back from learning what he could from some cop or a fireman; there was always somebody around who Gomer had known for years.

'So,' Bliss said. 'What *were* you doing at the bottom of Stanner Rocks on a night like this, Jane?'

Jane shrugged. 'We saw a fire on the rocks. *I* saw a fire. From the kitchen. Ben and Mrs Pollen went to check it out.'

'Why you?'

'Because . . .' Jane sighed. 'Because I was helping them to shoot a video, about Stanner Hall and . . . stuff. It looked kind of dramatic. And I had the camera with me.'

Merrily watched Jane. The kid had the camera on her lap. She was more subdued than Merrily had ever seen her in the presence of Bliss who, on other occasions, had brought out the worst in her. Merrily sensed a weight of suppressed evidence.

Bliss put his head on one side. 'And did you get some nice piccies, Jane?'

'Not really. The fire was more or less out by the time we got there. Because of the snow, I suppose.'

'Right, then . . . tell me how you found what you found.'

'Well, like I . . . got kind of separated from Ben and Mrs Pollen. Like, you stop to get a good shot of the skyline and stuff, and when you've finished they've gone. And then I saw a torch beam, and that turned out to be Mrs Pollen. Well, she found *me*. I like . . . I hadn't got a torch and I fell. In the snow. And I suppose she heard me and . . .'

'Nobody else about?'

'Er . . . no. Not as far as I know.'

'How long were you separated?'

'Only a few minutes.'

'And where was Mr Foley?'

'He'd like . . . Mrs Pollen said he'd gone part-way up the path towards the van and saw it was burning out and nobody seemed to be in there. So he just went down to the road to wait for the fire brigade. Would've been easy for them to miss the turning, especially with all the snow.'

'So just you and Mrs Pollen.'

'*She* must've told you all this.'

'Just you and Mrs Pollen. You saw nobody else.'

'No.'

'OK . . .' Bliss leaned back. 'I realize this is distressing, Jane, but what exactly did you see?'

Jane swallowed. 'It was like . . . half-buried in the snow. There was a lot of blood. And it was . . .' She looked up towards the cracked cornice around the ceiling. 'Bits seemed to have been torn away. Bits of . . .' Jane shuddered ' . . . face. And . . . like, tissue. Strewn about.'

Merrily put a hand on Jane's arm. 'How long had it *been* there, Frannie?'

'Foxes,' Bliss said. 'We figured foxes had been at it. Or

badgers. Doesn't take them long sometimes. 'Specially on a night like this, if there's fresh blood.'

'Do you know who it was yet?'

Bliss stretched his arms. 'Well, as it happened, I could've identified him meself. Except even I wasn't *entirely* sure, because, as Jane says, it was all a bit messy.' He leaned forward, hands on his knees, looked at Jane and then at Merrily. 'Reason I knew him is I'd had to give evidence a couple of times when he was on the bench.'

'Oh?' *Jesus.*

Bliss paused. He'd be wanting to see if either of them knew the name. Merrily said nothing.

Jane blew it, of course. '*Dacre?*'

'Sebbie Three Farms, as he's known,' Bliss said. He leaned back again, beaming at Jane. 'So where have you come across him? Not in court, obviously.'

'Gomer,' Merrily said quickly.

'*Gomer.*' Bliss beamed. 'What a useful little feller he is.'

'However, I don't suppose Mr Dacre was actually killed by foxes avenging all their relatives.' Merrily said, wanting a cigarette. 'Did he fall from the rocks, or what?'

'He almost certainly *did* . . . but whether it was accidental is open to debate. Would a local man, aware of the dangers, go for a stroll along Stanner Rocks in these conditions? If he was contemplating suicide, death would be far from a foregone conclusion – it's not all that high, is it?'

'Maybe he went up to see what the fire was?' Jane said.

'It's a thought, Jane. Or did he *start* the fire? Or did he catch someone *else* starting the fire?' Bliss stretched his arms luxuriously above his head, yawning pleasurably. 'It's a complete mystery, isn't it, girls? I do love a mystery.'

Except that he didn't. There was nothing, in Merrily's experience, that real detectives hated more than a complete mystery.

Which meant that Bliss knew what he was looking for and that it was only a matter of time.

On the village square, the Christmas tree lights had gone out, and the security lamps outside The Black Swan were fogged and feeble, like the hopeless eyes of someone bound up tight in white bandage.

Standing by the landing window, Lol felt helpless. He was stranded.

Canon Jeavons had been most disturbed to hear Jane's theory about Merrily and the Vaughan exorcism. A dangerously unpredictable situation. Give him some time to investigate this, think things out, and he'd be back.

In the meantime, Jane had called again.

'*The police are here now. Blue lights, I can see the blue lights out of the window. Or maybe more firemen. I'm up in my room. I've been sick again. I just ran straight up here to be sick in the toilet. Plus I didn't want to talk to any of them. I don't trust any of them. I want out of here. When you talk to Mum, just tell her . . . tell her I want to go home.*'

The phones went off in stereo, from upstairs and downstairs – bleeps and bells all over the vicarage, like the phones were crying out to each other. Lol ran down the stairs, through the hall, plucking the cordless from the kitchen wall.

'Hope I'm in time, son,' Lew Jeavons said. 'You wanna make some notes?'

'Hold on.' Lol moved to the scullery door, shouldered it open. 'I'll go in the office.'

The scullery was lit solely by the orange bars of the electric fire. He moved to the desk. The lemon sleep-light on the computer was swelling like something medical. He found a pen, sat down.

Sprang up again. 'Oh!'

'You OK, Lol?'

'Yes, I . . . Could I call you back?'

'Sure.'

'Right.' Through the window, Lol could see the snow-slumped apple trees and the flattened face of Dexter Harris, his jug-spout lower lip squashed up against the glass. 'Give me ten minutes.'

THIRTY-SIX

First Snow Casualty

When Jane realized how close she was to losing it, she backed away into the corner of the bedroom farthest from the window.

'Mum, he *couldn't*. He's gentle, he's entirely harmless. He's the only farmer round here doesn't even have a shotgun.'

'Look, *I* don't want it to be the truth either—'

Mum was sitting on the side of the bed, her face as grey as death. The two of them up here, with the lights out, exchanging information. Like spies, Jane thought, inside an enemy fortress. What she'd learned had, at first, just blown her away: the revelation that Natalie was the daughter of Hattie Chancery's child. Natalie Craven was *Hattie Chancery's granddaughter*.

That she was Sebbie Dacre's cousin. Jeremy's landlord. And that she was in fact called . . . *Brigid*?

So it looks like she's still doing it. They can't stop. It's a physical need. HOWARD. *I have been dreaming about her for about 20 years. she still makes me swet.* GAVIN

The implications would connect, at intervals, in a disjointed kind of way, and Jane would hug herself, the nylon parka crackling electrically.

'We should go home. We know too much.'

Meaning she didn't want to learn any more, not tonight, couldn't handle it. But Mum didn't want to go home. You could sense it in the way she was sitting – the duffel coat untoggled, hands on her thighs, resisting cigarettes only because it was such a small room and Jane was in it, too, and this was no night for opening the window. In some ways, Mum in the middle of something was no better than Bliss.

Avoiding the Foleys, Jane had brought her up two flights of stairs, along underlit passages, to this poky fridge, not imagining that things were going to get worse.

'You're a priest. You don't have to tell Bliss anything. It's like the sanctity of the Confessional. They can't make you. Not even in a court of law.'

'I don't actually think that applies in this situation. Anyway, that's not the point. God, it's freezing in here, Jane. Has it always been like this?'

'They can't afford luxury accommodation for the servants.'

They'd been talking about the camper van. The one that Nat and Clancy had arrived in, like gypsies. The van in which, according to Mum, Nat was said to have been seen, with a man. At first, Jane had refused to believe it. Stood to reason that when someone as good-looking as Nat arrived in a place like this, women would resent her on sight. When she had the brass nerve to hook up with an unmarried local farmer, the gossip machine would be white-hot, and all gossip machines manufactured disinformation.

'I'm sorry,' Mum said irritably, 'I wish I didn't even have to think about any of this. He's been in love with her for most of his life, even I could see that. Be nice to think love never had any negative side effects.'

'He wouldn't.' Jane pressed herself into the corner in despair. 'I don't know him well but I know he wouldn't. He couldn't. Clancy says he won't even send stock to market, because they have to suffer in pens, so they go direct to the slaughterhouse. He's an honourable farmer. He actually cares about living things.'

'He tried to hang himself.'

'That doesn't prove anything.'

'It poses questions.' Mum stood up and went to the window. A row of white-capped conifers stood like a primitive rood-screen between the hotel grounds and the long, pale altar of Hergest Ridge. 'And the other one is, where's your friend Natalie?'

Jane said, 'The last time I saw her, she was telling Ben she had to take Clancy to a neighbour's because the track to The Nant was blocked. Which it obviously isn't, so . . .' Jane felt sick. Somebody was lying.

'We know she took her to Danny Thomas's, but where did she go then?'

'All I know is she didn't come back here.'

'If she went to meet someone at the van—'

'Dacre? You're saying she was having sex with her cousin, right?'

'*I'm* not saying anything, flower, except that Jeremy and Dacre are not exactly mates, and if Jeremy happened to catch Dacre at the van with Natalie, then you don't know what might happen.'

'But *she* knows, right, and that's why she's keeping out of the way?' Jane felt her brain flailing around. 'A *lot* of people hated Dacre.'

'So it seems.'

'OK, listen – suppose she's having a thing with Ben? Don't look like that, Amber thinks it could be happening. She was like . . . she said to me the other night, kind of throwaway, that Ben would . . . that he'd be better off married to Natalie. Maybe seeing if she got a reaction, seeing if I knew.'

'Jane—'

'If Ben and Nat *did* have something on the go, they couldn't very well do it in the hotel, could they? And Ben was *so* anxious to be first on the scene of the fire. Without me there. Without video. Suppose he'd started it?'

'Why would—?'

'If *I* hadn't been in the kitchen at the right time, nobody would've spotted that fire, so like no wonder he was mad at me. No wonder he wanted to get up there to make sure it was fully destroyed. Because . . . DNA? Whoever was with Nat, they'd have left DNA all over the van, wouldn't they? Doesn't fire destroy DNA? Like at Gomer's depot?'

'And Ben killed Dacre as well, did he?'

'He nearly killed Dacre's shooter!' There was suddenly a hard sensation in the pit of Jane's stomach. It felt like certainty.

Mum's fingers were squeezing her knees. 'We should . . . stop speculating.'

'How do we do that, take sedatives? Like, Nat was even telling me she wouldn't be surprised if Amber walked out on Ben.'

'When?'

'Earlier tonight. She *wanted* Amber to walk out, didn't she? It's *blindingly* obvious. And also when Antony – Antony Largo, the TV guy? – was eyeing up Nat, Ben was *very* quick to warn him off. He's like, Keep your filthy paws off my house-manager, she's in a relationship. Well, yeah: Smoothie Ben and Foxy Nat? You gonna tell Bliss or shall I?'

'I don't think either of us needs to tell Bliss anything. I think he knows something already. He's too confident.'

'He's always like that.'

'In front of you, maybe. I think we should wait to see

what happens before interfering.' Mum sat for a while on the edge of the bed, rocking backwards and forwards. 'Wouldn't mind another chat with Jeremy, though.'

'That's your way of not interfering?'

'He talked to me before. He was still talking to me when Lol rang. Gomer and I said we'd come back and tell him what had happened.' She stood up. 'At least you'll be safe here with half of Hereford CID on the premises. Just don't . . . don't be alone with Ben Foley. Or anyone else, for that matter.'

'Am I stupid?'

'Don't tempt me.' Mum wrapped her scarf around her neck.

'Mum—'

'Mmm?'

'You'd better see this.' Jane dug *The Brigid Document* from her jeans, opened it out and tossed it on the bed.

They found Gomer in his truck on the edge of the car park. He jumped down, a half-inch of glowing ciggy slotted into his front teeth like a red jewel. He extracted it.

'Cops brought out the base of a paraffin lamp, Vicar. Likely the oil was used to start the fire, somebody emptied it over some bedding, whatever'd burn easy. Made a pile of it, set it alight, buggered off.'

Somebody opened both doors of the hotel porch and yellow light splashed out into the slush. 'Nothing left?' Merrily said.

A man in white leggings came out of the porch, carrying a bulky leather holdall, and got into a police Range Rover with orange traffic markings.

'Not much at all, Vicar. Only Sebbie, and he en't sayin' a lot.'

'Who did you get this from?'

'Les Thomas, Danny's cousin – one o' the part-time fire boys. Les also says—' Gomer lowered his voice. 'Says the cops is runnin' this big search for Natalie Craven.'

'On what basis?' Merrily asked.

'Mrs Watkins . . .' None of them had noticed Sergeant Mumford coming over; he moved quietly for a fat slob. 'Boss can see you now.' Mumford glanced at Jane. 'On your own.'

Lol had found deep footprints across the snowy lawn: two sets of them. One coming, one going.

Dexter Harris had come in through the old gate from the orchard, walked across to the lighted scullery window, peered in and then returned the same way before Lol could get round there.

Maybe the sight of Lol through the window had been a disappointment. If he'd seen Merrily here, alone, would he have come to the door? It was a disturbing thought, and something even more disturbing occurred to Lol when he was back behind the computer.

How sure was he that it had, in fact, been Dexter? Hadn't got a *very* good look at him in the kitchen earlier. Suppose, this had been the other one, Darrin? The bad guy. How alike the cousins were in appearance he had no idea, but he knew they were about the same age. The lower lip might have been exaggerated by being pressed against a wet window.

What must it be like here for Merrily now that Jane was away at weekends? For a house right at the heart of the village, it was surprising how isolated the vicarage seemed in conditions like these.

Something must be done.

Nothing, however, he could do tonight.

Lol sat down and rang Canon Jeavons back.

*

The lounge door was half-open and she could hear Bliss on the phone. He sounded irritated. 'Yes, I will. I already had. I'll ask her now.'

When he brought Merrily in, they sat this time at the table near the window, either side of the unlit Victorian oil lamp.

'The Ice Maiden's been called in,' Bliss said. 'Perfect night, eh?'

'Annie Howe? Is she coming here?'

'God forbid. No, she's on another one. This, er . . . this is something and nothing, Merrily, but you might be able to help us.'

'I heard you were looking quite seriously for Natalie Craven,' Merrily said.

'And where did you hear that?'

'She works here, Frannie, where else would I hear it? And she seems to be missing.'

'Yes, she is.'

'And you're looking for her.'

'Yes, we are.'

'And her daughter?' Would he know about Clancy being at Danny Thomas's?

'Her, too,' Bliss said.

'And the van that was set on fire was originally Natalie's, I believe.'

'Yes, it was.'

'You don't want to talk about this, do you?'

'No, I don't. Unless you can tell me where she is.'

'No, I can't. However, I do get the feeling that you know a lot more about her than you're saying.'

He leaned back. 'Oh?'

'Like that her real name's not Natalie Craven.'

'And what would her name *be*, Merrily?'

'Brigid?'

She could tell by the absence of reaction that Bliss was very surprised.

'You want to tell me about it?' she said.

'You little bugger,' Bliss said. 'Who else knows?'

'Who else knows what?'

'Right, Merrily,' Bliss said, 'we'll deal with this. But first let's get the other matter out of the way. Before Annie Howe arose from her coffin, I'd already heard from Melvyn at headquarters. The custody sergeant? Feller I consulted about your friend . . . forgotten the bugger's name, now . . .?'

'Dexter Harris.'

'Dexter. And his cousin, Darrin. Not Harris, Hook. Darrin Hook.'

'That's right.'

'Dead,' Bliss said.

'What?' Full-beam headlights blasted the window. An engine was revving on the car park.

'First snow casualty of the night. Run over by a van.'

'Where?'

'Ah,' Bliss said, as Mumford came in.

'Dr Grace, boss. Would like to see you.'

'Send him in. Excuse me a minute, would you, Merrily, been waiting for this.'

Merrily was half out of her chair when Mumford said, 'On site, boss.'

'Bugger.' Bliss stood up. 'All right, tell him I'll be there in five mins.' He nodded at the lights outside the window. 'For me?'

'When you're ready.'

Merrily put herself between Bliss and the door. 'What is this, Frannic? What happened to Darrin Hook?'

'Look, Merrily, I've just gorra— Can you—? All right, do you want to come with me? We can talk on the way.'

'Well . . . OK.' She stepped back and, pulling on her coat,

followed him out into the lobby, where he was stopped by a lanky detective in red Gore-Tex.

'This bloke Berrows, boss.'

'You've talked to him?'

'Not happy about him at all. Let us go through the house, no problem, but he'd got another guy there with him – Thomas – old hippy type, said he was on all-night snow-clearing. Said he'd been clearing Berrows's track. Tractor outside, fair enough, but something didn't feel right. Would've liked to bring him in, really . . .'

'Not yet. Not while there's a chance she might come home. You sure you checked all the buildings?'

'I'm satisfied she's not there, boss, but Mal and Ewan are watching the entrance, in case.'

'As long as the bastards don't fall asleep.'

'They fall asleep in this, boss, they'll never wake up.'

'They'll certainly wish they hadn't,' Bliss said. 'Come along, Merrily.'

Outside, new snow was falling in a careless, disdainful way, like the contents of God's shredder. The back door of a police Range Rover was hanging open. 'After you,' Bliss said.

She didn't move, both boots in a cake of brown slush. 'What happened to Darrin Hook?'

'All right.' He sighed. 'What's more interesting is *where* it happened. He was found on the A465 Hereford to Abergavenny road, halfway down the hill towards Allensmore.' He glanced at her. 'Yes?'

'I'm sorry—?'

'The proximity of a bus shelter leads Melvyn to think we may be looking at the exact spot where Darrin's little brother died. You coming?'

THIRTY-SEVEN

The Schizoid Border

The lights flickered again, the third time, and there was a crackle on the phone. In this area it was always the same with sudden heavy snow or any kind of extreme weather, including heat. The power lines and the phone lines were badly maintained, compared with the cities, and at some point they would go down and the centuries would drop away.

'*Black shuck, skriker, barguest, trash*,' Canon Jeavons said. It was like an incantation.

'Regional names for the phantom black dog,' Lol guessed.

'You dealing with archetypes. Heavy tribal stuff. The twelve priests, the snuff-box . . . and, of course, the black dog— The black dog is known all over these islands, and he's linked strongly to the landscape. He's *out there*.'

The lights dipped again, the reduced wattage reducing colours, giving the scullery the appearance of an engraving. Static cackled in the phone. Lol looked across at the window, convinced that he could still see the smeary impression of a man's face on the glass.

He was recalling Nick Drake's song 'Black-Eyed Dog', about the personalized depression at the door that had haunted him to death.

'Let's *talk* about the black dog,' Jeavons said. 'What is he? The shadow of fate? And why a dog?'

'Because a dog follows you?'

'Haw! Correct. The black dog that follows a family through the generations. And is always out there.'

Nick Drake had sung of the black-eyed dog that knew his name. 'Only, this one's described as demonic,' Lol said.

'A word open to many interpretations. I would say they are . . . representative of a layer of existence that it would be unwise to trust. I believe these images exist, I believe we should accept that but never attempt to relate to them. For there can *be* no productive relationship.'

'Unless you're interested in knowing about the imminence of death,' Lol said.

Bliss said to Merrily, 'You don't have to look.'

Sebbie Dacre's body was in a canvas shelter isolated on an island of white in a choppy sea of slush. There was industrial noise, industrial light and exhaust fumes coming from three sides. Nothing was silent, except for Sebbie Dacre in his shelter and the ruched and fissured rock face behind it, feathered and tufted with fresh snow.

And she did have to look. Because Jane had. Because Jane had been the first, after the foxes and the badgers, to discover this. She had to know what Jane had seen.

Two arc lights lit the area, powered by a small, chattering generator. Bliss lifted the canvas flap.

'Don't throw up here.'

The dead man's head sat on the corded collar of a withered old Barbour. His face, upturned to the ceiling of the shelter, was like the inside of a sliced tomato. The canvas also covered an ugly archipelago of blotchy things in the snow.

Enough. She turned away. Bliss let the flap fall.

'From the second ring of tape up to the hedge, it's all but useless,' one of the Durex suits said. 'Obviously, the fire brigade didn't help, trampling all over the perimeter, dragging bloody hoses. That whole area, up to the hedge, that's a complete write-off.'

'You'll get there, Jacko.' Bliss turned to Merrily. 'This is Jacko the Soco.'

'He just likes saying that,' Jacko said. 'Francis, I've sent the first set of stills and the video down to the hotel. You *have* got a laptop over there? Hey up, here he is.'

A man with a beard came over, scraping back the hood of his coverall. 'Francis, you little *turd*! Had a glorious long weekend planned, starting with me and my nursie tucked up by the fire with balloon glasses of Remy and a DVD of *The Blair Witch Project*.'

'It's a let-down, Billy,' Bliss said. 'You were spared a lot of disappointment. Go on, surprise me – give me a time of death to within two weeks.'

The pathologist unzipped his coverall and pulled out a Mars bar. 'Blood sugar comes first this time of night, matey.'

Merrily slid into the shadows. It was how they handled it – almost everything that didn't involve young children. Like wartime, she supposed. Frannie Bliss and Dr Grace lived in a permanent war zone, littered with hard jokes and Mars wrappers.

There would be a similar scene at Allensmore, if more subdued.

It was a big van carrying carpets, Bliss had said, that ran over Darrin Hook. The driver said he hadn't seen him. Which was understandable, as Darrin was already lying in the road amidst a lot of snow, his head two feet from the central white lines. In these conditions, with all the warnings and diversions, traffic was sparse, even on a main road.

Darrin had been sharing a rented flat with another bloke in a big former hotel near Wormelow, a few miles from where he was found dead. He might have been walking home or attempting to hitch-hike. There had been a half-empty bottle of Scotch in Darrin's jacket pocket, and the body smelled strongly of alcohol.

'Merrily, he was a scrote,' Bliss had said in the Range Rover. 'A toe-rag. A hopeless case. He got pissed, and disorientated. He fell into the road. Fellers like that, it happens to them all too frequently.'

'At exactly the same spot his brother died?'

'Life, Merrily, is full of accidental irony.'

'He killed himself, didn't he? He drank a lot of whisky and then he lay down in the road and waited for a lorry *at exactly the same spot*—'

'As he doesn't seem to have left a note, we may never know. But he'd been known to us for many years and appeared to have had connections with what we grandly refer to as the Hereford drug trade. So the Ice Maiden's looking at this more closely and wondering if *you* might know of any reason why Darrin might have been the victim of an intentional hit-and-run – on the basis that the carpet-van driver was not the first to squash his innards. That's the trouble with Melvyn – on a long night in the custody suite, he'll talk to strange women.'

'She's ruling out suicide?'

'Your theory's unlikely to have occurred to her. Perhaps you should talk to her. Sorry about that.'

On the edge of the disused quarry, Merrily turned her face up to the spattering sky. Darrin Hook was dead, and the location of his death linked it firmly to another death, seventeen years ago. And the chances were that Darrin, whatever kind of human detritus he'd been, would still be alive if some meddling priest had not suggested digging the whole thing up again by holding a Requiem Eucharist for Roland Hook in a – get this – *an attempt to cure his cousin Dexter's asthma*.

Healing and Deliverance: a creeping neo-medieval madness inside the collapsing ruins of the Church of England. She was feeling almost sick with self-disgust.

She wondered if Alice knew yet.

'Give me that again,' Bliss said to the pathologist.

'I'm not saying it's a fact,' Dr Grace told him, 'I'm saying it's worth looking at. Won't know a thing for certain till I get this chap back to the slab.'

'But it's probable, right?'

'It's *possible*.' Grace looked up at the face of Stanner Rocks. 'It's a substantial drop, but it's not exactly Beachy Head, is it? And he did fall into thickish snow. Now – and I believe one of your more athletic people has some of this on video from the top of the rocks – there *were* signs of disturbance. As if our friend tried desperately to clutch at outcrops and projections on his way down. Which would have slowed his descent considerably. Therefore – bottom line – broken bones likely, death far from inevitable. *Could* be he was awfully unlucky and his bonce bounced off a sharp rock at the bottom – you'll have a better idea of that when we move him and they can have a good sift around. But it very well may *not* be. Extensive facial injuries, even allowing for scavengers. That's as far as I'm prepared to go.'

'The alternative being that he was clobbered before he fell. That's what you're saying?'

'I'm *not* saying. But bear it in mind.'

'Oh, I will, I will.' Bliss was already heading for the Range Rover, lifting a hand to the pathologist. 'Nighty-night, Billy. Do a good one.'

Merrily was ringing Alice Meek on her mobile and not getting an answer.

It seemed to be some kind of guilt trip. Jeavons seemed to think that, having given Merrily some hasty and unreliable advice on the Harris/Hook issue, he had ground to make up.

He'd been researching intensively in his library and on the Internet, like it had become his responsibility to dispense wisdom on the Stanner case, details of which he'd gathered greedily from Lol. Family history, tribal traditions, race memories, curses – Jeavons's primary area of operation. Now he was retired, he said, it gave him a buzz to work all night.

'Does the black dog ever kill sheep?' Lol asked. 'Conan Doyle had his Hound ripping a man's throat out.'

'Seems unlikely, doesn't it, if the black dog is just a walking portent? And yet livestock are often known to have been attacked in areas supposed to be haunted by them. We may wonder if living canines, from foxes to domestic dogs, might in some way be influenced by the proximity of such entities.'

'Animals becoming possessed?'

'Another difficult word. Perhaps. In a way. I like you, Lol, you don't make light of such things, nor give the impression that you consider me to be mad and dangerous.'

'Oh, you're dangerous,' Lol said. 'But then, so are psychiatrists and psychotherapists.'

Jeavons did his *haw haw* laugh. 'And we share jargon with these professions – no coincidence. They are the new shamans, the smoke-and-mirror profession. The necklace of skulls under the suits and the white coats.'

'The twelve priests and the snuff-box,' Lol said. 'What's your take on that?'

'Archetypes, too, though less common than the black dog. The twelve priests represent the twelve apostles, and occasionally there may be mention of a thirteenth, the Man himself. This is widespread in folk-lore. And in fact the Vaughan exorcism itself is replicated further up the Welsh Border. At Hyssington, near Montgomery, we have a wicked squire who terrorized the area after his death. Like Vaughan, he appears in the local church as a bull. In this same church, the ubiquitous posse of parsons is waiting, with lighted candles. Like Vaughan, the squire gets reduced to something that can be accommodated in a snuffbox.'

'So what's that saying about the Welsh Border?'

'Borders are psychic pipelines,' Jeavons said. 'What you have here is a river into which streams of belief flow, from both England and Wales. This is a particularly interesting part because of the way Wales and England seem to inter-mingle. The original boundary was the Dark Age earthwork, Offa's Dyke, so how come we have an English town – Kington – which, according to my map, is on the Welsh side and a few miles away, a Welsh town – Presteigne – on the English side?'

'Schizophrenic,' Lol said.

'You have it! The Schizoid Border. Hey, we cookin' here, son. Consider the symptoms of the condition: delusion, hallucination . . . loss of identity, the withdrawal into a fantasy world.'

'The landscape of the mind is more important than the outside world and it becomes impossible to distinguish between them.'

Lol thought about isolated communities caught between two cultures, emotionally, politically and linguistically. Never sure where they stood in big national conflicts – like the Wars of the Roses, in which Thomas Vaughan was involved on both sides at different times.

The Schizoid Border.

'It's all bollocks, of course,' Lol said. 'You can make anything fit into psychology. It's why I packed it in and went back to writing little songs.'

But Jeavons wasn't letting go.

'Let's take this a little further. Localization of archetypes, OK? The appearance of the spectral bull up at Hyssington is immediately put into a local context – Oh, it must be the ghost of old so-and-so, he was a bad-tempered guy, he must have turned into a bull when he died. But – hold on here – as recently as the 1980s, a ghostly bull is seen in Kington Church by a woman visiting the area . . . whose name happens to be Vaughan. An indication that such phenomena can actually *become* personalized.'

'Yeah, but Thomas Vaughan doesn't seem to have been evil or tyrannical. So what's the evil that needs to be dealt with by this apostolic assembly of priests?'

'Can't tell you. The obvious target might be paganism, which I would guess survived in this area well beyond medieval times. The Christian Church lures the spirit of paganism into a holy place and relentlessly reads the scriptures at it until it becomes exhausted and shrivels into insignificance. It may simply be the spirit of paganism, or something more sinister . . .'

'Tonight, you could get the feeling of something more sinister.'

Lol told Jeavons about the discovery of a man's body at the foot of Stanner Rocks, torn about by some creature.

'Who is this man?' Jeavons said.

'Unlikely to be a Vaughan. The family died out in that area.'

The lights dimmed again, with a clicking from somewhere in the hollows of the house, and there was another dragged-out crackling in the phone.

THIRTY-EIGHT

Big White Bird

'I do, Jeremy,' Danny said. 'I remember.'

They had mugs of tea, another fat ash log on the fire. Danny was sweating, inside and out.

Yes, he remembered that summer. Because it was the Oldfield summer, the summer after *Hergest Ridge*, the album, came out, and the Ridge was world-famous as the tourists arrived to see where the celebrated composer had flown his model gliders. Only by then, Mike Oldfield was either leaving Kington or had already left.

Bitter-sweet memories. Danny never did get to hang out with Mike in his studio; however, that same year he *had* managed to persuade the gorgeous Greta Morris to go out with him.

He sat now, in front of the range, watching Jeremy Berrows fizzing into some kind of paranoid life in the wake of that visit from the police. The bloody hugeness of this. It was gonner light up this valley like SAS flares. Sebbie Dacre. *Sebbie Dacre*. Dead. *Killed*.

Danny had taken the call when the bloke rang for the vicar, to say that her daughter had found a body at the rocks. The idea of it being Sebbie had never even occurred to him, and Danny thought about him and Jeremy trying to look normal when the police had told them. Cops hadn't been fooled, he could tell.

And yet they'd gone. They'd looked around The Nant and they'd gone. They were looking for Natalie Craven and the child. He could've told them where the child was, but he'd held off. Didn't want to tell nobody nothing right now.

Had it occurred to the cops that Jeremy might have killed Sebbie and Natalie, too? Had they thought of that? Because Danny sure bloody had.

The lie about the track being blocked so the kid couldn't come home? The hurried note? The *hanging*, for God's sake . . .

Danny hung on to his mug, letting solid old riffs plash and bang in his head to hold him halfway steady. Let him talk, let it come out.

'We was only little kids that first holiday,' Jeremy said.

'I remember. Little blonde girl.'

'Playing around the farm, walking down to Kington for ice lollies. We never had a fridge back then, the seventies.'

Danny looked over at the dresser. 'That's you and her, ennit, in that photo? Don't recall seein' it before.'

'Always kept it in my bedroom. Kept it in a dark corner, so I couldn't hardly see it proper, most of the time, but I didn't want it to fade, see.'

Danny rubbed his beard. 'Jeremy, I just never imagined. Mabbe because she was real blonde then, and now her's dark.'

'Blonde as ever was, underneath. Nobody expects a blonde to dye her hair dark, do they?'

'Funny Greta don't know 'bout that. Bloody hairdresser's, that's the intelligence centre of the whole valley.'

'Does it herself. It was . . . the second time, see. The second holiday they had yere – that was when it really happened.' Jeremy was fondling the dog's ears, remembering. There was almost a smile on his face, over the ravages of the rope. 'Brigid's ole man, he was a nice enough feller. Quiet sorter bloke, but friendly. Wanting to know all about the farm, what this did, what that did. Tried to help with the shearing, made a bugger of it, but we told him he was doing well for a first-timer. Never talked about Paula. Brigid—'

Jeremy had to stop, tears in his eyes like broken glass. Danny remembered this time well: a damp, forlorn period, heralding the soulless eighties. Mike Oldfield had left the area for ever, and the world had already forgotten about Hergest Ridge.

'We was only about twelve. Too young for – too young to do much about it, anyway, although . . .' Jeremy flicked a sideways look at Danny, like, *What am I doing, talking like this to a bloke?* 'We was in the ole barn this day, sheltering from the rain. Brigid was . . . you know how they get sometimes, girls, women: moody. En't nothin' in the world that's right. No pleasin' 'em, no talkin' 'em out of it. So I suppose we kind of quarrelled, the way kids do.'

'*You* . . . quarrel with somebody?'

'Quarrel was with herself. Me as got hit, mind.'

'Where?'

'In the old barn.'

'No, you fool—'

'Oh. In the eye.'

'What did you do?'

'Nothing. What *could* I do? What would I want to do?'

Danny nodded. *Please, God, don't let him have done this.*

'Next thing, her arms is round me and her's sobbin' away, up against me, all soft. And then we kissed, real gentle. First kiss, Danny.' Jeremy looked up, flushed. 'Her fell asleep in my arms. And then I suppose, eventually, I fell asleep, too. Woke up with a black eye. And in love. You know?'

Danny smiled.

'Puppy love, my mam said. Be over it in no time at all.'

'They don't know, do they?'

'When she left, I didn't wanner live for a good while – you know how that is?'

Danny nodded. 'Course he knew.

'Couldn't sleep much, not for months. Used to creep out and spend whole nights, till dawn, out in the meadow with the ewes, then stagger off to school and fall asleep over the desk. Used to go up the church, times when there wasn't nobody else there, and I'd pray to God to send her back. Pray to God, Danny. Had a special prayer I'd wrote down. Figured if I kept repeating it, every day, real sincere, he'd bring her back.'

'God listen?'

'Not till last summer.'

'Bloody hell, Jeremy, poor ole Mary Morson never had a hope with you, did she?'

'Nice girl, mind.'

'*Mary Morson?*'

'They all got their ways.'

'Bugger me,' Danny said faintly.

'I wrote to Brigid, regular, she wrote back. Every week, more or less. The next summer I was thinking, *they'll be back*. Lookin' out for the caravan, you know?' Jeremy shivered over the fire. 'I remember, tried to phone her once. Got through to her dad. He said I couldn't talk to her. Her sounded different – harsh, wound-up. Said never to ring again.'

'And so you didn't.'

'How'd you know that?'

Danny sighed. Jeremy sank down in his chair, all the breath whispering out of him. The dog whimpered.

'Some'ing yere I en't getting,' Danny said. '*Why* couldn't you talk to her?'

'Danny . . .' Jeremy turned to him, full face, and Danny wasn't sure which caused the boy the most agony, the twisting of his neck or the thought of what he was saying. 'Some'ing *happened* . . .'

Danny had the feeling he ought to know, but he didn't.

'She was Brigid Parsons,' Jeremy said. 'That's what happened.'

Back at Stanner, the cold air dropping around them like a shroud, Bliss said, 'So how well do you know Natalie Craven?'

When Merrily had tried to raise the issue in the Range Rover, he'd nodded towards the driver and shaken his head, so she'd gone back to thinking about Alice, wondering if she ought to ring Lol, see if Alice had phoned. However Darrin Hook had died, it was going to damage Alice.

She followed Bliss into the porch. 'Don't know her at all. Jane's at school with her daughter. Which is how Jane got the job here – Clancy invited her over one weekend, and the Foleys were looking for cheap Saturday labour.'

'But you know who she is,' Bliss said.

'I know *who* she is . . . and I know . . .' She cleared her throat, swallowed. 'This is one of the things I was going to tell you in the Range Rover. We think – Jane and I think – that Natalie Craven may have taken the girl to Danny Thomas's house for the night, because they thought the track to The Nant could be difficult. Danny's the guy who was with Jeremy Berrows. He's . . . Gomer's partner.'

'What?'

'I'm sorry, Frannie. There was no reason to think—'

'Where?'

'It's a farm. Back off the Kinnerton road from Walton. Not sure what it's called, I—'

Bliss had surged into the lobby, leaving the door swinging back on her. *Hell.*

When she went in, the tall detective who'd been to The Nant to talk to Jeremy padded across the worn carpet.

'Mrs Watkins, could you phone the chief, please, in Hereford?'

'Annie Howe?'

'Not a happy bunny tonight, the chief.'

'Has she *ever* been a happy bunny?'

He grinned. 'Use my mobile.' He keyed in the number for her, and she sat down in a chintzy chair near the reception desk.

Annie Howe answered on the second ring.

'Ms Watkins. The fourth emergency service.'

Howe was an atheist, younger than Bliss, seriously educated, promoted over his head and on course for the stratosphere. She wore crisp, white shirts and pencil skirts and rimless glasses and smelled, Jane would insist, of Dettol No. 5.

'You wanted to, erm, talk about Darrin Hook?'

Merrily recalled the last time she and Howe had been together, in a derelict hopyard in the Frome Valley last summer, in circumstances that Howe was likely to have erased like a virus from the hard disk of her consciousness.

'Oh, yes,' she said. 'I'd like you to tell me *everything* you know about the late Darrin Hook.'

'Well, I . . . I only found out about him in a roundabout way – through his aunt, who lives in the village.' No harm in going into this; whatever you thought about Annie Howe, she didn't gossip. 'She was worried about a rift in the family, stemming from the incident you obviously know about, seventeen years ago, when Darrin Hook's young brother was killed. The other person in the stolen car, the cousin, Dexter, has suffered health problems ever since. Their aunt wanted me to . . . pray for him.'

'Pray for him.'

'I don't expect you to identify with this, Annie, but it's what we do.'

'After you've made a few inquiries, to make sure that God has all the relevant background information necessary to deliberate the possibility of intercession. Even though, as I understand it, omniscience is one of his—'

'Yeah, all right, you think my whole career has been founded on a tissue of myths. Fine. Strangely, I can live with that.'

'It *is* strange,' Howe said. 'But then the most unexpected people can fall prey to superstition. Like Hook himself.'

'I'm not following.'

'Darrin Hook was released from Brompton Heath Prison just under three weeks ago, having served less than half his latest eighteen-month sentence for burglary. The decision was made on the recommendation of, among others, the prison chaplain.'

'Oh?'

'Because Hook appeared to have undergone a conversion to your . . . faith.'

'Darrin Hook became a . . . *Christian?*'

'You didn't know that? Somehow, I'd expected that was how you came to be acquainted with him.'

'I'm *not* acquainted with him. I've never met him. And I certainly didn't know he'd been . . . When you say a conversion, what do you mean?'

'The usual absurd fanaticism. Bibles appearing in his cell . . .'

'Sent down from heaven?'

'Brought in by a prison visitor. A relative. Hook began to attend the Sunday services, throwing up his arms and yelling that he'd been saved and praise the Lord and all this tosh. I think even the prison chaplain became bored with him after a while – perhaps why he recommended an early release.'

Merrily was shaking her head. 'This is *all* news to me.'

The implications were startling. For a start, if this was true, Alice would have no reason to worry about Darrin's reaction to the idea of a Requiem Eucharist for his brother.

'You got this from the prison?'

'We haven't been in touch with the prison. The information came from a woman called Dionne Grindle, a cousin of Hook's living in Solihull. We found her phone number in his wallet. She turned out to be the relative instrumental in his seeing the . . . light.'

My niece, the one in Solihull, she did one of them Alpha courses at her church, did I tell you? Reckoned it d'creep up on you somehow . . . felt the Holy Spirit was in her heart like a big white bird . . .'

'She obviously didn't tell the rest of the family,' Merrily said.

'Apparently, Hook specifically asked her to say nothing to the Hereford side of the family. He said that he wanted to tell them in his own time and in his own way. He also, according to Ms Grindle, had plans to – and this is what interests us, of course – make an entirely new beginning by setting the record straight on a number of dark areas in his past. Now *I* assumed that, by this, he meant coming clean about previous offences for which he was never caught. And we'd have been, naturally, delighted to help him with the paperwork.'

'Wouldn't you have had to charge him?'

'Depends how serious they were. We can be fairly discreet, especially if it leads us to other offenders. And this, of course, is the point. If Hook *had* talked about his conversion and its implications, it might have been viewed as a rather worrying development by some of his former associates in this city's criminal underclass. Especially if he was indicating to all and sundry that he might be ready to put the record straight on certain matters – come clean, as it were.'

'You think he'd be a marked man?'

'It does rather sound as if he was bent on martyrdom.'

'Have you talked to his other relatives?'

'Only his mother, who lives in the city and knew nothing of any conversion. She thought the most likely person for him to tell would be the aunt, who—'

'So you *did* know about Alice.'

Howe didn't reply.

'Have you talked to her?'

'No answer when we rang. She's probably asleep by now. And we haven't been out there simply because most of the roads in that area are now closed. Anyway, I thought I'd talk to you first, somehow imagining you'd be able to tell me rather more than you have.'

'He really was killed?'

'He was certainly *killed*. But if you're asking if he was murdered, let me put it this way: there are some not-terribly-subtle textural differences between snow which has fallen naturally on to a body lying in the road and snow which has been kicked over it in order to conceal it from approaching vehicles.'

'Somebody . . . dumped him in a main road? *To be run over*?'

'Whether he was already dead, or unconscious, when he was placed in the road, only a PM can establish, so we won't know until tomorrow.'

Merrily discovered that she was pacing the lobby, loose shadows meshing in her path.

'Of course, the macabre aspect to this,' Annie Howe said, 'as one of our officers pointed out, is that Hook was placed in the road at the spot – or somewhere very close to the spot – where his brother died. Hook lived in a flat at Wormelow. A neighbour who was walking to the Tump Inn saw him leaving the building sometime around mid-evening, on foot. He may have been going to meet his killer and, unless this was a remarkable coincidence, we could assume the killer was someone who not only knew about the accident but also precisely where it took place.'

'I . . .' Merrily went back to the chintz-covered chair and sat down again. 'His cousin Dexter was driving. Which you know, of course.'

'Was Harris still close to his cousin?'

'Apparently not. There's been a rift in the family since the accident. We . . . *I* suggested the situation might be improved by holding a service – a Requiem Eucharist – for Roland, who was killed. Dexter said that Darrin would be dead against it. He suggested several times that Darrin was unstable . . . violent. He said, more or less, that he'd been scared of Darrin when they were kids. That Darrin liked to hurt people, cause trouble, had a cruel streak. I assumed, because Darrin had a prison record and Dexter didn't, that this was at least close to the truth.'

There was a silence. The door of the lounge opened and Bliss looked out, saw that Merrily was still on the phone, scowled and went back in.

'I'll tell you about Darrin Hook, shall I?' Annie Howe said. 'Because I arrested him once, you see, a number of years ago. He'd got into a factory on the Holmer estate, with some mates, lifting some computers that they didn't, of course, know how to get rid of – these particular models being part of a network system. So, when they tried to flog them to a nice chap who assembles PCs in his garage, we had the whole bunch in no time. Hook, it turned out, was the one who had got them into the factory, past quite an efficient security system. He's not bright, but he's remarkably good with his hands. And he does what he's told. You might say, I want to get into a chemist's shop, or I want a BMW Series 7, and Darrin will do the technical bits. You could call him an instinctive thief, a natural.'

'He was the one who broke into the car that night. When he was about twelve.'

'It's what he does. What he did. It made him popular with certain people. Won him acceptance.'

'Dexter indicated he was . . . you know . . . hard.'

'Mrs Watkins, all his convictions relate to basic thieving, never involving violence – not on his part, anyway. It doesn't surprise me at all that he was converted, in a very short time, to your religion. If he was exposed to someone with sufficient evangelical fervour, in a situation where he couldn't get away, he'd be a pushover.'

'Especially if he had something on his conscience?'

'I don't doubt that. You people are quite good at targeting someone's weak points.'

'You haven't talked to Dexter, then.'

'He wasn't at home, and we haven't tried to find him. It sounds as though he's either easily scared or he's been deliberately giving people the wrong impression about his cousin.'

'He was doing the late shift at Alice's fish and chip shop in Ledwardine, but I expect it'll be closed by now.'

'Long ago, I should think. Does he stay in the village?'

'I think he goes back to Hereford. Whether he could get through tonight, though . . .'

'We'll talk to him first thing in the morning, one way or another. He's not going to know we're looking for him. Well . . . thank you, Ms Watkins. We got somewhere in the end, didn't we?'

'I'm not sure where we got. If he hadn't told Alice about his conversion, I'm pretty sure he wouldn't have told Dexter.'

'We'll see,' Howe said. 'Good night.'

Merrily gave the DC his phone back and went out through the porch to avoid Bliss for a while. The implications here were horrific. Tugging up the hood of Jane's duffel, she walked out onto the forecourt, where the snow was falling hard again, like inside one of those glass things you shook.

I was bigger than Darrin, but he was real nasty, look. Stuck his knife in the back of my hand once. Had an airgun, shot a robin in the garden. Things people thought were nice, he'd wanner destroy.

It didn't fit. And yet these things must have actually happened, because Dexter Harris wasn't imaginative. It was just that Darrin hadn't done them. And if Darrin hadn't done them, then . . .

You're a fuckin' ole meddler, Alice, nobody assed you to start all this shit . . . what if everybody don't want the truth out?

Dexter didn't want it out.

She pushed back her hood, lifting up her face to the cascading sky, feeling the cold, stinging truth on her skin. Far from rejecting the idea of a Requiem Eucharist, a born-again Christian of the Charismatic persuasion – *throwing up his arms and yelling that he'd been saved and praise the Lord* – would see it as a sign, a response from God to his need to be cleansed of his sins.

Suppose Dexter was still in contact with Darrin? Suppose he knew about Darrin's conversion, guessed that, in Darrin's erratic mental state, it would all come flooding out, what had really happened that day, the things that Darrin had never talked about.

Never talked about *because he was afraid of Dexter.*

Dexter, the good boy. Not the most pleasant person, to

talk to, but he worked hard and he was a martyr to his asthma. And all he did that night, after all, was drive the car.

Merrily walked, with determination, back into Stanner Hall, pulling out her own mobile, ringing Alice again, letting it ring for over two minutes before giving up and ringing Lol.

THIRTY-NINE

What Brigid Did

All the time she was talking, Lol kept looking at the window. There ought to be curtains; maybe Merrily couldn't afford curtains on a starvation stipend. The snow was coming down vertically out of a windless sky, as if it had been directed to obliterate the village.

And unless it had been an apparition of the newly dead, that definitely hadn't been Darrin Hook at the window.

'So, not a word from Alice?'

'No,' he said, 'nothing. And it's not likely she's going to call now, is it?'

'You do know what's . . . implied here,' Merrily said, fifteen miles away and safe, thank God. 'You do realize what it suggests – about Dexter?'

'It suggests that Dexter might not be your problem any more,' Lol said carefully.

Merrily said, 'If he *is* responsible for—'

'Then you couldn't have known, you had no reason even to suspect it. You didn't know Darrin and, if what Howe says is right about his conversion, neither did Alice.'

'It was my decision. My solution to their problem.'

Jeavons's solution, Lol thought. He ought to tell her about Jeavons, but he didn't think she'd take it in.

'You gave them an option,' he said.

'The kind of option that someone like Alice was never going to refuse. When you think about it—'

'*Don't* think about it. There's nothing you can do about it. It's a police matter, out of your hands. Your only problem now is going to be Alice, and if you start blaming yourself, that isn't going to help. How's Jane?'

'Confused. Lol, why wasn't Alice answering her phone?'

'Probably because she hasn't got one in her bedroom. I'll go round and see if she's OK, if you like.'

'*No* . . . don't do that. If she hasn't been round and she hasn't rung, I suppose that means she doesn't know. If she's asleep, let her sleep. I'll call her in the morning, when she's better able to handle it, before the police can make a move on her. Damn – Bliss is making signals. What's it like there, now?'

He looked away from the window. 'Don't try and get back tonight, you won't make it. Not even in Gomer's truck. Is there somewhere you can sleep?'

'It's a hotel. But nobody's sleeping.'

'Call me back when you can, there's a couple of things—'

'Are you OK?'

'I'm fine.'

'I love you,' Merrily said, 'so don't—'

'Eirion rang, too. He's worried about Jane, and he—'

'I'm going to have to go.'

Lol sat staring at the hypnotic sleep-light on the monitor. He'd promised to call Jeavons back after he'd spoken to Merrily, but all that had been superseded now. He glanced at the window. He couldn't have told Merrily about Dexter looking in. He couldn't have done that.

Because it meant that Dexter had still been here an hour ago. Here in the vicarage garden. Out there looking in.

The fish and chip shop must have been long shut, but the chances of Dexter being able to get a vehicle out of

Ledwardine had, for a long time, been remote. Therefore, the chances were that Dexter was still here.

At Alice's? Obviously. Where else could he have gone? Lol picked up the phone. Maybe he should ring Annie Howe himself, let her know about this. Tell her that Dexter Harris, whom she would presumably like to question in relation to the possible murder of his cousin, was here in Ledwardine.

But then, it wasn't certain. Nothing about this was certain.

Ethel the black cat sat on the sermon book and watched Lol, as though sensing his indecision. Ethel had a red collar with a small round bell. The first time he'd been in this ancient house was when he'd arrived with Ethel, kicked and injured. And Merrily Watkins – 'one of my uncles used to be a vet, in Cheltenham' – had wrapped her in an old quilted body-warmer and laid her on the kitchen table examining her for internal injuries, removing bits of broken tooth. Lol often wondered if he'd fallen in love that night, when Merrily had said something like, 'God, these lights are crap,' explaining her belief that oaths were OK because they kept the holy names in circulation.

Without this cat . . .

'You're right.' Lol stood up and went to find his wellies.

Bliss led Merrily back into the lounge – his incident room – where a brass-stemmed standard lamp lit the scratched wood panels with a light that was thin rather than soft.

Over the fireplace, Sir Arthur's blue-tinted face gazed into places where Bliss wouldn't want to go. Bliss sat down in the easy chair near the flaking fire, one leg hooked over the arm, and motioned her to the sofa opposite.

'None of this goes out of this room, all right? And if it subsequently proves irrelevant to this case, it doesn't get spoken of again. Even Andy doesn't have clearance yet.'

Merrily sat down and closed her eyes. You could learn too

much in one night. She'd shown him the chat-room printout that Jane had given her, told him where it had been found. She wondered where Jane was, but at least Gomer had been with her.

'Best take off that sad old coat and have a coffee,' Bliss said. 'This could take a while.'

Jane looked up from making cheese toasties for the cops, watching Amber adding the herbs to her chocolate. Couldn't believe either of them was doing this. Keeping busy, knowing it was all coming to an end – shadows lengthening, ghosts emerging, moss and mildew reclaiming the walls of Stanner. Like being in the band on the *Titanic*.

'How can you just . . . go on?'

'It's what I do. I'm—'

'A cook, yeah.'

'Better than a conference, Jane,' Amber said bitterly, 'and without any dirty bedclothes. We'll even get paid.'

After a while, Amber said, 'She seemed such a godsend. A woman with all the management skills and diplomas and years of experience – a personable woman who was happy to work for a pittance and never minded scrubbing floors.'

Jane stopped grating cheese. 'Do you know where she is?'

'No.'

'Do you think . . .?' How could she ask what she wanted to ask? 'Do you think Dacre was killed because of her?'

Amber stopped stirring. '*Because* of her?'

Jeremy wouldn't come back and sit down. He walked into the little kitchen, with the dog at his heels, flinging open the back door, staring out across the yard, as if there was likely to be some personal message for him, scored out in the snow. When he turned round, back into the room, Danny saw pain passing across his face fast as a train over a level crossing.

'You thought it was me had him, din't you?'

'Jeremy, till them cops come, I didn't even know it was Sebbie dead.'

Danny pushed his fingers into his hair. It still wouldn't penetrate his brain that Natalie Craven was *the* Brigid Parsons, one of those names that nobody who'd read a paper or seen the TV news over the last twenty-five years would ever totally forget.

'How come we never knowed? How come nobody round yere knowed Paula's daughter was Brigid Parsons? Tell me that.'

'Nobody knew 'bout Paula, neither. They kept it quiet.' Jeremy came away from the door and went and stood by the paraffin lamp, looking down at the glass. 'Paula killed herself.'

'*When?*'

'Not long after giving birth. It was . . . pretty bloody horrible, Danny. Nobody talks about it. Nat'lie never learned about it till her dad was dyin'. Poor bugger blamed hisself, but it weren't his fault. It was in her.'

'So her mother killed herself, grandmother killed herself, and . . . It don't bear thinkin' about, Jeremy. None of it.'

'Brigid growed up thinkin' her mother died in childbirth. Which is true, in a way. Her dad, Norman, he had things to find out, too. Thought Paula was an orphan – which was true, like, but it was only when they come down yere he found out the truth about Hattie and Robert. The Nant was his now, see, but he felt it oughter be held on to for Brigid.'

'That'd been me, I'd have wanted to get rid, fast. Specially after . . .'

'He'd signed the lease by then.'

'But *you* knew. About Brigid and what she done. I mean you muster knowed, when it was all in the papers. You and Sebbie.'

'We never said nothin'. The two sisters never met. The

Dacres knew what nearly happened when they was little, swore her'd never get another chance. And were they gonner spread it round they got *two* killers in the family now?'

Danny didn't even like to think how Jeremy would have taken it. The girl he loved, the girl he'd prayed to God to send back. Jeremy in love with the memory of the monster who lured a boy of fourteen into an old railway shed with the promise of sex, and stabbed him and cut him and tore him to pieces with a little Kitchen Devil and her own nails. And the next night, while the police and the neighbours were still looking for the missing boy, did the same thing to his mate. *TEEN FIEND*, the *Mirror* said, when Brigid was convicted. This was the girl Jeremy had prayed to God to send back to him, and it didn't bear thinking about, none of it.

'I wrote to her,' Jeremy said. 'I wrote to her five, six times. Never had no reply. Figured mabbe her'd been moved and they never forwarded the letters. Turned out her dad wasn't passing them on.'

Poor little sod. Was some folk born unlucky or what?

'Wasn't until he was dyin', end of last year, that Norman sends for Brigid. Tells her the truth about who she was and where she come from. Tells her about Hattie.'

'And what good did that do?'

'Good?' In the lamplight, Jeremy, for once, looked his age and then some, his face full of dips and hollows.

'Must've seemed good for you,' Danny said, and then he thought about it. 'Bugger me, no wonder you rung me to come over when they turned up in that camper van. You was scared to death. You knew who it was gonner be all along. You just din't know if her was gonner have two heads and bloody claws.'

He turned and walked back into the living room, where the fire was burning low, tossing uncertain shadows on to the walls. Danny saw a dark and tragic tapestry forming.

'How long before Sebbie found out who the new woman was?'

'Dunno, Danny.'

'He ever ask?'

'Never asked *me*.'

'Just sent his Welsh shooters round to cause trouble. Put the wind up you. Let you know he was on the case. Cause a reaction. Was that it?'

'Mabbe he seen the Hound.'

Danny snorted, turning to face the boy who was standing in the doorway now, his face mottled by the fire.

'What he seen, Jeremy, was the curse of Chancerys comin' back to the Stanner Valley.'

Jeremy cried out, so sharp and sudden that the dog whimpered and cowered away from him.

'Why'd you take a rope into the barn?' Danny said.

And couldn't bear to hear the answer. He went and sat down by the fire, wishing to God he was at home with the cans on and The Queens of the Stone Age a satisfyingly numbing wooden mallet in his head.

'I begged her to go,' Jeremy said, like from a long way away. 'I begged her to leave. I *prayed* for her to leave, same as I'd prayed for her to come back. Now I'm praying for her to get out before it . . . I could feel it coming.'

'What?'

'The shadow Hound. Death.'

'Bollocks!' Danny roared. And yet remembered when he seen the two of them in The Eagle, thinking how soon romance died.

'And *you* seen the signs, Danny. Signs even you couldn't miss. And yet you did.'

Danny let his hands fall from his ears. 'What?'

'The night this Nathan got beat up.' Jeremy came to kneel down, side of Danny's chair, like a dog. 'You was there just before it happened, right? Think back, Danny – what was they saying?'

'I don't bloody know.'

'Yes, you do. You tole me.'

'They was . . . Like Foley said afterwards, Nathan called him a wimp. Then *splat, splat.*'

'No, words? What did he actually say? What did Nathan say?'

'Jeremy, for—'

'What'd he *say*?'

'Foley's telling him to get the hell off his land or else, and Nat . . . Brigid . . . her's like, *Better do what he says.* And then Nathan goes, *What you gonna do about it, you and that fuckin' little . . .*'

Danny stopped, the words booming in his head louder than The Queens of the Stone Age and The Foo Fighters live on stage, together. And a big part of the black tapestry got itself blocked in.

' . . . *That fuckin' little English wimp.*' The words shrank in Danny's mouth.

Quarrel was with herself, Jeremy had said earlier. *Me as got hit, mind.*

'Jesus Christ, Jeremy, he din't mean Foley was a fuckin' little English wimp, he meant . . . he meant *you.*'

He stood up, looked down at Jeremy by the chair, the boy's eyes full of a knowledge that he wished he didn't have.

'Foley never lifted a finger against Nathan, did he?' Danny said.

FORTY

Extreme

On the square, the Christmas tree lights had gone off at midnight, and now the tree was shapeless with snow and joined at the hip to the market hall. The falling snow was so dense that it was like passing through lace curtains, the few lights still burning in Ledwardine peering out at Lol like suspicious, muffled eyes.

Crossing into Church Street where the roadway and the pavements had become one, he passed the timber-framed terrace that included Lucy's house, its windows black, snow piled up on the step like a whole month of mail.

It was as if he was alone in the village. Everywhere, this white and quilted silence, like a chapel of rest.

A short way down the hill, the turning into Old Barn Lane was just another snow-flow now. But with hunched and crooked buildings either side, it was more sheltered here, the snow shallower, and Lol was able to hurry – as much as anyone could, moving like a wader in a congealing river.

In the months before he'd first met Merrily, when he was living in this village with Alison Kinnersley, he would sometimes walk down here for chips. Alice had lived over the shop then, and he vaguely remembered her moving out, into the first new home to be finished in Old Barn Close. Alice, it seemed, had always wanted a bungalow.

The shop was near the bottom of the lane before it fell

away into fields. Blinds were down, no light shining through the gaps, and no street lamps to identify the entrance to the Close, about fifty yards further on. He'd been holding the vicarage's black Maglite torch out in front of him, as if it was pulling him along. Now, passing the chip shop, its fatty miasma still in the air, he finally switched the torch on.

The Close was a so-called executive development of nine or ten houses and bungalows, architect-designed and well spaced between existing trees. Alice's home was at the end, backing onto the old orchard chain that curved around most of the village, ending up back at the church.

OK, then. If there was a meaningful light on in the bungalow, he was going to knock on the door. If Dexter Harris answered it, he'd say he was sorry to show up so late, but he was bringing a message for Alice from the vicar who was stuck over in Kington, had tried to phone and couldn't get a reply. It wasn't brilliant, but it wouldn't sound *too* suspicious on a night like this. If Dexter said that Alice was in bed, he wouldn't argue, he'd just go back to the vicarage and try to get through to Annie Howe.

If Alice was there, however, he'd have to play it by ear. His conversations with her, in the old days, had never got much beyond salt and vinegar, but he thought she'd remember him, and he guessed that, like probably everyone else in this village, she'd know about him and the vicar. Whether he told Alice about Darrin, if she didn't already know he was dead, would depend not least on whether Dexter was here or likely to return.

Lol stopped at the entrance to the Close, getting his breath back, brushing the snow from his glasses and the arms of his old army-surplus parka.

Why was he really here? Why was he doing this? Because he'd been unnerved by the face at the window? Even more by what Merrily had told him? Because he couldn't just sit there doing nothing until he fell asleep in some chair? Because he would otherwise have felt useless?

No – face it – it was essentially because he knew that this was what Merrily would be doing if she was here. Merrily – and he didn't like to contemplate this too deeply – would be afraid of what little fiery-faced Alice might have said or done and where it might have led.

Because of the relentless snow, he didn't see the light in the end bungalow until he was halfway along the close. All the others were either in darkness or had outside lamps as a deterrent to burglars. At Alice's, the light was in either the kitchen or the living room or both. Hard to say; curtains were drawn – cheerful red roses against a yellow trellis.

Both gates were open. A sign on one said *Orchard's End*. There was a white truck in the drive, with big tyres and a couple of inches of snow on the bonnet. Dexter? Lol switched off the torch. There was also a light on over a side door next to the truck. He went up and rang the bell, noticing that the snow had been roughly cleared from around the door, that footprints leading around the back were already half whited-out.

He heard the bell ringing inside, an old-fashioned continuous ringing, strident. He stopped and waited. No response. He tried again, keeping his finger on the bell push for about ten seconds.

Inside the bungalow the ringing died away. The lights stayed on. The snow kept on falling in its windless silence.

There was a slim glass panel in the door. When Lol leaned on the door to peer through it, the door swung open, and he wasn't expecting that at all.

Merrily lit a cigarette from the stub of the last. She never did this: it was chain-smoking, a sin. She hardly noticed until it was done and the smoke was curling up, past the waistcoat of Arthur Conan Doyle, like grey ectoplasm.

'How long have you known about her?'

'Me personally? Couple of months,' Bliss said, 'maybe longer. It's a routine thing, notifying the local bobbies when someone of her . . . status moves into your patch. Social workers and the Probation Service watching their backs.'

'How long did she serve?'

'Eight, nine years. The last year in an open prison. They come out, for lengthening periods, to get work experience, and she was taken on at a big guest house, and she did very well, got on with people. Which is how she got the taste for it. Like being on a permanent holiday, and most of the folk you met were on holiday too, or transient workers. Temporary. Passing through.'

'I suppose after being in one place for so long, it's hard to settle down.'

'She wasn't. She was in about six places all over the country. Different young offenders' institutions for the first years, and then two adult women's prisons. I don't think they knew what to do with her from the start. Smart, outgoing, quite good with people – long way from your usual moody psychos. But one of those young offenders' joints – Borstals, as was – she was in there with boys, and that could get inflammatory at times. She was a walking challenge for the hard lads – physically very mature for her age – and there were a number of incidents. And then she absconded and got caught quick and moved on. I think everybody was happy when she was old enough for Styall, partly because it was near where she lived but mainly because it was all women.'

Merrily said, 'Did the temporary employers know who she was?'

She was thinking, *Did* Jeremy *know what Brigid did*? But how could he not know? This was a national hate figure whose name, when it appeared in tabloid headlines, was almost invariably preceded by the word 'evil': *Evil Brigid should never get out, says victim's mother.* And then: *Evil Brigid pregnant. Evil Brigid freed in secret.* And the media hunt – *Where is Evil Brigid?*

Here.

'Not necessarily,' Bliss said. 'Some employers prefer not to know. And when she came out, she had a new name and new documents – driving licence, P45, all that. This is her second change of name – the first one, the press rumbled her at some hotel in Cornwall. That was when she dyed her hair. There was a rumour she'd had plastic surgery, but I don't think so.'

'The Probation Service are presumably still involved?'

'Oh yeh, they've always been there in the background. And also, in this case, the officer who nicked her, Ellie Maylord, who was my boss for a while when I was a youngster. Later, she became the first female operational DCI on Merseyside, ended up as superintendent. But she was just a little DC when she brought Brigid Parsons in, and she's always kept in touch with her . . . Well, I think she was fascinated, the way most people are, even coppers, by someone this . . . extreme.'

'Inevitably.' Merrily fingered her pectoral cross.

'So it was Ellie who contacted me, on the quiet, in October. My boss already knew, it turned out, but I was well off the need-to-know list. Ellie was worried about why, after managing quite a big hotel in Shropshire, Brigid had wanted to come here, to this – ' Bliss looked around ' – not terribly prosperous establishment. I said I'd make a few discreet inquiries, keep an eye on her. But, as you know, I've been a bit busy with one thing or another these last two months, so it got overlooked. Do *you* know why she came here?'

Merrily tipped her cigarette into a big metal ashtray,

pushing it away. Bliss didn't know, then, that Brigid Parsons was Hattie Chancery's granddaughter, Dacre's cousin. All he knew was that Dacre had been found dead and a convicted murderer was missing.

How come Hattie Chancery had failed to become part of the legend of Brigid Parsons?

Merrily retreated behind smoke; she'd need to think about this before enlightening him. 'She became pregnant in prison, didn't she? I remember reading a long piece in the *Observer* magazine some years ago – about a year after she came out.'

Recalling a photo of a woman's silhouette, shot from a distance, in a wide, empty field at sunset. A little girl running ahead of her. The little girl who was now Jane's unlikely best friend.

Jane's friend, the daughter of Brigid Parsons. No wonder she was quiet.

'Embarrassing,' Bliss said. 'It had to be either one of the male staff or someone she encountered on working days. But she never told, and she insisted on having the child. Toted the kid around with her all over the place. Admirable really, all the high-pressure jobs she managed to hold down and bring up a young baby. Something to prove, I suppose.'

'I see.' It all made sense now, what Jane had told her, about them moving from place to place, usually holiday resorts, lost in the anonymous army of migrant seasonal staff. Finally, travelling like gypsies. 'What about her parents?'

'The mother died when she was born. Dad supported Brigid, but then he got married again, had a new family. Didn't see much of her until he was dying himself, not too long ago. After her father died, that was when she came down here.'

'The head teacher at Moorfield, Robert Morrell – would he know who Clancy's mother was?'

'Might. I'm not sure. He'd love it, wouldn't he, the old namby-pamby liberal.'

'I'm just surprised he let her go near Jane.'

'Oh, I think we all tend to misjudge Jane,' Bliss said. 'She can be a pain in the bum, but she's from a nice home. Morrell might think Clancy could have worse friends.'

'You're being worryingly laid-back about this, Francis. Personally, I'm shattered.'

'That's because I know where I'm going. I'm accumulating background data for when we bring her in.' He smiled tightly. 'Which we will. We've got officers at the Thomas place.'

'You're making a few assumptions.'

'I'm looking at the evidence. A woman goes missing from work at a hotel just a few hundred yards from the spot where a man is found dead in suspicious circumstances? I mean, even if this *wasn't* Brigid Parsons . . .'

'Surely they wouldn't let her out without extensive psychiatric screening. I mean, how old was she when she killed those two boys – thirteen?'

'Killed *one* boy,' Bliss said. 'Mark Andrew Goodison. Stuart Petit survived, just. She *thought* she'd killed him, almost certainly intended to, but he survived to finger her. If he hadn't, I doubt she'd ever've been even questioned. The extreme savagery of it, nobody was looking for a girl. He lost an eye, Stuart, did you know?'

'I'd forgotten.'

'Most people just remember what happened to Mark – the bits of it the press felt able to print at the time. But whatever the shrinks say, I think there's a good chance that the child who did *that* – hasn't exactly gone away. Don't you?'

'I've never met her.'

'Stick around,' Bliss said.

*

They took the tractor, Danny and Jeremy – Danny realizing how much worse the conditions had got since he'd left home. But not being able to get *back* there, that was *not* an option.

Danny Thomas versus the worst winter for many a damn year, Danny Thomas versus *God*. No contest tonight.

When he got the engine going and the music started up, and this time it really was 'Bad Moon Rising', he got rid of it so fast he nearly broke the damn switch. And when Jeremy Berrows, hunched up in the other side of the cab, said, 'It's gonner be all right, I swear it'll be all right,' Danny couldn't find it in him to make any kind of reply.

Ahead of him, he saw the lights up on Stanner Rocks, National Nature Reserve and crime scene. He saw the heads in the rocks like some primitive, pagan Mount Rushmore in miniature, rimed with snow and secrecy, and he wanted to blow the whole enigma into the endless night.

'Danny, I know what it looks like to you, and that was why—'

'Why you never said a word?' Danny lurched in his seat, grinding the tractor onto the snowbound bypass, scraping his hair from over his eyes. 'I can't believe you never told me none of this, boy, I cannot *believe* it. I can't believe you let that woman leave that kid with Greta.'

'Danny, it—'

'I can't believe you'd *do* this.'

'Danny, I've known her for over twenty-five years. I know all her problems, I know why she done what she done, and I know the things she *won't* do.'

'You've known she was a bloody murderer for twenty-odd years, and you still wanted her. You brought her into the valley, and you never said a word. You knowed what she done to Nathan, and still said nothin'. You know it en't bloody changed, boy. That woman kills, and you let my Greta get involved in it, and you never said a word, and I thought you was my friend, and whatever happens I en't never gonner forgive that.'

In the clean, shiny, chromium kitchen, Lol saw things that bothered him, like a single cup on the kitchen table, half full of cold tea. Like a tin of assorted biscuits with the top off.

These things bothered him because everything else in here was immaculately tidy.

He didn't like to go further than the kitchen. He stood just inside the doorway, called out tentatively, 'Mrs Meek?'

On the wall by the door was a calendar of Peter Manders scraperboard etchings of Herefordshire scenes. Above it, two framed photographs, one of four grinning blokes, including Dexter Harris, hefting between them what looked like a tractor wheel. The other was a formula studio portrait of a small boy with close-cropped hair. Roland?

Roland and Dexter, only Darrin missing. The bad boy, the black sheep.

In fact, the weak boy, the easily led boy who could have used some support from a strong, self-sufficient auntie, if she'd ever been told the truth.

A door across from Lol was open to the dimness of perhaps a hallway, but through another door, opposite, he saw a stuttering light.

'Alice?'

A wide hall ending in an arched front door. From here, it was clear that the flickering was from a TV set in a lounge or living room. Lol went in.

'Alice?' In case she'd fallen asleep in front of the TV.

Leaving the back door unlocked, well after midnight?

On the widescreen TV, a black and white movie of *Gaslight* vintage was showing with the sound down: a woman in a doorway holding a lantern high.

This was a long room with a picture window overlooking the orchard, spectacularly snow-clad. The only light apart from the TV came from perfect red and yellow designer flames curling almost realistically from real coals on a gas fire in the bottom wall. The carpet was cream, the four-piece suite huge and expensive and vacant.

Lol went back into the hall. Doors on both sides, three of them slightly open. Bathroom: empty. Utility room with washing machine and dryer: empty. Toilet and shower room: empty.

He put an ear to the closed doors before slowly opening each of them. Two were bedrooms, with that room-freshener smell that told you they weren't in everyday use.

There was no sound, either, from the third bedroom. Lol went in, switching on the light. He saw a white dressing table, a built-in wardrobe. The bed was turned down and the room felt warm. There was a small en suite bathroom and toilet.

Alice's room. Nobody here.

The final room had evidently been intended for a study; it had built-in shelves and cupboards. There were cardboard boxes on the floor. On the wall opposite the door, by the window, was a framed local newspaper cutting showing a middle-aged man in an apron, holding out two bags of chips, a younger Alice looking on. The headline read: *Frying Start – Sizzling New Venture for Farmer Jim.*

Alice and Jim had been struggling for years on a small farm, not much more than a smallholding. Lol remembered someone saying that, by the time Jim died, the fish and chip shop in Old Barn Lane – the first chippie in an expanding Ledwardine – had proved to be the most lucrative business in this village, by a big margin, and that included The Black Swan.

A very worthwhile inheritance for somebody.

When Lol got back to the kitchen, Dexter Harris was sitting at the table, nibbling a chocolate biscuit. He barely looked up. The huge, solid greyness of him was reflected out of a chromium freezer door, a kettle, a Dualit toaster.

'Whatever you took, boy,' Dexter said, friendly enough, 'let's have it on this table yere. Else mabbe I'll make a start by breakin' your arm, see where we goes from there.'

FORTY-ONE

Living on the Edge of a Chasm

Neither Jane nor Amber noticed Beth Pollen until she was almost at the bottom of the kitchen steps.

'Would this be a convenient time to talk?'

Amber picked up the earthenware jug for the chocolate, defensive. 'Jane or me?'

'I think both.' Mrs Pollen looked tired, a bit frazzled. She said to Jane, 'And I *do* want to talk to your mother.'

'She's around.' Jane was embarrassed now about the way she'd clung to Beth Pollen at the rocks when the fox or the badger had run past.

'But I want to clear the air on some things first. Everything, in fact.'

Jane put down the cheese-grater and stared at Mrs Pollen, still in her sheepskin coat, open over a pale blue jumper and jeans, as she came down the final step into the kitchen.

'To begin with . . .' Mrs Pollen turned to Amber. 'When The Baker Street League cancelled their conference, that was entirely my doing. Neil Kennedy was actually quite amused, at first, by the idea of your husband trying to build a business around the dubious legend of Conan Doyle and the Hound of Hergest. And they were quite gratified with the terms he was offering – and the idea, if I may say so, of a weekend of your renowned cooking.'

Amber put the earthenware jug back on the French stove. 'What are you saying?'

'I had a long discussion with Neil Kennedy during the murder-mystery weekend. I told him Ben Foley believed he had conclusive proof that Doyle had been here, which he believed would finally discredit the Cabel legend, in Devon, as the source of the Hound. I said I understood Mr Foley, as a former television producer, hoped to use The Baker Street League to help him front a large-scale media campaign, particularly in America. And I told him . . . other things. Dr Kennedy was not terribly amused. As I'm sure you found out.'

Amber turned down the heat under the chocolate. 'You'd better sit down.'

'Thank you.' Beth Pollen took a wooden stool next to the island unit, and Amber dragged over two more, and put on the halogen lights. Jane stared into Mrs Pollen's weathered, guileless face.

'You deliberately screwed it up for Ben?'

'Yes.'

Amber said, 'I don't understand. Both Kennedy and you already knew there was proof that Doyle had been at Stanner. The document you mentioned . . . in the files of The Baker Street League?'

'That doesn't exist, Mrs Foley. I invented it. No article was written, as far as I know, for *Cox's Quarterly* or any other defunct magazine. There is no proof, to my knowledge, that Conan Doyle ever stayed at Stanner or came to this area. He *may* have – all the indications are there, the coincidence of names – but we'll probably never know. And if you remember, I said the other night that if anyone asked Kennedy about a handwritten document, he would deny all knowledge of it. Quite legitimately, as it happens.'

Jane felt like her head was filling up with a grey fog. She let Amber ask the question.

'Why? Why did you want to *do* this to us?'

Beth Pollen sighed. 'Because if Stanner had become, as Mr Foley had planned, a regular conference venue for The Baker Street League, The White Company would never have been allowed to set foot in the building. What I *didn't* lie about was the enmity between the two organizations, which, as a member of both, I've been able to observe, over the years, in all its incredible peevishness. I realize the League is far more prestigious, prosperous and influential, and I'm sorry, but I wanted *us* in here. I wanted Alistair Hardy here. He has a remarkable ability.'

'We don't understand,' Jane said.

Mrs Pollen sighed, her face coloured mauve by the halogen lights. 'We had to mislead The White Company as well. Doubt I'd have been able to persuade them if I hadn't been able to show there was evidence that Conan Doyle *had* been here at the critical moment. Alistair Hardy's fees are . . . sizeable. He's doing this for nothing because of the TV coverage.'

Jane felt herself exploding. 'Get me out of here! Everybody who sets foot in this place just *lies*.'

Amber said, 'Mrs Pollen, you said "we"?'

'Yes,' Beth Pollen said. 'The other person.'

The other person. The phrase seemed to bounce off the stones in the wall.

Natalie. It all added up, didn't it? When Ben had lost The Baker Street League conference, it was Nat who came up with an instant replacement and rescued the whole situation. OK, just a bunch of loony spiritualists, but better than nothing. The way Beth Pollen had turned up at the church, at just the right moment to impress Antony Largo. A set-up.

'I *was* going to get round to that,' Mrs Pollen said.

'Brigid?' Jane said.

'So you *do* know,' Mrs Pollen said.

Dexter had taken off his expensive biker's jacket, uncovering a grey denim shirt with epaulettes and a badge on the breast pocket with twin exhaust pipes on it. He stood in the middle of the floor, his hands half-curled, like ring-spanners.

'So you en't took nothin'.'

It was likely he'd recognized Lol now as the guy he'd seen through the scullery window. But he wouldn't know whether Lol had seen *him*, so he wasn't letting on. Hence the catching-a-burglar routine.

It gave Lol some leeway. He told Dexter his story about the vicar getting worried when Alice had twice failed to answer the phone. Lol walking over here to see if everything was all right, finding all the lights on in the empty bungalow, with the back door unlocked. No more than the truth.

'Sorry I came in like this, but anything could've happened.'

'Like what?' Dexter said.

'I mean . . . where is she?'

'How should I know? I come back from closin' up the chip shop, hour or so ago, she en't yere. Telly on and everything, no Alice. I been out lookin' for her. No sign. Dunno where she gone. Neighbour's, mabbe.'

'They all seem to be in bed.'

Dexter shrugged.

'You called the police?'

'Not *yet*. Her'd go through the bloody roof. 'Sides which, how's the police gonner get through with all the bloody roads blocked for miles around? Nah, her's likely wandered off. Her'll be back.'

Lol considered. He'd been honest so far, no call to deviate from that.

'She's had a shock. The vicar told me.'

Discovering that he was playing the Christian aide, the clergy groupie, the little guy in glasses who fluttered vaguely around the vicarage, a moth lured by the incandescence of its incumbent.

'Tole you what?'

'About your cousin.'

'Yeah. Tough.'

'You weren't that close?'

Dexter shook his head. 'Waste of fuckin' space, you want the truth. Never kept a job, always in trouble with the law. Brought the whole family into disrepute.' He leaned towards Lol, a bubble of moisture like an ornamental stud in the cleft of his lower lip. 'So what's with you and the vicar?'

'Friends. I'm staying the weekend with her. She was called out to talk to someone who attempted suicide.'

'Local?'

'Kington.'

'En't gonner get back from there in a hurry.'

'So I've got to ring her back about Alice. She's worried.'

Dexter stared at him blankly, like, *What do you want* me *to do about it*? He went to the chrome-fronted fridge/freezer. 'You wanner lager?'

'No, it's . . . Yeah, OK. Thanks.'

Dexter got out two cans of Stella Artois, tossed one to Lol. 'Wanner help me take a look around, is it?'

'That's a good idea.'

'Right, then.' Dexter put on a grim, knowing smile, snapping the ring-pull on his beer can. A smugness there, Lol thought, a satisfaction.

'Which way do you think she might've gone?'

'Put it this way, if you gets to Leominster, turn back.' Dexter had a swig of lager, took his leather jacket from the back of a chair, pulling a pair of black driving gloves out of one of the pockets. 'Never mind, boy, be a cold bed for you tonight, anyway, look.'

'Sorry?'

'Don't gimme that "friends" shite.'

Dexter clapped Lol on the back. It was as if he was on a roll and nothing could go wrong for him tonight.

Yes, Jane had heard of her. Although of course it had all happened long before she was born. She knew about her in the way she knew of, say Lizzie Borden, a half-mythical figure with a rhythmical, nursery-rhyme name and an underlying pulse of horror.

Brigid Parsons killed some boys.

There were others. There was Mary Bell, whose name you knew because it was such a nice, short, wholesome name, and the killers of little Jamie Bulger, whose names you could never remember.

But this was less horrific, surely, because only one of the boys died. And he was older than Brigid Parsons, so the element of cruelty was missing, or, if it was there, it was different. Different with Brigid Parsons.

Different with Natalie Craven.

You're asking me what I believe? I believe you don't let anybody fuck you about. That's it, really.

This was unreal, and it wasn't less horrific at all. Jane had an idea of how bad it actually was; she'd once read a colour-supplement feature: *Where Is Brigid Parsons?* Something like that.

Brigid Parsons could never call herself that again, in the same way that Mary Bell had had to lose her fresh, clean name – although apparently she was a nice woman now, not the same person as the child who'd killed two little boys and given herself away by asking to see them in their coffins.

Who were you kidding? In some ways, Brigid was worse.

For cruelty, substitute plain savagery. The magazine had revealed details that could not be published in the papers at the time, as those were days when family papers didn't go into details about . . .

. . . Mutilation.

Jane sat on her stool, looking down at her fingers, empurpled in the lights, then up at Beth Pollen, who had revealed the unbelievable. And then at Amber, who hadn't been able to speak for whole minutes, it seemed like, and when she did it was just to say faintly, 'Does Ben know?'

Jane looked back down at her fingers. The thing was that Natalie was just so. . . . *cool.*

Amber stood up and went and did a very Amber thing – she stirred the chocolate, although it was probably ruined by now.

Then she came and sat on the stool with her hands in her lap.

'*Does* Ben know?'

'I wouldn't think so,' Beth Pollen said. 'Though I suppose everyone will know in a short while, when they either find her or the media find out they're looking.'

Jane looked up at the high window, almost obscured now by layers of snow that, from down here, looked grey, like concrete. Christ, she thought, *Christ.*

This explained everything about Clancy: why she was so quiet, the tall, gawky kid behind the pile of books, why she'd been to so many different schools.

Why she'd leapt up from her homework in horror when Nat had walked down these steps with blood all over her arms.

The great revelation over, Beth Pollen talked about her and Natalie.

In the drab aftermath of his death, Beth had taken up her

husband's final research project, the previously unchronicled history of a great Victorian house on the very border of Wales and England. She'd thought it might make a small book, locally published, with his name on its cover, a fitting memorial. Sometimes she could sense him at her elbow as she typed, suggesting a better word, rebuking her for attempting to include some picturesque but uncorroborated anecdote.

Although the text would be tinted by her growing interest in spiritualism, the very sense of Stephen had made Beth more assiduous in her research. And that was how she'd met Natalie Craven, who also was awfully interested in the history of Stanner Hall.

'I suppose I needed a friend. No, that's wrong . . . I suppose I needed a different *sort* of friend. She could almost have been my daughter, but that's not how it was, either. She had this mature awareness of how things worked – how one might turn situations around – I suppose it was years of surviving in the prison system that made her like that, but of course I didn't know that at the time. She simply fired me, gave me back my energy.'

'She *can* make things happen,' Jane said. 'I think it's because she doesn't care whether they happen or not.'

'And I was intrigued by her relationship with Jeremy Berrows. Absolutely nothing *about* him – or so you thought at first. Only slowly becoming aware of a kind of native spirituality – the kind that you expect to find in farmers whose families have lived close to the land for centuries, but seldom do these days. Oh, I was *very* curious about Jeremy and how those two came to be together.'

'Especially after all those years apart,' Jane said.

'Well, the first ten she could do nothing about. And then, when you realize, approaching middle age, that perhaps you've never been able to connect with anybody as fully as the farm boy you met when you were *twelve* – that maybe you really were *two halves* of something – what do you *do* about it? Nothing. You don't really believe the validity of a memory that old, do you? It's like a myth.'

Two halves . . . Jane thought about Jeremy Berrows walking into his barn with a rope. She said nothing.

Beth Pollen said, 'We discussed it, after she'd revealed her real . . . her former identity.' She glanced at Jane. 'And if you're wondering how *that* came about, it was when we were researching Hattie, copying old photographs, and there was one of her as a girl, with her family, and I said, unthinking, "Oh, she looks rather like Clancy." Could have bitten my tongue off when I saw Natalie's face, but that's how it came out.'

'I think I've seen that picture. It's in her room now – Hattie's room.'

'So the next day we were due to go to Kington Church together. She didn't turn up. But the following day, early in the morning, there she was, awfully pensive. And just told me, quite simply, who she was and what she'd done. No attempt to justify or explain it, and she didn't swear me to secrecy – I hope she knew she didn't have to. I certainly haven't said a word to anyone . . . until now.'

'Didn't knowing about that, you know, alter things?'

'Threaten the friendship? Why should it? In some ways, it deepened it, because I felt this overwhelming need to understand her. I felt that no one, except perhaps Jeremy, ever had. And I felt that Stephen had brought her to me.'

'But she was a *murderer*,' Amber said.

'And she'd been punished for it.'

'And she was . . . that woman's granddaughter.'

'I'd be jolly stupid if I said *that* didn't frighten me. I remember that when I recognized the awful parallel between Hattie and the blood-weary Robert, and Natalie and Jeremy,

I was so *scared* for Jeremy. But in the end I realized that this, in some strange way, had only intensified the relationship. They were living on the edge of a chasm. I think, when she met him again, with the knowledge of what had gone before, she knew that if she didn't take that risk – seize it – then she'd just be . . . giving in to the past. And that's not how she is.'

Jane said. 'Let's get this out. You think that whatever made Hattie Chancery do what she did was also present in Brigid Parsons?'

'It's what *she* needs to know, and it's why she came back. She realizes there's a negative energy inside her that she can't always control. Her mother—' Beth Pollen took a breath. 'Natalie doesn't think, doesn't *want* to think it's a mental illness.'

'You and she think there's a . . . psychic connection with Hattie?'

'This is why I wanted Alistair here. People like you might demean spiritualism, but I think there *is* something to be discovered here, and it's nothing that we're going to find written down.'

'I'm sorry,' Jane said, 'I can't believe an intelligent woman like you really thinks that someone like Hardy can deal with something this . . . enormous. I mean, he . . . He's a phoney.'

Jane heard men's voices and footsteps at the top of the stone stairs. Two men were coming down the steps. Jane was expecting cops, or maybe Hardy and Matthews. She really didn't care if Hardy had heard her talking about him.

'He isn't a phoney, believe me,' Beth Pollen said. 'But I didn't say that I thought he could *deal* with it. A medium is simply what the word says. It's about communication, rather than solutions.'

Amber turned to Jane. 'I think she means *that*'s something for your mother.'

'Oh.'

It was Ben Foley who sprang from the bottom step. 'Amber, I'm sorry if I'm interrupting anything, but we'll need another room.'

The man with Ben bestowed on Jane a gracious smile.

'Jesus, I wouldnae like to do *that* journey again. Thank you, hen, you've got a hell of a nose for a developing situation.'

Nothing was ever simple, nothing ever painless.

Danny had been aware of diamond-bright blue-white vehicle lights behind them on the bypass, sticking with them after they turned off at Walton, using their tracks. But with snow fuzzed all over his wing mirror he couldn't be sure what it was, and by the time they pulled up at his place the lights had vanished.

It was when Jeremy got down to open the farm gate for him that the little black Daihatsu appeared, coming the other way, down from Kinnerton. Danny had the idea it had been waiting in the lay-by, about a hundred yards back, to see who was in the tractor. Now it stopped, hugging the hedge, wedges of snow collapsing onto its roof as someone got out, a woman in a blue waterproof. Then Jeremy was springing back from the gates, and he was locked together with the woman in the tractor's headlight beams.

And Danny was down from the cab, real fast, and in through the farm gate.

Greta had the door open before he reached it, standing there in a wash of yellow, and just for a moment it was like the first time he'd ever seen her, in a long floaty frock with little golden stars, like a dusty sunbeam.

'You all right?' Danny almost sobbing in relief.

Gret said, 'I couldn't do nothing, Danny. Had to let them in. Wasn't nothing I could—'

'What?' And then Danny heard another engine up on the road and turned and saw the blue-white lights hard behind the tractor at the gate, heard the jolt of vehicle doors opening.

'When they told me,' Greta said, 'about Sebbie Dacre . . .'

And then behind her, inside the house, a girl's voice was screaming out, in real distress, *No! Mum, go away! Don't come in!* And there were sounds of pulling and scuffling, and this long, rending wail of despair.

Greta said, 'You better—'

A copper came past her then, out of the front door, and Danny recognized his grey moustache: Cliff Morgan, sergeant.

'Don't get involved, Danny, eh?' Cliff said.

But Danny ran back with the coppers to the open gate, where meshing headlights had turned the snow magnolia, and Jeremy and Natalie Craven were boxed in between the tractor and Jeremy's old black Daihatsu, in the centre of all these beams of hard light, snow coming down on them, cops gathering in a wider circle, blocking the lane.

But they were separated from it. World of their own. Jeremy with his scarf wound around his neck, so she wouldn't see what he'd done to hisself, holding her hand real tight. 'Where you been?' he kept saying. 'Where you *been*?'

Natalie Craven pulled his head into the crease of her shoulder.

'It's all over,' Natalie said, long hands in his fluffy hair. 'All done now.'

FORTY-TWO

Alleluia

He didn't expect them to find her. That was clear. Dexter wasn't subtle, and he didn't expect them to find Alice.

They went up to the top of Old Barn Lane, back into Church Street and down to The Ox with its frosted front windows, a dim yellow glow visible from somewhere back in the pub.

'They used to drink yere, when Jim was alive,' Dexter said, as if they might see Alice peering in, thinking it was still 1979.

Dexter was going through the motions.

Lol wiped snow from his glasses with a forefinger. 'How did she find out about your cousin?'

'Eh?'

'You said you thought it was the shock that might've made her wander off.'

'I said that?' Dexter sniffed and slumped off round the corner, where an alley led to public lavatories. Lol followed him. A tin-hatted lamp on a wrought-iron bracket turned snowflakes into falling sparks.

'Check out the Women's, you reckon?' Dexter said.

'It's all locked up.' Lol could see an iron gate, a chunky padlock.

'Pity.' Dexter finished off his lager, tossed the can to the end of the alley. He came over, leaned down into Lol's face, his arms folded. 'You really poking that little vicar?'

'Not right now,' Lol said.

'Her go like *Alleluia!* when her comes?' Dexter burst out laughing. 'Just thought o' that.'

'Must remember to tell her,' Lol said.

'*Alleluia* when her comes.' Dexter laughed up at the sky.

'What do you reckon happened to him?' Lol followed Dexter round to the front of the pub, where they stood under its open porch. 'Just seems odd, a bloke falling in the road.'

'Pissed, most likely,' Dexter said.

'He hadn't given it up, then?'

'Uh?'

'Turning Christian?'

'Christian.' Dexter coughed and spat into the snow. 'He *never*. He just said what he wanted 'em to think – Alice, and fuckin' daft Dionne. I'll tell you, he was a weak bastard, always gonner go wrong. Too weak to hold a job down. Not like me, Alice knew that. I was all she got, look. Me as looked out for her. Sisters got their own lives and their families up in Hereford. Laughing their tits off at Alice, all this ole church stuff. I was all she got, daft ole bitch. Couldn't have no kids, look.'

'How long you been helping at the chip shop?'

'Helping? Cheeky *cunt*. When I'm in there, I'm running that place, look, reorganizin'. All these idle assistants, all this chit-chat, we don't need that. Get 'em served and on to the next one, don't give 'em too many chips neither. Where them customers gonner go, they don't like it? En't like there's competition. I says to 'em, these women, you do what I say, don't gimme no stress, look, and we'll get on. Where's your beer?'

'Must've left it on the table.'

'No fuckin' use there, is it, boy? Where you wanner go now?'

'Ring the police?'

'Waste o' time. Cops is shit round yere. They en't gonner look for an ole woman in this. What we'll do, we'll go round the ole bowling green and back up the square, see how it looks then. What's your name, I ask you that?'

'Lol.'

'Kind o' name's that?'

'A short one.'

'Got a job, Lol?'

'Bit of singing. Write songs.'

'That a proper job?'

'It is, actually.'

'All right, what we'll do, we'll go round the bowling green, but we'll come out by The Swan. That's what we'll do.'

Somebody who expected never to be contradicted or refused, due to being asthmatic and not looking for stress.

Lol remembered how, when he was working with Dick Lydon, the Hereford psychotherapist, Dick had this disabled client with the same attitude. You had to humour them to begin with, Dick used to say, and then, after a while, make it obvious that you were humouring them so they'd see a reflection of themselves.

That could take all night with Dexter. It could take all night, and it still wouldn't work. Whatever Dexter had done tonight, he was proud of himself. He kicked a lump of snow, hands punching out the pockets of his leather jacket, killing time looking for someone he knew they wouldn't find.

'What you waitin' for?'

'I'm just thinking,' Lol said. 'Where is Alice likely to have gone?'

'Coulder gone back home by now, for all I knows.'

'We'd have seen her. Unless she . . . We haven't checked out the orchards at the back of the bungalow, have we? There's a path through the orchards. Where people walk their dogs?'

'Alice didn't have no dog, never went for no walks.'

Past tense. Always past tense.

'No,' Lol said, 'but—'

'I *said* her never went for no fuckin' *walks*.'

Lol tightened up inside. Dexter didn't want him checking out that footpath.

'It's, er . . . also a short cut to the church, isn't it? And she was a church cleaner. The head cleaner. Be the quickest way for her to go.'

'Not at bloody *night*.'

'As head cleaner, she'd probably have keys. If she was very cut up about what happened, she might've got it into her head to go and . . . offer up a prayer?'

'At *night*?'

'Like you said, they do strange things, old people, don't they?'

The squeak of fists clenching in leather gloves.

Lol turned into the tracks they'd made, back up towards the square. 'Tell you what, if you go and check round the old bowling green, like you said, and I'll have a walk up to the church . . . Then I'll follow the footpath back the other way. You won't need the torch, will you?'

He wiped the new snow off his glasses and walked off.

After a few seconds, he was aware of Dexter following him. Not altogether a pleasant sensation.

'Mrs Watkins.' Merrily had been looking for Jane and he'd come down the main stairs, a man with a laptop and black-framed glasses. 'Matthew Hawksley. I suspect we may have exchanged e-mails.'

'Yes. I believe we did. Sorry about that. I just wanted to know what my daughter was getting into.'

'She isn't getting into anything. We try not to involve anybody under the age of twenty-one.'

'Well, that's . . . good.'

'Anyway, we're glad to have you with us,' Matthew said.

'Now *that* sounds ominous.'

'This place *is* ominous,' Matthew said. 'What's been happening tonight only underlines it.'

'A murder can make a children's playground seem ominous.'

'Oh,' he said, 'do they *know* it's murder?'

'It's a lot of manpower for a suicide, Matthew.'

'Yes.' He smiled. 'Look, I know how the clergy, in general, feel about spiritism, so I won't bend your ear on that, but – have you got a couple of minutes?'

'Maybe hours. I don't think I'm going to get home tonight.'

'You're probably right. Poor you. Look, I'd hate to say this in front of Ben Foley, but my feeling is that this place – this house, this hotel – should never have been built.'

'No, best not to say that in front of Ben.'

'Not built *here*, is what I mean. Not as if it was erected on the site of a former dwelling; there never *was* a house here.'

'On Stanner Rocks?'

'I'd probably argue that this site has a degree of psychic instability.'

'Jane would say pagan magic, and she'd put it down to the Border. Would that be in line with your thinking?'

Matthew grimaced. 'What you had was an obscenely rich family moving to a generally poor area. Perhaps they were warned, perhaps not. They were, after all, bringing wealth and employment.'

'And modern science to an area riddled with primitive superstition?'

'Spiritism.' Matthew smiled ruefully. 'I wish we had a better word for it. I'd be the first to agree that very few of the claims made by people like Conan Doyle have been substantiated. In fact we're no further forward now than we were then – except that we're less susceptible to frauds.'

'Wouldn't say that necessarily.'

'All right – ' he put up his hands ' – let's not go down that road. Let's get back to geophysics. I mean, look around . . . Even on a simple structural level, it doesn't feel right – damp coming through everywhere, woodwork rotting. I suspect the heating will *never* be adequate. Standing here, now, it's almost as if we're standing on the bare rock. Am I telling you things you already know?'

'You mean people didn't live here until we had an urban, industrialized society that believed man was destined to have full dominion over the natural world – i.e. the Victorians?'

'Bottom line is, Conan Doyle notwithstanding, Foley's going to go bankrupt here in no time at all, and he knows it. When I first heard that somebody had taken a dive off Stanner Rocks, I half thought it was going to be him. Hello—'

Merrily turned to follow his gaze. DS Mumford had come in from the car park and was standing just inside the entrance, bulky as a lagged cistern in one of those long, dark overcoats on which snow appeared to evaporate. Bliss appeared in the doorway of his incident room. Mumford nodded.

Matthew said, 'I don't know *much* about your side of things, but Beth Pollen tells me there's something you can do called an Exorcism of Place. Cleanses a place of bad vibes, the residue of unfortunate acts. Makes it a more amenable place to live and work.'

'It's not *feng shui*, Matthew.'

'I didn't—'

'Has anyone asked you to mention this?'

'I'm . . . just sounding you out, Reverend. But I think my colleagues – Beth, anyway – are getting a little nervous. The TV producer's arrived and he and Foley are intent on filming something tonight, as originally planned.'

'With all *this*?'

'With the police action as background. Sexy telly.'

Two uniformed police were opening up both swing doors to the porch and the tall detective who'd connected Merrily with Annie Howe moved to a vantage point near the unlit Christmas tree.

'Are they bringing something in?' Matthew asked.

'Some*one*, I'd guess.'

She heard doors opening behind her, sensed more people standing there. The electric current passing through the lobby could have relit the tree and doubled the candlepower of the chandelier. Everyone tensed for that first glimpse of Brigid Parsons. Even, presumably, the people who already knew her as Natalie Craven.

'Given what's happening, Beth now feels apprehensive about what we'd originally planned,' Matthew said. 'I think she'd be happier if there was a spiritual dimension to it.'

'Making it even sexier telly, right?'

Headlamps speared through the porch and then veered away – a vehicle stopping directly outside the doors. The two policemen moved to either side of the entrance. Mumford and a stocky policewoman in a dark blue jersey waited by the reception desk.

Presently, five people came in through the porch: two uniforms, two detectives, one woman.

'We appreciate you can't just exorcise a place willy-nilly. You'd need a focus,' Matthew said.

For just a moment, from about ten feet away, the gaze of

the killer, Brigid Parsons, met Merrily's. The eyes were brown and candid. What had she expected – cold, bleak, washed clean of humanity? Brigid was wearing a fleece-lined light-blue waterproof jacket hanging open over a dark shirt and jeans. Her head was held high, the dense dark brown hair falling back. As if she was finally ready to shed the years of dyes and deception.

Matthew said, 'We were thinking that the late Hattie Chancery might fit the agenda.'

FORTY-THREE

Tough Ole Bat

Merrily found Gomer in his truck, parked on the edge of the forecourt where the snow was churned up like cold custard. She'd climbed in next to him just as he finished talking to Danny on his old car-phone.

'How's Jeremy taking it?'

Gomer got out his ciggy tin, squinted at it, then put it back in a pocket of his scarred old bomber jacket.

'When things is bad, Jeremy just closes down, like he's been unplugged.'

'Where are they now, Gomer?'

'Back at The Nant.'

Through the windscreen, Merrily watched a policeman come out of the porch and look up at the flaking sky. The snow had become sporadic again, as if the weather was playing with them. One of the witch's-hat towers was wreathed in a pinkish vapour.

'And Clancy?'

'Still at Greta's, with a woman cop. Cliff Morgan, he reckoned they'd likely bring her yere tomorrow, give 'em some time together, 'fore her mam's taken to Hereford. Don't look like that's gonner happen till it gets light and they clears the roads. Any chance her'll walk away from this, Vicar? Light sentence? If her had good reason? Not a nice feller, Sebbie.'

Merrily shivered inside Jane's worn duffel coat, tightened her scarf. Clearly Gomer didn't yet know that this was Brigid Parsons and the chances of her getting out of prison *ever* this time were remote.

'Cops know her's Hattie's granddaughter, Vicar?'

'I think they'd regard that as a closed case.'

The curtains in the hotel lounge had been drawn now, for the interrogation of the prime suspect. A shadow rose against them: Bliss throwing up his arms in probable frustration, but it looked like he was dancing.

'Nothin' happens round yere's ever closed. You knows that,' Gomer said.

The church's main door was locked, and there was nothing in the stone porch apart from the side benches, the parish noticeboard and a rack of leaflets.

'Satisfied?' Dexter said.

Lol couldn't see Dexter, but the density of him made the stone porch feel claustrophobic. He bounced the torch beam around one last time.

'You're a funny bugger, Lol. What's she to you?'

'Alice?'

'Less it gets you brownie points with the vicar. Gets you into her, whatsit, cassock.'

'That must be it, then,' Lol said tightly.

He wanted to smash the torch into Dexter's face. Instead, he switched it off so that Dexter couldn't see him thinking. When Dexter had appeared at the scullery window, he'd come across the lawn from the orchard, and then gone back the same way, which would have brought him into the churchyard. Dexter had been this way before.

Lol looked out, down the churchyard path and found that he couldn't see the lych-gate. Normally it would be outlined in gold, from the lantern on the perimeter wall.

The lantern had gone out. Lol bent and peered through where the gate would be. Usually, you would see the lamps on the square and the partly floodlit profile of The Black Swan.

'Power's gone.'

'Big surprise,' Dexter said.

He was right; it was bound to happen. Sometimes it only lasted a couple of minutes, but more often three or four hours. And occasionally, in weather like this, two or three days.

Lol switched on the torch. 'Just hope the phone line's still up. You want to check that footpath, through the orchard, or call the police now?'

'En't your problem. You might as well go home. I'll call 'em from the bungalow, look.'

'OK.' Lol would call them, as soon as he got back to the vicarage. 'Well . . . I hope she's all right.'

'Tough ole bat,' Dexter said. 'Hey '

'Sorry?'

'Give the vicar one for me.' Dexter sniggered.

''Night, Dexter.' Lol walked back into the churchyard. The snow had slowed again, or maybe the loss of light just made it seem that way.

'Hold on – wrong way, boy.'

'I'll go through the orchard, into the vicarage garden.'

'Don't wanner do that this time o' night. Bloody dangerous, look, all this—'

'Done it *loads* of times. And I can check the other door, side of the church, on the way. You never know, do you?'

And now he did. He moved as quickly as he could through the untrodden snow, listening for the sound of Dexter crunching after him, like before, but it didn't come.

He adjusted the head of the torch to issue a wide beam, and the graves appeared out of the snow, like the stumps of a shorn forest, all the unsightly bits – the borders and the gravel beds, the pots of long-dead flowers – submerged.

The path, too, had vanished, and he had to guess his way through the wider gaps between graves and tombs overhung by the snow-bent branches of elderly apple trees.

He stopped when he heard the breathing.

Coming from somewhere in front of him, and it was very loud, theatrically loud and eerie – vampire breathing. Something alive among the graves.

Dexter. Dexter had done a circuit of the church and was waiting for him and letting him know. He'd lied to Dexter – been this way no more than once or twice, in high summer. He turned, and his foot stabbed into a squat gravestone, mostly buried. He pulled back in pain, shining the torch directly ahead of him, the beam hitting a wall of white, an impassable snowbank. Swinging the torch to the right he found one of the old toppled tombs, its cracks and cavities compacted with snow.

And what looked like a collapsed, eroded stone angel, breathing.

Antony Largo was in his denims and he looked invigorated and younger than Jane remembered him, and more cheerful. Pacing the kitchen, sizing things up. The stubble on his face was almost a beard now, and made his grin seem bigger and whiter.

'And how were you received, Matt?'

Matthew Hawksley considered. 'She was polite, courteous . . . but I'm not holding my breath.'

'She won't go near it,' Jane said. 'Even a minor exorcism takes a lot of preparation – days, sometimes. They don't go into it without long discussions with like *everybody*. In this case, she'd need the green light from the Bishop.'

'Ah well,' Antony said philosophically. 'If it's meant to be, it'll happen.'

But Jane knew that he wouldn't give up after all the trouble he'd taken to get here. After talking to her on the phone, he'd called up a guy who ran a film-unit resources business – called him up at home in the middle of the night and pestered him for something heavy and all-terrain within the hour. Whatever kind of money Antony had been waving around had brought him this monster Shogun, and then he'd done the journey the hard way, blasting up from London, through Gloucester and down to Ross. White-hellraiser.

'*Extremely* nasty in places, but I just plugged on. Miles tae go before I sleep.' He'd grinned. 'Sleep? When I fetched up here, it was like I was already there – *very* dreamlike. Damn cops wouldnae even let me in at first.'

'They thought you were a journalist,' Ben had said, glancing at Amber, who was back at the stove, making soup and resenting all these people in her kitchen. 'I think we'll have to play all this by ear.'

Seeing Natalie brought in for questioning had unnerved Ben. Jane and Amber had agreed not to discuss what they'd learned from Beth Pollen, if only because Antony was back. OK, *Women of the Midnight* was TV history now, but if he found out Natalie's real identity, nothing would stand in his way, like *nothing*.

The *contemporary dynamic*. The *now drama*.

'I don't know about the rest of you,' Ben said, 'but I'm just hoping this is some awful, *awful* mistake.'

'Well,' Antony said, 'whoever the hell this Sebastian Dacre was, he's given us a buzz we can*not* ignore.'

'Antony, everybody's knackered, everybody's fractious, everybody's upset . . .'

'Wrong,' Antony said. 'Everybody's *electrified*.'

*

In semi-darkness, the dining room was like a derelict chapel – a dead fireplace at one end, at the other this lofty stained-glass window fogged with night and snow.

'If you're getting feelings of déjà vu,' Bliss said, 'it doesn't hold any nice memories for me, either. As you know.'

He meant the time in October – although to Merrily, it still felt as raw as last week – when he'd asked her to talk to a particular man facing a murder charge, and she'd been dreading it and relieved when it hadn't come off. And then the situation had turned into a free-rolling tragedy, and the guilt and remorse had kicked in.

Which was why there was no way she could say no to this one, or even *think* no.

The door to the hall was open, and they were standing in a narrow alley of diffused light. Bliss had been waiting when she and Gomer came back into the hotel.

'We'll be outside at both ends, Merrily.'

'Tell me again. Give me all the details.'

'There *are* no details. We never got that far.'

'Then give me the outline again.'

'She admits killing Dacre – that's it. She keeps saying, "I killed him, what else do you want?" I say, "I want to know why." She says, "You wouldn't understand." And then, after a bit, she goes, "If you do a couple of things for me, I'll think of a full explanation for what happened, I'll write it all down, and I won't go back on it. I won't ask for a lawyer and I'll plead guilty." And I'm saying, "But, Brigid, it won't be the truth, will it?"'

'And she's saying, "Whenever did the truth matter to a copper?"'

'Words to that effect. People don't have much of an opinion of the police any more, do they? Not even convicted murderers. After I tell her I don't think she's actually in the best position to start demanding deals, we sit there in complete silence. Like, normally, I can sit quietly for as long as you like if I've got an excuse to keep staring at a lovely woman. But this one was somehow in control. Probably a status thing: the nationally famous killer and the obscure provincial detective. After about two minutes, I'm going, "All right, what is it? What are you after?" '

Mumford's shape in the doorway reduced the light to a corona around him.

'Sorry to disturb you, boss, it's as we feared: no chance of getting her into headquarters in the next four, five hours. Until daylight, in fact. Apparently, seventeen roads've been closed. Mostly this end of the county.'

'Shucks.'

'We can't even get the body away.'

'Where is he?'

'In the van on the car park?'

'You better tell all that to Howe, then.' Bliss didn't sound too unhappy. He turned to Merrily. 'The Ice Maiden's finally discovered who Natalie is. And consequently has decided the interrogation requires a woman's touch. Looks like you'll have to do. She'd hate that, wouldn't she?'

'Frannie . . .'

'Remind me to compliment the esteemed leader of Hereford Council on putting all our money into new shopping centres instead of winter maintenance. We have the lady to ourselves. Let's dance the night away.'

'What did she say when you asked her what she was after?'

'She said, "I'd like to see my daughter, alone, as soon as you can arrange it, and I'd also like, at some point, to talk to a Church of England minister called the Reverend Merrily Watkins." Naturally, I ask her why and naturally she declines to tell me. And when I write down this vicar's name I ask her to spell it because, naturally, we're unacquainted.'

'Why do I still get the feeling you engineered this?'

'It's what she said, Merrily, I swear to God.'

'She didn't mention Jane?'

'No, thankfully she didn't mention Jane.'

'It sounds as if she doesn't know I'm here.'

'Then let's surprise her,' Bliss said. 'For some reason that escapes me, despite all my training, experience and natural flair some people seem to prefer to unburden themselves to you. I'm not proud. It could save time.'

'And if she tells me things in strict confidence?'

'Then you can tell her what a basically nice, understanding person I am and how much better she'd feel sharing it all with me – as distinct from the cold-hearted friggin' bitch awaiting her over in Hereford, should she decide to hold out.'

Merrily looked at the connecting door to the lounge. 'Can I make a call before I go in? I need to . . . make sure things are OK at home.'

'We have all the time in the world,' Bliss said.

The sound of the breathing was like a recording, amplified, as though the tomb was an echo chamber, and something had reanimated the ancient corpse in there.

Most of her upper body was fused to the broken side of the tomb. Her legs were buried, and a weight of snow had collected in her lap like ice cream heaped in a bowl.

Only an inscripted slab of stone, long ago dislodged, had protected her face from the snow, and in the torchlight it was as florid as Lol remembered. Her tongue was out, and there was a spittle ring around her mouth, a dab of froth in one corner of her lips, bubbling when the breath came through.

Alive, though.

Tough ole bat.

Lol knelt down in the snow, brushing and pulling it away

with both hands, uncovering a pink, quilted coat done up on the wrong buttons.

Whispering, 'Alice . . .?'

All she did by way of reply was to go on breathing through her mouth, the air siphoned out in the gap alongside her protruding tongue.

Even her breath seemed cold.

She'd had a stroke. He'd seen this before – in one of the day rooms at the psychiatric hospital, a woman with schizophrenia having a stroke in an armchair in front of the TV, and her breathing filling the room. He remembered another patient going to turn up the telly.

He peered into her face: lopsided, like half of it had collapsed, her eyes closed. The colours of Alice's face, when you thought about it, had always suggested high blood pressure.

Her's likely wandered off. What they do, her age, minds start goin'.

Lol began furiously to shovel the snow out of Alice's lap with cupped hands, then began digging out her lower legs, cold as marble.

The woman in the armchair, the white-coats had been very careful how they moved her. That was in a centrally heated day room.

How long had Alice been here? An hour?

She should be dead.

He bent and put an arm under her shoulders, prising them from the tomb. He unzipped his parka, pulled it off and put it around her shoulders, digging with his other hand to find the crook of her knees, until she came up in his arms, shedding her shroud of snow.

Knowing, all the time, that Dexter Harris had to be watching him from somewhere close.

FORTY-FOUR

Sanctuary

The easy chair and the sofa had been placed at right angles under the brass-stemmed Victorian standard lamp, an intimate enclosure at the fireplace end of the long lounge. There was a coffee table with two coffees on it, served by the thickset policewoman whom Bliss had called Alma.

'I thought I could wait just inside the door,' Alma said to Merrily. 'It's a big room – I'm not going to hear anything you don't want me to. I can sit there and read the paper.'

Merrily took off her coat and folded it over an arm of the sofa. 'Wouldn't it be possible for you to leave us completely alone?'

'I still might have to keep looking in on you. Got my instructions.'

'Oh, for God's sake,' Brigid Parsons said from the armchair, 'what am I gonna do, hold her hostage? Strangle her with her dog collar?'

'Not wearing one,' Merrily said. 'You'd have to garrotte me with the chain of my cross.'

Alma didn't smile. Someone had thrown a fresh green log on the fire, making smoke and hiss and spiteful yellow flames.

'Blimey.' Brigid Parsons stretched out her long legs to the fireplace. 'You really *are* Jane's mother, aren't you?'

'If you want anything,' Alma said, 'don't come out. Call me and I'll come in.' She glanced over her shoulder before she went out of the lounge door. The fire cracked and let go a fusillade of sparks. Brigid Parsons stood up quickly and stamped on a firefly speck on the carpet.

'Ben Foley. Tight-arsed in all the wrong directions. I mean, come on – what's a bag of coal cost?' She sat down again. She wore tight jeans and a long-sleeved black shirt, with two or three buttons open, displaying a silver pendant in the form of what looked like an owl. A grey cardigan hung around her shoulders. She pushed back a strand of dark brown hair from over an eye. 'Jane finally got you in?'

'Indirectly. Which is the way it is with Jane. She doesn't *actively* work against you, she's just . . . indirect.'

'She's a good kid. I like Jane. She's got a lively mind. Unlike poor little Clancy, but whose fault is that?'

Merrily sat down at the end of the sofa, near her coat. 'Does she know? Clancy?'

'About me? Yeah. Yeah, she does. I wasn't going to tell her yet, I was gonna wait till she left school. I mean, I'd always found it surprisingly easy, *not* telling her – you walk out of prison into single-parent accommodation and a new identity, and that was kind of hard to get used to, so I used to practise on her. Telling her all about the new me before she was even old enough to understand what on earth I was on about. By the time she was two, the old me was history. Sorted.'

'Why were you going to wait till she left school?'

'Oh . . . because . . . Well, for a start, because Clancy isn't like Jane, who'd see it as a big challenge. But also, if I waited till she was eighteen she'd have the option to walk away.'

'From you?'

'If she wanted to.'

'Why *did* you tell her?' Merrily drank some coffee. It was good. Amber Foley, Stanner Hall's only asset. 'Did somebody get on to you – the press?'

'Nah, nothing like that. I mean, there *was* some of that, quite a few years ago – media trouble – when Clancy was little, and I had to change the name again – to Craven; when we ended up in Craven Arms, it was like a bad joke. It was a problem, for me, getting used to another surname. Less so for her. I think she thought it was something everybody had to do every few years. Excuse me, but are those cigs sticking out of your coat pocket?'

'Want one?' Merrily pulled out her Silk Cut and the Zippo.

'Thanks. It's a big thing when you first get out, not having to let one of the screws feel you up just to get yourself a fresh packet.' She took a cigarette and Merrily lit it for her. 'I'm sorry, I'm being flip. I don't feel flip. I feel like shit, naturally.'

'I can imagine.'

Brigid inhaled a lot of smoke and let it out slowly. 'Reason I told Clancy about Brigid, and the reason, basically, that we came here, was that a kid at school – a boy – was taking the piss out of Clan because she was quite a bit behind the others. We'd moved around a lot, with my jobs, and we'd just come up from Cornwall, and she'd got behind, and this kid was like, "Oh you're backward, you're ESN." Taunting her. I think he fancied her, actually – you know the oblique way they approach things at that age. How was he to know what a raw spot this was? So, anyway, she stuck a Biro in his eye.'

'Oh.'

'I mean, like *really* stuck it in. This wasn't one of your classroom semi-accidents. Some of the kids from school would go down the chip shop at lunchtime, and she walked up to him in the street while he was eating his chips and she just stuck the flaming pen in his eye. I mean hard. Hard enough that he needed surgery to save his sight in that eye. The police were involved for a while, but there was no charge. But word gets out, obviously, and I had a call from my old minder, Ellie, who was actually the detective who'd arrested me. And Ellie's like, what you gonna do about this? And she didn't know the half of it. She didn't know about Hattie. But she saw a dangerous parallel. I'm assuming you know what I mean.'

'I think so.' *He lost an eye, Stuart, did you know?*

'So we sat down one night last spring, Clan and me, and I told her. We sat there just like this, drinking coffee – only it was a bloody sight warmer, of course. It was after dawn before we went to bed – together, like sisters. And she never went back to that school, and that was when we came down here to live with Jeremy.'

Brigid Parsons sat up and looked around vaguely, then leaned forward and tipped half an inch of ash into the grate. Merrily realized that she'd hardly stopped talking since the policewoman had left them alone.

'That was a bit of an ice-breaker, wasn't it?' Brigid said.

Merrily felt very odd. It had been like two old mates catching up: the so-called woman of God and the woman who, as a teenager, had lured a boy into some derelict industrial building and inflicted upon him . . . was it *forty-seven* stab wounds?

'They haven't actually arrested me,' Brigid said. 'Or do I mean charged? Someone like me, they don't know how to play it. It's like asking the Queen if she needs the toilet. The red-haired Scouser said, "We've brought you in to ask you some questions, that's all." I just said, "I did it." He's like, *what?* And you could tell he'd rather I'd said, "Piss off, copper, you got nothing on me" like he presumably gets from everybody else. He looks at me like he can't wait to get my clothes off and into a plastic bag.'

'You told Bliss you killed Dacre?'

'Absolutely.'

'And did you?'

'Unless it turns out he had a heart attack on his way down, yeah.'

'Why?'

'It doesn't *matter* why. He's dead, I killed him. End of story. I'm not looking for absolution. Harold Shipman's banged up for killing about three hundred of his patients, but nobody knows why he did it.'

'That's because he hasn't even admitted doing it.'

'He's a doctor. Those bastards never admit killing anybody even by accident.'

'Was *this* an accident?' Merrily asked.

'Hey, listen, I've already been more cooperative than Dr Shipman. And I was also more selective. And I didn't want to talk about this to you, I wanted to talk about Clancy. Can I have another of those?'

'Help yourself.'

'Ta.' Brigid picked up the Zippo from the coffee table and lit her own cigarette this time, leaning back with it. 'Merrily – that's a very old-fashioned vicar sort of name, isn't it? Most women clergy seem to have these monosyllabic dyke-names.'

'I'm not.'

'I know you're not. You're with this songwriter guy who was mentally ill and isn't sure where he stands.'

'He wasn't mentally ill. He got sucked into the system. Would it have mattered if I'd been gay?'

'Don't look at me like that. I was inside for ten years, hormones squirting out everywhere. Yeah, maybe a little. She's had enough situations to adjust to.'

'Sorry?'

'Clancy. How much time do we have?'

'I don't know. I think the head of Hereford CID wants

you taken over there for questioning. She may get impatient. She may send a snowplough.'

'She?'

'She wouldn't want you talking to me. I think this is the only chance we'll get.'

'Female authority figures – like I need another one. OK, Merrily.' Brigid gazed steadily through the smoke. 'Here's the situation: I don't belong to any church, and I'm not sure what I believe. I've never seen the ghost of my appalling grandmother, and I've never felt her looking over my shoulder. Not, I should say, for want of trying. I'd love it if we could meet. Earlier tonight – Jane'll tell you – I mean, earlier tonight there I was lying up in her room, surrounded by creepy old photos of the bitch. The biggest one, I had to clean the glass and I did that by spitting in her face, over and over again. And then I lay there under her smeary picture, looking at both of us in the dressing-table mirror. Anything happen? Did it hell. No lights, no images, no sudden drops in temperature. Bitch.'

'Why did you want to see her?'

Brigid ignored the question. 'Last week – you've probably had this from Jane – Ben and I got into a confrontation with one of the shooters Sebastian hired, and he made some contemptuous remark about Jeremy. Blue light.'

She looked at Merrily for a reaction.

'You attacked him.'

'Ben was very gallant. He said at least people might stop calling him a poof now. He said he could understand it after the guy nearly shot Clancy at The Nant. Yeah, I . . . The guy wasn't expecting it, of course, and I think the first blow must've smashed his nose. What I didn't realize until Ben was pulling me away was that I had a rock in my hand. A jagged piece of what had been dressed stone, about the size of half a brick. I don't remember picking it up – I suppose it must have been a reflex thing when Ben and I first saw him coming towards us, and we didn't know if he was armed. And you still don't seem surprised.'

'What do you want me to say?'

'Feel free to be shocked. It still shocks me, when I allow myself to think about it. Which isn't too often, because I have to be at least halfway normal for Clancy. Naturally, I'm not unaware that this happened in roughly the place where my grandmother smashed the skull of my grandfather. But I stress that I did not feel anything. I didn't feel her *with me*. You know?'

'Does this sort of thing happen often? I mean, is it something you have to . . . control?'

'I don't think control comes into it. I'm not even an aggressive person. I mean, truly I'm *not*. When I was inside, nine times out of ten – no, hell, more than that – if someone had a go at me, I'd deal with it, and not in any extreme way, you know? Only on a couple of occasions in nearly ten years was there anything . . . And that's being banged-up, and being banged-up can be . . . trying.'

'What about the . . . thing that got you in there?'

Merrily recoiled. It was like two little steel shutters had come down over Brigid's eyes.

'I'd heard you didn't talk about it.'

'What's the point? You want some whingeing psychobabble? Psychiatrists and therapists . . . every so often, one would have a go at me. Sod that. I don't make excuses, I don't feel self-pity, and I don't permit myself to feel pity for . . . *them*. I did my time, I deserved it, that's it.'

It sounded like a litany, one she'd intoned many times.

'And I'm not mentally ill like my mother, and I'm not a drunk like my gran.'

'Your mother was—?'

'My mother, at the age of seven, tried to kill her sister.

She was rescued from a psychiatric hospital by my father. Not long after I was born, she slashed her wrists in the bath. Let's not talk about it. I'm not mad.'

What? 'You're probably too sane,' Merrily said. 'It's what's scary.'

'One of a number of things, actually.'

'You came here as owner of The Nant?'

'Done some homework, then. I've got a dossier on you, too. No, a lawyer and an accountant see to all that. I came because something had already happened. Well, two things. One, like I said, because Clancy stuck a Biro in a kid's eye. Two, because my dad was dead, but before he died he told me what he should've told me years before. Told me about Hattie and what happened at the big house we used to look at through the pines, Jeremy and me, when I was a kid on holiday.'

'Did your mother know about Hattie?'

'She'd cancelled Hattie from her history at an early age, but Hattie came through – or something did. My mother was diagnosed as schizophrenic. My dad was a male nurse who thought he could handle that.'

'And *you* really didn't know until—?'

'My *dad* didn't know until he brought me up here to look at The Nant, and Eddie Berrows told him.'

Merrily said, 'Clancy . . . the pen . . . was that the only time?'

'I hope so. Look, I said the shrinks never got anywhere with me, and that's true, but there was one guy. He was the chaplain at my last place – the open prison. He was ex-Army, and he went back into the Army as a chaplain a year or so later. He was very posh, but a bit of a rough diamond, and we . . . got on, you know? Mates, kind of. The last year, I'd go out for weekends and stay at his place, with his wife and kids. It was a laugh. He wasn't holier-than-thou, and he had his problems. And he'd keep saying to me, "You need a better priest than me." '

'What did he mean by—?' Smoke from under the green log belched into the room like dragon's breath and made Merrily cough.

'What he meant was a Deliverance priest, and he tried to explain what that meant, but I was like, "Sod off, Chas; what am I, demonic?" He . . . we still stayed in touch after I came out, and he must've been in contact with Ellie Maylord because he rang me a couple of nights after she did, about the biro incident. I'd spoken to my dad by then, and I told Chas about Hattie, and I said – even though I hadn't really made a decision at that stage – that I was thinking about coming back here to suss all that out, and he went a bit quiet. Well, what did he think, I was gonna be like my mother, run away, pretend it never happened? Even she finally realized that was futile. The next night he's on the phone again: "I'm going to give you the name of someone who can help you." I was still managing this hotel in Shropshire, and he faxed me some stuff over, and it said, *The Rev. Merrily Watkins, Ledwardine.* He said he knew you and he'd have a word with you if I wanted. I said, Forget it, no way, stay the hell out of it.'

'What's his name?'

'Chas? Charles Headland. The Reverend. You remember him?'

Merrily sank back into the sofa, an image coming up of an unforgiving, grey Nonconformist chapel below the point of Pen-y-fan in the Brecon Beacons, overlooking the valley of the shadow of death. An ill-assorted bunch of Anglican priests, most of them nervous, a couple over-confident, trying to see across the valley.

'I was on a course with him. *The* course – the Deliverance course. Where we were trained to investigate the paranormal and told where to sprinkle the holy water. I knew he'd been in the Army, but he never said anything about being chaplain of a women's prison. Where is he now?'

'He's out of it. He's not even a vicar any more. He had a breakdown.'

'I didn't know.' It happened. It happened to Deliverance ministers in particular.

'He faxed me a load of guff – where you lived, your phone number, the fact that you had a daughter about Clancy's age who went to Moorfield High School. Which was the only bit that was any use, initially. I didn't want Clancy to go to the school at Kington in case . . . well, I don't trust people, I didn't want any risk of it getting out. So I got Clancy into Moorfield, which was a safe-ish distance away. And I did ask her to look out for a girl called Jane Watkins, if only for Chas's sake. Not realizing Clancy was going to be practically *stalking* the poor kid.'

Merrily sat up.

Brigid smiled ruefully. 'She's quite good at not seeming to be doing it. She has a talent for appearing forlorn and vulnerable.'

Merrily remembered Jane telling her, half-exasperated, about the new girl who hung around looking all needy and alienated. Who was a year behind where she ought to be and therefore had to go into classes with little kids. How they had absolutely nothing in common, but she felt sorry for her and . . .

Merrily began to feel uneasy.

'It was me who got the Foleys to offer Jane a job,' Brigid said. 'I don't know why I did it, really. Except that I supposed it would guarantee Jane not becoming too fed up with Clancy, and I thought Jane was probably good for her. And Amber kept offering to pay Clancy to help out around the place, and frankly I didn't *want* her around this place too much. I suppose that while I wanted to find Hattie Chancery I didn't want Hattie to find Clancy. If that makes any sense.'

Merrily nodded, lighting another cigarette.

'I got to know a woman called Beth Pollen, whose husband had died, and the suddenness of it had thrown her into spiritualism. She was interested in Stanner, because he'd been doing a paper on it, and . . . she was OK. Somebody I could trust, amazingly. So I did. Beth became the first person outside the System I'd ever just told who I was and what I'd done. And she said that if there was an ancestral problem here – a curse, however seriously you want to take that as a decription – then we should address it from a position of knowledge. Between us, we uncovered a lot of stuff about the Chancerys and Hattie and what she was like. We went right back into it . . . right back to Ellen Gethin, who was the wife of Black Vaughan and killed this guy in cold blood after he killed her younger brother who—'

The lounge door opened a crack, and Brigid turned and waved, and the policewoman, Alma, came in. 'Everything OK?'

'Thanks,' Merrily said. Alma went out and the door closed.

'I still didn't want to involve you,' Brigid said. 'I didn't want us to have a half-arsed bloody exorcism – not after we found out about the crazy thing the Chancerys did, when the guy over the fireplace may or may not have been in attendance. I didn't want to resort to superstition, if there was any way . . . I don't know *what* I wanted.'

Jeremy? Did you want Jeremy?

The question had kept pushing itself into Merrily's head, and she kept pushing it back. She was aware that Brigid had mentioned Jeremy only in passing, only in relation to some other point she was making.

The log on the fire was giving up. There were no more

flames. Brigid shivered and pushed her arms into her cardigan. Her mouth was wide and generous, her eyes were warm, with deep, wry lines in the corners, and she talked like she was already back behind bars.

'I gather you've got quite a big vicarage in Ledwardine. Seven bedrooms?'

'Something like that.'

'Just you and Jane?'

'Mmm.'

'I won't dress this up. Would you have room for Clancy?'

'What?'

'That's my bottom-line question. When I go away again, can Clancy come and live with you?'

'I—'

'Jane's told Clancy all about you and your situation. Jane's done a lot of rabbiting, because Clan doesn't have much to say, except to me.' Brigid was talking rapidly now. 'Jane's told her about the big vicarage, and Lol, and how inhibited you are about that – not wanting anybody to know, not wanting to be seen as living in sin, and yet you're big on the concept of the Church offering sanctuary, and you feel guilty about all those bedrooms doing nothing, and . . . Look, I'm sorry to hang it on you like this, Merrily, but what other chance am I going to have?'

'Brigid, it's—'

'Natalie. It's Natalie. For the moment, it's Natalie.'

'It's a big step.'

'It could be the biggest thing you ever did. I mean it's too late for me, right? And yeah, I feel very bad about putting this kind of responsibility on anybody. But what happens if Clancy goes into the System? What happens if she goes into the System and somebody gets hurt, or somebody dies? Go on, tell me I'm being ridiculously superstitious. Tell me, from your vast experience as a Deliverance Minister, that I'm entirely irrational.'

'No. You're not.'

'Doesn't have to be a full-time thing – I realize that if Jane thinks Clancy's a pain in the arse now, that isn't going to improve. I thought maybe Danny and Greta, they got no kids . . . I thought they could have her some of the time, to take the pressure off.'

'That's why you sent her to Greta tonight?'

'It was an opportunity. I didn't realize, obviously, how tonight would turn out – this wasn't a set-up, Merrily, it wasn't cold-blooded. Listen, the other thing is that money won't be a problem. I know how pitifully little the clergy earn, and I can pay you ten grand a year, maybe a good bit more, until she's twenty-one. It's . . . all arranged.'

'It isn't about—'

'What it's about is spiritual security. And I know it's a huge thing to ask, and I promise that if it goes wrong for her, I will never, never hold you in any way responsible.'

'Natalie, how long have you been planning this?'

'Is that important?'

'And what about Jeremy Berrows?'

The door opened again, and Bliss's head appeared. 'Ladies—'

'Five minutes, Frannie,' Merrily said. 'Please.' Before the door had closed, she was leaning forward. 'What about Jeremy?'

'I've damaged him enough.' Brigid said. 'It's best if he doesn't see me again. Best if he truly forgets me this time, and that's all I want to say about it.'

Her face had become flushed and against the faded brocade of the chair she looked radiantly beautiful, lit up by this powerfully incandescent, raging . . . sorrow.

Merrily said, 'Tell me something: did you ever love him

at all, or was he just the only man you could be around for any length of time without wanting to take him apart?'

'That's not fair—'

'Natalie, we don't have time for fair.'

'What do *you* . . .?' Brigid Parsons dug her shoulders into the back of her chair, pulling her cardigan tightly across the opening of her shirt, as if it was a gash. 'What do you know about Jeremy, anyway?'

'I'm just trying to work out, from the bits you've let slip, whether you came back here for Jeremy or Sebbie Dacre.'

'You can't—'

'I mean, to kill him. Kill Dacre. And I don't really know where that came from. All I do know is how perilously close you came to killing them both.'

'What do you mean?'

'Erm, earlier tonight, Jeremy—'

Brigid Parsons stood up so suddenly that she knocked over the coffee table and both cups. '*What's he done?*'

Bliss and Alma exploded into the room, followed by two male uniforms.

FORTY-FIVE

Fatalist

It had stopped snowing again, but this only made the air seem colder and the sky darker. Alice was breathing up at it – a damp, soughing sound, like the wind through rotting leaves.

Alice was birdlike, but she was soaked and felt like dead weight as Lol waded through the orchard under the snow-lagged limbs of apple trees that he never saw until it was too late, because he'd had to leave the Maglite behind on the tomb, along with Alice's shoes buried in the snow.

It seemed strange that, when some snow-fuzzed twig scraped her cheek, she didn't wake up struggling and flapping, cawing at him, outraged. He wondered if she would ever wake up again and what state she'd be in if she did, how much of her would be functioning. *Salt and vinegar on that, is it, lovey?*

Or would the chip shop be under new management? *Get 'em served and on to the next one, don't give 'em too many chips neither.*

Lol stopped.

At the edge of the church's own orchard, the rhythm of Alice's breathing had fractured, the indrawn breath suspended like a roller-coaster car pausing on a peak before clattering into the long valley, and he thought, *Christ, she's gone.*

He didn't know any more about strokes than what the condition looked like. He didn't know whether the schizophrenic woman in the psychiatric hospital had lived or died, only that they hadn't seen her again.

Oh . . . *God*. Alice's breath shuddered back into the night, Lol quivering with relief.

The vicarage formed in front of them, lightless, just a different texture of night. Beyond it, you ought to have been able to see sporadic lights in the hills, but there was nothing there, nothing to convey space or distance.

Lol's hands and Alice connected with the wicket gate into the vicarage garden. He had trouble with the latch, had to put Alice down in the snow. Felt her sinking, but what else could he do? He was so soaked and freezing in his Gomer Parry sweatshirt that he could hardly pick her up again.

He carried Alice through the gate, across the lawn to the path that circuited the house and then round to the front door which, without a key, he'd left unlocked. He backed into it.

Completely black in here. Too risky to try and get her upstairs with no lights. Lol carried her into the kitchen, where the old Aga snored but where there was no sofa, not even a big chair. He was feeling for heat with the backs of his hands, holding Alice up. He knew there was a rug on the floor to the side of the stove, before you reached the window.

He found it with his feet and lowered her, and roughly rolled up his parka and pushed it between her head and the wall. Stood up and felt his way to the refectory table where there were chairs with cushions you could pull out. Collected four and took them back to where Alice lay, a small pile of clothes with a noisy pump inside. He began feeding two cushions behind her head against the wall.

Alice moaned, and he thought her hands moved.

'Alice?'

He felt her falling forward. *Keep her head up. Don't let her swallow her tongue.*

Alice said, '*Whosat?*'

'Alice,' Lol said, 'if you can hear this, it's . . . She wouldn't know him. 'I'm getting a doctor, OK? You're safe.'

'*Wangohome.*'

'You're safe.'

But she was still as crispy-cold as a sack of peas out of the deep-freeze.

'*Pummedown. Dexer, pummedown.*'

'Alice, I'm going to ring for some help. Just—'

'*Dowannago.*' A hand clawing at him, unexpectedly strong. '*Pummedown, Dexer!*'

'He's not here, Alice. It's OK. Dexter's not here.'

But almost as he spoke, he knew by the drifting odour of sweat and something else that he couldn't define – a gross swelling in the air – that he was wrong.

Left alone again, Brigid and Merrily gathered up the crockery from the burn-scarred carpet in front of Ben Foley's sour, hissing fire of green softwood. Merrily got out her cigarettes. There were only two left in the packet. She placed it on the arm of Brigid's chair. Brigid's face was candle-white.

'Why didn't I . . . *think?*'

'Danny's with him,' Merrily said. 'You know Danny – he'll stay there all night.'

'Can't stay for the rest of his life.'

'And would you have?'

'Given the chance,' Brigid said. 'I thought we were meant, right from the beginning. The one thing I could never forgive my dad for was intercepting Jeremy's letters. And – even worse – he found some way of stopping my letters to Jeremy getting out. I still don't know who he persuaded, or how he did it.'

'Because you did what you did soon after coming here?'

'And he found out about Hattie. He didn't *believe* . . . anything. And yet he obviously convinced someone that any correspondence from the area of Stanner would not be healthy.'

They sat for a while in a pool of quiet. Brigid didn't touch the cigarettes. The bulb in the standard lamp went dim and then stammered back to life.

'If the power goes, they'll probably handcuff me to the banisters at the bottom of the stairs.'

Brigid found a crumpled tissue in her jeans and roughly stabbed at her eyes with it. She stared into the dismal fire, and Merrily thought of the everlasting furnace in Jeremy's living-room range and was startled when Brigid said, 'I never changed a thing, you know. He kept on at me to move things around, have brighter colours, impose *me* on The Nant, but I never touched a single ornament.'

'Did you want to?'

'Every day.'

'But better it looked as though you'd never been there at all? If you weren't permitted to stay.' Merrily took a breath. 'Why did he do it?'

'It's not for me to . . .' Brigid dug her fingers into her forehead. 'He thought he was doing it for me. That's all I want to say.'

'People couldn't get their heads around it – you and Jeremy.'

'People are crass and stupid and superficial. Educated townies, with weekend cottages, tend to venerate country folk.'

'Touching, isn't it?'

'Always venerating the wrong ones. Never people like Danny Thomas and that little guy, Gomer. Certainly never

Jeremy Berrows. Always the loud bastards, who know everything and nothing.'

'Sebbie Dacre.'

'And the old Mistress of the Hunt.' Brigid looked up. 'I can *feel* her, can you? Over there, where that bookcase is – that's where the shelves were, where she kept the trophy stones for Robert Davies to look up at and eat his heart out. How do I *know*? I don't, actually, but when I picture that scene, this is the room. When the light faded a minute ago, I thought, that's *her.*'

Merrily said. 'I . . . I've been asked to help see her off the premises.'

'How do you feel about that?'

'I have to keep explaining to people . . .' Merrily looked at the cigarette packet, then put it out of her mind. 'You can exorcize evil in an abstract or spiritual form. With possibly-evil *people*, we run into problems. *You* hate the whole idea of Hattie Chancery. You want someone to come along and point a crucifix and send her, screaming, into oblivion.'

'And you can't?'

'Neither can I put her in a snuff-box, under a stone at the bottom of Hergest Pool.'

'You picked up on all that.'

'I don't know how relevant it is. It seems faintly daft sitting here, with you in your situation, discussing fairy tales.'

'Maybe you should talk to Beth Pollen,' Brigid said.

Frannie Bliss took Merrily into an office behind reception, steered her into the swivel chair at the desk, on the edge of which he sat, so that he was looking down at her. She felt for her cigarettes, realized she'd left them in the lounge.

'You want to know why she killed Dacre.'

'Call me a completist, Merrily, but that would be nice.'

This seemed to be Ben Foley's personal desk. It had gold

inlaid bits and a small, framed photograph of Amber smiling through the steam rising from two cooking pots.

'OK.' She knew that what she was about to tell him would, at some stage, take a slow turn away from the truth, whatever the truth was. 'We did a deal. She wanted two things. I . . . agreed to both.'

Bliss looked curious but didn't ask. She told him how Brigid Parsons had inherited The Nant, although everyone thought that Jeremy Berrows owned it. How the Dacres had been trying to buy it for years. How it had become a focus for Sebbie.

'And at some stage, quite recently, he appears finally to have discovered the true identity of the woman with Jeremy Berrows.'

'Finally?'

'He'd probably had his suspicions for a long time.'

'The printout pinned to the sign?'

'Could've been him letting her know that he knew,' Merrily said. 'And putting the name Brigid into circulation at Stanner Hall. Causing unease. Perhaps demonstrating how precarious things were for her. It must have gone up yesterday at the earliest, so . . .'

'So we're looking at blackmail.'

Merrily shrugged. It would do.

'Let's get this right,' Bliss said. 'Dacre threatens to expose her, explode her new identity, have the press down here in busloads unless she sells him The Nant.' He sat down opposite Merrily. 'Of course, the sensible thing would've been to flog him the farm for as much as she could get and then bugger off with the proceeds and change her identity again.'

'You're forgetting about Jeremy. Welded, body and soul, to The Nant.'

'And they're really an item, those two?'

'Think Romeo and Juliet twenty years on. In minor key.'

'They could always have gone off together.'

'Maybe half of him would go. Maybe not the half she'd want.'

'Jeez, what is it with this area? Scrubby land, lousy winters . . .'

Merrily said, 'You've heard about the shooters going on to Jeremy's land, coming on heavy? Those guys – from Off, right? Therefore less inhibited. I can't help wondering if that was less to do with terrorizing Jeremy than indicating to Brigid what life might be like for him if she didn't cooperate.'

'Clumsy . . . but very Sebbie, by all accounts. No, you're right, he wouldn't get the local shooting club to do some of that, would he? What about the final act?'

'Less forthcoming there, I'm afraid.'

'Yeh, well, to my knowledge, she's never said a word about Mark and Stuart in all these years. The *Guardian* once ran a story based on an interview with one of their former school-mates who reckoned Mark tried to rape her. Inference was, Stuart too, but Stuart's still alive and he's gorra lawyer. Nice opening for Brigid to make a statement – but not a word.'

'It's as if . . .' Merrily hesitated, tapping Ben Foley's blue blotter. 'As if the acts of violence are committed by a different person, and she isn't qualified to comment on them. You've heard all about Hattie Chancery, I suppose.'

'At length, from Mrs Pollen. I'm not allowed to be remotely interested.'

'No.' Merrily slowly shook her head; she felt very tired. 'Frannie, what can I say? I know what she did, and I liked her.'

'Merrily, I *fancied* her. What difference does that make?'

'None at all, I suppose, to you.' He had a case to build; the law was a pile of rough stones.

'All right, what do you *think* happened up there?' Bliss said.

'Well, we can assume she met Dacre at the van – to which she still had a spare key – to discuss the final arrangements in a place where both of them knew they wouldn't be seen together. Especially on a night like this.'

'And he *went*? Knowing who she was and what she'd done in the past?'

'*Distant* past. Plus, you're talking about a man who's not known for being afraid of much, certainly not the weather or a woman.'

Was this convincing? She wasn't sure it would be, especially if it subsequently came out that Dacre knew who had damaged Nathan, the shooter.

'And gets pushed over when he's not expecting it?' Bliss wrinkled his nose.

'Personally, given the conditions,' Merrily said, 'I wouldn't have ruled out it being, to some extent, accidental.'

'Did you ask her?'

'Wouldn't go into it.'

'What about the van?'

'I don't know.'

'We gather she was entertaining a man in there? Was that Sebbie? Might she have wanted to destroy any evidence of that? It'd make it worse for Berrows if he found *that* out.'

'She's Dacre's first cousin.'

'Merrily, if it wasn't for first cousins, there wouldn't be any population to speak of between here and Aberystwyth. Anything else?'

'Not really. If you ask her questions aimed vaguely towards those answers, that's what you should end up with.'

'So why – if you don't mind me asking – *did* she want to see you? When you came out of there, she looked bloody awful. She looked, for the very first time, in fact, like some-body who's about to be charged with murder.'

'Mmm.'

Merrily looked down at the desk photo of Amber through the cooking steam. There had been only one hard and binding agreement between her and Brigid, and that was a mutual silence about Jeremy Berrows's attempted suicide.

Had Jeremy known about the blackmail and decided – because he was afraid of what Brigid might otherwise do – to remove himself from an unsolvable equation. To make it so that she would no longer have any reason – or wish – to hold on to The Nant?

She still didn't know, and maybe the answer didn't matter. Merrily saw Jeremy growing old and silent, alone at The Nant, while Brigid spent the rest of her life hardening a new prison skin. It was desperately sad. She wanted to put her head on the desk and weep. And then sleep.

'Come on, what *did* she want from you?' Bliss said. 'It won't go out of this office.'

'She wanted me to adopt her daughter. More or less.'

'Merrily, you're *kidding*.'

'Doesn't want her in care, and she doesn't have any suit-able relatives. And she doesn't want to burden Jeremy Berrows or put him in a difficult position.'

'Bloody *hell*. I mean, you can't blame her for trying. But . . . cheeky cow.' He looked at her suspiciously as she pulled out her mobile. 'You didn't? Tell me you really didn't.'

She wouldn't look at him. 'I'm supposed to be a Christian? What was I supposed to say?'

Bliss let out a lot of breath in a thin whistle. 'For God's *sake*, Merrily . . .'

He didn't ask what else she'd agreed to.

*

As soon as Merrily was out of that office, she rang Lol again. No answer. This was starting to get worrying. She rang Hereford Police and asked for Annie Howe. They put her on hold and then came back and said they couldn't find Howe, would she like to call back?

Merrily found a local phone book. *Prosser.* Would that be a business number or private? Would it come under the name of the shop? She peered at the small print. She needed reading glasses; this had been obvious for a while, but you tried to resist it.

'Problem, Vicar?'

'Gomer. Sorry, I was looking for Jim Prosser's number at the Eight till Late. I need to talk to Lol, that's all, and the phone's . . . not working. I need somebody to go round. I thought maybe Big Jim, as he gets up early to see to the papers.'

And as he was big.

'Four two one three double six, Vicar,' Gomer said. 'But he en't usually up till five, and I knows for a fact they has their machine on all night.'

'Oh.' She shut the book hard.

'Trouble back home?'

'It's . . . possible.'

'Like to help, Vicar, but it's been comin' down like a bugger out there.'

'I know, Gomer, I wasn't suggesting anything.'

'Means we'd have to use Danny's tractor, 'stead of the truck. Take a while, with the ole plough on, mind.'

Merrily blinked. 'Is that feasible?'

'Ten minutes to get down to The Nant, pick up the tractor. 'Less, o' course, Danny comes straight yere. But then there's Jeremy – can't really leave the boy.'

'You could . . . always bring him here. If he'd come.' Merrily looked over at the two police on the door of the lounge where Brigid Parsons waited. Earlier, the WPC, Alma, had escorted her to the lavatory and back. 'Gomer, are you sure about this? It's not been this bad in years.'

'And all them bad years, I was in it, waist-deep.' Gomer beamed. There seemed to be more light in his glasses than in any of the bulbs around the walls.

'OK.' Merrily beckoned him towards the porch. 'I may be worrying unnecessarily, but you need to know what this is about.'

Merrily stood for a moment, watching the tail lights of Gomer's truck disappear. When she turned round, Jane was behind her in the porch.

'I saw you go in. Is she OK?'

'Not really. She's confessed to killing Dacre.'

The kid's face was threatening to crumble like biscuit. 'She's covering for somebody.'

'I don't think she is, I really don't.'

'But like . . . how could she think she could possibly get away with it?'

'I'm not sure she even wanted to. She's a fatalist.'

'But who'd want to go back to . . . grey walls and bitterness and bitchiness and gay sex? And dope smuggled in to take you out of it. What a terrible, totally heartbreaking waste of . . .'

'Two lives,' Merrily said. 'I didn't really believe in them at first, but . . . You said "go *back*".'

'I . . . heard something.'

'From Mrs Pollen?'

'Who told *you*?'

'Bliss.'

'It's unbelievable, isn't it? Bloody devastating.'

'Who else knows, flower?'

'Amber. That's it. I hope. Where's Clancy?'

'Still with Danny's wife. And a policewoman.'

'I'm glad she's not here. I know it sounds terrible, and I know what she's been through and what she must be going through now, but Clancy . . .'

'Yeah, I know, hard going.' The squares of glass all around them in the porch were glistening and opaque, like frosted ice-trays. 'I also talked to Matthew Hawksley.'

'I know. I'd already told them that you couldn't be expected to take that on, without weeks of preparation and back-up.'

They walked back into the lobby. It was quiet now, and gloomy. Merrily noticed that three of the bulbs in the chandelier had gone out, and it hung there, gleaming faintly like one of the roast-chicken carcasses an old neighbour of her mother's used to string up for the birds to peck at.

'What do we do now?' Jane said.

Merrily fingered her pectoral cross, nodded at the steps to the kitchen.

'Tell them I'll need another hour at least.'

Jane backed off. 'You *can't* . . .'

'I can try.'

'I told them you wouldn't. I told them you'd need . . . I told them you'd even have to talk to the Bishop.'

'I probably should, but I don't see there being time.'

Jane backed away, staring at her. 'You look *knackered*.'

'I'm fine.'

'*Mum?*'

'It's because . . .' Merrily took one of Jane's hands, squeezed it. 'Because Brigid asked me to do two things for her and this was . . . maybe the easiest.'

'Mum, I don't think she even believes in God.'

'She believes in love. That's got to be nearly as embarrassing.'

'What was the other thing?'

'We can talk about that later,' Merrily said. 'Can I borrow your room to prepare?'

'You do *not* know what you're taking on.' Jane's face was creased up with tiredness and concern. 'You don't know how far back this goes.'

'Do you?'

'All the time you go on at *me* about putting myself at risk, and you're putting yourself in the path of something . . . *unknowable*—'

'Jane—'

'Because you don't want to look uncaring and wimpish. The reason you're not waking up the Bishop is you know what he'd say.'

'Give me a break, OK?' Merrily tried to pull the kid closer, but Jane dragged her hand away.

What could you say? She was probably right.

'Is that, erm, Frank?' Jane packed herself into a corner near the porch, with the mobile.

'I don't know, I'm still half asleep.'

'Look, it's . . . it's Jane. From Stanner? We met at the murder-mystery weekend? I brought the chocolate?'

'I see. This is your revenge for being dragged out of bed to find a body.'

'Sorry? Oh . . . right. Yeah. No. Listen, I'm *really sorry* to wake you, but this is pretty urgent. I'll be dead straight and upfront about this. My mother's the diocesan exorcist for Hereford, and she's been asked to do something tonight to deal with the . . . presence . . . of Hattie Chancery. And I've seen the tape that Ben recorded with old Leonard, and you were there. And all I want to know is what Leonard said after Ben finished recording.'

'What makes you think he said anything?' Frank Sampson's voice acquiring focus.

'Just a feeling. And the way Ben's behaving.'

'So ask Ben.'

'Well, he's . . . he's been a bit funny lately. Honestly, Frank, I wouldn't bother you in a million years if I didn't think this was like crucial, you know?'

'Are you crying?'

'Of course I'm not. I just—'

'I'm not quite sure what you're asking.'

'Well, I'm not either. If I just . . . If I just tell what I'm worried about – I mean without going into the ins and outs of exorcism. If Hattie Chancery was in some way haunting this place . . .'

He chuckled. 'I think *something* is, don't you? Nobody's had any luck there.'

'Well, right. But *if* she was a presence there, what would be the significance of that? And how would it tie in with the really old stuff – Black Vaughan and everything – and the exorcism Leonard was talking about? What happened at that exorcism?'

'But was it?'

'What?'

'*Was* it an exorcism?'

'It was supposed to be a restaging of the exorcism of Black Vaughan, wasn't it?'

'But they had a medium, didn't they? Erasmus Cookson. Why would they need a medium at an exorcism? Perhaps they didn't want to *exorcize* Black Vaughan at all, but to *communicate* with him. Or someone.'

'Who?'

'Jane, I don't feel too happy about discussing this on the phone. I think you need to talk to . . . do you know Mrs Pollen?'

FORTY-SIX

The Living Dark Heart

In the kitchen, Lol was standing over Alice, blinking, focusing hard on anything that seemed paler than black, and Dexter's voice was curling out of the hall.

'What you gonner do now, Mister Lol?'

Alice's breathing was much louder in here, like an old steam train might have sounded in a station.

'Give us a song, is it?'

'How about you go and find the doctor, Dexter?'

'I don't think so, boy.'

'I'd better call 999, then.'

'You don't listen, do you, Mister Lol?'

Dexter's voice had a glasspaper rasp. Lol was sure that Alice could hear all this. He laid a hand on her shoulder. It was supposed to be reassuring. It was trembling.

'Look,' Lol said. 'It's like this: she's had a stroke and she's wet through and suffering from exposure. If we piss about for too long, she's going to die.'

He gently squeezed her shoulder, trying to convey that he was only trying to *scare* Dexter, and moved away from her, easing off his wellingtons, flexing his toes on the flags, putting his hands out to feel for the familiar and finding the edge of the refectory table.

'How quick?' Dexter said.

Lol stopped.

'How quick you reckon she gonner die?'

'I said she'd die if we didn't get a doctor.'

'Half an hour?'

'Kent Asprey, that's his name, isn't it? The local GP?'

'*Fuck* off.'

Lol went quiet. Of course, Alice had tried to tell him. Alice *had* told him. She hadn't wandered into the churchyard in search of solace and then collapsed; she'd had the stroke at home, and Dexter had come back from the chip shop and found her comatose and had dragged on her coat and outdoor shoes and carried her along the orchard path into the churchyard and left her to die there of exposure. Confident that nobody would go there until well after daybreak, by which time she would be long gone, frozen to the stones.

Go on: try and think of something more rational than that.

The banality of evil. Small-time, squalid, *local* evil, as huge and coldly bloated as the night sky.

'Where's the torch, boy?'

'Left it in the churchyard. Couldn't manage the torch and Alice.'

'You knob. Whereabouts you keep your candles? Where's the matches?'

'Don't know if there are any.'

'Naw, that little bitch smokes like a chimney. *Where are they?*'

Lol didn't live here. He didn't know where the candles were, or the matches.

'Get a doctor, Dexter.'

Lol saw a slice of grey, possibly one of the kitchen windows. He saw a tiny green glow in the air: smoke alarm, reverted to the battery when the power went off.

Dexter said, 'Her's goin' *back*, boy. Her's goin' back in that graveyard.'

Oh, no. No going back now.

'You can't put us both in the graveyard, Dexter.'

'Landfill site for you, boy. They'll find Alice – natural causes, no problem. They'll never find *you*. You're missin'. I got a mate in landfill. No problem. Back o' the truck. Easy-peasy. Got no choice, look.'

'Because you killed Darrin?'

Silence. Lol didn't move.

'I never,' Dexter said.

'Yeah, I know, it was a van, right? Like it was a lorry killed Roland.'

Alice whimpered. There was a movement like a great claw descending, then another – Dexter shifting handfuls of air to find him. He could smell Dexter now, a blend of beer, sweat and petrol. Lol moved behind the table.

'What did Roland do to you? Come on, what? Tell Alice – you owe it to Alice.'

'Little fuck.' Dexter moving slowly around the table towards him, the squeak of his leather jacket.

'He was gonna tell someone about the cars?' Lol moving round the table on the other side. 'All the cars you were nicking, you and Darrin?'

'I never nicked no cars.'

'No, OK, Darrin nicked them, because you wanted to drive them. Darrin was older, but he was smaller and weedier.' Lol sliding between the table and sink. 'Darrin did everything his big cousin told him because he was shit-scared.'

Thinking: *magnetic knife rack on this wall, row of kitchen knives in ascending sizes, butter knife to bread knife to carving knife*. Edging round the end of the table. Thinking, how could he use a *knife*, for heaven's sake?

'Bit of luck, Dexter, that crash at Allensmore . . . or what?'

Then Dexter went: '*Fuuuuuu . . .!*' Jarring sound of wood

526

scraping stone, jolting pain in both Lol's thighs as the table was slammed into him, jamming him into the sink.

'Who needs luck?' Dexter said.

A wrenching now – the table dragged aside, and where in God's name was asthma when you needed it?

Lol felt the breeze of Dexter's massive fist sailing past his head. He swayed – the wrong direction, and the next blind jab was into his left cheek, a knuckle stabbing up into his eye, dislodging his glasses. He slammed his fist into where he thought Dexter's gut was, hit leather, a metal zip.

Crap at this.

A fleshy hand around his chin, tossing his head back into the wall with a crack and a wild, white shooting pain. His glasses gone, the black air bursting. Torn from the wall, slammed down into the flags, kicked in the chest, in the stomach, the pain explosive, Lol retched. Curling into a ball, rolling and squirming until he came up against a leg of the table, his gut spasming. Christ, it didn't take long, did it?

'Best thing, look – ' Dexter's boot coming in again ' – is if you just lie still and think of fucking the vicar, or whatever you want. 'Cause I en't gonner stop, look. I en't got no choice, you knows that, and I en't got no time, with Alice to take back to her grave. So you just fuckin' lie there quiet and peaceful. And you takes it till it's over, all right, Mister Lol?'

'*Uhhh.*' Boot ripping across his face. Lol lay still – pain, fear, indignity, hopelessless coalescing in the air. He could hear Alice's hollow breathing. Then a singing in the air – Dexter's boot going for his head again, missing. He tried to haul himself across the floor, sensed the foot drawn back for the big one, pushed his head back into the flags, licked stone.

An indrawn breath, then a jarring crunch just above his ear, and Dexter grunting. He'd kicked the table leg, sounded like. Lol heard him backing off, boots scraping on the flags, and Lol rolled away, scrambling to his feet, bringing on pulses of pain, like being knifed all over. Fear overcoming agony. Thinking fast. Thinking Dexter would expect him to go for the main door into the hall.

So going the other way. Flattening himself into the far wall, looking hard into nothing. Across the room, the hall door slammed, Dexter cutting off the main exit.

Silence, now, except for Alice and the Aga, and Lol had the sense of Dexter moving very quietly around the room, eyes unseeing, hands poised. Figured if he could get into the scullery he could open the window, slide out into the strip of garden bordering the orchard, into the fresh, cold air and the kiss of snowflakes.

Dexter stumbled and hissed. Lol's fingers found the scullery door.

Shut. *No!* The sound of him bending the handle down would bring Dexter back here faster than he could open the door, and then it would all be over very quickly because he didn't think he could even stand upright.

Worst thing of all, even without his glasses, he could see Dexter's shape now, blundering towards the Aga like a prowling troll, outlined in the greenish sheen of the smoke alarm light, a little glow around it, and he knew that the alarm bulb, the size of the smallest pea in the tin, would soon be as good as lighting the whole room, and Dexter would have him again. Last time.

'En't nowhere to go, boy.' As if Dexter had seen his thoughts, neon-lit in the blackness.

Lol edged, very slowly, one foot at a time, along the wall to the second door. This one opened into the passage leading to the rear door of the vicarage and the back stairs. The rear door was always locked and the key kept . . . where? Couldn't remember. Jane had a key, because this had once been her private front door, the way up to her apartment, until using it got to be too much of a drag.

The second door was not quite shut and Lol rested his shoulder against it, knowing that it nearly always creaked. He could get through all right, but the noise would tell Dexter where he'd gone. If he could get upstairs, into Merrily's bedroom with its phone . . . if Dexter would just make some kind of covering noise . . .

'When I gets you . . . gonner make it all hurt real bad . . . I promise.'

It was enough.

Lol leaned back against the door to the back stairs and, with a creak even he barely heard, he was through. He went directly for the narrow stairs. No point in even trying for the back door. Tripping over the first step and going down on his hands, and then up the stairs that way, his hands finding the next steps, his bruised stomach screaming at him to stop.

He collapsed on the top step and just . . . just breathed, taking in real air, letting it come out in a rush, lying on his back. Hands out on either side, feeling the rough plaster covering the old wattle and daub.

When he tried to get up, he nearly passed out with the pain. Started to slide back down the stairs.

'Come on, boy.'

Sod it.

Lol said wearily, 'You're stuffed, you know that? They'll find your DNA all over her.'

'But mainly yours, boy. And you'll have gone. You'll have buggered off. They en't gonner find you.'

Lol looked back down the steep and malformed back staircase in search of light. This was the throat down which you dropped into the belly of the house. He saw a vague smear of grey, perhaps the small window alongside the back door. He sensed that the door at the end of the passage at the bottom of the stairs was still open to the kitchen.

And Dexter, somewhere very close.

He tried to stand up. A foot skidded off the edge of a stair and he shuffled down three of them.

'That's it, boy. Alice is dyin' to see you.'

Alice.

'*We needs it now, more than ever – the Holy Spirit, the Holy Eucharist.*'

Clear challenge there to the remorseless evil represented in Dexter Harris. They were going to drag him into a public place so that the born-again Darrin could publicly denounce him before God. Something in Dexter had sent him out in search of an answer to that.

'Why the churchyard, Dexter?' Lol croaked. 'Why did you take the trouble to bring Alice all the way to the church? Could've left her in the orchard, might have been days before she was found. Why the churchyard?'

Ritual behaviour. Dexter wouldn't understand why he'd done it.

'Why'd you take Darrin back to the scene of the crash?'

Dexter: one small greasy cog in the huge and complex machinery of evil.

'Poor Darrin,' Lol said. 'He could've had everything. The repentant sinner takes all. Including the chip shop.'

The voice roared up, like out of a wind-tunnel. 'That cunt? Pretend you changed your ways, sorry for what you done? That's how you gets out of jail quicker. *He* never found no fuckin' religion, he—'

'I think he did, Dexter. But if he was dead, who'd know one way or the other?'

'Come on, boy.'

'You can't get out for the snow, anyway.'

'I can get out.' Dexter was back on his high, everything

going his way, couldn't lose. 'Hey, guess what I found – nice set o' knives on the wall. You gonner come and have a look? How about I gives Alice a little prod, see if her's gone yet.'

. . . Real nasty, look. Stuck his knife in the back of my hand once. Had an airgun, shot a robin in the garden . . .

'No, I'm coming down.'

'Good boy.'

'Bloody hell, Dexter,' Lol said, 'where are you *from*? You're a walking curse. You're the living dark heart of your own family. You're a big, walking disease.'

Lol took the crooked, swollen steps steadily, a hand on each wall and his aching head way above everything – the attic, the snow-covered stone tiles – up in the teeming night sky. The last time it was like this, he was on stage in The Courtyard in Hereford, finding out that people still wanted to hear his songs after all these years. He was glad he'd done that.

By the time he was close to the bottom of the stairs, he could hear Dexter in the kitchen doorway, panting. It was rage, of course. Dexter had a limited emotional range. It was an encouraging sound, but it wasn't . . .

'Hey,' Lol said, 'that wouldn't be a touch of the old *asthma* coming on, would it? Can you manage to find your inhaler in this light, or will you have to suck your own—?'

He reached the bottom before he was expecting it and stumbled and twisted, and the agony from somewhere in his abdomen brought him to his knees.

'You . . . what are you, Dexter?' Lol whispered. 'What are you?'

He climbed back onto the third step and sat down, remembering the white high of just a few hours ago. Sitting barefooted on the rug in the scullery, in the orange glow of the electric fire, thinking about the woman in the kitchen with the lights turned down low. Warm love.

He closed his eyes, heard Dexter coming at him, all meat and malevolence, in the total night, and saw Lucy Devenish alongside him, with her poncho spread like bat wings.

You have to learn to open up, Lucy said. *Let the world flow into you again.*

FORTY-SEVEN

Losers

On the first landing, Merrily encountered a portly grey-haired man in a well-cut three-piece suit, very neat and compact and self-assured. The kind of man who *sauntered*. He was leaning on the banisters, gazing down the curve of the stairs, and turned as she came up.

'Mrs Watkins.'

'Have we met?'

He pointed at the pectoral cross. 'Can't be too many of those around here tonight.'

'Another eleven and we'd be ready to take on Black Vaughan.'

He laughed. 'Alistair Hardy.'

'I guessed. My daughter's just been telling me how you were in communication with an old friend of ours.'

He tilted his head.

'In a poncho?'

'Ah,' he said.

'Personally, I didn't think it was Lucy's style, but there you go.'

'You're sceptical about the spirit world?'

'Hell, no, I'm just sceptical about spiritualists.' She came to lean on the banisters next to him. The lighting down there was too dim; the walls cried out for huge portraits in ornate gold frames. 'Sorry, I'm not usually this rude. I think it must be past my bedtime.'

'Mine, too,' Hardy said. 'They even went to the trouble of fitting out a magnificent chamber for me. The one where Mrs Davies shot herself.'

'Whose idea was that?'

'I wish I knew. Have *you* been in there?'

'No.'

'Well, I'll tell you something, Mrs Watkins. I'm not a timid man, as you can imagine, but I have to tell you I could no more sleep in that room than on a bed of nails.'

She looked at him: fleshy, well fed, comparatively unlined. It was disturbing how untroubled some of these people appeared – coasting through life, the greatest fear of all having been removed.

'It's funny,' she said. 'I never think of spiritualists acknowledging the idea of evil. It's always seemed a bit . . .'

'Tame?'

'Not quite right, but . . . yeah. You never seem to accept the possibility of . . . risk.'

Hardy's eyes narrowed. 'Hmm.' He smiled and nodded and walked away.

In the centre of the great island unit, there was this small earthenware crucible in which incense was burning.

Fat candles sat in glass bowls placed at the cardinal points on the worktop and all the electric lights in the kitchen had been switched off, so that the ambience of the room was one of, like, shivery motion.

Jane thought of the fire on the rocks, how elemental that had looked, how basic it had turned out to be. Antony Largo had two cameras set up on tripods, both bigger and more technical-looking than the Sony 150 he'd given her.

And which he now gave her again.

'You're joking,' Jane said.

'Look, don't give me a hard time, huh, hen?' Just the two of them down here. Largo cocked his head, peering into her face. 'I never had you down as a prima donna.'

'*You* never had *me*—?'

'Look – a crucial set piece like this, I'd usually have three experienced people at the very least. Tonight, well, obviously Ben's gonna be in the movie – unless we get ourselves a spectral manifestation, he's gonna be the star, so *he*'s no help. Therefore, I'm gonna leave this wee implement with you. It's fully charged. You can choose to shoot stuff or not, but there'll only be the two of us. Maybe you'll see things I miss – I can't be in two places at once.'

Jane felt her hands closing around the Sony like they were betraying all her finer principles. She turned away as the first footsteps sounded on the stone stairs.

'Not yet!' Antony strode out, hands aloft. 'I'll tell you when.'

Jane held her watch to a candle. It was nearly four a.m. Antony waved her away into the shadows and moved over to the farthest tripod, bending over the camera.

'OK,' he said, 'in five.'

When they came in, even Jane could tell that most of them were rigidly self-conscious, didn't know where to look. You might have expected some small element of anticipation, but they were kind of shuffling like some ragbag band of medieval lepers in search only of relief.

Beth Pollen first, her white hair pulled back and secured with one of those leather things with a stick through it. Beth Pollen, who lost her husband and fell among spiritualists, but who had been a good friend to Natalie. Then Ben in his Edwardian jacket over a white shirt – not as dangerous as he'd seemed only hours ago, just badly wasted, the old sense of suave long gone. Amber . . . well, Amber was as normal, her gaze wandering to the big French stove, making sure that nobody had glued candles to her big steel hotplate. Matthew Hawksley was looking crumpled, his white jacket well creased. Alistair Hardy was in his conman's business suit, with his hands behind his back, looking like he'd come to value the place.

Losers, Jane thought, as they took their places on high wooden stools around the island unit, their faces shimmering in the candlelight. Hardy was at the top of the table. Missing was Natalie Craven, over whom a pile of circumstantial evidence towered like Stanner Rocks.

Nobody spoke. It looked like the set-up for virtually every phoney seance scene that Jane had seen on television, but maybe this was what Largo wanted. This wasn't a serious documentary, this was cheap, naff reality TV, coming from the same kind of factory as all that airport crap and the bollocks set in hairdressing salons.

True to his word, though, Antony didn't make them all go out and come in again more realistically. He wasn't invisible, but he was moving around unobtrusively enough, with another little hand-held Sony. Jane was aware of the tiny red light glowing on the second tripod camera. Long shots from two angles, then, with meaningful close-ups by Antony Largo.

He slid back to the tripod at the top of the room, refocused. Then he lifted a finger and brought it down, pointing at Ben.

Ben cleared his throat. 'Well . . . good morning. And I think it's a morning when none of us will be . . . altogether sorry to see daylight.'

Murmurs and smiles, Jane thinking, *Buggered if I'm shooting any of this.*

'Because of the weather, there are fewer of us than anticipated, but I think the essential people *are* here – most of them. To be honest, I think we've all been . . . shattered by what's happened tonight. And as we really don't know how it's going to turn out . . .' Ben looked directly into Antony's camera. 'I'm sorry, Antony, I really don't know how safe I am. I don't know how much of this is going to be *sub judice*, do I?'

'OK.' Antony stepped out. 'For anyone in doubt, here's the situation. The police tell me that someone is likely to be charged with murder sometime today. The whole thing then becomes no-screen until after the trial. If I'm any judge of anything, I would see this going out at the earliest possible opportunity after sentencing. In other words, you can all say what the hell you like.'

Beth Pollen said, 'And how do the police feel about us doing this now?'

Antony grinned, kind of piratical in the candlelight. 'If I may quote the Senior Investigating Officer: "Anything that keeps these weirdo bastards out of my hair for a couple of hours is perfectly fine by me." '

Nobody laughed.

'As long we understand where we are,' Ben said. 'I, um, was also given the impression that Mrs Watkins would be joining us. Is that—?'

'I'm here, Mr Foley.'

Mum was sitting on the steps like some sort of elf. Jane hadn't even noticed her. Instinctively, she switched on her camera.

'Super.' Matthew Hawksley stood up, pulling out another stool.

'It's OK,' Mum said. 'I'm not staying. I mean, very pretty and everything, but I'm sorry, I really wouldn't feel too happy about conducting a religious ceremony in, erm – ' she waved a hand at the candles ' – Titania's boudoir?'

'I'm sorry, too,' Beth Pollen said, 'but we were very firmly given the impression—'

'I'm not backing out,' Mum said. 'I'm just not doing it down here.'

Jane noticed Alistair Hardy straightening up on his stool, looking disturbed.

Mum smiled. '*Nor* in Hattie Chancery's room. I, erm . . . I thought we might use the dining room. If that's OK. It's a bit cold, but . . .'

'Mrs Watkins . . .' Antony abandoned his camera. 'Not only is it, as you so perceptively noted, a bit too cold, but it has absolutely no bloody atmosphere either.'

'It's got a stained-glass window.'

'Which, like all stained-glass windows, doesnae function as intended at *night*.'

Mum stood up, shrugging. 'I'm sorry, that . . . that's really not my problem.'

Antony Largo looked furious. Deep in the shadows, and in spite of Natalie and Jeremy and the whole depressing situation, Jane momentarily grinned.

'Carry on here, by all means,' Mum said, 'but if you want to join me . . . say, twenty minutes?'

Had this been an authentic castle or even a manor house, there would have been a chapel. The dining room, with its secular stained glass, was no substitute; the stained-glass window was thick as a boarded barn door, and the air felt milky and astringent. Worst of all, when Merrily knelt on the thin carpet and prayed, it was like tossing stones down a bottomless well.

But at least it was empty and it was dark.

She said The Lord's Prayer and St Patrick's Breastplate. She prayed for Lol, having tried the number again and found it continuously engaged and then, when it started ringing again, had no answer. Another bottomless well.

Blank minutes passed. She stood up, half-relieved, when the door opened and Jane slid in and waited there in silhouette, hands behind her back, ten years old again.

'You offended Antony.'

'I suppose that's going to screw us for getting DIY SOS into the vicarage,' Merrily said wearily.

'This is Channel Four.'

'I know. And I don't think I want to be on TV again.'

'You could say a flat *no* to Antony.'

'I don't think we'd have time for the row that would cause.'

'Time?'

The time is nearly up.

'What do you want *me* to do?' Jane asked.

'To be honest, flower, I don't really want you here at all, but if you've got to stay, sure, carry on with the camerawork.'

'I mean, do you want me to *do* anything?'

'Well, you could see if you could find me a jar, preferably one that hasn't had alcohol in it, and fill it with water.'

'You're going to bless it?'

'Uh-huh. But first, if you could give me a hand with these tables . . .'

They put on the lights and pushed two of the dining tables together under the stained-glass window. With the ceiling lights on, the glass was the colour of dried mud.

'Why here?' Jane asked. 'Why this room?'

'Oh, well, it's kind of neutral, isn't it? It's a big open space, no crannies, no cupboards. Unlike the kitchen. Also, the kitchen's too close to Stanner Rocks. I haven't seen it in daylight, but I get the feeling the kitchen's dominated by the rocks.'

'Isn't that the point?'

'Erm . . .'

'Mum, what's the matter?'

'Huh?'

'Listen, I rang this guy who . . . knows something about the history of this place.'

'At this time in the morning?'

'I apologized. Basically, he told me that what the Chancerys did – when they invited Conan Doyle – might not have been a simple re-enactment of the Vaughan exorcism. They . . . well, obviously, they had this medium there, so they might have been trying to *communicate* with Vaughan . . . in the spirit of the new – you know – secular science of spiritualism. Like, after all, there was nothing to suggest Thomas Vaughan was a bad guy. I mean, did he even need exorcising in the first place?'

'But why do it here? This is not Hergest Court, is it? Vaughan was never here.'

'He said ask Beth Pollen.'

Merrily thought of Brigid. 'Everybody says that.'

Frannie Bliss slipped in through the connecting door from the lounge. He stood there, taking in the rearrangement: the two candlesticks on the dining table, the holy water in a new decanter.

'Catholics allowed?'

'How do Catholics feel about spiritualism, Frannie?'

Bliss waggled a hand, conveying this way, that way.

'You believe in it?'

'Not when I'm on duty. Merrily, I accept that this is a private establishment that's been good enough to accommodate the police and we're in no position to question whatever else might be taking place here as long as it's legal . . . but your selection of this particular room . . .'

'Too close?'

'Frankly, I wondered if the proximity of our . . . guest might in some way have conditioned your choice of venue.'

'If you can find a room in this place that looks more like a church—'

'All right. Just . . . we're not talking about an actual exorcism, are we?'

'It's a word that functions on several levels.'

'Aw, shit, Merrily, you know what I'm asking. Looking at it from the angle that the law will not – to Brigid's advantage, I should emphasize – *allow* me to look at it, we have a number of close parallels here with the grandmother of the suspect. Now if, during the course of your activities here, my prisoner's eyes happen to turn blood red . . .'

'If only we had Annie Howe in charge,' Merrily said. 'Annie Howe simply would not believe that could happen.'

'So what *is* going to happen?'

Merrily perched on the edge of one of the dining tables, now pushed back against the walls, while the chairs had been arranged in a semicircle around the makeshift altar. A little like Sunday nights in Ledwardine Church.

'Well . . . the original plan by The White Company and Ben Foley appeared to be to try and contact whatever remains of Conan Doyle to find out if he really did get the inspiration for *The Hound of the Baskervilles* from the Welsh Border, rather than from Dartmoor. I wouldn't mind starting with that.'

'You're attending a seance?'

'It'll be an experience.'

'I don't like this. Spiritually, you've always been . . . conservative?'

'Lack of confidence, Frannie. As a teenager, I used to wear Goth frocks and black lipstick.'

'You're worried about something. You're nervous. When you're flip, you're nervous, I've noticed it before.'

'Detectives,' Merrily said. 'Always got to throw it in your face.'

When she walked back into the lobby, Jeremy Berrows was sitting in the chair by reception, with his scarf around his neck, staring at the lounge door like a dog outside his master's wake.

Was anyone better placed to hold up a small candle into the heart of the darkness? When Merrily had talked to him, at The Nant, Jeremy had obviously been guarded, fearing the worst. But now the worst had happened.

Nothing to lose.

Cheap phrase, never more true.

'The thing is, Jeremy, we're all from Off.' She'd pulled up a chair next to his. 'It's none of our business, really, and yet all the problems seem to have been caused by incomers who couldn't leave anything alone.'

'Incomers moved out, wouldn't be nobody left at all,' Jeremy said.

'Except you.'

Jeremy smiled probably the bleakest smile that Merrily had ever seen on anyone living. It was as if his suicide had been, in essence, a success. She had a stark image of him one day, years hence, being found dead by the postman or the feed dealer, half-mummified beside the ashes of his fire. A shell, a husk; it looked as if the process had already begun.

The image arrived so suddenly that it was as if he'd passed it to her. She was suddenly desperate to help him, to pull at least one person from the mire of myth and madness.

'Jeremy, they want me to try and . . . deal with whatever came through Hattie Chancery. To Paula, to Brigid . . .'

He looked at her. 'They knows?'

'Not all of them. Do you believe it came from Hattie Chancery?'

'Come *through* her, mabbe.'

'So where does it come from? How far back does it go?'

'Where's all evil come from?'

'For instance – have *you* ever seen the Hound?'

He glanced back at the lounge door. 'Just a shadow. A few folk seen him, time to time. It don't mean nothin' – no death, no disaster.'

'But if you were a Vaughan, in the old days . . .'

'So they reckoned.'

'What about now? Is there someone it still *means* something to? Who, if they saw it, would feel there was reason to be afraid?'

Jeremy swallowed. 'Dacre. The Chancerys.'

'It came to mean the same to the Chancerys, the Dacres, as it did to the Vaughans?'

Jeremy loosened his scarf a little. 'Sebbie Dacre's ole lady – Margery, her once come over to our place, hell of a state – my mam told me this, I was n' more 'n a babby at the time. Margery reckoned her seen it, twice. Next thing, Paula's died.'

'Margery connected that with the Hound?'

'Sure to. Her . . . said better all round if the child died, too.'

'She was scared of something being passed on?'

Jeremy nodded, swallowed.

'But it didn't affect Margery . . . *did* it?'

'Her never hurt nobody far's I know. But Paula was the oldest, see.'

'But Margery believed she'd seen the Hound. And Sebbie . . .?'

'Rumours. Zelda Morgan, one of his . . . lady friends, reckoned he seen some'ing made him real upset. And then he hires these boys from down Wales.'

'He didn't really think they'd bring him the Hound – dead, like in the novel?'

'Don't reckon he seen hisself partin' with seven grand, that's what you means.'

'But he kept sending the shooters up to Stanner . . . and across your land. And down to The Nant, of course. Because of—'

'Them's the two places Nat'lie was.'

'He connected the Hound with her? He knew who she was?'

'I don't reckon he knowed for sure. But . . . what was a woman that lovely doing with the likes of me? He wasn't daft. He was mad, but he wasn't daft. And I reckon he knowed the time was nearly up.'

'The lease.'

'Sure t' be.'

'And he wanted the ground. The idea of someone else occupying a farm right in the middle of *his* . . . this offended him. So possibly this was some kind of crude threat, maybe aimed at Brigid. Though you'd have thought it would have made him the very last person she'd want to sell to.'

'Well . . .' A sheen of sweat on Jeremy's forehead now. 'I think he reckoned it was coming off The Nant, see. Paula's land.'

'The Hound?'

'Whether he was really seein' some'ing *out there*, or he seen some'ing that wasn't outside of his mind . . .'

'Either way, part of him would believe a death was coming.'

'Likely.'

'His own?'

Jeremy looked down at the table. 'Or hers. It was him or her, I reckon.'

'*What?*'

'Thing is, see,' Jeremy said, 'he always figured he was out on the edge anyway, so he'd go around creatin' . . . situations. Trouble. And he'd get away with it – magistrate, Country Landowners. All this Countryside Alliance protest stuff – war in the fields and the woods, and the ole gentry right there in the middle of it, defendin' what's theirs. If there was anybody *exac'ly* like Hattie Chancery, my mam used to say, it was Sebbie – the huntin', the booze . . . he din't care. Never got nicked for drink-drivin' – cops liked him, their kind of magistrate: no mercy, no sob-stories, send 'em down, put 'em away. Robber baron, Danny calls him.'

'But when Brigid—'

'When Big Weale, the lawyer, died and Sebbie found out who really owned The Nant, that was when he got real paranoid. And the time was nearly up, he knowed that, but he couldn't *say* he knowed. What he'd do, way he was . . . he'd cause trouble, set up dangerous situations just to see what come out of it. Like them Welshies – troublemakers, off their patch, offer of big money. Explosive situation. Mabbe he figured somebody was gonner get killed.'

'Then there'd have been a death?'

'I dunno. He weren't right in the bloody head. Bad . . .'

'Bad blood?'

Jeremy's head went down into his hands.

'So when Natalie came back . . .'

'When her come back . . .' He looked up, through his fingers, really sweating now. ' . . . Half of me's the happiest man there ever could be in Kington. Other half's saying, *Make her go away . . . it'll all end bad*. Paula tried to kill Margery, when they was little. Now Paula's daughter's back . . .'

'Did you know that he was blackmailing her?' Merrily put a hand on his arm. 'And was that why you decided to . . . take yourself out of the situation. Take away the only reason

Brigid had for staying. You were . . . prepared to sacrifice yourself, in the hope that she'd come through?'

Jeremy looked to either side, back at the lounge door, anywhere but at Merrily. She was profoundly unnerved. It was terrifying how deep all this went. Rural isolation, paranoia. And a curse, like a virus in the blood.

'And thinking that . . .' She coughed, her voice so hoarse that it had nearly gone. 'Thinking *you* would be the death?'

'En't no way . . .' He started shaking his head, talking at the same time. 'En't no way out o' this.'

'Why?'

''Cause it goes too far back. It's built up.'

'*How* far?'

'To the Vaughans,' Jeremy said. 'They're *all Vaughans.*'

FORTY-EIGHT

Apocryphal

Danny parked the tractor on the square – not that you could see where the road ended and the square began. It had been a close thing whether they'd have enough diesel to make it, the way they'd run the ole tractor getting here.

'Power's off everywhere,' Gomer said, like it needed saying. It had been weird, Danny thought, the way Ledwardine had suddenly just appeared in the headlights, no warning, black and white buildings in a black and white night.

'That why the vicar couldn't get through on the phone, you reckon?'

'Makes no difference to the phones, do it?'

Danny and Gomer stepped down from the tractor into the thick snow. It had stopped falling now, like the sky had worn itself out.

'Behind there.' Gomer pointed to a hedge like a white wall, just down from the church.

'You ever have anything to do with this Dexter Harris, Gomer?'

'Big feller in the chip shop some nights, but he never got much to say and word's gone round he's tight with his chips so, if he's there, I goes home and makes a sandwich instead.'

'Makes sense.' Danny looked up at the windows of the

vicarage, all dark except for a small glow far back in one of the upstairs rooms. 'We putting this off?'

Without lights, what you could see of the rest of the village looked like a photo negative.

'Don't feel right, do it?' Gomer switched on the lambing lamp.

Dr Bell leaned away from the lamplight, his head pitched at an angle, as if he was listening to something that no one else could hear.

'Aye.' He nodded, his smile wry. 'He does urge me to point out that although he and I, at various times, both sought release and relaxation on the grouse moors of Arran, in later life he developed something of a conscience about such pursuits and came to deplore, in particular, fox-hunting.'

At the other side of the table, Matthew Hawksley half turned, to acknowledge the factual truth of this for the rest of them, and then faced the doctor again.

'Joe, did he ever shoot in this area? On the Radnorshire moors, for instance?'

Dr Bell took in two long and reedy breaths, his fingers steepled.

'He . . . thinks . . . *not*.'

His voice was high and precise, and scalpel-sharp. Posh Scots, Jane thought, was like posh Welsh – explicit in its enunciation and full of this clipped authority. It was clear that Matthew must have worked with him a few times before to get away with calling him Joe.

Jane blinked. *What am I thinking?* Gripping the Sony 150 – real and modern, hi-tech, digital, third-millennial. Bringing it up and shooting the scene just to *do* something, avoid getting drawn in, the way she had been at the climax of Ben's murder-mystery weekend in the lounge next door. This was a similar set piece, played out in the waxy ambience of an oil lamp with a frosted, globular shade – the same one that lit the scene when Sherlock Holmes confronted the Major.

And here, as Matthew had explained in his introduction, was the *real* Holmes, the prototype, the famous tutor at the University of Edinburgh School of Medicine who had initiated the student, Arthur Conan Doyle, into the basic techniques that Holmes would employ. *Dr Joseph Bell, born 1837, consultant surgeon at Edinburgh Royal Infirmary, life-long advocate of the employment of forensic observation in the diagnosis of disease*.

Jane glanced over at Mum: possibly her first experience of trance-mediumship.

It was more than acting, but . . .

Sometimes it looked as if Alistair Hardy had lost weight – or at least as if his body weight had been rearranged. But it *could be explained* . . . If he seemed taller, that was because he was sitting up so straight in his hard-backed chair. If his eyes seemed brighter and shrewder – almost piercing – that was because he'd become fired up by what he was doing . . . or thought he was doing.

And if his features looked sharper, his nose more like the beak of a bird of prey, that was . . . well, Merrily was willing to bet it wouldn't come over on the video.

Transfiguration. It was popular in Victorian times, but you didn't get much of it now when people were no longer easily fooled by clever lighting and special effects. She was half and half on this – half of her thought he was sincere in the *belief* that something was happening; half of her thought it was a total con. She wondered how convinced Matthew Hawksley really was.

Matthew said, 'As you probably realize, Joe, we're trying to solve a mystery.'

'In which case . . .' Dr Bell's lips tweaked in amusement ' . . . I cannot *think* why you would come to me.'

Matthew smiled. Apart from this intimate tableau, the room was in shadow. One of Largo's two static cameras was positioned in front of the altar, the other behind the semi-circle of chairs. Largo himself was crouching just a few feet from the table. Alistair Hardy had declined to be filmed going into trance. Maybe he didn't like the way his left side seemed to drop into spasm, his arm projecting from his body, his fingers curling.

Could be some kind of nervous condition.

'Would it be possible for you to ask Sir Arthur if he ever came here?' Matthew said.

'Here?' Bell snapped. 'Where is "here"? Be more specific, man.'

'Stanner Hall, in the County of Herefordshire, on the Welsh Border. Home of the Chancerys.'

'Not known to me.'

'Was it perhaps known to Sir Arthur? Would it be possible to ask him?'

Dr Bell went still. Alistair Hardy's breathing had altered its rhythm, was going faster, and he was blinking rapidly, like REM during a dream. Merrily saw Bliss sitting in the corner nearest the connecting door to the lounge, Jeremy hunched like a hedgehog nearby. She imagined Brigid Parsons in there, perhaps asleep in a chair, watched over by the police.

'Aye,' Dr Bell said after a while, 'I'm informed that it was.'

'Did he have relatives here? Members of his family?'

There was a longer silence this time, a blurring of Hardy's face as Matthew pushed his luck, maybe suspecting that he didn't have much time left.

'Was he aware of the legend of Black Vaughan and the Hound of Hergest?'

Dr Bell breathed gassily in and out through his mouth. 'Yes, yes,' he said, as if talking to someone else. 'Aye. Indeed.' He turned to Matthew. 'You touch on a most *vexed* issue, my friend.'

'In . . . what way?'

'I will not be . . .' Dr Bell sprang up. 'These people!' Forefinger pointing, accusatory, around the room. 'These people are a *disgrrrrace!*'

A plastic bottle of water labelled Highland Spring was sent spinning from the table. Merrily held her cross.

'The child.' Dr Bell's voice had deepened. It might – if you gave any credence to this – be considered a different voice. 'The infant. To involve an infant . . . *inexcusable.*'

You might now want to believe that this was the voice of Sir Arthur Conan Doyle. Hardy had his hands behind his back. There was a tremor under his breath. He looked up at the ceiling, and down at the audience. He didn't seem to see anyone.

Until his gaze collided with Merrily's – and it *was* a collision; she almost felt the jolt. She held the cross and didn't blink.

'They *tarnish* us.' Then Hardy looked away and sat down. 'They tarnish us.'

Matthew Hawksley retrieved the bottle of Highland Spring from under a chair and poured out half a glass, as Alistair Hardy coughed himself out of trance.

Merrily stood up. She didn't feel very priestly tonight, in her black cowl-neck jumper and jeans.

'Erm . . . did that suggest anything to anyone?'

'Oh yes,' Beth Pollen said. 'I think so.'

Merrily rather liked what she'd seen of Beth Pollen. A decent woman in search of some kind of spiritual truth. To what extent she was open to deception, however, was any-body's guess.

Merrily opened a hand. 'Please—'

Mrs Pollen stood up. 'The Chancerys . . . tried to build *themselves* into the fabric of the area. This area has always been overshadowed by the Vaughan legends, which have inspired pretty genuine fear over the years. The Chancerys were unlikely previously to have encountered the level of acceptance of hauntings, omens and curses they found here on the Welsh Border, even among fairly educated people. So they were saying, "Look, we're the heralds of a new age of enlightenment, we can deal with this. By recreating the circumstances of the exorcism, we'll summon the spirit of Black Vaughan, and then we'll talk to him rationally through a medium, and we'll find out what his problem is." '

'But it seems to have been a fairly cobbled-together affair,' Merrily said. 'And they certainly didn't have twelve priests.'

'But, as Sir Arthur correctly remembers, they *did* have a baby.'

Twenty years younger than Gomer, but a lot more cautious – he'd always known that – Danny went up the drive first, with the lambing light switched off. He did *not* like the sound of Dexter Harris.

He stopped halfway to the vicarage front door, where the bushes on either side had been turned into great white domes. There was enough reflected light to reveal deep foot-marks all over the path, as well as scuff-marks, drag-marks. *Hell.*

You got a weight of snow, there wasn't nothing couldn't happen in these villages. Used to be police stations every-where, now the dull bastards at the Home Office, never been west of Woking, figured cops could reach anywhere in minutes. But all it took was one big snowfall . . .

Danny switched on the light. It told him that the front door was ajar.

'Somebody been in,' Danny whispered.

'Well, don't bloody well hang around!' Gomer grabbed the lamp off Danny, planting his boot on the door, banging it open. 'Lol! Lol, boy, you in there?'

'Chrissake,' Danny muttered, Gomer blundering past him into the vicarage. 'Gomer?'

'Bugger,' Gomer said, dry-voiced. 'Oh, bugger.'

'What?'

'Better take a look.'

Danny stepped up into the hall. Could just make out a door on his left, then a staircase, a passage in front of him, and Gomer standing in a doorway to the right. Over Gomer's shoulder, in the lamp beam, he could see a big kitchen with a Rayburn or something of that order and a long table dragged to one side and, all down one leg of the table, long smears of red, unlikely to be ketchup.

'Blood in yere, Danny.'

'Take it careful, Gomer. I mean it.'

There was a door slightly ajar at the bottom of the kitchen.

'Lol!' Gomer shouted. 'You there, boy?'

'This en't lookin' good, Gomer. Don't touch nothin'.'

'Bugger that.' Gomer marched across the kitchen to the bottom door, hooked his boot around the side and dragged it open.

Some kind of short passage, with an oak beam across, a door and a small window on one side, a narrow stairway on the other.

On the floor, a body.

Merrily froze.

There were present, to help lay the spirit, a woman with a new-born baby, whose innocence and purity were perhaps held powerful in exorcism.

Today, of course, it wouldn't even be contemplated. The rule book said plainly, *See that all children and animals are removed from the premises.*

But that was then. And it was only a story.

'The assumption is,' she said to Mrs Pollen, 'that the baby in the story would have been newly baptized, otherwise it wouldn't be seen as a symbol of purity. In the medieval church, baptism itself was considered a primary exorcism. A baby would be christened as soon as possible because it was considered to be prey to satanic invasion, or even to actual possession by the Devil, until baptism.'

'That's how I understood it too, Mrs Watkins. A child who died before baptism would not be admitted into heaven. As well as having the sign of the cross marked on its forehead in holy water, its head was wrapped in a white cloth in which it would be buried if it died, as so many did, in infancy. The baby's immortal soul was then considered to have been formally saved.'

Merrily nodded. This woman had done her research.

'Well, then,' Mrs Pollen said, 'I don't know which account of the Vaughan exorcism you read, but the one in Mrs Leather's book does *not* say that the baby had been baptized.'

'No,' Merrily conceded, 'I suppose it doesn't. However—'

'And I'm certain Hattie Chancery hadn't been either, when her mother brought her in.'

'Oh.' Merrily sank down into her chair. She'd missed the obvious.

'For heaven's *sake*—' Ben Foley's chair legs screeched as he swung round. 'You're saying the baby was *Hattie*? How reliable is this, Beth?'

'Well, it's not actually documented anywhere, as far as I know,' Mrs Pollen said. 'It's what the original servants said.

We tracked down about four children or grandchildren of Stanner Hall staff who'd been involved in the ceremony. Three of them had heard the story, and two of them actually said their parents had been pretty jolly horrified when Bella Chancery proudly walked in with her new baby daughter.'

'And the baby was unbaptized?' Merrily said. 'Do we *know* that?'

'What we *do* know, from records, is that Hattie Chancery's baptism was delayed because she became ill. Although we don't have an exact date for the so-called exorcism, we know it took place in the winter of 1899, and the baptism is on record as having taken place in March 1900. I also know, from oral accounts, that Bella Chancery, during her spiritualist phase, was very dismissive of Church mumbo-jumbo and probably wouldn't have had Hattie baptized at all if Walter – much older, more set in his ways – hadn't insisted.'

'For God's sake,' Ben said, 'why on earth have you been sitting on this?'

'Because of the family.'

'But didn't Natalie *know*?'

'*Clancy* didn't know,' Beth Pollen said. 'I also felt that talking about it . . . I don't know what I felt, apart from a dreadful foreboding.'

'But just assuming we're all taking this on board,' Ben said, 'giving credence to . . . I mean, what are we *saying*? I can't even put this into words . . .'

'OK.' Merrily moved out towards the table where Matthew and Hardy were sitting. Into the light. 'When I was training for the Deliverance ministry, the key word was caution. You start with a prayer, build up as necessary. I've never done an actual exorcism of a person, and most diocesan exorcists will *never* do one. It's sledgehammers and nuts. If you overreact, you can open the way for something far worse, create a situation where there isn't one.'

Mrs Pollen was nodding fiercely.

'So,' Merrily said, 'someone staging a phoney exorcism, based on a *real* exorcism – OK, that may be apocryphal, but the techniques ring true – someone recreating that scenario risks inviting something in. Inviting madness, if you want to look at it psychologically. Or evil, if we're allowed to be spiritual. And evil loves a short cut. Evil takes the easy option.'

'The easy option being the unbaptized baby,' Mrs Pollen said.

FORTY-NINE

Requiem

'Except it wasn't intended to be an exorcism, was it?' Merrily said. 'Why don't you tell us about the original owner of Stanner Hall?'

Beth Pollen hesitated as the connecting door to the lounge opened and Alma's bulky figure squeezed through. Bliss stood up, Alma whispered something to him.

'Can I interrupt?' Bliss said. 'Mr Foley, do you have any more of these nice oil lamps? Or even – dare I suggest it – a generator?'

Ben stood up. 'Oh *no*.'

'I'm afraid so, sir. It was only a matter of time, wasn't it? Word is that all of Kington's off.'

'No,' Ben said, 'I'm afraid we don't have a generator. There are a couple more of these lamps, and a lot of candles, and I could probably get the gas mantles going.'

'Anything you can do, sir, would be very much appreciated.'

'Damn. Now?'

'Well, I'd hate to be a nuisance . . .'

'All right.' Ben walked across to the door to the hall. 'Oh – Antony has lights, of course. And batteries.'

'Not very much left, I'm afraid,' Antony Largo said. 'Best conserved, eh?'

Jane laughed cynically.

A power cut was going to cause problems, inevitably. Merrily sat and waited for the hall door to close behind Bliss and Ben Foley. At least it had given her some time to work a few things out, align what she'd just heard with what Jeremy had told her, surprisingly voluble once he'd got going.

'Sorry, Mrs Pollen,' she said. 'I think we were talking about the original builder. I mean, I gather you'd know more about this than anybody, from your husband's preliminary work. As I understand it, the architect who designed Stanner Hall for his own use had done quite a lot of work for Walter Chancery.'

'Yes.' Beth Pollen sat just in shadow, looking down at her hands in her lap.

'And his name was?'

'Rhys Vaughan. However—'

'I know much of this is rumour, but we ought to hear it, don't you think?'

Beth Pollen sighed.

'I mean, as far as I can make out, nobody knows for *certain* whether he was a direct descendant of the Vaughans of Hergest, but *he* certainly thought so,' Merrily said.

'Well, he was a Welsh-speaking Welshman, and the Vaughans were a very important family, descended from the Princes of Brecknock, supporters of a great Welsh cultural tradition, I mean, in the Middle Ages the whole of Kington was actually Welsh-speaking. It must have been important to Rhys that when he built the house it should be on a significant site as close to Hergest as possible. He did originally try to buy Hergest Court, and when he failed he was determined to build something as impressive as Hergest had been in its great days.'

'And where better than the famous Stanner Rocks?'

'They weren't very famous then, Mrs Watkins. The rare

plants were only discovered quite recently. But yes, it was an impressive site and he was able to buy a good deal of land. Land wasn't terribly expensive in those days. It all took a long time because he'd keep running out of money and have to go back to the Midlands and design industrial buildings for people like Walter Chancery.'

'This would be what interested your husband, who worked for Powys Council.'

'The great Welsh mansion that never was, yes. Rhys was a very romantic figure. A great patriot. He obviously loved the idea of dominating the border, as he believed his ancestors had.'

'And working for Walter,' Merrily said, 'meant he had quite a lot to do with the much younger Mrs, erm, Chancery.'

'Oh dear,' Mrs Pollen said. 'This is all rumour. Steve absolutely abhorred this kind of gossipy, anecdotal—'

'It was a bit more than that at the time, though, wasn't it? According to my information, Hattie Chancery bore very little resemblance to Walter, and the only person who couldn't see it was Walter himself.'

'*Bloody hell!*' Jane said.

'The word is that this was more than just a passing dalliance. Bella was seriously in love with Rhys, and when he died she was in a terrible state. Which I suppose poor old Walter put down to her being pregnant.'

'Mum, where the *hell* did you get this?'

Merrily raised an eyebrow at Jane and hoped that she could make it out in the lamplight. *They're all Vaughans,* Jeremy had said. Hattie and Paula and Margery and Sebbie and Brigid. All Vaughans, with all the Vaughan baggage.

'So Bella, in her grief, carrying Rhys's child, desperate for her lover's vision to become reality, put the arm on Walter to put in a bid for the unfinished folly.'

'It was *almost* finished,' Beth Pollen said. 'All that Bella had to do was bring one of her interior-designer friends up from London. Cost Walter so much money in the end that I think he had to sell one of his companies to meet the final bills. Which I suppose was the beginning of the end for the Chancery fortune. Seems to be what this place does.'

Merrily looked at Amber Foley, who sat as still as a mannequin, her face a mask of dismay. The darkness beyond the lamp-glow seemed more real, now that everyone knew it was a darkness shrouding the whole mid-Border.

'Which brings us to the seance,' Merrily said. 'I'm calling it a seance, because I think the Black Vaughan exorcism thing was probably a cover story, possibly for Walter's benefit. Would that be close?'

'It's all conjecture, isn't it?' Beth Pollen said.

'Is it OK if I go on?'

Beth Pollen spread her hands. Of course . . . this was the part she would have identified with, as a woman who'd lost a much-loved husband, a soulmate.

'If we assume that Bella read the Vaughan legend, what would have stood out?'

'The baby,' Jane whispered.

'And she now had one of her own. A little Vaughan. A genuine heir to all this – the whole huge tradition. A tiny descendant of the Princes of Brecknock. And she could *never* admit it. I don't know anything about Walter Chancery, but taking over the house built by your tame architect is one thing . . . living in your wife's lover's mansion with his child . . . *very* different.'

'This is totally mind-boggling,' Jane said.

'And may not be true,' Beth Pollen said, rather desperately now.

'But she was a serious follower of the big new fashion for spiritualism.' Merrily took a long breath, wishing it carried nicotine. '*I* think when she read about the baby, she conceived the idea of somehow – and we can't know the details – of somehow presenting the child, Hattie, to her heritage. And more specifically, to her father. The medium . . .'

'Wouldn't the medium have given it away, Mrs Watkins? If her father had spoken through Erasmus Cookson?'

'*No.*' Jane was on her feet. 'Because Cookson was from London. Bella had him brought in. He just *had* to have been a mate, someone she could trust not to pass on anything indiscreet until afterwards.'

'But the priests . . .'

'Window dressing, I suspect,' Merrily said. 'This is a woman who was secretly bereaved, desperate for psychic contact with her lover. Suppose she'd planned, at some stage, to leave Walter for Rhys Vaughan? Perhaps he'd told her that when the house was finished . . . I don't know. We *can't* know.' She glanced at Alistair Hardy. 'And where Conan Doyle comes in, I've no idea at all.'

Beth Pollen sighed. 'We might as well try and finish the story. My researches suggest that it was Walter who invited Conan Doyle. I think . . . I think it was probably true that Doyle, a man with a strong sense of what was right and wrong, would have been appalled to find a baby brought into something like this. And I suppose that, being the man he was, he wouldn't be able to rest until he'd found out what was behind it. Perhaps Bella begged him to keep quiet, and so . . .'

'That was why he switched *The Hound* to Devon?' Jane said.

'Impossible to say, isn't it? It could have been something fairly shocking that happened at the seance.'

'The baby starts croaking in Welsh?' Jane smiled malevolently.

'I suppose we were all hoping something might be confirmed this weekend,' Beth said.

Alistair Hardy was sitting upright, like Dr Bell, with his arms folded. 'You didn't tell me any of this, Beth.'

'No,' Beth said, almost distantly, and Merrily guessed that this had been a test for him. That Beth's commitment to spiritualism was less unquestioning than her colleagues in The White Company had supposed. That Alistair Hardy had perhaps conveyed messages from her husband that she *wanted* to believe and yet . . .

Poor woman. If Hardy, as Dr Bell, Conan Doyle or even himself, had been able to reflect any aspect of a story which was unsupported by anything in print, his stature would have been confirmed, at least in Beth Pollen's estimation. As it was, he remained iffy.

'That's all I know,' Merrily said.

Beth Pollen said, 'Perhaps it's best if we leave it there.'

'Is that what you want?'

'No. We can't, can we? There's a woman behind that door over there who's either a totally evil human being or a human being to whom evil was . . . bequeathed. We can't alter what happens to her, but we *can* try to stop it here.'

Merrily nodded.

'Hattie was unbaptized,' Beth said. 'I'm sure there's a psychiatrist or a geneticist somewhere who can put it into terminology that wouldn't cause anyone any embarrassment, but it seems likely that that night she acquired what we poor country folk can only describe as The Curse of the Vaughans.'

Merrily looked across the room at Jeremy Berrows, who knew.

'Why don't we see what Arthur Conan Doyle had to say? Go back to the Baskerville curse. Who invited evil into Baskerville Hall?'

'Hugo,' Jane said. 'A wild, profane and godless man, in the seventeenth century, at the time of the Civil War. Hugo promises to "render his body and soul to the Powers of Evil" if he can catch up with the wench. No real parallel there, Beth.'

'Oh, I've tried jolly hard to come up with one. The nearest I can get is Ellen Gethin. I often wonder if Ellen didn't offer herself to the Powers of Evil if she was granted the opportunity – and the physical strength – to avenge her brother.'

'But did she?' Merrily wondered. 'I mean, did *she*? That's a very familiar story. I bet you'll find slightly different versions all over the country.'

'Well, yes, and Ellen does seem generally to have been a good and faithful woman, who mourned for her husband, buried his headless body, never married again. Nonetheless, what we're looking at, surely, is a curse, a genetic disposition, what you will, following a *female line*. Hattie killed her husband, Paula killed herself and . . . Natalie . . .'

'Natalie may also have been involved in the death of her cousin,' Merrily said. 'We can speculate for ever about where it came from, but three generations that we *know* of . . .'

'So. What do we do, Mrs Watkins?'

The big question. Alice: *We needs it now, more than ever – the big white bird.*

Ancestral healing. The healing of the dead.

Dexter: *Should never've gone round askin' questions, rakin' it all up.*

Jeavons: *It's how we develop within ourselves – by suffering through our failure and trying again and suffering some more. We suffer, Merrilee.*

The globe of the table lamp was shining like a full moon. Merrily walked over to it.

'We can only apply actual exorcism to something demonic and believed to be . . . not of human origin. Perhaps that's why, in the old story, Vaughan describes himself as a devil. Makes it legit. Hattie Chancery, however . . . I mean, she might not have been a terribly nice person for part of her life, but . . .'

The TV producer, Antony Largo – egalitarian denims, wide and sceptical smile – said from behind his camera, 'This sounds like what my old man would've described as namby-pamby liberalism.'

'No . . . basic Christianity.'

'Oh, right.'

'However, I don't want to *under*play it. What I had in mind was to wait until first light and then hold a Requiem Eucharist, for Hattie Chancery. For anyone who isn't conversant with this, it's basically a funeral service, with Holy Communion. And the aim, essentially, is to bring peace to Hattie and bring Jesus Christ into this place.'

Antony Largo smiled at Amber. 'Story of your life here. Never get the ones who pay for the rooms.'

Merrily sighed. 'Just a guess, Mr Largo . . . you're not a Christian, right?'

'Astute of you to notice, Mrs Watkins.'

'And honest of you to admit it—'

'Oh, I'm actually quite proud of it.'

'—Because it kind of rules you out.'

'I'm sorry?' Largo frowned. 'Rules me *out*?'

'And, in fact, anyone else who isn't a Christian. We can't afford to take this lightly. It's not like the Chancerys' exorcism, with fake priests. Has to be the real thing or it's not worth doing.'

'The *real* thing?'

'Normally, with a history like this, I wouldn't even attempt it without back-up . . . maybe two other priests. There at least has to be what you might call a solid front. No weak links in the room. Anybody else unhappy about commitment? Mrs Foley?'

'Well . . .' Amber looked uncertain. 'Ben and I had our

marriage blessed in church. I was christened, I was even confirmed at fourteen.'

'Fine. As the owners of this place, it would be good to have you both here, but you do need to think about where you stand, whether you have faith that this is going to make a difference.'

'I'd agree with that,' Antony Largo said. 'I'd say you need to think very hard indeed about where you stand. For my part, after driving all this way through the white hell, I'm no' being fucked about any further by the only organization with ratings falling faster than anything on the box. Either I'm in the whole way or I'm outta here.'

'That's up to you, Antony,' Amber said quietly.

'Well . . .' Merrily went back to her chair. 'We've got an hour or two to think about it. I was thinking maybe six-thirty, for seven a.m.? So that, by the time we finish, the sun's up. Whether we can see it or not.'

FIFTY

Free Coward

There was a white linen cloth over his face.

He lay as if he'd fallen backwards down the stairs. Very narrow and secret-looking, these stairs, Danny thought, specially by lamplight, like the steps was creeping quietly up into the bones of the building.

There was this fat black oak beam across, like a great wedge holding the walls apart. This was likely where a small door had once hung to conceal the stairs, keep the cold out. Very old house, see, Ledwardine Vicarage, and this part didn't look to have changed much since little Tudor fellers, size of Gomer Parry, was busying up and down the steps.

Must've had its share of dead bodies over the centuries, and mabbe this was the way they was brought out.

Not like this, mind. God almighty, but Danny felt sick.

This one, it was like he'd been flung back by a sudden angry blast of wind, his head near enough back in the kitchen, his arms thrown out, his hands reaching the walls on either side, with scabs of dried blood on the fingers of the left one.

There was blood, too, underneath the linen towel over his face – blood and other moisture that had sucked the thin cloth around his head, so that you could see the rough form of his features. Like the mould for a death mask, Danny thought, holding the lambing lamp with both hands, realizing that he was doing this because he was shaking.

Dear God, you could only take so much of this in one night.

He was already backing off into the kitchen when he saw Gomer bending down to peel away the cloth from the dead man's face.

'*No!*' Danny jerking the lamp away in horror, him and the bloke in the darkness of the kitchen shouting out together.

Gomer straightened up, shrugging his shoulders.

'Police en't gonner want you to touch nothin', see.' Danny felt like he was chewing cardboard.

'And you don't want to see that, anyway,' Lol Robinson said. 'Take my word for it, Gomer.'

Gomer sloped back into the kitchen, feeling for his ciggy tin.

'Can we shut that door now?' Lol Robinson said.

When they were both in the kitchen, he closed the door firmly on the back stairs and the body, and then he led them into another room where the first things Danny saw were the amber eyes of a black cat lying on a desk, washing itself by candlelight.

'I'll . . . make some tea, soon as the kettle boils on the stove,' Lol Robinson said.

'That'd be good.' Danny had a proper look at him for the first time, taking in the glasses with one lens missing, the thin track of blood from the edge of an eye to the point of the chin. Thinking this Robinson was five or six inches shorter than the late Dexter Harris, mabbe three, four stone lighter. Thinking, how? *How?*

When they'd walked in, Lol Robinson had been shut away in here, on the phone to the doc, checking how this poor woman was, this Alice. Seemed no ambulance could get through on the roads and the air ambulance wasn't allowed to land at night, snow or no snow. So the doc and the community nurse had taken this Alice to the little clinic at the surgery.

The police hadn't got through yet, but they was on their way.

'Them ole beams,' Gomer said, thoughtful. 'Harder than steel girders. Older the oak, harder it gets. Walked into one once – just walking, mind, normal pace – next thing, I'm flat out, din't know what day it was.' He looked at Lol Robinson. 'That be it?'

'He . . . came in like a mad bull,' Lol said. 'Roaring. Pitch black in there, of course. When it happened . . . not a sound I'm ever going to forget. You know?'

Oh hell. Danny winced. *Of course. Jesus.*

'Bugger me,' he said. 'Muster near took his head off.'

'Something like that.' Lol was holding himself real funny, like there was some physical injury you couldn't see.

'He was comin' for *you*,' Gomer said.

Lol nodding. And but for this power cut, Danny thought . . . Hell, this was the only feller he ever met with reason to be grateful to the power company supplying Herefordshire.

'Right, listen now, boy.' Gomer lit a ciggy. 'Piece of advice yere. I reckon what happened, you was runnin' *away* from this feller.'

'Well, that—'

'No, *listen*! Any suggestion of you deliberately goin' this way in the dark, on account of *you* knowin' 'bout the beam, while *he* en't been this way before . . . Know what I'm sayin'?'

Lol smiled faintly, shaking his head.

'Ah . . . now! Don't you bloody look at me like that, boy! You gets some clever buggers in the cops nowadays – university degrees, New Labour. Feller breaks into your house nowadays, you gotter make him a pot o' tea, order him a minicab. Bottom line: better to be a free coward than a hero behind bars.'

'Specially as you was wearin' a Gomer Parry sweatshirt when you done it,' Danny said.

Then he noticed the way that Lol's hand was shaking, on the edge of the candlelight, as he tried to stroke the cat.

'Bastard of a situation to be in, mind,' Danny said. 'Real bastard havin' to wait here for the cops, with . . . him in the next room.'

'Reckon I'd've covered his face up, too,' Gomer admitted. 'Must have a dent in his head you could prop your bike in.'

Lol Robinson laughed a lot at that, leaning back against the desk.

Wasn't normal laughter, though, even accounting for the physical pain, and Danny didn't reckon somehow that the dent in the head was the reason Lol had covered up the feller's face.

It was the right thing. The primary rule, always hammered home with a couple of tragic case histories by Huw Owen in the Brecon Beacons, was this: never leave without doing *something*. This was more than something.

After half an hour, the lamp was sputtering, its oil level running low, the colour of even the nearest walls changing from magnolia to a dingy nicotine yellow.

And the confirmed congregation for Hattie's Requiem stood at: Beth Pollen, Jeremy Berrows, Jane – pagan Jane, for heaven's sake – Amber and Ben Foley and possibly Francis Bliss.

She needed one more, maybe two, specific communicants to make this work.

Bliss was initially helpful. He agreed to put a Range Rover and driver at the disposal of Beth Pollen, who'd offered to go down to St Mary's Church to borrow the Sacrament. Just when you needed another priest, the vicar of Kington, it seemed, was away; to obtain the sacrament they'd need to disturb the verger.

But there was a limit to Bliss's cooperation.

'Merrily, are you like *totally three sheets?*'

'No, I'm serious. It's important.'

'God knows, I've stuck me neck out a lorra times for you and, God knows, I'd do it again. And you've been good to me. But there are places I *will not go*. Not with the legendary atheism of the Ice Maiden and that bastard around with his little Handycam.'

'He won't be there, Frannie. Neither will Annie Howe. And if the lure of money wins out, and Ben Foley shows us the door, I'm ready to hold this service in a clearing in the woods.'

'So I can tie her to a tree?'

'Bloody hell, Frannie, I think she'd even be allowed out of *prison* to attend her granny's funeral. Don't you?'

'Merrily.' Bliss stood in front of the door to the lounge, as if she might suddenly charge it. '*No*.'

This was when Mumford came in to say there was a call for her, at the reception desk.

It was coming up to 5.15 a.m. when Jane found Mum sitting by candlelight in Ben's office under the etching of Sherlock Holmes's most despicable moment. She looked – face it – shattered. The crow's-feet seriously in evidence, her fingers dancing unevenly on the desktop.

'Mum, why don't you like go upstairs and get some rest?'

'It's OK, I need to . . . meditate.'

'It's not going to be easy, even I can see that. She still thinks she owns this place. She isn't going to want to leave.'

'Sorry, who?'

'Jeez. Hattie Chancery?'

'Oh.' Mum smiled strangely. Fatigue. Halfway out of it.

'Who was the call?'

'Lol.'

'He's *waited up for you*? You don't realize the kind of guy you've got there, do you?'

'The picture's forming, flower.'

'What did he want? Is he all right?'

'In a manner of speaking.'

'You're not going to tell me about this, are you?'

'Not now. But I *will* tell you. I will tell you everything. Bear with me, flower.'

Jane felt excluded, apprehensive, insecure. 'There's nothing wrong between you and Lol, is there?'

'Absolutely not,' Mum said. 'Can you give me a few minutes to sort something out?'

Jane wandered away and came back quietly a couple of minutes later and didn't go in, just stood outside the door. Expecting to overhear a phone call. Instead, listening in utter dismay to the sobbing and unable to work out whether this was relief or total despair.

The phone at reception called her away.

'Jane?'

'Irene! Haven't you gone?'

'I'm not going. I was on the Net for a couple of hours. Anyway, I decided not to go to Switzerland. It's no problem. It means Lowri can take her mate from school and I can have pizzas instead of bloody turkey.'

'Irene, this is—'

'Shut up, Jane. You know who this Brigid is, don't you?'

'I . . .'

'It's bloody Brigid Parsons. That stuff's from a nasty little site called *veryverybadgirls.com*, on which sick bastards all over the English-speaking world discuss their masochistic obsession with women who like to damage men or boys. Or kill them, in most cases. You know who Brigid Parsons *is*, don't you?'

'Er . . . yeah.'

'And that's not all,' Eirion said. 'That's really not all. I do not *like* this, Jane.'

FIFTY-ONE

Of the Midnight

Merrily had never felt more grateful at being permitted to cry, let out this great vomit of emotion. Because there really was no way you could sit down and reason it all out, analyse your own reactions, from the initial blinding love and relief, through the horror and the pity, all the way down to the guilt and remorse and the residual dread that settled in your stomach like sour wine.

After attempting to repair her face with wipes from her shoulder bag, she'd come out of Ben's office to find Jane waiting with a candle on a tin tray and the laptop she'd borrowed from Matthew Hawksley.

Jane had been on the phone to Eirion whom Merrily kind of thought had gone away for Christmas. And what was he doing up at this hour, anyway?

Nothing was normal.

Jane placed the laptop on the counter at reception and plugged it into the phone socket. Merrily stood and watched the savage colours rise on the flat screen.

www.veryverybadgirls.com

'This isn't the important one,' Jane said, 'but you need to see it first.'

Ben Foley looked as if he'd been holding his head under a cold tap to revive himself.

'We should've talked.' His swept-back hair was damp and lank, his long, thin face still glowing with towel friction in the haze of the Tilley lamp. 'We should've talked ages ago. Now you think I'm some kind of conman and Jane hates me.'

'My emotions change with the wind,' Jane said.

They went into Ben's office. He shut the door.

'Before you say anything, Amber's told me about . . . Brigid Parsons.'

'You really didn't know before?' Merrily said.

'I swear to you I didn't. And I'll tell you something else – if I *had* known I'd still have offered her the job.'

'Of course you would. Probably for the same reasons she'd have turned it down if she thought there was any chance you knew. What I'm more interested in, however . . . How long have you known Antony Largo?'

'Ha.' He pulled out a chair. 'You'd better sit down.'

Jane opened the laptop on the desk, brought up the first downloaded file: *www.veryverybadgirls*. He looked at it with distaste. 'Is there a name for men like this?'

'I'm sure we can think of one,' Merrily said.

'A name . . . or a man like this?'

'Both?' Jane brought up the second site. 'OK,' Merrily said. 'This, as it happens, was a cross-reference or whatever they call it, from *veryverybadgirls*. Which was how Jane's boyfriend found it – although I think it was the other way round. He'd already checked out Antony Largo when he found out Jane was working with him. Finding this.'

the official women of the midnight website

'Ah,' Ben said, with no great surprise.

'You've seen it before?'

574

'No, I'm not much of an Internet person, but I'd have been surprised if there hadn't been one.'

'Seems to have become quite a cult, doesn't it? Video editions with extra footage, all the unpleasant details you weren't given in the original.'

'Never liked that sort of thing myself – director's cuts. When a production's finished, it's finished.'

'I think we're looking at prurient rather than artistic interest. What emerges from this – and from the *badgirls* site – is this particular producer's . . . would obsession be too strong a word? . . . with bad girls generally and Brigid Parsons in particular.'

Ben Foley sighed. 'Yes. I knew about that. Antony's, ah, had a thing about her for quite a long time. Since he was a junior researcher at the BBC – *Panorama* or some such. Around the time we first met, as it happened. They were going to make a film about Brigid, when she was not long out of prison with a young baby. Idea was they'd follow her progress back into the world – all back views and silhouettes, of course. Antony was part of the team – very minor role, so there was no way she'd remember him, but he . . . fell for her in a big way.'

'Fell for *her* . . . or what he thought she was? I mean, when you say he had a *thing* about her . . .'

'She's a rather beautiful woman. A beautiful *dangerous* woman. I'd like to think he was a little more sophisticated about it than the poor pervs on that website.'

'I don't remember the Panorama programme.'

'Because it never happened. She pulled out in the end. Probably realized there was absolutely no way they could do it without identifying locations, at least. Current Affairs were furious – these were the early Birt years, when the pennies had to be accounted for.' Ben shuddered. 'Antony never forgot her, however, which I never found entirely healthy, or indeed his apparent obsession with women who'd killed men and boys. When he was making *Women of the Midnight* he did his damnedest to get Brigid. She wouldn't meet him or any of his team, and she made sure they never found out where she was. So all they could do in *Midnight*, in the end, was tell the story – as they had to do with Myra Hindley – without an interview with the subject. Still made compulsive viewing, though.'

'So when you invited him here—'

'I've told you, I had no idea Natalie was . . . anything other than another woman on the run from a bad relationship. I thought my secret weapon in persuading Antony was going to be the story of Hattie Chancery. Antony saw Natalie, looked at her the way he looked at all attractive women, and I warned him off. He must've recognized her at once, didn't say a word to me, but then he wouldn't. From that moment on, he was evidently following his own agenda.'

'Does he know you know . . . now?'

'No. And I'm going to choose my . . . my moment. The little *bastard*.' Ben struck the desk with his fist; the laptop vibrated. 'The minute Amber told me, the truth of everything blew up in my face. That shit. He did it *so* well, continuing to resist my arguments, letting me woo him, finally relenting, oh so reluctantly. And now he's going to shaft me and walk away. I want to kill him, Merrily. When Amber told me how he treated you like dirt in there . . . He *wants* to be thrown out. He doesn't need me or Stanner any more. He's got what he wants.'

'Has he? I'm sorry . . .'

Ben stood for a few moments staring at a picture of the young Mary Bell on the laptop. 'You'd better have a look at this,' he said.

*

He pulled a dust cover away from a TV monitor with a nine-inch screen. 'Hope there's enough juice in this battery.'

From a cupboard under the desk, he produced a video camera like the one Jane had been using. He connected it to the TV, switched on, turning the sound down low. Video channel, cool blue screen.

'I was rather surprised when Antony turned up tonight, having apparently driven from London after talking to Jane on the phone. I did a check with the AA – the route he was claiming to have taken was blocked in several places, even to a Mitsubishi Shogun.'

Jane looked up. 'You mean he was . . . *here all the time?*'

'Not here, but somewhere close. For at least a couple of days. When he came in tonight, he had his usual bag of cameras, but no room to go to. Took out what he needed, asked me – in view, as he put it, of all the thieving police around – if I'd put the bag in the safe. Naturally, when I found out what I found out, I had a poke around in his case. Found this.'

Brigid Parsons was on the screen, in close-up, unsmiling, no make-up, hair untidy. She seemed to be in a vehicle; there was a metal-framed window behind her. She was talking about her father.

' . . . *When he married again, I was fine with that, yeah. I mean, the poor guy deserved some kind of life. With my mother, he was husband, nurse, minder. I think he did love her at first . . . or maybe not, maybe it was just infatuation – and some kind of need. She was undoubtedly a beauty, and she needed him, and it was his job, what he did. I suppose there was a buzz in that, being needed . . . for a while.*

'*When she was pregnant, it was, undoubtedly – he'd tell me this, time and time again – the happiest time of his marriage to Paula. So full of the happy hormones. But after I was born – whether it was like with her sister I don't know . . . whether she was jealous, but . . . I do think that if she hadn't killed herself she'd have killed me.'*

Ben snapped off the sound. Brigid mouthed silently on the screen, her hands weaving about, her face contorted, those lush lips writhing in distaste, actual tears in her eyes. She wiped a hand across her eyes, and there was a streak of what looked like drying blood on one wrist, and livid, open lacerations.

Merrily turned away, to Ben. 'He's been here recording, with Brigid?'

'Duplicitous little *bastard*.' Ben switched off the set. 'How did he persuade her? I don't know. But he's got an interview there maybe fifty minutes long, nearly all of it usable and worth a small bloody fortune. While my piffling Conan Doyle doco . . . well, that will *never* be made, will it? Now you know why I want to kill him. Amber said restrain yourself, think things out, and that's what I've done so far.'

'Have you told the police?'

He looked puzzled. 'Why should I? Hasn't broken the law, has he? I must say it did occur to me that if the police were building a case against poor Natalie, this was something they might like to impound – which would screw his exclusive, let the whole thing out of the bag. But that seemed rather unsubtle. I've told *you* because you raised the issue with me, and I want to be honest with you. But I'd be glad if you'd keep it to yourself for the moment. I am, I regret to say, unashamedly looking for a way to shaft him back.'

'I'd like to ask Brigid about it.'

'So would I, if I had the chance,' Ben said. 'But I don't see it, do you? I don't see any of us having a chance to talk to her again for about twenty-five years.' He put the dust cover back over the TV monitor. 'Look, this . . . Vaughan thing. I don't know what to think. *Is* that woman . . .?'

'I don't know, Ben.'

'We don't even know if any of it's true, do we?'

'It makes a lot of sense, though.'

'Inherited evil?'

'Most of what I do, I can't prove . . .' Merrily suddenly felt so tired that she had to stand up to stop her head falling forward on to the desk ' . . .anything.'

When she went alone in search of Bliss, Mumford pointed her to a door that she hadn't noticed before, near the foot of the stairs. Mumford put a finger to his lips as she went quietly in to find a small room furnished as a study, with bookshelves. And Bliss slumped over a desk, with his head laid on an arm.

He sprang up instantly.

'It's allowed, Frannie,' Merrily said.

'Must be getting old. Used to be able to do all night and all the next day on black coffee and cheese-and-onion crisps.'

'The adrenalin of crazed ambition. Listen, when Danny Thomas gets back, I'm hoping to get Clancy brought over. You could at least give me Brigid for half an hour.'

'You were trying to nobble me before I was properly awake, weren't you? Listen, I've been to me share of Requiem Masses. I know the kind of emotion all that can generate. Blood on the altar I do not want.'

'Blood on the altar?'

'Gwent police have been talking to Nathan – Bowker, Bowdler? Anyway, the cowboy with the big gun and the small brain who was savaged by Ms Parsons for the crime of trespassing with intent.'

'Oh.'

'I'm assuming this is news to you, naturally. But he's only just back on his feet and the first thing he did, when he was able to talk without pain, was to telephone Mr Sebastian

Dacre with a view to obtaining compensation for his injuries in return for his silence. The way you do.'

'When was this?'

'Last night, shortly before seven. Nathan said that when they were first let loose, Sebbie had talked about the woman living with Berrows. Nathan was a little coy on this, according to Gwent, but they had the feeling that it had been suggested that Nathan and his mates needn't be overly polite to her. No suggestion from Sebbie, of course, that she might *retaliate*, so the lad was gobsmacked in every sense of the word.'

'And you think this was what sent Dacre up Stanner Rocks in a snowstorm? Confirmation that this was Brigid Parsons and she hadn't changed?'

'We'll be looking at Sebbie's mobile, to see who he rang last night, who he might've made an appointment with. Unfortunately, the thing was smashed on the rocks, so it'll have to go to the boffins. But, yeh, you're right, I reckon. Puts paid to any doubts he might've had that the lovely Natalie was indeed his little cousin Brigid. And it gives him more leverage. Being arrested for GBH, if you happen to be Brigid Parsons, it's not gonna be a smack on the wrist, is it? Also, think of the publicity. Sebbie gives her an ultimatum, re sale of farm . . . she sends him on his last journey.'

'Frannie, would anybody in his right mind attempt to blackmail somebody known to be violent while standing with his back to a cliff edge?'

'Who says he was in his right mind? Have *you* spoken to anybody thinks he was in his right mind? He was probably in an alcoholic haze. Besides, it didn't end there. Just pushing the feller off the cliff, see, that wasn't very Brigid. A bit perfunctory.' Bliss rubbed his eyes. 'I shouldn't be telling you this, I don't know why I'm—'

'Go on.'

'Zelda Morgan? Matrimonial ambitions?'

'I remember.'

'Zelda was at her mother's seventieth birthday party in Kington, didn't get back to Sebbie's till just before we talked to her last night. Checked the answering machine but she didn't get round to checking the voicemail on her mobile till an hour or so ago when she woke up in the armchair. Bit of a shock, out comes Sebbie's voice, being very Sebbie. "Get your" – excuse me, Reverend – "get your fat arse over here. Get the police. Fucking madwoman's pushed me off the fucking rocks, and I can't move." '

'What?'

'The voice of an injured man, possibly, but certainly not the voice of a dying man. Billy Grace was right. The facial injuries were not entirely consistent with a fall. She followed him down and beat him to a pulp. She's not a pussycat, Merrily.'

'Can I talk to her again?'

'And would you like to tell me why?'

'I don't *know* why.'

'About this Vaughan connection, yeh? What's that mean to you?'

'Frannie, this could take a while.'

'Never mind,' Bliss said.

At 6.30 a.m. Merrily went up to Hattie Chancery's room with a Gideon Bible and the decanter of holy water.

Pictures of Hattie in the mustardy light. What struck her was how pale the woman had been, skin like white fish-flesh, anaemic.

There was a picture of her with the Middle Marches Hunt, which presumably provided regular infusions of blood.

Merrily shivered. Hardy was right: the entire room was a cold spot, the atmosphere thick with something she could only interpret as loathing. It could be Hattie; it could also be Brigid.

I was lying up in her room, surrounded by creepy old photos of the bitch. The biggest one, I had to clean the glass and I did that by spitting in her face, over and over again.

Merrily loosened the stopper on the decanter.

When she came down, Bliss was in the lobby, putting down the phone. There was concern in his eyes when he saw her; she must have looked something like she felt.

'You've gorra tell me, Merrily.'

'What?'

'Oh, come *on*.'

It was up to Ben to tell him about the video, so what she told him, in the end, was about Lol and Dexter. What Dexter had done to Darrin and to Alice, what he'd tried to do to Lol, how it had ended and what lay on the floor of the inner hall of Ledwardine Vicarage.

Stuck out here in the snowy wastes, Bliss hadn't caught up with the Hook inquiry. By the time Merrily finished, expressions were shifting around his face like jigsaw pieces in search of a picture. He walked away across the lobby and then back again. He stood in front of Merrily, chewing his lip, and then he turned his head and nodded at the lounge door.

'Yeah, OK. Go in. Tell Alma I said you could have her.'

'Well . . . thanks.'

It was time, then. No excuse.

As the C of E Deliverance manual kept underlining, when you conducted a Requiem Eucharist in an exorcism context, it was advisable to have at least one other priest there and preferably several. This was for a normal service, with full preparation taking place over several days. This was with a congregation of carefully vetted Christians.

With no back-up, and a congregation including two spiritualists, a trance-medium, a Roman Catholic, a teenage pagan – kind of – and a murderer, you just tossed the book over your shoulder and prayed for survival.

FIFTY-TWO

These Things Happened

It was better in here now. Clouded with damp mist and shadows, but the candles were glowing brightly on the make-shift altar, unexpected stars in a murky sky, and the murmured *amens* were rising to join hers, this soft miasma of voices, a fuller response than she'd expected.

It was as if the ritual itself was controlling the conditions, making rough but perfectly symmetrical interweaving shapes in the void. The living and the dead, and the holy. One small circle of light.

Or maybe she was delusional through lack of sleep, and this was autopilot.

Before the others had even come up from the kitchen, she'd done some sprinkling of newly sanctified water, the routine blessing of the room. Haunted-house procedure. Then a short prayer, once they were all inside. And then a repeated blessing after the Dr Bell episode and the Vaughan revelations – all this probably helping *her* as much as anyone, calming her nerves, setting up a receptive state of mind.

Careful devotional preparation before the service is recommended for every communicant. And also for the priest, naturally.

Oh sure . . .

There was a white cloth on the altar, a small chalice for the wine, a saucer for the wafers. Beth Pollen had assisted here. Merrily glimpsed Beth sitting next to Jane, staring straight ahead with focus and determination.

There seemed to be twelve of them now, including Brigid and Bliss and Alma. Antony Largo, wherever he was, had made no attempt to come in and his cameras were gone. The one she knew least was Clancy: school skirt, white school blouse, dark golden hair overhanging her eyes, her mouth sullen – eerily like the young Brigid, whose same picture, from a school photo, had been appearing in the papers for years and years.

Twelve of them. Twelve and Hattie. More holy water sprinkled in Hattie's room before leaving. *Lord God, our heavenly Father, you neither slumber nor sleep. Bless this bedroom . . .*

Merrily connected now with that. It was the beginning. She stepped out with her Bible and her service printout.

' "I am the resurrection and the life," the Lord says. "Those who believe in me, even though they die, will live, and everyone who lives and believes in me will never die . . ." '

We have all got a sporrit something like a spark inside we, said the old man to Mrs Leather.

The brown mud in the stained-glass window began to clear in the early dawn, suggestions of colour rising like oil in a puddle.

'So this is a service with Holy Communion to bring peace to Hattie Davies – Hattie Chancery, who died by her own hand before the Second World War. But I'd also like us to remember, in our prayers, Hattie's daughter, Paula, who was also a suicide, and Paula's daughter, Brigid who is . . . with us.'

With the aid of a car battery provided by Ben, she'd managed to print out the order of service from Common

Worship on the C of E website. Close to the top of the service – and lest anyone forget what this was about – she'd brought in a serious Confession that she made them repeat after her, line by line.

'We acknowledge and bewail our manifold sins and wickedness which we, from time to time, most grievously have committed.'

There were candles on tables amongst the congregation, establishing that they were part of it, not an audience. Brigid Parsons sat next to one, with Jeremy and Clancy. Brigid's hair was freshly brushed and some of its long-ago colour was shining through, in strands of fine gold, as if in acknowledgement that she'd soon be able to wash it all away because anonymity wouldn't matter any more, where she was going. Her face was dark and strained, the wide mouth turned down, with lines either side that looked as if they'd just been pencilled in.

> 'We do earnestly repent,
> and are heartily sorry for these our misdoings;
> the burden of them is intolerable.'

Merrily had tried to talk to Brigid in the lounge, but Brigid, who had slept for a couple of hours on the sofa, had been unresponsive to everything except the idea and purpose of the Requiem. *'Please, just . . . take the bitch away.'*

'This is not about revenge.' She focused on Brigid now, in the near-white candlelight. 'It's not about hitting back, it's not about *laying a ghost* . . . it's about forgiveness. We're looking at Hattie and what she did, and, sure, there were a lot of evil elements there . . . *but that does not make Hattie evil in herself.* We have to search, in this service, for a depth of forgiveness that we perhaps wouldn't be able to reach in everyday life. We're always saying, I can forgive anybody anything but *That* . . . Today, we have to say – and mean it – I can forgive anything, *including* That.'

In her own mind, she saw the woman in the picture over the bed, a woman with fair hair twisted and coiled like a nest of pale snakes, and eyes like white marbles. She could hear wild laughter, the smack of stone on flesh and bone.

Whoop, whoop.

It wasn't easy, was it?

'Fortunately,' she said, 'we can count on some help.'

She opened the New Testament: John, Chapter Twelve. At a later stage, she'd have to say, *'Let us commend Hattie to the mercy of God.'*

It was clear that nobody was ready yet to consider mercy. Not even Jeremy Berrows, the natural farmer, the quiet farmer, innocent face under hair like dandelion clocks. Giving Brigid an occasional sideways glance, their shoulders touching. Jeremy Berrows, who firmly believed the evil that arose in Brigid had been bequeathed to her by Hattie.

And maybe it had. Maybe Bella Chancery, led here by a twisted path of deception, had opened the door to . . . something that Jeremy was now being asked to forgive. Now. Within probably an hour of losing for ever his main reason to go quietly on.

John 12, verse 27. *'Now my soul is in turmoil, and what am I to say? Father, save me from this hour? No, it was for this that I came to this hour . . .'*

Canon Jeavons's point entirely. *It's how we develop within ourselves – by suffering through our failure and trying again and suffering some more. We suffer, Merrilee.*

If Merrily could take on Jeremy's suffering she'd do it. She felt a low-level tingle in her spine.

Behind Jeremy was Alistair Hardy, rotund and bland and

– a phrase you didn't hear much these days, but it suited him – clean-shaven.

The psychic? She didn't doubt it, but there *was* a lot to doubt. The Lucy Devenish thing, for a start. Also Dr Bell's 'revelation' about the use of a newborn baby in that dubious ceremony. Because Beth Pollen had almost certainly known of the suggestion that the baby was Hattie, had almost certainly told Hardy.

Smoke and mirrors.

' *"The crowd standing by said it was thunder, while others said, An angel has spoken to him. Jesus replied, This voice spoke for your sake, not mine. Now is the hour of judgement for this world; now shall the Prince of this world be driven out . . ."* '

Driving out evil, it was hard not to personalize it.

Brigid Parsons . . . Paula Parsons . . . Hattie Chancery . . . Black Vaughan and Ellen Gethin. To what extent could this possibly be said to go all the way back to Black Vaughan? Who seemed to have been only a fall guy, anyway. A story to blacken Vaughan and his tradition – the Welsh tradition in an area becoming rapidly Anglicized.

She looked at Ben Foley, his sleek head bowed. The original destructive haunting was said to have threatened the whole economy of Kington; Ben had been hoping it would revive his.

She wondered if she ought to have included Sebbie Dacre in this.

A Vaughan thing.

Had Dacre been told that he was a Vaughan? Did that explain his robber-baron mentality, his need to reclaim what was his, to dominate the valley? But the threat Dacre perceived was a threat from within his own family. The worst kind. Look at Dexter Harris.

Merrily looked around the cold room with its tiny spearpoint flames. Looked around, flickering face to flickering face.

Where are you, Hattie?

Of all the things she hadn't intended to ask . . .

'Dying, you destroyed our death. Rising, you restored our life.'

He's here. *Christ.* He should be here.

Here now.

Everything is all right.

The tingling in the spine.

But she felt so utterly tired that the candles blurred and the faces fused. She shook herself very lightly.

Not everyone took communion. Beth Pollen was first, looking up at the rising cold blue in the stained-glass window. Then Jane, with a wry and slightly apprehensive smile.

> 'Every time we eat this bread
> and drink this cup,
> we proclaim the Lord's death
> until He comes.'

Brigid, when her turn came, had her eyes closed.

'The bread of heaven in Jesus Christ.'

If she'd done this before, it had not been for a long time. Her hands came up, reaching for the chalice, the cuffs of her black shirt unbuttoned, falling back over her wrists so that Merrily could see deep, fresh scratches, the blood barely dry.

God . . .

She was so knocked back by the significance of this that she barely noticed Brigid moving away afterwards and Clancy taking her place.

Had Ben noticed it? Had Jane? Had she imagined it? Was it an hallucination? In the context of the Eucharist, These

Things Happened. Immediately, she began to pray for guidance, for back-up, over Clancy's dull gold hair.

Becoming aware at that moment of Jeremy Berrows, sitting back in the front row – Jeremy's eyes wide, lit from two sides by candles. Jeremy's eyes widening. Gazing beyond Merrily, upwards, back at Merrily.

'*The cup of life in Jesus Christ.*'

'Mum,' Jane said faintly.

Merrily turned and saw, maybe, what Jeremy saw.

Its outline *might* have been conjured from the snowbanks joining the rising hills, and the jagged pine-tops, shadows against the first light. But yes, oh God, she saw it crouching there inside the leaded glass with its black haunches in the blue and its shadowy snout uplifted into the red where the first light was bleeding through. She saw it, and it was poised to bound.

No!

A coarse sucking sound sent her spinning back to the altar and the thick, dark blonde hair and *the cup of life in Jesus Christ* – Clancy's hands around the chalice, Clancy's lips . . .

She just stood and watched, her mind whirling, as Clancy trembled hard, as if in orgasm, and threw back her head and drank all the wine and smiled horribly up at Merrily with her black-cherry, glistening lips and eyes like small mirrors, a little candle-flame, a spark, *a sperrit*, in each of them.

In the very cold silence, Clancy burped and the wine spouted out of her.

Whoop.

FIFTY-THREE

No Smoke, No Mirrors

It was like one of those Victorian clockwork-tableau automatons that you wound up and things started happening, everything interconnected: Brigid Parsons pulsing to her feet and Alma, long practised in restraint, preventing her from moving from the spot, as Jeremy and Jane and Bliss converged and one of the altar candles self-snuffed.

Merrily was putting herself between all of them and Clancy, and shouting, *'Baptized?'*

Shouting out to Brigid, *'Has she been baptized?'*

Becoming aware that she hadn't actually shouted it, just mouthed it, and Brigid was shaking her head.

'That's OK,' Merrily said calmly. 'That's not a problem. We'll see to it now.' She smiled at Clancy and Clancy smiled faintly and vacantly back. 'Clancy, you up for this?'

Keeping it casual. Playing down what was going to be something very big and crucial, because if this kid got spooked and took off . . .

Clancy didn't respond, but she didn't move away, just stood there like she'd been summoned to the head teacher's office. Stood there in get-this-over mode. Not sullen or antagonistic, just tuned-out.

Which was dangerous, of course. Merrily lifted up her hands and felt a rush of adrenalin, endorphins, the electricity crackling.

Don't get carried away. Concentrate.

'Shush,' she said softly bringing her palms down, trying to lower the energy level in here because it was becoming negative – too many warring agendas. It was only a hotel dining room, it wasn't a church, nothing to amplify emotions but no weight of worship to soothe them either. A playground for Hattie Chancery and whatever moved her, but the kitchen would have been worse.

People were back in their chairs, the clockwork winding down. Some hadn't reacted, like Alistair Hardy, watching her with his head on one side, one arm apart from his body, the hand twitching, fingers flexing. Did she need him out of here? No, let it go. He wasn't interfering; she had the sense of a spectator, no agenda.

Merrily turned to the altar and gathered up the decanter. This was about the essentials. No fuss . . . stripped down . . . clean and simple . . . the basics. It mustn't be rushed, however. Keep it casual, but get it right, because this . . . well, this was a medieval baptism. This *was* the exorcism.

She was looking into Clancy's face now – the kid avoiding her stare, which wasn't hard; she was a good bit taller than Merrily. But this was what Clancy did, she avoided, retreated, did not get involved. The inherited curse of negative celebrity.

In the name of the Father, the Son, the . . .

When Clancy finally knelt, it was like hands were pushing her to her knees. Merrily was aware of Brigid Parsons drawing in a thin ribbon of breath and the placid, unmoving eyes of Jeremy Berrows. When she closed her eyes momentarily, she could see a ring of candles, tiny snail-shells of light.

She held on to the sense of assurance rising from her abdomen, her solar plexus, as she approached Clancy and the half-perceived form of the woman standing close behind her who was in dark, nondescript clothing, perhaps a two-piece suit, bust like a mantelpiece, close-curled hair, eyes like white marbles.

Taking the stopper from the bottle. Time passing. If there was a preamble, Merrily wasn't aware of it.

'Do you . . . reject the Devil and all rebellion against God?'

Nothing.

'Say, "I reject them." '

Say it, for God's—

Clancy looked confused. Her face was damp and florid in the crimson glare suffusing the room.

'Clancy, say, *"I reject them."* Say it, if . . . if you want to.'

Clancy rocked, losing her balance, the words tumbling out.

'Do you renounce the deceit and corruption of evil? Say "I—" '

'I . . . renounce them . . .'

The cold sun hung in the red portion of the stained-glass window, like a blood-blister. When Merrily finally drew the cross on Clancy's skin, she almost expected the water to boil and sizzle. It didn't.

Anticlimax. No smoke, no mirrors.

It was always best.

Clearing away the remains of the Eucharist, after the baptism and the commendation, Merrily's hands were weak, but there was still a dipping and rising in her spine, something finding its normal level.

Jane came to help her. At some point – good heavens – she actually squeezed Merrily's hand.

'Hey . . . not bad.'

'Erm . . . thanks. Only it wasn't—'

'Yeah, I know. It wasn't down to you. All the same, you could easily've blown it. Mum . . .' Jane began to fold up the white tablecloth with the wine stains. 'Is this . . . I mean, you know, is this *it*?'

'No chance. I'll probably be back three or four times. Could you . . . leave the cloth there, flower. Call this superstition . . .'

'Oh . . . right.'

Clancy was at the bottom of the room with Brigid and Jeremy, Bliss and Alma a few yards away, giving them some space.

Merrily shook her head as the old concertina radiator began gonging dolefully behind her, squeezing a little heat back into Stanner Hall.

'What happened to your wrist?' Merrily said as they filed out into the lobby, she and Brigid side by side with Bliss in front, Alma close behind.

Brigid said nothing.

'Happened on the rocks, didn't it? Last night.'

Brigid shrugged and it turned into a shiver. Brigid was very pale now, pale enough to faint. They moved towards the reception desk, Mumford standing there, his face grey with stubble and no sleep. In the half-light, the lobby looked as dismal as an old hospital waiting room.

'Brigid,' Merrily said. 'Tell me . . .'

'All right, it happened on the rocks.' Brigid turned to her, still walking. 'Look, I just want to say, you know . . . thanks. I don't know what you did, but maybe . . . maybe something happened. Even I think that. And I'm not impressionable. Not for a long time.'

'Something probably did happen,' Merrily said.

'And I wanted to say . . . if you could maybe stay in touch with Jeremy, because he . . .'

'I know.'

'It could have happened for us. We were so close to it.'

'I believe you were.'

On the reception desk, the phone was ringing. Mumford picked up.

'I wish I'd known earlier,' Merrily said. 'I wish somebody had felt able to say something.'

She looked at Jeremy, who must have said more in the past few hours than in his entire adult life.

'And Clancy . . .' Brigid said.

'Don't worry.'

'I'm not going to cry,' Brigid said. 'It's not what killers do.'

Mumford said to Bliss, 'It's the DCI, boss.'

'Tell her we've had word that the snowploughs've been through and we're on our way.

'Boss—'

'Tell her we've gone.'

Merrily said, 'That was Annie Howe, the head of Hereford CID. If you don't make a full statement she's going to give you a very hard time.'

'That'll be something to look forward to.'

Merrily said, 'You see, the point is, that wrist injury – I saw it on Largo's video.'

Brigid stopped. Alma said, 'Keep moving, please, Brigid, directly to the porch.'

Then Clancy Craven was there, dragging on Alma's arm, face all twisted up.

'You're not taking her! You're not! *You can't take her away!*'

Clancy started to scream. Merrily saw Jane behind her, looking upset, unsure how to respond. Jeremy watching her too, with an expression that, if you didn't know him, you might interpret as anger. Jeremy turned and walked away towards the entrance as Brigid pushed in front of Alma, hugging Clancy. 'Clan . . . it'll be OK. It . . . Everything's taken care of.' Over Clancy's shoulder, she said to Merrily, 'Where did you see that video?'

'Ben has it. Ben thinks it was shot a couple of days ago.'

Bliss was listening now.

'But the fresh blood shows it had to have been between whatever happened on the rocks and you being brought in, right?' Merrily said. 'Did you get it when you beat Sebbie to death at the foot of the r—?'

'*Merrily!*' Bliss snarled.

Brigid said, 'What?'

'For fuck's sake—' Bliss spun round, ran to the door to Ben's office behind reception, flung it open. 'In! In there *now!*'

FIFTY-FOUR

Reichenbach

When Bliss said, 'Clancy, would you and Jane like to fetch us all some of Mrs Foley's incredible coffee?' Clancy looked at her mother like this was some cheap trick and when she returned with the coffee all the police cars would have gone from the forecourt.

'I promise you, Clancy,' Bliss said, 'we won't leave the premises without you get another chance to see your mum, yeh?'

Clancy wouldn't look at him but she went off with Jane. She hadn't looked at Merrily either since the water had dried on her forehead. This could take months – years – of after-care. It wasn't magic.

Merrily put a new cigarette packet, open, on the desk, with the Zippo. On the front of the packet it said *Smokers Die Young*. Alma brought in a third chair and an ashtray, and Merrily sat facing Brigid, watching her smoke with a cautious relish, as if she was already banged-up.

'Right.' Bliss sat next to Merrily. 'Where's this video?'

'You don't need to see it now, Francis. Its existence is enough.'

'Men just bloody lie to you all the time,' Brigid said.

'Meaning Largo?'

'Some of us, on the other hand,' Bliss said, 'though we may seem like crass twats only looking for a result, have a profoundly spiritual core. Some of us might even be deeply shocked to think that a woman who's just left a feller horribly unfaced should allow herself to be whisked away to be interviewed about it for the box. Something doesn't ring true, in other words, Brigid.'

'Could I talk to Merrily on her own?'

'No, but you *can* talk to DCI Howe, who is also a woman – so I've been told. Can we cut the crap? I sometimes feel that a service like the one we've just attended can blow away the need for an awful lot of unnecessary evasion. Which goes for you, too, Reverend. In fact, you can start us off.'

'OK.' Merrily took a cigarette.

'And make it quick while I can still breathe in here.'

'Well, essentially, Antony Largo has been after Brigid – in at least one sense, maybe more – since he was a young researcher with the BBC. Antony Largo likes – sorry, Brigid – vicious women. He made a well-known documentary called *Women of the Midnight*, which—'

Bliss leaned into the smoke. 'He made *that*?'

'While still in his twenties, apparently. And never looked back.'

'As I recall, Merrily, that programme caused a flap by being a bit . . . well, it looked closely at the sexual side of things, didn't it? We heard from past lovers, in considerable detail.'

'And you can apparently get the rest of the detail on video through the Internet, as long as you claim to be over twenty-one.'

'Well, well,' Bliss said. 'So you knew Mr Largo then, Brigid.'

'No, I didn't, actually. I didn't even remember his name. Only anoraks know the names of TV producers. Didn't recognize him, either, when Ben brought him in, though I'd apparently met him at Ellie Maylord's, when these guys were after me for *Panorama*. As he reminded me the other week.'

'In what circumstances did he remind you?'

'After he was here with Ben that first time, he didn't go back to London. He booked into the Green Dragon at Hereford, and he phoned me.'

'Must've been a shock, Brigid.'

'Yeah, it was. He said could I meet him. He said as soon as he saw me he was thinking, like, what if Ben finds out?'

'You'd appreciate talking to someone who really cared.'

'You wouldn't believe some of the men I've met who really cared,' Brigid said.

'I may even have arrested a couple. So, you met Mr Largo?'

'I met him in the camper van.'

'Aha.'

'Was a refuge for me, that van.'

'I thought you'd sold it to the nature lads.'

'Lent it. Said I might need it back at some stage.'

'Oh?'

'In my situation, the kind of refuge you can drive away is sometimes useful. It's also better if you don't keep it at home. That way, visiting reporters, or other people you don't want to get involved with, don't get to see it in advance. I have bad memories of driving out of Looe at the head of a cavalcade.'

'So you entertained Mr Largo in your camper van, even though—'

'In this case, because I didn't dare meet him anywhere public, and I wasn't having him anywhere near The Nant. And I didn't *entertain* him, thank you.'

'You can't blame people for embroidering – man and a woman in a camper van on a remote clifftop. And with what we know of his tastes . . .'

'That was on his second visit, I assume. The first time he

suggested I might like to cooperate in a sensitively made documentary. The second time, it was to offer me a percentage. Which he said could run to well over a hundred grand, including US rights.'

Bliss leaned back, eyebrows going up. 'Tempting?'

'Not to me. This might be difficult for you to get your head around, but money doesn't mean that much to me or Jeremy. As long as we're in a position to earn enough to keep going.'

'Money means a certain amount to everybody, Brigid.'

'Ask Merrily what means more.'

'Peace of mind,' Merrily said. 'In a very particular sense.'

'Did you like Mr Largo?' Bliss asked.

'I didn't feel very happy being alone with him, if that's what you mean.'

'In what way?'

'Buy the video, Frannie,' Merrily said.

Brigid smiled and extracted another cigarette.

'You turned him down?' Bliss asked.

'I put him off. You see, the danger here is that this was one of a very small number of people who would actually have been close enough to me as an adult to recognize me. Only, things had changed a lot in the last couple of months. I'd found a man I wanted to spend the rest of my life with, and he was living in a place he needed to spend the rest of *his* life *in*.'

'Having you around could be pressure for a serious introvert,' Merrily said. 'It's a big secret to keep.'

'I think we'd've started to tell local people in time – the ones who could handle it. Guys like Danny Thomas and Greta. You get a group who know, and you have this level of protection that you wouldn't get in a more populated area.'

'True. They like to know all about you, but once they *do*, they can be very loyal. And very good at secrets, of course.'

'Sometimes too good at secrets.' Brigid lit her cigarette. 'I'll buy you another packet of these before they take me away.'

Merrily smiled. She was getting that feeling in the spine again.

'You led him on?' Bliss said.

'I said I'd need an absolute assurance that my appearance would be disguised and also my location, and I didn't think he was going to be able to promise that. I also said that if I did it I wouldn't want any money, but I *would* want right of veto or whatever. You see, I've never seen *Women of the Midnight*. It's not the kind of thing I watch, strangely enough. He said a solid, *sensitive* programme like he was planning would take the heat off and also allow me to have my say. Well, I didn't want my say, but I didn't want him shopping me, either. Not yet.'

'Did you never think of going to court for special protection?' Merrily asked. 'Make it so the media weren't allowed to identify you, for Clancy's sake?'

'I didn't want special protection. I didn't deserve special protection. Clancy, maybe.'

Bliss said, 'Can we talk about Sebbie Dacre?'

'I'll only go so far.'

'He was blackmailing you, right?'

Brigid laughed.

'What's so funny?'

'He wouldn't have the . . . I dunno what word I'm looking for, but he wouldn't have it. I'm sorry. I didn't want him to die.'

'You killed him, Brigid.'

'I wanted . . .' Brigid blew out a lot of smoke, turning away. 'What's the bloody point?' The smoke drifted up and mingled with the smoke around the muzzle flash from Sherlock Holmes's pistol in the picture.

'Please,' Merrily said, 'don't stop now.'

'Look – he was out of it, he really was. Hell, there's enough insanity in my family for that to surprise nobody. Somebody told him about this website where all these saddos were drooling over what women had done to men, and he printed stuff off, pinned one to the sign at the bottom of the drive so I'd know that he knew. He was dangerous. He was a risk. Sure. At some stage he was going to tell somebody who'd take him seriously. But he still didn't know, for certain.'

'You think he was genuinely mentally ill?' Merrily said.

'I think it was the booze, mainly. The toxic combination of booze and being a Chancery.' Brigid flicked her cigarette towards Bliss. 'What's that *sound* like? I don't know why I'm bothering – this guy isn't going to believe the half of it.'

'Try him. He's a Catholic.'

'But I just want to make it clear – *again* – that I've never . . . I am *never* gonna blame whatever I've done on being a victim – my mother's daughter, Hattie's granddaughter. I will live with being a bad and vicious person – a monster – and getting punished for it, rather than take one miserable step down Sebastian's road. I'll be an old lag with a filthy mouth. I'll be an evil monster for *Sun* readers to wish dead and sick kids to wank over, and that's *it*.'

'And yet you came here to find out about it. You cooperated with Beth Pollen and The White Company . . .'

'It was about closing doors, Merrily. And it was about Clancy – I've explained all that. It wasn't about me.'

'You know,' Merrily said. 'I don't think I'm buying that. You understand—'

'No, listen—'

'You understand too much about Sebbie's problems. And

he denied it too, didn't he? I mean, people who talked to him—'

'If you talked to him, you'd think he didn't give a toss. "Load of old drivel" – I've listened to him in the pub, spouting off – maybe for my benefit, just in case I was who he suspected I might be. Just so I'd know he wasn't scared of anything, particularly me, and the past.'

'Why scared of you?' Merrily said.

'Not for me to say. Ask Jeremy.'

'Because your mother tried to kill his mother when they were little? Because Ellen Gethin—'

'Why did he come to the van last night?' Bliss said. 'And why were you there?'

Merrily said, not quite knowing where the question came from, 'You were trying to help him, weren't you?'

'Where did you get that idea?'

'I don't know.'

'I was . . .' Brigid ground out her cigarette in the metal ashtray. 'He wasn't blackmailing me, OK? He was saying to me, "I've been expecting you, and you're . . . trouble." Something like that. I was a threat. Jeremy said he'd been seeing the Hound of Hergest, like other drunks see pink elephants. He never said that to me. He said he wanted Brigid Parsons to sell him The Nant, and he'd give a fair price for it, and that would be the end of a long, bad period. He thought I could take Jeremy with me and buy him another farm a bloody long way away. He didn't *actually* try to blackmail me . . . not then. But I didn't want to go, you see, and Jeremy . . . nothing was going to get Jeremy out of The Nant, so I . . . said why didn't we meet?'

'Usual venue,' Bliss said.

'Look, I honestly didn't think. How naive was that, for someone like me? See, the thing is, we were never going to like each other, but he wasn't going anywhere, he owned everything in a big circle around The Nant, and he could make things very difficult if he wanted to – I mean he gave us a taste of that with the hired guns, like this Wild West situation. I still thought there had to be a way we could coexist.'

'What were you gonna offer him, Brigid?'

'Not The Nant and not sex. Peace of mind? A way of making peace with the past? On one level, that seemed very naive, but, yeah, it was worth a try.'

'Good God.' Merrily sat up. 'You were going to invite him to the White Company gig.'

'I did. I told him there were some people who'd like to help him with his . . . paranoia. I said we should attack it. As a family unit. Bite back.'

Merrily nodded. 'You and him.'

'And The White Company. And you, maybe. Deal with it – for Clancy's sake. And by then, I'd also been made aware that I needed help on a personal level if I was going to survive here.'

'Nathan?'

'That was a shock. It happened quicker than I could think.'

Bliss leaned back, arms folded. 'What exactly happened with Sebbie, Brigid?'

'In Sebbie's view of things,' Merrily said, 'there would be only one reason for a direct female descendant of Hattie Chancery to invite a man to Stanner Rocks.'

'I thought we'd got way beyond all that,' Brigid said. 'Twenty-first-century Chancerys. I didn't realize, even then, how far he was sunk into it.'

'Jeremy said Sebbie was resigned to there being a death in the wind, and he thought it was going to be either him or you.'

'I don't believe these hicks,' Bliss said.

'We use words like "superstition" in a loose, disparaging way,' Merrily said, 'but when superstition meets mental instability it can get way out of hand. And that's why neither you nor Howe is going to get a motive that makes complete sense. That is, of course, unless—'

'What?' Bliss said.

'Sebbie was drunk when he arrived, right?'

Brigid nodded.

'Did he attack you?'

'Not in any . . . I don't know. It got stupid, all right? It was never really civilized from the start, but it got . . . When I said to him that there were these people who were trying to follow the whole curse thing back to Vaughan and wanted to deal with it once and for all, he just . . . exploded. Went totally berserk. This is in the van, right? How *dare* these fucking outsiders think they can come in and meddle, take over other people's lives, other people's pasts . . . ? And it's snowing heavily now, I'm standing in the door of the van, trying to stay upright, and I'm going, "You stupid, drunken pig, we *ARE* the outsiders who came in and meddled and took over . . . *it's our fault!*" '

Brigid closed her eyes.

'The Chancerys,' Merrily said.

'Yeah.'

'Do you think he saw what you were proposing as an attempt to destroy his whole . . . power base, if you like? The Vaughan in him?'

Brigid nodded. 'All the baggage that history and folklore had inflicted on the Vaughans, including an exorcism, a snuffbox and a big black ghostly dog – he disowned it all, and he loved it all. It was everything. It was who he was. Mr Sebastian Dacre, JP, Master of the Hunt, Sebbie Three Farms. He needed it like Hattie did. If there *is* a curse, they gave in to it, they clutched it all to their bosoms. *Whoop* fucking *whoop*.

It's like hunting – they know some of it's vile, but it's part of their . . . yeah, their power base.'

'But it took a lot of booze to live with a curse.'

'Yeah.'

'What happened on the rocks, Brigid?' Bliss said quietly.

'Well, he started by breaking up *my* humble power base, as he saw it. He threw the oil lamp at the wall, and it went on the bed. He was set on a course by then, he made sure it all caught fire. After that, I don't even . . . I don't even remember how we got there . . .'

'At the edge of the rocks?'

'He was pretty drunk. I was thinking, what if he goes up with the petrol tank? Selfishly, I assure you, because I'd get the blame . . .'

'What happened, Brigid?' Bliss said again.

'What happened?' Brigid started to laugh and then choked on the smoke. 'The last of the Chancerys – the last of the Vaughans – out on the edge like Holmes and Moriarty at the Reichenbach Falls, that's what happened. And the snow's coming down heavily – you couldn't even see where the edge was. And he's going, "I'm having you out of here!" He's going, "I'll have the whole of the fucking press here by the morning, if not before. *You* can't go anywhere, you can't get out in this weather, but *they*'ll get in when they know. They'll hire helicopters." This kind of madness. Then he just starts backing away towards the edge, and he's shouting, "What you gonna do now? Gonna push me over like our esteemed granny?" And I'm like, "Are you crazy?" 'Cause the snow's built up this kind of ledge that projects beyond the edge, so you think it goes back further than it actually does.'

'And he *was* crazy,' Merrily said.

'Oh yeah. But I mean, me too. I pushed the bastard over.'

'You pushed him or he slipped?' Merrily said.

'I pushed him. I'm Brigid Parsons, granddaughter of

Hattie C. What do you think, I'm going to try and *save* him?'

'Yes,' Merrily said.

Bliss said, '*Merrily . . .*'

'He grabbed at your hands, your wrists, and you tried to hold on, and his nails tore your wrist . . .'

'I don't remember.'

'You don't *want* to remember.'

'Merrily, this is not what we do,' Bliss said.

'This is not the interview room, I can do what I like.' The heat was in Merrily's spine again, all the way up. 'This is Brigid taking responsibility again. She's putting her hands up and she's saying, "Yes, it's me, I take full responsibility, it's me, the flawed human being . . . it's not *the other thing*."'

'Merrily,' Bliss said gently, 'you're forgetting the rest.'

'No, I'm not. Brigid, did you go down that slippery, treacherous path to the bottom of the quarry in the blinding snow and beat Sebbie Dacre's head in with a rock? Did you do that?'

Brigid rocked back in the chair, eyes tight shut.

'I don't remember.'

'She doesn't remember,' Merrily said to Bliss. 'You need to get Ben Foley in here.'

FIFTY-FIVE

Sky's Come Down

On the TV monitor, watched by Bliss and Ben Foley, Brigid was talking about life in a detention centre for young offenders where her peers regarded her with a kind of awe.

'I was pretty much heartbroken for months. Couldn't talk to anybody for fear of breaking down. That was seen as me being aloof and cool and dangerous. Nothing's ever how it looks, is it?'

Merrily, crouching next to Brigid at the desk, murmured, 'Mark and Stuart. *Did* they try to rape you?'

'Get off my back, Merrily. Why would I give the parents any reason to like evil Brigid any small amount better while thinking less of their sons?'

'You're not evil, Brigid.'

'Natalie,' Brigid said.

'Brigid . . .' Bliss was sitting on the edge of the desk. 'Do you say anything about Dacre on this video?'

Brigid shook her head. 'He didn't want any of the spooky stuff.'

Merrily saw Ben Foley wince.

'I meant his death,' Bliss said. 'The death that occurred not long before you recorded this.'

'No. Of course not.'

'All right, I've seen enough for now, thank you, Mr Foley. Hang on to it, though. Can you make a copy?'

'I did that before the power went.' Ben was looking nervous, Merrily thought, his skin pale and porous.

'Tell me how exactly you encountered Mr Largo last night, Brigid,' Bliss said.

'Well . . . I knew he was supposed to be coming back, to shoot The White Company experiment. Antony said he'd wanted to see me again before it all got going. He said he was on his way to Stanner Hall for The White Company.' Brigid looked apologetically at Ben. 'Actually, I don't think that was his intention. I don't think he'd have come back here at all last night if the snow hadn't made it impossible for him to get out of the valley.'

'You're probably right,' Ben said. 'He was just going through the motions. I misunderstood his glee.'

'He said he saw me in the Daihatsu, taking the track up to Stanner,' Brigid said. 'But then he saw this Range Rover coming up a bit later. When he saw that it was heading the same way, he decided to wait at the bottom, near the quarry, so whoever it was wouldn't see us together. After . . . what happ—' Brigid's face tightened. 'After I pushed my cousin off the rocks, when I was stumbling down, Antony must've seen me from his Shogun, and he came out to meet me, with a torch. He said he thought he'd seen somebody falling. Next thing, we both saw Sebastian lying in the snow, and it was . . . you know, it was pretty obvious he was dead.'

'What did Mr Largo say?'

'He said, "Christ, Brigid, what've you done?" And I was . . . stunned, I suppose. It was a bad dream. To find I'd . . . done it again. Killed somebody. Happening just like that – so fast, so *unstoppable*. You're looking round to see if the world's the same place you were in a few minutes ago. It's like the whole sky's come down on you. Like all the sides of everything are coming in on you. You can't believe it happened, you want to turn time back. You can hardly breathe.'

She's talking about the first time. Merrily's fingers were clasped around the pectoral cross.

'I really didn't hate him, I pitied him. And there he was, killed so quick. Here one minute and ranting . . . and then just a piece of bloody meat. And you think . . . how *can* it—? And . . . and then you turn around and all your future's gone as well.'

Bliss said softly, 'And Mr Largo said . . . what?'

'He said, "Oh my, Brigid, you're in the shit here." '

'He didn't ask you what happened?'

'He just said that. And then he said best not to go too near. He said I was obviously in shock. We moved the Daihatsu back to near the roadside, and he took me back to the Shogun and drove me off up towards Presteigne or somewhere. We went into this fairly big pub I'd never been in before, where there were quite a few people, and he found us a table by the fire and he bought us brandies. And he was trying to explain how it was going to be if they got me for this . . . like *if* they got me. I knew it was as good as all over, and I was hardly listening, just sitting there in front of that fire, thinking about Jeremy back at The Nant and *his* fire. That lovely fire. Thinking we'd never sit in front of that again, together. Thinking about Clan, what was going to happen to her now. Thinking how, when the Social Services got hold of her, there'd be nobody who could remotely understand what she was carrying around, and Clan, she doesn't help herself, you know?'

'He was right, though,' Bliss said. 'You *were* in a mess.'

'He said, "Look, I want to help. I'm not going to tell you there's nothing in it for me, that it's any kind of selfless act, but I'm willing to up the percentage considerably." And I'm like, "What's the use of that, you can't have a murderer taking a cut, there's some law against it." And he said no, the money would go to Clancy, in trust, or whatever. However I wanted to do it.'

'And now the money you didn't care about, suddenly that was meaningful.'

'It was meaningful because I haven't really *got* any money. I've got a farm and a man who belongs to it, so I haven't got a farm to sell. And to keep Clan out of the System, that would take big money, to pay for somebody . . .'

Bliss glanced down at Merrily, then back at Brigid.

'So you agreed.'

'He said he had a contract already made up and he'd make some quick changes and put his signature to them, and that would legally oblige him to pay a third of the action to Clancy. He took the contract out of his pocket and he put it on the table in the pub. It looked legit, but how would I know? What was I going to *do* here? What would *you* do?' Brigid did a swift sweep of faces, her hair swinging. 'Any of you?'

'So you recorded the interview.'

'He said if we didn't do it now, it'd be down the pan . . . which was pretty obvious. So we drove into New Radnor, and we parked off the bypass, which was still pretty clear, and he set up a camera with a light inside the Shogun. He had two cameras going – one he held, the other on a short tripod in the back of the car, shooting like a profile of my face. He had loads of batteries and stuff, and he clipped a personal microphone to my coat and we . . . we just recorded it in one go.'

Like it was being done at gunpoint, Merrily thought.

'I just babbled on, I wasn't really thinking about what I was saying. He asked questions and I just said the first things that came into my head, except when he asked about Mark and Stuart and I just said I hadn't got anything to say about that. We must've gone on for nearly an hour and a half, with a couple of breaks so he could move the car a bit to stop us getting blocked in by the snow.'

'And you were sworn to secrecy about when it was done?' Bliss said.

'He said it had to be kept under wraps or we wouldn't make a fraction of the money. He said he'd be compromised if it came out he was a witness to the murder.'

'Interesting,' Bliss said. 'What would this be worth, Mr Foley?'

'A lot. Even now, Brigid Parsons is still big box office. Brigid Parsons back in the headlines with – I'm sorry – another conviction for a similar crime would be huge. Mega.'

'Even an interview knocked off in a car?'

'Makes no difference these days. You can get perfect quality anywhere. Gives it more of a sense of authenticity. By the time he's dressed it up with other interviews, old news footage, comments from a shrink – you've got to have a shrink these days, and most of them will say whatever you want. Yeah, he's looking at big bucks. *Enormous* bucks.'

Merrily said, 'So how important *would* it be for Brigid to have done another murder?'

'Like I said – mega. Court case of the year. Questions asked in Parliament about the monitoring of murderers who've been let back into society.' Ben looked at Brigid, as if he still couldn't absorb the idea of her as a serious killer, as anybody other than Natalie, his manager. 'But most importantly, she's out of the picture. This is the only interview anybody will ever get.'

Bliss said, 'I know where you're coming from, Merrily, but . . .'

Merrily looked up at Ben, saw his eyes go wide and still with sudden comprehension.

Bliss chewed his lip, then he said, 'How successful *is* Mr Largo at present, Mr Foley?'

'He . . . seemed to be on top. But then, in this business, nobody ever goes around telling people their careers are on the slide. I don't really know where he is in the pecking order, I've been out of it for too long. Been out of it so long I trusted him. Thought he was a mate.'

'But even if he *was* still successful,' Merrily said, 'something like *this*, that would still be the summit of his career . . .'

'God, yes,' Ben said. 'Most independent producers would k—' He swiped back his hair with both hands. 'Figure of speech.'

Merrily wondered if Largo had heard Sebbie on the phone to Zelda Morgan from the bottom of the rocks, where he'd fallen. Probably not. Had he even thought of the risk that Sebbie's fall could be ruled out as the cause of death and, if he had, might Sebbie still be alive? Or would he have taken a chance, anyway? She was a notorious convicted killer. Who was going to believe her denials?

She waited for Bliss to ask something, but Bliss was staring up at the window, chewing his lower lip again.

'What would Largo's state of mind be?' she asked Ben Foley. 'He's waiting in his car, say at the entrance to the quarry. He's seen Brigid going up there. He's seen a Range Rover taking the same route. Perhaps he's in the car with the headlights on, or perhaps he's out there with the torch. But suddenly he sees a body tumbling down from the rocks through the snow. What's he feeling? Shock? Incredulity?'

'What do I say?' Ben's attempt at a smile was loose and nerveless. 'Shock and incredulity aren't in Antony's repertoire.'

'What, then?'

'Seeing what looks like a murder happen before his eyes? A murder on a plate? A murder committed by a high-profile killer he's been . . . lusting after – for reasons most of us wouldn't like to contemplate – since he was a graduate trainee?'

'In your own words, then, sir,' Bliss said.

'I would say barely controllable, very dark sexual . . . excitement.'

'I see.'

'Of course, the man *has* used me, lied to me, cut the ground from under my feet and left me humiliated, so I may be a *tad* prejudiced . . .'

'Brigid,' Bliss said, 'when you came down from the rocks, what did Mr Dacre say to you?'

'He didn't say anything.' Merrily was aware of Brigid drawing in a thin thread of a breath. 'He was dead.'

'All right.' Frannie Bliss stood up. 'I can't let you go anywhere yet, Brigid, you realize that. But I won't send you to Hereford. I'll say we've had new snow. I'll say something.' He turned to Ben. 'Where is he, Mr Foley?'

'He's gone, I think. Can't have been too many minutes ago.'

'Back to London?'

'He said he'd phone me.'

'When?'

'Sometime. Actually, it may be sooner than sometime. After I copied his video discs to VHS, I, ah, put blank ones back in his case.'

'Naughty. What've you done with the originals?'

'They're here. I may put them under a stone at the bottom of Hergest Pool for a thousand years.'

'Sorry, sir?'

'Local joke,' Ben Foley said.

Bliss thought for a moment. 'Sod it, let's get the bugger stopped on the road and brought back. I want his clothes.'

*

They went out for air, Merrily and Brigid.

They stood at the highest point of the forecourt. The view was immense and blinding under a surprising glaze of gaseous early sun. No snow had come down since dawn.

'Is it safe?' Brigid was staring at one of the small farms lying under Hergest Ridge like a trinket fallen from a shelf, and Merrily realized that this must be The Nant, tilted into the hillside, half submerged in snow. 'Is it safe to tell Clancy? Is it safe to tell Jeremy?'

You could see something crawling slowly towards it like a beetle, perhaps the loyal Danny Thomas going in his tractor to see to Jeremy's animals.

'I think Jeremy already knows.' Merrily gazed over the snowy forestry to Hergest Ridge: thick white icing on an old fruit cake, rich and spicy, dark and bitter and soaked in alcohol. Where was the Hound? Out there, somewhere, or existing only in the collective consciousness of mid-Border people, a shadow on the retina of the mind's eye?

'Can I stay here?' Brigid said. 'If it . . .?'

'Can you?'

'It's a challenge, isn't it?'

'Everywhere's a challenge.'

She was thinking about something Gomer had said about Jeremy's island of calm in a sea of noise and blood. She wondered what would happen now to Sebbie Dacre's three farms, whether some other robber baron would come riding over the horizon in his Range Rover, unable to spot the symptoms of history until the disease had set in. It was important to guard the island.

Behind them, a shout went up.

'That,' Frannie Bliss said, 'is outrageous. They think they're a bloody law unto themselves, these bastards.'

'It's a remote area,' Mumford said. 'Always been self-sufficient. Half of them have got their own snowploughs.'

Merrily stood at the bottom of the steps, below the hotel porch, as Bliss followed Mumford down.

'Who we looking at here, Andy?'

'I'll give you three names, boss. Berrows . . . Thomas . . . Parry.'

'Damage?'

'The van with Dacre's body in it had a headlamp smashed. That's the only police property. However—'

Merrily hurried over. 'What's happened?'

'Your little friends,' Bliss said, 'decided, for reasons of their own, to reverse all the sterling work done to clear tons of snow from the bottom of the drive, thus allowing us all to return to comparative civilization.'

'They . . . put the snow back?'

'They put it *back*, Merrily, even better than nature had done it in the first place.' Bliss's voice acquired some heat energy. 'They seem to have created an impacted wall of snow harder than the sides of the fucking Cresta Run. So that the first vehicles, thinking the road was clear, just piled into it.'

'I think it was Berrows started it,' Mumford said. 'He was . . . in a bit of an emotional state. Especially after the girl came down. Then Thomas and Parry arrived in the tractor with a plough, and it escalated. They can go a bit mental, sometimes, Border people.'

'Nick them,' Bliss said grimly.

'And the other bloke's talking about legal action,' Mumford said.

'Sorry, Andy?'

'The Scottish bloke.'

'Scottish bloke.'

'In the Shogun.'

'I see.'

In the silence, a little smile landed like an insect at the corner of Bliss's mouth.

'The impact seems to have dislocated his shoulder,' Mumford said.

'Did you tell him how sorry we were?'

'No, I thought you'd like to do that yourself, boss. As the SIO.'

'Yes,' Bliss said. 'That would be correct procedure. I'll come now.'

FIFTY-SIX

Christmas Eve

Killing for a chip shop. Killing for what Jane had described as a *contemporary dynamic*.

Small doorways for big evil.

'Most motives for murder seem ridiculous,' Merrily said, in front of the parlour fire as the daylight slipped away. 'But all that tells you is that the reasons – the motives – are usually irrelevant. For most of us, they wouldn't *be* motives. We hope.'

You hoped. You hoped you had an immune system, a natural defence – Christianity, whatever – against all the evil in the air around you. You hoped there was no such thing as an evil person, only someone with a weakened immune system.

She'd been to see Alice this afternoon. Alice had come out of hospital. Alice was at her sister's house in Belmont – Darrin's family, Roland's family. A whole male generation wiped out.

Alice couldn't move her left side much, but she could communicate, just about – verbal soup dribbling from the right side of her mouth. You could get the sense of it, mostly. For instance, the family's discovery that no doctor had actually treated Dexter Harris for asthma in over ten years. Since the Family GP had become part of history, such things didn't come out.

How long had Dexter been feigning attacks to get himself out of various situations and responsibilities? *Don't give me no stress.*

Mostly, Alice had just wept, a fiery little woman doused by life. There would be a lot of weeping in that house this Christmas. It was what Christmas would become, for them, for the foreseeable future.

She'd promised Alice and the family some healing. From the Sunday-evening service. The, erm, *healing* service. Well, what could you do? A forum to discuss setting up a spiritual healing group in the diocese had been arranged for mid-January, at the Cathedral. The Bishop himself would chair the meeting. The idea of having Lew Jeavons as guest speaker had been ruled out.

'I need to ring him,' she said to Lol. 'Do I mention the twelve priests? Or do I wait for him to bring it up?'

'He may not want to explain.' Lol was sitting on the rug with his back against the sofa, his head against Merrily's thigh. 'Some things just . . . evolve.'

Just before she and Jane had left Stanner, Alistair Hardy had taken Merrily aside. *I'm uncomfortable about this, Mrs Watkins, knowing how you feel about people like me. But after what you said when we met on the stairs, about the twelve priests and Black Vaughan . . .*

He'd counted them, he said. This was just after the incident with the girl during the Eucharist, before Merrily had initiated the baptism. He'd counted all twelve.

And what were they wearing? Merrily had asked, legitimately sceptical. *Kind of . . . monk's robes? All carrying candles?*

Yes, Hardy said, they did have a candle each. But none of them wore monks' robes. And two of them were black, and one was a woman.

Just thought she might like to know.

Lol had told her that Jeavons had felt bad about the way the Dexter thing was turning out. Asking Lol to ring him as soon as he could find out what time the Stanner Eucharist had been arranged for. He hadn't said a word to Lol about his international database of over three hundred healing and deliverance priests.

After being given the approximate time, he'd asked for the location. And a map reference.

Hardy said he'd noticed that Merrily's aura had appeared brighter and more vivid. As the dark essence of Hattie Chancery hazed into something palely grey.

Probably still there, though, Hardy said. *There's probably more to do. You'd know about that.*

Aftercare required.

Before lunch, Bliss had rung. DNA tests on Antony Largo's clothing had proved inconclusive. Maybe he'd managed to dump some. This was not, Bliss said, going to be easy. Antony Largo was not in custody, and he had the worst kind of lawyer. The Crown Prosecution Service, as usual, was demonstrating symptoms of irritable bowel syndrome.

However, Strathclyde Police had been helpful. Largo had formerly been known as Anthony McKinnon. Born in the fairly sedate seaside resort of – wait for it – Largs, north of Glasgow, McKinnon, aged sixteen, had been one of several juveniles questioned in connection with the alleged gang rape of a prostitute, who had eventually decided that she didn't want to appear in court. It wasn't much, Bliss said, but it was a start.

Brigid Parsons had made a full statement at Hereford and had been released without charge. It was a delicate situation, and its satisfactory resolution depended on Bliss nailing Largo. Bliss wouldn't give up.

Meanwhile, Natalie Craven and her daughter had returned

to The Nant. Former DCI Ellie Maylord had been consulted and would be travelling down. Bliss thought it would be a good idea if she and Merrily met. Merrily agreed.

Aftercare needed.

But Dexter Harris, Bliss said, had been more or less textbook. A black bin-liner had been found in a roadside litter-bin, inside it a claw hammer coated with blood and hair. By this time, Dexter's truck had been forensically examined. Truck/hammer/Darrin/Dexter. A formality. Lol's part in the final act had not been made public, but he wasn't looking forward to the inquest.

Lol's theory about Roland? Well, that was never going to be proved one way or the other. Lol was convinced that when Dexter had made Darrin take the car that night, it had been his intention that Roland wasn't coming back. Everything that Dexter had laid on Darrin – the brutality, the cruelty – was probably down to Dexter. All that and more.

Howe, it seemed, had been unconcerned. It was all academic now. Forensic psychology would say that Dexter was formula-psychopathic – the lies, the cunning, the remorseless cruelty. Merrily recalled a report that suggested over one per cent of the population was, to some extent, psychopathic. Most psychos didn't kill. Most killers didn't make a habit of it.

'The thing is,' Lol said now, 'Dexter was . . . let's be honest, he was dull. An extremely dull person. Unbelievably self-righteous, limited intellect, all that. But as a killer, he was imaginative. He was instinctive . . . creative. He had *flair*.'

'Christ, Lol!'

'Like, when he decided I needed to be killed he had it all worked out in no time. Disappearance . . . some landfill site. My DNA all over Alice. He walks in and finds Alice has had a stroke, he acts on it, he uses the whole situation, including the weather conditions, just like he did with Darrin – I mean, both of those could have *worked*. And he'd have held out against interrogation because he'd have resented it. The cops would have been *in the wrong*. *He* wasn't a criminal. He was a working man with a clean record . . . well, since the age of twelve, and you couldn't hold that against him.'

'But some of his family did.'

'And he resented it. His family had treated him badly. Whatever happened to any of them, they deserved it.'

'What's the betting that the damage inflicted on Dexter's family's property by Darrin was not in fact done by Darrin at all?'

'Dexter.' Lol nodded. 'Makes sense. Dexter seems to have created a whole new image for Darrin within the family. Alice swallowed it, anyway. Maybe she didn't see much of Darrin.'

'But Roland's death – accidental? Engineered? How good a driver *was* Dexter?' Merrily remembered Bliss's reconstruction.

'*Unfortunately, Dexter panics, stands on the brakes and the Fiesta stalls on the kerb, directly in the path of the oncoming lorry.*'

'Try not to think too hard about it,' Lol said.

'Where does it come from, then?' Merrily said. 'What was feeding his imagination?'

'Your guess may be better than mine.'

She slid down to the rug, next to him. Although the snow was almost gone, he hadn't left Ledwardine since Dexter's death. She hadn't yet asked him what the estate agent had told him before the office had closed for Christmas, an hour or so ago.

'I kept wanting to confess to Annie Howe.' Lol looked at her, his glasses faintly misted. 'Maybe it's something about her that withers your resolve. But then I hadn't got much resolve anyway.'

'Much more than you used to have, sunshine.'

'I mean, *I did it*. I killed him.'

'Why do people keep throwing false confessions at me? You didn't touch him.'

'Which makes it worse. Like hiring a hit man.'

'You didn't hire the beam.'

'Every time I walked under it, I instinctively ducked,' Lol said, 'although I knew I could walk under it upright, with three or four inches to spare.'

He'd followed Gomer's advice, told Howe that Dexter was coming after him and he just ran upstairs. In fact, Lol had sat on the stairs and insulted Dexter, building up Dexter's fury to the point where . . .

'But if he'd *suspected* there might have been a low beam there,' Merrily said, 'he'd have bent his head, and then he'd have . . .'

'Taken me apart.'

'And you didn't know the beam was going to *kill* him.'

'Well, that's the point. I didn't care.'

'Lol, look at me,' Merrily said. 'With Alice lying there, *I* wouldn't have cared.'

Prayer and cleansing in the inner hall. Some savage scrubbing of the floor. She'd offered to conduct Dexter's funeral at Hereford Crematorium, but the Bishop didn't think it was wise under the circumstances.

'I wonder where he got his inhalers.'

'I think he or Darrin would know people who did chemists' shops. Not that Dexter would personally associate with that kind of low life . . .'

In the village – this made him feel even more uncomfortable – people smiled at Lol now. *'Ow're you, Mr Robinson?* Scary.

'Do you think I should ask Jeavons over for Christmas lunch? I know it's a bit late, now, and with Eirion coming over . . .'

'Lew's going to his mother-in-law's.'

She looked at him suspiciously. 'You've become very friendly with Jeavons . . .'

'I don't understand it either. Normally I don't get on with priests at all.'

'All right,' Merrily said, 'what did the estate agent say?'

She knew the agents had been trying to get hold of him because Prof Levin had called to pass on the message.

'It's not *necessarily* good news,' Lol said. 'The people who were buying the house called yesterday to pull out. The husband said he was very annoyed that nobody had told them. He's a lawyer in London. He said there'd been a precedent and someone had received a considerable out-of-court settlement as a result of a similar failure to disclose a problem of this nature.'

'Huh?'

'They have a five-year-old son, and he was playing about upstairs and he came down in tears and said he wanted them to have their *own* house. Said the same thing the next time they came. They got it out of him that he kept meeting an old woman on the landing. In a cloak.'

Merrily sat up.

'The wife went into Jim Prosser's shop and asked him a few meaningful questions. The agent said Jim told them about Lucy, the poncho. He said she was well known as a witch.'

'Jim said *that*?'

She thought, *'Ow're you, Mr Robinson?*

'The agent said normally this sort of thing didn't put people off any more. Kind of added to the charm of a house.

624

She said, "Of course, I know you were a friend of the late Miss Devenish." '

'Meaning it wouldn't bother *you* . . .'

'It wouldn't have bothered these people either except that the kid suffers from . . .' Lol hesitated. 'He's got asthma.'

'I don't like this,' Merrily said.

'I knew you wouldn't. I asked for some time to think about it.'

'If I told Huw Owen about this, he'd say it was some kind of occult trap.'

'He's away, though.'

'Yes.'

'You want to consult Jeavons?'

She looked at him in his Gomer Parry sweatshirt, his spare pair of glasses, a bruise around his left eye.

She leaned her head back against the sofa.

'Nothing's bloody simple in this job, is it?'

Early evening, she had a phone call from Beth Pollen, calling from the Stanner Hall Hotel where she and Jane were helping out. Jane said the atmosphere there was definitely better, although that might be psychological. Amber, she said, was usually cheerful; Ben was quiet and contemplative.

'I went to Stanner Rocks this afternoon,' Beth Pollen said. 'Martin Booth, who's in charge of the botanical survey, took a group of us up there – the first since the police removed their tapes and things. The naturalists were jolly worried about damage done to the site by all that activity. Have you heard of the Early Star of Bethlehem?'

'Is that the unique . . .?'

'The plant that's unique, in this country, to Stanner Rocks. It's just flowered.'

'Oh.'

'Despite the name, this doesn't normally happen until

February. Personally, I'm taking it as a sign of something. Jane thought you'd want to know. She wanted to bring you a sprig, but they wouldn't let her touch it.'

Merrily smiled. 'I should think not. Erm, have you spoken to Alistair Hardy?'

'At length.'

'Right. Well, about the twelve priests . . .'

'I'm sorry?' Mrs Pollen said.

'Oh. Well.' Merrily watched Lol playing with Ethel the cat. His sweatshirt had ridden up. An area above his waist was still purple and black. 'Well, I hope you have a good Christmas,' she said.

Afterword

Allowing the paranormal limited access to a mystery novel is a perilous business. All I can say is, I've lived not far from all of this for a long time, and there are some aspects of it that nobody in the area even tries to explain away.

The central theme was founded on fully-documented (as well as some original) research. Some years ago, there was a programme I wrote and presented and which Penny Arnold produced for BBC Radio called *The Return of the Hound*, investigating the origins of Arthur Conan Doyle's most famous novel. The quotes between the text, from people with experience of the so-called Hound of Hergest (and, of course, the bull in the church), are taken from that programme. It would be hard to doubt the sincerity behind any of these interviewees, so thanks to all of them, and also to Susan and Ken Reeves of Kington Museum, historians Bob Jenkins and Alan Lloyd, Alun Lenny and Roy Palmer, author of *Herefordshire Folklore* (Logaston Press) the very worthy successor to Mrs Leather's classic, *The Folklore of Herefordshire*, which is still around (would that *she* were) in the Lapridge edition. Incidentally, I've heard other intriguing stories relating to the Hergest mystery from people unwilling to be quoted, and you get the feeling that the spirit of Sebbie Dacre may also still be abroad in the Kington area.

However, the legend of Black Vaughan doesn't always add

up and leaves much to be unravelled. It would have been easy enough to add or alter a few details to make it more fiction friendly, but I didn't like to touch it.

In the late 1980s, there was amused press speculation about the return of the Hound of the Baskervilles, when a mystery predator was said to be at large in the area of Clyro, in Radnorshire, where the Baskerville family had a country house and where the village pub is called the Baskerville Arms. Nothing was ever caught. The recent Beast of Llangadog also had its curious aspects.

You can see the remarkable double tomb of Thomas and Ellen in the Vaughan Chapel at Kington Church, and you can also see Hergest Court from the road, although it's not open to the public. You may have difficulty finding Stanner Hall (or any trace of the Chancery family) although the Rocks are very apparent from the bypass. Thanks to Fred Slater, author of *The Nature of Central Wales*, and Andrew Ferguson, custodian of Stanner Rocks. Seriously, *don't go up there without permission*; the ascent can be dangerous and some unique plant life is at risk. Besides, it's more intriguing from a distance, and you can spot the body parts.

On healing and deliverance, many thanks this time to Peter Brooks (who provided much technical assistance and a timely copy of *Is Spiritualism of the Devil?* (1919) by Rev. F. Fielding Ould) and John Woolmer, whose penetrating book, *Healing and Deliverance*, I discovered thanks to its publisher Tony Collins of Monarch Books. *Healing the Family Tree* by Dr Kenneth McAll is published by Sheldon Press.

Recommended biographies of Sir Arthur are: *Teller of Tales* by Daniel Stashower (Penguin) – very strong on the spiritualist years – and *The Doctor, The Detective and Arthur Conan Doyle* by Martin Booth (Hodder and Stoughton).

Thanks, for technical assistance, to Tim Green and Julian Carey, of BBC Wales, John Mason, Pam Baker and Jane

Froud of the Original Cloak and Dagger Company, deviser of murder-mystery weekends. To Prof. Bernard Knight for hangings. To editors (in order of appearance) John Jarrold, Peter Lavery and Nick Austin, for crucial tweaks. To Stefanie Bierwerth for smoothing paths.

Finally, the contribution over six solid weeks during the final rewrite by my wife, Carol – editor, director, inspired plot-doctor – was unparalleled and rescued this book from that familiar abyss. No one else could have done this with such perception and precision.

PS. A short while ago, when the Hergest Pool was drained for cleaning, a large stone was found in the centre. Historian Alan Lloyd, who was quite interested to find out if there was anything underneath it, said no local farmer could be persuaded to use his tractor to find out.

PHIL RICKMAN

The Wine of Angels

PAN BOOKS

The Rev. Merrily Watkins had never wanted a picture-postcard parish – or a huge and haunted vicarage. Nor had she particularly wanted to walk straight into a local dispute over a controversial play about a strange seventeenth-century clergyman accused of witchcraft . . . a story that certain old-established families would rather remained obscure.

But this is Ledwardine, steeped in cider and secrets. A paradise of cobbled streets and timber-framed houses. And also – as Merrily and her teenage daughter Jane discover – a village where horrific murder is a tradition that spans centuries.

'As if an episode of *The Vicar of Dibley* or
The Archers had suddenly turned into *Cracker*'
Sunday Times

'Escalates with all the excitement of a good
thriller and races breathlessly towards the climax . . .
a wonderful, enthralling read'
Daily Express

OTHER PAN BOOKS

AVAILABLE FROM PAN MACMILLAN

PHIL RICKMAN

THE CURE OF SOULS	0 330 48756 6	£6.99
A CROWN OF LIGHTS	0 330 48450 8	£6.99
THE WINE OF ANGELS	0 330 34268 1	£6.99
CRYBBE	0 330 32893 X	£6.99
CANDLENIGHT	0 330 32520 5	£6.99
THE LAMP OF THE WICKED	0 330 49032 X	£6.99

All Pan Macmillan titles can be ordered from our website,
www.panmacmillan.com, or from your local bookshop
and are also available by post from:

Bookpost, PO Box 29, Douglas, Isle of Man IM99 1BQ
Credit cards accepted. For details:
Telephone: 01624 677237
Fax: 01624 670923
E-mail: bookshop@enterprise.net
www.bookpost.co.uk

Free postage and packing in the United Kingdom

Prices shown above were correct at the time of going to press.
Pan Macmillan reserve the right to show new retail prices on covers
which may differ from those previously advertised in the text
or elsewhere.